AEGEAN LAND
THE FOURTH C...

KRITI

Ionian Sea

Kritan Sea

PELOPONNESOS

Sparte

KORINTHOS

MESSENIA

LAKONIA

ARGOLID

ARKADIA

ELIS

Athenai
ATTIKA

AKHAIA

Thebai

BOIOTIA

LOKRIS OZ.

LOKRIS OP.

PHOKIS

EUBOIA

AITOLIA

Aegean Sea

MALIS

DORIS

AKARNANIA

Adriatic Sea

Pherai

Larissa

THESSALOS

EPEIROS

Thermaic Gulf

ELIMIOTIS

KHERSONESOS

Aigai

ORESTIS

Strymonic Gulf

KHALKIDIKE

LUNKESTIS

Pella

THRAIKIOS

MAKEDONIS

PELAGONIS

PAIAONES

DARDANIS

ILLURIS

A BLOODLINE OF KINGS

A Novel of Philip of Macedon

Thomas Sundell

Crow Woods Publishing

Published by: Crow Woods Publishing
                Post Office Box 7049
                Evanston, IL 60204
                Email: crowwoods1@netscape.net
                Web address: http://sites.netscape.net/crowwoods1/

Cover illustration of the assassination of Alexandros by: James Mesplé

Publisher's—Cataloging-in-Publication Data
Sundell, Thomas.
  A Bloodline of Kings: A Novel of Philip of Macedon / Thomas Sundell.
  p.   cm.
  ISBN 0-9665871-8-9
  1. Macedonia—History—383-356 B.C.—Fiction.   2. Philip II—Fiction.
I. Title.
  PS3569.U63B56   2001
  813'.54—dc21

Library of Congress Control Number: 00-090162

Contents

AUTHOR'S NOTE

This is a work of fiction. The path it takes steps upon the stones of fact and crosses gossamer strands of scholastic interpretation. Yet it is my interpretation, however much it owes to scholars like:

I. Akamantis, M. Andronicos, M. Austin,
R.A. Billows, E.N. Borza, A.B. Bosworth, A.S. Bradford,
J. Cargill, G.L. Cawkwell, P. Connolly,
H.J. Dell, A. Despinis, S. Drougou,
C.F. Edson, J.R. Ellis, D.W. Engels, R.M. Errington,
J.V.A. Fine, A. Fol, R.L. Fox,
R. Ginouves, P. Green, G.T. Griffith, A-M Guimier-Sorbets,
N.G.L. Hammond, V.D. Hanson, M. B. Hatzopoulos, J. Heskel, S. Hornblower, et al ...

Is history only entertainment, a story to be told? No, history is a profound current flowing through all that we think and say and do. Compare the words said by the new Macedonians and the modern Greeks on the new republic being named Macedonia. Ask yourself why this matters so deeply to them.

I hope my story told here is true to the past. Years ago I spoke of writing this novel to the late Brendan Gill, of New York literati fame. He declared that a historical novel could not be historical. That we can never relive what was thought, said, and done then. And he was right, but missed the point. Though we couch the past in terms of our own times, we must seek to know and understand the past.

If my story is not true enough, I know that Philippos will admonish me in my dreams. This is a good story to tell.

I write this story because I must. Still, you are able to read this story only through the patience and efforts of my wife, Ivy. This story is dedicated to my children—Virginia, Nathaniel, Cara-Alexandra, Victoria, and Valentia.

My thanks to Dr. Elias Kapetanopolous and David Castlewitz for their advance reading of the manuscript and their cogent comments.

ARGEADAI MAKEDONES KING LIST

Argeadai Dynasty

Kharanos
Koinos, son of Kharanos
Khurimasos, son of Koinos

Temenidai Dynasty to 358 BC

Perdikkas I
Argaios, son of Perdikkas I
Philippos I, son of Argaios
Aeropos I, son of Philippos I
Menelaos, son of Philippos, regent for Alketas
Alketas, son of Aeropos I
Amuntas I, son of Alketas
Alexandros I, son of Amuntas I
Perdikkas II, son of Alexandros I
(Philippos, son of Alexandros I, pretender)
(Alketas, son of Alexandros I, pretender)
(Alexandros, son of Alketas, pretender)
Arkhelaos, son of Perdikkas II
Aeropos II, son of Perdikkas II, regent for Orestes, then king
Orestes, son of Arkhelaos
Amuntas II, son of Perdikkas II
(Pausanias, son of Aeropos II, pretender)
Amuntas III, son of Aridaios
(Argaios, son of Saturos, pretender)
Alexandros II, son of Amuntas III
Ptolemaios, son of Amuntas of Orestis, regent for Perdikkas III
Perdikkas III, son of Amuntas III
Philippos II, son of Amuntas III, regent for Amuntas IV
Amuntas IV, son of Perdikkas III
(Argaios, son of Saturos, pretender)
(Arkhelaos, son of Amuntas III, pretender)
(Pausanias, son of Pausanias, pretender)
Philippos II, son of Amuntas III

TEMENIDAI DYNASTY OF THE ARGEADAI MAKEDONES:

From Alexandros the First to Philippos the Second

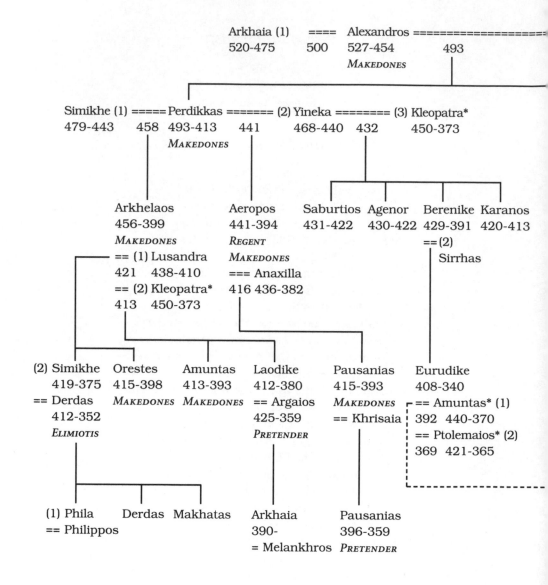

Arkhaia (1) ==== Alexandros =====================
520-475   500   527-454   493
                   MAKEDONES

Simikhe (1) =====Perdikkas ======= (2) Yineka ======== (3) Kleopatra*
479-443   458 493-413   441   468-440 432   450-373
            MAKEDONES

Arkhelaos   Aeropos   Saburtios Agenor   Berenike Karanos
456-399   441-394   431-422   430-422 429-391 420-413
MAKEDONES   *REGENT*   ==(2)
== (1) Lusandra   *MAKEDONES*   Sirrhas
421   438-410   === Anaxilla
== (2) Kleopatra* 416 436-382
413   450-373

(2) Simikhe Orestes   Amuntas   Laodike   Pausanias   Eurudike
419-375   415-398   413-393   412-380   415-393   408-340
== Derdas   *MAKEDONES* *MAKEDONES* == Argaios *MAKEDONES* == Amuntas* (1)
412-352   425-359   == Khrisaia 392 440-370
ELIMIOTIS   *PRETENDER*   == Ptolemaios* (2)
                                                               369 421-365

(1) Phila   Derdas Makhatas   Arkhaia   Pausanias
== Philippos   390-   396-359
                                 = Melankhros *PRETENDER*

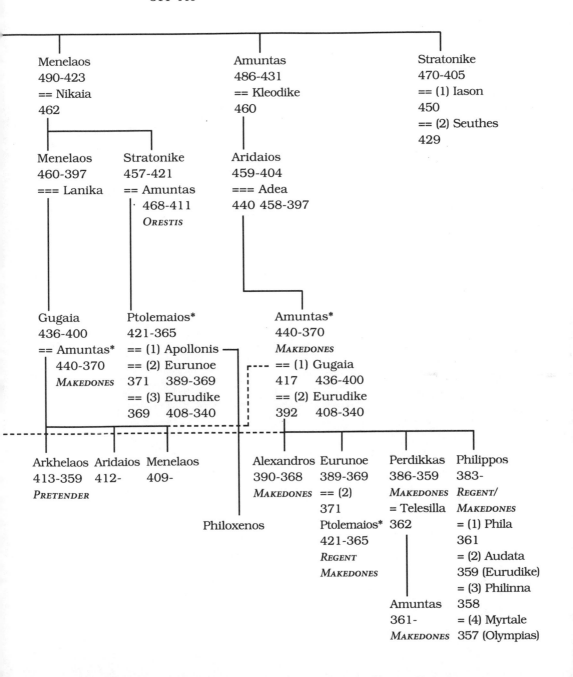

==================== (2) Andromeda
                          511-440

Menelaos   Amuntas   Stratonike
490-423   486-431   470-405
== Nikaia   == Kleodike   == (1) Iason
462   460   450
                                                == (2) Seuthes
                                                 429

Menelaos   Stratonike   Aridaios
460-397   457-421   459-404
=== Lanika == Amuntas   === Adea
            · 468-411   440 458-397
              ORESTIS

Gugaia   Ptolemaios*   Amuntas*
436-400   421-365   440-370
== Amuntas* == (1) Apollonis   MAKEDONES
 440-370   == (2) Eurunoe   ┌--- == (1) Gugaia
 MAKEDONES 371   389-369   ┆   417   436-400
            == (3) Eurudike   ┆   == (2) Eurudike
            369   408-340   ┆   392   408-340

Arkhelaos Aridaios Menelaos   Alexandros Eurunoe Perdikkas Philippos
413-359   412-   409-   390-368   389-369 386-359   383-
PRETENDER   MAKEDONES == (2)   MAKEDONES REGENT/
                                          371   = Telesilla MAKEDONES
                    Philoxenos Ptolemaios* 362   = (1) Phila
                                421-365   361
                                REGENT   = (2) Audata
                                MAKEDONES   359 (Eurudike)
                                                              = (3) Philinna
                                          Amuntas   358
                                          361-   = (4) Myrtale
                                          MAKEDONES   357 (Olympias)

PART ONE

Of the Temenidai Blood
383 - 370 B.C.

CHAPTER ONE

Fourth Child

383 B.C.

α

She lifts a hand to wave off the swarm of gnats, as the cart plods along the dry rocky path. Marnike, seeing her wave as a summons, rushes over the stones to her side, "Madam, is there something I can get for you?"

"No, no, Marnike, unless you can shorten this ride, get this incubus baby out of my belly, or..." but Eurudike's voice trails wearily. "No, Marnike, there is nothing I need."

The cart jerks as the mules pull it forward across a seam of rock. "Maman, maman, are we there?" The voice of a six-year old girl calls from inside the cart.

"Shush, Eurunoe, don't wake your brother. You must nap a while longer." Though how she can nap under the still heat of the cart's canopy is beyond Eurudike.

Beside Eurudike, the driver shifts, spits to the side of the road, "Your pardon, Madam, but while we're moving slow, we are moving steady. We should make the city before nightfall. And we'll be stopping at the wood-men's village when the sun is at zenith."

Eurudike knows her present condition is temporary. After four months away in Larissa, she should be pleased at the return to Aigai. But she feels anger. This is not the return for which she longs. Rather than trudging back to ancient Aigai, she would have them all marching on Pella to regain the whole of their lands.

How can anyone be angry for two long years? But she is. Two years in which they have held only the rump of their kingdom, while others have despoiled their wealth. Two years of hearing condolences, excuses, patronage from official friends—like the Aleuadai of Larissa, that rich, large ruling clan, the proudest of the Thessaliotes, yet unable to offer more than sympathy. Two years of plotting revenge on Argaios or, more importantly, since he is a mere puppet, on the Olunthians.

3

And when they reach Aigai, the sight of her husband, the king, won't assuage her anger. True, she will learn the extent to which his separate mission to Epeiros has succeeded, and his latest letter claims much, yet he is ever optimistic. In her view, he will remain who he is, the fumbler who lost them their throne.

When she was young, and her father gave her to Amuntas to seal the alliance between the highlands and the lowlands, her expectations had been grand. She knew she would face the scorn the lowlanders feel towards the highlanders, especially for those highlanders whose lands march to the borders of the Illurian tribes. But wasn't her blood from the royal houses of Lunkestis and Orestis? What were these Temenidai, for all their pretensions, but latecomers from the far south to the Argeadai clan of the Makedones? And are not the highlanders true Hellenes? True to the ethos of an older time?

Yes, high expectations. Though she was young, barely of an age to marry, and Amuntas, even then, was past his prime, still he was the new king. And she was the wife of his kingship, the queen. Her children would rule. Not his first family, despite their pure Temenidai blood. Those great dullards, having too many cousins as ancestors.

Eurudike smiles wryly at her reveries, tries to imagine that eager girl she had been. To be honest, she despises the bitterness in which she dwells. She had been a happy child. She longs to feel meaning for herself more than being simply a vessel for her male children.

The baby moves within her, perhaps pricked by her thoughts. *So you're a manchild, too,* Eurudike thinks. Three children already, and now a fourth. Well, this will be the last. The image of Amuntas' lined, sagging, hairy body comes to mind. Yes, the last. He doesn't have it in him to father more, not like that bestial Bardulis in his mountain lair, still fathering warriors even though the Illurian was an aged man, older even than Amuntas.

Tiny fists pummel inside her, and she gasps. Marnike, trudging beside the cart, reaches up a hand to steady her, "If not today, then tomorrow, I think this child will come."

Silently she agrees with Marnike. The baby has dropped, ready now to push its way free of her. Well, she will be glad to be free of him, even if it means pain. Isn't pain of some kind always part of being alive?

The baby becomes quiet after its shifting, and Eurudike returns to her memories. Amuntas always maneuvering, trying to hang onto his throne, needing some outside power to prop him up, to hold the kingship around which all the wolves circle. Now it is the Spartans he courts, the revulsion flowing within Eurudike. Spartans to counter the treacherous Olunthians. Before the Olunthians he had sought support from the Athenians. And it had been the Thessaliotes who had rescued them in their first year from the depredations of Bardulis and his tribesmen. Always someone to help.

4

This need is because he is no more than the first among equals within his own lands. All the lowland chiefs quarrel incessantly. What leadership can you expect from a family that kills its own brothers, nephews, cousins? Still, Amuntas is a survivor; one of the least branch of the Temenidai, yet king late in life even if he must wrestle with distant cousins.

A memory of Amuntas laughing and proud at the birth of their first son, Alexandros, comes to mind. Laughing, head thrown back, bristly beard jutting, his favorite horn mug with its mouth of gold raised high, "Madam, madam, you do me honor. We will secure our children in these lands down through time." A vain boast he had made. But even in her bitterness, that phrase from her husband the king, "Madam, madam, you do me honor..." has the power to please her.

Up ahead a rider comes slogging back down the pathway, past the struggling column of carts, peasant spearmen, and retainers. She can see the rider is not from the column but is one of her own people from Aigai. As the rider comes closer, she realizes it is Ptolemaios, and her interest quickens. He has seen her party and urges his mount forward.

"Queen Eurudike, the king has asked me to see to your welfare."

"Ho, cousin, you come alone. Is it your sword that is to see to my comfort or is your command more sweeping than mine?"

Ptolemaios laughs, "Neither, dear lady. I am only the token of the king's good earnest, and could not for myself think of anything more pleasant than to see to your care."

"I fear you spent too much time in Athenai learning to compliment women."

"I assure you, cousin, that the men of the south think of good women only in terms of bloodlines."

Thinking it little different in the north, Eurudike responds, "And what do they think of bad women?"

"If accomplished, as charming companions; if not accomplished, then they don't think about them at all."

Ptolemaios' good humor refreshes Eurudike, making her feel both queen and woman despite her stomach's gravid girth. Yet why good humor, knowing how much he, like her, resents this near exile? "So, how do you propose to help our journey along?"

Ptolemaios waves in the direction of Aigai, and Eurudike sees his servant coming leading fresh horses. "If your maid assists you, I thought we might mount you on that gentle mare. I have food and drink awaiting at the village which is just beyond the bend, down the hill and out of these trees. From there, we can make Aigai earlier than this cart."

"Perhaps you are god sent, Ptolemaios." Turning to her woman, Eurudike says, "Marnike, tell Kleipha to come up and stay with Eurunoe and Perdikkas. Then you help me ride with Lord Ptolemaios."

β

"I tell you, Amuntas, these Spartans will make harsh taskmasters," Derdas mutters.

"Derdas, you are young," the king smiles easily, nodding in the direction of the porch, where Eudamidas, the Spartan commander, is in council with his officers, "they are powerful now, and will do to break the Olunthians for us. You know what they have done in Epeiros. Alketas is driven out. Yet they do not understand the north; do not understand what makes the Epeiriote king an ally of Athenai. In time, Alketas or another of his family will regain his throne and rule Epeiros. So, in time, we will regain Pella, riding on Spartan backs. Yet they will not remain command in strength in the north, and in due course we prevail because we are the north."

"I would still feel better if Medeios had been able to lend his family's strength."

"The Aleuadai must face their neighbors in south Thessalos. They have enough on their hands. Before long you will hear them pleading for our help against their cousins." Amuntas smiles again, thinking of the pleasure it will be to aid Medeios of Larissa, both to repay the kindness of the past and to possess the strength to help friends. "So long as you and I stand together, Elimiote and Makedone, we will outlast our enemies."

Eudamidas abruptly dismisses his men. "Set a smile on your face, Derdas, we must again pay court to the might of the south," says Amuntas.

The Spartan commander comes striding across the large reception room, his boots rapping their progress on the floor's mosaic. "My officers tell me that inadequate ground has been allotted for our encampment."

"Our apologies, Eudamidas. Let me have one of my companions arrange that your force stay on the grounds of Herakles' temple. I fear we have been too casual for you," Amuntas suggests brightly.

"Wherever, so long as the ground is well drained yet clear water is within easy reach."

"Certainly. That is what recommends the temple. You will experience some strong winds at times, but in this warmer weather your men will find it refreshing."

Eudamidas nods, "So it may be." He turns to Derdas, "You have riders out scouting as I directed?"

"Yes, my own people. I have also sent a body of mercenary foot to the crossing at the lower Haliakmon. They might as well earn their keep."

"Good," a tight smile crosses Eudamidas' face, "We could use a stronger force. We can't expect our main body this year."

"I'm sure they could be here this year if you Spartans didn't feel required to overawe the Boiotians," comments Amuntas.

Eudamidas grimaces, "We've been through that. We are enough for what we intend now. You doubt that you will regain Pella this year?"

"Please don't think my observation a criticism, commander." Amuntas smiles readily, "For my part, I can no more stop speculating than water can stop flowing downhill." Yet Amuntas knows that the Spartan is thinking who is Amuntas to complain or, even, scheme. Given how useless the Makedones are at war, with their heedless gentry horsemen and their cloddish cowardly peasant foot. Spartan valor, discipline and arms give Sparta the right to decide fates and command others. "I realize the advantages you bestow by assisting us to regain what is ours. And the advantages you also gain by preventing Olunthos and its allies from becoming overmighty."

"As the first state of the Hellenes, we have a responsibility to assure stability," responds Eudamidas.

"Certainly, commander. And a stable north gives no leverage to Athenai while offering Sparta a safe road to Persia," smoothly agrees Amuntas. *How little the Spartans understand the north*, thinks Amuntas.

Derdas, restless with these trite niceties, interjects, "I will rejoin my troops tonight. You can count on the weight of my horse to screen the army. In two days, I will want to cross the Haliakmon to secure new grazing. That will also put more pressure on Olunthos."

"Excellent. We will be able to follow you once Amuntas' foot and his queen have arrived." Eudamidas is pleased.

"Derdas, you will stay long enough to greet Eurudike?" asks Amuntas.

Derdas laughs, knowing how nervous Amuntas is over the smoldering Eurudike. "Cousin, I am at your side through whatever food you serve to feast your companions, but then I depart."

Feeling relief, Amuntas is again struck by how much he relies on Derdas. How strange are ways of the gods, who determine where friendship will rest. Derdas is a contrast to Amuntas—for the Elimiote king is intense, dark, brooding, easy to anger. Physically, Derdas is short, bright eyed, full of energy, and at age 29 almost thirty years the junior of Amuntas. Ten years ago, Derdas killed the then king of the Makedones in answer to an insult. In so doing, he made way for Amuntas. They have stood by each other ever since.

A clatter of sandals follows the pattering of bare feet in the corridor. In a moment, the boy, Alexandros, rushes in followed by his panting tutor. "Ho, father, the column is in sight and mother is in the lead with Lord Ptolemaios."

γ

Kleopatra watches from the recesses of the stairwell. Torches light the feasting room where Amuntas offers to his guests boar haunch, pigeon, roast deer, and lamb with the breads, cheeses and fruits of his lands, all awash with wine and ale. Amuntas himself is roaring with laughter, as the clan leader Iolaos leads the group in a bawdy lowland song.

Contradictory emotions move in Kleopatra. Satisfaction that the servants are efficient, for they are under her hand. Mild derision at the foibles of men in drink. Pleasure that Amuntas is again in Aigai. Resignation that Eurudike will again assert her own management of the household. Certainty that Amuntas must be told that his wife is in labor. Yet none of these emotions are for others to see or know. For Kleopatra, it is enough if those who are not Temenidai feel awe for her and that those who are Temenidai feel either reverence or dread.

Was she not the wife of the last two strong kings of the Makedones—father and son? And her own boy, son from the second marriage, briefly enthroned only to die. Yet she made certain her granddaughter was given to Amuntas, even as he sheltered Derdas, her son's killer. Her boy, really a fool, so young, arrogant, certain of himself and his authority as king—as if kingship alone created authority when, if truth be known, a king must expend great effort to gain and hold authority or he won't be king for long. Yes, she knows what kingship is. Thus, Amuntas needs her, as she needs a king.

Still she watches, not ready to interrupt. Amuntas is doing one of the things required of a king. He is charming the powerful into obedience. However much Eurudike writhes in producing this child, it is only a fourth child. If a girl, then a coin for alliance. If a boy, he is a long way from the throne and, possibly, trouble for the successor, as her first husband's brothers were for him. She admires Amuntas, though he probably doesn't know it. Others, like Eudamidas the Spartan or her granddaughter, Eurudike, may feel contempt for Amuntas, but Kleopatra knows that Amuntas will hold the throne as long as he has life. Beneath that bulk, that gray, that smile—he is tenacious and guileful. He will ride the wild horse that is the Makedones. If thrown, he simply remounts.

The long song is over. Amuntas, beaming, yelling obscenities, is bringing Iolaos two mugs abrim with red wine. *That's right*, thinks Kleopatra, *bind Iolaos to you.* His family has been a pillar for the Temenidai since the first when the three brothers came down from the mountains. Iolaos, who tries to knock some skill and bravery into those crowds of peasants you summoned; Iolaos, whom you need to secure your rule.

Kleopatra steps forward. On seeing her, the men quiet, like sheep under the shepherd's gaze. Ptolemaios points Amuntas in Kleopatra's direction. "Lady Kleopatra, what news?" shouts Amuntas.

"Queen Eurudike's labor has begun, my king."

Immediately, Ptolemaios, Derdas, Iolaos and the others raise a cry, "King Amuntas, may Zeus protect you and your own; may the child of your loins be born strong and with the favor of all the gods." Those without cups in hand quickly grab up theirs and in near unison the northerners in the hall down their drinks, then scream a piercing war cry. Eudamidas and his officers, not to be outdone by a barbarous libation, declare their own praise of the father and his child—but in the refined phrases of southern Hellenes. Laughter, jokes heavy with sexual humor, soon wash through the room.

Throughout, Kleopatra stands regally, waiting. Slim, erect in posture, tall for a woman, hair piled high in silver abundance, she is an arbiter of behavior.

Amuntas breaks away from the group of couches and its crowd of men. He is drunk but not far gone. "Well, Kleo," he says softly, familiarly, "how does my lady bear up?"

"Eurudike will bear this child as well as the first three," dryly replies Kleopatra. "You may want to visit your children and let them know your concern."

"Yes, she is a good bearer of children. Yet Gugaia died hard trying to give birth to our fourth child," Amuntas reminds Kleopatra of his first wife. Those words leave much unsaid. Three boys of that first union, estranged from their father. Not any father, but a king. Not boys any longer, but men. Men who gave covert support to their father's rival, Argaios. A fact that Amuntas has chosen to ignore, though the sons have been secretly warned to be gone from Pella, back to their rural estates, before their father arrives with his Spartan allies. Amuntas' words usher to mind the contrast of his two families.

"Eurudike is not Gugaia," asserts Kleopatra. "She is a tough mountain woman for all that she is queen and lives in the lowlands. Come, leave your drinking companions. Find your children. Be ready to see your wife when her ordeal is done."

δ

"Kleipha, Kleipha, bring more hot water. Hurry, girl, hurry," Marnike calls impatiently to soothe her own misgivings. Eurudike is at a crest of hurt, loosing inarticulate exclamations of feeling. Then, the trough beyond the crest, a moment to gasp air, and the pain starts rising again.

"You're doing well, dear lady, doing well," croons the midwife, "the baby is coming, not much longer, push now lady, push, that's it, harder now, push."

Marnike joins the chant, her mouth by Eurudike's ear, "Push, push, you're almost there, push." A wild hand of Eurudike's is grabbed and squeezed, held, while the queen's moaning climbs. Push is the pulse beat of pain.

Then the baby is in the midwife's hands, red, seeming wizened, slimy. The cord is cut. An angry, furious cry proves the baby's health. Though Eurudike takes little notice, as her body pushes out the after-birth.

"You have a boy, dear lady," coos the midwife. The women in the room raise the cry of a manchild. The goddess Hera is invoked, as is the kindness

9

of the Moirai. The midwife sprinkles herbs in a cup as Kleipha pours the steaming water. The cup is given to Eurudike's lips. Other herbs and water are mixed to begin sponging mother and child.

Eurudike lies aching, her genitals, hips, legs numb in parts and in parts throbbing, but all distant now. Sweat cools. She is tired, ready to rest. But a part of her mind is still active. She had known, a boy, another boy. Three boys of hers to secure the throne in her line.

A small wet mouth is put to her swollen breast. The sudden touch creates happiness, relief. No longer queen, she is mother.

ε

Amuntas sits on the floor of his daughter's room. Alexandros and Eurunoe sit on the day bed facing their father. All are dressed in white wool chitons. They are waiting for the nurse to finish dressing Perdikkas. They are also waiting for Kleopatra to summon them.

"What name will you give the baby?" asks Eurunoe.

"Well, if the baby is a girl I thought Adea after my mother or Berenike after your mother's mother. If a boy, then Philippos."

"Why Philippos, father?" asks Alexandros.

"Do you remember the history of our family?"

"Yes," says Alexandros, though there is doubt in his voice, "Wasn't Philippos the enemy of King Perdikkas the Second?"

"That Philippos was both brother and enemy to Perdikkas. And brother to my grandfather. But I am speaking of an earlier Philippos. The kings of old were from Perdikkas the First to Argaios to Philippos to Aeropos to Alketas through the regency of Menelaos to Amuntas the First to Alexandros—your namesake and a great king—to Perdikkas the Second to Arkhelaos to the time of troubles and pretenders to now, my reign." Amuntas pauses, smiles, proud of being king, proud to be of this bloodline of kings. "That earlier Philippos is the one whom I would honor. Let me tell you a story of his time."

"In those days, we ruled the regions of Pieris and Emathis from here, holy Aigai near the Haliakmon river. The same lands that have stood by us while Argaios pretends to be king in Pella. When Philippos ruled, it was before we defeated the Eordi. Our firm allies then, as now, were our cousins, the Elimiotoi. And, in those days, we could count on the other cousins, the Lunkestoi and Orestoi, your mother's people, for then, of course, we were all more closely related."

"A people named the Almopes lived in the basin of the Upper Astraios River, bordering Emathis. There had been many disputes over grazing, hunting, feuds and rapes. As always, we Makedones were growing, thriving, while the Almopes were an ancient, barbarous people still clinging to dying gods. The disputes gave rise to war. Philippos led our people against the Almopes. He cleared the basin, forcing the surviving Almopes to disperse. A part of these people climbed the mountains of Barnous and, reaching the other side, were welcomed by an Illuroi tribe."

"The Illuroi, learning from these fugitive Almopes of the wealth of the Makedones, made common cause. A combination of Illuroi kings and a prince of the Almopes led countless warriors into the Astraios basin. Philippos had returned here, to Aigai, to lead the purification ceremonies. A general named Kallias was overseeing our new settlements when the wild tribesmen swept into those lands. Many of our people died. Kallias rallied our fighters and held the valley mouth long enough for many to escape, but then was overwhelmed."

"The Illuroi entered Emathis for the first time since we had joined Pieris and Emathis into our kingdom. Panic reigned. Many fled. King Philippos sent word to our cousins for aid but did not wait. He rode forth, with his infant son, leading a small band of companions. As he rode, he held up his baby boy Aeropos to be seen by all the fleeing bands of country folk. With each passing *stade* as each group of refugees was met, they, seeing their king with his infant prince, stopped running. Men, women, boys, and, yes, even girls, turned, stripping limbs from trees, picking stones from creek beds, they followed their king."

"Soon they were a host, angry, righteous, determined. Near Mieza, they found the Illuroi and Almopes. And with the sight of the enemy, the day, which had been gray, rainy, saw the clouds part, letting the sun of the Makedones pour down, blinding our enemies. Philippos and our people did not hesitate. Though the Illuroi are terrors as fighters, berserk in their glorying of Ares, that day Herakles joined his children, the Makedones, and we slaughtered the heartless raiders, pursuing them to the very banks of the Astresos."

"And so Philippos regained all that was lost. And the people had a new pride and sense of being favored by the gods. For the remainder of his days, Philippos ruled wisely over a peaceful land."

Kleopatra, standing at the door, claps her hands in praise. Having the attention of the trio, she says, "My king, your queen is ready to receive you. I have Perdikkas waiting for you as well."

They follow Kleopatra and her servant, who is holding a torch, down the corridor. At the door to the next room, the sleepy three-year old Perdikkas, in the firm hand of his nurse, Toli, joins their procession.

Together they reach the birthing room where all is now placid. The women of the household have dispersed, their duties and ceremonies over. Amuntas enters the dim lit room. His wife is tired but alert, lying on the couch, the infant asleep beside her. Marnike sits on the floor next to the bed, smiling. "Ho, little mother, you are well?" asks Amuntas. Seeing Eurudike nodding, he adds, "So, have you given us a boy as you expected?"

"Yes, Amuntas, you are a begetter of men," even now there is an edge to Eurudike's response, for the compliment references his first family as well as the royal family.

The children crowd in. Perdikkas is least inhibited and quickly touches the infant, "Ma, me not the baby any more; now me have a baby." The claim is greeted with laughter from all.

ζ

Marnike sits carding wool in preparation for spinning. Eurudike lies quiet on the day bed, thankful she had ordered it brought out to the porch so she could feel the breeze. Beside her, tucked into a cradle, the baby Philippos sleeps. Distantly, they can hear young Kleipha playing hide-and-seek with Eurunoe and Perdikkas. But this scene of domestic lassitude is a facade, for within Eurudike feels turmoil.

She relives in her mind the departure of Amuntas. There stands her husband, big, bluff, hearty with the assurance that Pella will be his within days. The Spartan, Eudamidas, is mounted, looking down on Amuntas with that air of an eagle disdainful of a crow. Yet it is Ptolemaios, lifting her son Alexandros easily into the saddle of his mount, who seems the brightest, clearest. It is this realization that makes her tense: that if any one of them should die in the coming attack, she does not want it to be Ptolemaios.

Ptolemaios of Aloros. Whom she has known since she was a child. Ptolemaios, her cousin. Why him?

Has she ever known Ptolemaios not to be right? Not to do what needs doing? Not to be certain of himself? Not to be able to command others or, if junior in rank, not to lead by example?

Eurudike thinks back over the years. When she was twelve, her uncle had come visiting with his family. At the evening meal, the betrothal of Ptolemaios to Apollonis was formally announced. The men talked of Apollonis' dowry; how well her lands in Orestis matched the lands held by Ptolemaios. In addition to lands already granted in Orestis, Uncle took that moment to grant Ptolemaios his great estate in Aloros. Wealthy through his father, wealthy again through his wife's dowry, handsome through the grace of the gods, with the blood of the Temenidai in his veins through his mother, he could easily have been a distant, haughty prince. Yet to her, he was attentive, finding as much pleasure in their conversation as in the conversations of his peers and seniors.

Eurudike's father, Sirrhas, was a prince, warrior and hunter of high renown, so his regard for Ptolemaios, both as nephew and as a man, spoke well for Ptolemaios' future. The day after the marriage announcement, before the men departed to hunt, Ptolemaios asked her to display her riding skills. Skills in which she trained for her indulgent father. Despite her anxiety at performing before the men, especially Ptolemaios and her father, she still controlled her horse exquisitely, putting the animal through intricate steps then racing over hurdles as if she, too, were a hunter and warrior. Their praise had warmed her, for her childhood was not long in praise. Ptolemaios had helped her dismount, holding her hand firmly as if she were to be his bride.

Now, in her late twenties, married herself, she believes there is a connection between the two of them that goes beyond kinship. Perhaps the warmth of her feelings is no more than sympathy, for Ptolemaios is recently a widower. Only one child survives his marriage to Apollonis, an eleven year-old boy named Philoxenos. She has no strong impression of the boy.

Perhaps Apollonis had too little northern blood and too much of her mother's people. The mother, a southern Hellene whose father had played court to old King Alexandros. Perhaps that explains the early deaths of all but one of Ptolemaios' children.

"Madam, will you want to dye this lot red?" Marnike interrupts her reverie.

"Yes, if we use the alkanet roots that came from Miletos it will give us a brighter red than the madder."

Marnike nods, "There is enough of this fine wool for several garments. Are you thinking of clothes for the children?"

"Well, no. Perhaps a matching chiton and himation for the festival of Dionysios."

"All red?"

"Accented with black piping and tassels. For the fibula, my heavy gold pin that has the enameling of a raven."

Marnike mutters something softly disapproving to herself, and settles back into the rhythm of her work.

Smiling inwardly at Marnike's doubts, Eurudike is again struck by how few want to think beyond tradition. Perhaps it's that the passage of days seems unchanging and unending to them. For herself, she sees ceaseless change. Rarely dramatic, but constant. A philosopher might argue that she catches only the surface of things and that behind the surface are principles of trueness that never vary. Well, she lives in the world of men. Men and gods. Their living, struggling, dying are her concern. What exists beyond death or beneath the surface of life she will learn in time. She will leave that until then.

Beside her, the baby stirs. She hopes he will not wake for he seems greedy for her milk. She touches a finger to the swollen nipple beneath the fabric of her robe. Tender but not sore. Within an hour or two her breasts will want that hungry little mouth.

She is glad that he is the last child. She can see an end to the constant demand of children, to the drag of them upon her skirts, upon herself. There is wonder in how they grow. Aleko now off with his father to wars and not yet eight years old. Aleko who is so solemn and big eyed. Eurunoe with her wavering cries, her shyness, her desire to hide. Perdikkas who is into everything, whose chubby legs are always in motion from the moment he wakes until he collapses in sleep. Perdikkas the impetuous—how she loves the boy. If she had been a boy she would have been Perdikkas.

Now this one. She looks at the baby, restless in his sleep. *Who will you be, Philippos?* Like Perdikkas, he seems active, alert. With only a few days out of the womb, who knows who he will be—if he will even survive the wilderness of childhood ills. Well, with Aleko and Perdix in front of him, he will be no more than a princeling if he proves himself useful and an exile somewhere if he isn't.

CHAPTER TWO

Kleopatra's Stories
375 B.C.

α

Philippos is running downhill as fast as his legs will carry him. His brothers and their companions are pulling further ahead, their longer legs giving them the advantage. He keeps his short spear held high to avoid entangling it in the tall grasses and low bushes. He leaps a water runnel and nearly falls but balances and keeps to his downhill rush. At the bottom of the hill his father and the other men yell encouragement to the racers. Philippos realizes that Alexandros has the lead but it's shortening as the clot of runners pursue the tiring prince. He doesn't see Perdix, though his brother must be somewhere in the pack of older boys. Grimly Philippos slows to a stride he can sustain rather than a breakneck speed that will wind him long before he reaches his father and the warriors.

He concentrates on his footing, on keeping an even step, on breathing regularly. He concentrates on using the lessons his athletic instructor has taught. He picks up his pace again as the rhythm of his run takes over from the exhilaration of that first reckless burst. His mind seems to float. The spear, which had become heavy, is now light again.

He is aware of the moisture that glistens his body. He feels the stretch and pull of leg muscles. His mind has time to see an ant hill and to note, in passing, the clarity of his vision in picking out the busy creatures. He is motion itself, yet alert to the uneven ground.

Not until he overtakes the first of the older boys is he again conscious of the race. Now he is among the laggards, those who had stumbled and fallen or who winded themselves too early. The emotion flooding him now as he runs is an elation, for he is the youngest, the smallest.

When he reaches the end he arrives among sprawled red-faced boys, some walking unsteadily as their legs react to the run. Alexandros is drenched with wine, having come through to win the race. Yells and cheers reach Philippos as he slows to a walk. Among the confusion of the racers are their fathers, uncles, older brothers, cousins. Each praising or criticizing or jesting with some fatigued runner. Amuntas, his father, stands by Aleko and Perdix, beaming at their performance, calling to retainers to bring fresh clothes.

At fifteen, Aleko is tall and slender. One of the royal pages. Perdix, four years younger, is heavier of body for his size. They are talking with keen gestures and high voices, obviously retelling the race. A surge of affection sweeps Philippos as he looks at his kinsmen. He is glad Aleko won, only momentarily wondering if some of the runners allowed the crown prince his victory.

Looking over his shoulder, back up the long field, he is surprised by the litter of spears. The realization strikes him that he is the only one to arrive at the bottom with his spear, still unwinded, still ready to hunt or fight.

"Ho, Philpa, here boy." His father sees him, calls Philippos to him. Perdix waves wildly, happy at being accepted among the older boys and men. Philippos shoulders his spear, pleased with himself, pleased with the sunny day, pleased to be part of his family.

β

"Take your time, master, and listen well." Philippos' man, Skaros the Thraikiote, holds up his hand, head cocked to one side, "Hear the hounds carefully and you can pick out their individual voices."

Philippos listens to the distant baying of the dogs in full chase.

The servant observes, "There is Khlippa. Now, Laevi. She has that clear bell voice."

From among the many baying voices, Philippos can now pick out the deep boom of Khlippa and the higher clear note of Laevi. "But what does it mean? Where are they going? What are they chasing? Can the horsemen be up with them?"

Skaros waves toward the northwest, "There. They are out of Deep Valley, on the ridge leading toward Apollo's shrine. Your father and the others should be gaining on the hounds again. As to their chase, well, they were after foxes tonight but I think it's something bigger they're chasing now. A fox would have led them tighter. This must be a boar or wolf—or a man."

"A man?"

"Mayhap. Whatever, it's bigger than a fox and not so artful."

The two listen hard. Philippos' sense of grievance at being left out of the hunt is lost in the wonder of reading distant events from the sound of the dogs.

As the wind shifts, carrying away the voice of the hunt, Skaros rises, stretches, picks up a stick and stirs the fire. Further back, at the encampment in the dell, other followers are preparing the meal that will welcome the tired riders. Their conversations rise with the new wind as a soft accompaniment to swaying trees and the high moon.

"Skaros, before you were captured, when you were young, did you hunt often?" The boy's question is not wholly idle.

"Aye, in that time and place I was a promising hunter. I still have more forest sense than most, and then I was keener. The hunt is almost as good as war."

"What do you mean?"

"A hunt calls for endurance, stealth, skill at arms, and, at times, prowess. Those are the same virtues called upon by war. But these virtues are heightened in war by the greater danger and sacrifices. When you kill an animal, you feast. When you kill a man, you exult."

The boy nods, thinks about what Skaros is saying, and considers if the sentiment is purely Thraikiote or in keeping with the beliefs of the Makedones and the Hellenes. "How did you know when to go to war? If war is better than hunting, why not war always?"

Now it is Skaros who considers. He is concerned not only to represent his past truly, but to frame a response that will please his master. No matter how young the master, it is important to please him. And the Questioner, as many in the household refer to Philippos, is not pleased by flattery but by what is true. "The shepherd of our people, our chieftain, called out a war. Though he would consult with the other grandfathers, unless war was obvious from an enemy's attack. Sometimes war came to avenge an insult or to remind our neighbors that they should not trifle with us. Those wars were simple affairs, fun, though some died, of course."

Skaros sits back, remembering. "There are other wars, though, desperate wars, and not glorious. Those are the wars that come from famine or when suddenly some people, traveling in multitudes, driven from somewhere else, enter your lands. Then more than warriors die. Then there is no generosity to a foe. Then you fight to placate the gods, to secure your kinsmen, to assure that your son or even just a daughter survive."

"So, is war better than hunting?"

"In some ways they are alike. You hunt for food, especially in the fall so there is meat through winter. Or you hunt to keep predators off of your goats or other herd beasts. That is more like war against men. Keeping predators away." Skaros stirs the fire again. "What is apparent, though, is that men fight back in ways the wiliest animal predators cannot achieve. No animal is as cruel, as persistent, as unrelenting as a man."

"So when you kill a man, you kill the mightiest of foes?"

"Yes. Though killing men—or women and children—is unpredictable. The gods cause some to accept their fate and offer their throats meekly. Others will not stop striving even while their lifeblood empties from them."

The two are silent for a time until Skaros picks up the thread of his musings, "When I was captured, we were raiding into the Paiaones. No doubt we were the predators then. But the Paiaones would encroach on the lands of my tribe. Anyway, I took an arrow in my leg." He runs a finger along the scar. "There was a boy of the Paiaones about your age. Maybe a year or two older. He walked among our wounded dispatching each with his mattock. I could see him coming closer and tried fervently to crawl into the brush to hide. For me, he was not a boy, he was Kharon the Ferryman."

"You were afraid."

The old man laughs, "Afraid? I have seldom been more frightened in my life. Men laugh at cowards, but there are times when fear is your best friend. I have never fought without fear. Fear has kept me alive, kept me struggling and awake to all around me. Fear is a friend so long as you do not let it be your master." Skaros stills immediately, feeling he is saying too much.

"My athletic instructor says much the same. As does the philosopher assigned as my tutor. They both speak of being master of yourself. The first to get the best from your body, the second to get the best from your mind." The boy chuckles softly, "Of course, they dislike each other and would be amazed to think they teach the same moral."

Again the wind shifts, and the baying of the dogs is heard. Both sit up and listen intently. A smile of satisfaction graces Skaros, "They are almost on their prey. Hear their excitement."

Listening, straining to hear, the two are silent. Distantly, a high yelping reaches them. Whatever is chased is now being killed.

Skaros sighs, "The huntsmen will be back before dawn."

"I'm hungry now." The boy quiets Skaros' reaction, "No, Skaros, I will wait. At least I can share hunger with the hunters. You know you did not say what happened to the boy, when you were captured?"

"In crawling, I reached the body of a dead bowman. His quiver still had arrows. My intention was to kill the boy. Instead the Paiaones returned from their pursuit at that point. Their chieftain saw what the boy had done and berated him loudly for behaving like a woman and spoiling likely slaves."

"And is slavery better than death?" Philippos asks deliberately.

"For me life is better than death. Being a slave does not change who I am, only the condition in which I live. But I was lucky. Instead of being sold south to the Hellenes, I came to the Makedones to work in the fields of an old couple. Since you Makedones don't truly abide slavery like the Hellenes, I became more son than servant. After they died, I was taken on to serve the young king Orestes. The king who died so young. Lady Kleopatra saw to it that I joined Amuntas' house since I had caused the Regent Aeropos to dislike me. With Aeropos king at Orestes' death, it was best if I was out of his sight."

Without thinking, Philippos reaches across to touch Skaros. The first time he has ever touched this man on purpose. "And now you serve me," he asserts.

"Yes, master," Skaros answers.

Then Philippos laughs in full mirth, and Skaros finds himself joining in the laughter. They sit by the fire together laughing at the humor of the fates that twine an eight-year old to the life of a fifty-year old retainer. Affection for Skaros floods Philippos. This man is truly his tutor, not Agemilaos, that dry spouter of Homeric tales his father hired.

γ

After days in the hills hunting, being back home seems almost unreal. Suffocating. All the routine of the palace, of the women, is around them again. The court is astir. More than is common.

Philippos knows that his father is preparing to receive a delegation from Athenai. The war against Olunthos ended four years earlier. The cost to Lakonia—to the Spartans—was dear, and included one of their two kings. Since then Sparte is less interested in the North. Now the pressure from Athenai to join the alliance they are building is intense. Olunthos and its allies, all the minor cities of the Khalkidike, are showing signs of renewed strength. If Athenai and Olunthos come to agreement without Amuntas, then the pressure on the Makedones could be too much. If, on the other hand, Amuntas makes agreement with Athenai, then Olunthos is isolated and must be content with the existing status. But what will be the cost of friendship with Athenai?

Already when they returned from the hunt other notables from the kingdom and from the highland chiefdoms had gathered at Pella. Many Philippos had met or seen before, but this gathering casts a wider net than any he remembers. The palace is full of strangers, as is the city.

There is much to see, more to learn. Is he not a prince? Has he not hunted with the first men of the kingdom? Yet here is his tutor telling him it is time for bed. Bed!

"There is nothing more I can say to you, Little Centaur. If you will not do as I direct, I must send for your Lady Mother." The rotund man is clearly exasperated, but still speaks slowly to underscore his dignity.

"My Lady Mother has more important activities than her fourth child," Philippos answers sarcastically.

The pudgy philosopher knows the boy is right and is at a loss. These days Philippos heeds him less and less. A cough interrupts the squabble. Both turn to see Lady Kleopatra at the door, "Agemilaos is right, you know, Philippos. The shadows of night are here. Tomorrow you must compete in the running and wrestling, but here you are wasting the rest you will need to succeed." The austere lady, tall and in a dark robe, seems like a prophetess.

19

Agemilaos the Tutor bows. Kleopatra enters the room, "With your permission Prince Philippos." Who would deny the ancient Kleopatra entrance?

"Of course, Philippos is right as well, friend Agemilaos. His mother, Queen Eurudike, is called by her duties to the court. So it is up to you to persuade the prince, and are you not practiced in persuasion? Philippos is a prince and a prince must have sound advice from his counselors. A prince must learn what is right and, more importantly, what makes sense, what is practical. So he must weigh the advantage of staying up later than usual this night to observe the activities of the court and the ways of the notables against the advantage of being well rested and able to show skill in competition with his peers tomorrow. Neither choice is better or worse in and of itself. The choices are better or worse depending upon what Philippos wants to achieve." Kleopatra bows her head stiffly to Philippos.

Somehow Kleopatra has accomplished what Agemilaos could not. Philippos knows that it is better for him to sleep, and his resentment at being excluded, as ever it seems he is excluded by being the youngest, is dispelled in understanding that Kleopatra has given him the choice. "I will prepare for bed," he says.

"Thank you, Philippos," Kleopatra smiles briefly. Then she turns to the tutor, "Agemilaos, I believe I shall flout tradition a bit more and ask that you leave Philippos and me alone together."

The idea that there could be any impropriety by Kleopatra with her great-grandson is absurd, and so Agemilaos bows, "The lesson you have taught tonight has been learned by both Philippos and me. Thank you, Lady Kleopatra." The tutor withdraws, dignity intact.

"Now, Philpa, ready yourself to sleep. I will wait."

Philippos feels some embarrassment in disrobing and using the bowl before Lady Kleopatra, but the occasion demands he sacrifice his pride. That done, he lightly sprinkles water on the corner altar and bows his devotions to Zeus and Herakles.

"Philippos, light a taper and stand it by the images. As you do, think of the flame's aspect as both the sun of your clan, the Temenidai of the Argeadai Makedones, and as father Zeus. Know that through Herakles, and down through your royal forefathers, you are both man and divine."

Startled, Philippos obeys the ancient queen. His earlier devotions were hurried, unthinking. These new devotions make him consider his origins and the line of blood in which he shares. Done, he turns to receive his next instructions.

Kleopatra smiles, beckons him to the bed as she seats herself on the nearby bench. "Philippos, who am I?"

Her question puzzles him, "You are the Lady Kleopatra."

"Am I a woman?"

"Yes," he says hesitantly, "but not as other women."

"Why?"

"You are a queen. You command the royal household." Silently, he thinks, *you are old, you have seen more than most. You were the wife of the last great kings.*

"Does not your mother, Queen Eurudike, rule the household?"

"Yes, no," he waves his hand impatiently, "she does but through you."

"Is there more?"

Philippos thinks about the position Kleopatra holds. He tries to see it clearly and express her power. "You have the ear of my father. Mother hides away from father. I mean, she has her own little court and only shares those things she must share."

Kleopatra nods, thinking, *so bright a boy, to understand and not take sides.* "Your father prepares Alexandros to be king. That is proper. Your mother favors Perdikkas. Neither take the time for you that they might. Does this anger you?"

The boy ponders the question. "Yes. Not father. But I do get angry at mother. Why does she always go a different direction than father? Shouldn't she care for all of us, no matter if father gives the most time to Aleko?"

"I could tell you that it is hard to be a queen. Maybe it's even harder to be a woman. Yet those are not reasons enough." Kleopatra gazes at the bronze lamp, "Your mother believes she knows better than your father how the kingdom should be ruled. But your father is the king." The old woman stops, and decides to take a new tack.

"Philippos, would you honor a bargain with a queen?"

"With you, Lady Kleopatra, of course."

"You are not likely to be king. Only a series of calamities would cause that end. You could, though, be a strong arm for your brother. And if, by happenstance, the kingship should fall vacant, then having been that strong arm, you will possess the qualities to rule ably. For that, the notables and the citizen army would acknowledge your right to rule gratefully."

She pauses, considers her words, not certain how well the boy understands her. "If you will accept instruction from a woman, I propose to teach you what I know of kings and of ruling. I will do this by telling you of my life and of what I have learned. Do you accept?"

Without knowing why, tears glisten down Philippos' cheeks. For as long as he can remember, this high-born crone has frightened him simply by her singular presence even though never has she been unkind to him and always her watchfulness has benefited him. He clears his throat, "You are not as other women, Lady Kleopatra. I would take your words to heart."

Suddenly feeling a resurgence of joy, Kleopatra briefly smiles, "Take my words to mind. Consider them carefully. Decide for yourself what value they have. We start now with a story from my past." Philippos nods his assent.

"I was born in the reign of Perdikkas the Cunning or Perdikkas the

Second as some call him. As you know, my family has Temenidai blood, as well as blood of the highland kings and of the lowland first families. We were foremost in Mieza, with well favored lands and many supporters and retainers whom we could bring to the aid of the king."

"When I was born, Perdikkas and his two older brothers were sharing the kingship, as they had for more than a year. Their father, Alexandros, had many sons. King Alexandros possessed many true qualities and was able to achieve much for the Makedones. It was Alexandros who was first acknowledged by the highland kings as their overlord and so is the source of the Argeadai Makedones claim on the highlands."

"Still, sometimes even true qualities can lead a king astray. For Alexandros, it was his inability to deny his many sons that caused the kingdom grief. In addition to Perdikkas, the sons numbered Philippos, who was the eldest and who came to hate Perdikkas, seeing Perdikkas' cunning as treachery and weakness; Alketas, also older than Perdikkas, who was powerful and usually seconded Perdikkas; Menelaos, who was ever careful to stay out of harm's way but was an inspired stockman who improved the qualities of our herds; and Amuntas the Amiable, your father's grandfather, who was generous and clever and never on the wrong side. There was also a sister, Stratonike, who was eventually married off to the king of the Odrusai Thraikiotes, Seuthes. During Alexandros' life, all of his sons held large estates and each held positions of importance in their respective corners of the kingdom. When Alexandros died, as he had wanted, the citizen army elected the three eldest sons kings."

"For a time, some years actually, the arrangement of three equal kings existed. The truth is that Alexandros recognized Perdikkas as the most able of his sons, but could not bring himself to set aside the older two. The division of authority weakened the kingdom, for Philippos would never agree with Perdikkas and both maneuvered Alketas. Finally, the notables and army intervened, deposing Philippos and Alketas in favor of Perdikkas. Alketas accepted the change, but Philippos never could."

"Among the women of Alketas' household was a beauty named Simikhe. Her name is often besmirched as if she had been low born or even a slave. Politics can vilify any name. Simikhe was the daughter of a well-enough born man, though not of a great family or even a family with more than an average holding of lands. She had beauty and enough courage or fool-ishness to become Perdikkas' wife. And she bore for Perdikkas his son, Arkhelaos."

"Our kingship goes to who is able among the Temenidai. Whispers and gossip can be as damaging to reputation as outright failures. Long before Philippos declared against his brother Perdikkas, he attacked by innuendo, gesture, secret act and silver. Chief among the slurs was the question of the legitimacy of Arkhelaos."

"When Simikhe died, Perdikkas went for some years without a wife.

After all, he was past fifty at her death. Who could have foreseen how long he would live? He confounded all his enemies. Then he married Yineka, daughter of a Paiaones king. From her, his son Aeropos was born."

"The notables were not happy over a son by a Paiaones, even if she was one of the city Paiaones and not a pure tribesman. True, Arkhelaos was grown to manhood, but as a warrior he was vulnerable. Pressure mounted on Perdikkas to secure the Temenidai line without resorting to Aeropos. Most thought he would force Arkhelaos to take an additional wife, perhaps an Aleuadai from Thessalos or maybe an Epeiriote princess. Arkhelaos' wife seemed barren."

"Instead, Perdikkas took himself a Makedone. He married me when I was eighteen and he was sixty-one. A measure of caution on his part—to avoid too much power in Prince Arkhelaos' hands. I say measure because it was my family more than myself that was important to his interests."

"Perdikkas took a second measure that surprised everyone. He began to get children on me." Kleopatra pauses, remembering. Then chuckles warmly, "The old rogue discovered how much he liked young breasts and firm buttocks." She looks sharply at the boy, "Do my words shock you? Do you understand their meaning?"

"N-n-no, I'm not shocked," stammers Philippos, who clearly finds her language unexpected.

"Put aside your preconceptions of who I am and how I sound. I was not always as I am today. Be certain you understand what I say. Ask questions if you don't. Now, do you understand these words?"

"Yes, Lady Kleopatra, my brothers and their friends use them," he admits.

She nods and continues, "Perdikkas liked me. First, he liked that I did not cower from him. Second, he liked that I was beautiful and willing to give my beauty to him. Eventually, he liked that he could teach me without doubting my trust of him or his trust of me."

"Despite his age, like the Illurian Bardulis, he continued to get me with child. First, Saburtios, was born. Next Agenor, named after my father. Then Berenike, your grandmother. And finally, Karanos, who was a sweet boy. Sadly, Saburtios and Agenor died in childhood in the year when the sweating illness swept the land. In some ways, though, you remind me of Karanos." Philippos is not sure he likes the comparison.

"As I bore children for Perdikkas, his brother Philippos grew more alarmed. Perhaps if there had been one child there may not have been trouble. Then Philippos could imagine he and his sons would remain important to the kingdom. But Philippos was jealous of Perdikkas— believing Perdikkas too timid and too cunning by half to be a good king. Philippos believed himself to be a bold direct man, though, in truth, he was devious and crooked. His face was hearty, but his heart was vengeful. Each child born to Perdikkas was another child for whom the king would provide. For Philippos, each of our children seemed a mouth eating into his own patrimony."

"Trouble occurred through the interference of Athenai. Their League wrapped itself around our coasts. They had founded Amphipolis a few years earlier. Most of the Khalkidike cities were forced into membership with the League. Methone, on our Pieric coast, had been made a member."

"When Perdikkas attempted to forestall Athenai, he was unable to gain the confidence of the Khalkidike cities. Except for the citizens of Potidaia, and they only due to being ordered by Athenai to raze their walls. Perdikkas supported Potidaia against Athenai. He was bold because he expected the southern cities of Sparte and Korinthos to give him aid. Korinthos had agreed, but did not come through."

"The Athenians created a federation among the Khalkidike cities, appointing Olunthos as its capital. Worse, their gold and promises caused Philippos to come out in open revolt against Perdikkas. Our cousin, the Elimiote king, also supported Philippos. The Derdas of that day led his tribesmen against Perdikkas."

"Philippos should have known better than to rely on the word of southerners. As the Athenians became alarmed over Korinthos and Sparte, they had second thoughts. Philippos and Derdas had taken Therme and were besieging Pudna when they were betrayed by Athenai. Athenai re-allied with Perdikkas and gave him Therme for which he dropped his support of Potidaia. That city then fell to the Athenians. Derdas retreated into Elimiotis. Philippos was isolated, then killed during the pursuit following a skirmish. So ended that threat to my husband and children."

"Then all was well, great-grandma?" asks the yawning Philippos.

"Nothing is simple, boy. Another time I will tell you how Philippos' son fled to Thraikios and gained support of the Odrusai king, Sitalkes, and how Sitalkes invaded our lands. But that is for another night."

"All right, great-grandma."

"Sit up a bit longer, Philippos. Now is the time for questions. What have you learned from this tale?"

The boy looks owlishly at the old woman. He considers the story he has heard. "Well, that the cities of the South are powerful and can stir up trouble." He grins, "That an old man can like a young wife." He ponders, "That brothers can hate each other, but I knew that since my father's first brood hates us." Then brightly, "And never trust the word of the southern cities, especially the democratic Athenai."

Kleopatra nods gently, "Make none of those truths into axioms. Consider why they were true then and what might have changed that truth. What could have bound the brothers together to support each other? We Makedones are only strong enough to withstand our neighbors when we stand together. Notice that a king's first responsibility is to maintain his rule and protect the integrity of his lands. For Perdikkas also betrayed Potidaia.

Perdikkas had to come to terms with Athenai. Perdikkas walked a line that shifted between Athenai and Sparte. That was the start of when those two cities were locked in their great conflict. To Philippos, his brother Perdikkas never seemed consistent. Had Philippos been sole king, he would have lost the kingdom. Perdikkas was always consistent. But his consistency had nothing to do with Athenai, Sparte, Potidaia or other allies. His consistency was to the survival of the Makedones as an independent people."

The two sit silently for a moment. "You loved Perdikkas, great-grandma," says the boy.

"He was a good king," replies Kleopatra. The boy recognizes that she has given Perdikkas her highest compliment.

δ

Philippos sits on the wall, hugging his knees, shivering even with a towel draped over his bare shoulders, watching the intense contenders on the field, the hooting, pushing mass of onlookers, and the hurrying servants, always fetching and carrying. For as far as he can see the broad meadow is filled. On the far margins are the tents and pennants. Off to the right are the enclosures with the excited whinnying horses. To the left, on the hillside, are the dedicatory altars. But before him are the playing fields, each with its burst of athletic striving: the track with runners racing; a wrestling ground, where two men circle, grapple and heave; a fairly clear space, where, one after another, the javelin throwers try their hand at the mark. Beyond this front line of events other activities are in motion, deeper in the meadow. The ever-shifting bustle of men and boys fills his senses with noise and movement.

Realizing he is shivering, Philippos consciously controls his body. Though the breeze gives a touch of coolness as the sweat dries on him, the shivering is part excitement over the day and part reaction as his muscles respond to the labor he has expended. So far, he has participated in six competitions in his class of boys. His wins were for wrestling and long distance running. He placed among the top three in throwing the javelin. He was no more than one of the top quarter of competitors for short distance running, for the long jump, and for throwing the discus.

His father will not permit him to compete in boxing. He is too young yet for the chariots. But in less than an hour he will be racing on his favorite horse—the small yet surprisingly strong gray mare, Peplaia. At the thought of the horse race, he smiles.

The morning results are good. He had not expected to do so well. Still, he feels a mild dejection. Perhaps from fatigue or perhaps because no one especially urged him on save Skaros. The events for the boys mostly attract the younger fathers or the occasional older brother. His brother, Perdikkas, had watched him wrestle.

Philippos is pleased he won that series. His last opponent had been Eurulokhos, who is almost three years older. Not only older, but taller and heavier. But Philippos is faster. Thinking about it now, Philippos guesses Eurulokhos was tired from having faced four strong opponents before Philippos. Certainly he had been slippery with sweat. Still, Philippos had also wrestled four others before facing Eurulokhos. Philippos is unable to decide whether his victory was truly his own or only the cumulative effect of five wrestlers.

"What are you brooding about?"

"Eurunoe? You're not supposed to be here."

The girl laughs, "How am I to find a husband if I don't look over a field of men?"

"You aren't old enough for a husband. You must be with Arsinoe and that crowd from the hills."

"I am not," the young woman throws up her head haughtily. "Mother is up at the shrine with her ladies. She wants me to join her."

Philippos looks up to the altars on the hill and sees a knot of women and old men preparing a sacrifice or some other dedication. "What's that about?"

"A ceremony for Apollo and Artemis. I think it's really a welcome for the Pelagonoi and Lunkestoi. Apparently father wasn't certain they would travel this far to participate."

"Eurunoe, it wasn't the distance; it's their politics. They must be scared of the Illuroi and they aren't certain what support they might get from Epeiros or from the South."

"How would you know?"

"I listen," he says with disgust at his sister's naivete, "and I think about what the men say."

"You're just in love with war like all boys your age," is her rejoinder.

He grins, "And you're in love with men's bodies like all the girls your age."

A chuckle of delight at their expense causes them to look up from their argument at a man sitting on a horse near them. The man is handsome and well dressed. The horse is of good quality and has been carefully groomed. "Excuse my eavesdropping, but you were talking about my people." The words have an accent to their ears, the language more proper and stilted than their own speech and possessing the accent of the west.

Seeing their stares, the man continues, "Let me introduce myself. I am Parmenion, son of Philotas. We are Pelagones. And no, we are not afraid of the Illuroi. They are afraid of us. As for the Lunkestoi, well, sometimes it can be difficult to determine who is Lunkestoi and who is Illuroi." He smiles engagingly.

"You are modest, prince. You are more than a Pelagone, you are *the* Pelagonoi," simpers Eurunoe.

"There are two branches of your family here, are there not?" asks Philippos.

Parmenion continues to smile but his eyes appraise the boy. "Yes. As with the Temenidai, uncles, brothers, nephews, cousins can all be one family or can splinter into many branches. For now, our royal family has two branches."

"So you know who we are."

"Of course. Your brother, Alexandros, pointed you out, so I came over to become acquainted," Parmenion answers Philippos. "As I came closer, I recognized you from the early competitions. You run well."

Philippos feels surprise that this man, whom he takes to be in his early twenties, would be interested enough to watch the boys' competition. "Did you have a son competing?"

"Goodness, no." Parmenion waves his hand over the natural stadium of the meadow, "You see all around you the lords, leaders and principal followers—and their heirs—of both the highland and lowland Makedones and many of their neighbors. You know, Pelagonis is a few valleys and some mountains. On one side, to the south, we have the Lunkestoi; on our north side are the Paiaones. West of us are the Dardanoi and other Illuroi. And to the east, beyond Mount Boras, are you, where the Almopes used to be before your ancestors destroyed that people. So we must be here. Not because we are afraid, but because we are practical. Yes, a few valleys, but they are our valleys, and we are the valiant Pelagonoi. We would know our neighbors well, especially those civilized neighbors with whom alliance is logical."

"So you watch boys run?"

"Not simply run, but how they prepare to run, how they react to their run. How they behave when they win or when they lose. How they behave with their friends and with their servants. I am curious about everyone and everything. And I am curious about you, Princess Eurunoe and Prince Philippos."

Eurunoe blushes, taking the words as a compliment. Philippos takes them for what they are: an honest statement of purpose in protecting the self-interests of the Pelagonoi.

"Have you competed?" asks Philippos.

"Yes, but there will be more events for my age class in the afternoon."

"What is your best event?"

Parmenion studies Philippos before answering, "I am good on my feet, whether wrestling, throwing the javelin or running. What I like best is not the formal events—it is stick-ball. My team has not been defeated. We play aggressively and are strong in the melee, but without forgetting our purpose in putting the ball over the line."

The statements are said matter-of-factly, so there is no hint of boasting. Yet Philippos feels a challenge is implicit in the words, not an athletic challenge, rather a challenge to understand why a common game is important to a prince of the Pelagonoi. "You are the lead player of your team?"

"Yes," smiles Parmenion, "but my forward players are bigger men. I command from the second line. That way I can best direct the play."

Philippos nods and smiles inwardly, wondering if this proud prince has obliquely warned Philippos' father and brothers of the prowess of the Pelagonoi. Clearly the prince and his family intend to negotiate as equals in any alliance with the Makedones. "You play today, after the marking ceremonies?"

"We'll be one of the teams playing at day's end. Will you want to watch to see if we win?"

Philippos drops down off the wall and reaches up to pat the flank of Parmenion's horse, "I will be there, Prince of the Pelagonoi."

*   *   *

Now, up on his horse, Peplaia, all thoughts of Parmenion and stick-ball have fled Philippos' mind. There are twenty-six horses on the line, each with its serious self-absorbed rider. The horses shuffle, snort, take half-steps, feeling nervous tension from the riders, intensely aware of the other horses, especially those to either side.

The stallion next to Peplaia keeps sidling toward the mare, though its rider, a boy whom Philippos does not know well, jerks his mount back in line each time. Philippos smooths his hand down Peplaia's neck, stilling the animal's fear of the stallion.

The crowd quiets as the race flag is raised. Philippos concentrates. As the flag swishes down, he digs in his heels and releases Peplaia. They are quickly in the front rank of riders. Philippos keeps Peplaia from running full out, knowing that speed will be needed only after the knot of riders has thinned into a length of contenders.

There is nothing Philippos loves more than this. The boy and horse are as close as two creatures can be to becoming one. Their wills and purpose are the same.

The race is a third of the way along. Philippos begins their advance that should give them the lead before the finish line. Peplaia is running well. She is eager, strong with the surge of her own muscles, confident in the guidance of her young master.

Philippos recognizes the back of the boy next ahead, the court physician's son. In seconds, he and Peplaia will be passing them. Then from the corner of his eye, Philippos becomes aware of trouble. A large black horse is out of its rider's control. The animal is careening away from the inner track, across the paths of oncoming horses. There is an instant to decide whether to pull up or urge Peplaia faster. Philippos kicks in his heels. The mare stretches forward, moving easily into her fastest motion.

The boy ahead of Philippos turns his horse away from the wild black.

Philippos swerves as little as possible. Peplaia smashes on by the turning horse, causing the physician's son to tumble. Ahead another horse is down, its rider rolling in the dust. Philippos tightens his grip with legs and knees, lifts his seat, and gives Peplaia her head. The horse jumps cleanly over the fallen boy. Philippos is in the clear with Peplaia striding evenly, straining to take the lead.

But too much time has been lost. Philippos and Peplaia come across the finish line in fourth position.

Philippos lets Peplaia walk off her excitement. Skaros comes running to take the mare. "Too bad, master," comments the old man, "you might have taken the lead. You timed your push just right."

"Thank you, Skaros," the prince grins, "even without winning, the finish was rousing." He dismounts, leans briefly against Peplaia and whispers to the horse, "You did well. You have great heart, Peplaia."

"You father wants you to join him."

"Where is he?"

"You'll find him under the yellow tent top, over by that copse of tall beech trees," Skaros waves toward the west end of the field.

Philippos strides quickly through the crowd. He is glad he's done competing for the day for he can feel his fatigue. Responding to the sudden upset during the race took a toll on top of all his earlier events. Still he hurries, as he always hurries to a summons from his father. At the pavilion, he must push and twist his way through the talkative men clustered there.

"Father, here is Philippos," calls out Perdix.

Philippos reaches the knot of his menfolk. "Good, you came fast, boy," his father is grinning. "I hear you did well in the race, coming through when others went astray."

"Yes, father." As usual someone has brought word of the boy's deeds to King Amuntas. The eyes of others are always on the Temenidai.

"Good, good. Well, we will all be going from here to the temple of Herakles. A thanks offering will be given for each of my boys." The father is beaming.

A loud voice from nearby calls out vehemently, "Not all of your sons."

Philippos turns and is shocked to see his half-brothers. The three men stand together with several of their friends. Heat rises within Philippos as his mind whispers their names: Arkhelaos, Aridaios, Menelaos. Anger springs out of his fears at the sight of them.

His father—their father—steps forward, his arms wide, smiling, "My boys, you are welcome to join us in this ceremony. I am delighted you have come."

Philippos looks to his brother, Alexandros. Their eyes exchange the knowledge of their emotions, even though Alexandros' face remains impassive, as is their brother's, Perdikkas. King Amuntas will be generous with

29

his older sons, but will never trust them. The younger sons are his heirs, provided they are old enough when he dies. Philippos, Perdikkas and Alexandros know that for now their father's good health is their protection.

ε

Late now, the lamplight is guttering, low. Kleopatra is seated next to the bed on which the boy lays at ease. Their voices are as soft as the lighting.

"Great-grandma, why must we fear Arkhelaos and his brothers?"

"You know why, Philippos."

"Yes. They are excluded yet believe their rights precede ours. So they will ever be our enemies. All that I know." The boy twists to look at the old woman, "I mean why is the world this way?"

"I could tell you that the gods made the world this way, but that is not an answer is it?" She sighs, "Philippos, I cannot fathom the gods. I use to think the gods meddled as part of their own mysterious concerns. Then, when I was older, I believed there were no gods at all. That all there is, is what we see. Later, I came to believe the gods are likelier than not —that something set all this in motion—though their own concerns make them largely indifferent to us and our affairs. Eventually, I came to believe that the gods are intensely interested in what we do but that they meddle less than is supposed. Instead, a god or goddess adopts you or you adopt a god. I'm not sure which." She smiles faintly, "Somehow there grows a personal affection—an attachment—between you and a god. The god sees farther into the future, knows more, certainly knows you in your entirety, can reach down through the ages. Knows your forefathers and your descendants. Maybe you are even a reflection, a piece, of your forefathers. And the god sets you challenges. Sometimes the challenges are big, momentous, but more often they seem incidental, a trivial part of each day, yet cumulatively your responses to these challenges determine how you grow."

"Do you mean your personal god guides you?"

"Yes. Guides you and helps you shape your self into more than you can become on your own. On the other hand, if you are blind to the god, if you do not receive the god, you take on your own shape and it can easily become stunted or, even, twisted. It is hard to grow straight for there are never ending winds, storms, blight, if you have not the protection of your god."

Philippos considers these ideas. He likes the idea of a personal god rather than the pantheon of gods who are busy with their own feuds and purposes. Still, he's not sure that answers his question. "Do you mean that all the troubles of the world come from those who have not let themselves be divinely guided?"

"There are troubles and there are troubles. When a storm crosses the mountains and ladens our lands with winds and rains, a bird may be dashed from the skies. To the bird, the storm has brought calamity. The same rains let the thirsty soil drink, so that grains and grasses sprout, allowing a mouse to be fed. Allowing all of us to feed—the bird, too. The storm is trouble for our bird and a blessing for the mouse. Some troubles are like that. Some happenings are, in a sense, neutral—and the calamity or blessing depends on where you are and how you act."

"What about men? What about Arkhelaos?"

"Men must struggle for there is never enough for all. At their best, men struggle side by side, lending each other strength. Among men, there is inequality. No one has all the strength, all the ideas, all the nobility—but strength, ideas, nobility have been shared out unevenly. Part of the challenges we are set, I suppose."

She stops, trying to form her thoughts into words, "So, while men may struggle side by side, someone must lead their work, give it direction. In Athenai and some other cities, the leaders are chosen by the citizens. This is unusual, for in most of the world leaders come from among the handful who make up the noble families. Both ways can give rise to weak leaders and strong leaders. The times may call for a weak leader, someone who lets events play themselves out when troubles are few, or for a strong leader, someone who controls or channels events when troubles are many. Too often, though, the wrong kind of leader is in place for what the times demand."

She waves her hand in a gesture of dismissal, "I am being too theoretical. You ask about your half-brother, Arkhelaos. When your father was younger, he married his cousin, Gugaia. Then the king was Perdikkas. Both your father and his bride's lines of the Temenidai were outside the central power. Gugaia's mother, Lanika, was of a minor family. Her father, Menelaos, had married cautiously within the backwater region where his principal estates lay. That branch of the family was content to be the big frogs in the smallest of ponds. Of all the Temenidai, they seemed least to possess the fire of our nobility."

Urgently, suddenly, Kleopatra reaches and grips the boy's hand, "What is nobility, Philippos?"

"Nobility? It is the lineage of a family chosen and favored by the gods." The boy thinks, "It is also how one behaves, acts. In that sense it is how one honors himself and his forefathers by acting in keeping with his heritage."

"Those are good answers. Let me add that nobility isn't simply reverencing the past, the forefathers; it is reverencing today and tomorrow by possessing the vision and energy to alter that heritage to meet the challenges that arise. Some say that the world is forever the same. I believe that the world is forever changing. In my life, nothing has stayed the same. Thus challenges are endless."

"The boys your father had of Gugaia possess no fire, no vision, no nobility. They cannot be proper kings. Part of the bargain I made with Amuntas when he married Eurudike is that he disinherit his eldest sons."

The boy is startled. In all he has heard of his father's first family, he had not known it was this woman who determined that Alexandros would become a king, and that he and his brother, Perdikkas, would share in authority and responsibility.

"Now, boy, the hard part of what you said about nobility is how it becomes accepted that a family has been chosen and favored by the gods. Not only must you know that truth of the Temenidai, but it must be believed by all the Makedones. And the one who is chosen king by the family, magnates and citizen army is that member of the Temenidai most able to be king when the kingship becomes vacant. Not always is this the first born son."

He nods his understanding, and yawns.

"Are you tired, boy?" she asks kindly. "Is this enough for one night?"

He had been tired. Earlier, before Lady Kleopatra came into his room, he had been drowsy, hoping to sleep. Now, though, his mind is speeding. "Great-grandma, let's talk longer yet," he says.

She smiles at her young descendent. Night after night, whenever possible, without the explicit knowledge of the family, Kleopatra pours herself into this vessel of a boy, this younger son. For he never fills. He is eager for whatever she will give—the only person for whom she opens her persona, the only person who appreciates—no, loves—her and knows her mind fully. How imperfect this partnership. How much can a boy so young understand? Does she do wrong to feed him ideas so demanding that he will be old before his time? What choice does she have, for he is the vessel that will carry her soul into the future, to his sons in his every thought and deed. That is what she fervently believes.

So she nods her assent, "Let me tell you of my Arkhelaos." Gathering her shawl around her shoulders, letting her mind cast back, she begins, "Your half-brother was named after my Arkhelaos for Gugaia gave birth to your half-brother just after the coronation of Perdikkas' son. Of course, I was the widow of the old king, the father. Arkhelaos had been crown prince for a long time and was not a young man. He had a family: a wife, Lusandra; a son, Orestes; and a daughter, Simikhe, named for his mother. He had married quite late to a girl too young. I suppose the bitterness of the fighting between Perdikkas and his brother, Philippos, had much to do with the nature of Arkhelaos. Or being born to a mother he loved yet who had been looked down upon by all the high notables. Even the king, in the years after Simikhe's death, seemed ashamed of having married low. I don't know," she sighs, wistful even now.

"When a king dies, especially a king who has ruled long, long beyond the years of most of his people, there is great uncertainty. Though the uncle, Philippos, had been dead for years, Arkhelaos had not forgotten the lesson that his right to the throne could be disputed. His uncle never accepted being deposed. Hard fighting and a near loss of the throne were required before the line of Philippos was eliminated. Yet another line, that of Alketas, had become the true power in the land. This occurred in the last few years of Perdikkas' life, as the king was ailing. Though publicly supporting Arkhelaos, in private Perdikkas favored his brother. And why not? For Alketas had been his staunch ally since childhood."

"If Alketas was as much a king in his own estates and among whole regions of the kingdom, then his eldest son was as much a crown prince. Arkhelaos' first act as king was to have his uncle and cousin killed. His second act was to put aside his wife, Lusandra, and marry me."

"While Perdikkas had favored Alketas, I had favored Arkhelaos. Favored, what a word. We were already lovers. I can say that now, out loud, to you, but only to you. You hold a secret of mine, a piece of me." She looks at the boy sitting up in his bed, eyes big and round. "Nor was he the first. A southern man, black hair and red skin, Demetrios, was a lover. There were whispers that my youngest, Karanos, was not the son of Perdikkas. Perdikkas believed him to be his son. Maybe he was. Or maybe the son of Demetrios. Or even the son of Arkhelaos. I do not know." She shakes her head ruefully, "I was in my mid-thirties with a husband in his late seventies when Karanos was conceived. Right now, at your age boy, you do not know what fire can exist in the loins. But you are a Temenidai and you will know."

Strange, how she wants this boy to believe in her. She feels like crying at the trust in his eyes. But she has not cried for many a long year, even when alone. "The third act of King Arkhelaos was to give my son, Karanos, his death." Her words raise the hair at the back of Philippos' neck, even though said softly, with little emphasis.

The old queen does not falter, "There has been no one more fierce than Arkhelaos. He killed my boy. We were married but it did not matter. I would not let him touch me, would not talk to him, would not see him. My daughter, Berenike, acted as go-between. Arkhelaos would have no barrier. He was impatient, in a rage. Not against me but against himself, against the fates that required him to harm what he loved, at the supreme folly of being a plaything for the gods. He burst in upon me, scattering my women, sending them away. I can see him now, the doors flying open, crashing against the walls. The women in a stir and he yelling, setting off panic among them, his guards trailing in behind him, and he raging, cursing, flailing, pushing them all out. While I sat there, cold, numb, unable to move, feeling only stone in my heart, unafraid. He came and knelt before me, tears streaming down his face, stretching his hands out to me, not touching me, and talking, wildly, then softer, and all the years of his life, all his hopes, sins, remorses, desires, all of him poured out as he begged my forgiveness even before the gods."

"Somehow it touched me. This warrior, this hard demanding lover, this man of forty-five was at my feet, asking for what I could not give him. I could love him, I could resume my life with him, I could understand the insanity that sometimes worked in him, but I could never forgive him for Karanos. Still—in the early dawn—we conceived my boy, Amuntas. Somehow I accepted Arkhelaos and returned to life myself." She falls silent, musing.

"Great-grandmother, I thought Arkhelaos was a good king. How could he murder Karanos, your son, maybe his son? He had made you his wife." Philippos had never heard this story of the boy, Karanos.

"Arkhelaos believed Karanos was the son of Demetrios. He could not abide the rumors and remarks of the court. All of the nobility were suspect." The old lady pauses, "How can I convey those times to you? Perdikkas had lived too long. The conflicts between Perdikkas and his brother, Philippos, led to compromises, to securing the loyalty of the high families with lands and privileges. The long decline of Perdikkas ensured the power of those he favored. They were entrenched, unassailable, or so they thought. And with few exceptions—important exceptions—they underestimated Arkhelaos. He would not give them a wedge, a lever to use against him. You see, he had twenty years to think about how he would reign, twenty years in which he was the designated successor by his father, twenty years to chafe. In killing his uncle Alketas and his cousin Alexandros, Arkhelaos served notice that no one was too high, too power-ful. Killing Karanos, even after taking me as his wife, told everyone plainly that he would act on the slightest suspicion of betrayal or lack of respect."

"You could be his wife, be loyal, knowing he killed your son?"

Kleopatra sits back, trying to face pains and decisions made long ago. "Philippos, both the birth and the death of Karanos were caused by me. Death surrounds a king. I knew that. Had Arkhelaos not loved me, become my lover, he would have had me killed for betraying his father with Demetrios. Maybe I wanted power too much myself to turn my back on Arkhelaos. I had been queen for twenty-four years then. I was numb at first, then hated Arkhelaos for a long time, even as I loved him. Hate and love are not opposites. Through it all, I knew what kingship demands. Few kings of our people have been as capable as Arkhelaos."

"To him, we owe Pella, this city with its temples and palaces. To him, we owe the ties to the Hellenes forged in his reign. What other king has attracted the likes of Euripides, Timotheos, Zeuxis, Agathon, Khoerilos to our court? To him, we owe the organization of the kingdom. He began a true army. He introduced new crops, improved stock. He built roads, bridges. He founded the festival of Olympia at Dion. He rebound the high-landers to us, defeating Arrhabaios and Sirrhas of Lunkestis, after the humiliations that occurred under his father. The strength we have today comes from the renewal of our mutual reliance on Elimiotis. Would Derdas be your father's stalwart ally if it were not for Arkhelaos? The friendship of the Aleuadai of Larissa, of all of northern Thessalos, began with Arkhelaos. Never have the people prospered more than under his kingship. Never have the Makedones gained greater respect from the southern Hellenes." She stops, feeling nearly faint from the burgeoning emotions within her. With stopping, with silence, with memory, comes a fresh stab of pain and guilt over Karanos. The slain boy will never stop reaching out for her.

Quieter now, she reaches out to touch the boy's arm, to seek understanding from him, the understanding she never asks from anyone else. "The tragedy of our people is that Arkhelaos did not reign longer."

"He was murdered," says Philippos tightly.

"Yes," wearily she responds, "the conspirators wanted his death to appear as an accident. He was out hunting with the men of his court, his companions. We know that at least three of them worked his murder. I believe there were others involved, more senior, who used the petty slights felt by the three to twist them into killing Arkhelaos. How else could he have become separated from the main body of his companions with just those three nobodies accompanying him? Supposedly a lion surprised them and in the wild tussle a knife went into Arkhelaos which was meant for the lion, as did an arrow. But the lion was dead before they reached the glen. The claw marks and torn flesh came after the knife. Probably the arrow was shot first. It no longer matters. Krataios, Hellenokrates of Larissa, and Dekamnikhos. The last was the boy Arkhelaos had flogged for deriding Euripides. The three died painfully but never admitted any other conspirators." Her bitterness stills him, "Never trust the carrion eaters that surround the throne."

Kleopatra thinks back, "Krataios had been a favorite. At one point, Arkhelaos considered him worthy of being the groom to his daughter, Simikhe. Before a betrothal was announced, Arkhelaos changed his mind. He discerned some flaw in Krataios." She waves her hand dismissing her ghosts, "Krataios brought ruin on his family."

Looking at Philippos, she adds, "Arkhelaos ruled for almost fourteen years. Had a strong successor followed him, we would have avoided the troubles that came instead."

"But then my father would not be king," he answers.

Kleopatra chuckles, feeling some relief, "You're right, boy. Nor you a prince." She tousles his hair, "At least that is good. Your father is not an ideal king but he achieves what is needed for our people and lands. In addition, he gives us a strong line of male children so that his succession will be secure. The people love your father," she smiles. Smiles with her eyes alight. She is truly pleased at the thought of strong king succeeding strong king, of a kingdom safe in its kingship.

"Do you know, Philippos, that I bore one son to Arkhelaos and named him Amuntas? Most thought I named my baby for King Amuntas the Good but it wasn't so. I named him for your father, who was then a golden warrior of twenty-seven. Even then, your father was my favorite of all the Temenidai, after Arkhelaos. How ironic."

"Orestes was acclaimed king on Arkhelaos' death. I was shut out in my grief. A seemly choice you would have thought. Orestes, eldest son of Arkhelaos. Yet only sixteen. Too young. So his half-uncle, Aeropos, became regent." She shakes her head, "Had I been myself I would have worked against that solution. Aeropos. No one was more devious. I could barely comprehend him and I knew him all his life. Ambition consumed him. He was thirty-seven then. In those few years, he came into his own."

"Orestes was dead within two years, before he could reach his majority. I believe he was poisoned. He wasted away almost from the moment he was proclaimed king. Aeropos was made king in his own right. And ruled adequately if despotically." She laughs derisively, "I am not unbiased. He retired me to a country estate in his keeping."

Philippos touches his great-grandmother's arm, for her face is working with emotion. Though no tears flow, her sorrow is plain to see. "We can stop, great-grandma. We can talk again another day."

The old lady straightens and her face resumes its normal serenity, "Only if you are too tired to continue, Philippos."

"I want to know more, great-grandma. A lot of things I've heard said, only in a jumble. When you tell how things happened, it makes sense to me and I can see it in my head." Wistfully, he adds, "Father used to tell us stories of our forefathers, too. I always liked the one about King Philippos. But his stories seem no different than the stories of the Trojans or the legends of Herakles. When you talk to me, it's like you are telling me things I must know if I am going to grow up and be an arm for Alexandros—to take my place as a Temenidai."

"You are right, boy, I am telling you of things you must know." For the first time ever, Kleopatra leans over and kisses the eight-year old on the cheek. "Now, let's continue. Remember that when Arkhelaos became king, he stifled many of the old families. In moving the royal court from Aigai to Pella, he physically moved away from the priestly families and many clan heads. Aeropos was not so foolish as to put himself back in the hands of the priests. The capital stayed at Pella—after all, in little more than a decade it had become the chief city of our lands. Still, Aeropos had to make many concessions to the notables, the big landowners. The money and goods flowing into the king's hands dwindled. The royal foot soldiers were disbanded. They had been one of the principal tools Arkhelaos used to make himself independent of the notables. We were back to aristocratic horsemen and their followers as the basis for Makedones' strength."

"Aeropos held the throne, but a throne less powerful than the one held by Arkhelaos. Next, he made a mistake in his dealings with Sparte. You know enough of southern history to know that about ten years earlier, the Peloponnesians, led by Sparte, finally forced Athenai and her allies to surrender themselves. From that time, Sparte's arrogance had grown. Especially under Agesilaos, when he became one of the Lakonians' dual kings. Agesilaos was the Spartan king who led the expedition into Asia Minor to free the Asian Hellenes from Persia. The resentments of Athenai, Thebai, Korinthos, Argos and others against Sparte were supported by Persian gold. All that Agesilaos was attempting came to nothing when these cities revolted. Agesilaos marched his army back—crossing into Europe, marching down through Thraikios, until approaching the Strymon River, the Spartan army was refused entrance into our lands by Aeropos."

She pauses, wets her lips, "I believe Aeropos hoped that the money he received from Korinthos would enable him to assert himself against the old families. To succeed, he must delay Agesilaos long enough for the revolting cities to re-establish their power and provide him with support. Aeropos was a fighter of some skill, but not as skilled a general as Agesilaos. He also failed as a diplomat, for he could not persuade the Thraikiote tribes, in particular the Odrusoi, to attack Agesilaos' army. Without direct allies and without sufficient mercenaries, he was forced to rely on the very families against whom he was maneuvering. Agesilaos seized the crossings of the Strymon River. Instead of stopping at Amphipolis, he marched quickly across Bisaltis and Mygdonis to confront Aeropos. The King of the Makedones gave in." Her voice is dry, yet satisfaction at that humbling of Aeropos is discernible.

"Now that the southerners are more balanced in their power again— with Athenai, Thebai and Sparte each needing supporters—it's hard to remember how reckless a gamble Aeropos made. The defeat changed him. Within months, he was dead. Before the goddess Atropos cut the thread of his life, she frayed it. He suffered progressively, losing the ability to use his left leg and arm, then losing the ability to speak, and finally losing his life."

Philippos asks, "Do you believe the gods were punishing him?"

"Some people see the gods in every event, every action. I believe that we can be in touch with the gods at all times. If we cut ourselves off from the gods, if we betray ourselves, then the gods step back and let our own actions destroy us. I think Aeropos helped to arrange Arkhelaos' death. I think he had Orestes murdered. He reached for the kingship but paid too dearly for it, so that what he took was empty. I think he did this himself, for the gods stepped back. Once he understood his failure, then the gods rendered him impotent and stopped his life."

They sit silently together, contemplating the fate of Aeropos. Finally, Philippos rouses Kleopatra from her reverie, "What happened next, great-grandma?"

"Aeropos' son, Pausanias, was declared king by the adherents of Aeropos. He was just of an age to make that possible. Yet the opponents of Aeropos put up as king an even younger candidate—a measure of their desperation. He was my son, Amuntas. Even then there was a third candidate,

Argaios, the last male member of Alketas' line of the Temenidai— he is the son of Saturos, Alketas' youngest boy. For a year the candidates tried to outwit each other. Argaios faded, and saw fit to support my son against Pausanias. Amuntas held Pieris and Emathis. Pausanias' power was in the north, in Almopis, and in the east. If the stalemate had continued much longer, who knows what might have become of the Makedones."

"I loved my boy, Amuntas," she sighs. "Still, he was not fit to be king. He took his position for granted, held himself as better than those around him, not simply as a king but as himself. The years of my retirement, the years which formed him into a man, were under the shadow of Aeropos. And Aeropos made sure that his half-brother's boy was good only for show."

"I have told you before that the strength of the Makedones comes from combining the lowlanders and the highlanders. As Pieris and Emathis are the heart of the lowlands, the support of Elimiotis is the key to the highlands. Derdas—the Derdas you know—was then young, perhaps nineteen, but had succeeded in Elimiotis two years earlier. He is a hot-tempered man whom my son made the mistake of irretrievably insulting. Derdas killed my boy in his rage." She shakes her head sadly, "He had been such a good little boy. Had Arkhelaos lived, had this whole thread of happenstance not occurred, he might have been so much more." She looks up, "Was not to be."

"One thing my son, Amuntas, did do while he was king was to bring me back to the court. I was appalled by the chaos that threatened our people. His murder would not end the strife for Pausanias was too taint-ed by faction to be accepted across the land. We needed a new king who could knit us together."

"Derdas had fled to your father's house. I intervened, going from fam-ily to family to bring peace. First to your father, then to Iolaos and other principal men, like Korrhagos. They formed a bedrock. Some from court, some from country, and not only from Pieris and Emathis, but from all over, even Almopis and Eordaia. Pausanias' party shrunk. And in that fortnight of talk, Pausanias was struck down by one of his band of companions. I suspect your father's hand in that doing, but I am not certain to this day. However it occurred, it cleared the way. I married my granddaughter, Eurudike, to your father and saw to it that he was declared king. The third named Amuntas to take the throne. As you know, his descent is from the youngest brother of my first husband, Perdikkas the Cunning." She nods with self-congratulation, then looks intently at the boy. He is drooping.

"Well, Philippos, that's enough for one night," Kleopatra pats the head of the sleepy boy. "We have reached the point where your father is king."

"Yes, let's stop now," he yawns. "I do want to hear how Argaios usurped the kingdom and how father got it back. And how the Illuroi attacked us while we were weak. Also, great-grandma, another time can you tell me more about Bardulis, the king of the Illuric Dardanoi?"

"Yes, all that and more. I have talked long enough tonight, my throat is dry. We must have our questions and answers from this lesson another night as well."

"All right, great-grandma," his sleepiness stealing over him. She rises, picks up the lamp, and looks down as Philippos settles comfortably under his coverlet. She is thankful for this boy, for this chance to redeem a lot of sadness.

ζ

"What are we, Iolaos, to the southern cities?" asks King Amuntas.

The grey-bearded magnate responds, "Let my son answer your question." Iolaos extends a hand to his eldest, Antipatros. Amuntas considers the young man and nods assent.

"To them, we are barbarians," says Antipatros. Seeing that his answer is not enough, the young noble says further, "We are their source of timber and pitch for their ships. So we are a resource they want to control. We are also the buffer between the wild north and their civilized lands. So we are useful to them. They believe we are stubborn and willful for not bending their way." In proceeding, Antipatros words come with increasing heat.

"Excellent. All true," exclaims Amuntas. "Now, how can we use their beliefs to our advantage? All of you, your thoughts," commands the king to the circle of his close companions, the nine men and one boy, Alexandros, standing close to the throne.

Ptolemaios of Aloros states clearly, ticking his points off his fingers, "Look about us, King, for we are alone. There is no support from Thessalos as Iason of Pherai overawes our traditional friends in Larissa. There is no support from Epeiros, as their two new kings decide how to rule jointly. Olunthos is treachery itself. The allies of Athenai are all about us. Sparte no longer contends for the North. We must seem to bend to the wind. For now, the wind blows from Attika. Let ourselves be cordial, amenable, thankful to Athenai for the opportunity to sell them our forest harvest."

"The key, I think, King Amuntas, is being the buffer Antipatros spoke of," interjects Antiokhos, cousin of Amuntas through the king's mother.

"Please expand your theme."

"Is Athenai really interested in us? Yes, they want our timber. Yes, they want us to acknowledge that Amphipolis is their city and to enlist our aid in returning it to their dominion. Yes, they want us as a balance against the cities of the Khalkidike. And, yes, they want to own our coastline so that they own our commerce. But most of all they want us to exist. To have sufficient power, but no more, to keep the Illuroi, Paiaones, Thraikiotes and other tribes away from the civilization that exists south of Mount Olympos or fringes the Aegean Sea here in the north. If we let them believe we are weak, they will help us to be strong. If they believe we are strong, they will seek to humble us."

"Well said, Antiokhos," responds Amuntas. Seeing his son's disappointed face, Amuntas asks, "And what say you, Alexandros?"

"Father, you have told me of the strength our kingdom held under King Arkhelaos. Why can we not again be strong and ignore the grasping Hellenes?"

Amuntas is silent, considering his son. How to make the boy understand how tenuous is power in this land? Perhaps it would be enough if the boy understands the careful favor that makes the nine men in this room the king's adherents. "The source of our strength lies in the mutual support between the king and his companions, as well as between the Makedones as a whole and the Temenidai family of the Argeadai clan. We are favored by Herakles and, through him, by Zeus only so long as we are true to one another. King Arkhelaos created many new customs; he invented a new army relying on smallholders instead of magnates. This gave the Makedones a sunrise of strength, true, but in so doing he antagonized his fellow nobles and other holders of broad lands. He sowed a harvest of hatred. The strength was an illusion and disappeared by sundown when he died under assassins' blows."

Several men call out, "Hear him, prince. Hear your wise father."

Alexandros' face becomes an opaque mask, "Thank you, father, for your instruction."

Amuntas feels a spurt of exasperated affection for his dejected son, for he understands the frustration of wanting to act directly but always having to follow a crooked path. Still, he continues, "We meet the Athenian envoys tomorrow, my companions. Would anyone else care to make a suggestion? No? So, as we decided a sennight ago, we will make an alliance on terms generous to Athenai but will not surrender the ties we've made with the citizens of Amphipolis." The king surveys the nodding heads, "The alliance to last ten years and be renewable."

"No reason for a fifty-year alliance," laughs Iolaos, referencing the earlier failed alliance with Olunthos.

The king smiles, "Ah, the measures we go to in desperation. Who knows, if they had honored their part we still might be in alliance."

"Having the lands we had pledged to them is better than any help Olunthos offers," argues Antipatros.

"So, let us adjourn. Remember that we meet with Philotas, Parmenion and the rest of the Pelagonid delegation after midday." Amuntas smiles gleefully, "I'm for a swim before our meal. Would any of you care to join me?"

η

Eurudike gazes intently at the fountain's spray of water as it catches the light before falling to the pool below where it plays over the surface in ever-changing ripples. For the moment, all of Eurudike is focused on the water's transition at the touch of light. There is a spectrum of color in that instant. There is divinity.

Her concentration falters. She re-enters the world of mortals and is no longer with the goddess, Aphrodite. Still, the memory of that minute clarity, where she felt herself to be water and light and nothing else, gives her deep pleasure. How reassuring to know that if one reaches out with all one's senses, then one can cross the boundary of mortality and for a moment share in the life lived by the divine. Breathing deeply, she let's herself feel joy.

"Mistress," interrupts Marnike.

"Yes, Marnike?"

"You asked me to let you know when it is time to return to the palace. The king should be at the gymnasium now. We will avoid his entourage if we leave now."

"Have you had any message from Leandros?"

Marnike flushes slightly, not liking the subterfuge that Ptolemaios' servant is her lover. "Yes, madam. He will see me at the yard of the shrine to Hestia."

"Then I must pay my respect to Hestia. Perhaps I will stop at Poseidon's temple, as well. That will give you more time with Leandros. Yes, you go on ahead. I will meet you at Hestia's later, after the midday meal."

"Yes, madam," Marnike does not pause, but departs quickly. She has served Eurudike since she was a small child. As she hurries to her false assignation, she thinks about the dangers in Eurudike's actions.

She knows that sometimes it is the servant or slave who is sacrificed to protect or obscure the real betrayals of a mistress or master. Her preservation in this affair weighs heavily on her. Her life revolves around serving and pleasing Eurudike. If all goes well, she will be released in the next few years into a marriage arranged by Eurudike. She will both regret leaving a mistress whom she cares for and be eager to start a life with someone new, for she is certain her mistress will find a good husband for her, someone with whom she is well matched. Though Eurudike is not an easy mistress, she is always fair with Marnike and often confides her own fears, amusements, speculations and ideas to the young woman. That is, until recently. Until Eurudike's attention was caught by Ptolemaios of Aloros. Now she is more distant, more manipulative, more purposeful.

What matters to Eurudike is almost solely Ptolemaios. Her lack of caution could cause deadly trouble. Yet in all of this, Eurudike expects Marnike to act the innocent, to not realize that Eurudike is infatuated with Ptolemaios. Marnike snorts in derision. What is amazing is how few realize the queen's obsession.

As she hurries down the slope, she spies Eurunoe and her friends on the grounds below. Eurunoe sees her and waves. Marnike waves back, grinning. She likes Eurunoe, though Eurudike's daughter is often too timid and, when bold, always when it is inappropriate. Such an awkward darling, yet liked by all. Marnike wonders for a moment whether she ought to confide in Eurunoe, but instantly dismisses the thought. Though Eurudike is consumed by Ptolemaios, Marnike does not know for certain that any impropriety has actually occurred. Possibly, Ptolemaios simply enjoys the attention of the queen and is true to his king. Likely he's not enthralled by the same passion.

Anyway, Leandros is waiting. Who knows? Maybe the task of spending time with her is not unpleasant to the man.

θ

"What I liked best during the game was when Parmenion saved the goal by diving across the Stagiran forwards, tripping them both," exclaims Perdikkas.

"He broke Kleisthenes' leg. My father splinted him up and had to sew the tear in his shin," responds Aristoteles.

"Did your father minister to Parmenion as well? The Pelagone broke two ribs," asks Philippos.

"No, father was attending his fellow citizens of Stagiros only."

The three boys lay side-by-side on their backs talking idly about the stick ball games and watching the occasional cloud and more frequent birds in the sky. As predicted by Parmenion, the Pelagonid team had triumphed over all opponents.

"Do you think the other teams will adopt the Pelagonid style of play?" asks Perdikkas.

"Shush, look over there. See the three small birds chasing the raven," Philippos is up on one elbow, pointing toward the horizon.

"Can you make out what type of bird are the small ones?" asks Aristoteles.

"Not from here. If they veer closer, we can tell."

"An omen, do you think?" grins Perdikkas. "The raven is Athenai, and the little birds are Makedonis, Elimiotis and Pelagonis."

That fancy starts Philippos laughing, "You are right, Perdix. Only I think the little birds are Aleko, you, and me."

"Well, the three little birds are some variety of finch," comments Aristoteles. "If they come closer I could say with more certainty."

"Ari, how is it you know all the different birds or bugs or flowers?" asks Perdikkas.

"By observing, seeing the differences and similarities. And I ask those who know. My father. The old woman who lives out by the marsh edge, the one they call Old Zoe. Do you know Ahtmoses? He's the Aegyptian that lives three houses down from the two-sisters stele. He knows a lot and has many scrolls. I met him accompanying father."

Across the meadow they can see Alexandros coming their way.

Faintly, they can hear him calling them. "Ah, well. Must be time to eat," Perdikkas stands up and waves to his brother.

"I am getting hungry," says Aristoteles. "I'll leave you 'til later." He stands, brushes of the grass and nettles, "See you at the gymnasium?"

"Alexandros and I are supposed to attend the Pelagonid delegation with father later," answers Perdikkas.

"What about you, Philpa? Or ... you could come eat with my family."

"Is your father still angry because I tumbled you in the horse race?" asks Philippos, also standing and brushing himself off.

"Maybe we should meet later."

Philippos grins and lightly punches Aristoteles on the arm, "Well, I think I want to watch how father deals with the Pelagones, but after that would be okay."

"Okay, then, see you later." Aristoteles strides off just as Alexandros reaches them.

"You two are spending too much time with the Stork," states Alexandros, watching the back of the departing boy and thinking that his brothers should be with their peers among the nobility. He turns to his younger brothers, "You'll need to eat fast and get presentable. Phew, Philpa, how much time did you spend down at the stables this morning?"

Philippos laughs at Alexandros, "Wait until you're king, Aleko, then you can order us about."

"A king doesn't order, he commands," says Perdikkas with mock solemnity. The three boys laugh, for Perdikkas is quoting their mother.

"Okay, okay," smiles Alexandros, "I can take a hint. But we do need to hurry. I don't want to miss any part of the meeting with the Pelagones. I want alliance with them."

"We're with you in that," says Perdikkas.

The three boys walk quickly across the meadow, talking about Philotas and his son, Parmenion. As much as any one thing it is the string of victories by the Pelagonid stick ball team that has convinced the princes that they want Pelagonid friendship in the future fights with the Paiaones and Illuroi. "With the Pelagonoi linked with us, even the Lunkestoi will feel pressure to heed the Makedones," asserts Alexandros.

"Aleko, something more important than the Pelagonoi or even Elimiotoi is the three of us," says Philippos.

"What do you mean?"

"The lands held by King Alexandros were torn apart when his sons fought each other. We Makedones have not been as prominent since then. Before father's reign, brothers and cousins killed each other over the throne. When you are king, Aleko, your right arm should be Perdikkas and I should be your left. While we are together, no one can split the kingdom."

The older boy stops, eyes shining at his little brother, "I so pledge," and he holds a hand out to Philippos.

"And I," says Perdikkas, stretching his hand forward.

"And I," responds Philippos, joining their common grip.

"We are the Temenidai!" whoops Alexandros, saluting the sun in the sky, and declaiming, "sons of Temenos of Argos, of Herakles, of great father Zeus himself. From ancient Argos come the Hellenic Temenidai. We three bear a finer distinction for we descend directly from the first Perdikkas, who, with his two brothers, was adopted by the Argeadai clan and led the Makedones out of the highlands onto the plains of Pieris. What is more wondrous than to be a Temenidai of the Argeadai Makedones?"

Philippos laughs with exultation at the pride and joy Alexandros displays. What, indeed, is better than to be one of these three brothers?

CHAPTER THREE

Mother's Love

371 B.C.

α

 karos is exasperated at his master, "Prince, will you stand still!"

Philippos laughs in excitement, "We need a more delicate hand than yours to arrange a garland, Skaros."

"True, true, but I'm all you've got while the women fuss with Eurunoe," grumbles Skaros. He finishes tying the knot at the back of the tall boy's head, "Now, turn around. Let me see if the robe is hanging properly."

The sight of Philippos so formally dressed almost takes the servant's breath away. A handsome lad, just age twelve now. How he has shot up in height these last two years, with more growth to come. Still broad-shouldered. Not classically good looking, but he will turn an eye. The men will watch him closely for the next five years or so, then it will be the turn of the women. "I guess you look all right, master," concedes Skaros.

Perdikkas pops his head in at the door, "Philippos, are your ready? We have to hurry if we're going to help father walk to the groom's house. My, don't you look sweet."

"You should talk, Perdix, I can smell your perfume from here."

Perdikkas' face turns red, "I knew it was too much. Labi said his hand slipped but I think he did it dcliberately."

"At least you're not wearing any more perfume than he would wear," laughs Philippos.

With a parting wave to Skaros, Philippos joins his brother. They hurry along the corridor and then down the stairs. "How is father doing?" asks Philippos.

"Aleko says he's better this afternoon, more like his old self. Maybe winter has just been hard on him."

"He seemed well during the ceremonies but I thought he'd be too tired for tonight."

Perdikkas answers, "He wouldn't miss the procession. Not only for

Eurunoe's sake. He wants to show everyone that he's still physically capable."

"Good. The fact that he's able to walk without support and participate in all the ceremonies shows he's recovering," responds Philippos, with a sense of gratitude to Asklepios or Apollo or whoever of the gods is responsible.

"Let's make sure he doesn't overdo. If he thinks he's strong enough, he'll attend every honor feast and go from house to house. Then tomorrow, he'll be flat on his back again. Aleko says we're to watch over him."

"What's mother doing?"

"She's taken it on herself to counsel both Eurunoe and Ptolemaios," Perdikkas cannot help smirking.

Philippos stops, grabbing Perdikkas' arm, "What do you think, Perdix? We're alone. You can talk plainly. Why is mother so intent on marrying Eurunoe to Ptolemaios? Sis is barely eighteen and he must be fifty."

"What does that matter, Philippos? You know Ptolemaios heads the Athenian faction in our lands. All these years, father has toed a careful line between Sparte, Athenai and now Thebai. In recent years he's generally favored alliance with Athenai. Ptolemaios heads the timber interests and they always favor Athenai. Tying him closely to us serves the Temenidai —he shares some of our blood. More than mother if the truth were known," Perdikkas speaks earnestly.

"Do you like him?"

"Like him? No, I never liked him," clearly Perdikkas does not give any weight to his own personal feelings about Ptolemaios.

"Eurunoe could marry Ptolemaios' son, Philoxenos. They're closer in age. Wouldn't that tie them to us as much?"

"Philoxenos? That weakling. His father doesn't like being in the same room with him," Perdikkas dismisses the possibility. "Look, Philippos, today is the marriage day. We are going to make it a great day for Eurunoe. Make no long faces. As it is, Eurunoe is marrying later than many girls. Look at Arsinoe, she married that old fart Lagos when she was even younger." Perdikkas adds, "Ptolemaios may not seem the best brother-in-law, but there is sense to this."

"You're right, Perdix. It's just that Eurunoe is so dreamy."

"Yeah, as mother would say, our purest lamb." The boys chuckle and hurry on.

* * *

Ptolemaios' town house is not far from the palace. By the time the end of the procession leaves the palace gates, the front of the procession, with Ptolemaios and Eurunoe in the bridal chariot, has only a few hundred feet more to walk. Perhaps seven hundred people make up the marriage procession.

When the chariot reaches the house, an older cousin from Ptolemaios' Orestes lineage serves to welcome the bride. After all, Ptolemaios' mother died long ago. Philippos watches with amusement as Ptolemaios hands Eurunoe down from the chariot to his cousin, then leaps to his bride's side. With a quick heave, Ptolemaios lifts Eurunoe up in his arms and carries her across the threshold of the house. A cheer is raised and the crowd pushes to follow the couple. Despite his age, Ptolemaios shows himself to be vigorous and strong.

The many who are attending the princely wedding are too much for a house even as grand as Ptolemaios', so only the first third of the procession gets inside. The rest mill around outside, raising their voices in song. Ptolemaios' servants scurry through the outdoors crowd passing out drink, tidbits of food and small gifts.

Like all the others in the forefront, Philippos is propelled along by the good-natured thrusting and pushing of family, friends and other guests. He sees Ptolemaios carry Eurunoe across the inner courtyard, past its altar, and into the kitchen. There Ptolemaios gently sets her down by the hearth which has its workaday appearance curiously heightened by the contrast of festive flower wreaths tied around it. As the nuptial couple join hands to light the fire, Philippos, like all the others, lightly tosses a handful of almonds, honeyed candies and dried cherries over the pair. With the traditional offerings raining all about them, Ptolemaios and Eurunoe laugh as the flame rises quickly, brightly from the dry kindling. Another cheer greets their happiness, "To your good fortune and prosperity."

Philippos can tell that Eurunoe is nearly giddy with the events of the day and in anticipation of the bridal chamber. Ptolemaios is boisterous, making much of his adoption into the king's family, swearing his faithfulness to family and friends. By the long standing favor of the king, by his many acts of courage, counsel, and confidence, he stands today with a princess as his wife. King Amuntas puts his arm about the man's shoulder and holds his daughter's chin up in his other hand as he gives a brief speech in the couple's honor.

Forgetting his doubts, Philippos takes pleasure in seeing Ptolemaios as joyous as his wondering young bride. In less than three months, the marriage has been arranged and taken place, with its consummation in a bedroom of this house as its next step.

On the far side of the room, Philippos catches sight of his mother. Her face is a study in calm. Philippos knows that face, that calmness. Knows that it is a mask. But what feelings does it mask? Why isn't she displaying the same delight as all the rest? Perhaps she is simply tired, for with the king's illness, she has shouldered all of the arrangements and tasks, asking only that Alexandros care for his father.

A tug of his robe brings Philippos around to Perdikkas' grinning face, "We're going to the bridal chamber. Eurulokhos and Hipponikos have brought the noise makers. We'll hide in the draperies. Come on." Philippos follows, wanting to be in on the joke.

β

The assembled men turn and wait in silence as King Amuntas makes his way across the audience chamber, leaning heavily on his son, Alexandros. With the weeks since Eurunoe's wedding, Amuntas has regained his good color and much of his bearing, though he tires easily. He loses breath with very little exertion. He is thinner, still. The men, the king's companions and other notables, near thirty in all, watch and assess the king and his designated successor.

Seated on his throne, and made comfortable by Alexandros, who tucks a fine wool cloak over the old man's legs, Amuntas begins the session, "You know why I've summoned you. Sparte has called a conference, which all states must attend. I want your advice before deciding who will attend as my representatives and what instructions they will receive. I believe we can safely say that Persian gold is again in Spartan coffers." The sarcasm is so likely that it gives the men no amusement. "I propose that my delegation be three individuals. Athanaios watches over Thebai. Ptolemaios does the same for Athenai. Antiokhos is a Lakonian in spirit." At this jibe the men do laugh good-naturedly, for while Antiokhos is known for valiance he is also known for indolence when at peace. "Does any one propose another? Do any of the three of you choose to withdraw?"

"Good king, I would ask that you name another to my place. I do not feel that now is the time for me to be absent from the kingdom on a lengthy journey." Ptolemaios pauses, "I suggest Iolaos or Philippos, son of Makhatas, go in my stead."

"Hasn't the bridal bed worn out yet, Ptolemaios," calls out Antipatros. At this sally, most of the men laugh.

Ptolemaios grins, showing that no insult is taken, then raises his hand to still the laughter. "Antipatros, son of Iolaos, I wish my reasons were as simple as the pleasures of mating. What I say is said in respect to our king and is something we all fear." Turning back to the man on the throne, Ptolemaios states, "You have been deathly ill, sire. We all praise Apollo and rejoice at the progress you make in recovery. Yet you know you are not strong enough now to lead us in battle." Indicating the crown prince with a lift of his chin, Ptolemaios continues, "Prince Alexandros is coming of age and will, in time, take your place in war. For now, though, we are vulnerable. We are surrounded by enemies." His voice rising in power, Ptolemaios turns to appeal to the other men, "Bardulis of the Dardanoi has been occupied for a number of years in controlling the Illuriote tribes west of him. He has accomplished that work and again turns his greedy eyes on the civilized world. Agis has succeeded to the leadership of the Paiaones. He is a treacherous neighbor at best. Kotys, king of the Odrusai, now dominates all of Thraikios, from the Strymon to the Propontis. These are our barbarian neighbors, and they have never been more dangerous."

Several men call out, "Hear him, King; hear Ptolemaios."

Ptolemaios holds up his hand again and the others still, "What of our civilized neighbors? We have watched Thessalos turned from its habitual disunion into a subject land of one city, of one man, Iason of Pherai. What does that mean for us when we have traditionally supported the Aleuadai of Larissa? Can we imagine Iason as our friend? How do we face this tyrant? I see the potential there for a state stronger than Sparte's Lakonia." Murmurs rise from among the men. Ptolemaios points from one man to another, "Do you doubt the possibility? Think of a Sparte on our borders. What then becomes of the Makedones?"

He wheels back to face the king, "Have I mentioned Olunthos yet? Do you doubt that we are surrounded? Should I tell you of that city's plots with Pherai?" He begins ticking off his fingers, "Stagiros, Mende, Apollonia, Akanthos, Sane, Argilos, Sermyle, Torone, Singos, Skione. Which of these cities does not follow Olunthos' lead? How many times must we fight the Khalkidike?" He shakes his head, as if in anguish, "Of course, there is Epeiros. Neoptolemos is a good man, but he has a viper in his brother, Arubbas, as fellow king. Still, if we continue in our friendship with Athenai, we can count on Epeiros not to lend support to our enemies. Any friend of Athenai is a friend of Epeiros. And what is the price of Athenian friendship for the Makedones? We all know it—to acknowledge that Amphipolis is their city."

Ptolemaios sighs, "Many times I have acted as your envoy to Athenai. This time, King Amuntas, let someone else go in my stead."

Amuntas begins coughing, harshly, bending over. Alexandros leans down patting the king's back. A servant hurries to the king's side with a mug, but the king waves it aside. He straightens, "Pardon my malady, cousins." He pauses, continues in a hoarse voice. "Ptolemaios has expressed his view of the situation. In general, I concur, though with a touch less of his drama." Again, the men chuckle. "We have an uncertain future. Though we look to the gods and have our seers, all of the dangers enumerated are real. Keep in mind, though, that only Iason of Pherai and a Bardulis stronger by his conquest of his western neighbors are new to us. My condition is more frail than I would like. I am unused to illness. Even were I strong enough, I am not the best general here. Derdas, Iolaos, Ptolemaios—you have been my chief generals. Let it remain so. Philippos the Elimiote, if your cousin Derdas can spare you, would you join the delegation?"

"Aye, cousin."

"Good. That's settled." The king sits back. For a time he seems to brood. The men exchange glances. Amuntas raises his head, "What I am going to declare will not please you. I believe we need to count on one of the three chief cities of south as an ally. Of the three, Athenai most relies upon us, since our timber makes her fleet. We have tried Sparte." The king grimaces, "They ask too much and provide too little. Thebai is not a well-known

49

quantity. True, they succeeded in throwing out the Spartans and the league they enforce over the Boiotians grows in strength. Still, I doubt those farmers would ever understand anyone's concerns save their own. Their new strength will prove ephemeral." He looks from face to face, "I believe our only choice is Athenai. For what it's worth, we have a pact of friendship with Iason of Pherai. All to the good, but he intends to be hegemon of the Hellenes. He'll honor the pact for as long as it takes him to secure Larissa. We need a counterweight. Who else can it be than Athenai?"

All are silent. Each is thinking through the king's line of reasoning, and they all see where he is going. One by one they realize and look to him. He nods, "Yes, we give up our recognition of Amphipolitan independence. What do we lose? Amphipolis won't like us much. That won't stop trade. They still block the Thraikiotes, especially King Kotys, from invading west. True, Athenai will next ask us to aid them in enforcing their rights over the Amphipolitans. Though not for some time. Who knows whether we will ever need to field an army for them? To sew up an alliance with Athenai, what better market for announcing our change of heart than Sparte's conference on a Common Peace?"

"Father, Athenian seizure of Amphipolis would put the wolf's head inside our door," exclaims Alexandros.

"First Athenai must succeed in taking Amphipolis. Public recognition seals our friendship with Athenai, but does not prevent us from working through friends in common with Amphipolis to ensure her continued independence." The king smiles slyly.

Iolaos speaks up, "We'll get no real aid from Athenai without giving her real help against Amphipolis."

"True, old friend," responds the king, "but I'm not sure we want their aid so much as the public knowledge that their arms would be forthcoming if we were attacked." Certain he has the men with him, the king adds, "Now, let's debate the full instructions for our three envoys..."

γ

She shivers as a draft whistles around the inner columns of the temple. *A cold spring this year*, she thinks. She hears the clatter and blowing of a horse. *Good, he's here.* An inner flame made up of desire, excitement, anger, fear, guilt and love bursts within her. She feels alive again.

"Euri," the whisper of his pet name for her penetrates the sanctum, "where are you?"

She steps from behind the pillar. At the sight of her, he rushes over and pulls her into his arms. "Oh, my huntress, I have missed you." The warmth of his kisses raises goose bumps along her neck.

"Ptolemaios, I didn't know it would be this hard."

"My queen, my heart, please know that I am with you at all times no matter where I physically must be." His emotions seem to choke him, and he grips her harder.

Still she does not return his kisses, stands rigid within his embrace. He releases her and holds her at arms length, "We have been through this before, Eurudike. It was you who suggested that marrying Eurunoe would divert suspicion and allow us to be together more often."

"Yes, yes," she answers wearily, "I know what I have done. I also know how heart-sore this makes me. What kind of mother am I? What kind of wife?"

"You have not felt affection for Amuntas, let alone love, for nearly ten years. You have long since barred him from your bed. By rights, I am your husband. By the love we share, I—am—your—husband!" This last he says fiercely, through clenched teeth.

"We should have waited." She catches up his hand, "The king is dying. We all know it." She shakes her head sadly, "If I had realized last autumn how quickly he would fail, I would not have had you marry my daughter. We could have waited, and I would marry you in my own right."

He strokes her cheek gently, "Do not reproach yourself. We do the best we can. No matter the sacrifice made, the future is uncertain. Amuntas is a tough old man. He is dying, yes, but his dying could take several more years."

"What of Eurunoe?" she asks.

"Ah, she's a moon-calf." He smiles, "I am gentle with her. I do not ask much of her. I'm not sure this isn't still dress-up for her."

"And in bed?"

He doesn't let his thoughts show in his face. The truth is that Eurunoe has surprised him. She is a demanding lover—endlessly finding touches, strokes, holdings she's never tried before. He has been surprised by his own response to her. What he thought would be an occasional duty has become an enlivening focus of their lives together. He hopes no word of this has reached Eurudike. To Eurudike, he simply says, "Your daughter is healthy and dutiful."

"I shouldn't have asked," she says dryly. For a moment she leans her forehead against his shoulder.

The thought enters his mind of having the girl and this woman together. The idea excites him. Is there any way he could persuade mother and daughter to share him? He sees no ready solution. Still, the fantasy tickles him.

"I do not want to stand here much longer," she says with a hint of her royal manner. "What arrangements should we make?"

"I have had one of my people secure a house that sits back behind the marketplace. You can reach it discreetly by way of the women's gate. The garden abuts onto the precincts of Hephaistos' temple. If you are there, leave a shutter to one of the upstairs windows open. Most afternoons are mine to do with as I please." Seeing she understands, he adds, "Later in

51

the month, in a fortnight, I will be leaving to make a circuit of my estates. Eurunoe will go with me as far as Edessa. If you will travel to your farm outside of Europos, I will join you there for the festival of Hekate."

She nods assent, then pulls him close. No longer rigid, her mouth seeks his. His hands roam her body, until she takes hold of one to cup her breast. They lean into each other. She whispers in his ear, "Ptolemaios, I hate this subterfuge. Somehow there will come a time when we can openly be together, as husband and wife. Until then, please put up with my moods. I love you so, yet feel such sorrow at how we must twist and turn."

"Eurudike, I am yours until death." They kiss, chastely, and break apart. He turns abruptly and strides out into the dark.

δ

"No, no, Philippos, your shield must come up and move left in a sweep, like this," the old soldier, Lusias, demonstrates the move. "Then thrust with your spear. Not weakly, but with force. Directly against your opponent's eyes. When he flinches, drop to his throat and you have your blood-sacrifice."

The boy executes the move again. "Lusias, what happens if I fail to catch his spear with my shield?"

"Well, you're dead, of course," Lusias starts laughing, heartily, fully. "So there's good reason to practice." The man wipes the tears of mirth from his eyes. "Ah, what's the use, boy. You're no footman. You will be leading horsemen, stabbing at backs when the enemy breaks."

Philippos feels a spurt of anger at the words, "Teach me properly, Lusias. Teach me all of it—all that you know of fighting."

"Yes, Prince, you'll get your full measure worth." The soldier turns and bellows over the field, "Alkimakhos, get over here. I want you to take on Philippos. Bring your pole and shield." The boy leaves the group practicing with swords, grabs up his equipment and comes running.

Lusias sets the two boys opposite each other. "Okay, now, I want the two of you to square off. Don't hold back. Push, shove, do your best to make an opening and go for a kill. The winner will be the one that takes three out of five touches. On my signal, you start. Go!"

Shield batters against shield. The boys grunt with exertion, seeking a touch. Weighted poles act as spears, thudding against shield and helmet. Suddenly Philippos steps back, throwing Alkimakhos off stride. With a quick sidestep forward, Philippos nails Alkimakhos at the center of his breast plate.

"Not a very likely step," criticizes Lusias, "remember, you'll have the pressure of seven men behind you. This isn't fighting barbarians in the hills. This is how Hellenes fight in phalanx. Get back at it."

Again, the boys struggle. A quick downward thrust of Alkimakhos pole tangles Philippos' feet. Falling, Philippos grabs at his enemy's pole with his shield hand to keep the pole from withdrawing. Using his own body weight, he snaps the pole from Alkimakhos' hands and thrusts up from the ground with his own pole. Alkimakhos fends off the thrust with his shield but is now unarmed.

"Good response," praises the soldier. "You have learned early the danger of tripping an opponent, Alkimakhos. Still, it was a good move. But you must be quicker. Philippos should not have been able to trap your spear. Let's start again."

Again and again, the boys work at becoming skilled in killing. Philippos prevails at the fifth touch. Both boys stand breathing heavily. Philippos can feel a bruise forming on his cheekbone from Alkimakhos' last touch. The two boys are grinning.

"Okay, let's step up the pace," grunts Lusias. He brings the rest of the boys over to join the two. At Lusias' direction, the boys form two squares —four across and six deep—to make a small phalanx for each side. The soldier appoints Philippos the captain of one team and Alkimakhos the captain of the other. He gives them five minutes to talk with their fellow team members to decide on strategy. He even allows a perfunctory sacrifice before the contest begins. Then at his signal, the melee is on. Lusias and his assistants follow the action closely, calling out advice, encouragement, and objections.

Seeing the scrimmage, passer-bys stop and come over, so that a thin crowd forms around the battling phalanxes. More advice, catcalls, comments are screamed out to the boys.

Within the phalanxes, little of Lusias or the crowd is heard. Those in front are thrusting frantically, wickedly, with their poles, while anxiously taking their enemies' thrusts on their shields. Those in back are adding their weight by pushing their column leaders forward on the opposing team. Some are cursing, some sobbing, but all are caught in the rhythm of the shove and recoil. The weak sun of spring seems to bear down hotly. The field that had been muddy now seems dustier.

Philippos begins calling the chant. First Hipponikos takes it up, then boy after boy on their side. For a time, the rhythm of the chant and the rhythm of the push fuse. Then with a mighty shout, Philippos yells, "Now!" breaking the rhythm. All on his side crash into their opponents. Philippos doesn't touch his immediate opposite with his pole, instead, he jumps on the enemy's shield and simply runs over the boy. The opposing phalanx reels, breaks apart, with some boys down, and those in back and on the edges backing off to escape the disaster. The center holds briefly, then collapses as it is overwhelmed. Having won, Philippos' companions break into dance and song.

Lusias calls them all to order. Point by point, he goes over the mistakes he's seen or the occasional proper thrust or action. Finally, running down, he has them ask questions which he answers before dismissing them.

Seeking out Philippos, Lusias asks, "Well, Prince, was today's lesson worthwhile?"

"Yes, friend, but we need to expand the class so we can try larger maneuvers."

Lusias shakes his head, smiling, "You do not rest do you, Philippos?"

"There is no time," the boy laughs. "Tomorrow, Lusias. Let me catch up with the others." He runs after the other boys who are heading for the swimming pool.

ε

Spring turns soft, then eases into summer. Not yet the daunting heat that can stride in from the south, instead summer is still fresh, inviting.

Arriving with summer is a plea from Elimiotis that King Amuntas arbitrate a dispute with the Perrhaibic town of Dolikhe. A representative soon follows from this north Thessaliote community. Normally, they would have turned to the Aleuadai of Larissa. But the times are not normal in Thessalos with Iason of Pherai prowling. So Dolikhe is willing to take its chances on the fairness of Amuntas despite his ties to Derdas of Elimiotis.

Dolikhe is the leading town of a district within Thessaliote Perrhaibis called Tripolis. The district is important as it controls the southern entries of two passes through the mountains that divide Elimiotis and the Makedones from the south. The eastern pass, Petra, crosses into Makedones Pieros between Mount Olympos and Mount Tifaros, which is the southern most outreach of the Pieric mountains. The western pass, Volustana, separates the Pieric mountain chain from the Kambounos mountains. This western pass, whose road rises from the Tripolis valley and crosses into Elimiotis, is the center of the dispute.

As often happens, the dispute is over grazing rights. Then it escalated into an issue of tolls at the pass. Ultimately, the question is who owns the pass? Elimiotis or Perrhaibis? While real differences exist, neither side wishes to see the argument degenerate into bloodshed. Nor does either side want to see the dispute become an excuse for Iason's intervention.

Derdas has opted not to represent Elimiotis, as his long personal friendship with Amuntas might make any possible judgment the king makes in Elimiotis' favor seem unfair. The other chief man of his lands, his nephew Philippos, son of Makhatas, has yet to return from the Spartan conference. So Xenokleitos, the noble most concerned from the Elimiote viewpoint, is to state their case.

For Dolikhe, the town's citizens have elected Philomides to speak.

Conscious of the honor such an appeal for arbitration makes, Amuntas is dressed at his most resplendent. The court behavior is formal. Following the opening rites, the two opposing representatives have exactly half the morning apiece to state their cases and may refer to any testimonial witnesses, documents or precedents their assistants have assembled. Amuntas will then recess to ponder the arguments, as well as to discuss the merits of each case over meal with any three of his chosen counselors who are not Elimiotes. In mid-afternoon, the court will re-assemble to hear his judgment. The decision is to be taken down in writing by scribes so that copies of the judgment can be housed in the temples of the goddess Dike in the cities of Dolikhe, Aiane and Pella.

To Philippos, listening with his brothers to the high carrying voice of Philomides, the Perrhaibic argument seems strong. Yet would Amuntas really surrender the pass to the Thessaliotes? He nudges Perdix and whispers, "If father grants the pass to Perrhaibis, won't that put it into the hands of Iason of Pherai?"

Alexandros leans over, "Maybe. Perrhaibis is an independent land within Thessalos, but the Aleuadai of Larissa have generally run things there. Though under King Arkhelaos, just before his murder, we held Perrhaibis. If father decides for Perrhaibis, the Aleuadai will be thankful as well as Perrhaibis. Perhaps it's a good idea to strengthen Larissa in a way which does not defy Iason of Pherai."

Perdikkas adds, "Not only that. Derdas has already indicated to father that he will accept the decision truly, either way that it goes. He knows he can force the pass if it ever comes to that. What he wants to be sure of is his share of the tolls from traffic traveling north to either Eordaia or Orestis."

"Then father won't decide just on the merits?" asks Philippos.

"There's little to choose between the arguments. Father could reasonably decide for either party," responds Alexandros.

Several individuals around the boys try to shush their conversation as Philomides reaches his conclusion. Upon the ending declamation, a polite round of applause for the skillful rhetoric sweeps through the great hall.

Xenokleitos stands, stretches, paces back and forth in front of the king. Time begins to stretch and still the man says nothing. As the audience waits, the echoes of Philomides speech cease to sound in their minds. Tension builds, though some fear that the highland man is too intimidated by the city politician's speech to know how to respond.

Finally, he begins, "King Amuntas, I will speak plainly for the facts are simple. For generations, we have been at peace with our neighbors across the mountains. Depending on the favor of the gods, grass is green on both sides of the mountains. There have been times of need when one people or the other borrowed sustenance for their herds from their neighbor. Who can say where rights extend? Is it not sufficient that the north side is Elimiotis and the south is Perrhaibis? Is that too simple an explanation? Do we need to send out officers to survey these crags and steeps, when the herders will still wander from one to another? Let those decisions of where a man may graze his sheep and goats be left among the locals. Let them be admonished to be tolerant of a neighbor's needs. If fairness is demanded, let a sacrifice be made and a coin tossed."

"What of Volustana Pass itself? If a stone wall runs between the lands of two farmers, can they not both agree to maintain the wall? If we know that Elimiotis runs up the north side of the Kambounos mountains and Perrhaibis the south, can we not agree that tolls from those going south belong to Perrhaibis, while tolls of those going north belong to Elimiotis?"

"Why do we have this dispute? Did it not start with one small valley lying high in the mountains which herders from each people could reach? Isn't the right answer—the peaceful solution—to say that the valley is in the possession of the spirit of the Kambounos, and that the goddess allows us all to use the valley? Shall we occupy the valley in alternate seasons or years? Shall we split the valley midway? What solution do you suggest, King Amuntas?" And with that question, Xenokleitos bows and sits down.

The audience stirs, surprised by a speech of mere minutes after the hours-long exhortation made by Philomides. Is the brevity a mockery of the king's justice? Is Elimiotis shrugging its shoulders, surrendering the argument to Perrhaibis?

The king stands and the court is instantly silent. "In one hour, assemble here to receive my judgment," says the king gravely.

"What will father do for an hour if he can't eat?" laughs Perdikkas. "The servants won't have a meal ready yet. It's too early."

"He'll rest," says Alexandros. "He's still not strong."

Philippos considers the strange twist in which Elimiotis advances no argument but simply appeals for fairness, "Is there a dispute at all?"

His brothers turn to him. "I mean aren't all the chief people of Perrhaibis here?" Philippos continues, "By showing that Perrhaibis relies on the King of the Makedones to come to an accord with Elimiotis, are they not demonstrating that the three lands exist in friendship. That our three peoples are only a step away from formal alliance. What does that say to Iason of Pherai?"

"You're right, Philpa," says Alexandros excitedly. "They no longer can be certain of support from Larissa, so we become their patron. Maybe it's not enough to scare Pherai, but it does tell him that he can't just have his way in Perrhaibis without considering our reaction."

"So what father is probably doing is meeting privately with Derdas of Elimiotis and the Perrhaibic clan heads," says Philippos. "If not now, then during the course of this visit."

Alexandros begins laughing in appreciation of the subtlety of the show, "You can bet that Philomides wasn't in on the secret."

"Nor were you," says Perdikkas to sting his brother.

"The fewer that know a stratagem, the likelier it will succeed," retorts Alexandros.

"This coughing illness may be dogging father's body, but not his mind," comments Philippos.

ζ

Philippos slows his weighted wooden sword as he watches a palace servant running down the distant street toward the practice field. A jarring pain recalls Philippos to the exercise. Stesidamos is delighted with his win, not realizing that the cause is approaching from behind him.

"That was inexcusable, Prince," storms Lusias. "You can keep Stesi at a distance all day."

Philippos interrupts Lusias by gesturing beyond the crestfallen Stesidamos to indicate the runner, "A message. He's coming for me."

"In battle, a messenger may be coming for you, too. That should not cause you to drop your guard or keep you from finishing your enemy." Lusias is unmollified. "Probably some ceremony or palace claptrap that you're called to attend," he growls.

"No," says Philippos, "he's running too hard and he's shouting something."

Lusias and Stesidamos watch closely. "You're right, Philippos," says the boy. Others practicing on the field notice the runner and pause to see what's happening.

"He's calling something about the Spartans," adds Lusias.

"Yes, yes," grins Philippos. "The Spartans are beaten!"

"Who did they fight?" asks Stesidamos.

"Has to be the Boiotians," answers Lusias.

"Epaminondas of Thebai thumbed his nose at the Spartans at their peace conference. The Spartans authorized one of their kings to chastise Thebai. King Kleombrotos has an army of ten thousand," Philippos stops talking as the now panting runner reaches them.

The man's chest heaves up and down, and he gulps in a breath, "Sorry, sir. Your father summons you. The Thebans and their Boiotian allies have destroyed a Spartan army at a place called Leuktra. Spartan King Kleombrotos is dead. Your father has ordered the seers of Ares to conduct a sacrifice. You are to attend. There will be a counsel following."

Philippos is delighted. Though age twelve is the earliest he could be considered a man, he did not expect to be called to a counsel yet. He has not killed a man in battle or taken a dangerous animal, like a lion, bear or boar, in a hunt. In a couple of years, he might become acknowledged anyway, but this summons surprises him.

"I will come immediately. Lusias, will you see to my things here?" Not waiting for a response, Philippos hands the trainer his shield, helmet and wooden sword. "Stesi, please, help me untie my thongs." With Stesidamos undoing the breastplate ties on one side and the messenger on the other, Philippos is standing nude quickly.

Already alerted, Skaros is coming at a run, carrying a toweling cloth and clothing. Within minutes, Philippos is ready. Together, the boy, his man, and the palace servant jog toward the temple of Ares.

* * *

"Let me relate to you what is clearly known. The dispatch from Athanaios was sent both by ship and by messenger-relay. The ship had fair sailing and has arrived first. The battle was fought five days ago. The Boiotian army was commanded by Epaminondas and Pelopidas. The Boiotians were outnumbered five to three. According to Athanaios, the main battle was preceded by a fight between the horsemen. When the Theban cavalry routed the Peloponnesians, the fleeing horsemen disrupted the lines of Lakedaimonian and Peloponnesian phalanxes. The Theban and Boiotian phalanxes advanced immediately. Epaminondas had deepened the lines that faced the Lakedaimonians and Spartiates. When an outflanking move was attempted by King Kleombrotos, Pelopidas led Thebai's Sacred Band into the gap. More than four hundred Spartiates were killed and thousands of Lakedaimonians. Kleombrotos is dead. The remaining Peloponnesians retreated to a fortified camp," Amuntas pauses, surveys the extra large counsel he has called. The counsel members are tense, attentive, intent.

"What is as important as the battle itself is the alignment it reveals. Athenai has backed off from supporting Thebai. She's scared silly that Thebai could prove more powerful than Sparte." Many of the men nod their understanding. "Iason of Pherai is mobilizing forces to support Thebai. Obviously, he shows less fear of his neighbor. Also, he doesn't panic as he has only his own decisions to mind, unlike the democrats in Athenai. Sparte, of course, is sending another army to support the remnant of the first."

"You all know that the path I've followed for a number of years is friendship with Athenai. I still feel her interests and ours will coincide more often than the interests of the other major states. Not that we should ever cease to be vigilant of any encroachment she might make on our patrimony," Amuntas pauses again, catching his breath, as he no longer has the lung capacity to sustain an audible speech for long to so large a gathering.

Clearing his throat, then coughing into the ever present cloth he carries, Amuntas resumes, "We will know more of events in the south in time. For now, though, I want to discuss the situation in Thessalos. Athenai is timid. She may prove less than reliable if intervention were needed there. Our traditional friends, the Aleuadai of Larissa, are cowed. What does Leuktra mean for Thessalos? What do the events of Thessalos —our neighbor—mean for us? This fighting between Thebai and Sparte may prove a ladder that allows Iason of Pherai to climb higher than either Thebai or Sparte. Should we re-align? If not, should we actively seek to forestall Pherai? If so, how do you propose to do so? Let me hear your views. Iolaos, why don't you start?"

Before Iolaos steps forward, Ptolemaios is in front, "King Amuntas, please excuse my taking precedence. Would you ask Iolaos to start by giving us his assessment of the military strength of the Makedones?"

MOTHER'S LOVE (371 B.C.)

Amuntas nods his assent, and the debate begins.

For Philippos, what interests him is the interplay among the roughly seventy men in the hall as much as what is being said. Probably as many more notables of the realm are not present as are here. Most of the absentees are on their estates or about their business far from Pella. The court and the lowland Makedones of Emathis and Bottiaia are over-represented, but he is certain that is typical of a counsel. Even so, before a half-hour is out, he identifies four discernable factions in the room.

The timber people are all with Ptolemaios. Perhaps he has the traders, as well. Iolaos represents the country nobles—those whose wealth is in large-scale farming, breeding and stock. Mostly conservative. Not inclined to look outside the borders. Antiokhos and his son-in-law, Lagos, seem to head what can only be called the court faction. They seem to be trying to represent the king's point-of-view, without being certain what the king is thinking. The fourth faction surprises Philippos for it is headed by his brother, Alexandros. The senior prince seems to be fascinated by Thessalos. His supporters are generally younger, and many are highlanders.

Philippos looks at his father, the great sagging bear of a man, silvered, lined, ancient. His father turns his head and spies Philippos watching him. The old man winks, then is again attentive to the loud argument Lagos is making. Philippos can see the old man trying to hide his amusement.

Amuntas interrupts the speech, "Hold, please, Lagos. You can continue in a moment. Keep your thought in mind. Alexandros, would you state your view again, please."

"Certainly, father. I feel we should respond graciously to any overtures from any party in the dispute. To the extent possible, we should observe neutrality. In the meantime, we should take steps to strengthen our borders with Thessalos. We should also work to assist the Aleuadai of Larissa. A standing force should be maintained." Alexandros is ticking off his points rapidly, when Amuntas raises his hand to stop the flow.

"If I understand your last point from your earlier diatribe, I gather the standing force would combine a partial callout of the nobles and their followers, supplemented by units of phalangists made up of mercenaries and a trained core of smallholders?"

"Yes, father. We could apportion the year in sixty-day segments and rotate duty among the nobles and smallholders. That way it would not burden anyone greatly and all would gain experience."

"Good. Keep standing." The old man turns his head and calls out, "Perdikkas, son of Amuntas, what say you?"

"Father, I agree with Alexandros."

The king grunts, smiles slyly, "Philippos, son of Amuntas, are you of like mind?"

"Yes, father." Philippos is proud of being called on in the counsel. It is the first he's spoken.

"Now, youngest of men, the phalangists were your idea, were they not?"

"Well, father, all three of us agreed that we need a Makedon phalanx and not just mercenaries."

"Just so, boy, you all three agreed." The king is smiling broadly, "Now, Lagos, what were you saying about the uncertainty of the kingdom's future?"

η

Lying in bed that night, Philippos is lonesome for Lady Kleopatra. He would dearly love to share with her the news of his first attendance in a formal counsel. Though she died more than a year ago, she often comes unbidden into his thoughts. What would she make of Thebai's victory over the Spartans?

Only lately has he begun to realize how remarkable was the friendship they shared. He can barely remember how it began. He does know that he had been frightened of her when he was little. Yet her kindness to him had been steadfast. Once he got past her stern appearance, he found her endlessly caring of him. Not in some cuddling, unmanly manner, as you would expect from a woman, but in a demanding expectation that he understand and think about his birthright and governing, about war and trade, about ... well, about anything a king must consider.

She is the only adult who treated him as a person in his own right. Until today. Until his father called on him, as on any counselor. He hugs the new knowledge of his manhood to him.

Why did Kleopatra choose him? Why not Alexandros or Perdikkas? She might have advised Eurunoe—as most women would have done. Philippos concludes that being female had become irrelevant to Kleopatra. Certainly, she is the only female he has known for whom that state, her gender, did not matter to him. Is that why she chose Philippos, because for his brothers it might have mattered?

She told him once that Alexandros had his father, Perdikkas his mother, and so she would have Philippos. Philippos does not believe it was that simple.

He wonders which of the gods she had especially reverenced. There were manifestations of Zeus that she honored, he knew. And, of course, she honored Hestia. But from clues and odd comments, he suspects it is Helios, the sun. Not just Helios, but Helios as the particular embodiment of the Temenidai. She believed firmly that the best thing was a strong, able king who guarded and worked to assure the prosperity of the kingdom. A shepherd king. Maybe even more, a succession of such kings. Of all things Kleopatra might have wanted, it would have been to be such a king. Denied by her sex, she did the next best thing—helped form Philippos to be the kind of king she would want to be. A puzzling, troubling thought, for Alexandros will be king, not Philippos.

When she died—quietly, in her sleep—he felt such grief. But because their friendship had been theirs only, he had tried to keep the grief locked inside so no one would know. Some weeks later, at the daily libation in the courtyard of the palace, he had broken down. Sobbing. All it had taken was a memory of Kleopatra standing by while his father conducted the kingly ritual. Perdikkas had led him away, comforted him without mockery, never asking why Philippos wept so.

Kleopatra. Skaros. Perdikkas. Father, of course. And then Alexandros. And all the others, Eurunoe, mother. People important in his life, for whom there is meaning and caring.

His mind returns to Kleopatra. If he tries to imagine her face, to reconstruct her image, it is elusive. But when she comes to mind herself, she is clear and present. Sometimes, in dreams, they talk. Almost as in the past, except he seldom remembers what they talk about in those dreams.

He slides out of bed, kneeling, the floor cold. He appeals to Hermes to take a message to Kleopatra, whether she is in the Asphodel or Elysian fields, for he is certain she is not in Tartaros. *Please, great lord, let her know of the events of this day; please, let her know that I miss her and that I honor her memory.*

Climbing back in bed, he thinks of the god Poludeukes, whom he has adopted as his special god. Often, he thinks of himself as Kastor, the god's mortal brother. Though chosen by Philippos because Poludeukes is principally the god of horses, Philippos knows that the god and his hero brother are held in high regard by the Spartans. In becoming a man on the day the Makedones learn of Sparte's defeat, could that be an omen that it is time to seek a new guardian among the gods? He decides that tomorrow he will ask the seers at the shrine of Poludeukes to make a sacrifice. Perhaps the god will direct him.

Settling back down, Philippos has one last thought of Kleopatra before drifting into sleep. She is sitting by the bed in the dim light, as of old. She leans across and kisses him on the check.

θ

Idly Ptolemaios lets his hand play over the queen's shoulder, breast, stomach, and inner thigh. She catches the errant hand, "You're tickling." She stretches, rises, and gives him a hand up.

"Whew," says Ptolemaios. "It's been some time." He surveys the trail of clothes from the door to the bed.

Eurudike laughs weakly, "I should say so, we didn't even eat yet."

"I ate," he leers at her.

She brushes his hair into place, liking the grizzled mix of gray and black. They nuzzle. She runs a hand over the muscles of his back, "When do you leave again?"

"Not for ten days." He yawns, then adds, "Some of the smallholders near the upper Loudias lost their crops to flooding. They will appreciate grain from my estates. I could have my stewards act for me, but I prefer they see the largesse come directly from my hands."

"Yes, they will know not only that you are their benefactor but that your interest in them is personal."

He touches her nose with his forefinger, "Let's eat. I'm starving."

"The fish will be cold."

"No matter," he smiles. He likes the idea of the queen having prepared the meal for him, just as when he possessed her all he could think of was how she submitted herself to him. Apart from the rush of his own sensation that is. Yet that thought was enough to give flame for an extraordinary lust and an exquisite climax.

While Eurudike cuts the bread, she notices the scratches on his upper arm left from her nails. "I marked you as mine, Ptolemaios," she remembers her passion. *With this man I could lead a peaceful, happy land. Our names would echo through generations as the benefactors of our people.*

"You are a lioness, Euri," his eyes alight, he pops a scrap of fish in his mouth.

She asks, "What do you think of this wild scheme of Alexandros'?"

"To tie Thessalos to us and use our combined strengths?"

"Yes, that and the reorganization of the nobility's military service?" asks Eurudike.

"A lot of men are against an innovation that would obligate them to strengthen the kingship." He takes up her hand and kisses it, "Are you opposed because Alexandros is the author or because his schemes could divide opinion?"

"Amuntas dotes on the boy. I think Alexandros holds too high an opinion of himself. That can only lead to tragedy. He should learn to rely on you and the other chief men. As much as I differ with Amuntas, at least he knows what he does well and what he should leave to others."

"Your son is young."

"Yes," she answers pointedly, "and headstrong. He has no regard for me and little regard for anyone but himself."

Ptolemaios considers, "Alexandros does make light of Iason of Pherai. I don't understand your boy's confidence. The rest of the Hellenic world does not make light of the tyrant."

"Much of Iason's forces are made up of mercenaries. Aleko believes mercenaries can be suborned. He thinks a loyal force of Makedones would be stronger than mercenaries if they are well led. I think Derdas of Elimiotis has a hand in this. He has made a disciplined force of his horsemen."

Ptolemaios steeples his fingers and rests his chin upon the tips, "Fighting barbarians is one thing. We Makedones can be good at that, especially the highlanders. Facing trained phalanxes is another thing. I don't mean the old rushed together citizen bands that train four days a month and respond to emergencies. Their day is long past. I mean the rigorous phalanxes of Sparte, of Thebai, of Iason's mercenaries. They would be too strong for us. And the horsemen of Thessalos are no less capable than our own people." Ptolemaios shakes his head, "I think the ventures Alexandros proposes are madness. Instead, we should husband our strength and maintain our alliance with Athenai."

"That's why it's important for your voice to be the strongest in the land. Build up your adherents so none can gainsay you. Let us stay the course with Athenai. We cannot allow Alexandros to plunge the kingdom into some witless adventure so that he can think of himself as a latter day Akhilles." The mother is fierce in her condemnation of her eldest son.

He nods, "We need to expand our allies within the kingdom beyond those who identify their interests with my policies. I believe Antiokhos is as alarmed over Alexandros' militancy as we are. Can you learn more about the views of his faction? I need details: what this man wants, what that man fears. And you might set a scribe to trace all the family connections. I don't want to misstep because I've forgotten that someone is someone else's second cousin. Once I have enough information in hand, I'll get a meeting with Antiokhos."

"I can do all that. Arsinoe, the wife of Lagos, may be a starting point. She's too bright and too young not to be restless with so dogmatic a husband."

"Lagos is a good man in a fight. He will follow his commander into any fray, always protecting his leader's back. In counsel, his words always protect his father-in-law, Antiokhos."

"No doubt there is a need for strong followers." She leans over and kisses his lips. They taste of fish. Straightening, she says, "I prefer a man who can lead."

He chuckles, "Come, sit with me. Let's eat together."

ι

"Philippos, I don't see much of you any more," complains Eurunoe.

"You are a married woman now, sis. Soon you'll make me an uncle," laughs Philippos.

The slight woman looks at her youngest brother sorrowfully, "I'm not so sure."

Realizing that Eurunoe has sought him out for more than company, Philippos asks, "What's this, Eurunoe? Why are you unhappy? You've been wed for six months and this is the first I've seen you sad."

"When did we last see each other?"

He feels uncomfortable. He guesses, "Six days ago?"

"Philippos, son of Amuntas, you know it's been longer than that!" She sighs, "Never mind. It was at the banquet for the Attalidai—that family from the Anthemos region."

"You're right." He takes his sister's hand, not use to the role of confidant, "What is the matter, Eurunoe?"

She looks closely at Philippos. Tries to see him fully, to assess him, feeling uncertain about unburdening herself. She drops her gaze from his eyes, her voice whispers, "Ptolemaios loves another."

Philippos almost smiles in his relief, thinking *what man does not have many loves*. He doesn't smile, though. Even at twelve, he knows enough to treat his sister's concern seriously, "Is it a boy or a woman, do you think?"

"I wouldn't be upset if it were a boy," she exclaims.

"How do you know he loves some other woman?"

"Philippos, I am not foolish. Oh, I know I bumble a lot, make mistakes, get people laughing at me. That's okay. But I am no fool. I am a Temenidai," her voice has strengthened.

He responds respectfully, "Why have you not seen mother and talked this over with her?"

Eurunoe looks away from her brother. Distantly, gardeners are working. Beyond the shadow of the porch, the sun beats starkly. Helios is king. She considers her words carefully, "Ptolemaios is the most powerful man in the kingdom after father and Alexandros. He and mother are cousins. They have known each other since she was a child. If there is anyone she admires, it is him."

He listens intently. There is more here. Something his sister has not voiced.

Eurunoe turns her gaze back to her brother. A tear glistens by one eye. She whispers, "I cannot go to mother."

Instantly, he knows her thoughts. It is mother she suspects. The image of his mother's face beyond the hearth on the wedding day snaps into mind. He knows Eurunoe is right without knowing why he knows.

"What should I do, Philippos?" she asks.

Anger is in him. He stills the anger consciously. It will not help. He thinks about the predicament. Thinks analytically—as clear of feeling as he can be. "Father will not live a lot longer. Mother and he have not been husband and wife in deed for a long time—maybe they never were except to create us children. If Ptolemaios and mother love each other, there is no crime if they do not act on their love. They would be wise to conceal their feelings." A new thought comes to him, "Has Ptolemaios been unkind to you or heavy handed?"

"No, not unkind. In truth, he's more than dutiful," her voice holds some pride. "But I am a cup he uses. Maybe a cup he treasures, but still just a cup."

Philippos nods his understanding, "Do you think they are lovers? Not simply that they share a love for each other?"

"Yes, though I have no proof. What if I did? What would I do with it? Do I want to cause that kind of suffering?"

"Can you accept your part as well as theirs?"

"No," the word is hissed. Then she steps back, looks away again, "Yes, I can accept so long as I think only about my life with Ptolemaios. It's like a scab on a sore, I keep picking at it. What hurts is what mother did. How could she have me marry Ptolemaios?"

Truthfully Philippos answers, "I don't know." He pauses, thinking about their mother, knowing how kind she can be, how smart and certain of herself, but also how centered on her own concerns. "She loves you, Eurunoe, in her own way. Maybe she saw this as a way to tie Ptolemaios to us, knowing he would not be unkind to you."

She stares at him, "If I get proof that they are lovers, should I go to father?"

"Father could have them both executed for treason. If it's made public, he might have to."

"I do not want that," she replies. "I know you boys don't like Ptolemaios, but he is a good man. And how could I be the cause of mother's death? Father is her husband in name only. I think it's Ptolemaios and mother who should have married." Eurunoe straightens, reaches and touches Philippos' shoulder, "I shall weep no more. Say nothing. Let the Moirai decide."

Philippos thinks of the Moirai, the fates. Sometimes they are depicted as kindly spinners of life's thread; other times as fanged crones swooping down to carry off the newly dead. "I will not say anything, Eurunoe."

She pulls him to her for a brief hug.

CHAPTER FOUR

Old Man

370 B.C.

α

The horsemen pause on the ridge above the farmstead. Below is a house and its outbuildings sitting in a muddy yard. They can see the figure of a thickly wrapped man leading three horses to the stables. Several other men stand at the yard's gate, all bundled against the cold. From the height of the ridge, only the forms below can be discerned, not the features.

One of the group at the gate spots them. He's pointing up. The others stir, and one runs heavily to the low sprawling house. He must be calling to the house for several men spill out the front door. They are waving to the watchers on the ridge.

"Well, Arkhelaos, it looks like your brothers have succeeded in assembling the men of the district, despite the cold," though muffled by scarves, Ptolemaios speaks loud enough for all his companions to hear.

"The people here know us; we know them. They come when we call." The words possess a menacing quality of which Arkhelaos is unaware—he thinks and speaks as he feels.

At Ptolemaios' gesture, the lead horseman begins the descent on the rutted track that will take them to the valley. As they ride, Ptolemaios reflects on the role he must play here. He must emphasize the innate virtues of the Makedones and not disclose his fine appreciation of the southern Hellenes' city-state culture. He must be warrior, hunter, horseman, and farmer. He must seem as blunt, yet as crafty, as these rural folk. He must be one of them, yet have them recognize that he is more than any one of them. He must cause them to want to serve him and, through him, themselves. Ptolemaios rides down into the valley supremely confident.

Soon they are through the yard-gate and are dismounting. More than a dozen men surround them. Some are silent, but most shout greetings. Arkhelaos is well thought of here. His younger brother, Aridaios, gives him a bear hug as welcome.

"Ari, Ari, hold. Where's Meni?" asks Arkhelaos of his brother.

"I sent him over to Old Thalik's. We have people staying there as well. They'll be coming here shortly."

"Are we too many to meet in the house?"

"There'll be room in the hay barn. I set men to clearing the lofts. We'll have more than a hundred, all told. I've had a speaker's box built for Cousin Ptolemaios, so everyone can see and hear him. After the talk, the women will serve a meal in the house. We'll be a mite crowded then, but we'll eat in relays. Ptolemaios can wander from group to group for more private conversation." Aridaios is clearly pleased at his preparations.

Ptolemaios has been listening. He claps Aridaios on the shoulder in thanks, and leans close to say, "I'll want to know not only who is here, but who is not here. Any smallholder or more prominent person. Especially if their absence is due to affection for Alexandros, particular loyalty to King Amuntas, or animosity to you and your brothers. For all who've come and for all who've stayed away, I want the names, particulars and pertinent facts noted by my scribe, so talk with him. All right?"

"Aye, cousin, we will be thorough," Aridaios grins. Calling the group together, he leads them to the hay barn.

*　*　*

The opening rituals are done and the priest has stepped back. Ptolemaios mounts the small platform and takes a good look at the crowd. His scribe has already whispered to him that one hundred and twenty-three men are present. Apparently twenty-eight citizens are absent, although only twelve due to alleged reluctance. Ptolemaios nods somberly to the several faces he recognizes. Easily a dozen of the men have campaigned with him in the past. He holds up an arm and the talking quiets.

He begins, as he has begun at other communities and rural gatherings throughout the region, "Men, you are here because your neighbors, Arkhelaos and his brothers, invited you. Those of you whom I have met before are here because we hold each other in mutual respect. Most of all, though, you are here because we are going to talk about matters that vitally affect you."

"Our good King Amuntas has ruled the Makedones for more than twenty years. Some of those years were turbulent; some of the time parts of our land have been disaffected. On the whole, though, he has and does rule wisely and well. The civil strife that followed the death of old King Aeropos was put to rest."

"For many years now, the king has designated his son, Alexandros, as his successor." There is a growl from many in the crowd, and Ptolemaios motions to quiet the muttering. "Yes, the king may state his preference, but the citizens pronounce a man king. And many of us here feel that the king errs in barring his sons by Gugaia. By what custom can the king be made to disinherit his eldest sons when he marries a new wife? Though Queen Eurudike possesses the blood of Orestis and Lunkestis and some measure of the Temenidai, does that justify this stricture?"

Gesturing to the three brothers, Ptolemaios adds, "True, these men are not sons of his kingship, still they are King Amuntas' eldest sons. True, that when the Argeadai clan arranged to present Amuntas to the citizens for the kingship, he made an agreement that any children born of Eurudike would take precedence. Still, you know the worth of these sons of Gugaia. Rather than retire able men to their estates, at a minimum the king might employ them in the running of this realm so that they may represent your interests. Interests that Arkhelaos, Aridaios and Menelaos know well and share with you." Nods of assent can be seen among the audience.

With a dramatic sigh, Ptolemaios says, "Its not to be. For Alexandros is the designated heir. And many of you know the animosity that exists between the younger sons and the king's first born sons. The time is coming when this difference is critical. As some of you may know already, the king is in ill health—has been in decline for over a year. There will come a day in the not too distant future when the god Hermes will accompany his shade to the River Styx. When that day occurs, Alexandros will be called to the throne."

"What is the nature of Alexandros? That is the crucial question. Is he a man of strong character and worthwhile experience? I believe, in time, he could be a good king. Though age twenty now and possessing the headstrong ways of youth, time and the careful guidance of his father would temper him. But I fear his father will not be there long enough, and the kingdom will come into the young man's hands before he is ready to rule well. He will be no shepherd to his people. He is hot to make his mark in the lands to the south. Hot to be accepted as the foremost Hellene." Some in the audience shake their heads in disapproval.

"We Makedones can be hardy fighters. You there, Bruges, you fought with me at the Three Stones Ford against the Paiaones. Aratos and Putheas, you were part of the men I led when we repelled the Dardanoi raiders near Lake Bigorritis, sweeping them out of Eordaia. We can be tough fighters when well led. When protecting our lands or raiding into the barbarians to keep them off-balance."

"What I fear, though, is that Prince Alexandros will spend the resources of the kingdom on mercenaries. I fear he will lead our young men on adventures in the south. That he is seduced by a dream of southern acclaim, and that, in pursuit of his dream, he will offend those southern cities which buy our timber, our grains, our horses. What I fear is that in his pursuit of his personal dreams he will diminish the patrimony of every man here." The sidelong looks and muttering among the crowd increase. They share the dismay being expressed by Ptolemaios.

Again, Ptolemaios motions for quiet, "Friends, cousins, I draw a picture more bleak than it needs to be. That is why I am here. Prince Alexandros can be reasoned with. If he understands your concerns, understands that what is important to you is the safety of your families and holdings, understands that you need markets for the produce of your lands, understands that the security of our borderlands is more important than southern adventures, then we can redirect his energies. To understand, though, he will need it clearly stated. He will need to see that his people hold their concerns in common. Once he sees what is important to you, once he understands the gravity of your purpose and the firmness of your resolve, he will surely act the good shepherd king that we all want."

"Queen Eurudike, myself, other companions of good King Amuntas, ask you to have faith in our efforts to channel and teach the young prince. We ask your support. Hold your young men to their tasks on your estates and farms. Do not give consent to the strangers who come among you from the court at Pella to recruit for southern adventures. Hold your purse strings tight. If we should need some among you to travel to Pella or Aigai or elsewhere in the kingdom to show your solidarity with us, then come join us gladly, well-provisioned and armed. Appoint among yourselves those who would lead such a gathering. Pick stalwarts, who share your enthusiasm and strength of purpose. Stand ready to take your place in keeping our lands strong and self-reliant. Together, we will tame this impetuous prince."

Then piously, he prays, "Oh, gods, bless us in our good purpose. To you, belong the first fruits of the kingdom—bull calf and grain, stallion and timber, ram and metals. No king shall squander for pride and mercenaries what is owed you. We are your servants, and we accept our duty to safeguard the kingdom."

Ptolemaios steps down and Arkhelaos takes his place to announce that food is ready at the main house and that there Ptolemaios will be available to take individual questions or to hear requests or concerns.

While Arkhelaos is speaking, Aridaios nudges Ptolemaios, "That was good. Not too long. Enough to alarm them but not cause them to act prematurely. You sounded loyal but worried."

"I've had practice at this these last few months. Things are shaping well." He smiles at Aridaios, "You and your brothers are the key to this part of Emathis. There are key men in other regions, as well. We will be ready when Prince Alexandros starts making mistakes."

β

"I tell you the Thebans have turned the world upside down. Sparte, Persia, Athenai will not put it right side up. Look at this new city the Arkadians are raising. Its foundation marks their true independence. The federation that Lukomedes of Mantinea is creating among the Arkadians is possible only due to alliance with the Boiotian League. Epaminondas of Thebai is as much the architect as Lukomedes. The Peloponnesos will never be the same. Thebai is shackling Sparte. This is more important than any peace conference hosted by Athenai that excludes Thebai. Artaxerxes of Persia might as well play host as Athenai." Athanaios is arguing before the king and his companions for closer ties with Thebai. A number of men present feel that Thebai could be a better friend than Athenai, especially since it's become apparent that Iason of Pherai pursues his own goals apart from Thebai, not only in Thessalos but further south.

Philippos, as the youngest, stays quiet, even though his thoughts are racing. His sympathies are with Thebai, for she acts out of strength. A new strength, that's younger than the prince. Who does not rejoice when the underdog becomes the top dog, save the dog that was on top?

Athenai is as fickle as ever, since its leadership must react to every wind that blows through the minds of its citizenry. Yet, he believes in Athenai in a way that Thebai or Sparte or Pherai or any other Hellenic city does not inspire. The very maddening, elusive, contradictory quality of the people of Attika is as much the strength of Athenai as it is her weakness. When other states falter and fail, they seldom recover. But Athenai rises up, repudiates its past leaders, elects new, and sets forth again. Whether it be drama, rhetoric, philosophy, pottery, leather, metalcraft or statuary —it is Athenai to whom a Hellene must turn for the ultimate expression of quality. A cowardly wretched state on one hand, it can also act brilliantly, heroically, generously. Sometimes the city is foolishly belligerent, other times as crafty and subtle and cruel as a wealthy peasant. Truly it is a city of the goddess Athene.

Amuntas raises a hand to stop Athanaios' flow of words. The king appears hollow, shrunken, weary. "Enough, good Athanaios. You argue well but to no purpose. I am decided in continuing our friendship with Athenai. Not that I wish to make an enemy of Thebai. If Thebai remains in the ascendance so that Sparte can no longer balance the power of central Hellas, then now is not the time to turn away from Athenai."

"Father," calls out Alexandros, "we have seen how often the Athenians waver, first bold, then timid, then arrogant again. How can they be a weight in the balance?"

For a moment, the king smiles. Smiles broadly, his famous smile of old. "They panic like sheep, it's true. Much depends on who is their shepherd. The men who lead them now will not sustain their place. The wheel turns and the Athenian people will seek out their past leaders. Watch and you will see Timotheos guiding them again." A murmur passes through the room. "Yes, I concluded an arrangement with Timotheos. He will be the factor for our timber in Athenai and the coins he earns will serve him well. Under him, you will see a less hesitant, confused and vicious people in the Athenians."

OLD MAN (370 B.C.)

Stiffly Alexandros responds, "You are firm in your decision, sir, and it was taken before we assembled. There seems little for your companions to consider here. You are king. The forests are yours to dispose of."

Angry at his son, Amuntas states harshly, "Yes, I am the king. I am the Makedones, young prince. Not only the forests, but the earth itself and all its minerals, the rivers that flow to the sea, the sea as far as the eye can see—these are mine. They are mine for I am the Temenidai *basileos* of the Argeadai of the Makedones. It is through me that Zeus gives the Makedones dominion to these lands. You are mine, as well. Know the truth I am speaking for there will come a time when you will guard our patrimony as jealously as I."

Alexandros is as angry as the red-faced king, "I hear Lord Ptolemaios' advice in your decision. Your policy looks to the past while Thebai creates a new future. How does Athenai act as a balance against Iason of Pherai? Is he not a threat to us and a threat to Thebai? Is not Thebai our natural ally now? Is not our enemy's enemy our friend?"

"Do not force a neighbor to be an enemy, Prince. Iason of Pherai has much to contend with in Thessalos. There is no need to provoke him. I know you believe we can divide the Hellenes with Thebai. You would grant the entire south to Thebai, and have us dominate not only our own lands but also those of Thessalos. You do not understand the limits of our strength."

While the two argue, Perdikkas leans over Philippos' shoulder and whispers, "I wish they would stop. Look around you. Every one of these old men is thinking how he can take advantage of the rift growing between father and Aleko."

Philippos nods somberly, and whispers back, "It is Ptolemaios who opposes Aleko."

"You know the rumors that Ptolemaios is raising forces in parts of Emathis and further north?"

Again Philippos nods, "Eurunoe tells me some things. Aristoteles has heard more. Aristoteles says that Ptolemaios is careful to say nothing treacherous even as he rouses the fears and angers of the country men."

"Yes," Perdikkas places a hand on Philippos' shoulder, turning the younger brother to face him. "Ptolemaios is in league with Arkhelaos."

"Who do you think Alexandros can count on?"

"Iolaos and Athanaios. Derdas and his kin. Antiokhos is less certain. He will bow to whomever seems strongest to preserve his privileges. And where he bows, so will Lagos. Of course, Antipatros will agree with his father, Iolaos. Iolaos is old, too. Once he's gone, Antipatros will lead the strongest block of citizens."

Philippos raises a finger to Perdikkas' lips, "Not here. We should talk with Aleko away from here. We must court Antipatros."

The whispering boys have drawn the attention of the nearest nobles. The shift in focus catches the eye of Amuntas, who stops his tirade. The

71

boys turn back with a start at the sudden silence. "Do you wish to share your thoughts with all of us?" bellows the king, expecting more opposition.

Perdikkas calls out, "Father, Philippos and I agree that there is weight in both views. We are glad that in counsel we can examine each side of an issue to be certain that all its probable consequences are considered. This also provides you the opportunity to expound on the purposes of your decisions."

Amuntas stares at Perdikkas. Then he laughs merrily, "Who would have expected you, Perdikkas, to become so politic?" The majority of the men join in the good-natured laughter with some relief. "No doubt, Philippos, you would echo your brother regardless of what you were actually whispering?"

"We are all concerned for the kingdom, father, Alexandros as well as you. I think it is good that we can argue here, even grow heated in defense of our ideas, so long as when you dismiss those from whom you've asked advice, all of us support your decisions in full."

Several of the king's companions call out their approval of the sentiment, "Hear him, hear him, King Amuntas."

Alexandros smiles. The large attractive smile he has inherited from his father. "Father, my brothers are correct. Excuse me if I become vehement as I pursue the line of my argument. You are king, sir, and we abide by your decisions."

The king is willing to accept the accord offered. None of this by-play has escaped him. He knows full well his mortality. Knows full well the speculation that must occur when a new king will soon reign. He has lived through the deaths of many kings. While the opposition to his policy is real, his sons are not so foolish as to force a breach. Amuntas is pleased with their restraint. Perhaps Alexandros will make a good king with the abler support of his brothers. The king smiles warmly, "I am well satisfied. You, Prince Alexandros, have raised many good points. No policy is a statue of stone. We must always be vigilant and willing to reconsider. For now, though, we will proceed as I have directed. Timotheos of Athenai will be our factor for the timber of the Makedones."

γ

Tasting the watered wine, Amuntas sighs. He debates calling for honey and herbs but making the concoction would be more of a stir than he wants—no matter how soothing to his ravaged throat. He coughs, sips, coughs again. His servant hovers. He waves the man off, "Go, Ikanthos. I will call you if I need you."

Amuntas watches the old serving man shuffle away. Thinks, how very much alike is the shuffle of old men. I move with much the same staggering, sliding walk. How much longer, oh god Hermes? He tries to decide whether he wants to die. All his ailments, all the pains, will end. That surcease may not be enough. To become a shade, does it follow that he will fade in the memories of his sons, of his companions? Was there once a king named Amuntas? Amuntas the what? Strong? Good? Wise? Or maybe just Old Amuntas.

Sitting here, alone, is a relief. Lately, he has discovered solitude. He, the hearty one, the boon companion, the talker, the one who gathered friends and family, who greeted, consulted, took the lead, who are well, drank better, who was every man's friend. Grasping the kingship caused him to make enemies, but it had made many more want his friendship.

Now, though, with this dogged, killing illness, there is less to do, less he can do. And, to be expected, there are fewer who are his peers in age, rank, and understanding with each passing year. After a lifetime of active, boisterous purpose, he finds he wants time to reflect. No longer to calculate what others want, and how he can use their wants to his advantage and to the advantage of the Makedones. Now he can try to assess himself, flaws and failures against virtues and achievements. In the end, what else matters but the character of a man? How will Minos, Rhadamanthos and Aiakos judge his life when he comes to the Underworld?

A spell of coughing shakes his frame. He sips again. Six boys and a girl. He smiles to himself. He knows of his son-in-law's speeches. Knows the frustrations that make his three older boys bold. But he is certain of the mettle of his younger sons.

Long ago he dispossessed Gugaia's boys, and knew then that it would be future trouble. Had there been no children by Eurudike, the bargain would have been moot. As it is, he bartered his three eldest to gain the throne. What do they have to complain of? Had he not made the bargain, there would have been no throne for their longing.

Kleopatra had known how strong the flame burned in him to be king. Perhaps the Makedones really got the best of the exchange. Has he not ruled for twenty-four years and put an end to the fratricide among the Temenidai?

A soft knocking comes from the door to the anteroom. He does not respond. He does not want intrusion. The knocking grows louder, more insistent. The door is opened without his consent. His irritation spurts into anger until he sees that it is Eurunoe standing there, beyond the apologetic face of his guardsman. "Father, I must see you," she says.

He stands slowly and waves her in.

The girl—woman, really—is hesitant, but when is she not? "Father, I must ask you to hear my petition." Eurunoe drops to her knees before him.

Reaching out a hand to touch her head, Amuntas realizes that the girl has been crying and remains quite distraught. "Say what you will, daughter," he states gruffly. Inwardly he quails, not wanting to learn whatever she would reveal.

"Please spare mother and my husband, Ptolemaios. Their passion for each other is out of their control and in the hands of Aphrodite. That they must make amends, I understand. Know, though, that I am with child. My boy or girl will need a father." Eurunoe lifts her eyes and sees bewilderment on her father's face harden into anger.

"What do you say? Do you know how painful is your accusation? What repercussions could result?" Before they can continue, loud voices can be heard in the anteroom and again the chamber's door reverberates to heavy pounding. Amuntas lifts Eurunoe's face, "What is this now, my sparrow?"

"Alexandros," she sobs, "he knows and will take their infidelity to all your close companions."

"How long have you known?" asks the king.

She twists her head away and whispers, "For a long time, sir."

Amuntas bellows, "Come in, come in." He stands, rage coursing through him, not so much for the betrayal, if that is what it is, as for this eruption of dramatics when he would rather be alone to deal with the fears in his own soul. Yet he is still king, and even as Alexandros and his three attendants stride in, his mind is racing. Is this the opportunity to quell Ptolemaios? Does Alexandros need Ptolemaios as a balance weight to keep from taking the kingdom on a wild ride that must fail? What does Amuntas owe to Eurudike, or to the shade of Kleopatra?

Alexandros barely pauses at the sight of Eurunoe kneeling by their father. He is grim faced, as are his three companions: his friend, the noble Parrhasios, his chief officer, the mercenary, Teikhonos, and his steward and confidant, Ephrastos.

Amuntas holds up his hand when they are eight paces away. "What is it you have to say, Prince Alexandros?"

"Father, I have proof that Lord Ptolemaios conspires against your life. He is also mother's lover. They betray you and Princess Eurunoe."

"Do you have proof that your mother is part of a conspiracy or only that she takes her pleasure with Ptolemaios?"

Alexandros glances at Ephrastos, then looks to the king, "Only of her infidelity, sir. Though, that itself is treachery."

Amuntas holds up his hand again, and all are silent. The king thinks to himself that there is no purpose in Ptolemaios seeking his death, for he is already a dead man in just a little more time. That Eurudike and Ptolemaios are lovers, he knows—and has known—though he hoped the marriage to Eurunoe had ended their liaison. Alexandros has already made the scandal too public. If there is a deadly plot by Ptolemaios, the only sensible aim is against Alexandros. On the other hand, it's to Alexandros' purpose to see Ptolemaios executed or banished. Whatever evidence exists must be in the hands of Ephrastos. The king addresses Parrhasios, "You, sir, what is your purpose in being here?"

The startled Parrhasios replies, "Why to support my oath-brother, Alexandros."

"What do you know of these events, independent from these gentlemen? Is there anything you can add to what they will tell me?"

"No, sire," Parrhasios' face flushes red.

"Then be good enough to leave."

Parrhasios looks to Alexandros, then bows his head to the king and departs.

"Aleko, is your officer here to execute any orders given or does he have independent knowledge of these events?"

"He is here solely at my command should I give orders for his troop," responds Alexandros reluctantly.

"Then, Teikhonos, see to your troop. Have them stand down. As you depart, ask my guardsman to send for the Princes Perdikkas and Philippos. Thank you." The king sits down abruptly, "Now, then, Aleko. I assume your evidence has been gathered by Ephrastos?"

"Yes, father."

"Then is Ephrastos of sufficient value to you as a counselor that we should spare his life?"

Both Alexandros and Ephrastos react with shock. Alexandros stammers, "Father, what are you saying? It is Ptolemaios who acts criminally."

The king's hard voice demands, "What is this man's value to you?"

"Ephrastos sees things clearly and speaks his mind to me truly. I rely on his abilities," hotly responds the prince.

"I have no quarrel with him supporting you in that role. So long as I am alive I order that he speak to no one other than you. You will give me your oath, Alexandros, that the moment you learn that Ephrastos has spoken to anyone other than yourself, you will put him to death."

Alexandros is silent with rage and no little puzzlement. He stands staring at his father, unwilling to be twisted from his purpose. He tries to understand why the old man is quashing the accusations against Ptolemaios. The only reason that comes to mind is that the accusations embroil his mother, Eurudike. He starts to protest, "Father, Ptolemaios is a threat..."

"Not to me," says the king. "Now, give me your oath or I shall call in my guards and make certain that Ephrastos is voiceless."

Reluctantly, the prince raises his palms outward to the gods and lifts his voice, "Before the sacred twelve, I, Alexandros, son of Amuntas, prince of the Makedones, do swear that should my servant, Ephrastos of Pharsalos, speak of these events to anyone but me, I will ..."

"No, Aleko, not only about your accusations and evidence. I mean what I say. If Ephrastos speaks to anyone but you," the king's voice is gentle, though his intent is hard.

After a quick look at Ephrastos, who nods his agreement, Alexandros begins his oath again, "Before the sacred twelve, I, Alexandros, son of Amuntas, prince of the Makedones, do swear that should my servant, Ephrastos of Pharsalos, speak to anyone but me—while good King Amuntas is alive—I shall put Ephrastos to death." He stares defiantly at the king, daring comment on the condition he's added.

Satisfied, Amuntas says, "You and I are witnesses with the gods to this oath, Eurunoe." He turns to Ephrastos, looking at him fully. The servant drops his eyes, then bows his head to the king. "Go now, Ephrastos. I honor you for being a true servant to my son. I only wish you were wiser," says Amuntas, gently.

The king waits until Ephrastos leaves the room. Then he turns mild eyes on Alexandros, "Well, Prince of the Makedones, please sit on the dining couch. Eurunoe, join your brother. No, Aleko, say nothing until your brothers are here, then we will talk about the doings of our family."

The old man closes his eyes, sits back and waits. The prince sits brooding. Eurunoe is still, but within her she feels elation that her husband will escape punishment. She knows that she is a pale flame against the fire that is her mother. She can both resent and love Eurudike. What Ptolemaios gives Eurunoe is enough, believes the girl. Most men share themselves with many women. Some take boys as lovers, too. At least Eurunoe shares only with her mother, and for that she is grateful.

A discreet knock on the door announces the brothers. Amuntas calls them in and they come quickly, clearly puzzled and concerned by the summons. The king waves them to another of the dining couches. They draw it up close.

Amuntas looks over his four offspring. They are a handsome quartet. At twenty, Alexandros is tall and thin. His beard is soft, dark. He is eager to make his mark on the world, eager to succeed his father, yet not so eager that he can't be reined in and directed. Eurunoe is a year younger. Having been told, Amuntas can see that the slight roundness is pregnancy. The king wonders why she has said nothing of the affair until now. She is a beauty, yet without the headstrong vivacity that was her mother at the same age. Perdikkas is a boy who makes the old man smile. Just sixteen, he seems suddenly gangly when he had always been stocky, even pudgy. A boy into everything, loud, funny, popular. Perhaps Eurudike is right, perhaps this is the child with the most potential. And Philippos, the thirteen year old. Probably the most handsome of the four, though he will not be as tall as Aleko. He is good-humored, like Perdikkas, yet more purposeful. Not well liked by Eurudike, who finds him too calculating. Maybe they are too much alike.

A coughing spell distracts Amuntas. Eurunoe hands him the cool watered wine. He catches his breath. As the tightness in his chest eases, he begins, "Your brother, Alexandros, has proclaimed, outside the family, the infidelity of your mother with your brother-in-law. He has gone further and accuses Ptolemaios of plotting my death." The king shakes his head sadly, "I fear I have not instructed you well in kingship, Aleko. Perhaps I have been too sparing of all of you."

"Let's start with family. We are the Temenidai and of the Temenidai, we five are now the heart of the oak. Your elder brothers are set aside. Your mother, Ptolemaios, other distant cousins, like Argaios or Pausanias the Younger, are not in my direct line of descent. As you know, having my blood and blessing are important but do not guarantee your kingship, Aleko. To become king, you must be more than one of the Temenidai. You must have the support of the wider family—not only those who are pure Temenidai but the clan leaders of the Argeadai and the several leading families with whom we are tied by marriage, present or past. And to remain king, you must strengthen those ties and ties to other great families of the kingdom. Make their interests, yours; make your interests, theirs. To be effective as king, you need something more. You need the Makedones as a people wanting your kingship, seeing your kingship as their best bulwark against the many enemies who would tear apart our people and their lands. My lessons of this truth came hard. Let me assure you that I learned those lessons well."

"Jealousy, rivalry, infidelity, murder, rebellion have in the past riven our family. My reign has knit together the kingdom. I do not want the scandals of the court strewn across the land like seeds for suspicion, distrust and hate. We will settle our affairs behind closed doors among ourselves." Amuntas pauses, on the verge of more coughing. He sips from his cup and controls his body.

"At most, I have a year or two of life remaining. I am older than most men. The gods have been kinder to me than I might have expected. In the four of you, I see that Herakles and his father Zeus have not abandoned our family. For twelve generations or more, we have been kings of the Makedones. Our line extends through the founders of Argos to Herakles to supreme Zeus himself. The watering of the divine with mortal blood is not so great that Zeus forgets his children." Amuntas slows, realizing that he is losing the thread of his purpose. Age does cloud the mind.

"Your mother and Ptolemaios have been lovers for ten years or more. Aphrodite knows I no longer wanted to continue in that position with your mother," says Amuntas dryly. The statement causes the children to sit straighter, not having known the extent of the outrage. "If I can turn a blind eye to it, then you must. Ptolemaios is a power in his own right in our lands. He and your mother are the principal ties to the royal families of Orestis and Lunkestis. Those highland branches of our people are the wall against which the Illuriote sea of barbarians lap."

"I know of Ptolemaios' travels and speeches. He skirts treason. There is little doubt, Aleko, that he sees himself as your rival for the kingship. You must curb him without losing our friendship with the highlands."

"Understand what I say, kingling. Curb him—not banish him, not execute him. You must find the way to control him and direct him to your purpose. If you do, he will be far more valuable to you than Ephrastos. He has been of great worth to me."

Amuntas turns to Eurunoe, "Daughter, you have concealed from me more than you should have. When I am dead, Ptolemaios and your mother will want to wed. Do not stand in their way. Retire with your child to the estate you most favor. In time, perhaps, a new husband will be found for you by your brother. If that is what you want."

"Father," asks Philippos, "is that how you would curb Ptolemaios, by giving him mother?"

Amuntas looks carefully at his youngest, then he laughs. The laughter becomes coughing. When again under control, Amuntas nods sagely. "Boy, you do know your mother. Yes, she is one part of the halter we place on Ptolemaios. We must balance his power with that of the Argeadai—of Iolaos and his boy, Antipatros. In turn, Antiokhos, Athanaios, and the others. They all must be placed like stones in a wall. Derdas is also key. He is master of the passages to the south, and his principality balances Ptolemaios' ties west of him."

"Most of all, though, Aleko, you must embody the security of the kingdom. Talk with my companions and the notables, like your oath-brother, Parrhasios. Learn not only what your friends want, but what your enemies want, and the wants of the many more who sit on the fence between you. Go out among the people. You can speak as effectively as Ptolemaios. Let the people know how you will safeguard them as king. Give them a taste of the future so they can identify their wants with yours. Build your strength among more than your friends, for your friends will not be enough."

Amuntas turns to his younger sons, "Perdikkas and Philippos, do not suppose you are too young to help your brother. Be seen as strong supporters of your brother. If differences are perceived among the three of you, then some will work to widen those differences so they can take advantage of any split among you. More of our people, though, will simply be frightened that the differences could lead to bloodshed and weakness, as has happened in the past."

Perdikkas pledges, "Father, Alexandros has my loyalty. He, Philippos, and I have already bound ourselves by oath."

"Good, boy, good. Do you see, Eurunoe, your brothers and you are the Makedones? Never make the mistake of thinking that the favor of Zeus does not require sacrifice. In time, you must give up your marriage to Ptolemaios. Be certain that each of your brothers will, in time, give up some part of themselves. Will you follow my command without protest?"

Mutely, the young woman nods her assent.

Amuntas pushes himself up on his feet again. His breathing is heavy, rattling. He clears his throat and spits into the pot by the chair. Slowly, yet firmly, he stretches to his full height—still a bear of a man. "Eurunoe, go and summon your mother. Perdikkas, send for Ptolemaios. We will agree on the future tonight. Alexandros, you will be king. Ptolemaios will end his campaign to vilify you. In return, he will gain your mother, keep his life, and remain a power. Tomorrow, we will bring together all our companions who are now in Pella or who can reach the city in time for an afternoon banquet. I will demand their concurrence in your succession to the kingdom, Aleko."

δ

The breeze touches the leaves at the height of the trees, but beneath the canopy all seems still. The four boys and the aged servant are quiet, intent. The five are hunting. Pointing ahead, Skaros reveals the fresh wild boar droppings beside the faint path left by the passage of forest beasts.

Down slope, through the trees, is the glint of water. A sizable pond and larger marsh fill much of the vale below them. The five hunters expect their prey to be rooting by the pond's bank or wallowing on the farther side where the pond's margin becomes indistinct as it merges with the land.

Skaros pats Philippos on the shoulder and points toward the far side of the path. Turning to Alkimakhos, Skaros indicates that the young noble should move fifteen paces beyond Philippos. To Antigonos, the boy giant, Skaros assigns a place five paces away on this side of the path opposite Philippos. Finally Little Korrhagos is placed fifteen paces ahead of Antigonos. With the boys in position, Skaros waves them forward.

Spears at the ready, the boys move as silently as they can through the undergrowth. Skaros trails to the left of Philippos. He has guided the boys well but all hunting is part chance. He wants Philippos to have the kill, for the king's son will not truly be accepted as a man until he kills either one of the dangerous forest creatures or an enemy.

Ahead, at the forest edge near the pond, birds are calling. Their calls are simple gregarity. None are calling alarm even as the foes of nature stealthily approach. Not until Korrhagos stumbles over a half-buried log does a bird fly up in alarm. Without command, the boys stop and wait, wanting the forest to regain its calm. Each listens. Then together the uneven line steps forward. Not until they reach the end of the trees, do they pause again. No boar can be seen. By silent agreement, the boys step out into the sunlight.

The boys gather and Skaros joins them. Nothing is said. Skaros waits to see if Philippos will take the lead. As if Skaros' thoughts have entered Philippos' mind, the prince points Alkimakhos and Little Korrhagos to follow the pond's left bank, while he and Antigonos turn right. Skaros follows Philippos.

Not until they reach a place where the bank is broken and the vegetation less dense, do Philippos and Antigonos see a clear fresh boar print. Philippos sends Skaros back on their trail to fetch the other two boys. The prince and Antigonos follow the boar sign down the bank. Scrambling to the bottom, they find that the verge of boggy ground widens here, allowing room to walk between the bank and the pond. Antigonos squats down and with his finger traces the edge of one of the boar's hoof prints. Looking up at Philippos, Antigonos grins and indicates with his hands an estimate of the size of this larger than normal boar. Philippos nods back, his eyes alight with the same pleasure that breathes in Antigonos.

Eagerly the two go after the boar. Stepping around a corner of the bank, they come on the creature rooting in the foliage by a rivulet that feeds the pond. Startled boar and startled boys rear back. The boar is a great shaggy creature, yet for all its size, it reacts faster and with more agility than the boys. With a snort, it scrambles up the further bank to escape. The dry dirt at the top gives way, and the beast falls heavily with a squeal. Instantly, it's on its feet again and whirls to face its danger.

The boys had started to rush after the boar, but as it turns on them, they separate to divide the animal's attention. Tossing its head and snorting loudly, the boar charges Philippos—for beyond him is the path and escape. The curved tusks of the boar are twin knives that can slice a man easier than they rend the earth. Philippos holds his spear low, with its butt planted in the mud and his back foot atop the butt. The boar zigs, then zags, as it charges. Philippos swivels to stay in true line facing the running beast. The force of the boar as it hits the spear head sends Philippos sprawling. With a shout, Antigonos sends his spear into the boar's side. The animal's legs thrash wildly, then stop. For a moment longer its sides heave, then it is dead.

Philippos gets to his feet, unconsciously brushing at his mud and blood spattered legs. His spearhead and shank are sunk deep into the boar's chest. Blood runs down the cracked length of the shaft. Antigonos puts a foot on the carcass and pulls his spear out of the boar's belly. Blood spurts and is accepted by the boggy ground no more eagerly than the muddy water.

"You got your boar, Philpa," laughs Antigonos.

"He's as big a boar as you are a cadet, " says Philippos in awe.

"She, Philippos, or haven't you learned the difference?" Antigonos jokes.

"Wouldn't you give praise to catch the male that mates her. He would need to be colossal."

"She's past mating, now."

"Help me get my spear free."

"You'll have to cut it out."

Philippos unsheathes his knife and starts cutting to widen the boar's death wound. Antigonos disembowels the beast to begin its butchering.

*   *   *

With fingers laced behind his head, Philippos gazes up at the patterns forming and reforming in the clouds. Beyond the fire, Korrhagos belches with uninhibited delight, "What a meal," he exclaims.

"There was a moment there, when the she-boar rushed the embankment, that I cursed us for not bringing the dogs," comments Antigonos.

"There is more purity to hunting without dogs," interjects Alkimakhos.

"Purity, maybe, but we almost lost our quarry," rejoins Antigonos.

"Hunting with dogs can be a joy if they are well trained," adds Skaros.

Philippos turns on his side and looks at his companions. He is mellow with good feeling. He is now a man. The kill was clean. His stomach is full. His friends are true friends. He would have liked his father and brothers to see the kill, but so what, he will bore them with the tale. Or, better, let his friends bore them. He can remain modest and let his friends enlarge upon the feat. "Korrhagos, you have a good voice. Do you know the praise-song to Artemis that begins with As moon light through the forest gleams?"

Korrhagos raises his head and in his clear voice begins the song. Hesitantly, then with increasing confidence, the others join in. Korrhagos continues with another hymn, then a third. Antigonos picks up by leading a satirical piece that mocks hymn singing. Alkimakhos is upset by the blasphemy, but quiets as Philippos begins a drinking song. That piece causes Skaros to offer a Thraikiote fighting song, which he quickly translates and teaches to them. Before long they are bellowing Thraikiote war cries, which causes Skaros to start laughing.

"We've had a good day," says Philippos. "Shall we stay out the night or is it time to start back to the main camp?"

"I'm for staying out and seeing what Artemis allows us tomorrow," answers Alkimakhos.

"I told father we could be gone two days," mentions Antigonos.

Skaros comments, "We have plenty of provisions."

"What say you, Little Korrhagos?" asks Philippos.

"My father will follow the lead of Antigonos' father."

There is a moment of silence as Philippos considers the truth of Korrhagos' words. "The two have been close of late."

"You know it took my family a long time to win the king's acceptance."

"Aye, that was the cost of following Argaios instead of my father."

Korrhagos nods, "My cousin will marry Antigonos' brother. His family has given surety for mine with the king."

"I like your cousin," throws in Antigonos.

"Stratonike is a beauty," agrees Korrhagos.

"I wish the same could be said for my brother, Demetrios," laughs Antigonos.

"What do you know of Argaios now?" asks Alkimakhos.

"Nothing," says Korrhagos quickly, "we have no contact with him or his ilk."

"Argaios is a guest-friend of the Bouzugai family in Athenai. He is living in the home of Lakhes Demokharous. And there he may stay, Hades willing," Philippos voices his contempt for the Temenid pretender. "Alexandros has been acknowledged as the king-in-waiting. There will be no succession dispute."

Alkimakhos stretches, then settles back for the kind of talk he enjoys, talk of families and power, "Since Old Onomakourgas died there's no one left of prominence in Pella who supported Aeropos when he was king. His lineage is no threat to your now."

"His grandson, Pausanias, is lurking in Olunthos. Pausanias flits between the Khalkidike and Thraikios. First at Abudos, then at the Odrusid court, then back to Olunthos, and so forth. With him are some few companions whose lands have long been forfeit. All that holds them together is the hope of vengeance and the dwindling silver Pausanias has left from the treasuries of his grandfather and father." Philippos pauses, "I say to all of you, and you are to repeat what I say to your fathers, my father presented Alexandros to the assembled nobles as his successor. Alexandros is acclaimed. Our line of the Temenidai is the source of the kings of the Makedones."

Korrhagos adds eagerly, "Periandros represents the families that Old Onomakourgas held as his faction. And Periandros is firmly a supporter of the king and you princes."

Alkimakhos begins ticking clan leaders off on his fingers, " Iolaos and Antipatros are yours; Athanaios, of course; Antiokhos, and with him, Lagos; the Antigonidai; Periandros..."

Antigonos cuts in, "You're all talking around the point. The only real question is whether the king has bridled Ptolemaios of Aloros. What say you to that, Philippos?"

"The noble Ptolemaios is a member of our family by virtue of his marriage to my sister. He is ambitious, and holds himself as more experienced than Alexandros. He holds himself a better successor than Alexandros, a better fit for the kingship. Some few may share that opinion. All that said, Ptolemaios will accept Alexandros as king on my father's death. That bargain is made. His alternative is exile." Philippos smiles, "Father is ill but still commands. He is as wily a fox as you are likely to meet. Ptolemaios the hunter is the one who is snared."

Philippos continues, "Remember, Ptolemaios is useful and serves my father well. His experience does have value. In time, he will come to see that he can succeed in the same way with Alexandros. There is no other way he can succeed."

Korrhagos grins in agreement. Alkimakhos nods slowly. Antigonos stares into the fire. Skaros is looking up at the few early stars of dusk. Waving a hand of dismissal, Philippos says, "But enough of this talk, I liked this evening better when we were singing. Alkimakhos, do you have a raga you can offer? Maybe something the shepherds sing?"

"Let me get my *auloi*. Did anyone bring a *timpanon*?"

"Aye, masters," offers Skaros, "I have the flat drum."
"Then let us sing," directs Philippos merrily.

ε

Eurunoe stands on the portico watching the light fall of snow. Snow has always pleased her. She pulls her fur closer around her shoulders and smooths it over her round belly, so that both she and her child within are warm.

She worries over the child growing within her. She hopes it is a boy, for then Ptolemaios may again delight in her. She rarely sees him now, and when she does he is moody and abrupt. Not unkind. More indifferent to her. She's uncertain whether his interest waned with her inability to continue lovemaking or with his disappointment over the kingship. Or, maybe it's simply his frustration at no longer being her mother's lover, as well.

How odd it must seem to others that she and her mother were his lovers at the same time. Could both she and mother become Ptolemaios' wives after father's death, she wonders. There are men who have several wives. Few among the Makedones, it's true, but more commonly among the Illuroi, Paiaones and Thraikiotes. She has heard of two sisters married to a man, but she has never heard of a mother and daughter. Besides, they are the Temenidai. Their lineage is Hellenic. The mores of the South are what they follow, not the ancient practices of the North. And the South does not understand multiple marriages. Still, it's possible. What if the family is purely Argeadai and the descent from Temenos only a story concocted in the reign of the first Alexandros? Why must the family be Hellenes?

Father said she could have another husband. Perhaps that would be better. Let mother have Ptolemaios. A feeling of loss swells within her. No, she does not want to give up Ptolemaios. He can be so merry and wonderful. He made her feel so cared for during the many months after they first wed. He could hardly look at her and not want to bed her. She will share him if she must, but she will not give him up.

She shivers and starts to go in when she sees a runner coming from the direction of the palace. She waits, curious. The man takes the steps at a run and stops easily before her. She recognizes him as one of the King's runners. Somberly, the runner says, "Lady Eurunoe, your father asks that you hurry to him. Is Lord Ptolemaios within? He is summoned, as well."

"My husband is not here. You may find him at the house of Lord Antiokhos." She opens the door and calls to her servant, "Kalliopi. Come, bring a wrap, for we must go to my father. Hurry, woman."

*   *   *

Amuntas lies on the day bed, breathing heavily, painfully. Sweat beads his forehead. He opens his eyes, seeing those around him. His servant, Ikanthos, is weeping. Silly man. The king tries to speak but not even a croak comes out. He struggles to sit up. Perdikkas drops to his knees and helps his father.

Supported by his son's arm, Amuntas manages a few slurred words, "Not much longer. Aleko ... you know ... what to do." The words trail off. The harsh breathing seems to be all that exists in the room. The king rallies again, "Aleko, come closer."

The young man kneels by his brother. The king's breath is foul. Amuntas re-opens his eyes, sighs, "I entrust ... our family ... and our people ... to you, Alexandros. Be moderate ... in your actions, ... balance sternness ... with generosity. Be a king." Amuntas closes his eyes. His mouth opens, as if to add something. Nothing more comes. He turns his face away. Perdikkas lowers his father's head.

Time passes slowly. Notables and household servants come and go. Iolaos, looking aged himself, whispers to Alexandros, "You have put your guards at the treasury?"

Of all who wait on the king, only Eurudike seems calm. Calm and strangely beautiful, almost luminous. She beckons to Eurunoe.

"Yes, mother," the woman asks softly.

Her voice at a normal pitch, Eurudike asks, "Is it wise for you to stand so long? Shouldn't you rest?" Lightly, Eurudike touches her daughter's swollen belly.

"I am tired, mama," agrees Eurunoe. At the queen's gesture, a serving man brings a low stool.

By the far wall, Philippos paces. He's not certain what he feels. They all had anticipated the old man's death for so long. The old man himself has divested most of his powers, assuring the succession, preparing for this day. All Philippos feels inside is emptiness, a great suspense, maybe a touch of panic, though he cannot consciously acknowledge that fear. He is reminded of Kleopatra's death. His stomach growls in hunger, and the boy feels distress that his body doesn't recognize the gravity of this event. Why is the body not respectful of the meaning men place on their lives?

The king is the chief priest of the land. Soon it will fall to Alexandros to carry out the proper rituals. Does each passing generation dilute the descent from Zeus? Will the intercessions of Alexandros possess the efficacy of Amuntas?

Philippos turns away from the room, and stares out the narrow window. Beyond the palace yard, he sees the people of Pella, crowding the gate, waiting, hungering after each rumor, hoping the king will regain strength, that he can delay death. Despite the cold, they gather, their numbers continuing to grow through the hours.

Antipatros comes to stand by Philippos, placing a hand on the youngster's shoulder. He gestures at the people, "You know what they're saying? They want a miracle. They fear your father's death. Only a few will openly talk of his dying. Some will talk of great Hades and the lands he rules in the underworld. Others will speak of Orpheos. They will say that Orpheos will guide the king's spirit after the body is dead."

The boy thinks about Orpheos, legendary poet of the Thraikiotes, who wandered these lands before the Makedones came down on Pieris. Orpheos taught that life continues, that here and now is but one of many abodes. Amuntas followed the Orphic rituals.

"What will they say of father after he is dead?"

"The common man respects your father. The years of strife are past. They will call him Amuntas the Wise."

Nodding, absently, Philippos considers his father's achievements. The man who reknit the Makedones into a nation after the confusions and disunity caused by the mad succession of kings that followed the murder of King Arkhelaos. Orestes, Aeropos, Pausanias, Little Amuntas, and Argaios —all of them holding the throne briefly. What turmoil. As for Amuntas, son of Aridaios, he has ruled for twenty-four years. Perhaps he is not as wily as old King Alexandros, perhaps not as expedient as King Perdikkas, certainly not as militant as King Arkhelaos. Still, Amuntas is a king loved by the people. Amuntas, a king who never forgets that, as their chosen shepherd, his first task is their well-being.

Thinking of these things, Philippos replies to Antipatros, "They will make him a companion of the gods."

There is a push among the notables by the day bed. The king's rattling breath is gone. Then it comes again as a strange sucking sigh. And is gone. Moments cling to immortality. Amuntas Aridaios Temenidon of the Argeadai Makedones is dead. Prince Alexandros will be king, upon the affirmation of the citizen army and its veterans.

*   *   *

Later, by himself, Philippos allows his grief to spill. Convulsively, it wells within him. Wave after wave, until finally he is conscious of his body again, that vessel of reality, which has made his face slick with tears and snot. Wiping his face dry, Philippos raises his eyes to Zeus, and thanks the great god for his father, Amuntas.

ζ

Alexandros stands stiffly, while his companion, Parrhasios, laces the king's cuirass. The young king grunts at the tightening, then gives way to his impatience, "No, Philippos, you will not accompany us. You and Perdikkas will remain behind. If this should go wrong, then you two must be here in Pella."

"Perdix must stay, Aleko. He's your heir, not me," responds the boy.

Antipatros rumbles, "I like your spirit, Philippos, but King Alexandros is right. The Dardanoi are treacherous scum. We may buy them off or it may come to a fight."

85

The dozen or so men in the room are armed or in the process of arming. Only the two young princes are defenseless in tunics. Their fascination with the expedition to the Dardanid king, Bardulis, is heightened by their exclusion.

"If the Lunkestoi were not so craven, we would spend Illuriote blood and not Makedones silver," comments Parrhasios.

"We've been through all that," states the king curtly. "Why should the Lunkestoi protect our lands? Anyway, I do not want to waste lives now. We will husband our strength. For now, this is the better way. Our tribute will stop the Illuric Dardanoi at our borders."

"The Lunkestoi are Makedones, too," offers Perdikkas.

"Maybe. If so, they have forgotten their kinship," answers Antipatros.

"What of the Pelagonoi?" asks Philippos.

"Cousin is fighting cousin there. Anyway, when have we been successful cooperating with those northerners?" responds King Alexandros.

"Father thought they were worth cultivating. I think Prince Parmenion would be an able ally," answers Philippos.

"Enough!" exclaims Alexandros angrily. "My decision is made. We will buy off the Illuroi now, and fight them another day. Maybe we need to strengthen our ties to the Lunkestoi and Pelagonoi first. Maybe the kingship needs strengthening here at home first. Now is not the time to let Bardulis stampede us into crisis." He pulls away from Parrhasios, grabs up a spear and stalks out of the room.

The other armed men follow, although Antipatros lingers a moment, grinning through his beard at the forlorn princes, "This time your brother is right. But I like your ideas." Then he turns and strides out.

η

Eurudike reaches across the table and smooths the hair away from her daughter's face. Both women have been crying. "I do not know what to say to you, Eurunoe. Why does Aphrodite cause us to love the same man? He is so much a mixture of fire and ice, of pride and competence, of manliness and caring."

Eurunoe covers her face with her hands, "Mother, I am bearing his child. I am his wife."

"Yes, child," the mother nods in understanding, "yet I have known him all my life. He is sun and moon to me. Marriage to your father was forced on me. I know love only through Ptolemaios."

"Why did you marry me to him?"

Eurudike bites her lip, turns her face away. *Why? To avert suspicion. To have Ptolemaios close. To make access easy. What obsession is love.* Shame fills Eurudike for using her daughter. What can she say to Eurunoe? Turning to face her daughter, she says, "It seemed best then."

86

"What do we do now mother?" asks the young woman.

"We can supplicate ourselves to Alexandros in hopes he will grant our dual marriage to Ptolemaios."

Eurunoe shakes her head, "Aleko hates Ptolemaios."

"Alexandros needs Ptolemaios."

The two stare at each other. Finally, the older woman smiles and takes her daughter's hand, "You are a good girl, Eurunoe."

Wearily, Eurunoe responds, "Yes, mother." Her voice trembles as she holds back her anguish.

θ

The young king's laughter fills the hall. His companions stand smiling, waiting to understand his mirth. Alexandros stands and holds out the scroll in his hand, "Iason of Pherai is dead. He's been assassinated— murdered in his own court by a group of youths."

"Who rules in Pherai now?" questions Antipatros.

Alexandros glances at the dispatch, "It's not clear yet. Maybe Alexandros of Pherai. The Aleuadai appeal to us to help throw off the dominance of Pherai."

A commotion at the door interrupts the king, as Ptolemaios of Aloros and his followers enter the hall. "Wait, now, friends. Let us welcome my brother-in-law," says Alexandros magnanimously.

"Ho, Ptolemaios, congratulations on the birth of your son," calls out Alexandros.

"Thank you, King Alexandros. The naming ceremony for your nephew will be held at Aigai so your mother can participate," answers Ptolemaios easily. Gesturing to all, Ptolemaios adds, "You must join us. You and every man of rank not present. My steward will send notice."

Alexandros' face shadows a moment, knowing that in retiring his mother to Aigai he hoped to end the scandal of his mother and sister. "Shall we all leave together and make a procession there? If we go in ten days time, we should be there when the time comes."

"That will be good. Your sister should be able to travel then. Her fever keeps recurring, but she's a strong girl."

Never having heard Eurunoe described as strong gives Alexandros pause, still his elation causes him to say, "That will be fine then. The stewards can arrange things. You hear, Ephrastos?" At the slave's nod, the king continues, holding out the scroll in his hand, "Have you heard the news?"

"About Iason of Pherai? Yes, that's why I came so quickly," answers Ptolemaios.

"This gives us the opportunity we need. The Aleuadai want our aid," the king is grinning.

"Have you given thought to Thebai?" asks Ptolemaios.

Parrhasios breaks in, "What of them? What attention have they given the north?"

The older man looks coldly at the younger, "I was speaking to King Alexandros." At the rebuke, Parrhasios' face flushes. "Perhaps, Alexandros, we should discuss this opportunity in Thessalos among your senior advisors?"

"Who is available?" asks Alexandros, turning to Ephrastos. "Call together my counselors. Antipatros, how is your father?"

"Ailing, sir," Antipatros looks grim, "I believe he must miss the session."

"Will you stand in for him?" asks the king.

Antipatros looks at Ptolemaios, knowing that the session will be divisive. The king is seeking his supporters. "Certainly, sir." Looking at the king, Antipatros thinks, *The magistrates will accept Alexandros supporting the Aleuadai, and the move will be popular with the people. What if Alexandros intends more than that?* Ptolemaios looks smug. Alexandros remains pleased. *How can they both see this turn of events as opportunity?* Antipatros feels disquiet.

PART TWO

Brothers in Arms
370 - 358 B.C.

CHAPTER FIVE

Alexandros

369 B.C.

α

Parrhasios runs his hands along Alexandros' spine, the oil of the unguent spreading evenly beneath his fingers. Slowly he kneads the muscles of the king's shoulders. Alexandros grunts his appreciation, and turns his face to look at Antipatros, who sits nude on a side bench. "The key is to strike while the situation remains confused. Which of Iason's relatives rule Pherai? Polupheron or Alexandros? Medeios of Larissa says this is the time to act. I do think Perdikkas and Philippos may be on the right track in training our smallholders to be something less than hoplites and something more than peltasts. Unfortunately, I cannot wait on their results. We must move quickly. The two troops of hoplite phalangists we trained over the winter will secure Pella. For Thessalos, we take all our foot mercenaries, our own horsemen, and the horse of Derdas and Ptolemaios."

Antipatros wipes his face with a towel. The room is steamy from the nearby pool. "You want a council called tonight?"

"Yes. Aristippos of Larissa will be here tomorrow."

Antipatros nods, "What do you want for helping the Aleuadai?"

Alexandros considers, "If we give them the strength to restrain Pherai, why shouldn't I be made *tagos?* As the military leader for life of Thessalos, I would gain the resources to withstand the Illuroi or, even, Athenai, if it came to that."

"They're not going to want to change masters. The Aleuadai see themselves as the foremost family of Thessalos."

Parrhasios interrupts, "Good thing for them the banquet hall fell on the heads of the Skopadai of Krannon or they wouldn't be the first family."

"Ancient history," says Alexandros dismissively. "You're right, though, that there are many fine families that could see themselves as rivals of the Aleuadai." The king rolls over and sits up, "Thank you, Parrhasios, what you may lack in skill, you make up with care." The two grin at each other.

Antipatros waits for the king's answer to his statement. He realizes that he would rather be at his stud farm on the Axios than striving for patience with this king. He keeps such thoughts to himself and his face impassive.

Alexandros returns to the discussion, "So I promise them self-rule. And the price of my support is their support in future campaigns against our enemies. They needn't actually send troops, I'd rather they provide money."

"Wouldn't it be best to have something tangible now?" asks Antipatros.

"They will need to pay the costs of this campaign." Then slyly, grinning again, "And affirm our primacy in Perrhaibis."

"Good. That is a motive they will understand and believe. It gives Derdas good reason to join the fight with us. The council will be enthusiastic about gaining first rights in Perrhaibis." Antipatros is pleased. His fear that Alexandros would demand too much of the Aleuadai is gone.

"Now, another problem," the king pulls at his lip in thought. "How do we get Orestis and Lunkestis to commit strong forces to us without appointing Ptolemaios to lead them? I'd prefer our fine lord be left at home."

"Isn't it better to have your enemy close by where you can watch him?"

"Yes, Antipatros, that's the conventional wisdom. He will be watched in any event. No, I want the Orestoi and Lunkestoi to get used to a Makedon king leading them."

Antipatros thinks the idea over. He curls a tuft of his beard over his finger. The solution lies in the necessary security of the kingdom he muses. "Who will you leave as regent?"

"Perdikkas."

"All right. If you are leading the campaign in Thessalos, and Perdikkas is in Pella, then you still need someone watching the Thraikiotes and Paiaones. Someone else will need to watch the Dardanoi and other Illuroi. Why not leave Ptolemaios commanding the border with Thraikios?"

"He'd rather be with the queen-mother," suggests Parrhasios.

"Here's how it will be," says Alexandros decisively, "I will lead in Thessalos, with Derdas as my principal general. Ptolemaios will be responsible for the eastern march. Perdikkas will remain in Pella, with you, Antipatros, as his general. I will send Philippos Arkouda and Periandros to the northwest—they can bolster Lunkestis. I won't draw warriors from Lunkestis, only from Orestis and Elimiotis, as well as Makedonis."

Antipatros thinks it unlikely that Aeropos of Lunkestis would agree to participate in any event. He says, "Let Arkouda and Periandros take your little brother, Philippos. The boy will gain good experience. No doubt Arkouda will take his sons, Demetrios, Antigonos, and, maybe, Polemaios. You three royals will then be in different places."

Alexandros likes Antipatros' suggestion. He comments, "Philippos is always going on about Prince Parmenion. Maybe it's a good time to remind the Pelagonoi of our alliance."

"Who else on the council needs persuading before tonight's session?" asks Antipatros.

"Let's have a small gathering at supper. The three of us can guide the others. Parrhasios, you'll need to be serious tonight," says Alexandros with a touch.

"I can be, you know," responds Parrhasios. The young man looks steadily at Antipatros, expecting a challenge. Antipatros simply nods his agreement.

β

Like the king, Philippos watches the different mercenary captains exercise their hoplite companies on the marching field. All nine captains know they are under the eyes of their employer, so the competition is intense. Today they feel no patience for any laggard in the ranks. Though few laggards exist among the professionals they lead.

Observing, Philippos realizes that six of the companies or *lokhos* are Peloponnesian mercenaries organized in the Spartiate fashion, having 144 men to a unit. Two are organized more traditionally, with 48 men in each subunit, making 192 in a *lokhos*. These men are recruited out the central Hellenic cities or from the Hellenic tribes further west. The ninth *lokhos* is Kretan, and is the largest at 224 men. In all, there are about 1,500 heavily armored fighters. With their attendants, servants and camp followers, the cost of supporting them is high.

Besides the armored warriors, Alexandros has assembled several mercenary bands of peltasts or lightly armed foot men. They will protect the flanks of the hoplite phalanx in battle with their bristle of javelins. Most of the peltasts are Thraikiotes, although one band is all Paiaones.

When the army is fully gathered, the Makedones, Elimiotes and Orestiotes will provide the horsemen. They will number better than 600 riders, perhaps as many as 800. Their followers will act as *psiloi* or skirmishers, using slings, bows, and long knives. In all, something over 3,000 fighting men will make up Alexandros' army.

The marching men are raising a cloud of dust. Their loud trumpets sound commands that can be heard over the din of clanging armor, stamping feet, and hoarse cries. They maneuver in patterns too intricate for the battle field. Still, such training must build cohesion, thinks Philippos, though he wonders if using battle tactics wouldn't be more useful.

Perdikkas walks over to Philippos and points at the marchers, "Alexandros has the army he wants and the opportunity to use it in Thessalos."

"Why so glum, Perdix?"

"You get to go off to the borderlands. Alexandros goes to war. I sit here."

"You could argue that you have the greatest responsibility," answers Philippos.

"What do you mean?"

"You and Antipatros watch over Ptolemaios."

The seventeen-year old Perdikkas scuffs the dirt with his foot, "Why do you think Ptolemaios accepted his task so easily?"

"He's getting a little long in the tooth for active campaigning?"

"He's as hardy as ever. Whatever we say about him, he's never shirked a fight."

Philippos considers again, "This isn't a fight he believes in."

"Even if so, you'd think he'd want to be in Pella. If Aleko dies in Thessalos, Ptolemaios will pounce on me."

"He's realist enough to know Aleko won't let that happen. That's why you have Antipatros at your side." Philippos tosses a pebble at a blade of grass, "Anyway, Aleko is giving Ptolemaios a plum. Holding the frontier is an important responsibility."

Moodily, Perdikkas sighs. Then he grins, "Have you seen the wife of Mikuthos, the mercenary captain?"

"No, which one is she?"

"She's less than four feet tall, but perfect. You want to put her on your lap. They say he's extremely jealous of her."

"Perdikkas," says Philippos in a warning tone.

"I like women. I have to kick around Pella while you two are doing something," explodes Perdikkas.

"You can hunt. You can train Makedones to be phalangists. You will be administering the kingdom as regent. The shipments of timber to Athenai will be your responsibility this year."

"Yes, yes, little brother."

"Hasn't Alexandros granted you two new estates so that your lands along the Haliakmon are continuous?"

"Yes, he's given me my bribe." Perdikkas grins, reaches out and tousles Philippos' hair, "I'll be all right. I have a district of Pieris to rule directly, you know. You're right, there's a lot to do as regent. I'm just feeling restless. This is the largest army assembled here since father and the Lakedaimonians faced Olunthos."

"Father would have been pleased to aid the Aleuadai." The memory of Amuntas is a strong chord in Philippos.

"Yes, for all father's fears, Alexandros' ambitions seem reasonable. Perrhaibis fits nicely, and there is precedent for our rule."

"I wouldn't count on Perrhaibis while our hold on Elimiotis depends on the friendship of Derdas."

"Derdas is a friend," exclaims Perdikkas stoutly.

"Of course. His friendship was with father. He is our ally, true, but not with the same heartfelt attachment. Derdas has two sons. Will Elimiotis always be friendly?"

The brothers stare at each other. Perdikkas says slowly, "Derdas has a daughter, too. Maybe she should marry into the Temenidai when she comes of age."

"You're closer to marrying age than me," laughs Philippos.

"At you age, you have to watch out for men," responds Perdikkas. "No, Phila is young. Maybe in a half-dozen years or so, she'll be ready for marriage." He smiles, "I will be married before then."

"Who to?"

"I haven't decided. I need to talk it over with Alexandros. There's a few years yet. I'd like one of the old families, a hearty Makedon girl. Aleko may see that as a threat and only be willing to see me marry an outsider." He shrugs and grins, "Aleko ought to get a Thessaliote if this campaign is successful. One of the Aleuadai is likely. If it's not successful, he'll need a Makedone or maybe some highland royalty, like father."

"You've thought about this."

"I told you I like women," Perdikkas laughs.

* * *

On the far side of the field, Alexandros confers with Derdas and the mercenary general, Diodotos Kokinos. The Makedon king is arguing, "I know there are logistical constraints. But I want us to move as early as possible. So I propose shipping the foot along the coast to the Vale of Tempe. The horsemen can use the Volustana pass. Derdas, you tell me, how soon could the horse reach Gonnos from the time you leave Phulakai?"

"About 45 to 50 miles, that is by way of Dolikhe and Olooson, and if the way is open through the pass to Phalanna. Otherwise, we add 15 miles or so," muses Derdas. "I want the horses and men in good shape. Much of the ride is up-and-down hill. We will need to push harder once we're out of Perrhaibis and into Hestiaitis. We'll need to rest the horses before the push. Let's call it four full days, since we can't count on Phalanna being clear. You'll want us ready for action at the end." He grins at Alexandros, "I'm surer of being there in four days than you are by riding the waves. A calm could set you back as long, and the wrong winds or a strong storm could make it longer."

"Load the day before, then a day at sea, counting the unloading. And a march of a day to Gonnos from the coast," comments Diodotos Kokinos.

"You may march your mercenaries in a day from the beach. The rest will take longer," amends Alexandros. Turning to Derdas, he asks, "When can you have everything ready at Phulakai?"

"Give me fifteen days from now."

"Can you do it in ten instead?"

Again Derdas grins at the impatient young man who is king, "Twelve days." Derdas likes the directness of Alexandros. Where Amuntas would take time to consider every possibility, looking long at the potential causes of failure, Alexandros already sees himself succeeding, and wants to find the quickest path to his success. Still, things Derdas did willingly for Amuntas, he gauges carefully before committing to Alexandros. The death of Amuntas awoke ambitions in Derdas. He now thinks on the idea of controlling Perrhaibis from Elimiotis. Perhaps, even, adding the neighboring Epeiriote province of Tumphaia. A greater Elimiotis would allow Derdas to give each son a worthwhile legacy.

Alexandros nods, "All right, you leave Phulakai twelve days from now. In sixteen days you are in Gonnos. We will be there waiting for you." Pointing to the columns of exercising hoplites, he adds, "Before the month is out, I want the Aleuadai feeding this lot."

"At Gonnos, we'll be a long day's march from Larissa," states Diodotos Kokinos.

"Yes, we'll be met by the Aleuadai, their retainers and their allies at Gonnos. That should add about three hundred horsemen and two or three times as many foot. Call it a thousand to be safe," calculates Alexandros. "When we enter Larissa, we can expect another thousand foot to rise and join us, from the city and countryside."

"Mostly rabble, though. Not worth much," says Diodotos sourly.

"Still, an army of 5,000 or more will be enough to assure the Aleuadai regain their freedom," Derdas considers the results certain.

Alexandros agrees, "Once Larissa is secure, we can think about other possibilities."

γ

The stand of beech trees gives shade that cools Philippos after the climb up the hillside. From here, he can see out across the valley floor. The broad valley below is like a funnel that allows the Illuroi to pour into the lands of the Makedones and their highland cousins. No wonder the Lunkestoi are as often in alliance with the Illuroi as opposed to them. At least the Pelagonoi, further north and east, can withdraw to their mountain havens. Here, the Lunkestoi would be hard pressed to make a stand.

Seeing the valley lying below is inspiring. It seems a woven blanket spread in loose folds over a bed. No wonder the gods inhabit the highest mountains. The impulse to climb the hillside, to be alone and away from the traveling party, to seek a moment with Zeus or, at least, the spirit of this grove and hill, is rewarded. *Oh, Lords of eternity, thank you for the loveliness of this day, for the blessing of my kindred. Dear Apollo, beautiful Artemis, thank you for these trees, for the breeze, for this ecstasy of a pure day that I breathe in, for my good health. Oh, great god Zeus, thank you for your help, aid me to be worthy of my ancestors.* The prayer, the thanks, welling up and spilling through his mind, feels fitting and heartfelt to Philippos. Though he does not think of himself as pious, he knows what he owes to the grace of the gods.

Somehow this whole journey, this ride through these lands, the companionship of Antigonos and the others, this being apart from the weights and considerations of the court, cause Philippos to feel an elation, as though some goddess, perhaps the Kourete of this grove, has entered his mind, his being.

Straining his eyes, looking as far north as he can, Philippos seeks to impress upon his memory all that lies before him. The purple hazed distant mountains seem to call him. The vital greenness of the valley beckons. The glint of stream and lake ask for discovery.

Having taken his fill of the vista, Philippos turns to find his way down to the men below. There remains a three-hour ride today before they reach the next fortified Lunkestoi town. There they are to meet Aeropos of Lunkestis who rules these lands.

*   *   *

The grizzled beard on the face of Aeropos of Lunkestis is braided into four thick strands. That and the tawny lion hide he wears around his shoulders make him seem the rudest of barbarians. Yet his three boys stand dressed in the most civilized of clothes, as though sons of a wealthy patrician of Athenai. The contrast is a purposeful statement. Despite their clothes and their youth, the boys are sturdy images of their father.

"Welcome, cousins," declares Aeropos, "We meet at last. My men and I have been up north. With the unrest among the Pelagonoi, I am concerned to show the Dardanoi that we are alert. The evil-spawned ridge runners might excite themselves into thinking this is a good time to raid."

As leader of their expedition, Philippos Arkouda acknowledges the welcome, "King Aeropos, we are well met. Your valiance is widely renowned. Our party can strengthen your numbers as you display your vigilance." Clasping hands with the king, he adds, "Your boys have grown since I was last in Lunkestis. Yet I would recognize your sons anywhere."

The king laughs proudly, "They do bear the likeness of my line. Alexandros, Heromenes, and Arrhabaios, invite our guests to join our banquet." The boys lead the newcomers into the hall.

Seated, with a shank of lamb in his hand, Philippos is content to listen while the men argue the rights in the royal feud occurring in Pelagonis. The Lunkestis *basileos* Aeropos had graciously but briefly received his presentation as prince of the Makedones and brother to the lowland king. To Philippos, it seemed as if Aeropos' acknowledgment said no more than *yes, princeling, you are of a rank with one of my younger sons*. Philippos is still amused at the presumption. The Lunkestoi are always the most restless of the highland Makedones.

"My father knows he must demonstrate the strength of the Lunkestoi to you and your family if he is to win your respect," says Alexandros of Lunkestis, as he takes a seat next to Philippos. The two are of an age, Alexandros being about a year younger. His smile is friendly.

"Do you sing?" asks Philippos.

"Who does not?" replies Alexandros of Lunkestis.

"There is a song from your grandfather's day that was sung by the Lunkestoi in defiance of Arkhelaos, who was then king in Makedonis. Do you know it?"

The Lunkestoi prince grins, "Yes."

"Good. Now, we'll need some others for the chorus." Philippos picks up a piece of bread crust and throws it Antigonos, "Titan, I need your voice. We're going to sing *Valley men rally*."

Antigonos starts laughing. "You give away the game," says Philippos. He bangs on the table with his cup, getting the attention of the boys at the table. "Now, listen, the highlanders will sing their *Valley men rally*. We give them three parts, two high and one low. Then we come in with our version, *Valley men folly*. Little Korrhagos, you take our high part, Antigonos and Demetrios the low, and I'll take the mid-voice. After the first three verses, we switch. Alexandros and his companions take the lowland version and we do the highland version. All agreed, all understand?" The boys all nod. "Okay, then, on my count. One. Two. Three. Skip. Five."

A Lunkestrian youngster leads, his high voice cutting through the rumbling voice and clatter of the hall. Korrhagos comes in, letting his voice twine around the other. Then another Lunkestrian voice counters. The hall begins to still. Soon the six parts, sung by more than twelve voices, climb and twine, fall and counterpoint. The contrary verses of the two versions somehow complement, underscoring both the vanity of the words and the commonality of the bravery they profess. When the lowland voices change to the highland version, and the highland accents lift the lowland mockery, the essential unity of that past bloody experience is emphasized. As the final verse is sung, the voices drop off, part by part, until the last low pitched solo ends. The hall erupts into cheering and laughter.

Young Philippos stands and raises his cup, "To the valiant Lunkestoi." All drink deeply.

Then Aeropos stands and bellows, "To the cunning Makedones, our cousins." Antigonos howls like a wolf as all drain the wine in their mugs.

δ

In Larissa, the banqueting is in its fourth hour. King Alexandros is drunk. The victory had been absurdly easy as the Pherai garrison fled. Too easy a victory—for the citadel is now held by the Aleuadai and not Makedones. The celebration feast offered by Medeios, Aristippos and their kinsmen while lavish tastes too much of bitterness for Alexandros. So he is drinking heavily.

By contrast, the general Diodotos is all smiles. A mercenary likes bloodless victories that earn good money. A battle with few deaths but ample opportunity for looting would have given him greater pleasure. Still, he is philosophical. His master would have forbidden looting an allied city anyway.

Derdas raises a mug, calling out some toast that doesn't reach the mind of Alexandros. Obviously Derdas is pleased too. He gains the administration of Perrhaibis without losses among his precious horsemen.

The worm twisting in the king's mind is his hunger for Thessalos. A warrior's victory would have impressed his power on both his own subjects and the Thessaliotes. If Alexandros gains the mantle of *tagos*—the military overlordship—of Thessalos, then all the Makedones, hill and lowland, must recognize his superiority.

Though drunk, swaying and outwardly inarticulate, in his core voice, in his inner ear, where the gods speak to a man, he is sober and calculating. The scene about him blurs easily, save whatever minute item takes the full focus of his remaining attention. Within him, relentless, is the worm, the ambition, the fixed idea. Pherai is not beaten, only withdrawn. The fight must be carried to Pherai. First, free more of Thessalos. Build strength. Then come crashing down on Pherai. Destroy the city and he is the power in Thessalos. King Alexandros. Alexandros the Great.

Belatedly, Alexandros realizes that Medeios is talking to him. He hopes he's not given voice to his thought before Medeios. Medeios is offering him another cup of wine. Blearily, he accepts.

*　*　*

"They want us to leave," Derdas states flatly.

"Yes, I daresay," Alexandros lounges on the couch, eating olives and spitting the pits into a small clay pot. "They welcomed us readily enough to begin with." *Derdas counsels withdrawing so he can enjoy Perrhaibis,* thinks Alexandros.

"They'd want us here the moment Pherai threatens," comments Parrhasios.

"Perhaps we need to persuade Pherai to offer a threat," suggests Diodotos.

"How do you propose to do that? We've been here a month. Pherai isn't about to advance against us." Derdas shakes his head in frustration, "We've done what we came to do. If we pull out now, taking our thank gifts, we retain our influence on events in Thessalos. If we anger the Aleuadai and their allies, then why did we come here?"

Diodotos is unwilling to let go of the campaign. His men are idle, not a good state for mercenaries. "We need to give the appearance of weakness. You could spread your forces wider. Make it appear difficult for us to assemble. Let the agents of Alexandros of Pherai reach the democratic faction of Larissa."

Parrhasios is growing excited, "We could begin to withdraw. Derdas to Olooson. Diodotos to Gonnos."

"No, I won't withdraw," says Alexandros angrily. "The elders of Krannon invite us to share our protection with them. My agents are further south, in Pharsalos. We are sure of a welcome there, too. With Larissa, Krannon and Pharsalos as partners, we could move against Pherai herself."

"Will the Aleuadai continue as partners?" asks Derdas.

"Why not? Isn't Pherai still a power? With the bulk of our forces moving south, doesn't that end the irritation of seeing strutting mercenaries about their city," responds Alexandros.

Derdas is silent, considering. Maybe it's worth the risk. But what's the gain? If Thessalos is stable, then Elimiotis' southern border is secure. If Alexandros builds a balance between Larissa, Krannon and Pharsalos does that guarantee stability? Pherai will continue to dominate the ports on the Pagasai Gulf, making her the economic powerhouse of Thessalos. And what of the western Thessaliote cities, especially Trikka, Gomphi and Aiginion? Alexandros wants to be *tagos* of Thessalos. How does he achieve that? Thinking carefully, Derdas knows he does not want this boy having that much power. Still, he'd best moderate his opposition until he is in touch with other clans among the Makedones. Perhaps it's time to sound out Ptolemaios. "You make an interesting argument, King Alexandros. What would it mean in Thessalos if Pherai is truly humbled and not simply embarrassed until it sorts out its leadership?"

"If we humble her, we become the source of order in Thessalos," states Alexandros triumphantly.

"Save for Thebai, of course," muses Diodotos.

"What has Thebai got to do with it?" scornfully asks Parrhasios.

Looking startled, Diodotos answers, "Thebai wants Thessalos to be weak. She's not forgotten Iason of Pherai. So long as the Thessaliote confederacy squabbles, she's no threat to her neighbors."

"You're jumping too far ahead, General. The lands of several peoples lies between Thessalos and Boiotia," says Alexandros peremptorily.

Inwardly sighing at his paymaster, Diodotos thinks of the roughly 130-mile march from Thebai to Pherai. Seven days. Much less for Theban horsemen. Nonetheless, Diodotos recognizes the need to support the king's notions, "A move to Krannon would be good. The horses need their grass and fodder, and the men could use a march."

"I think it best if I remain in Larissa to keep my eye on the Aleuadai. Parrhasios, you will accompany Diodotos to Krannon as my personal emissary. Take the Peloponnesians and the Kretans. They seem to be causing the greatest difficulties here. I will retain the Makedones and the remaining mercenaries. Perhaps the Orestiote horse should join Diodotos? What do you think, Derdas?"

"Yes. My boys and the Orestiotes keep brawling with each other. What do you want me to do?"

"I think you continue to put pressure of Pherai with your horsemen. Be more aggressive with your patrolling. See if you reach Skotussa without opposition. If need be, do some skirmishing but don't press too hard yet. Withdraw north if the Pheraienes come out in force."

"What do you intend to tell Medeios and Aristippos?" asks Derdas.

"Their continuing freedom from Pherai depends on their ability to build up strength. We are keeping Pherai off-balance to give the Aleuadai time."

"Good. What if they are successful?"

"In the battles to come, we give the Aleuadai the privilege of holding the center of our line," smiles Alexandros. "And I think it's time we had Antipatros, I mean, Perdikkas, dispatch additional men south to us. Antiokhos or one of his senior kinsmen can lead the column. I think we need another thousand men. If they march down the coast road, that will allow Antiokhos time to shape them into a cohesive force."

Derdas, like the others, realizes that Alexandros has no intention of loosening the bridle he is placing on Thessalos.

ε

Tapping the shaft of his writing brush against his teeth, Ptolemaios considers what further to write to Eurudike. The letter outlines the steps he's taking to secure support against Alexandros. He is cautious in his expressions in the event the letter goes astray. He knows he has the queen-mother's love and agreement. Still, however much she resents Alexandros' kingship and desires that Ptolemaios lead the Makedones, she is the boy's mother. Much he might say to her in person that he cannot commit to writing. There is much more that he does not reveal to her at all. Why test her loyalty to him unduly?

Sighing, Ptolemaios signs the letter and seals it shut with his signet ring. He will see her in a fortnight. By then he should have further word from Thessalos about the king's mismanagement of the Aleuadai. "Leandros, you will place this letter in the queen's hands and no others. The maid Marnike will see that you have an audience with Queen Eurudike." Ptolemaios smiles at his man, as he hands over the folded letter, "Tell the queen that I am in good health and eager to see her. On your way out, send in my secretaries. I will dictate the remaining letters."

Waiting, Ptolemaios feels satisfaction. The king's failures are coming to light much as he expected. He takes pleasure in commanding the Thraikiote border. Not only are the borderlands safe, the command gives good reason to raise horsemen and even bodies of foot. His adherents are in place throughout the eastern marches.

He chuckles to himself, thinking of the watchers he has set to watch those whom Alexandros planted among his men to watch him. Of course, some of the watchers report back to Derdas, Antipatros, or others rather than Alexandros. All the care taken by the magnates in gaining reports of each other's doings. What a strange combination it is of necessity and absurdity.

His early caution when sounding out support against the king has passed into boldness. The king does not play the game of intrigue well. More important, many of the companions of the deceased Amuntas are alarmed at Alexandros' transparent effort to dominate Thessalos. The old men who run this country want stability and security, not adventures that threaten all they have gained over the years.

An exception might be Iolaos. Or, rather, given the old man's ill health, his son, Antipatros. Antipatros follows his family's custom of promoting the kingship of the Temenidai. That has been their path to prominence and position for generations. Tradition has it that their family was the earliest to rally to the first Perdikkas, founder of the royal line. Antipatros is a clever man, though he hides his intellect in a manner cruder than his father.

Ptolemaios does not want to lock horns with Antipatros. Better to counterbalance that family's influence. He is confident that Alexandros will make mistakes that will give him opportunity to offset Antipatros' loyalty.

A knock at the door announcing the secretaries interrupts Ptolemaios' considerations. The thought formed—a desire really—for the loyalty of Antipatros is dismissed as unlikely, "Come in, come in, I do not have all day."

ζ

Nervously Philippos changes his grip on the lance. He tries to seem calm. All he can think of is the likelihood of dying in the midst of someone else's feud. His horse snorts and shakes its head, uneasy at its rider's fear.

The days in Lunkestis seem like a dream now. Why didn't they stay there instead of coming to Pelagonis. How did Arkouda join them to this raiding party led by Philotas and Parmenion. At that thought, Philippos is embarrassed at his cowardice for it was due to his urging that they were with the raiders.

In the valley below are the three villages they will attack. Parmenion's cousins have taken refuge in this valley, their last stronghold in these lands. Parmenion said the enemy strength could be no more than eighty men plus the villagers. Altogether, maybe three hundred fighters are below.

Arkouda leads twenty men. The royal Pelagones consist of about 120 warriors. They will succeed only if they take the enemy by surprise. Their approach to the valley has been accomplished skillfully. During the night, their scouts guided them into place. They have found no enemy sentries. As soon as the sun clears the eastern hills behind them, they will ride down on the villages. Are the villagers truly asleep or is it all a trap?

A rider is slowly coming back along the column of waiting horsemen. He stops to say a word here or there. Philippos discerns that it is Parmenion, making certain of his men's readiness.

Just ahead, Arkouda shifts in his saddle. "Philippos," he whispers,

The boy touches his heels to his mount and steps forward beside the clan chief, "Yes, Lord Arkouda?"

"You remember my instructions? The Pelagones will hit the main village first. They will send a party to cover the lower village. We will cover the village at the north end of the valley. We are to let the enemy escape north but not in any other direction. Is that clear?"

"Yes, sir."

"I am responsible for your safety. You are the king's brother. I know your impetuous nature, but I want you to stay behind me," Arkouda's voice is gruff with affection. Doubtless he is wondering how he got talked into this adventure, and what will be the king's reaction if the boy is killed or maimed.

The surge of good feeling for Arkouda washes away Philippos' nervousness. The fear is still within him, but it is obedient to his will.

Parmenion reaches them, "Makedones, your sun will be rising at your back. Its rays will be in the eyes of my cousins. Be assured, they will run, and you will help us herd them out of Pelagonis." His voice is cheerful, "Let us do the killing unless you can't avoid the work. Prevent any one from the north village from entering the fray. Let any go who flee north, out of the valley."

He reaches across to grip Philippos' arm, "Dear brother prince, thank you for bringing your people to our aid. Now I think it's time we strike. Father will lead us out any moment."

Parmenion stays by the side of Philippos. This seems to reassure Arkouda. Within the time of a few deep breaths, the column moves out. Slowly the horsemen pick their way down the narrow trace of the wooded slope. As the sun lightens the hills behind them, they reach the valley floor and form twenty wide and eight deep. They trot through the grain fields toward the middle village. Distantly, the lowing of cattle can be heard as the village boys lead them forth. They pick up their pace, and a detachment of twenty Pelagones peel away to block the small south valley village.

Arkouda calls for the Makedones to follow him. Parmenion touches Philippos' shoulder in farewell, and heels his horse to hurry to the first line.

Now the Makedones are alone and riding north. The barking of dogs can be heard. The enemy will be alarmed, realizing their danger.

Philippos tucks his lance between his upper arm and his chest. The shaft rests easily in his right hand. The lance point seems to lead him to the enemy. Reins are held in his left hand. His heart beats as fast a tempo as the horses' hooves. Soon the huddle of the north village is in sight.

Arkouda raises his lance, motioning them to slow and spread out. Periandros leads five riders to the right, cutting the pathway south to the middle village. Demetrios, Antigonos' older brother, leads another three riders to the left, to cover the track to the stream that cuts through the valley. Arkouda motions Philippos, Antigonos and Little Korrhagos to join him. Then Arkouda, the boys, and the remaining half-dozen riders walk their horses slowly toward the small village. Behind them, faintly, they can hear shouts and war cries where the Pelagones are attacking the main village. Even against the wind they can smell the smoke of the fires.

For a moment, Philippos thinks about the distant strife, his mind's eye seeing Philotas and Parmenion directing the raiders. Reeling anti-Philotates and frightened villagers are being cut down. Yet for Parmenion, these people he is killing are relatives, are his family and their followers. Even the villagers are his people. Kleopatra would say some trenchant remark about the needs of power. Still, there is horror to this. Philotas will rule Pelagonis, but at sad cost.

The advancing line of Makedones rein up at Arkouda's command. They are close enough to see men, women and children hurrying, frantic, in the little village. Across the fields, Periandros halloos and points north. Arkouda calls back, seeking clarification. Periandros pantomimes that some villagers, at least, are fleeing north.

Philippos is keenly disappointed, his pent-up excitement and fear plummeting. Now he wants to do battle. Wants to find out how he will behave. Suddenly, he's certain he is brave. A thousand times he has imagined himself at war, fighting some anonymous opponent, vanquishing some evil warrior. Today it could have been real. Nerved up and now nothing. They sit on their horses and watch panicked villagers run. Children crying. Possessions grabbed or lost. Like an anthill stirred with a stick. There is no glory here.

Antigonos leans over and spits, then straightens in his saddle, "I feel like a fox watching a hen yard that smells my scent."

Little Korrhagos laughs, "More like a wolf that's already eaten its mutton and can't be bothered to catch another sheep from the flock."

From behind them, on their left, comes the drumming of hooves. They turn to see a group of riders burst up from the stream bed. In an instant, they realize the riders are escaping from the middle village. To be ahorse and so well armed, they must be the cousins Parmenion is hunting.

Arkouda shouts to let them pass but to the fleeing Pelagones, the Makedones are more warriors they must defeat to survive. The dozen or so riders gallop directly at the boys, seeing the weakest link in the enemy line.

Philippos couches his lance, adjusts the brim of his flat helmet, and braces himself for the shock. Just as an enemy rider comes within reach, Philippos dances his horse aside to avoid being bowled over and strikes with his lance. The burly rider wheels and is inside the arc of the lance head. The big bearded man strikes with his sword, but the blow falters as he is skewered under his raised arm by the lance of Antigonos. In turn, Philippos blocks the blow from another rider intended for Antigonos.

Without thought for safety, with the urgency of his adrenaline, Philippos hurls himself into the action. His lance crushes past an enemy cheek-guard into the orbit of an eye. As quickly the dying rider is past him as the horses carry the combatants apart.

The Pelagonid survivors are through their line. Arkouda's men wheel to pursue. From both flanks, Periandros and Demetrios lead their horsemen after the escapees. More horsemen are coming from the south. Through the dust, Philippos can make out Philotas' royal banner.

An arrow takes a Makedon rider through the neck and a saddle is empty. More arrows fly into their ranks. Arkouda turns them to ride down the village archers who have chosen to intervene. Demetrios and his men have already reached several archers. The few others are running for the shelter of the stone huts. None of the archers reach the buildings.

No enemies are in sight. Philippos reins up. Dust marks the passage of the royal troops beyond the village. Looking about, Philippos realizes Periandros and his fellows must have joined the pursuit.

Demetrios canters over, "Any losses?"

"I don't know. Some. One of us took an arrow."

"Who?"

"I'm not sure," Philippos turns back. Across the field are clumps of standing horses, several bundles of clothes and flesh lying on the ground, one horse down and struggling.

"Looks like your lance found someone," grins Demetrios.

Remembering now the impact of hitting the passing Pelagones, Philippos nods, "Yes, one of them rode onto my lance."

Slowly they walk their horse toward the scattering of fallen men. Antigonos walks over to meet them, his face streaked with tears, "Korrhagos is dead." A lament swells in Philippos' breast. What a fine voice had Little Korrhagos.

Arkouda is looking grim. In addition to Korrhagos, one other Makedone is dead. Another is not expected to live. Several have lesser injuries. Five Pelagones lay about the field. Demetrios and his men killed the archers, another four or five opponents, not that they count for much. One wounded Pelagone is a prisoner.

Philippos Arkouda will need to account for Korrhagos. Will the boy's death, while in Arkouda's care, strain the alliance Arkouda is seeking with that family? An alliance which is to be sealed by the marriage of Demetrios to Stratonike. Still, the prince is well and has made his first kill, as has Arkouda's son, Antigonos. The gods have shown kindness.

Philippos dismounts to stand with Antigonos. Despite the sorrow over Korrhagos, Philippos feels intensely alive. The air tastes clean. The sun is up enough to see that the day will be dazzling. Antigonos smiles, together the two friends clasp hands.

η

Ptolemaios strides into the quiet room, "Out, out, all of you, out. Let me be with my wife."

Eurunoe struggles to rise from her bed, as her maids and the priestess of Athena all hurry to escape the exuberant authority of Ptolemaios.

The armored husband reaches her bedside and quickly kneels, gently helping Eurunoe to sit up. She feels damp and feverish to his hands. "Ah, Chickadee, I pray Apollo sees you well," he says gruffly, and kisses her softly on the forehead.

"I feel better with you here," she responds. And her words are true.

"I came as soon as I heard," his voice contrite.

"Thank you," tears well in her eyes. She weeps easily, the baby's death making everything seem such an effort. She exhausts as readily as she weeps. "I wanted our son to grow strong and proud like his father, and be part of his father's pride."

Ptolemaios is humbled as he thinks of his line of descent. The gods take as much or more than they give. For all his personal vigor, there is only the fey young man, Philoxenos, to carry on.

Eurunoe whispers, "You are the great-grandson of good King Alexandros."

"I am more Orestid than Temenidai." He derides himself, "I am the most sophisticated uplander in Makedonis. Grandfather Istros to my father, Amuntas of Orestis, to me to my son, Philoxenos. See how it slips away when we come down out of the hills? In four generations, we go from rough tribal chief to a pottery and dance dilettante."

Eurunoe is crying, grief for her son, pity for herself, and a lassitude of sorrow. A sense of foreboding enfolds her, not so much for herself as for Ptolemaios. She dabs at her eyes with the blanket to blot her tears. She smiles weakly, "You look good, husband. Riding the borders agrees with you."

He pats her hand, "Yes, being out on the trail, training our fellows, all of that pleases me." He tries for a heartiness that rings false.

"You bring the breath of outdoors with you. You are in good enough cheer despite our sorrow."

For a moment he thinks of the news from Thessalos. How Alexandros is besieging the citadel at Larissa. How the Aleuadai have appealed to Thebai for intervention. The boy-king is making a muck of it. Throughout Makedonis there is disgust at the king's failures. Ptolemaios is at heart in good cheer, despite the sick room, and having, in the days riding to their estate, adjusted to the babe's death. Babies do die often enough, after all. "What would you say if we carry your bed outside? The day is sunny, bright and warm. Give the sun of the Temenidai a chance to heal you?"

"I would like that," she smiles up at him. "Would you stay with me today? Tell me about your adventures?"

To care for someone ill is not his nature, yet the guilt and odd love he feels for Eurunoe compel him to make amends. He does not believe she will survive her ailment. He brushes the hair back from her face, "I am yours to command this day, Chickadee."

Their eyes search each other's. Her fingers touch his lips. He kisses her fingertips. They are as close as they will ever be. Abruptly, he stands and bellows for her servants to come and fetch her so she may enjoy the sun and breeze.

* * *

In the evening, Ptolemaios dictates dispatches to his secretaries. He must make up for the many hours spent by Eurunoe's side. They had talked of everything, except her health and the baby—from the last time they saw Euripides' old play, *Arkhelaos*, to the relative merits of bronze, leather and linen cuirasses to the variety of barley best planted in Orestis. That the hours had passed pleasantly surprised Ptolemaios, for he had initially regretted his promise to Eurunoe. Now he realizes that he never enjoyed her company more.

So, work this evening, a hundred tasks to do, arrangements to make, for he intends to march on Pella. Eurudike will be by his side. So will almost all of King Amuntas' companions. True, he will denude the border of armed men. Coordinating the arrival of his Orestid adherents from the west will be tricky. He is not positive which way Aeropos of Lunkestis will side. This embassy of Philippos Arkouda seems to have impressed the Lunkestoi and Pelagonoi. His thoughts and ideas are running fast. His two secretaries are catching his instructions as quickly as they can, but from time to time, they ask him to pause, while they catch up. He paces.

Suddenly, from the far wing of the house comes an unmistakable keening. His secretaries look up. Ptolemaios closes his eyes, head down, sighs. *Lord Apollo, why today? Why give us only today together?* And as quickly as these thoughts are formed, the god's answer comes to his mind, *You were given many days, but it is only this day you consecrated.*

Leandros is at the door, "Lady Eurunoe is dead, sir."

Ptolemaios nods his acceptance, turns away, trying to hide his tears, feeling amazement at how his heart is torn asunder.

θ

Parrhasios fears for Alexandros. The king is stropping the blade of his sword, working furiously to bring the edge to its keenest sharpness. The suppressed rage and frustration felt by the king is apparent in each tightly controlled motion. "Aleko, what good do you do offering yourself to Ares? Let Diodotos Kokinos lead the assault. That's what you pay him for."

The king raises his eyes to Parrhasios. Eyes that bulge slightly in fury. "We must succeed," Alexandros' emotions make it difficult to express his thoughts. He feels his humiliation so damningly. "Derdas will slow the advance of the Thebans from the south. We have today, Parrhasios. By seizing the citadel today, we make ourselves secure. We vindicate ourselves before our kin in Makedonis. If we fail, then our only choice is to retreat from Thessalos. All we have done here will be for nothing. Worse than nothing, it will be plain failure."

The word failure echoes in Parrhasios' mind. He dare not say what he thinks, that they have failed in any event. Though he loves Alexandros dearly, Parrhasios knows he does not want to die in an assault that is useless even if it succeeds. "I believe the advice you received from Antiokhos is correct. What Ptolemaios is doing in Makedonis is more important for your future than what is happening in Thessalos."

Alexandros closes his eyes. He seeks to clear his mind. He does not want to see the anxiety on the beautiful face of Parrhasios. In his heart, he knows he is being foolish. This assault, this throw of the knucklebones, means nothing. Yet to withdraw—to flee Thebai and run home—he must face the scorn of his mother and the notables. The cautioning words of his father come to mind. He knows he has attempted too much and so failed at all. He summons the visage of Ptolemaios to mind. *What will that crafty man do? Does Ptolemaios really think he can gain the kingship in my stead?*

Opening his eyes, Alexandros faces the truth. Sadly, he says, "Cancel the assault in my name, Parrhasios. Kokinos must block the citadel while we ready the army for withdrawal. Send a messenger to Derdas. By morning, we must be gone from here. Send another messenger to the coast to ready the ships."

"The ships are on alert, Aleko."

The king nods, absently. "As of the ninth day, Antipatros and Perdikkas still held Pella," sighs Alexandros. "We can be there in three days if Poseidon smiles. Perhaps we should count on six days."

The wryness in the king's voice sounds good to Parrhasios. There had been precious little humor here since the twin calamities had been announced —the march north of a Theban army under their master general, Pelopidas, and the rising in Makedonis against the king's authority.

Alexandros stands and attempts a smile, "Quickly, good friend, there is much to do."

The king's immediate resolution and cheerfulness astonish Parrhasios. Only now does he understand how uncertain the king has felt in Thessalos. Smiling back, Parrhasios responds, "I am yours to command."

*　　*　　*

Alone, now, Alexandros thinks about who he can count on to support him. There is not much money left for the mercenaries. He is certain Pella will be his, for there he can rely on the loyalty of Perdikkas, and the opposition of Antipatros to Ptolemaios. So he will have a base. From all reports,

Philippos will keep Arkouda and Periandros true to his cause. Their families form a strong block. Here he has Parrhasios. He cannot trust Antiokhos. Derdas is becoming less certain.

Bitterness engulfs him at the thought of his mother. As always, she would deny him. His mind shies away from her. He does not like thinking about his mother.

For a moment his mind touches on his sister, Eurunoe. His sorrow over her death is a mingling of grief for her and irritation over the loss of restraint on Ptolemaios. Not that Eurunoe ever was much counterweight for the old noble's ambitions. Alexandros feels he could better have used another loyal brother, than the weak sister she was. Still, he will miss her.

For months, he has felt inadequate to his task as king. For a long time he envied the easy times his father had. The truth slowly reached him, that King Amuntas never had an easy time of it and learned to balance the contending powers and factions within the kingdom from hard experience. Curiously, that truth has given Alexandros hope. He has come to admire his father. The knowledge that his father failed many times but always came back, and ultimately succeeded, is a source of strength for Alexandros.

Humiliation gives way to determination. He will not lose his throne. The times ahead will be difficult. He does not yet know how he will tread a path through all the pitfalls, he is only certain that he will find his way.

As a start, he must rejoin his army, and lead them out of the trap Larissa has become. Coming here had been too easy.

He finishes strapping on his boots. Outside the room he can hear the movement and murmur of his officers and servants. *Father Zeus, help me make the right choices. Let Herakles and my forefathers guide my actions. Lend me the shade of my father, Amuntas the Good, to counsel me. I have been heedless all too long. I am the Makedones; I am king; I am your son. As you have entrusted me, give me the guidance I need.* Pulling open the door, Alexandros strides firmly across the threshold.

ι

Picking out the left forefoot of his horse, Philippos is feeling pleasure in the task. Grooming the animal is both necessity and release. While this horse, Grizos, is not a favorite among the fourteen beasts kept by Philippos, he is a patient, enduring animal. Philippos likes more temperamental horses. But for this long trek with Arkouda, he chose his three mounts carefully. They are traveling animals more than battle steeds. Letting the hoof go, Philippos pats Grizos on the shoulder, "Good boy. Skaros will have a treat for you, then you can graze."

Skaros takes the horse's lead, "Will you make an offering again tonight?"

Philippos shakes his head no, "I am done grieving for Eurunoe. Her shade is beyond the underworld's river." He looks out over the encampment.

Arkouda called an early halt tonight. Tomorrow will be a short ride to the rendezvous where they join the three clans, Arkouda's, Periandros', and Korrhagos'. When together, there will be nearly three hundred riders, and they can proceed safely to Pella. "Tonight we rest. Who knows what we contend with after tomorrow."

Arkouda and his sons, Demetrios and Antigonos, come heavily up the slope, two big men and a large youth. Though the youngest, Antigonos gives promise to becoming the tallest. "Philippos," calls out Arkouda, "I think it's time we talk."

"Yes, Lord Philippos Arkouda, son of Theotimides?" asks Philippos.

"You know that every magnate, every clan, even every smallholder, is deciding whether to support King Alexandros or Lord Ptolemaios and the queen mother. I know you will support your brother. You have my support, and that of my sons and all my kinsmen." Arkouda's scarred face looks grim, "You understand, Philippos, the distinction I am making?"

"You are pledging yourself and your clan to follow my lead, rather than my brother's, though you know I follow my brother, the king," answers Philippos. Though his voice is matter-of-fact, inwardly Philippos is astounded by this act.

Demetrios adds, "You have proven yourself truly a prince of the Temenidai." Unspoken is Demetrios' rebuke of Alexandros.

The Theotimidai do not approve of Alexandros, given his actions since called to the throne. Still, they are not traitors. Arkouda is proffering the clan's fealty to the Temenidai in the person of Philippos, confident of the prince's loyalty.

"This is a time of crises," says Philippos, "when the enemies of the Makedones could take advantage of our disarray. My intent is to reconcile Alexandros and mother. If they make peace, then I believe Ptolemaios must choose to submit or lose the moral advantage. Little blood has flowed, yet. We must succeed before bloodshed makes their differences too bitter." Though prince, he is a teenage boy with less experience than the clan chief. Philippos sighs and says, "I need your advice, Philippos Arkouda, now and as we proceed."

Arkouda hesitates, then offers his view, "Only you and Perdikkas can reconcile your brother and mother. That is a necessary start." The warrior pauses, then adds, "I doubt that anything less than overwhelming might will bridle Ptolemaios. Periandros and I have talked. We believe Pelopidas of Thebai will not halt in Thessalos. He will want to ensure that your brother does not meddle there again. Pelopidas must take some time to settle affairs in Thessalos to his liking. If in that time, we Makedones settle our own affairs, then we can present one face to the Thebans. More likely, though, we will not agree in time. Pelopidas will come with his army and force a decision on us. We are uncertain whether the Theban will uphold Alexandros, raise up Ptolemaios, or create some other solution."

The idea of Thebans deciding the fate of Makedonis is frightful. Philippos burns at the thought, yet his own hopes sound naive before the logic of Arkouda and Periandros.

Demetrios speaks up again, "We believe Ptolemaios has sufficient strength to balance the king's. Still, many of us are opposed to Ptolemaios. We do not think he can impose himself entirely. He must find some compromise or some way to win more of us. You are right in thinking your mother is one key to his power."

"You have offered your support to me, Philippos Arkouda. Would you bind yourself and your family to me by oath before the twelve gods?"

"I will, Prince," answers the chieftain, "and though I cannot speak for Periandros or Korrhagos the Elder, you can expect their offers to support you."

The gratitude Philippos feels momentarily threatens to cloud his eyes with tears. With a catch of his breath, he states, "Know before you make your oath, that I am pledged to my brothers, Alexandros and Perdikkas. No matter what occurs, they are my chiefs, they command my allegiance."

Arkouda looks steadily at the boy before him. He is a good looking youth, not pretty or too fine featured. True to his word. Brave in a fight— not heedless—fearful yet mastering his fear. A quick mind—knowing the value of his thinking, yet valuing the ideas of others. Arkouda had not known as much of this boy as of his brothers before this journey. The god Hermes must have guided their steps, giving them adventures that revealed the boy's mettle. Arkouda counts his clan blessed that he did not decide their loyalty before learning the character of this prince. "I would expect no less of you, Philippos, son of Amuntas. Let us make a ceremony of our oath this day. We Theotimidai would be your first adherents, and set an example for Periandros and Korrhagos."

CHAPTER SIX

Ptolemaios

368 B.C.

α

Ptolemaios peers out at the new day. Mist fills the hollows, cling-ing to trees and undergrowth. The road to Pella is obscured. Still, his army is stirring. He can hear the servants call and dogs gruffly barking. He turns from the tent flap, "How many slipped away last night do you think?" His thoughts are bitter.

Eurudike sighs, "Be patient. The decision is out of our hands for now. In the meantime, you learn who are your truest friends."

He laughs ruefully, "Ah, woman, you are resilient."

"I am a queen. I know how intricate are the paths to power." Realizing how boastful her words sound to this man, she adds, "As I grow older, I realize how wise and strong was the old queen, Lady Kleopatra. I should have listened to her more instead of resenting her skillful management of the king's household."

"If that's your chief regret, you are a wondrous child of fortune." Ptolemaios sits down beside Eurudike and takes her hand, "Were it not for Alexandros' opposition, we would be man and wife." He looks into her eyes, but already his thoughts are passing into speculation, "Pelopidas will decide for Alexandros. How could he do otherwise? Alexandros was acclaimed king. He is pure Temenidai. And he no longer poses a threat to Thessalos, and consequently none to Thebai."

The frown on his face eases as he considers the counter argument, "Still, I too possess Temenidai blood. The nobility follows me—most are following me. The Thebans cannot be certain how erratic Alexandros may prove, whereas I'm a man of maturity, committed to stability, even if known as a friend of Athenai." Catching the look on her face, he asks, "Why are you smiling?"

"You labeling yourself a Temenidai. All this talk of that family and the Argeadai clan, tracing descent from Herakles and its favor to Zeus. Yet with each passing generation the line to the golden age of the gods lengthens.

Their bloodline thins. There always comes a time when a dynasty fails, and a more vigorous family prevails." Not wanting to pursue the thought, she sniffs, "They are latecomers to the Makedones, these Temenidai. You and I are from the older royalty of the mountains. We are uplanders. The only reason the Temenidai pretensions matter is the extent to which the common folk accept their legends."

He knows she is right, truly the Temenidai are upstarts compared to his own royal lineage among the Orestoi and Lunkestoi. He is proud of his ancestry. Still, her disparagement of the Temenidai misses the point. No one denies the Temenidai came late to the Makedones, perhaps a dozen generations back counting Alexandros. The story of the three brothers from the south, exiled from Argos in the Peloponnesos, is well known. How they broke away after serving a highland chief for years. How the three gathered the lesser sons, outcasts, and wanderers of the Makedones and led them down from the hills. They became champions of the migratory sheep herding clans by defeating the Thraikiote tribes of the Pieris. Then, being adopted into the royal clan of the Argeadai, they went on to snatch the prize lands of the mysterious Bruges. That strange people moved en mass from Emathis to Asia, leaving a hole in the fabric of people surrounding the Thermaic Gulf. A hole filled by the first Perdikkas in the face of Paiaones, Almopes and others. Isn't that success the very proof of divine favor? That the outcasts succeed where the chieftains fail?

"You would make a better king than Alexandros," asserts Eurudike.

For the first time that morning, he smiles, "I know. Do the Thebans want the Makedones ruled by a capable king? We both know they want us just strong enough to hold back the savage dark north and just weak enough never to venture into the sunlit south." He shakes his head, "It does not matter what they want. If Pelopidas decides against me, as I expect, the matter does not end there. A time will come when you and I rule the Makedones."

*   *   *

Shame is a mantle Alexandros wears. Outwardly he displays confidence; inwardly, he feels humiliation at allowing himself to become the Thebans' puppet. At his core, he is angry, but also relieved that so much is now out of his hands. The relief also feeds his shame. Before his companions, he strives for equanimity, "Break your fast with us Antipatros. Sit down." He gestures widely to the morning foods, and to Parrhasios, Perdikkas and the others.

The austere Antipatros stands at the door, wanting a private word with the king, "Is there space by your side, good Alexandros?"

Cheerfully, Alexandros calls, "Amuntas Plousias, shift your bulk aside. Antipatros seeks my ear." The agreeable Plousias does as the king bids.

Once seated, Antipatros bends to the king, "You need have no fear of Pelopidas. I am reliably told that he decides in your favor. The Thebans are still hashing out the details, but the main point is agreed. Still, expect their support to bear a price."

Knowing that Antipatros has capable agents, the king is heartened, though he anticipated the outcome. At Alexandros' gesture, Parrhasios and Perdikkas join the discussion, "Antipatros brings word that we are vindicated." Turning back to the older man, the king says, "They will require alliance, of course, which pins the tail on our Athenian friends. Must we publicly forswear Athenai?"

"I believe they will seek stronger guarantees of your good faith," states Antipatros.

"They know the treasury is empty," comments Parrhasios.

Alexandros snorts impatiently, "A temporary problem so long as we have the forests and mines."

"What do you know of Pelopidas' re-organization of Thessalos?" asks Perdikkas.

Antipatros is pleased that Perdikkas is thinking deeper than the moment. "Pelopidas abolished the office of *tagos*. He makes certain that Alexandros of Pherai will not dominate Thessalos. As counterweight, he created a new office, the *arkhon*. Agelaos of Pharsalos was appointed, at Pelopidas direction. The Theban general wants to end the rivalry between Larissa and Pherai, and strengthen other communities. Note that he gains the Thessaliote votes in the Delphic Amphiktyony for Thebai."

"How does the *tagos* and the *arkhon* differ?" persists Perdikkas.

"The first was tribe based, with power to levy the clan notables and their followers. The *arkhon*'s powers are city-based. Dues must be paid by each city of the league. The *arkhon* has greater authority, at least, in theory." Antipatros pauses, his voice thoughtful, "Agelaos is a good choice. He possesses high rank among the clans, yet clearly identifies himself with his city, Pharsalos. And he's old enough that he won't be *arkhon* for too many years."

Interrupting, Alexandros asks, "Do you see a parallel between what Pelopidas did in Thessalos and what he's likely to demand of us?"

Grinning for the first time, Antipatros says, "The kingship is yours, he won't attempt abolishing the sacred office. So, no, no direct parallel. The pattern to seek is Theban self-interest." Leaning back, Antipatros scratches at his beard, "Consider their actions. For a second year, Epaminondas of Thebai leads the Boiotian army into the Peloponnesos to bolster their allies, Arkadia, Argos, Elis, and Messenia. He invades the lands of Korinthos, seeking to isolate Sparte from her allies. That's the Thebans major effort for this year. So, what is their intent in sending a second expedition into the north under Pelopidas?" He has the king's full attention, "Is it really Thessalos and Makedonis that concern the Thebans, or is it, as always, Athenai?"

"Why not all three?" replies Alexandros.

"Oh, he intends to settle all three, only at minimal cost. Pelopidas does not take on Alexandros of Pherai directly. True, the Thebans dominate Thessalos while their army is there, but no real effort has been made to dismantle Pherai's power. Now, he is here. We can smell the campfires of his army. Does that cause any of us to think we are his primary objective?"

Only Alexandros considers the possibility, though he doesn't voice his fear.

Antipatros continues, "I believe the object of all this is to deny Athenai aid from Thessalos and you, and to make the Athenians as concerned for the north as they are for the Peloponnesos. Iphikrates is at Thasos with an Athenian fleet. Soon he will start his siege of Amphipolis. Our existing alliance with Athenai requires us to give him support, not that any of us want her to succeed at Amphipolis. Coming north with his army, Pelopidas ensures that Iphikrates will fail. The Theban threatens the line of stations that guard Athenai's access to the Euxine Sea, and the grain supply necessary to feed her people. For Athenai, it's more important that her fleet protect the grain than it is that they gain Amphipolis."

Alexandros considers the argument, "You're saying Pelopidas secures Thessalos and Makedonis, and creates a base that allows the Boiotians to march through Thraikios and attack the Khersonesos." Alexandros can see why Iphikrates tries his desperate bid for Amphipolis. Were Amphipolis to fall to Athenai, they'd have the stopper to bottle the Boiotians in Makedonis. "Pelopidas will require us to repudiate Athenai, not simply ally with Thebai. He'll want our timber shipments to Athenai to end, or maybe redirect them to Boiotia. He may demand silver and men for a march into Thraikios."

"Much depends on how the Thebans fare in the Peloponnesos. I doubt Pelopidas has the means or authority to march on the Khersonesos this year," observes Antipatros. "We can expect him to return. Like all southerners, he is suspicious of kings. Nonetheless, as a Theban oligarch, he respects traditional hierarchy. You are secure, Alexandros."

*　　*　　*

The finish line is not far ahead. Philippos is running easily, as are the other boys running with him. They are only exercising, not racing. Across the field, Philippos spots Lusias, busy putting a dozen young men through their paces with spear and shield. Pella owes its defense against Ptolemaios these past months as much to the old mercenary as it does to the determination of Antipatros and Perdikkas.

As he runs, Philippos considers the city's predicament. On one side is Ptolemaios, mother, many old nobles, and their followers. On the other side of the city is Pelopidas, with his smaller but better disciplined force. Within the city are Alexandros and the royalists.

The professionalism of the Boiotian army, and the reputation of

Pelopidas as a commander, allow them to dominate. A familiar event to the Makedones. Some army crosses the border—Spartan, Illuriote, Thraikiote, Athenian, or, now, Theban—and all comes to a standstill. Talk and money become the weapons of the Makedones. The common people hide away. The notables slink off to their estates. The king and a handful of companions negotiate.

Philippos is disgusted at their weakness. So he works himself hard. He tries to ignore their situation and pour his energies into athletics. Running. Swimming. Wrestling. Javelin throwing. Riding. Whatever will occupy his mind and make his body sweat. And with him are his companions, more than a dozen sons of Makedon nobles or foreign envoys to the court.

His mind cannot cease speculating, no matter the distances he runs. His mind picks at the scab of their weakness. How can it ever change? What will it take to make the Makedones inviolate within their borders?

Largely together, the boys cross the finish line. Philippos slows to a walk, puffing, purposely drawing big drafts of air into his lungs and expelling them. He likes the sensation of his worked muscles. All around him, the others are chattering and walking to avoid their muscles stiffening. They honor his silence and do not address him.

Philippos stops and looks around at the boys, Alkimakhos, Eurulokhos, Stesidamos, Hipponikos, Antigonos, Aristoteles, Hegesias, and the others. A feeling of sadness sweeps him at the memory of Little Korrhagos. He would be here were he alive. A resolve blossoms within Philippos at the sight of his friends. These companions and he will found the phalanxes needed by his brother and the Makedones. All of them have trained under the eyes of Lusias. All of them could train others to wield the long spear in tight formation, shield protecting his neighbor. There will come a time when the Makedones will no longer be trifling.

β

Pelopidas and his officers stand on the steps of the small temple that is dedicated to the four daughters of Zeus and Themis. Before them, on the temple grounds, are the supplicants. The king and his companions are to the right. Ptolemaios, the Queen Mother, and the notables who support them are on the left.

The temple, being outside the city gate to the northwest of Pella, is a convenient meeting point as far as the Thebans are concerned, though that's not why it was chosen. Sacred ground assures a peaceful assembly, and agreements made before the four sisters—Dike, Eunomia, Eirene, and Horai—are dedicated to justice and order.

Despite resenting the Thebans, Philippos is intensely curious to see Pelopidas. Standing with his brothers, Philippos studies the Thebans on the temple steps. Which one is Pelopidas? He must be physically attractive since he was one of the seven Thebans who redeemed their city through the ruse of disguising themselves as women to gain entry into the Spartan occupied citadel. Of course, that was ten or more years ago. Since then, his leadership in the fighting at Tegura and Leuktra was brilliant, even if his friend Epaminondas has a greater reputation for strategic thinking. Which one is he? The man most prominent on the steps bulks large, giving the impression of a fighter more than a leader.

The priest and his assistants complete their ceremony. The meeting is blessed. As they withdraw, among the Thebans a slim man takes a pace forward and raises his arm. The big man that had drawn Philippos' attention stands by the slim one's side. Perdikkas whispers to Philippos, "Pelopidas is in front. The big fellow's name is Ismenias, the second-in-command and a formidable fighter. The two have led Thebai's Sacred Band for years."

Pelopidas' voice booms out from his slender frame, "King Alexandros, Queen Eurudike, Lord Ptolemaios, nobles of the Makedones, you have asked me to arbitrate this dispute that threatens the accord in your lands. As a senior representative of the Boiotian confederacy and the city of Thebai, I am honored by the trust you place in me. Know that what I decide here has the full weight of my city and my fellow countrymen."

Perdikkas whispers again, "Fine words for Theban coercion." Alexandros turns and lightly cuffs his younger brother into silence.

Oblivious to the interplay, Pelopidas continues, "I have carefully considered the arguments and see no merit in the dispute. Lord Ptolemaios, I command that you submit yourself to your king. King Alexandros, you are commanded to put aside any ill will toward Ptolemaios, his family and friends. The followers you both have gathered must disperse—send them back to their homes. To assure the cooperation of both parties, each party will give into the care of Thebai fifteen youths. These youths must be from your leading families." A murmur runs through the crowd. Pelopidas turns to the royal faction, "King Alexandros, who do you select as guest-hostage from among the Temenidai?"

Alexandros calls out, "My brother, Prince Philippos." He turns and gestures to Philippos. Their eyes meet. With a shock, Philippos realizes that this was pre-arranged but nothing had been said to him.

The remainder of the selections and the Theban's closing speech are lost to Philippos. Though he realizes he should have guessed this outcome, Philippos puzzles through his reaction. His anger and dismay at Alexandros is already fading. Perhaps there had been no time to prepare him. Perhaps the Thebans insisted none of the selected be informed in advance. Philippos acknowledges that it's logical he should go. Perdikkas is the heir if Alexandros were to die. And a principal member of the Temenidai is required, not some cousin. A thought to the older half-brothers is instantly dismissed. Pelopidas knows enough of our affairs to know sending one of the half-brothers would have offered no surety. Still, it would have been amusing to think of Arkhelaos in Thebai.

Thebai. He will be traveling to Thebai, to the south—through all Thessalos and on south to the most powerful city of the Hellenes, Thebai.

Excitement begins to grip him. He will be far from home, but not alone. Surely, he will have retainers. And some of the king's fifteen must be Philippos' companions. He will be treated as a prince. True, the circumstances are demeaning to Alexandros and the Makedones. And as a hostage, there exists some threat to his person. Yet the opportunity to see and learn, there is so much he might gain. He resolves to himself that whatever befalls him, whatever he learns, will be experience gained to the advantage of his royal house.

A feeling of being watched steals over him. Philippos raises his eyes and looks about. Across the courtyard stands his mother. Her gray eyes stare steadily at him. He cannot tell what she is thinking. The absurdity of this situation, this day, of their divided family, strikes home to him and he grins at her.

To Eurudike, her youngest child's grin seems more a baring of teeth than a smile. She realizes that Alexandros did nothing to prepare the boy. That Philippos is being sent south is hard, though not nearly as heart wrenching to her if the choice had been to send Perdikkas. Given the hazards of life, the possibility exists that any child sent south won't return.

The loss of Eurunoe is fresh. Although Eurudike has never allowed her children to prevent her from leading the life she wants, each is a piece of her, each has a call on her heart. Yet to her mind, all of this—the humiliating terms dictated by Pelopidas, the son sent south—she counts against Alexandros. He is king in name but not in strength.

γ

Alkimakhos kicks at the tree root dejectedly. Several other boys squat around the old tree. Some sit on the raised roots, sisters to the root absorbing Alkimakhos' abuse. Little is being said, for there's nothing they can do about the loss of so many companions and kin. The thirty who will travel south to Thebai tomorrow will be missed. From their circle of friends go several boys in addition to Philippos—Stesidamos, Antigonos' young brother, Polemaios, a cousin of Eurulokhos, named Kleitos, another of the Korrhagos family, Lamakhos. Alkimakhos complains, "Are any highlanders going or are the Thebans only taking royal Makedones?"

Hipponikos answers, "I hear that some go from the Orestid and Lunkestid clans that support Ptolemaios. No one is surrendered from Elimiotis. Mostly it's our clans." Then, in a flash of pride, "Ours are the principal families of the Makedones."

"Here comes Titan and Stork," calls out Eurulokhos, "They'll have word of Philippos."

The awkward pair comes up the path to the tree, the six foot tall Antigonos and the thin knobby kneed Aristoteles. To the other boys the friendship between the two seems odd, the hearty brawling Makedones and the graceless Stagiran wonder. "What say?" asks Alkimakhos.

"It's as we feared," answers Aristoteles. "Philippos is caught in a round of farewells. He's at his mother's house now." Antigonos makes a face to mimic the famous Eurudike. The others laugh.

One of the younger boys reminds them, "Stesi's family has invited everyone to join his parting feast."

"Ever since his father's ships came in with their Aigyptian and Tyrian cargoes last year, that family's been making a display," states the severe Alkimakhos.

"Oh, don't make a face. Who would not do honor to a departing son? Besides, you'll likely drink as much of their wine as the rest of us," replies Antigonos. The truth gives the boys more mirth, since Alkimakhos is known to become silly when drunk.

Eurulokhos comes to the point, "So, Philip can't join us for our last hunt together?" Their plan is for a final night out with all their friends, non-hostage and departing hostage, running the dogs in the forest to see what they scare up, then building a bonfire, drinking 'til morning, singing and carrying on, so that tomorrow and for many tomorrows, they all share good memories of one another.

Aristoteles nods, ticking off the hostages on his fingers, "Philippos is out. Stesidamos can't get away from his family. Antigonos' mother has Polemaios close to tears. What of Kleitos? He's your cousin. Has anyone heard whether Lamakhos can come?"

"Kleitos thought he'd be able to get away late to join us," says Eurulokhos. "If caught, he was going to say Prince Philippos requires his presence."

"Lot of good that would have done him," comments Hipponikos. "I doubt we'll see Lamakhos. He's also stuck at the palace, since Parrhasios is his uncle."

Surveying the glum faces, Antigonos starts laughing, "What a bunch of sour grapes. We're going to have to go hunting without them after they're gone, so what's one night earlier?"

"You think we should go anyway?" asks Alkimakhos.

"Why not?" grins Antigonos. "Isn't the wine already hidden? Skaros and the other are readying the dogs. So we do it in their honor instead of with them. We can tell stories about them at the night fire, and be suitably maudlin."

δ

Ptolemaios stares into the fire, watching the dance of flame and glow of embers. He is glad to be away from Pella. The past weeks taste bitter with failure. Still, as Eurudike pointed out, there is much they are gaining. Many nobles and landowners openly declared for them. These Thebans are like a flood that temporarily alters the landscape. When the flood recedes the land's form is the same. Pelopidas has healed nothing, the division among the Makedones exists.

Being on the border again feels good. Here choices are simple. Any marauding Paiaone or Thraikiote is killed when caught. Any that come in peace to trade are tolerated. The closest thing to ambiguity is keeping Amphipolis independent while not offending the Athenians.

He eases the belt at his waist, and runs a hand down the calf muscles of his thigh. Muscles that stiffen too easily. He hates aging. Being older, knowing that much more is good. But fading strength is an affront, for which in his secret heart he blames the gods. He turns his mind back to Amphipolis.

The city was founded some seventy years earlier as an Athenian colony. The success of Amphipolis under its founder Hagnon was not inevitable. An earlier Athenian attempt to dominate the mines of nearby Mount Pangaion and trade of the Strymon valley had failed. The Edonoi, a Thraikiote tribe, defeated the prior generation of Athenian settlers. Defeat at the barbarians' hands must have seemed cruel since the Athenians had already beaten the Thasians at sea and besieged their city on the island of Thasos, ending Thasian exploitation of Pangaion's gold and silver.

The original community was called Ennea Hodoi—nine ways. Local stories say that in ancient times the Persians sacrificed a white horse, nine boys, and nine girls when their army under Xerxes crossed the Strymon River. The gods of Thraikios can be demanding. Ennea Hodoi became Amphipolis under the Athenians.

In reality, Athenai erred in how it settled Amphipolis. Too many of the settlers were not Athenian. Many were allies, and the majority of these were from the island of Andros. During Athenai's great war with Sparte— about fifteen years after Amphipolis was founded—the Spartan general Brasidas seized the city with the help of its citizens from Andros. These people were outraged by Athenai's treatment of Andros, as the Athenians coerced their allies to support them against Sparte. Ever since, Amphipolis maintains its defiance of Athenai, and its citizens consider Brasidas the city's true founder.

For the Makedones, Amphipolis is both gemstone and millstone. Sitting on its hill overlooking the river crossing, and guarded by its great wall that stands on the margin between hill and river, the city is a market and a bastion. Grain, timber, pitch, and slaves flow down the river from the Paiaones and Thrakes. Metals come from Mount Pangaion to the east. This same commerce sustains the Thraikiote tribes of the region—Edonoi, Bisaltiones, Odomantoi, and others—making them strong enough to fear. That wealth makes difficult the Makedones' efforts to overawe these people.

PTOLEMAIOS (368 B.C.)

As much as the Athenians, Ptolemaios covets the city. Though his greed does not possess the bitter lust of the Athenians. Their loss of Amphipolis was the start of their decline in the great conflict with Sparte. Athenians will intrigue, will fight, will sacrifice to regain the city. Even now their fleet under Iphikrates—friend and adopted son of old King Amuntas, and, for that matter, guest-friend of Ptolemaios—hovers, waiting for any opportunity to snatch at or, at least, embarrass the Amphipolitans.

The flames of the fire leap, crackle, and curl. Ptolemaios' face glows in the reflected light, absorbed in his thoughts. There is no possibility in the current situation for the Makedones to control Amphipolis. So it is best that no one controls the city save the Amphipolitans. Still, with Alexandros forced into alliance with Thebai, it may be to Ptolemaios' advantage to aid Iphikrates. Not so much help as to truly harm the Amphipolitans or to catch the Thebans' attention, but enough to secure Iphikrates' appreciation. Yes, having Iphikrates beholden to Ptolemaios could be useful in the future.

After all, Ptolemaios and Iphikrates know each other well. The Athenian has spent much of his career in the north, even marrying into the royal family of the Thraikiote Odrusai. A hint or, better, some useful advantage would be well received by Iphikrates. Ptolemaios considers. If an Amphipolitan grain convoy were betrayed into Iphikrates' hands, that would be sufficient. Or, if the timing of the Pangaion bullion train were passed to him, so he could ambush it before it reaches the city. Iphikrates likes gold as much as any barbarian dynast.

Deciding, Ptolemaios calls to the officer of the watch, standing at the campfire down the slope, "Telestes, have the scouts, Takhos and Lukon, brought to me." He stands and stretches, again massaging his leg muscle. He steps away from the fire and looks up at the sky. The night is clear and alive with the light of thousands of star. No moon out. He searches for his favorite, the bright star to the north. *Are you ice or fire, a soul or spirit? Are you impartial to my fate or set in the sky to inspire me?*

Arrival of the scouts interrupts his reverie. Takhos is a Thrake from the deep inland, where their mountains are high. Lukon is an islander, from Samothrakos. Their comradeship is improbable but constant, seemingly built on mutual reliance rather than friendship. One is guile and the other is force. They wait for him to speak.

"You will travel to Amphipolis. Be inconspicuous. I need to learn the schedule of the next three shipments from Krenides to Amphipolis of Pangaion's bullion. Bring word to me quickly. Start with the inspector of the city's horse and mule stock. To identify yourself to him, tell him you follow the North Star. And give him this coin." Ptolemaios hands a silver piece bearing an image of Herakles to Lukon. "Let me hear from you not later than five days hence."

In silence, the two depart. Watching, Ptolemaios waits until they are gone, then calls to Telestes again, "Send for Apollophanes of Pella." While waiting, he decides that Telestes may be the very officer to carry word to Iphikrates once Takhos and Lukon report back. Telestes is a discreet man, wholly loyal, son of a man beholden to Ptolemaios. Yes, Telestes will do nicely. *Has the tact to suggest possibilities to Iphikrates without stating treasons.*

Telestes comes in sight with the handsome Apollophanes. Ptolemaios waves the young man forward. Wryly, knowing his purpose, Ptolemaios is amused at the waste vanity has made of this youthful aristocrat. "Greetings, Apollophanes. I apologize for bringing you so late to my side. I can plead only the press of matters on which the king insists. Still, isn't it appropriate that pleasure is saved for last, so it can be savored? How can I be of service to you?"

Visibly heartened by Ptolemaios' kind tone, Apollophanes answers, "It is up to me to put aside any annoyance at the delay in greeting you. Your generosity in setting aside your duties to see me is fully appreciated. You know that I have ever been your admirer, and it is on that knowledge that I presume in bringing to you my grievance."

"Please be seated. I would hear the concerns that burden you." Turning, Ptolemaios motions to a servant to bring wine. As a preliminary, Ptolemaios inquires about the young man's family. Apollophanes offers polite reassurances and further expressions of long-standing family support for the views espoused by Lord Ptolemaios and Queen Eurudike. With wine in hand and the servant withdrawn, Ptolemaios touches Apollophanes lightly on the arm, "Now, let me hear what it is that troubles you."

The man leans close, "While my father, uncles, and elder brothers have always shared your hopes for a proper balance between the powers of the kingship and the rights of landholding Makedones, for a time I was misled." Apollophanes sighs dramatically, "I am of King Alexandros' age group. We were royal pages together, and for years I was part of his set, joining those who spited his father, King Amuntas. I do not think I flatter myself to say that in those days, Alexandros relied on me to bring my friends into his faction. I had his confidences. He was eager to enlist me and mine in his cause." Leaning in closer to Ptolemaios, breathing his words in the older man's ears, "In truth, I was besotted by him. I could think of little else than Alexandros. Were we barbarians, I would suspect some spell or monstrous enchantment used to entangle me."

His face displaying serious sympathetic concern, inwardly Ptolemaios feels mirth. He gives careful attention to Apollophanes, "Say nothing, sir, that you might regret as an indiscretion later. Though potions and spells are not unknown in our rude land."

"You are kind in your advice, Lord Ptolemaios, but I would have you know all, know the worst. I am certain your wisdom will discern my truth worth." Continuing, Apollophanes says, "I would have given my life for

Alexandros. There was nothing he could not have asked of me. I am ashamed to say that in my folly, I did not perceive how the prince used me for his purposes while bearing me no goodwill. Only later did I realize that he viewed me with contempt as a mere creature of his. All this time it was Parrhasios who held his affection, and who had influence."

"For the time that Aphrodite befuddled me, I thought that Alexandros saw me as his finest friend. Yet, in an instant, the goddess tore the veil from my eyes when Alexandros granted preferment to Parrhasios. My brothers laughed at my delusion."

As the words are spoken, Ptolemaios hears what he has been waiting to hear, the hatred of Apollophanes for Alexandros. The favored, pampered, youngest son was laughed at by his coarse older brothers. And the hatred is born. They say that Aphrodite may choose to ruin a man for amusement, but in Ptolemaios' experience it's more often the gross indulgence and over-affection of a mother or the brutal faultfinding or even sheer indifference of a father that weakens a man's character. Apollophanes is filled with vitriol. Ptolemaios holds back, hearing out the young man's confession, so that when he offers his absolution it will be all the stronger.

After Apollophanes begins to repeat particulars, Ptolemaios again grips the man's smooth muscled arm. The flow of bitter words stops. "What would you have me do, fair Apollophanes?" asks Ptolemaios.

"Accept me into your service. I know, we all know, that when the Thebans depart, you will again be the rightful strongman of the Makedones. Alexandros is king only so long as others prop him in place. I would be by your side when you take your vengeance."

"Possibly, young sir, you are the very sword I have awaited. You are a man of immense promise, and I do not hesitate to believe that you can be of such service to me that I would be ever grateful." Ptolemaios smiles and raises his hand to the youth's shoulder. The answering smile of Apollophanes is hungry for regard. "Yes, Apollophanes of Pella, I am glad you have come to me. Your heartfelt allegiance will gain reward as it is expressed in action."

ε

For Philippos, the house of Pammenes is both guest-home and cage, as is the city of Thebai. Pammenes himself, a politician and general as important to the Thebans as the illustrious pair, Pelopidas and Epaminondas, is cultured, gracious, and kind within the bounds of his responsibilities. Despite his princely upbringing, Philippos is reminded daily by the very attributes of his distinguished host that the Makedones merely ape culture that comes readily to a southern aristocrat. Or so it seems to young Philippos. Of course, an Athenian might snort in derision at the idea of a Theban farmer being held up as a cultural icon.

The house itself is airy and light, with its large central courtyard. Despite his rank and being male, Philippos has a second-floor room. Apparently the need to secure the prince is greater than the possible scandal of having him associated with the women's quarters. A new wall blocks any untoward access to the women, and a new staircase gives him a private entrance. The room is good-sized. With only Skaros as his servant, the room is plenty for the two of them.

Sitting on the railing of the second-floor walkway, Philippos watches the activity in the courtyard. Two household slaves are knocking the dust from wallhangings and tapestries gathered from the women's wing. Their methodical thumping provides a basic rhythm beneath the scurrying and screams of the smaller children as they play tag around the family altar. Philippos likes the liveliness of this household. The tensions and subcurrents that exist at the palace in Pella are absent here.

Pammenes' oldest boy, also named Pammenes but called Cricket by his parents and Insect by his sisters, steps into the courtyard and calls up to Philippos, "Some of us are going to the gymnasium. Do you want to join us? Bring your boy if you do."

"Great, I'll come down," responds Philippos. Inwardly he is amused at the thought of calling Skaros 'his boy.' The Thraikiote would be surly for days. Southern Hellenes make much of the distinctions between classes for all their vaunted democracy. Calling into the room for Skaros to follow with oils and cloths, Philippos goes clattering down the stairs.

Philippos joins four youths and their servants. In days past he has met them all and has sorted out their friendships and relationships. Cricket's best friend is the stalwart Kleomenes, called Five for being the fifth son in his family. Kleomenes' affable cousin is Pindaros Milao. The antic Kratulos, a neighbor and the clown of the group, completes the foursome.

As they start out, Cricket's whining younger brother comes hurrying up. "You were leaving without me," he says accusingly.

"Why are you always late?" replies Cricket.

"You know it takes me longer," answers Pamesias, counting on his malformed leg to excuse all he does.

In mock solemnity Kratulos asks, "Five, surely you can carry Pammikins so he won't tire?"

"I wouldn't want to be mistaken for his lover."

The four boys burst into laughter. Indignant, Pamesias aims a kick at Kleomenes, but his brother intervenes, tousling the youngster's hair and pushing him out into the street. "Come on, let's get there before the place fills up," urges Cricket.

Striding through the streets, with the noise of their progress bouncing off the walls of the houses, the group receives equal shares of greetings, taunts, and scowls from various passer-bys. The boys are well known. The route they're taking is already familiar to Philippos, since the gymnasium is one of the few locations he regularly visits. Much of Thebai remains unknown to him. He is not permitted to venture alone or solely with other exiles.

While he walks with the others, exchanging gibes and ribaldry, his mind is on the day their column arrived at Thebai. The citizenry and other inhabitants had turned out in finery to welcome their general and hero, Pelopidas. They'd marched to the central market, dust of the column and the multitude settling over the festive decorations. There they disbanded. First, the mercenaries were paid off and dispersed. Second, the hostages were allocated among the city households, with rank determining which household received a hostage. Third, the citizen soldiers stood down and mingled with the crowd, joining their families and friends.

For the Thebans, the day became a festival. For the Makedones, the parceling out of the hostages rekindled anger and humiliation. Philippos had felt exposed, burned, as if being sold in a slave market. During the long walk south, there had come a mutual acceptance and shared feeling among the companions of the march, Theban and Makedones. That regard dissipated in the sunshine of the marketplace. As each household head claimed a hostage, Philippos writhed with shame. Yet he was treated with courtesy and tact by Pammenes, who invited him to join his home, as if they were natural guest-friends.

Since that day, Philippos has only occasionally met a fellow Makedone. Usually they see each other at the gymnasium, or occasionally on the street or at a feast in the home of a Theban notable. Despite the rarity of meeting, the thirty hostages stay in touch through messages carried by servants and retainers, whose movements are not restricted by the Thebans.

Last night Skaros told Philippos that he could expect Stesidamos, Kleitos, and maybe Lamakhos at the gymnasium if he went before mid-morning. Philippos is pleased at the thought. He hasn't seen Stesi since the first *dekades* of the new moon.

As usual, Cricket's route skirts the walled Kadmeia, the citadel and ritual center of Thebai, which sits on a low hill. There are more direct ways to the gymnasium, but Cricket uses this route to visit the lion statue dedicated to Herakles. Philippos doesn't mind the longer path, since daily obeisance to an ancestor seems proper.

Some understanding of Thebai and its political factions has been filled in for Philippos by Skaros, based on the Makedones' servant grapevine. Philippos surmises that the real reason for the roundabout route to the gymnasium is to keep to safe neighborhoods, away from the conservative party. Cricket would expect to face gangs of boys whose fathers are opponents of Pammenes, Pelopidas, and Epaminondas if he took the direct route.

For a time as they walk, Philippos puzzles at the Heraklian legends celebrated by Thebai, and the demi-god's earlier identification with the city of Argos in the Peloponnesos. Surely the Argolid connection is older and its tradition purer. Of course, Herakles traveled far and wide. That he may have lived in Boiotia for a time is reasonable. Even the slaying of his children when he was overcome by madness is possible. Still, Philippos does not trust the Boiotian tradition. The stories passed down within his own family are clear on their Argolid origin and of Herakles as their progenitor. After all, why else would the Makedones accept the Temenidai as the royal family if not for the blessings of Zeus and the ancestry of Herakles.

Shouting up ahead breaks into Philippos' thoughts. Cricket and his friends have halted where the street widens into an open square. Philippos pushes through the servants to the front. Cricket is talking to some boy Philippos does not know.

"They followed us from the market, throwing pebbles and cursing the barbarian," says the boy. He is young, flushed and uncertain what to do.

Beyond them, Philippos sees a dozen or so boys laughing and jeering in a circle. Some are even older youths approaching manhood. "What are they doing?" he asks.

Cricket turns, embarrassed, "Those are the Lakedaimites. That's what we call them. Their fathers favor Sparte. A countryman of yours is in their midst. They're giving him a scare."

Angrily, Philippos blurts, "What are we standing here for. Let's charge them."

"We can't. Brawling is forbidden. Our party doesn't want to give theirs any excuses just now. Epaminondas is still away, and with him are many of our supporters."

"Well, I'm not with any Theban faction," asserts Philippos, and with that he runs at the enemy circle. Breaking through the surprised Lakedaimites, he rushes to the side of the scared but resolute Polemaios. With a Thraikiote war cry, old Skaros follows Philippos. Now the three stand back-to-back facing the circle of youths. Within Philippos is a wild elation. All these days of humiliation, of fighting down his pride, are gone. He taunts the taunters, "Come on, try us now. You're still four to one or better. Watch out though, the sun of the Makedones is up."

The circling boys look to one another. Their leader, a tall heavy youth, is unsure. Before him are three barbarian Makedones, and at his back are an unknown number of opponents. One of the bolder Lakedaimites throws a stone, but Skaros catches it in his hand and hurtles it back, striking the thrower in the shoulder. With that, the fight is out of the Lakedaimites. The leader leads his gang at a run out of the square toward their home territory.

Philippos hugs Polemaios and Skaros. Together they sing a paion to Herakles. Turning, the three grinning, they see Cricket and his fellows still standing at the street corner. Philippos calls out, "What is it, Little Pammenes?"

"I don't know whether I should send to father with news of this," answers Cricket.

"Surely there's no concern every time boys scrap?"

"Your safety is my responsibility."

"Come, don't be concerned. Let's go on to the gymnasium," urges Philippos. Most of the others agree. Outnumbered by the voices around him, Cricket is persuaded and the enlarged group jovially walks on. Within Philippos, all the self-pity and frustration of these past months is gone. He leads the boys in rousing choruses of scurrilous songs.

*   *   *

Stripped for wrestling, Philippos waits his turn. His opponent will be a Theban named Hermiodos, who is the same age. The boy is taller than Philippos but narrowly built. While the others watch the current match, Philippos watches his opponent, trying to discern as much as he can about Hermiodos' skills and temperament.

There is a shout and a chorus of cheers and jeers, as Stesidamos is thrown and pinned. The noise echoes in the large hall of the palaistra, despite the many similar groups engaged in wrestling, long jumping, discus and javelin throwing along the length of the hall. Studding the main hall are doors to other rooms or to outside. Changing rooms, swimming and bathing pools, massage room, ball courts, boxing and exercise rooms, the long stadium for running sprints, vendor rooms for food and drink, lounging and meeting rooms, storage rooms—the complex is larger than anything in Pella. Outside are tracks for long runs, the archery butts, and playing fields. This is the main gymnasium of Thebai, where boys, youths, and men flock. The gymnasium is as important to the social and political life of the city as the marketplace, council hall, temples, and theater.

Hermiodos stretches, loosening muscles. An older friend whispers in his ear and the two laugh companionably. Philippos assumes that Hermiodos is relaxed and feels no anxiety about their match. Is it not important to him or is he so certain of success? According to Cricket, Hermiodos is a keen wrestler, noted for using his body length for leverage. Cricket's advice is to get behind Hermiodos quickly rather than advancing against the tall boy's reach.

Several men join their group, greeting the Theban boys they know. Pindaros Milao salutes one of the men affectionately. Cricket's brother, Pamesias, comments caustically in an aside to the Makedones, "Pindaros could be charged with prostitution for the number of men he likes."

"Nothing wrong with friendship," answers Polemaios.

"Pindaros sees nothing wrong with accepting their gifts, either," adds Pamesias maliciously.

Philippos thinks that the bitter, young cripple is jealous. He knows Pamesias is an adequate swimmer, and excels at archery. For other activities,

Pamesias is unsuited due to his deformed foot. Yet he is not unattractive physically. His bitter runaway mouth and his quick evasion of responsibility make him unpopular.

Skaros taps Philippos on the shoulder, "You're up, Prince. Show them what the Temenidai can do."

Philippos grins. Not counting Skaros, five of his countrymen are here today, an unusually large number. They cluster about him, as they had clustered about Stesidamos before his match. Their encouragement provides an armor as he steps into the circle of dark sand. Their expectations of him make the match more than casual.

From the far side of the circle, Hermiodos acknowledges Philippos with a nod and begins to slide to his left. Both are crouched, arms extended, their feet gliding easily. They are alert to each other. Philippos feints toward the center, then moves quickly to flank Hermiodos. The boy is not deceived, and moves as fast. Then their cautious gliding steps resume. Each tries an additional feint, then suddenly they are gripping each other's arms, testing each other's strength. Philippos sidesteps to the right and is behind Hermiodos. Before he can tighten his hold, the tall boy flips Philippos across his hip. For a moment, Philippos is vulnerable. He recovers before Hermiodos can take advantage.

Again they glide slowly, facing each other. Another rush and they embrace, trying to crush the breath from each other. Neither has succeeded in throwing the other off his feet. Philippos slips his grip down, pulling up Hermiodos' leg. Without realizing how it has happened, Philippos feet are swept out from under him and he is hoisted in the air. Hermiodos is much stronger than Philippos realized. Reaching down desperately, Philippos grabs Hermiodos about the chest and squeezes with all his might. Both collapse to the sand, and are instantly up, circling each other.

Sweat is pouring off Philippos' body. This contest is taking more out of him than most matches. Soon the two are grappling again, each straining for an advantage. Hermiodos' hand slips. Philippos bends the hand back. Hermiodos moves quickly, and his elbow jars Philippos in the mouth. Slippery with sweat and now blood, they attempt a series of holds on each other. Muscles bulge as they heave and strain. Philippos bores in, but again feels his feet lifted from the ground. Rage boils within him and he longs to gouge Hermiodos' eyes or chew off his ear. Instead, he grips and squeezes. Nothing will shake him loose of the tall boy. Again they collapse. This time Hermiodos is on Philippos before the prince can escape. Philippos heaves up like a demi-god parting the ocean's waves. Hermiodos' sweeping leg cuts down Philippos as grain before the scythe. Again, Hermiodos is on Philippos. This time there is no freedom, and Philippos is defeated.

Hermiodos stands slowly, gasping for breath, but smiling. He extends a hand to Philippos, "You are amazing. I thought you had me more than once."

Cricket and his companions crowd forward, slapping Philippos on the back, "You came closer than anyone to beating Hermiodos." All around other Thebans extend their congratulations. The frustration at losing subsides within Philippos, and he can think rationally again. That Hermiodos is the Theban champion in his age group is obvious now.

"Let me treat you to a massage and a swim," offers one of the Theban men to the prince. The man is tall and handsome. "I am Hermarkhos Oreos, cousin of Hermiodos," he says, smiling brilliantly at Philippos.

"That would be kind, Hermarkhos," answers Philippos. The prince calls to the others, "Who's for a swim?"

*   *   *

Pammenes the Elder is seated by the window, reading a scroll, as Philippos enters the study. The man closes the scroll and places it to one side on the sill. He pats the bench on which he is sitting, "Come, join me, Prince Philippos."

The anxiety at being summoned quiets within Philippos at his host's friendly tone. He crosses the room to sit beside Pammenes. "You asked to see me, sir?"

"Yes, there are several questions we should consider," Pammenes pauses to look his guest over. "I wanted you to settle into the routines of the house before posing these questions. I recognize how awkward it must feel to be a guest in my house yet a hostage for the good behavior of your brother. Does my home begin to feel comfortable for you? Does the companionship of my sons begin to feel natural?"

With sincerity, Philippos can answer, "You and all in your home are most gracious. I feel fortunate in Cricket's, I mean, Little Pammenes', willingness to share his friendships and to introduce me to Thebai. I would not want my status as guest to unduly burden you."

"I heard about the incident with the Lakedaimite boys today," states Pammenes. "I suppose it's inevitable that you Makedones become another point of contention between the factions here. Thebai is not a bloody city, like so many. We have rivalries, though rarely do they give rise to riots, murder or other mayhem. We are justly noted for the stability of our families and traditions. I doubt you or your tribesmen have much cause for concern. Still, a little discretion is in order. I do applaud your quick defense of Polemaios. I ask that you abide by the counsel I have given Cricket to avoid, so far as possible without negating honor, situations that excite factional rivalries. Properly you have demonstrated that being a stranger in Thebai is no excuse for allowing others to treat you less than as an honored guest." He smiles, "Enough of that."

Philippos is heartened by Pammenes, and his admiration for the man increases.

"I would raise another issue which, in its way, may pose a greater hazard to your reputation," Pammenes looks a touch embarrassed. "I am told that Beauty approached you today. I mean Hermarkhos Oreos."

"Yes, sir. He joined our group with several of his companions while we were wrestling. Afterwards, we shared a massage and swim, and talked 'til past noon."

"Philippos, I do not know what sexual experience you possess. Were I truly your father, and not his substitute, I still might not know," the man chuckles. "I do feel I should warn you that a certain notoriety surrounds Hermarkhos. Many men and boys establish liaisons as you know. Normally, these relationships last for some years and have meaning for their whole lives. That is well and benefits the youth who learns and the man who mentors. Beauty, I fear, may give too freely and taste too widely. He is an attractive man and well-liked. You are capable of forming your own judgment as to whether he is a man of your preference. As a newcomer, I want you to be aware of his lack of restraint."

"Thank you, sir. I confess I found him convivial but no more than that."

"You are a discerning youth," replies Pammenes. "Finally, I believe it my responsibility to see that your education continues while you live in my home. The tutor who instructs Cricket and several other boys is well suited to instruct you, too. Pamesias continues with his grammarian, musician, and coach. You are ready for advanced topics, like Younger Pammenes. Your teacher, Kerkidas, was taught by Kebes, who was, in turn, taught by Philoloas, who was a disciple of Puthagoras. Though not an old man, Kerkidas is thoughtful, well-versed, and good-humored for a Puthagoran. I expect you will do well by him. I will introduce you to him tomorrow, and lessons begin the next day."

"I appreciate your care, General Pammenes," says Philippos honestly. "There is a subject I would learn more of that I doubt good Kerkidas can teach. You are the instructor I seek."

"How so, Philippos?"

"Would you tell me of your campaigns and battles? Explain to me how you handled emergencies and contingencies? Give me your views of other commanders, like Pelopidas and Epaminondas? Or, go beyond Thebai, to tell of Spartans—Agesilaos, Brasidas, and others—or of any noted Hellenic generals."

Pammenes is silent, considering. There are so few who ask earnestly rather than in flattery. Fewer still who understand that warfare is changing. He is pleased by the admiration. He would rather it were his son asking, or one of his son's friends. Prince Philippos is as close as one can be to being a barbarian and still be called a Hellene. His family rules a rude land. Perhaps, taken in hand, this boy could become a life-long ally of Thebai. The boy is promising, a delight in his curiosity and eagerness. "Study hard with Kerkidas, and from time to time, you and I will study the ways of war, Philippos. Know that my time is limited, so I can offer only one evening in ten for your instruction."

Philippos is elated, and the two clasp hands to seal their bargain.

ζ

"Well, mother, you asked for this meeting. Here I am. Are we going to continue to exchange pleasantries or are you going to tell me what you want?" Alexandros' tone is amused but he is not.

Eurudike looks her son over. His intensity is reflected in his gaunt cheeks and brittle manners. "Since when is it a meeting when a mother asks to see her son?"

He snorts his contempt, "I am not Perdikkas. You and I are political opponents."

"For you, everything is black or white, Aleko. For all the time you spent with your father, you fail to see the nuances of life. I can be your political opponent, as you call it, and still care for my boy."

Alexandros is becoming exasperated. He shakes his head, "No, mother. You cannot be my caring mother and be my enemy. You made a choice in favor of Ptolemaios of Aloros. I know he has long been the man in your life, not father. Whatever your heart says, your duty is to me as your king."

Anger is rising in Eurudike, but she controls it, "Aleko, you do not believe that I can disagree with your policies and still love you as my son?"

"That you can do, mother," he grants her. "Disagree in private with me. Even let me know you disagree. Even offer me the advice you are so capable of giving. Be part of my household. Support me in public. Act as the queen mother, as the keeper of my household. As a woman, as the mother of the king, you can do these things and still love your son." Setting his cup on the floor, he stands, "What you cannot do is embrace my mortal enemy, scorn my policies in public, seek allies among my opponents. Don't you understand that this is life or death? While I am king, Ptolemaios cannot be."

She bows her head under his onslaught. "Aleko, I want us to be reconciled. Though you may not understand, I do care for you while loving Ptolemaios. We cannot go on divided. Perdix is after me night and day to end the differences between us. Your brother is eloquent on your behalf." She looks up, and smiles gently, "You three boys have always stood together. I feel shame that Philpa is held in Thebai."

Alexandros nods soberly, "We will get him back. From all that I hear, he does well at the house of Pammenes." He considers his mother carefully, "Perdikkas is right, you know. We should not quarrel. Mother, I can accept your criticism if you speak it directly to me, and not to every noble or smallholder Ptolemaios tries to recruit. Let us again be mother and son." He extends his hand to her.

She reaches and clasps his hand in both of hers. Unexpectedly, she is crying. She turns her face away, ashamed, as the tears continue to flow.

η

Selecting a javelin, Ptolemaios balances it in his hand, then in a smooth half-turn and throw sends the light point into the target post.

"Eight for ten," applauds Apollophanes.

"Do you want another set of ten, sir?" asks Telestes.

Ptolemaios smiles, "I believe I'll let my shoulder rest." Putting his arm across Apollophanes back, he says, "Come, let us go down to the house. My other guests will be arriving soon. In coming ahead, I expect you want some privacy."

Leaving Telestes to supervise the clean up, Ptolemaios and Apollophanes stride arm-in-arm to the country house. "Tell me, good friend, how are the ways at court?"

With a question in his voice, Apollophanes says, "We were surprised when Queen Eurudike resumed responsibility for the king's household."

"Yes, I'm sure that caused a stir," Ptolemaios says with a hint of irony. "Women can be a mystery as all men know. Often to our regret. Still, the queen is also a mother, and quite naturally feels pulled in more than one direction. I think we might acknowledge Perdikkas for this reconciliation. The lad can be persuasive and his mother has always favored him."

"You feel no concern, then, at her return to the king's fold?" asks Apollophanes anxiously.

With a brief chuckle, Ptolemaios declares, "None. You see, Queen Eurudike has not changed her view of the king's foolishness. We think, though, at this time—given the impositions of Thebai—that her opposition can be more effective as a member of the household, rather than as an avowed adversary."

With a slight wistfulness, Ptolemaios continues, "I will miss her by my side. We await better times to be together."

Apollophanes is reassured. "You want me to continue as before?" he asks.

"Certainly. Keep your face open and admiring of Alexandros. Know in your heart, though, that your time is coming. The people who matter increasingly feel that Alexandros is a petty, vindictive tyrant, and no true king. When the time is right, they will acclaim you savior of our country."

Apollophanes smiles at the vision, "I look forward to the surprise that Alexandros will feel."

CHAPTER SEVEN

Thebai

367 B.C.

α

hen we first began our classes, I told you that there was much you could learn from me, and more that you could learn from each other and from yourselves. What is our purpose here?" asks Kerkidas of his young students.

Cricket responds immediately, "To question?"

Kerkidas looks about the room. Philippos fears to make an incorrect answer. He has heard too much mockery of rustic Makedones. Pindaros Milao ducks his head, as well. Kleomenes makes an attempt, "To think, master?"

"To learn the answers Kerkidas wants to hear," calls out Kratulos.

Kerkidas grins, but also lightly raps Kratulos on his head with his stick for the levity. "Perhaps all your answers are correct. I prefer to think of it as 'To search' as in to seek the truth. Knowing that we will fail yet recognizing that in so doing, in the search itself, there is value for us." The teacher is dressed garishly, as is the practice with certain Puthagoreans. He is a philosopher in the Puthagorean sense; that is, a lover of wisdom. Where ever wisdom appears. Though he is thin and abstains from meat that does not mean he is austere. He looks for wisdom in ecstasy as readily as in contemplation.

"Philippos, we've not heard much from you today. Tell me what you believe is true about the number one," orders Kerkidas.

"Kerkidas of Tanagra, you taught us that behind everything that we think we know through our senses there is a wholeness, which is the One. What we experience are but changing glimpses of that One. We ourselves are small patches on the surface of the One. That change itself is an illusion of our perception—the shimmer from the surface of the One."

Kerkidas holds up his hand and Philippos stops. Gently, the tutor says, "I did not ask what it is that I teach—and without being too critical, I think you need to listen more acutely to my words—I ask what you believe is true."

Philippos looks down at his toes. He wiggles them. Within, he feels his usual humiliation at his inability to get at the truth as truth is understood by Kerkidas. His toes look dirty from their early morning exercises. Softly, he answers, "Sir, do you see my toes? They are the truth I know. I think to move them and I move them. If I stub my toe, it hurts. If I bathe my toes, they feel refreshed. I understand my toes, sir." He looks up. Kerkidas eyes him with encouragement. "I know that you will ask me about my thoughts and feelings. Can I see them as I see my toes? No. Still, I experience them. They are better known to me than you are. Everything that I know comes to me through my perceptions. Yet you teach that our perceptions are false. That truth lies beyond them. I grant that perceptions can be deceived. I grant that my perceptions can be limited, and even that there are ways to perceive that I cannot experience and, perhaps, cannot conceive. If my eyesight were more acute, could I see things that are beyond my ken now? Yes, I think that is true. The sighted man sees things that a blind man cannot."

Philippos falters unsure where to take his line of reasoning. Kratulos starts to interrupt, but Kerkidas holds up his right hand to the boy and beckons Philippos with his left.

The young prince looks away, his eyes are unseeing as he looks within, as he attempts to grasp and say what he knows is truth. "The diversity of life is all about us. I know my thoughts but cannot know yours, even if you try to tell me. Though I can form an opinion of you, I can never reach the essence of you. So my perceptions are limited, and there is truth that is unreachable for me. Yet, though things seem separate, I do sense that there exists a unity to them. The analogy you used of the fire seems proper to me. Do you remember when Pindaros asked about the gods? You said that the gods might be tongues of flame that flicker from a fire but that the fire is a wholeness. The flames are both separate and one."

Momentarily there is silence as Philippos runs dry. From outside come the noises of the day—the chirping of birds, the distant calls of the street, within the house the rhythm of a loom. Still gentle, Kerkidas asks, "You say that you sense a unity. How can that be?"

Philippos' face is strained by his thoughts. "Consequences," he says. "Whatever happens, there are consequences. Everything connects. Once a wise woman told me of the storm that the bird perceives as a calamity while the grain finds its rain life giving and the mouse perceives it as a blessing."

Kratulos starts to snicker and is soundly rapped by Kerkidas. "Continue, Philippos," says the teacher.

Red in the face at Kratulos' ridicule, and fearing more polite amusement from the others, Philippos doggedly pursues his thoughts, "I mean that the creatures' perceptions are not false for themselves but are incomplete for the whole. Unity is that whole. Any one view is imperfect, and the whole lies still beyond our collective views. I think we hope that the whole has purpose since it is more than any one of us can understand, yet it affects all of us. We are like sailors in their hammocks. If one shifts position, they all must shift. What I do, touches you, and from you to another. Our actions are raindrops on a pool of water, with each small splash interleaving with a myriad of other splashes."

"Tell me about our hope that the whole has purpose," asks Kerkidas. By now the other boys have ceased their bids for the teacher's attention and are, like him, listening to what Philippos is trying to express.

"If there is no purpose to the whole, then no matter how long the chain of circumstances, all is chaos. Our individual attempts to create order around ourselves are immaterial at least and foolish arrogance at most. Though we fear that all this may be chaos, we cannot afford to believe that. The more we believe there is purpose, the more it becomes evident. For as we believe, we are attentive to how each thing is connected to all other things. At a minimum, there are causes and consequences, and maximally, there is purpose. There are those who say the golden age existed when the gods walked the earth, and man was born and acted with the gods. Beyond myths, I see, I feel no evidence of a golden age. Instead, I see a working out on earth, and across the universe, even what's beyond my ken, the results of our corporate actions. We are a carpet, constantly frayed by the treading of many feet, yet as constantly reknit so that we never come undone completely. We are responsible for the reknitting. That is what we do as mankind. We labor to build, to create, to summon order into being."

Not holding back further, Cricket bursts into argument, "Aren't we as destructive as we are constructive? Don't we war incessantly? Isn't there plenty of heedless violence and impulsive breakage?"

Philippos looks at Cricket with careful consideration, "Yes, certainly. Aren't those acts in reaction to something else? Resentment of another's wealth and good fortune, a selfish effort to stop others from having what you do not. An infantile act. Or, an act of desperate need, to secure survival, to pre-empt another's fortune to make your own. However violent, the destruction is not groundless, though it may be misdirected."

Philippos waves a hand as if swatting at gnats, "I'm not sure, and I don't seek to excuse murder and mayhem, but always there is a larger vista. Sometimes things are torn down to make way for larger edifices. Long ago, in the lands my people occupy, there was another people, the Bruges. Somehow their time ended. Some of them traveled on, into Asia Minor it's said. Some few stayed and disappeared into the growing numbers of Makedones. Others went who knows where. Many in our lands believe that the gods caused that people to disappear so that ours could grow. This favor of Zeus is seen in the preeminence of my family. Maybe there will come a time when we Makedones must give way. You see, we see so little because we are, of necessity, so intent on ourselves. Our lives, the lives of our family, of our whole people, are too brief to know truly what the gods or the One knows."

β

Sitting on the garden bench, Perdikkas watches Alexandros play the *kithara*. The tones of each plucked string rise in melancholy. "Don't you ever do a cheerful song?"

The king attempts a quick complicated passage, but fails. He frowns and stops.

"Well, I can see why you like slow dismal tunes," comments Perdikkas.

"You play it. You're better at this than I am," says Alexandros, handing the twin necked instrument to his brother.

"Neither of us will ever make a profession as balladeers," says Perdikkas, with a chuckle, as he accepts the *kithara*. Soon he has a simple yet fast paced melody in the air.

Alexandros grins at Perdikkas, "So you're bored, aren't you? Ever since you handled last year's timber shipments, you've been wondering what to do with yourself." Perdikkas nods his assent without looking up from his quick fingered plucking of the strings. The king continues, "What would you say to riding to Lunkestis or, even, Pelagonis? The word I get is that Bardulis and his Dardanoi are stirring again. Maybe he wants to renegotiate our payments to him."

"How long will we pay him his blood money?" asks Perdikkas.

Alexandros looks away. From the garden he can see the precincts of Ares Polemos, with its white columns standing out against the dark green of the nearby cedar trees. He sighs slightly, thinking that he would like to light the fires in that temple, "I'm not ready to take on the Illuroi. We need this quiet to continue; we need to build our strength."

"Ptolemaios and his cronies are behaving themselves," comments Perdikkas. "Fighting the Illuroi is traditional, like keeping wolves off a flock. Not like fighting the Thessaliotes. Maybe a campaign against Bardulis would heal some of our internal wounds."

"No," says Alexandros sharply. "Calling out the nobles and their men would increase Ptolemaios' authority. We need a counterbalance."

"You could go back to Philpa's idea of creating a phalanx of heavy foot from each region of our lands. You've got a good start with the two companies of hoplites we raised for Thessalos."

"I miss Philippos," admits Alexandros.

"How do we redeem Philippos and the other hostages?" musingly asks Perdikkas. He considers his own question. "If the Makedones are united, we end the excuse used by Thebai to intervene. How do we demonstrate our unity?"

The king shakes his head, "It's only an excuse. They would find another public reason to continue their interference. They want us dependent on them."

"Still, if the notables are in accord, at least, for the sake of any outsiders, and if we actively police our borders, they have no choice but to ease their hold. If we create a standing armed force, they must treat us more respectfully."

"Unity?" snorts Alexandros. "Beyond Ptolemaios, there is still Pausanias the Exile and Argaios, with their pretensions for the throne. And we have our dear half-brothers to think of."

Perdikkas shrugs, "What state in all Hellas does not have its own exiles? Pausanias and Argaios are not threats. As for our country brothers, no one would follow them. No, it's only Ptolemaios to be concerned about. We have to secure his cooperation." Perdikkas broods, knowing the course of action he's going to suggest, but knowing also that his brother will be opposed. Still, for mother, who won't stop nagging at him to mediate with Aleko.

Deliberately, Perdikkas sets the *kithara* down, stands, walks over to his brother, and sits opposite him where the grasses are shorter. "Aleko, permit mother to marry Ptolemaios. Father said long ago to use her as a snare for that son-of-a-bitch. Use the snare Aphrodite puts into your hands. You would gain their gratitude, and in giving the queen mother publicly to Lord Ptolemaios you demonstrate that the breach is healed."

Alexandros' face turns red. He stares into his brother's eyes, on the verge of an angry rebuff. Yet he pauses, for this idea that he has forbidden has played in his own mind. Perhaps there's more merit than demerit to it. Perhaps his spite is blinding him to Aphrodite's gift. "I want the Boiotian confederacy off my back. I'd rather see Ptolemaios dead, but barring that event, I'd rather use him to further my own ends. As for mother, maybe getting what she wants will open her eyes to seeing him as he is. And I want Philippos back."

He looks away from Perdikkas, "Every month, mother formally requests that I allow them to wed. Maybe I've been embarrassed by her choice long enough. Maybe it's time to put her heart to use." The king nods, "All right, Perdikkas. Let it be so. I do not want the ceremony seen as a victory for them over me. Have it done quietly, and let it be known that a loving son can be generous and grant his mother's lover pardon."

"You should tell mother, not me. Do it when she makes her request this time."

"No, it's up to Ptolemaios to ask me for mother's hand," states Alexandros. Suddenly, he smiles, "Let him do it properly, Perdix."

At the garden gate, the guard calls out an inquiry. Alexandros acknowledges with a wave, and smiles again at his brother, "We are discovered and our privacy lost." Through the gate come a dozen or so young men, led by

Parrhasios, all laughing and rough housing. A cheerful group enjoying the raillery between Parrhasios and Apollophanes.

γ

The marketplace is a profusion of people, produce, and animal stock. Cricket is laughing at a swineherd's efforts to secure a huge sow. The sow is squealing and leaping with amazing agility for its size as the swineherd swears blasphemously and swings his staff. Philippos longs for a spear. The sow would not escape then. Chuckling, Cricket grabs Philippos' arm and shouts in his ear, "This is really what makes Thebai great." He waves his hand at the whole scene of market stalls, from turnip sellers to horse corrals. "Ask my father. Our walls, all the roads that lead to Thebai, our position in the center of Boiotia, the steadfast courage of our warriors— all are important—yet they're nothing if the populace is not fed. Here you see our foodstuffs. The people of Thebai never go hungry. The plains of Boiotia bear the fruits of our labor. The Athenians can scoff that we are all farmers, but it is they who are dependent on their ships to bring wheat, barley, and oats from distant lands."

The two are on their way to the Iolaic gymnasium. Like the *agora*— the marketplace—the gymnasium of Iolaos is on the eastern side of the lower city. Some days, they walk as far as the smaller gymnasium that lies just outside the city's southern gate, the one dedicated to Herakles. Cricket had not been to the Herakleian gymnasium before Philippos joined the household. They go there when they have time, since Philippos prefers to honor his forefather. Today, though, Philippos must return to the house by late afternoon for his lesson from Pammenes.

"Should we eat now or later?" asks Cricket, pointing to the stall of a meat pastry cook.

"Your mother is a better cook than any in the market," answers Philippos.

"True, that's because her family's from Aulis. They spice their food more," agrees Cricket seriously, while still eyeing the food stall. "Still, some things she doesn't make."

Philippos laughs, "A sausage or two wouldn't hurt us provided you're paying. My allowance hasn't reached your father yet this month."

A wealthy boy, Cricket regularly pays the way for Philippos. Yet it is a sticking point for Philippos. He resents his frequent poverty. He is a prince, yet he is dependent on the vagaries of dispatch riders from Pella. Cricket has no idea how deeply Philippos feels his failure to reciprocate his companion's generosity.

Soon both are walking along with grease on their hands and chins, and savory meat pie filling their mouths. Cricket's muffled voices says, "Kerkidas would have a fit seeing us eat meat", the idea increasing his pleasure.

"That's one of many points on which I differ with our Puthagorean. We need flesh, fish, and fowl every bit as much as bread, fruit, and vegetables. Ask any coach at the gymnasium." Philippos shakes his head, "I like better his theory of balance. That applies to food as much as any issue of philosophic harmony."

"Why don't you argue more in class? Between you and Kratulos, there's more comic quips than reasoning."

Philippos hits Cricket lightly on the arm, "What's wrong with laughter?"

"Maybe it's good in its place, but sometimes you exasperate Kerkidas."

"Sometimes, he exasperates me."

*　*　*

Lying stretched out on the massage table feels good to Philippos. The exercises and running stretched his muscles; swimming and massage restored their balance. Now, he feels lazy. Cricket is off meeting some of his friends. The masseur is gone. Philippos is thinking about Lusias, his old weapons coach. There are enough Makedon hostages to make a decent practice phalanx. If Cricket and the other Theban boys could be persuaded to form an opposing team, they might have fun. Probably, though, the city fathers would view a Makedon practice phalanx with alarm, even one made up of boys as young as nine.

"You look superb, lying there."

Philippos lifts his head. He had not heard Hermarkhos Oreos enter the room. Had he dozed? The man is handsome, his smile welcoming without a trace of irony. The flutter spreading within Philippos at the flattery is a surprise to the boy. "You possess the reputation to make a good judge," answers Philippos.

"Ah, then others have warned you about me?" laughs Oreos. "What can I say? You have the strong thighs of a horseman. They mark you clearly as a youth of noble bearing. And I, a horseman of some repute myself, cannot help but love a youth both noble and with good thighs." Leaving the doorway, Oreos comes to Philippos' side.

Catching his breath in his throat, Philippos feels the warmth of the man next to him, "Perhaps there are too many boys with muscular thighs in Thebai."

"Believe me, Prince of the Makedones, there are not too many. Indeed, there are no others as strong and able as you." Oreos' voice has thickened slightly. He steps back, as if to gain composure, but reaches out to turn Philippos' face his way. Fingers follow the prince's jaw line. "You have an uneven face, Prince. How intriguing is your lack of symmetry. The difference is slight enough to add interest to your face rather than oddity."

"I'm not in the habit of examining my face."

"No, of course not. Who would expect that of a rugged Makedon warrior?" replies the man with just enough mockery to show he is sharing the jest.

"And you need not, for I have done you the service. I like the quality of your features."

Taking a step forward, Oreos' hand touches Philippos behind the knee and runs slowly and with increasing firmness up the length of the boy's thigh and ending in a long caress of the naked buttock. "Your skin is warm, and the musculature is exquisite."

Philippos does not know whether to be offended or compliant. He welcomed the man's attentions these past two *dekades* of the month. Philippos has been gruff with Oreos, not wanting to appear easy. The man's teasing only increased. Until now, Philippos has been careful not to be alone with Oreos. This open display of desire by Oreos is new.

The boy wants to jump up and run. He remembers Pammenes' counsel. Philippos is afraid, mostly of doing the wrong thing, of appearing ridiculous. Still, he likes seeing the man's desire. He wants the passion. He hasn't known it yet, while boys younger than he already have their mentoring lovers.

"You see what you do to me, Philippos," whispers Oreos.

Philippos is staring at Oreos' erection. Straight on the view is intimidating, yet seeing the swollen member is also somehow comical, like the attachments worn by clowns in a priapic skit. Philippos stifles a snicker. And with his amusement comes his own self-control. He decides to take on Hermarkhos Oreos as a lover, to gain the experience. The man is good-looking, a member of a leading family, and fully infatuated. Philippos is confident now that he can dominate the relationship.

"I am no woman or soft boy, Hermarkhos Oreos. I let no man use me, giving gifts that cannot be reciprocated. Though I am younger than you, if you want us to share love, you will follow my lead."

Oreos is taken aback. He visibly wilts. "It is I who should teach you," he stammers.

Swinging off the table and standing, Philippos says, "Between friends, companions in mind and body, what matters is how the heart feels. That which you admire and yearn for in me is the same aspect that demands of me that I lead. You can recognize the blood of Herakles in me. As your family is descended from Herakles' companion, Iolaos, so it is natural that there exists a strong attraction between us. Yours is the part of Iolaos, and mine is Herakles." Reaching, Philippos grasps Oreos' penis firmly and, pulling the man to him, kisses Oreos on the lips. For a moment Oreos resists, then he seems to melt into desire.

*   *   *

Though only eight boys and fewer servants, the tumult they make as they walk home bounces off the stone walls of the houses on each side of the street. They are loud with exuberance, mutual badinage, and the gossip of the day. For Philippos, this daily routine seems something apart from him even as he participates fully.

A part of his mind is puzzling over his feelings about Hermarkhos and their tryst. He feels oppressed now, while at the time he'd felt elation. He'd successfully played the part of the man. His orgasm had been a heady rush, more piquant than any masturbation. Yet he is troubled. Does he want to sustain the obligations he is creating with Hermarkhos? Has the impulse of the moment betrayed him into acting incautiously? Of the love-making, he has no concern. Instead, it is his insistence on switching roles, on taking the man's part rather than the youth's, that seems too pride filled. What must Hermarkhos be thinking? The man cannot boast of his conquest. Of course, that was part of Philippos' intention. Hermarkhos likely feels demeaned, his seduction robbed of its worth. Yet he demanded promises that they meet again soon.

"Hey, you aren't listening," calls Pindaros Milao, tapping Philippos.

"What are you talking about?"

"Kratulos says that there's no true accounts of your origins, of the line of descent of the royal Makedones. He says there are only stories from Xerxes' time on."

Keeping his temper, Philippos asks, "What do you mean, Kratulos? We trace our line from Herakles."

Kratulos stops and turns, grinning, and the boys cluster, "I heard that long ago, in your great-great-grandfather's time, there was a contest held in your sacred city. Bards, wise men, storytellers were all invited. Your king and queen of that time offered honors and wealth to the best poet. The one who proved himself the finest would be asked to learn all the legends, heroic tales, and history of the royal Makedones. So men from many lands, not just Makedones, competed. They sang of the gods. They sang the tales of the wars with Troy as purely as ever the blind hostage Homeros. They sang of heroes—Herakles, Theseos, Iason, Odduseos, and others."

"At last, only two men were still competing. One knew every story, from beginning to end, but spoke dryly, dully. The other was all drama and pathos—he could make you weep, laugh, seethe, sigh, exclaim in wonder—tailoring his words to his art and not concerned if a story's path was ever the same twice. The queen chose the first man, while the king chose the second. The royal pair grew obstinate with each other. Finally, the king invoked his royal command, and the poet of drama won over the poet of truth. For the king believed that only a tale well told would be worth hearing. The queen, though, was right. While famed for colorful stories, often of fantastic possibility, no one among the Makedones can attest which of the many versions is true. And so your people's past faded from memory."

"I think whoever told you this tale was just such a one as you describe, full of nonsense," asserts Kleitos angrily.

Philippos is laughing, "Do you know, Kratulos, that is the story we tell of the royal Thraikiote Odrusai. And my man, Skaros, tells me that the Thraikiotes tell a similar tale of the kings of the Skuthos or Sakas, the people who ride the steppes north of the Euxine." He smiles merrily at his fellows, "Like any fable, the story is not concerned with common truth. Look at us, there is too much truth. Polemaios has buckteeth. Kratulos, you always laugh when you fart. Cricket sighs whenever Pamesias calls his name. All these are common truths. Like your fable, we could argue the merits of accuracy and artistry. For me, make the chronology, the sequence true, and fill-in with what is notable, of value, but let the dross fall away."

"Well, whoever heard of an ancient Makedon hero?" counters Kratulos.

Remembering the Lady Kleopatra, Philippos grins broadly, "I could tell you more history of my family than you could hear in a *dekades* of the month. I'll give you one such story for the walk home. Let me tell you of the days when we defeated and expelled the Eordoi." The boys begin walking again. "Fighting began in the time of old King Aeropos, not the Aeropos who held the throne in the time of Spartan king Agesilaos. This Aeropos was king when you Southern Hellenes were fighting for control of Delphoi, and Solon was *arkhon* of Athenai. When Aeropos died, his son, Alketas, inherited the hostilities with the Eordoi. Now all this fighting began when ..."

*　　*　　*

Dusk is falling outside. Within the study room, Philippos sits quietly, in reverie. He is weary within himself—not from the fatigues of the day. He is weary of pretense, of playing the exuberant northern prince. He knows it is better coloration than being the brooding boy, as he was when he began his stay in Thebai. Still, it is hard to shoulder aside all the slights and injustices of being a hostage. No wonder Kleitos walks around sucking his fist in frustration and sullen resentment. The insults Philippos can answer, can turn aside by mocking the mocker. What weighs on him are the unthinking slights, the assumption of northern inferiority made by these southerners, the constant deprecation all unrealized by these Theban cocks. His spirit is dragging.

He yearns for those days when he had no greater concerns than avoiding his tutor and obeying his coaches. He smiles to himself thinking of Lusias. The aging mercenary would have no sympathy for the prince. *If you are a prince, act like a prince*, was a saying Lusias offered him whenever the contests left him bloody and close to tears. Lusias taught him to ignore pain.

A soft knock at the door announces interruption. "Come in," calls Philippos.

Skaros stands there, an oil lamp flickering in his hand, "No need to sit in the dark, master."

"It has grown dark, hasn't it?" responds the boy.

"Pammenes is coming now for your evening lesson." Skaros lights a standing lamp from his hand-held flame. The room is no longer obscure. The two benches on which the boys sit for their morning lessons with Kerkidas are pushed back against the wall. Philippos sits on a stool by a narrow table. A slate with his chalk sketches of the palace at Pella is revealed on the table. Across the room is a wall hanging depicting Kadmos with the exhausted guide cow in the foreground and the established citadel of the Kadmeia in the background. Kadmos, founder of Thebai, is said to have come from Phoenikis, across the sea. His wife, Harmonia, was the daughter of Aphrodite. Harmonia reconciled those living in these lands with the people of Kadmos, and together they settled Thebai. More interesting to Philippos than the ancient legend is the portrayal of the modern Kadmeia. He had felt challenged to draw his home city, Pella.

Skaros picks up the slate, "A good likeness of Pella, but not for now." Deliberately, he wipes his sleeve over the slate, causing Pella to disappear.

"You are right, Skaros," says Philippos, "we won't give them a glimpse into ourselves."

Down the corridor comes Pammenes. His voice booms, "I see you are ready for me tonight, Prince." In his arms he is carrying three helmets. The bronze metal gleams. The horse hair crest on the top helmet becomes red from black as Pammenes enters the light of the room. The man sets the three helmets on the narrow table.

One helmet, for an officer with its high crest, is old fashioned, and of Khalkidikian style. The second is a traditional Boiotian horseman's helmet, flaring out over the ears and face. The third helmet is from Thraikios, with its high bell, open face and hinged cheek guards.

"What do you think of them? Which would you choose if you were going into battle?" asks Pammenes.

Philippos hesitates, then picks up the Thraikiote helmet.

"Why?" asks Pammenes.

"Because I could still see and hear, but have sufficient protection to make wearing the helmet worthwhile."

"Are you fighting on foot or horseback?" asks Pammenes.

"On foot."

Pammenes picks up the horseman's helmet, "What about this helmet?"

"It's good for its purpose, but not strong enough for phalanx fighting." Philippos continues, "You have seen the helmet the Thessaliotes use? Just like their sun hats only of bronze? They wear them straight on their brow rather than back as you'd wear a hat."

"You mean the *petasos*. Yes, it's good against sword slashes since the rim is out so far. Though it's even weaker than our riders' helmets." Pammenes shrugs, "You see how I spent my afternoon. The board debated the merits of different helmet designs. The question to be resolved is what design we adopt so we may order the thousand helmets we need to stock the city arsenal. We are depleting our supplies with these annual campaigns."

"What have you decided?"

"Oh, it will take several more meetings before there will be consensus. Of course, it's not just helmets. Cuirasses, spear points—for footmen, for horsemen—greaves, or maybe no greaves, it goes on and on." The general smiles, "Some days I wish I were back when a man brought his own armament."

"Don't many of your people supply themselves, especially the federated troops from other Boiotian cities?"

"We must field a well-trained force. You don't defeat Spartiates without thorough training. Our citizens train for two years in their youth, though we may extend that period to four years. The backbone of our army, though, isn't the common citizenry. It's the elite, the men we pay to train year in and year out, whether in phalanx or on horse. Them we supply. I don't mean mercenaries, foreigners. I mean our best men, our Sacred Band." Pammenes pauses, "Besides, if the city provides the weaponry, then our men are armed uniformly. That makes less confusion on the battlefield. It allows consistency in training and in action, and eases supplying the men when they're in the field."

Pammenes pulls up a stool and sits down next to Philippos. He stretches his legs, causing the leather of his belted boots to creak. "We pay a lot of attention to details. Most cities put men in the field who fight barefoot. The Lakonians pride themselves on their tough feet. Not us. We wear boots. And we endure a lot of chafing from our allies. But boots are tougher than feet for a stand up, all day fight."

"There are arguments for and against footwear," comments Philippos neutrally.

"Yes, usually a question of speed versus endurance." Again Pammenes smiles, "A Boiotian—especially a Theban—always comes down on the side of endurance. Who else would mass fifty men to a column? You don't move columns of that size hastily. Yet who can resist the weight of our push? Not even the finest Spartiates." Pammenes waves his hand in dismissal, "Sounds like Theban boasting to you, doesn't it?"

"Not after Leuktra, sir," answers Philippos truthfully.

"Yes, Leuktra—the end of Spartan invincibility." Pammenes takes Philippos' hand, and says earnestly, "That's all that mattered about that fight you know. Oh, others have defeated the Spartans in battle. The Athenians at Sphakteria, say. Only there the Lakonians were badly outnumbered. They were overwhelmed as much by swarms of light troops— peltasts, archers, *psiloi*, and slingers—as by hoplites. And to what end? But Leuktra is different. We killed one of their kings and every Spartiate we could reach."

Pammenes sighs, "Look carefully, Philippos. Did we destroy their army?

144

No. They retreated, they held. What mattered is the sense of victory. What mattered was that other states became our allies, offered to join their forces to ours. Battle is a terribly chancy thing. We took a fearsome risk. Oh, we trained. We were ready. We mastered the details. And every detail is important. Yet no detail is as important as the whole. What matters is what we have done with our victory. That matters far more than the victory itself."

The man is intent on the instructions he is offering the boy. "Sparte will never be a power again. That is what we are making sure of. That is why each year we send an army into the Peloponnesos. We strengthen the Arkadians as they form their confederacy—modeled on our Boiotian confederacy. We give birth to a new Messene. We support the factions in Elis, Akhaia, and the Argolid who oppose Lakonia. No more will Sparte dominate the Peloponnesos. No more will she interfere north of Korinthos."

"Never forget, Prince, that the outcome of war, of a series of campaigns, is more important than the outcome of a battle. You must know what it is you want to attain. Sometimes it is wiser to decline battle, even if you feel you could win it. The lives of our people are too precious to waste. We are not so many, and training takes years. So never waste a life. Make it count. Give battle when the result you want is more than simply defeating your enemy."

Pammenes sits back, relaxes, and loses the intensity of manner, "I have some news for you. I meant to talk about it first but my mind was on helmets and warfare. First, the dispatch rider came in and you again have money deposited with Nikolaos the merchant. Second, the rider brought the news that your mother and Lord Ptolemaios are wed. King Alexandros has formally requested the return of the hostages, with your name at the top of the list. He cites the stability of the realm and the reconciliation of all factions as epitomized by this marriage. Here is a private letter to you." Pammenes pulls the note from his sleeve.

"Do you mind?" asks Philippos, wanting to open the letter.

"Of course, son, go ahead. News from home is a lifeline."

Philippos opens the note with his thumbnail. Holding it up to the light, he reads:

Philippos, prince and brother,

Before opening this letter, you will probably hear that Alexandros has granted mother permission to wed Ptolemaios. We hope this act and the steadiness of the kingdom will end Thebai's excuse for holding you and the other hostages. We petition for your return.

Alexandros is coming into his own. There is a greater sense that he will be a proper king. Ptolemaios remains a power. I think that is a fact we must accept so long as he publicly supports our line.

The sum sent to you is greater than in the past. We want you to take ship to Pella as soon as the negotiations for your release are completed.

> *By the by, your friend, the Stork, will be traveling to Athenai to study philosophy.*
> *How can such a good mind go to such waste?*
> *Aleko and I await your return eagerly,*
> *Perdikkas, Prince of the Makedones*

The words summon the image of Perdix clearly. Philippos grins despite the stab of longing he feels for home.

Pammenes touches Philippos lightly, "I truly hope you can be restored to your family."

δ

The festival garlands brighten the streets of ancient Aigai. The ritual capital of the Makedones is filled with country folk come for two days of pageantry combined with revelry. The fact that the king attends, as do so many magnates from throughout the king's lands, adds to the excitement. Following the festival, the king will hear complaints and rule on the disputes that have arisen since his last visit to Aigai.

The dual festival is of great antiquity. A seasonal festival marking the end of winter, it possesses a dark fearful side and an orgiastic incautious side.

On the first day of the festival, the birth of Zeus is enacted. His mother, Rhea or, perhaps, Gaia herself, suffers greatly in giving birth. Yet she keeps silent in her agony, lest she alert her violent husband, Kronos, who would hide away the child or, so some say, expose the child and end its life. Kronos fears the prophecy that the child will be the death of the father. The only part of these first rituals enjoyed by the people are the dances of the three Kouretes and, later, the three Daktuloi. The Kouretes are three youths, guardians of Rhea, who dance with sword and shield around the newborn Zeus. The noise of their dance masks the cries of the infant so that Kronos remains unaware. Some say that the Kouretes sprang from the infant's tears falling to the earth.

The Daktuloi arise from Rhea digging her fingers into the soil as she writhes in her birth pains. These ten youngsters also dance. Elsewhere, in Samothrakos or on Lemnos as examples, the Daktuloi are depicted as smiths. In Aigai, the tradition is different. Here they are five boys and five girls. Their dance is gentle, following the war dance of the Kouretes. Each of the ten Daktuloi represent some knowledge or skill of mankind. One is a smith. Another a herder. A third a healer. A fourth a weaver. And so on. For it is from Zeus that the time of man descends.

Unlike in other lands, at Aigai it is the herder who is central. He is the only one of the ten to dance twice within the circle. And in his second dance, the last formality of the first day, he dances with a goat. The humor of the last dance presages the theme of the second day.

Fecundity is celebrated the second day. Now the Daktuloi children are gone, replaced by older youths. The males dance in costumes supporting huge phalluses. The females are personifications of Kore—of young women on the threshold of marriage and sexual maturity. Aphrodite commands this day. Other lands would make Dionysios have primacy. In Aigai, some of the older clans still hold that the goddess central to the second day is not Aphrodite, but Hekate.

Despite the abandon of the second day, with its humorous play depicting the god Priapos or the loosing of the goat herds to run through the town, there is a darkness within the day, for another trio of goddesses are present throughout the rituals. These are the Erinues, who watch from the sideline so that if abandon becomes scandal there will be retribution. Their presence is accounted for as being children of Kronos like Zeus or, in another version, of Ouranos like Aphrodite. At best, the three Erinues—Allektos, Tisiphone, and Megaira—are as watchful maiden aunts. At their worst, they are bitch furies pursuing errant men to their deaths. Still, Erinues aside, for the town's people and the country folk there will be merriment and much winking at behavior unacceptable on other days.

Echoing the temple events will be many impromptu dances and skits. Goats sacrificed will become goats eaten. The festival has always been a favorite of King Alexandros. His father, Amuntas, brought him every year as a child. Of course, Aigai was their citadel, their key to retaining a hold on the Makedones, with Amuntas as king and chief priest. Even in the years that Argaios held Pella with aid from the city of Olunthos, Aigai remained true to Amuntas.

Riding with Parrhasios now through the crowded streets—bowing, acknowledging, waving to familiar faces, whether notables or commoners, among the throng—Alexandros is elated. He turns in his saddle to his companion, "You know, last fall, at the beginning of the year, I vowed that this year would be better than the last. Here it is the month of *Xantikos* —just over five moons from *Dios*—and I feel that the tide has turned in my favor. We are as unified now as when my father held the throne."

"What do you have in mind, Alexandros?" asks Parrhasios, for he knows when the king makes such statements it's after mulling over some idea or plan.

Catching the warning look on Parrhasios' face, Alexandros laughs, "No, I don't intend to entangle myself with Thessalos any time soon. I do think, though, that we need a successful campaign in the fighting season. The common folk need to see their king as their protector."

An old crone steps in front of the king's horse, halting their progress. She is waving a walking stick or, maybe, a branch from an olive tree. A middle aged man, poorly dressed, grabs at her arm, trying to pull her out of the king's path. She ignores the man, probably her son, and addresses the king, "Hey-oh, you King, you givin' judgments on the third day?"

"I am, madam," answers the smiling king, glad to have an opportunity to show his accessibility to the commons.

A toothless grin is the response he receives, and she pats him on the leg, "A true Temenidai you are, sir." A small crowd has stopped to watch the exchange. The shrewd old woman plays to the street as well as the king, "I be no Arsinoe, Berenike, Kleopatra, or Eurudike, or none of them noble ladies. Just plain Doris. And my clan be not high like your'n, though it be as old or older. And that be important. We Briagiades hold our lands of mother Hekate's grant, from the beginning of time. So when you come to judgment in the row betwixt that priestly set who fawn on Hermes, you remember that my people hold the creek's bottom lands since before them priests their temple built."

In her excitement, the old woman is pointing her stick at the king. Even with her son hauling at her, and calling desperately, "mother, mother," she has no comic appearance. If the day were not bright with promise, the king would ward her off with a sign against the evil eye. He can well believe she is descended from the goddess Hekate. This sudden disquiet he keeps hidden, and in a booming voice to reach the outskirts of the crowd, Alexandros answers handsomely, "Be assured, madam, that I will hear all you and your family have to say as well as the argument of the other disputants. I will consult the elders and the precedents. And I will render a judgment that is as fair and just as I know how."

She cackles in delight, "Aye, you grow like your da', old King Amuntas, day by day. I seen you as a small boy, ridin' abumpin' by his side. You be just, and to those lying priests you be terrible." With that, she allows her son to pull her away.

The king and his companions urge their horses forward. Alexandros pats the shoulder of his mount, to ease its nervousness of the crowd or, perhaps, to quiet his own feelings. Parrhasios comes up to ride beside the king again, "I swear, Alexandros, if you don't do right by that old woman, she'll curse you with all the powers women can summon." He shudders.

Alexandros chuckles, "She was fearsome. I'm glad it was her smiles she gave me today."

"The great gods may hold across the lands of the Hellenes, but to dark hills and darker caves, the old ways still cling. There are tales you hear of the Erinues and other triple goddesses that would still a man's blood."

"Don't grow superstitious on me, Parrhasios. I am through Herakles, a son of Zeus. We are of the sun, the light, and we need not fear the moon." Alexandros smiles again, pats Parrhasios on the arm, "Before she gave us such a start, I was telling you that I intend to announce a border campaign. As always, we have a choice. I am inclined to leave the northwest alone. We'll continue to pay tribute to Bardulis. We could thrust north against the Paiaones. But it is the east and southeast that interest me more. The Khalkidikians, Thraikiotes, or even Amphipolis could readily challenge our grip on the Bisaltai lands. Whoever might challenge us there would do so at the secret bidding of Athenai. Or, we could better define the extent of our power in Anthemos. That would make Olunthos take notice that we are no longer distracted by internal factions."

Parrhasios nods, considering the options. "By leading a force to the Bisaltai, you counteract whatever influence Ptolemaios built in that area when he commanded the border."

Alexandros grins in acknowledgment, "There's that, too."

"Have you considered the heart of his power in Orestis?"

The king shakes his head no, "That would re-open wounds."

"Think about this. Since Thessalos, the Elimiotes have not supported you as strongly as you would like. Derdas claims to be occupied with his duties in Perrhaibis. If you took a force west, to Tumphaia, you could assert Makedon primacy there over the interests of Epeiros, of the Molossi tribe. You would be on the borders of Orestis and Elimiotis. You could directly call on Derdas for support and impress the highlanders that you are truly the over-king of the Makedones. You would win renown among the Orestiotes as much as among any of our semi-barbarian cousins."

"Why couldn't we do both this year, there's time?" asks Alexandros. The idea intrigues him. "If we move on the Bisaltai just after planting, say in early *Daisios*. Say we allow three months for that campaign. Then in mid-*Gorpiaius*, we cross the kingdom and march into Tumphaia. We allow a month there, not aggravating the Molossi too much, and be back in Pella for the New Year."

"Have you sounded out any one else yet, about a spring campaign?"

"Only some of the younger men, like Antipatros. Enough so I feel comfortable summoning a campaign for some future month, without being specific about its target."

Parrhasios smiles, "After the temple events, we should play Kouretes and join in one of the war dances. We will dance the war dance, the *telesias*, in earnest."

Alexandros laughs in agreement, his face alight with the idea of taking action again. With once again directing events, instead of having events control him.

*   *   *

Having kicked off his boots and stripped down to a loincloth, Alexandros grips the shield he's been offered. Like most older shields, it is heavier than his own. Today, armorers are able to float the bronze cover thinner. The extra weight will limit how long he dances. He practices a few thrusts with the Keltic sword.

Around the king, nine of his companions also prepare to dance. Others stand by, calling encouragement and passing cups of watered wine to the ten. Already the beat of the timpanon and the shrill cry of the pipes, the *auloi*, are calling to them. Slipping on his helmet, Alexandros looks about to see if their entire group is ready. Philippos Arkouda is the oldest dancer; Apollophanes is the youngest. As the oldest, Arkouda will be in the inner circle with the king and Parrhasios. They are the Kouretes. The others will dance the outer circle.

The master of the musicians calls the summons. On that signal, Alexandros leads his troop through the crowd and onto the dance ground. The king gives a wavering warcry. Like a chorus, his men answer.

Soon, Alexandros is weaving the intricate steps of a Kourete. The deeper drums have come in to reinforce the beat. The wine has loosened his mind, so that he dances without being self-conscious. His steps are flawless. He accents the high notes with his warcry. He and Parrhasios and Arkouda are like three parts of the same being—whirling, sliding, slashing, leaping. At each final beat of the measure, they clash swords against shields. Encircling them are their seven companions, equally agile and fierce.

The pace of the music is quickening. Sweat slicks Alexandros' face. He feels exalted.

Opposite him is Apollophanes. As Alexandros begins to turn away, Apollophanes crosses from the outer to the inner circle. Catching the fast motion with his side vision, the king starts in surprise. Before another thought is completed, pain engulfs him. Doubling, turning, falling away, he can hear the shriek of the crowd but does not recognize it. Apollophanes' second sword thrust ends all thought within Alexandros.

ε

Ptolemaios commands the council's silence, "We are agreed, then, that Perdikkas is not ready to assume the throne. Though eighteen, he behaves younger than his age. Who here would entrust the kingdom to his care? Have we not seen already in Alexandros the folly of placing too much responsibility on the shoulders of so young a man?"

"Arkhelaos and his brothers are grown men," objects one of the older magnates, "Through them flows the blood of the Temenidai. Perdikkas could be set aside in Arkhelaos' favor."

"What you say is true, Agathokles. Consider, though, that Arkhelaos sided with Argaios against his father, Amuntas. Consider that Amuntas, in his wisdom, set aside his older sons for his younger. Consider that while we here have been active partners of Amuntas in ruling the Makedones, those sons have run only their own estates. I will ask for Arkhelaos, as well. Who here would entrust the kingdom to the care of Arkhelaos?"

While Ptolemaios' arguments are telling, he has no concern that the name of the dark, angry Arkhelaos has serious support. Agathokles only seeks to secure his own voice and power in these deliberations.

Antiokhos stands and addresses his fellows, "Why spend more time in debate? The solution is obvious. Ptolemaios, through his wife Eurudike, should be acclaimed king."

Weakly, with support from the arm of his son, Iolaos rises. All the others fall silent. They wait on the frail, senior councilor. Iolaos clears his throat. His wizened face is impassive against his body's pain, "I do not urge others. You must decide for yourselves. I say only that my house stands by the rights of Perdikkas. We do, though, recognize his youth. If Ptolemaios is willing, we support him as regent for his stepson, Perdikkas. If Ptolemaios is not willing, we seek a regency council, with its chief appointed by Thebai."

An intake of breath from the others, and silence. None like the solution, but there is no solution without Iolaos and Antipatros.

The soft spoken words twist inside Ptolemaios' mind, though he forces himself to smile, "Iolaos, you may speak only for your house, but, as always, your words are both admonishment and advice to the rest of us. I put it to you all, shall I act as regent during the minority of Perdikkas, son of Amuntas?"

What really are the choices before the fifty-eight men assembled in the hall? If Iolaos offers his support to the elevation of Ptolemaios, then the kingdom's two strongest factions are together. And whatever else might be said of Iolaos, he is always on the winning side. Some few here may hold out against Ptolemaios, and many more may be resentful of his dominance, but what alternative is there? Better a regent than a king. Better a Makedone, than more interference from Thebai.

Lagos stands, "For Ptolemaios, as regent for Perdikkas." Others stand and declare. The support grows until it is a thicket of men. Now there are smiles. The strain is over. Whatever they may truly think of Ptolemaios, all prefer the certainty of acclamation over the uncertainty of indecision.

ζ

"You make a mockery of me, Eurudike," protests Ptolemaios.

The queen turns to look at her husband. There are new lines in her face, "I do not want to, Ptolemaios. Is it not usual to offer to the goddess Eukleia?"

Ptolemaios stands abruptly, "You know my meaning. An offering to Eukleia in the marketplace before we wed is one thing. Commissioning a statue to Eukleia at Aigai is another."

Eurudike looks searchingly at her husband, "Tell me again, how it is that your guards were at the Pella treasury the same night that Apollophanes killed Alexandros?"

"Apollophanes killed your son, not I. The traitor has been executed," Ptolemaios paces, his hands clasped behind his back.

"Answer my question, husband," asks Eurudike with unnerving softness.

151

"I've told you before. Why do you harp on this? I had word of a conspiracy, but it wasn't specific enough for me to act to prevent it."

"You knew enough to risk Alexandros' wrath by relieving his men and posting your own guards," she says quietly.

"Yes, I knew enough to take elemental precautions. You know I sent riders to warn the king. They did not reach him in time." There is pleading in Ptolemaios' voice.

"Your spies are not careless, for their master is not. Yet all they discover is what is obvious, Apollophanes killed my son. Did your riders not reach Alexandros in time, or were they not sent in time?"

"When the god Hermes causes me disquiet, I take measures." He throws his hands in the air, "From two reliable sources I heard that someone was boasting that he would kill the king. Yet the sources heard not the boasting, only word of it. A third source said that one of the king's boon companions was filled with hatred for imagined slights. A fourth source offered that the king was in danger when at Aigai. That was it. Four whisperings that were it not for my disquiet, no rider would have been sent. You know there are always whisperings, always rumors, someone told someone who told someone else. And when you trace it all back, that wasn't what was said at all." He sighs, comes up to her and places his hands on her shoulders, "Eurudike, please, put this behind you. In time, Perdikkas will be king. For now, I guard his heritage. The killer and his menfolk are dead, the womenfolk sold, the estates seized. It is done."

Eurudike is unresponsive. Formally, she states, "Eukleia was the virgin daughter of Herakles. Her renown is her good reputation, her honor. And so we Temenidai honor her. As do the Boiotians, Lokrians, and other southern Hellenes. I will give her a statue at Aigai so all may know that whatever lethal conspiracy existed around my son, I was no part of it. Who would invite the wrath of the gods by claiming innocence in Eukleia's name if, in fact, they were guilty? Husband, you may subscribe your name or not to the dedication." The mother's words remain soft, but firm in resolve.

Ptolemaios throws up his hands, again, "And so you imply that I was a party to the conspiracy." Ptolemaios would like to strike the queen. His frustration almost overcomes his caution.

"Ambition drives you, Ptolemaios. I've always known this. Indeed, I admire you for it, as well as for your decisiveness." Eurudike touches her husband's cheek, "Guard my son, Perdikkas, well. See to his welfare in every way. Prepare him to be king. Let no harm befall him. And you shall have my unqualified support in ruling as regent." Her eyes harden, "I could not bear the loss of another son."

They stare at each other. Ptolemaios turns away, "Put up your cursed statue at Aigai. You need not fear for Perdikkas." He strides from the bedroom.

η

The sky is clear and there is no sense of an impending storm in the market of the small city of Anthemos. The town is the economic center of a narrow region of the same name that runs along the valley north of Mount Kalauros. To the south of Mount Kalauros march the lands of the Khalkidike, the three-fingered peninsula held by a confederacy of cities led by the strongest among them, Olunthos. Anthemos, region and city, was a pawn in the wars between King Amuntas and Olunthos. Ever since the Spartan aided restoration of Amuntas, the region is counted as part of the Makedon king's realm.

Today seems like most days in Anthemos. Twelve years have passed since Amuntas, Derdas, and the Spartans defeated Olunthos. For twelve years, Anthemos has been at peace. The talk in the town is of goat and sheep stocks, of cheeses and wools, of specialty woods from Mount Kalauros, of barley grown on hillsides. Pella, the Makedon capital, seems a distant place, being nearly 380 stadia by road or two days of walking or four days if leading a donkey. The citizens of Anthemos think in terms of their rivals at Kissos further down the valley. Or of Strepsa, on the coast, that serves as port for the valley. Up the coast a bit from Strepsa is the larger port of Therme, which is a city of some size. But Pella—well, as long as the border is quiet, Pella hasn't much interest in Anthemos, nor, truth be known, does Anthemos in Pella.

Today, though, if a citizen of Anthemos is paying attention, he would notice more strangers than normal attending the market day. The townsfolk do not notice, until a dozen strangers gather on the steps of the fountain house that centers the market. Cloaks thrown back to reveal armor, swords now in hand, the strangers are impossible to ignore.

"Anthemites, Anthemites, gather here. Gather, citizens," loudly bellows a burly man atop the steps. A few cooler heads among the citizenry look to the town gates, but it is too late. More strange warriors are there. Through the gate can be seen a cloud of horsemen, followed by a column of spear-topped footmen, rushing up the road to the city. "Anthemites, stop your business and come here." The call has become a command.

The tall straight-backed man standing next to the bullnecked herald raises an arm to motion for silence. The murmuring stills. The noble Hellene calls out, "Citizens of Anthemos, you and your families need not be alarmed. We wish you no harm. Anthemos is honored, for today begins my campaign to end the parasitic rule of the blasphemous Ptolemaios and his Illuroi wife, Eurudike. Ptolemaios, killer of King Alexandros, has betrayed the trust given him by King Amuntas. Taking the woman, Eurudike as lover, he thinks he can seduce the whole kingdom. He is not a true Temenidai. I am the Temenidai. I am the true king of the Makedones. I am the son of a king, grandson of a king, great-grandson of a king. Through me flows the blood of the Temenidai. I am Pausanias, son of Pausanias, grandson of

Aeropos, great-grandson of Perdikkas and on through Alexandros the First, his father Amuntas the Good, back to Herakles and Father Zeus. I am the Temenidai."

The astute in the market have already whispered to one another that Pausanias the Exile stands before them. What matters most is the many mercenaries in his employ. Someone is providing their pay, and it isn't Pausanias. Some of the high folk among the Makedones must be supporting the pretender. Still, they can't be paying for an entire army, even if it isn't large. Who else supports Pausanias? Olunthos and the Khalkidike cities? A southern power? A Thraikiote king? Persia?

On the steps, the commanding voice continues, "You will allot one in ten of your citizens to serve in this sacred army of retribution. Each ten will provide the bread, oil, and wine needed by him and two others for a period of thirty days. After thirty days, and as other cities, towns, and villages join us in restoring legitimacy to the Makedones, your men may return to Anthemos. My officers will instruct ..."

And so Pausanias begins his fight against Ptolemaios.

θ

Pushing his bowl aside, Ptolemaios leans forward to make his point clearly, "Telestes reports that Therme has fallen to Pausanias. We confront his forces a day's march away. He's got that ruffian Diodotos Kokinos leading his men. My forces are weak without the support of the kingdom. Derdas doesn't come. He sends a troop of twenty horsemen under Xenokleitos. Twenty men for all of Elimiotis! And Aeropos of Lunkestis sends us his prayers to Zeus and his fifteen-year old son, Alexandros, with an escort of five. At least Orestis gives me three hundred men. Only they're at least three days away. We cannot count on the highlands. We save the kingdom with the lowlands."

Antiokhos looks away, embarrassed by the king-regent's desperation. Lagos pulls at his lip. Athanaios folds his arms across his chest, feeling scornful since his advice to appeal to Thebai was rebuffed. Arkhelaos scowls darkly, but has offered no ideas other than the prowess of himself, his two brothers, and their followers. He drinks deeply from his mug.

Calmly, Iolaos answers, his voice soft and low, "You have thirteen hundred men facing maybe twice that number. His strength is in his footmen. Your horsemen can delay him. Philippos Arkouda is a devious leader and will make Pausanias and Kokinos contest every *daktyloi* of land. My son is raising men on our estates. I know that Korrhagos the Elder and Periandros do the same. Some, though, are reluctant, like Agathokles, for any number of reasons. You have exiled good men like Parrhasios and Amuntas Plousias leaving the lowlands unnaturally weak. You disbanded the phalanx established by Alexandros. Still, if we gain time, we can more than match Pausanias. He succeeds only if he's fast."

Sitting slightly apart from the men, as if an observer and not a participant, Queen Eurudike has been attentive to their debate. For several of the men, it is shocking that she is here at all. Yet she has as much at stake as any man in the room, so she insisted on being here.

In her mind, only Iolaos has made sense. To rely on Iolaos and his clan solely, though, would be the height of folly. If the challenge to Ptolemaios had come from the Illuroi or Paiaones, the highlands would have rallied quickly to join the king. The highlanders have no interest in this squabble over which of the Temenidai is high king. Orestis alone has reason to love Ptolemaios, and even that tie is frayed. Ptolemaios has been distant from his highland origins for too long.

"We will not have gathered our strength in time, I fear," Ptolemaios answers Iolaos. Grimly, he continues, "I am perfectly aware, as is Pausanias, that I have not had time to reconcile the kingdom to my rule. I will be blunt. You five gain nothing from a victory by Pausanias. You may think you have something to gain from my defeat, however. I am certain you have it in your power to raise the men in this kingdom in numbers and with speed that would readily overawe Pausanias and his paltry hoplites. Great Zeus, the bulk of the troops facing them now come from my estates alone!"

Before her husband can say more to damage his standing in the eyes of these magnates, Eurudike interrupts, "Of course, we all stand by the regent, and by Prince Perdikkas. There is no doubt our rule will be sustained. Consider, though, how much might be lost, how much the people and land might suffer, until our strength is ready to face Pausanias. You have already decided to forestall the zeal of Diodotos Kokinos with silver. Adding that payment to what the kingdom gives Bardulis the Dardanoi yearly, could beggar us or, at the least, make us weaker for the next alarm. Is there no other answer?"

Her tone of voice tells the men that in fact she has an answer. Eurudike looks from one to another, her eyes lingering longest on Iolaos before returning to Ptolemaios. She smiles, "As you have talked an answer has occurred to me."

Seeing again the resilience of his wife, Ptolemaios feels hope, and some pride in her, "My dear, please?" ˙

"We are blinded by the power of Thebai. There is another power in Athenai. Now that we know the Khalkidike confederacy funds Pausanias, I think we can appeal to our long-standing friendship with Athenai. She will be eager to detach us from Thebai, and will not want the king of the Makedones to be beholden to Olunthos. Given the urgency, we need not appeal directly to the city. Instead, we appeal to my foster-brother, Iphikrates, who, as you all know, commands the Athenian fleet that stands off from Amphipolis. He possesses an independent streak and will not feel he must wait on word from Athenai before acting. The fleet is more than strong enough to break Pausanias. And at little cost to Makedonis."

Athanaios asks, "Why would Iphikrates leave off his responsibilities to curb Pausanias?"

Feeling a surge of confidence, and knowing the greed of Iphikrates from old, Ptolemaios responds, "I have no doubt that an appeal to the mutual regard he bears the Temenidai will be persuasive. He will be gifted for his trouble, and can easily argue that putting down Pausanias is necessary to his responsibilities of securing Amphipolis. Is he not our guest-friend? Is he not the adopted son of King Amuntas?"

"He will remember me fondly," states the queen. "He will honor my request, and will come in haste and strength." Her certainty silences the others.

ι

Philippos leans against a tree. Behind him, Hermarkhos Oreos places his hand on Philippos' shoulder. The boy shrugs it aside and steps away. "Can you not accept my care at your grief? I would take your grief on my own heart if I could," says Oreos.

Philippos turns, his eyes cruel, "Oreos, were you to know my brother, you would have your own grief. And if it were as mine is, it could swallow you whole. My grief does not swallow me whole only because my vengefulness makes a granite mountain impossible to swallow."

Seeing the hesitation Oreos feels, Philippos waves him off, "Now is not the time for us, not the time for idle pursuits. It would be best for you to leave."

"When can we meet? I will come whenever you say."

A sense of disgust invades Philippos at the man's need, perhaps heightened by the anger Philippos is feeling at all things Theban, by the frustration of being held hostage when he should be home with his kin, "Go, Hermarkhos Oreos. Give this some time."

"I depart, handsome Philippos, with a measure of grief that is my own." Oreos flings his cloak about himself and strides off.

Exasperation with the fop is lost immediately at his departure for the ache inside Philippos is a thousand times more compelling. Alexandros is dead. Philippos remembers Apollophanes. Another fop. Perhaps remembering the vanity of Apollophanes makes it impossible for Philippos to tolerate now the vanity of Hermarkhos Oreos.

Philippos knows that Apollophanes could be no more than an arrow sent from someone else's bow. Who else but Ptolemaios? Philippos shies away from thinking about his mother. Yet the question remains a corrosion in the back of his mind. *Did she know? Did she have a hand in Aleko's murder?*

If only the god Apollo or even Ares would turn him into a spear and hurtle him across the breadth of Hellas to skewer Ptolemaios through his evil heart.

Skaros comes up the slope to stand before his master, "They will be here soon. I'll stand watch here in the grove. You had best wait at the tomb."

Philippos nods and takes the path to the shrine and tomb of Linos. In the forecourt where the ceremonial flax is flailed during the annual festival, he quickly offers a prayer, then enters the tomb's hall. The gloom within is chill.

For a time he muses about the gods, wondering if they truly exist or whether they are no more than the comfort and the terror that men need.

"Philippos, Prince of the Makedones," calls the voice of Kleitos.

Philippos faces the outside light streaming through the doorway of the small shrine. "Here," he calls.

Kleitos ducks his head and enters. Stesidamos and Polemaios follow him in. The boys are somber.

"Skaros is still on guard?" asks Philippos, to break the silence. Kleitos nods assent. Philippos questions, "Are any others coming?"

"Yes, but not until after dark," answers Stesidamos. He leaves unsaid the danger of discovery if the Theban authorities learn that the Makedon hostages gather.

"Have you heard, Prince Philippos, that Pausanias the Exile has invaded Makedonis?" asks Polemaios.

"We think that will split us further. Some more won't come now," says Kleitos.

"I want to know what is thought within the community of hostages. Who stands by Alexandros and sees Perdikkas as his heir? Who stands by Ptolemaios? And, if the rumor be true, who stands by Pausanias?" commands Philippos. "Polemaios, you are the youngest. It should be easiest for you to ingratiate yourself among those for whom we have doubts."

Kleitos looks about at the dark shrine and the tomb of Linos. "This is a dreadful place," he comments.

"A women's place," says Stesidamos with disdain.

"The dirge's of Linos are famous. Who else played a lute with greater melancholy, Apollo excepted?" asks Philippos. "And he was an Argive, whatever they say here in Thebai. An Argive killed by Herakles. So, you see how appropriate is this tomb? Besides, no one comes here this time of year."

The ache is still within Philippos, but seeing his companions, speaking the language of home, sharing the concern for their people and land, eases the immediate pain that is so maddening to the prince.

"Have you eaten, Philippos?" asks Kleitos. Seeing Philippos shake his head, Kleitos pulls bread and cheese from the fold of his cloak.

"I'll fetch water," says Polemaios, eager to succor Philippos.

Philippos holds the bread in one hand, staring at it, uncertain whether to break his fast. Stesidamos reaches out and hugs his friend, "Eat, my prince. Let the gods give you strength for there is much ahead."

"Swear to me that you will hold true to the Temenidai. We will see my brother properly mourned, as king and kin. And we will have vengeance in time," says Philippos fiercely.

"I swear to you, Philippos," states Stesidamos solemnly.

"I swear," says Kleitos.

Philippos tears the bread, placing a piece in Stesidamos' mouth, and another in Kleitos', and a third in his own. Somehow this spontaneous act becomes a ceremony of commitment. Within Philippos is the sullen fact that he is bound to Thebai as long as the crisis continues in the north. Maybe longer. Mourning for Alexandros has begun, vengeance will have to wait.

CHAPTER EIGHT

Pelopidas
366 B.C.

α

Standing in the dark on the hillside, at the sentry line, the two men can see across the valley plain to the campfires of the opposing army. The pricks of light are in an arc that extends for at least ten *stade*. Along the river line the enemy has his outposts and pickets. Toward the coast are the Athenians and Thraikiotes; inland are the Makedones.

Iphikrates and his force had marched into view at mid-day. News of his coming had reached Pausanias two days before. Tomorrow, perhaps within an hour of dawn, Pausanias can expect Iphikrates and Ptolemaios to attack.

Pausanias turns away from the bitter sight of so many campfires. "I expected Thebai to intervene eventually, but not Athenai. At least, not so quickly," grimly states the pretender.

"So, you miscalculated. We still have strength enough to withdraw unscathed," Diodotos Kokinos is unfazed at the turn of events. True, he would much prefer a new king beholden to him for attaining the throne. Still, his men are well in hand. He has been paid. There has been some fighting and plunder: enough of the former to give an edge to his warriors, enough of the latter to make them glad to fight.

Pausanias is suddenly eager to put this failure behind him, "Proceed to withdraw. Let the *psiloi* disperse to their homes. They will be glad to leave us. You and I, with your hoplites and peltasts, will march tonight for Strepsa. We can be aboard the ships by dawn. Pray for fog so we may slip through the Athenian fleet."

When word first reached Pausanias of the Athenian ships riding the estuary to Pella's port, he was uncertain whether the reports were true or a stratagem of Ptolemaios. He had clung to hope and his army. And who knew the intentions of Iphikrates? Athenians are as dangerous to their friends as they are to their foes. Soon it became apparent that this time they or Iphikrates, at least, was supporting Ptolemaios.

No matter what the Athenian demos believe, Iphikrates is as much a mercenary as Diodotos Kokinos. Ptolemaios spends his money well. Or, if reports are true, Eurudike, who now rides armed by the side of Iphikrates and calls him brother, wooed the Athenian general's service as persuasively as she had wooed Amuntas and Ptolemaios. *The barbarous bitch stops at nothing to rule the Makedones*, thinks Pausanias savagely.

For a moment the fury at being thwarted makes thinking impossible. I am the rightful king, his thoughts scream. Followed by a whispering haunting thought, *Did not grandfather murder his way to the throne? Do not the gods smell injustice down the generations seven lengths?* He grabs Kokinos' upper arm and draws him close, "Our friends in Olunthos and Makedonis miscalculated as well. Their investment is lost this time. They can be certain, though, that the opportunity will come again for Ptolemaios cannot last. We will march again, and I will be king of my people."

Smiling sourly, Kokinos answers, "Of course, Prince Pausanias. You know you may engage me when next the opportunity arises." The words are hollow. Kokinos doubts that Olunthos would dare flaunt Athenai if she makes formal an alliance with Ptolemaios. "I must be off, Prince, if our withdrawal is to be done properly."

Releasing Kokinos, knowing the doubt the older man leaves unsaid, Pausanias looks back one last time at the campfires of the allied army. He knows he is right. Ptolemaios cannot hold the kingdom together. No, it is not Ptolemaios he need fear. If it's anyone, it's Eurudike.

β

Iphikrates belches softly, full of the celebratory meal. He hears a giggle behind the curtain. He smiles faintly in the dusky room. The Makedones have quaint customs, though he is pleased that they have sent the young dancer to him. Queen Eurudike is intent that he be served.

Running callused hands over his beard and face, Iphikrates wonders whether all the drink will preclude his performance with the dancer. Shrugging, he knows it does not matter. Tonight or morning, it will be sweet. *Great gods, these Makedones do drink*, he thinks to himself. *Barbarians, not true Hellenes, despite their pretensions.* Though that matters little to him as well, since all his career he has managed barbarians for the service of Athenai, and himself. Is he not son-in-law to the king of the Odrusai, the ruling Thraikiote tribe?

He wishes he liked Ptolemaios better. The man acts the part of a lion, but is no more than a weasel. Well, Ptolemaios has a borrowed throne and a wife who can put it to good use. Now that Olunthos and the Khalkidike know their place again, the Makedones can help Iphikrates accomplish the goal that has eluded him—the subjugation of Amphipolis. The general smiles at the thought of surpassing Timotheos and all the other great men of Athenai.

A discreet cough interrupts his musings. The curtain rustles. The dancer is wanting attention. Laughing inwardly at himself, Iphikrates thinks, *Well, let's see if anything can be done to reward the little beauty's eagerness.*

* * *

The victory over Pausanias is sweet. Especially, thinks Eurudike, the part she has played. These last twenty days she feels she is coming into her own. She commands and men obey.

Stretched out on her bed, her mind racing, she cannot sleep. The wine should have made her drowsy, but it is nothing against the exultation she feels. Her husband is subdued in her presence, bowing to her suggestions. Iphikrates follows her advice and does as she wishes. The others, like Lagos, are lapdogs. Well, not Iolaos and Antipatros, they remain as they are except more watchful.

The question is whether this ascendancy will continue. Certainly it is born of the crisis created by Pausanias, and on her ability to enlist Iphikrates in their cause. What Iphikrates will want now is help in taking Amphipolis. Ptolemaios wants to be king truly, but she will deny him. She will not let him touch Perdikkas. Philippos is safe in Thebai.

Her mind returns to Iphikrates. If Iphikrates conquers the Amphipolitans, he becomes the most important man in Athenai. As it is, few rival him—at most a dozen Athenian senior politicians and generals. The Athenians are impatient with him now for his failure last year in the Peloponnesos against the Thebans. He needs his victory over Amphipolis. The Makedones can be the key that unlocks victory.

If she gives Amphipolis to Iphikrates, what does that do to her position, to the dynamics of alliance among the nobles who allow Ptolemaios to be regent, and to the future of the Makedones in facing Athenian and Theban ambitions? Iphikrates is satisfied and goes home to Athenai to turn his victory into power. The Athenians no longer worry over the thorn Amphipolis is to their pride. Instead, they are strengthened in their self-imposed mission to make the Aegean Sea an Athenian lake. With Amphipolitan independence gone, the Makedones will have lost a sometimes ally in their dealings with Olunthos and the Khalkidike, with Athenai, and with the Thraikiotes.

Iolaos and his clan could turn against her. So, Amphipolis cannot fall. She must do what the Makedon kings have traditionally done, seem to aid the Athenians while ensuring that Amphipolis remains independent.

Somehow in providing that sham aid to Iphikrates, she must find the means to continue her power. The germ seed is in the joke itself, colluding with the magnates in creating a subterfuge that Iphikrates does not penetrate.

A concern is Ptolemaios. He is unhappy with her, that she can feel. He is too withdrawn, too silent. She needs him, though. The nobles would never agree to her holding the throne as sole regent, so Ptolemaios is necessary.

What does she feel for him? She does not know the answer to her own question. The word love is so difficult, has so many meanings. She desired him for years, wanting to be openly beside him, pursuing him, gaining him. And he, her. Why is it less than either wants? That long trail of desire and want was a curse of the fates. How she has prayed to Aphrodite and Artemis to intervene, to make into good the object of such longings. But what goddess has power compared to the spinning thread of the fates?

He arranged the murder of Alexandros, she shudders. Her own acquiescence stones her soul. She is brutal enough with herself to acknowledge that she makes a better king than did Alexandros. And in that she takes pride. Could the boy not have died honorably fighting in Thessalos? The repugnance she feels for Ptolemaios, and the sorrow at the deed, torment her. Yet she takes advantage of her son's death—and cannot feel any more virtuous than her husband. And what does virtue have to do with power, with kingship?

Her son's death. Her son, once a boy she loved enough to make the stars jealous, with whom she became estranged. As distant and cold as if he were her husband, King Amuntas, himself. Alexandros, whom she thought of as Amuntas' boy. To know, now, that she loves him still, and there is no way to make amends or to even reach into Hades to seek forgiveness.

Her thoughts come back to Ptolemaios. Strange how, despite everything, the physical passion still burns between them. She runs her hands roughly over her body, ending with one hand cupping a breast, the other smoothing the skin of her throat. Still good, she thinks. Though old, in her forties, her body is strong. Not weighted down. No mustache grown over her lips. Four children, and she competes successfully with women twenty years younger for the looks of men. The very delight she feels in these facts is mingled with a measure of self-disgust. How she feels about her body, about herself, is very much like the ambivalence she feels for Ptolemaios.

Perhaps the most important question about Ptolemaios is whether she can control him.

*   *   *

Ptolemaios paces. His relative importance among the trio who defeated Pausanias curls bitterly in the bowels of his mind. He puts a good face on it in the councils and riding to war, but he seethes. He imagines the words said between Athanaios and Agathokles, or between Iolaos and Antiokhos —*Ptolemaios rules so far as his wife directs.*

He will put up with this for now. He must. The moment will come when her high-handedness will undo her.

Iphikrates is almost as bad. He is so understanding, so accommodating, so willing to aid his foster sister in her distress—so long as it affords him the support he needs to deal with Amphipolis.

If Eurudike gives Iphikrates the means to seize Amphipolis, then their rule as regents won't last the year. Well, she's not so foolish. And with the thought comes the feeling of admiration he has always felt for her resilience and vitality. He remembers the young girl who rode so well before her father, uncle and cousin many, many years before. He loved her from that time on, wanted her for his wife instead of the woman his father had him marry. Eurudike—who but she would have wedded old Amuntas, father of grown children already, on the possibility he could end the dynastic bloodshed and create a stable reign.

Ptolemaios aches with the wish that it had been different. That the cousins had wed. That they ruled together as king and queen, legitimately chosen by the Temenidai family, the Argeadai clan, and the majority of the magnates and the citizen Makedones. That they had an accomplished son to succeed them. That the Makedones would honor them and prosper under their rule. *How life makes mockery of our ideals,* he thinks.

Well, he won't turn weak now. He is not so old. There is time yet to regain the respect of Eurudike. Time yet to overawe the nobles, and teach them to look for their leadership in him. He will dominate. If the Athenians saved him from Pausanias and the Khalkidike confederacy, then maybe the Thebans can save him from Eurudike and Iphikrates.

γ

As the two clatter up the steps of the council hall, Pammenes turns to Philippos, "Prince, I ask again that you give us as much information as you can. Since time is short, Pelopidas travels as the city's envoy with only a meager escort. He can do more than persuade by oratory. Whatever you can tell us about Ptolemaios and your mother will help."

Philippos does no more than nod. He is uncertain whether he should aid the Thebans. Despite his increasing admiration for Pammenes, what matters to him is what's good for his clan and the Makedones. Perhaps their current alliance with Athenai is for the best? What are the ambitions of Thebai in the north? Perhaps there are questions he should ask these generals.

They stride through the portico and main hall to a side chamber. Even in the full heat of summer, the chamber feels cool. Pelopidas is seated at a table, his spare frame well muscled. Beyond looms his friend, Ismenias. Pelopidas stands in welcome, "Thank you for joining us on such short notice. Please, gentlemen, be seated." He waves to a slave standing at a side door. "Refreshments," he commands.

As the slave brings in a jug of watered wine and a plate of sesame cakes, Philippos takes a seat on the bench opposite the table. He folds his arms across his chest, still uncertain of his course of action.

Pammenes, helping himself to a cake, asks, "How can we aid you, Pelopidas?"

"As you know, the burdens on our city are many. Yet the cry from the north cannot be ignored. There is not time to assemble and victual a strong force, so Ismenias and I go to Makedonis with a few companions." Left unsaid are the political arguments that filled this hall for several days. Pelopidas possesses a command because he is avid in his contention that Thebai cannot ignore the north. But the command is hollow. Those politicians who fear the dominance of Pelopidas, Epaminondas, Pammenes and their faction were strong enough to prevent a second army commanded by the faction, for Epaminondas has an army in the Peloponnesos.

Addressing Philippos, the general adds, "I must succeed in safeguarding the interests of Thebai and the Boiotian confederacy in Thessalos and Makedonis. Our interests and yours are joined, in that I go to ensure the continuation of the regency and the ultimate succession of your brother, Perdikkas. To do this, I can only rely on my friends."

Ismenias interrupts, "You can count many friends."

"True," smiles Pelopidas, "I am fortunate, may the gods be pleased. Many volunteered to ride with us. We must make haste, and so only a few select men accompany us. Yet our efforts could be wasted for lack of adequate—of current and accurate—knowledge of the situation among the Makedones."

"Well, we are practical men here," states Pammenes, "working to solve a problem. You are seeking advice from Prince Philippos. I think it only fair, despite the assurances of friendship between Thebai and the late King Alexandros, that you offer sound reasons why advising you benefits the kingdom of the Makedones."

Philippos is not fooled by Pammenes taking his part. He knows these three are close allies. Still, it is pleasing that they have the intelligence and sensitivity to recognize his concerns and to acknowledge them this way. He begins to relax, "Yes, Pelopidas, son of Hippoklos, what are the interests my family and Thebai share?"

Pelopidas turns serious. His eyes bore into Philippos. The youngster is reminded that this is the man who with six others freed Thebai from the Lakedaimons, and who led the Sacred Band at the battle of Leuktra. Pelopidas says in measured tones, "The kingdom of the Makedones is fragile due to the differences among members of your royal family. The land lies under constant threat from the Illuroi, Paiaones, and Thraikiotes. Even her civilized neighbors intervene, as does Olunthos and the Khalkidike. Traditionally, the Temenidai king has balanced in turn the demands of the south—of Athenai and Sparte. Only recently is Thebai a factor in your calculations. We check and eliminate Sparte from your concerns. The Athenians, though, are on your doorstep. Indeed, if you consider their dominance of Methone and Pudna on the coast, they are already a step across the threshold."

Pelopidas sighs gently, "We Hellenes have witnessed before how the friendship of Athenai leads states to be incorporated into the hegemonic designs of the city's citizens. What starts in good faith, ends in the tyranny of the Athenian demos." He shrugs, "What is the proverb? If you fear the robber come in the night, have your mastiff wait by the door. Thebai can be the mastiff that guards your door, Prince."

Ismenias leans in to join the argument, "In exchange, Prince, we prevent the Athenians from dominating all commerce with the Makedones. So long as you have reasonable alternatives, you gain a reasonable price for your timber and metals. We, too, gain. Horses from Thessalos and Makedonis keep our Boiotian stock strong."

Pelopidas takes up the refrain, "Is the cycle of drought and flood twelve years long? Three lush years, a meager year, three arid years, two flood years, two meager years. Whatever the cycle, husbandry is demanding. Whether it's grasshoppers or other blight, the farmer must plan for disaster. When the wind is in his favor, the rains gentle and lasting, the sun at the right time, and his crops and animals grow well, then is when he sets aside for the days when water cannot be found or when the mud is endless and everything rots." Pelopidas pauses, considers his metaphor, "Now, Thebai sits brightly in the sun. We who are responsible for her care cannot expect warm sun and gentle rain endlessly. How does a state store its good fortune? We believe we set aside for the future by assisting our friends and dividing our enemies. We would be a friend to the Makedones, knowing that there will be times ahead when we will need our friends."

Philippos shifts on his stool, "If I were going to describe the Makedones, I would say we are an ancient rock, thrust up out of the sea. Waves crash against us regularly, perpetually. Sometimes, when there is a great storm and the winds create rogue waves, we are awash—as when the Persian host marched through our lands in the days of our great-grandfathers. Sometimes mighty Zeus launches a lightening strike, and some part of the rock is cleaved—as when we war among ourselves over a bloody throne. Sometimes, though, the sea is calm. Our high rock can be seen for miles and is the host for any passing seabird or migratory fowl—as when King Arkhelaos sheltered Athenai's exiles and invited talented men from all of Hellas to enjoy his bounty." Metaphor unraveling, Philippos scowls, yet the image is clear within his mind's eye. The Makedones are that great rock standing alone surrounded by hostile elements.

Abandoning his construct, Philippos smiles, "Perhaps the picture I paint is too bleak. What people do not want their lands prosperous and their children safe—food in the belly and a fair prospect ahead? You are right, safety comes only through friendship, through alliance." Though the thought that treachery can come the same way echoes in his mind. "What would you know?"

"I know that whatever word of the Makedones reaches Thebai, whether by letter or from visitor, you learn what is said. You have established your own power over the hostages and their servants. Even those of the factions opposed to your brother and you give up their secrets to your spies. That is right in your eyes for you are a prince and have a prince's obligations." Pelopidas smiles gently, "You are an enterprising young man." He continues, "How do things stand between the regent and your mother? Who among the nobles are fully committed to Ptolemaios, who to your mother, who to your brother, Perdikkas, if distinct from your mother, and who only to themselves? Ptolemaios was the spokesman for Athenian interests when your father was king, just as Athanaios was his agent to us at Thebai. Does that make Ptolemaios irretrievably committed to Athenai, like the exile Argaios? Judge the regent for me if you would."

Philippos looks away from the compelling eyes of Pelopidas. He is surprised at feeling desire for the man. How like a lodestone must Pelopidas have been in his youth. His thoughts turn from the general to his own family and lands. *Judge Ptolemaios. Gladly. As guilty as were the killers of King Arkhelaos,* thinks Philippos. *I would execute him slowly and scatter his ashes on the wind over an enemy's lands where the curse of Ptolemaios' being could poison the soil.* "Ptolemaios is vanity. Not like some fop in clinging clothes or jewelled skin. In his soul. He knows few doubts. The very certainty of his righteousness feeds immense frustration and anger that others do not see as readily as he his overwhelming worth. Know that he is cunning and ruthless, not easily fooled when someone seeks advantage from his weaknesses, even his vanity. Flattery is not a path since his certainty makes flattery a matter of indifference."

"His only vulnerability is mother. Men ask if the gods take a direct hand in our affairs as they did in the days of Agamemnon and Akhilles. I can explain in no other way the love between my mother and Ptolemaios. Some lovers are blind to one another's faults. Not mother and Ptolemaios —they see each other clearly yet still must love what they see. How else can I explain my mother loving the murderer of my brother?" The bitterness within Philippos is abiding.

"Perhaps what I have said of Ptolemaios' vanity applies as readily to my mother, Queen Eurudike. She believes she would be a better king than was my father or my brother, and probably, better than is Ptolemaios as regent, were she only a man. She wants to be the first woman to rule the Makedones." He pauses, trying to assess his feelings over his mother. Is she a harpy flying over the land? Deep inside he aches, wishing he could love her better. Knowing there is much worthwhile in her. "I believe the key for you, Pelopidas, is the unnatural ascendance of my mother through the help of Iphikrates. Ptolemaios must resent this. Nor can all the other proud magnates be ready to follow her lead. They may have enjoyed her tweaking the nose of Ptolemaios, but no more than that. Ptolemaios will seek to redress the balance, and most will be sympathetic, ready to see mother reduced to a proper role. Of course, Ptolemaios will overplay his hand, striving to be foremost in all their eyes."

Pelopidas taps a finger against his forehead, "Much as I have guessed. What of the nobles, where does each stand?"

"If you look to the lowlands only, there are some seventy men who hold significant lands and power. They are a conservative group as a whole. Some have lineages as long as my family's. Although the people feel reverence for the Temenidai as the family chosen by Zeus to lead the Makedones that does not mean they blindly follow the senior member of the family. To be king, you must be a Temenidai of the Argeadai and you must win the trust of the people. Though it is the citizens who acclaim, do not discount the womenfolk as a voice at the hearth which the king must reckon. Among the high families, trust of the king is requisite if they will support him. Though the Temenidai corporately have the respect of the nobles, the one elected king is the one Temenidai who secures the greatest strength in support among the nobles. The key to this, in normal times, are the faction leaders, like Iolaos. The lesser nobles usually follow the lead of these great magnates. Together they determine who is the candidate for kingship. When notables present the kingly candidate to the army and veterans, they either affirm or deny the candidate his kingship."

"You could be describing the Molossi in Epeiros or any other Hellenic tribe ruled by kings," comments Ismenias.

"Perhaps," answers Philippos cryptically. "I suggest that you ought never make the mistake of thinking all the Hellenic tribes are alike and that all are inferior in power or politics to city-states like Thebai." He purses his lips, considering, "From time immemorial the Makedones have stood between the barbarian peoples of the north and the Hellenic tribes and states. You, Athenai, and Sparte, and other proud cities like Korinthos and Argos, may think yourselves the spearheads of our civilization. Never forget, that we Makedones east of the Pindos mountains, and the Molossi to the west, are the shields."

Pammenes intervenes, "No need to bristle, Prince. I think Ismenias simply was seeking more detail."

"Yes," asks Pelopidas, "let's take each of the great nobles, one by one, and think through how they must feel about the events of the past year. Let's ask ourselves why they agreed to the regency of Ptolemaios. Let's explore their motives. Ismenias, in this debate, I wish you to take the opposite stand from Prince Philippos. Challenge his reasoning. Pammenes, I want you to support each statement the prince makes by adding other reasons that agree with his arguments. I will reserve to myself the role of questioner. Prince Philippos shall have the role of presenting the primary thesis for each noble. Shall we begin with Iolaos? ..."

δ

Pacing back and forth along the upper verandah over the courtyard, Philippos is in turmoil. He wraps his cloak tightly around himself. For more than a month, he has lacerated his spirit, despising the weakness in himself that allowed him to be seduced into opening his thoughts to Pelopidas on all his family and connections at home. How could he be so silly, so girlish? Flattered into sharing his counsel with the great Theban, he had said far too much.

His behavior since has not been a credit to him either. Out of sorts, he is surly with Pammenes, with Kerkidas, with the boys, even with Skaros. The young children of the household have begun to avoid him. And in this time he's taken four different men as lovers, one each *dekades* of a month. Burying himself in sensation so that he has started to disgust Kleitos and Polemaios. Each of the men "honored" by his favor are as startled as he feels by the suddenness of his attentions. He does not understand this driving need to fondle and be fondled. Add to that the drinking, as if wine were a river he must swim across.

Now he can hardly abide himself.

On waking late today, he had escaped the house before others knew he was up. All he wanted to do was walk. And so he had, for hours, through the city, out the gate, far into the countryside. He had gone further south of the city than he had ever been before. Until the gathering storm had so darkened the path that he abruptly turned about and began the long walk back.

Well before he reached the city gate the rains drenched him. At one point, he stopped walking, looked up to the heavens, water streaming down his face, and thanked Zeus for waking him to his shame.

Slowly, then, he returned to Pammenes' house. Skaros, for one, was glad to see him, worried over what had become of him. Who was shivering more, Philippos in his wet clothing or Skaros in his fright for his prince?

A quiet evening followed. A light supper, some non-consequential talk with Skaros. Not a direct apology to the man, but Skaros knew his master well enough to realize that this bad time was done. Philippos recognized now that his moods and abandon had been hard on Skaros. The servant's color was off and his appetite meager. For once, Philippos helped Skaros to bed. Suddenly, the always robust Skaros seemed old and fragile.

Out on the verandah, the night is clear. The stars fill the heavens with a tracery of light. Philippos stops his pacing, leans well out on the rail and gazes up into the night sky. A prayer to rough strong Herakles does not seem enough for such a clean night. If he is to cleanse his soul and make amends for these past many days and the misery of his betrayal to Pelopidas, he must direct himself to the power above who can forgive him his guilt. Though Zeus has shown him his errors, it is to Hera he asks for love. Not Hera as mother—though mother's love is something most people want—but to Hera as the epitome of understanding for human failure. Mothers, traditionally, forgive and love whether they understand their children or not. How can that be good enough? The forgiveness Philippos seeks must know him at his worst as well as his best. Though his thoughts go to Hera, the image forming in his mind is of Lady Kleopatra. The ancient, practical, wise realist—perhaps the person he most admires, most loves, most misses.

*　　*　　*

Morning brings no relief to Skaros. Instead the fever gains a stronger grip on him. His skin is hot and dry to Philippos' touch. "I will bring you water, Skaros," the prince promises.

Hurrying down the stairs to the well, it occurs to Philippos that this past month he has heard others mention this person or that person ill. They say the fevers burn bright until the person is consumed and turns to ash. Not Skaros, surely. Always Skaros is the strong companion, bearing whatever load of burden or vexation Philippos heaps on the good man's shoulders, and sharing whatever lightness of laughter or well-being Philippos encounters. No, fall to illness? Not Skaros, certainly not Skaros.

Back in the darkened room, Philippos kneels and holds Skaros' head up so the man can drink. Philippos whispers, "Pammenes promises that the physician will see you as soon as he is done seeing to Perrinna and two of the children. Simmias is a great healer, Skaros. He is a wise man often sought for his counsel." There is no acknowledgment from Skaros.

Alternately through the day Philippos paces or bathes Skaros, trying to cool the burning fire. From time to time, Philippos makes the trip to the well. The jug the prince uses is chipped at the rim, and it is decorated with the figures of Odusseos confronting the suitors. They gleam wetly when Philippos slops water from the bucket to the jug. Soon the jug is empty again, a quarter of its contents dribbled down Skaros' throat, three-quarters sponged over his body.

A knock sounds at the door. Philippos admits the physician Simmias and Pammenes. Pammenes is haggard. Simmias is intense. "How is Skaros?" asks Pammenes. The healer does not wait for a response, going immediately to the task of examining the fevered man.

Philippos has the presence of mind to ask after the others who are ill. "We've lost one, the other two continue to struggle. We think Pamesias is coming down with it," answers Pammenes. The older man is weary and resigned. "You may not be old enough to remember past epidemics. For a year or so, then after a break, for another year or two, the land is swept. This happens maybe every twenty years or so. Maybe the gods winnow their human crop. Usually it's the young and old that are taken. Some years it's the coughing illness, other years, something else. Now it's fevers so fierce that ..." he breaks off his monologue, embarrassed.

Completing his examination, Simmias rises. The gaunt old man is grim-faced, "Too far along. There's little more that can be done. Continue as you are doing, Prince. Help him rest easy. Talk to him, keep him interested in living.

169

He will either rally some time tonight or he will die." Seeing the fear in Philippos, the physician adds, "I'm sorry. I must attend Pamesias. If I intervene in the early stages, I can sometimes help. There is nothing I can do here."

Philippos continues his rounds—bathing Skaros, forcing the semiconscious man to drink, and descending the stairs to get water. All the time he is with Skaros he talks quietly, mostly of his own boyhood and of all that they have shared. He tries singing songs Skaros' taught him. He feels like weeping. Each time he drags the water up from the well, he says prayers to Apollo and Asklepios. Apollo knows, though, that Philippos is not his admirer. Philippos even tries praying to some of Skaros' outlandish Thraikiote gods. The young prince can hear their mocking laughter at his fumbling ritual.

Late, how late Philippos does not know, Skaros begins keening softly. After a time Philippos can make out words, slurring, disappearing, resurfacing, whispering as they sing-song along. Sounds like a childhood tune. Philippos is crying as he listens, his ear close to Skaros' lips, his sponge smoothing Skaros' hip. The song or songs end, muttering replacing the thin tune. Maybe an incantation, maybe Skaros is praying to his gods. Skaros moans, turns over, and his eyes open to Philippos. Their faces are less than a hand's palm apart. Skaros smiles and whispers dryly, "My prince, you are afraid? Don't be. We are born to die. I will miss you until we're together again." The eyes of the servant unfocus, and his spirit moves on.

For a while longer, for some small piece of eternity, Skaros' body breathes shallowly. No more muttering, no more sighing songs, no more moans, only the small fluttering breaths, that hesitate, then flow. For that time Philippos can scarcely breathe himself for the hope that moment of lucidity in Skaros gave the prince. In the end, though, Skaros' body lies unmoving, cold. The fever is gone with the death of the man.

Here is your sacrifice, Apollo, rages Philippos as he smashes the water jug against the post of the door. Later, huddling in the corner, Philippos tries with all his might to recall the proper funeral ceremonies for a Thraikiote of Skaros' tribe and standing. From within this sorrow, a determination grows. Sobered in spirit, this past twenty-four hours have erased within Philippos the wasteful self-pity of the past month or more, he stands and is again a prince of the Makedones as Lady Kleopatra would expect him to be.

ε

The robe is beautiful—the weaving so fine, the colors full and rich, the cloth both soft and strong. Held in the hands of the merchant, Assurrkos, the robe seems to say the man who wears me is a man of wealth, of honor, of power. Ptolemaios cannot resist the robe. Still, he asks, "Could you fashion fur trim along the neck edge? Something deep black, like the tip of a stoat's tail? And what do you have as a pin? Gold certainly, but I want fine work."

Assurrkos smiles and in his curiously accented speech says, "Let my assistant show you. We have many styles and sizes. The workmanship is excellent in all. Would you have the style of Skuthos or Aigyptos, Phoenikis or Ephesos? I have others as well." He waves his hands to his servant who spreads a dark cloth on the floor. As he unwraps the cloth, a dozen or more pins and fibulas gleam on the cloth's field.

"Or, you may want to consider this pin," Assurrkos holds in his hand a moderate-sized brooch of a lion-faced sun, its eyes picked out with small gems of brilliant blue. Lapis lazuli—the Persian stone—has long been favored by Ptolemaios. A fact known to Assurrkos from past dealings.

At the sight of the brooch, Ptolemaios begins chuckling, "Ah, Assurrkos, you know me too well. Why do I bother myself when you could decide for me? All right, the robe, the pin, all of the items you recommended."

"Certainly, sir. As you desire, majesty," the merchant bows deeply.

Ptolemaios waves his hands and walks away, "Speak to my steward, he will pay you. Other matters call my attention." Striding now, he calls to the guard-officer at the door, "Serapion, are the scribes waiting?"

"Yes, Lord Ptolemaios." The officer hesitates, then adds, "The queen's maid brought a request from Lady Eurudike that you meet her before dictating the summons for the council."

Ptolemaios scowls, "She is stubborn, is she not, Serapion?"

"Sire," the officer bows his head.

"Accompany me to the queen's chamber," growls the regent.

The two men walk in silence to the opposite wing of the palace, the officer a step behind the regent. Retainers and servants bow their heads as the regent passes by along the corridors. He greets none of them. At the queen's door, Ptolemaios waves Serapion forward, "Announce me to the queen." With his officer before him, the visit becomes official.

Serapion knocks smartly on the door. A serving woman opens it and bows low at the sight of Ptolemaios. Serapion calls out, "Lord Ptolemaios is here. Prepare the way for his presence."

"Well, come in, come in. What are we here, satraps of Persia?" Eurudike's sarcasm mocks the announcement formula.

Ptolemaios enters the bright-lit hall, with its south facing windows. From his somber rooms to this colorful chamber alive with women and their activities is a contrast. Spindles and looms fill the length of one wall. Eurudike sits where she can supervise the work of many ladies and servants. Here a pair are weighing wool. There several are carding. Others spin, and yet others dye the yarn in large clay pots. The most skillful ladies weave. Everywhere he looks, Ptolemaios sees the queen's industry. He ignores them all, except the queen, "You asked to speak to me, Eurudike."

"Yes, as you were filling your time with the fripperies offered by

Assurrkos, I knew you have no duties so urgent as to preclude seeing me."

Warily, Ptolemaios raises his hand in acknowledgment, "Let us not spar, when we could argue about something of substance."

The admission invokes a genuine laugh from Eurudike, "I do enjoy it so when you are willing to be real." She claps her hands abruptly and waves all of her companions out of the room. With murmurs and lingering glances they depart to other rooms of the suite. Eurudike waits.

Ptolemaios turns to Serapion, "Stand outside the door and see that we're not disturbed. Send a runner to inform my steward and the scribes that I am delayed." Bowing, Serapion closes the door behind him.

Ptolemaios crosses to a second chair and hauls it close to Eurudike. Leaning forward he kisses her lightly on the forehead, before sitting, "Well, wife, what is it you want to say before I summon the full council?"

"So you intend to go through with it? Take the offer of Pelopidas and betray Iphikrates?"

The regent stares at his wife, the queen, before answering. His look searches her face, "You just said that you prefer it when I'm real. Well, we have been unreal with each other too long. You secured us the aid of Iphikrates. With his aid, we ended the threat from Pausanias. All good." He grimaces, "You and I both know that the price wanted by Iphikrates for his help is too much. We cannot give Amphipolis to Iphikrates, to Athenai. You would temporize and stall. Well, you overestimate your charm. Iphikrates will not be toyed with. You know the man, probably better than I do. He has only two passions, his ambitions for himself and his ambitions for his city. I think it well if you continue publicly as his friend. Let me take the onus for siding with Pelopidas and Thebai. But let's not pretend between us. There is no choice in the matter. We need the support of Thebai, and they are no long-term threat to us like Athenai." Ptolemaios reaches a hand out and Eurudike accepts it in hers.

"Did you have Alexandros killed?"

The shift of subject is truly no shift, as Ptolemaios knows. The death of her son is the principal barrier between them. He decides not to lie, "I helped create the conditions that led Apollophanes to strike. I could have warned Alexandros, but did not. Perhaps I could have stayed Apollophanes, but I did not. The laxity of Alexandros' security is his own responsibility. I believe if not Apollophanes, someone else would eventually have killed your son. A weak king attracts contempt. I wanted the kingship, which could only come to me through Alexandros' death. I am not sorry that Alexandros the king is dead, though I am sorry that he was your son and that you are grieved."

She nods her recognition that he is being truthful.

He ventures more, "I believed, perhaps mistakenly, that some part of you knew what was necessary and expected my willingness to accept the benefit of his death."

She looks away, a single tear glistening her cheek. Softly, hoarsely, she says, "It's past. It cannot be undone. I was wrong in opposing his kingship. I had hoped there was a way that would see him deposed or abdicating."

"Unless he fled in time, any combination of men who forced his removal would see him blinded, at least." Ptolemaios sits back, "I believe if Alexandros were still with us, you would find him as intolerably arrogant and foolish now as then."

"So I should continue to favor Iphikrates and express distress to him at your actions and loyalty to you as responsible for the kingship." Her mind is clear again.

"That would do nicely, dear. And for my part, I will publicly embrace General Pelopidas. I will summon the full council, wearing my fripperies from Assurrkos and looking regal, and assert the continuing independence of the Makedones while re-affirming our abiding friendship with Thebai and the Boiotian federation."

"What further hostages will Pelopidas take south with him?"

"Philoxenos for one, my son will finally be of use to the kingdom," says Ptolemaios dryly. "Pelopidas will leave the bulk of his small force with us. The loss of hostages and the presence of even a few Theban hoplites should cloud the extent to which I am coerced into cooperating with Thebai. A little doubt in Iphikrates' mind about this new alliance should help."

They become silent. Husband looking to wife, wife to husband. They continue to hold hands.

Finally, he leans forward again and kisses her softly on the lips, "I must go. I do have duties, no matter what you think."

She smiles gently, "Of course you do, as do I. Come to me tonight, Ptolemaios."

"I will, dear Eurudike."

ζ

The forests of the Makedones rise tall and dark all around the small party of horsemen and baggage carts. The rough road disappears from sight, as it wends through the trees, no more than seventy paces further on. Ismenias touches the flanks of his gray mare and trots forward to catch up with Pelopidas. Pelopidas turns in his saddle at the clatter of the swift moving hooves. "Great place for an ambush," bellows Ismenias.

"We have outriders ahead," answers Pelopidas. "I doubt there is danger to us between here and Larissa. Enjoy the beauty of the way, Ismenias."

"You split our party into three parts, and we were no great number to begin with. How do you expect me to find joy in that?"

"I know you're uneasy, my friend. Leaving Thumokhares and sixty men at Pella was necessary to give substance to our alliance. True, we could have traveled with the hostages and their escort if we were willing to dally at their slow pace. I doubt if their numbers would add materially to our safety. We are best relying on speed for safety. For once Ismenias, you will be a hare, not a lion."

"I know your reasoning," grimaces Ismenias. "If we're going to rely on speed, we'd be better off with pack mules instead of carts."

Pelopidas nods agreement, knowing that Ismenias' worries are well enough founded. "We exchange these carts for mules at Larissa. The Aleuadai will accommodate us. If you prefer, we could sidestep and go by way of Elimiotis. Derdas would also aid us."

"Bah, you're right, Pelopidas. Our only real concern is in south Thessalos. Alexandros of Pherai would love to cause you grief. We're all right, for now. No side trips to barbarian chiefdoms, let's go directly to Larissa. You might dispatch several riders ahead to make arrangements with the Aleuadai so the transfer is speedy. Lingering in Larissa could see word of our travel reach Pherai."

"We're moving steadily. In Larissa there will be a feast and discreet discussions with Medeios and his family. There will be time enough to make arrangements. We will let them do us a favor. It's far easier to bind someone you who does you a favor than to bind him that you do a favor for."

"That was not the policy you followed with Ptolemaios," comments Ismenias.

"You're right. There we relied on mutual back scratching," laughs Pelopidas.

Ismenias smiles, "He did seem eager. Young Philippos was right."

"That boy is smart. He called it right with the regent, his mother, and every notable we needed." Pelopidas considers, "The question is, do we let the boy return to his people? Is it better for Thebai if he remains with us?"

"Well, you needn't be concerned for now. Ptolemaios made it clear he doesn't want the boy back."

"Eurudike watches over Perdikkas like a she-bear with a cub. Ptolemaios will meet his future there, long before Philippos is a threat to him," says Pelopidas, thinking aloud.

"These Makedon kinglets do like to kill each other."

"Yes, but look at these forests, Ismenias. Every fifth tree could be the mast of a ship. Add to that the horses, the silver, the grain—there is great wealth here. Be glad they kill each other. If they didn't, they might be killing us." Then Pelopidas laughs again, "I'm glad the future is in the hands of the fates. For all that we plot and scheme, we should know the limits of our abilities."

The two ride side by side. The forest can seem silent, dark and forbidding. For these city-bred men, the forest is wealth only. Denying ship masts to Athenai is deeply satisfying.

η

Thebai is not as volatile politically as many of the city-states. For more than a dozen years now, its governing has been firmly in the hands of the seven men and their friends who freed Thebai from its Spartan garrison. Many of those in the city who had supported the Spartans and Lakonians back then were slain at the time of the restoration. Yet, fewer were slain or exiled at Thebai than would have been the case in like circumstances in Argos, Athenai, Eretria, Korinthos, Megara, Olunthos, Sikyon, or any other city or federation.

Yet politics and faction appear even in a city ruled by a stable oligarchy. The seven saviors became six at the death of their leader. They age. Differences of opinion arise.

For now three men largely direct the power of Thebai, due to the working agreement they have made together. These three are Pelopidas, Epaminondas, and Pammenes.

The task of Pelopidas is to manage Thebai's northern and eastern interests. While Athenai looms extra large in these considerations, Thessalos is taken very seriously, too. Beyond Thessalos, the north is seen mostly as a part of Athenian concerns since the North Aegean is the roadstead to her food supply.

Epaminondas manages the southern and western interests—primarily the Peloponnesos, especially Sparte and her allies. Keeping the Arkadians and Messenians in harness against Sparte is crucial. Occasionally, Epaminondas has time for the west, for Phokis, Aitolia, Akarnania, and Epeiros.

Pammenes has the hardest task, in some ways. His is primarily a political role. He holds the center, the factional maelstrom of Thebai herself and the confederacy of Boiotian cities.

Political opponents exist and are concerted in their efforts to diminish the influence of the trio. Other than for that one purpose, their opponents lack unity. The citizenry are landowners of independent mind who generally follow the trio's lead in foreign affairs but as often side with various opponents on issues involving solely the city or confederacy. The trio agree that too often the citizens look to their own short-term advantages rather than the long-term security and prosperity of the city. To retain their influence, the trio must temper their requirements to a narrow, winding path through the thicket of their fellow citizens' often emotional, sometimes trivial, demands. Neither Pelopidas nor Epaminondas envies Pammenes his role.

Still, to the population at large in Thebai, the three are heroes. Others of their companions, like Ismenias, rank with them in the eyes of people. So the news of the capture of Pelopidas and Ismenias by Alexandros of Pherai is a lightning bolt striking to the heart of the city's politics and to the spirit of the people's affections. The immediate expedition sent north to rescue the pair is more enthusiastic than well advised. Its defeat and failure does nothing to daunt the resolve of the citizenry.

Instead, a determined Thebai recalls Epaminondas, its foremost general, to lead a second relief army. The time is taken to organize an army appointed with experienced officers and file leaders, and largely made up of veterans. This army epitomizes the modern war making capability of an Hellenic state. Even the mercenaries employed by Alexandros of Pherai cannot prevail against the full strength of an aroused Thebai and Boiotia.

While Epaminondas concentrates on honing the true strength of an army, its discipline not its swords, Pammenes initiates correspondence with Alexandros to determine what the tyrant wants. Though sharp spear points and polished shields give grim delight to the Theban people, for they like vengeance, Epaminondas and Pammenes do not want a fight. All these warlike preparations are necessary, but their sole use would likely mean failure. Pelopidas and Ismenias are needed alive, not revenged. The two leaders put their faith in private negotiations to free the pair. Punishment of Pherai will come only if Pelopidas and Ismenias are harmed.

Philippos, seeing and hearing the two great men, is excited and intrigued. The frequent visitors to the house of Pammenes, coupled with the real urgency of the crisis, make Philippos feel he is at the center of events. Pammenes willingly includes Philippos in the talks, as part of his tutoring the boy in real politics and as a tonic for the boy's grief over Skaros. The prince realizes that here he is gaining an education that complements what he learned at his father's court and at Lady Kleopatra's knee.

This afternoon, Philippos and Cricket—who now insists on being called by his name, Pammenes, though designated *Neos* or younger—are copying the letters to be sent to Theban agents in several Thessaliote cities. Scribes could do the task, except for the confidential content. By entrusting the boys, no one from outside the household need be involved. Each is down to his last letter.

"Philippos, have you been to Pharsalos?" asks Pammenes *Neos*.

"Briefly. We marched through the city when I came south. The city fathers had us camp fifteen *stade* further along the road. Pelopidas and the senior men dined in the city that night."

"This letter goes to a man whose name seems more Asian than Hellenic. Are there a lot of Asians in Pharsalos? Lydians, Karians, or people from further east?"

"No, the people seemed the usual Thessaliote mix, at least where we passed through. We didn't go through the *agora*, maybe there's a merchant enclave from the Persian lands."

"Praise Nebbos," exclaims Pammenes *Neos*.

"What is it?" asks Philippos looking up from his scroll. Already the young Pammenes is blotting his work.

"I spilled the ink."

"How bad is it?"

"I think it'll be all right if I scrape the area with a blade. I'm not starting over."

"Who is Nebbos?" asks Philippos.

"He brought writing to Thebai. He was a companion of Kadmos, of course, and came from the east. Everyone knows the story here. Of course, only the literate call on Nebbos." Pammenes *Neos* looks sharply at Philippos, "I suppose you Makedones have never heard of Nebbos. Who brought writing to your people, who do you honor?"

"That depends. Some who live in Pella and the ports honor Sesat. She's an imported goddess. In the country and in the older cities they honor Apollo, and attribute writing to his inspiration. Still others, mostly the mountain Makedones and neighboring highlanders say it was Daidalos who brought writing to men. Different stories depending on where you're from."

"What do you think?"

"I haven't given it much thought. I suppose we must look to Apollo ultimately. Who he inspired or how many he inspired to introduce writing to men would be hard to say. Probably there were different people in different lands who received his favor."

Pammenes *Neos* considers the idea, "That sounds reasonable. There are different forms of writing." He shrugs, "Anyway, here in Thebai, we know it was Nebbos."

"I'm done," announces Philippos. He stretches his fingers, "My hand was cramping. Worse than holding a sword or spear, don't you think?"

"I need a bit more time."

"Have you thought about what we're copying?" asks Philippos, picking up the short scroll.

"Yes, I doubt our agents will be successful in persuading their cities to aid us against Pherai."

"I'm not so sure your father or Epaminondas expect that." Philippos smooths the scroll with his fingers, "It's enough if Alexandros of Pherai understands how isolated he can become if he continues to oppose Thebai."

"Your family has agents in all the Thessaliote cities, don't they?"

Philippos laughs, "More likely every member of the family and every senior magnate or clan head has agents in those cities."

"Do you?" asks young Pammenes pointedly.

"Not on my allowance, but my brother Perdikkas certainly does. Since my brother and I act together in all things, then I guess I have agents there, too."

"Could your brother's agents help ours?"

The deep voice of the elder Pammenes comments, as he enters the room, "Good question, son. How are you two doing? Done with the dispatches?"

"Just now, father," answers the boy.

"So Philippos, do you think we can persuade Alexandros to give up Pelopidas?" asks the man.

"Absolutely, sir. The only real question is what you will have to give in return."

The older Pammenes stares at Philippos and weighs his response, "You're right, of course. When Athenai sent Autokles and his army to support Pherai that changed the game. Now is not the time for war with Athenai. We have too much to do yet in the Peloponnesos. Epaminondas suggests we could clip Athenai's wings by becoming a sea power as well as a land power."

"How will your Boiotian confederates view such a move?" asks Philippos gravely.

Pursing his lips, Pammenes *Palios* says, "So you are aware of restlessness in the League."

"The point was raised at dinner the other night."

"So it was, so it was," Pammenes sighs. "How does a city protect itself and prosper without impinging on its neighbors? Our population grows, and so our needs grow. Always there is contention. If Boiotia fails, it won't be for lack of effort by Thebai. What do we do with cities like Orkhomenos, Plataia, and Thespiai who refuse to ally? From Tanagra, Lebadia, Koronia, Kopai and the smaller towns we receive loyal support. Not from those three proud cities. They would rival us if they could, even though it's been evident for generations that Thebai is the pre-eminent city of Boiotia. And yet I understand their fears. Who would stand by and watch his city decline without struggling to reverse its fate?"

Philippos adds, "The Persian king sought a Common Peace in all of Hellas, using Sparte as his hammer. You and your friends did not accept Thebai being overshadowed by Sparte."

"Strange isn't it, how Persia wants peace here so it can hire our mercenaries to be the iron in their own armies," comments Pammenes *Palios*. "Perhaps if Sparte had been content to allow others to prosper, a Common Peace would have been accepted. Sparte's ethos has always been too narrow for any state save Sparte."

"Here are the letters, father," says Pammenes *Neos*, handing him the stack.

The general looks through the stack briefly, "You've been exact, you've done well." He looks up, smiling affectionately at his boy and Philippos, "Come, let's take refreshment. Some of the council members are due here shortly. We'll get these letters off to the riders once Epaminondas adds his seal. He's waiting in the *andron*."

He claps an arm around his son and beckons Philippos, "So, Prince, what do you think will be the price Pherai sets for the return of Pelopidas?"

"Alexandros of Pherai wants a free hand in Thessalos."

"A stiff price, for can Boiotia permit a strong Thessalos?" The eyes that look at Philippos are intent and intelligent. "If we agreed to stay out of Alexandros' way, do you think Ptolemaios would be willing to be our catspaw in Thessalos?"

Softly, Philippos states, "You have already proven that the Regent Ptolemaios will act on your behalf. You may be the sole prop to his position. Only don't trust him to extend himself beyond what works to his own accord."

CHAPTER NINE

Homecoming

365 B.C.

α

Daily life in the household of Pammenes settles back into routine in the months that follow the return of Pelopidas from Pherai. For Philippos that means lessons from Kerkidas, athletics at the gymnasium, confidential meetings with his fellow hostages, and occasional evening conversations on war and diplomacy with Pammenes. He is past grieving for Skaros. Somehow he is stronger emotionally. A fact noted by Pammenes *Palios*. The period of abandon is past and, for now, Philippos has ceased his sexual aggression. That is not to say Philippos is happy in his exile, but he is patient.

Today, on rising, Philippos finds himself whistling, pleased to feel the heat of the new day. He is hungry for the hot flat loaves of morning bread and the accompanying figs and cheese. He is up well ahead of Pammenes *Neos*. The slave who has been providing for both boys since Skaros' death brings in a fresh tunic.

With quick decision, Philippos holds out a large silver coin to the man, "Phrunis, accept this with my thanks. You have been doing double duty for some time now. From today, it will not be necessary. The slave market is being held today and I will purchase a body servant. I would appreciate your helping the newcomer by instructing him in the ways of the household once he's here."

Phrunis bows, "Certainly, Prince Philippos." Setting the folded tunic on the bed, he continues, "I hope my service to you has been satisfactory."

"Of course, Phrunis, and I will assure your master of the same. As a prince of the Makedones, I should have my own staff. A recent dispatch from home provides the coins to make that possible again." Splashing a bit of water on his face from the bowl, Philippos dries himself quickly with the towel handed to him by Phrunis. As quickly, Philippos throws on the tunic, belts it, and grabs up his sandals, "Is the day as good as it seems, Phrunis?"

"Why any day without trouble is a good day, sir. I do think it will be quite hot later." Pausing on his way to the door, Phrunis adds, "You may want to get to the slave market right after your lessons. The best often go quickly."

Mumbling a swift prayer to the images of Zeus and Herakles in the corner, Philippos hurries out the door in search of breakfast. If he gets there before Pammenes *Neos* and Pamesias, the cook will give him an extra wedge of cheese.

* * *

Pammenes *Neos*, Kratulos, and Pindaros Milao accompany Philippos to the slave market. The boys are at that age when they are sometimes treated as adults and sometimes as overgrown children. In truth, they can be either. The question they debate as they walk to the market is whether Philippos can make a valid purchase without Pammenes *Palios*.

"Father is responsible for you. He stands in place of your parents as your guardian here in Thebai. You cannot act without his consent," insists Pammenes *Neos*.

"Philippos is not Theban. Who knows what customs they follow in the north. For all we know, there he could buy a whole tribe if he had the money," answers Kratulos.

Philippos comments with mock severity, "For a whole tribe, it's not a question of money. It comes down to having enough armed men."

"We are not in the north," states Pammenes flatly.

"Still," interjects Pindaros, "everyone knows Prince Philippos. He's not any scion of a Theban family. He may be able to do what we cannot."

Stubbornly, Pammenes says, "The slavers will not accept his money. Father must be present."

"He can buy fruit or sausage without your father. He can gift a temple without your father. He could buy a horse without your father," taunts Kratulos.

"We are here," says Philippos mildly. "Pammenes *Neos*. I will purchase my slave on the approval of your father. Believe me, the slave masters will accept my money."

The slave market is crowded today. They edge through the avid throng until they reach a good vantagepoint on the steps of an old temple. In the center of the market is a wooden platform on which the slaves currently being auctioned are paraded. Around the rear perimeter are cloth-shaded enclosures where additional slaves sit. There prospective buyers examine them. Occasionally a private purchase occurs at the enclosures.

A dozen or so slavers are augmented by their overseers, slave handlers, and guards are selling from a handful to several score slaves apiece. Perhaps as many as a thousand buyers and onlookers mill about the market—talking, eating, bidding, comparing views on the slave flesh, exchanging news, appraising particular slaves. The hubbub is loud, though not as loud as the auctioneer. He is another Stentor, his loud high-pitched voice cutting through the noise, like the Hellenic herald at Troy.

The boys stretch to better see the slaves. A fat man also standing on the steps leans their way and asks, "You there. Are you here to see the girls? If that's all you want, you should be gone. Your families would not approve your being here."

"No, sir. Our companion is buying a slave today," replies Pindaros Milao, indicating Philippos.

"Not without a man to represent him, he isn't," states the fat fellow. Then considering, he adds, "I could make your purchase for you for a small commission."

"He is making the purchase contingent on my father's approval. My father is Pammenes," says the son proudly.

"I thought I recognized you," comments the fat man. "Your friend should speak to the dealers before he bids, otherwise the auctioneer won't acknowledge him."

"Thank you for your suggestion," responds Philippos.

The boys enter the crowd and snake their way to the enclosures. There Philippos introduces himself to each dealer and asks the provenance of the slaves being offered for sale. Some are local stock representing the regular turnover occurring among the estates of Thebai and central Boiotia. The excitement today, though, is over two assemblages of slaves. One group is from the north, mostly Thraikiotes, with a sprinkling of Illuroi, Skuthos, and more distant people. The other group is from the west—Sikuloi, Sikanoi, Italiotes, and even exotic peoples from the markets of Aigyptos. Slaves such as these are rare in Thebai. More often they would be sold in Athenai's port of Piraios, or in Patrai, Korinthos, Delos, or at the mercenary mart on Kythera.

Philippos speaks what he knows of Skaros' dialect, trying to see if others of that worthy's tribe are for sale. The sound of the language causes such nostalgia in Philippos that he desists. Eyeing the many slaves, Philippos spots several that look promising. He points to a youth and asks the dealer if he might look more closely to determine the state of the young man's health. The dealer waves the youth over and provides a guard to assure docility.

"I don't think you should buy anyone so young," says Pammenes. "You should have a mature valet. Someone used to our ways. Why look at these wild slaves? Most will end up working the land. Consider the slaves raised in good homes here in Thebai."

"Pammenes *Neos*, I will not be staying in Thebai. I will need a man who can live readily in the north, who knows the rigors of the hunt and the raid. Our winters are more bitter than yours. Allow me the courtesy of knowing the type of individual I need."

Carefully Philippos probes the slave's mouth, examines eyes and ears, tests the muscles of back, legs, and arms, touches firmly the groin looking for hernias or other oddities. Finding nothing amiss, Philippos waves the man back. He continues on down the line of enclosures, picking an occasional individual to inspect. Only once does he look over a person not of the general type he is examining. The young woman caught his eye, and she must undergo the same searching investigation as the various youths. Finally done, Philippos is ready to join in the bidding.

Kratulos eagerly asks, "Who will you bid on?"

"There are a number of possibilities." Philippos nods toward a tall red-haired man he had examined, "That one, the Illuriote, is my first choice. Let's see how the bidding goes."

"Why did you pick out the girl?" asks Pammenes curiously.

Philippos smiles, "She seems different from the rest, not as sullen or resigned. I like the look of her."

"You're not considering buying her surely?" stammers Pammenes.

"Oh, probably not," sighs Philippos, already regretting the whimsy that caused him to look her over. Still, he liked the direct defiance of her eyes when he ran his hands along her legs and buttocks.

Back at their old stand on the temple steps, they wait for the slaves in which Philippos is interested to reach the auction platform. Kratulos goes off in search of something to eat. Philippos idly bids on one of the lesser possibilities, more to test the process than to seek a buy. The slave goes to a farmer from northwest Boiotia. "He'll be worked hard," is Pammenes' only comment.

Philippos comes alert as the girl he's fancied walks to the center of the platform. The bidding starts low enough. Soon it settles into a pattern of three bidders, each making cautious small increases over the prior bid. Pindaros says, "Looks like she's going to one of the brothel keepers. She'll lose her freshness soon enough."

On impulse, not wanting for her the future predicted by Pindaros, Philippos raises his hand to bid. He adds a meager increase, but his offer surprises the other bidders. The bidding quickens. The competition feels Philippos' desire for the girl. His bids become bolder. Soon it is only himself and one other man. Then even the opponent goes no higher and Philippos wins the girl.

"Good thing your buying is contingent on father or you'd be stuck with her," says Pammenes.

"No, she's mine now," says the prince haughtily.

Kratulos returns with four skewers of roast goat and enough coarse bread to feed them. The boys discover how hungry they are.

"This bread is like kollura, the bread of the Thraikiotes. Their women offer bread to their goddess of mercy," comments Philippos.

"If that girl is Thraikiote, she should be offering you bread today," says Pindaros with a grin.

Pammenes explains sourly to Kratulos, "Prince Philippos bought a girl instead of a valet."

"I heard. Some of the men at the meat vendor were laughing about it."

Philippos grunts, his mouth full. By now he is used to the gossiping of Thebans and the fact that he and his fellow hostages evoke frequent curiosity. Chewing thoughtfully, he considers for the first time what he will do with his purchase. Will Pammenes *Palios* be angry? He jingles the coins in his purse. Will there be enough for a valet, too? He stands on his feet, eyeing the platform to see who is being offered for sale now.

Kratulos suggests, "Philippos could wait until the end of the day when the remnants are sold in lots. He could end up with a tribe after all."

"Anyway, what tribe is the girl?" asks Pindaros.

Distracted Philippos answers, "She's a Paiaone—from one of the north-country subtribes, not an urban Paiaone. They live north of the river Axios between the Illuroi and the Thrakes."

The redheaded Illuriote stands in line on the platform. He should be up for sale soon. The crowd has begun to diminish, which is good. Many are off seeking food. Others have made their purchases for the day. Prices have started coming down from the early sales of the day. *Maybe there's enough money left to buy the Red*, thinks Philippos.

When bidding starts on the redhead, Philippos waits to see how it develops. A couple or three farmers are bidding, not a lot of interest. Not many want the effort in breaking a northerner's will. Philippos enters the bidding. Immediately the man who Philippos bested in acquiring the girl starts bidding. The brothelkeeper doesn't even bother looking at the red-head. He stares across the marketplace at Philippos.

"Looks like you offended Drupetis," says Pammenes. "He's a distasteful man. His money supports political opponents of father."

Grimly Philippos continues bidding. He knows he's lost if Drupetis is determined. Doubtless the brothelkeeper can better afford the slave, espe-cially after Philippos' purchase of the Paiaone girl. Still, the redhead will go as dear to Drupetis as Philippos can make it. Within a half-dozen more bids, Philippos can go no further.

Drupetis tops the boy's bid. There is silence. The crowd and auction-eer wait on Philippos. The prince hates his defeat and looks away.

Then Pammenes whispers, "Keep bidding, I will back you. You can owe me."

Philippos looks into Pammenes' eyes. The boy smiles encouragement. With renewed purpose, Philippos makes a strong bid. After another four exchanges, Drupetis drops out disgustedly. Philippos has his redhead.

"Well, now, master Philippos, you have your own household," crows Kratulos.

Philippos clasps Pammenes' hand in thanks. The Theban murmurs, "I could hardly allow an enemy of father to embarrass a guest-friend of our house."

The boys share in the triumph. Together they march to the enclosures to pick up the purchases.

β

A burly man, warmly dressed for the wet night, knocks heavily on the door to Amuntas Plousias' town house. Holding a torch, another strong man stands next to the slim Perdikkas as they wait for welcome from the owner of the house. Behind them, in the dark, is yet a third guard protecting the back of the Makedon prince. Perdikkas no longer leaves his safety to chance.

Hearing the rasp of the door bolts Perdikkas steps forward. The heavy door swings open easily on oiled hinges and there is Plousias smiling broadly, his steward by his side, servants with lit oil lamps behind them, "Holy Aphrodite! Perdikkas, it's good to see you. Come in, come in, get out of the rain."

"Amuntas Plousias, you look the same as ever, prosperous and happy," answers Perdikkas as he follows his first bodyguard across the threshold. Perdikkas hugs his friend. "Welcome back to your home land, Plousias. I want to hear all about your travels."

"You will, you will. Let us join our friends," Plousias leads the prince and their retainers around the covered perimeter of the courtyard to the dining room. Seeing the glint of armor under the cloaks of Perdikkas' bodyguard as they walk, Plousias raises an eyebrow.

Seeing the glance, Perdikkas explains, "Mother is superstitious. She feels the loss of one son is enough and insists that I give thought to the security of the realm. Don't be offended when Andros here tastes my supper before me."

"Your mother is wise. As we both know, there is evil in the world," answers Amuntas Plousias jovially.

Entering the dining room, they bring with them a gust of wind and chill. The other guests rise to greet the new arrivals for Perdikkas is, in truth, the guest of honor even though the feast celebrates the return of the host to Pella after an exile of more than two years. Five men and a boy comprise the other guests: Antipatros, Philippos Arkouda, Periandros, Agathokles, Xenokleitos who is representing Derdas of Elimiotis, and the boy, Alexandros of Lunkestis, representing his father.

As servants gather the wet cloaks, greetings and pleasantries are exchanged. Soon all are reclining on their dining couches and the first course is brought in. Despite the compliments offered to Plousias for the beauty of the setting, the fine taste of the dishes—this of lamb, that of partridge, this with apples and cherries, that with a sauce of cheese, eggs, and spices—and the high quality of the wine, no one's mind is on the food.

Instead they feel a collective euphoria in Plousias' return, and in the confidence flowing from the maturing Perdikkas. While the regent, Ptolemaios, knows of this gathering, his very impotence in the face of their common purpose is a third source of their pleasure.

"Korrhagos the Elder is chagrined that he was unable to join us tonight," offers Antipatros. "He, like my father, is less able to get out these days. He sends you his blessings, Prince Perdikkas."

Plousias, who is irrepressible tonight, says, "So who does Ptolemaios dine with this evening? Grim Arkhelaos?"

The others laugh, and Agathokles adds, "You are right to crow, Plousias. Here you are back in Pella. Ptolemaios has learned that you understand money better than he does, better than any of us. So he needs you." More soberly, the older man says, "Still, he has friends. He counts on Lagos, Antiokhos, and perhaps Athanaios. They're not here."

"All of Orestis supports Ptolemaios," comments Xenokleitos, his tone conveying his contempt for the neighboring highland state.

"No longer Lunkestis," interjects Alexandros, son of Aeropos. "And if you were to ask Philotas of Pelagonis, you would find that he and his son, Prince Parmenion, support you, Prince Perdikkas."

"That's the doing of you, Arkouda," acknowledges Perdikkas, "you and my brother, Philippos." Across the room the old warrior smiles and nods acceptance of the recognition.

Pushing a plate aside and combing crumbs from his beard, Antipatros states, "We have broken bread together. Good as was the food, it's now time to talk about larger matters. Plousias, tell us of your exile."

"You may recall that Parrhasios and I and the others went south to Larissa initially. We found the Aleuadai less welcoming of Makedones than they once were. Some of our group stayed in Larissa, but most of us traveled on to Pharsalos. Agelaos of Pharsalos was attempting to enforce his role as *arkhon.* He is largely accepted in the western reaches of Thessalos. In the east, he could do little in the face of Pherai's opposition, despite the support of Pelopidas of Thebai. As you know from your own agents, Thessalos is a sea of internecine feuds. Anyone who raises his head above the interests of his own farms and estates is likely to find an early death. Alexandros of Pherai is consolidating his power. Many Thessa-liotes are deciding that his tyranny and its stability is better than the destructive feuds, better than the uncertainty and sudden murder." Plousias shakes his head in wonder, "What a power Thessalos could be. Only Alexandros is not Iason, he lacks the finesse, the grasp of strategy, the sheer attraction of his uncle. Even with this victory of his over Thebai, I doubt he will succeed in unifying the cities and rural clans of Thessalos." The others mutter or nod in agreement.

Plousias continues, "I think in the long run, we Makedones would do better to support Pharsalos over Pherai or Larissa. Let the latter cities exhaust themselves fighting. Pharsalos can be the arbiter in that land if she has our support."

"Why?" asks Agathokles.

After considering a moment, Plousias answers, "Pharsalos is a city in which a number of clans share power. They have learned to cooperate to control trade with western Thessalos. They possess long-standing and far-reaching ties to the rural people. The rivalry between Pherai and Larissa causes most Thessaliotes to hold both cities and their great families in disdain. Often they must mask their contempt for fear of the long reach of the Aleuadai or Alexandros of Pherai, but the contempt is there. Pharsalos and its leaders are generally respected as a community where reason and debate are possible, where there is recognition that prosperity derives from the common good."

"When will the Makedones—and I take you to mean all the Makedones, not just the lowlanders—possess the purpose and means to support Pharsalos?" asks Xenokleitos mockingly.

"Only when we are unified ourselves," rumbles Antipatros. Scratching at his beard, he continues, "You highlanders enjoy your independence when the lowland throne is weak and there is no trouble in the north. I tell you that the throne will not be weak when Perdikkas bestrides it. And my eyes and ears tell me that Bardulis the Dardanoi is about done putting his house in order, and will be looking to loot our houses again before long."

"How long do you think we have?" asks Perdikkas.

"Maybe a year. Maybe a bit more."

"He's very old, though," offers Alexandros. "My father believes his tribal alliances will fall apart on his death."

"Bardulis has been looming over us all of our lives. The Illuroi are like the snows of winter. Just as we complete a harvest, they come to take their share. Each new year begins with payment to the Illuroi. Yet we say, if Bardulis is a man, then he must die. We say this year after year, yet he lives. He fathers sons and they grow to manhood and become greybeards themselves and yet he lives. He believes he cannot die. Who can throw the lie in his face? What other warrior rides to war generation after generation? No one knows how old he is. Is it 80 years? Is it 90 years? Are you going to count on the safety of Lunkestis by waiting for Bardulis to die?" No one expected a speech from the taciturn Arkouda, least of all himself. Smiling self-consciously, he eases himself back down on the dining couch. The point he makes is vivid in their minds.

"Agis, king of the Paiaones, is nearly as old," offers Periandros. "They don't have the numbers of the Illuroi, but man for man they are as fierce."

Agathokles waves a hand in dismissal, "Illuroi. Paiaones. Thraikiotes. We face barbarians always. And in Olunthos, Athenai, Pherai, Thebai we face wilier foes in our Hellenic cousins. What is important is that we have on the throne a man who can lead us. Someone who takes advice from his nobles and companions, then decides what's best and acts on that decision. Perdikkas, you are that man."

Perdikkas considers his words carefully. The support of these men and those whom they can rally are crucial to his gaining the throne and in ruling successfully. Yet he senses that the realm is too divided. There are influential men not represented here—it is not enough that Korrhagos sends his blessings. And there is his mother and the power she wields. "Your faith in me as your future king, as the rightful Temenidai, strengthens my resolve and purpose. The gods approve the covenant we make."

He looks about the room, considering each man and the boy, "Yet the time to act is not now. I will reach my full majority in a matter of months. Then no one can dispute my rights. Our task is to be ready for that moment. If Ptolemaios is going to strike me it must be soon. Queen Eurudike is a restraint on him. But he knows that to survive he must act." Perdikkas gestures to the guards standing at the margins of the room, "These men of mine are likewise restraints. I am not so foolish as to believe that the queen and a few swordsmen are sufficient. The real safeguard is you. If you are with me, if you bring others to our sides, we cannot fail. If by attacking me, he attacks all of you, he knows he is already beaten."

Periandros speaks up, "We would follow you now. Why wait? Why give Ptolemaios any more opportunity?"

Perdikkas holds out a hand and ticks his reasons finger by finger, "I will not give Thebai cause to intervene. I will not create anarchy that Pausanias the Exile can use. I will not give Athenai an excuse to forward the candidacy of Argaios. I will possess my mother's full support. You will gain more adherents to my cause the closer we are to my majority."

"These are good reasons, Prince Perdikkas," states Antipatros flatly. His eyes challenge the others in the room, "You see that he thinks like a king. Yes, there is danger waiting, but we can aid Perdikkas in assuring Ptolemaios that his death comes if he reaches for the prince."

"We could see that Ptolemaios suffers an accident," says Amuntas Plousias bitterly, the hatred of the regent flaring out from his habitual affability.

"No," commands Perdikkas. "I will kill Ptolemaios. I want no accidents. When I reach my majority, he is dead." The clear menace within Perdikkas dominates the room, even Antipatros.

The stillness is broken as Alexandros asks, "What of Orestis?"

"Orestis is hemmed in by Derdas of Elimiotis to the south and your father in Lunkestis to the north. So long as we prevent Ptolemaios from fleeing to Orestis, they will submit once he's dead," explains Perdikkas.

"Parrhasios and I left Pharsalos when we realized we were being stalked there," interrupts Amuntas Plousias. "We went to Dodona in Epeiros. Parrhasios remains at the court of the Molossi king. He can bring a hundred horsemen to support Derdas in cowing Orestis."

"Who were the stalkers?" demands Arkouda.

"Mercenary killers, maybe sent by Ptolemaios, maybe by Alexandros of Pherai. We were never sure."

HOMECOMING (365 B.C.)

"Amuntas Plousias, you and your people will be responsible for the treasury when the time comes," says Perdikkas. Turning, he looks to Antipatros, "Can you secure the gates of Pella? The city, its environs, and hinterlands?" The big man nods acceptance. Perdikkas continues, "Xenokleitos and Alexandros, son of Aeropos, you must coordinate our support in the highlands. Agathokles, you will rally Aigai and all Pieris. Philippos Arkouda, your task is to secure Almopis and Eordaia. Periandros, you go east. You must undo the influence Ptolemaios has built from the river Axios to the frontier." Smiling his confidence, Perdikkas raises a kylix of wine, "All of us must work to bring in Korrhagos and Athanaios, and to isolate Antiokhos and Lagos. Let Arkhelaos be the regent's sole prop. Are we agreed?"

Antipatros stands and raises his mug, and the others follow—together, smiling broadly to each other, they call out, "We are agreed, Prince Perdikkas of the Makedones." And the deep voice of Arkouda adds, "King-in-waiting, we are yours to command."

γ

Kneeling on the dung and straw-strewn floor, Arkhelaos tosses the sheep anklebones. He groans as the four bones come up with two pairs. His brother, Aridaios, grins at his elder's discomfiture. The youngest brother, Menelaos, intently waits his turn.

From the horsestall where he is grooming his favorite mare, Ptolemaios calls out, "Why don't you three quit gambling? You just pass the same handful of coins back and forth to each other."

There is laughter in the stable among the regent's companions and even among the grooms and stablehands. They quiet as Arkhelaos stands and stares. The grizzled face shows no humor. "You all laugh, but these are not ordinary coins. We have them from the soothsayer, Tiamat the Khaldean. There are six coins. One for me, another each for Ari and Mene. The other three are for father's other sons. Whoever holds all six coins from one winter solstice to the next will gain the favor of the dark gods for the year that follows."

"How many coins do you hold, Arkhelaos?" asks Telestes, who commands Ptolemaios' bodyguard.

"Four," states Arkhelaos flatly. "Ari and Mene hold one apiece."

Curious about the gullibility of the brothers, Ptolemaios asks, "What did you give this Tiamat for the coins? And how did the coins come to be so blessed?"

Already regretting the candor caused by his resentment of the laughter, Arkhelaos is hesitant to explain more. Aridaios speaks up, "We each gave him a silver drinking cup and two sacrificial lambs. Only an old-fashioned *skyphos* cup would do."

Someone in the back calls out, "Certainly, they're larger than a *kylix*." Again, many laugh.

Menelaos interrupts defensively, "We saw the sacred fire and the dark gods through the blue and purple smoke. They gave the blessing and promise. How often do the dark gods get twelve perfect lambs?"

"Twelve?" asks Ptolemaios, "so your half-brothers were with you?"

"No," says Aridaios, "we did it for them. That way they never saw the coins."

"Six silver cups, each one a *skyphos*," says Telestes wonderingly. "Sounds like your soothsayer did well by the exchange."

Furiously Arkhelaos barks out, "You all may laugh now, but you will see that the ancient gods, the gods before Zeus, still have power."

"You mean the Titans? Or the witchery of Hekate? The fates themselves? Some foreign gods of the Khaldeans? To which ancient gods do you appeal?" asks Telestes, his broad bearded face smiling in jest.

Already angry, Arkhelaos shakes off the rapid questions, "Why act the fool, Telestes? I honor Zeus and make no attempt to say for him where his powers leave off and the powers of other gods begin. But we all know that beneath the bright existence of the twelve gods and their companions, there are older beings whose will works through the world. The fates are but one set of god-beings whom we must acknowledge. There are others."

Glaring at the courtiers and stablehands alike, Arkhelaos raises his head proudly, "Menelaos tells you true. We saw these beings in the sacred fire of the Khaldean." He holds up one of the coins so that all can see it, "This is no didrachm, stater, daric, or even shekel. This is like no coin you have seen. Not silver or gold, it is made of both. These coins are ancient, yet each bears its own likeness and a symbol. The one I hold up has my likeness on its face and the symbol of a bull on its reverse."

"May I see it?" asks Ptolemaios, stepping forward and holding out his hand.

Thinking that the Ptolemaios has begun to believe him, Arkhelaos hands him the coin. The regent turns the coin back and forth, examining its appearance. The likeness is odd, strange to see a man depicted and not a god or a city emblem. The profile does seem to have Arkhelaos jutting chin and heavy brow. The coin is not shiny, not newly minted. Heavier than silver, it has an odd oily feel to it. Ptolemaios is puzzled. He hands the coin back. Turning to his men he raises his voice, "Let's not question the brothers further. We all know there are mysteries in the world that cannot be satisfied by mortals such as us. Perhaps the Khaldean's prophecy is true. As Arkhelaos says, we will know when the six coins are in the hands of a brother for a full year. We rely on oracles and sacrifices. Some oracles, like at Delphoi, are protected by Apollo or another of the twelve gods. Other oracles are older than the twelve gods. They say that of Dodona. Dark gods or other sacred beings may voice the truth."

In his mind, Ptolemaios dismisses the story of the coins. Likely the brothers have been hoodwinked. Still, strange happenings can be true. What matters to Ptolemaios is that he has quashed the argument between Arkhelaos and Telestes. The alliances that keep Ptolemaios alive and in power are wearing thin. He must be vigilant. Arkhelaos and his brothers hold the loyalty of rough countrymen like themselves, men from rural estates more used to stock animals and crops than the ways of the court. Telestes guards the regent's back. He is a creature of the court. Ptolemaios needs them both.

The regent raises his voice again, "Who's not yet done caring for his horses? Let the stablehands take over. This morning's hunt was good. Our feast should be ready. Who else is hungry?" Taking their assent for granted, Ptolemaios leads his companions from the stables.

As they walk the path up the rise to the palace, Ptolemaios motions Telestes to his side. Quietly he asks, "How does our campaign go?"

Telestes leans close and says softly, "Perdikkas is well-guarded. I have a man in the kitchens and another as gardener. One of his bodyguards may be turned. My people are working on it. If all goes well, I will meet with the man before the new moon."

"Is that all?" asks Ptolemaios.

"Queen Eurudike is invited to the estate of Lagos and Arsinoe for the lunar festival. Her people become lax when she is away. Then we need only concern ourselves with Perdikkas' own guards. I expect to strike then."

"Not yourself surely? Nothing can be traced back."

"No, I have two competent dupes. They are sure to succeed and will be well-rewarded, although they will not enjoy their rewards long. You need not fear a path." Telestes laughs gently, "I do love these games."

"Who will they be traced to?"

"I toyed with discrediting Antipatros or even Queen Eurudike, but thought it best to have several lines of possibility. Yourself, Prince Philippos, and Alexandros of Pherai."

Startled, Ptolemaios looks at his captain. Then considering, he nods, "You are right, one line needs to trace to me or none of it will be believed. Philippos and Alexandros are good. Why not make an unsuccessful attempt on my life as well. Trace a line to Olunthos. That will confuse the issue of Perdikkas' death adequately. It's a shame he has no jilted lovers. The common folk like to believe in scandals."

"If I do that, I may need to delay another month to reset the trap."

Ptolemaios weighs the danger. He would prefer to take the time to think through all the dangers, but his instincts tell him that he will fall from power unless most Makedones believe both he and Perdikkas are targets. "Then you must delay. Take two months if need be. Set it up well. You may even add a third target, maybe the queen, though be sure any attack on her is foiled. Think carefully, Telestes, and come back to me with a plan." He grasps his captain's arm, "I am confident in your skills. If others prove to be traitors attacking their betters, their estates could fall to you."

Telestes smiles—the smile has warmth and humor, it is his eyes that glitter.

δ

Philippos sighs, barely listening to Kerkidas the tutor. Lately lessons seem to drone. Life in Thebai is endless, as if they were insects in amber, immured forever. He is too old for tutoring. When will he return to Makedonis and take up the duties of a man?

With a start, Philippos realizes that the other boys are grinning at him. "I repeat, Prince Philippos, is a man moral because of an innate goodness or is a man moral because he has been taught to be moral?" Kerkidas is impatient with Philippos.

"A man learns to be moral," answers the youth.

"If two brothers are reared together and receive the same training, yet one leads a life of virtue and the other a life of depravity, how would you explain the difference?"

Considering, Philippos says, "Perhaps the same customs and ideas have been presented to them, but their own observations cause them to interpret the ideas differently. The elder is the heir and is treated with pride by the father. The mother dotes on the younger son and calls him her own. Both are told that virtue brings its own reward, yet one hears truth and the other hypocrisy."

Kratulos breaks in, "And when they go out in the wider world their experiences diverge even more. One is landed and the other must seek his fortune."

"So experience is more powerful than either formal teaching or physical birthright?" asks Kerkidas.

Pammenes *Neos* pipes up, "Formal teaching can add skills—intellectual or craft skills—and is one part of experience."

"What about me?" asks Pamesias. "My nature includes this foot." He kicks forward his twisted clubfoot. "Everything I do, everything I am, must take this foot into account."

"Because of its limiting effect, you are pushed into directions you would not have gone had you been born with two sound feet?" probes Kerkidas.

"I will never follow my father's way of life and stand as a hoplite within our city's phalanx against our enemies. Instead, I can place an arrow in the eye of a rabbit at three hundred paces." Sorrow and pride mix defiantly in Pamesias' voice.

Trying to comfort his brother, Pammenes adds, "You are an able rider. On a horse with a lance, your foot does not matter. You are a noble, Pamesias. You will serve Thebai in the saddle."

Kerkidas guides them back to the discussion, "So, we start life with a set of potentialities. Some are physical, some are social—having to do with the status of the family into which we are born—and some are mental, our raw intellect. On that uneven yet blank wall experience etches a picture. Together they form the character of the wall. If you are that wall, then are you only the wall as built, as it started, and as things happened to the wall? Are we so inanimate? Are we only a wall? Where are you in all this?"

Exasperation in his voice, Kleomenes exclaims, "I'm no wall. I think, I act."

Pammenes echoes his friend, "There is a me that's more than slate and happenstance." All the boys are nodding their agreement, and universal agreement is unusual in the classroom.

"So you can decide to be more or less than your nature and your experience?"

Pindaros calls out, "Certainly. We all know stories of people who overcome the obstacles in their lives. The fables are full of such tales."

"Oh, Pindaros, only you would cite fables as evidence," says Kratulos in mock reproof.

"How many do?" asks Philippos in sudden vehemence. "How many men take control of their lives? Aren't most men logs in the water, riding wherever the river current takes them?"

"Maybe you don't control your life all the time. Maybe you try, but there are too many pushes and pulls that override your efforts. Sometimes, if you keep trying, you succeed. Sometimes you are alert enough to make a critical decision at the right point." Pammenes is in earnest.

"Then you are saying that the virtuous man is the man who is not defeated but keeps making the best decisions he can in any given circumstances," replies Philippos.

"Not self-defeated," suggests Kleomenes as modification.

"Surely there's more to virtue?" asks Pindaros.

"Let's see where we are," intervenes Kerkidas. "At the moment, we have a man who starts with a given nature, the potentialities I stated before. The man suffers experience, things happen to him. He interacts with these happenings, setting up counterinfluences. As a thinking being, this man considers his experiences. He acts from decisions rather than fixed reactions. Now we add a value judgment. We say the man makes the *best* decision. What causes a decision to be *best*? From whose point of view is it *best*? Does the question of virtue rest in that word *best*?"

"Virtue resides in making the best decision. I would stress the making over the best. There is no virtue in being solely passive," says Philippos with certainty.

"Sometimes it's good to let the world go its way," disagrees Kleomenes.

"Yes, but only if you decide that the action you will take is not to act. There is no virtue if you take no action because you cannot take an action or because it doesn't occur to you to take an action," answers Philippos fiercely.

"Non-action is an action?" queries Pindaros.

Kerkidas smiles, "As a result of decision, yes."

Maliciously Pamesias asks Philippos, "When you bought your wild man Pikoros and the beautiful Petalouda, were you making virtuous decisions?" Kratulos and Pindaros laugh out loud.

"I don't know yet," says Philippos stiffly. The household has been astonished by the introduction of Philippos' two slaves. Pammenes *Palios* grudgingly permitted the purchases and admonished Philippos to keep his slaves well in hand. Fortunately for Philippos, these past months Pammenes *Palios* has continually been embroiled in the crisis between Thebai and Athenai over the city of Oropos. Consequently, the master of the house is unaware of the tensions arising from the pair of slaves.

Pikoros, the redheaded Illuriote, is deft with horses and outdoor work, and clumsy with resentment and frustration when required to do anything indoors. A failure as a valet, he answers the jeers and jibes of the other servants with anger. Blows have been exchanged and more than one member of the household has possessed a bloody nose or blackened eye. Now Pikoros is banished to stable, gardens, and orchard.

As for Petalouda, it is her beauty and supposed wantonness that cause jealousy among the household staff. None of the female servants will speak to her, all the adult and almost adult males think of ways to bed her, though none succeed. Indeed, none try other than by sly remark and innuendo for it's known that Philippos does bed her. Still she cares for her master ably and, in consequence, he is cleaner dressed than ever before in his stay at Thebai.

Only Philippos and Petalouda know that while she accepts meeting the prince's sexual needs, she does so with little enthusiasm. For Philippos, this is a problem to be solved. He has no interest in forcing himself upon her. He thought that her early reluctance would yield to a mutual pleasure. Not so. Only rarely now does he comfort himself with her. She does not seem to mind, taking what pleasure she wants. Her reaction indicates mild interest and occasional annoyance. The truth is, his pride is hurt, though he is sufficiently detached to find his own hurt pride amusing.

Kerkidas latches onto Pamesias' question, "Let's not be abstract. Pamesias asks a question that ties us to reality. And Philippos answers truly that he doesn't know whether his decisions held virtue. He did make a series of decisions. He acted. His actions have consequences felt by many beside himself. Were the decisions he made the best decisions he could have made? Were his decisions virtuous?"

"Don't we have to ask about his intentions?" offers the stolid Kleomenes.

"You mean that his intentions could be virtuous but his actions not?" asks Kerkidas.

"Or even the opposite," says Pammenes *Neos*. "Certainly the consequences of his actions may have little connection to his intentions."

Philippos stands up abruptly, "I am sorry but I am unwilling to have you examine my intentions. You will draw your own conclusions in any event—of my intentions, my actions, and of the consequences. I have answered Pamesias fairly. I do not know whether my decisions were virtuous. I think we make decisions with many motives, some virtuous and some not. I could not allow Petalouda to go to the brothel keepers. I judged Pikoros as the best man among the slaves available to meet my needs. He is no valet. In the north, I will have less need for a valet than for a man—slave or not—whom I can trust to carry out the tasks I set him." With that, Philippos walks out of the class.

The boys leave Kerkidas with the puzzle of virtue's source.

ε

A single oil lamp illuminates the room. A bare room, save for a narrow table in the center of the room with two stools and a low bench. On one stool sits Telestes, chafing his hands together against the coolness of the room. With the sun down, the temperature has dropped. Telestes is not thinking about the cold. He is waiting, listening for steps in the outside hall, and hearing his own thoughts as he runs over the plot in his mind. If he is successful tonight, then the plot to kill Perdikkas will be in motion. All he need do is neutralize one guard close to the prince. Tonight will show how that guard will be enrolled or negated.

He hears the outer door of the building opening. He loosens his sword in its scabbard and keeps his hand on its hilt. There is the noise of quiet movement in the hall. Softly the signal is rapped out on the unlatched door to the room.

"Enter," says Telestes in his normal voice, which sounds loud to him against the stillness.

The door opens and Telestes' sentinel ushers in the man Telestes is courting, along with Telestes' agent, Lukon, who plays cook's helper in the prince's household. Telestes stands and welcomes them both with a glad smile, "Lukon tells me good things of you, Onetor."

With the door shut and the sentinel gone back to his post, Telestes waves his visitors to their seats. Onetor appears suspicious and uncertain, but he sits on the bench. Lukon pulls up the other stool. "Onetor, here, ain't so sure this meeting's safe," explains Lukon. "That's right, ain't it?" says Lukon, nudging Onetor.

The big man doesn't like being nudged, but he shrugs and says, "Look, you want something done and I want the money. That's simple." He thrusts his head forward, "I just don't want to be left taking the blame. I want to be sure there's a way I get out and go south."

"Which of the islands are you from?" asks Telestes.

"Rhodos," says Onetor grudgingly.

"If we see that you join a crew bound for Khios or Samos, would that do? You'd be on your own from there."

"Aye, but I'd rather go the inner route, down to Andros or Tenos."

Telestes does not answer, simply stares at Onetor. The silence grows lengthy. Lukon stirs but says nothing. Telestes considers the man before him. Why should this man betray Perdikkas? He's paid well enough by Perdikkas. Even were he to escape, having a hand in the killing of a prince of the Makedones would become known. Who would trust him again?

Lukon says that the hulking man bears the prince some obscure grudge. Takhos, Telestes' second agent in the prince's employ, reports only that Onetor is a loner among the prince's bodyguards. Onetor is the only Dorian among the guards. His speech is thick with the accents of his home.

Maybe the simplest way is to kill Onetor tonight.

On a hunch, Telestes asks, "Have you ever been to Sparte?"

"No, but I've taken their pay in the past." Onetor grimaces, "They're arrogant bastards. I left them."

"Is Perdikkas an arrogant bastard?"

Surprised, Onetor says, "No, not like them."

"So why do you hate the prince?"

"Who says I hate him?" Onetor demands. "It's not a matter of hate."

"What is it a matter of then?"

"Lukon here says you'll pay ten gold darics if I turn my back. I don't do nothing. I just let it happen. Is that right?" demands Onetor forcefully. "Perdikkas is nothing to me. He's only silver that pays my way. You pay more."

Telestes is not satisfied. What good is a man anyone can buy? He could sell the plot to Perdikkas. Yet, Telestes can tell there's something more to this than money. Lukon is right, Onetor wants to see this done. He wants Perdikkas dead. What's being left unsaid?

Lukon nudges Onetor again, "Tell him about the boy."

Onetor flushes and looks away.

"What boy?" asks Telestes gently.

Onetor doesn't answer. He's grown sullen.

Lukon sighs in exasperation. "Onetor here had his eye on this lad. A likely boy. You know," he winks at Telestes. "Anyway, the boy admires Onetor until Perdikkas notices. Well, Perdikkas ain't as even-handed as the rest of his family. He sticks to women. Anyway, he says somethin' about the boy bein' very young. And Onetor gets told his duties are outside now. Ain't that right, Onetor?"

"What concern was it of his?" asks Onetor plaintively. "Look at me. I'm an ugly man. Who cares for a stranger who is an ugly man? A man who takes money to fight? But that's not what the boy saw. We did nothing. The boy simply took to me."

Now Telestes thinks Onetor will fit his purpose after all. He offers a small smile, "I understand. I believe you will earn your ten darics and a ship ride home." Telestes nods to Lukon and stands, "Lukon will let you know when the time has come."

Lukon gestures Onetor out. As the door opens, Onetor suddenly embraces Lukon. Behind him, through the door, crash three armed men. The bench, stools, and table are shoved aside as the assassins reach for Telestes. Lukon is down, disembowled by Onetor's knife. He is screaming. Telestes fights desperately, seeking to keep the three blades away. Onetor joins his comrades in attacking Telestes. A sword chops into Telestes' arm. Another stabs into his thigh. Knowing he is going to die, Telestes hurtles himself against Onetor. The two slam down to the floor, as a sword slices into Telestes' shoulder and neck, grating across his collarbone. As quickly as it started, the fight ends. Onetor rolls Telestes body off him. He staggers to his feet, helped by his fellow guardsmen. Blood oozes through his tunic with each breath he takes. He croaks to his companions, "Let's go, I don't want to die with these pigs." One of the men leans down and stabs again into Telestes' back. Then tugs at the body, turning it over. A search finds a leather bag of coins and a fine dagger. Both are taken as the men leave—Onetor supported by a brother-in-arms. The room is quiet again, only now it is painted in clotting red and stinks from death's release.

*　*　*

The great hall resounds with laughter. The storyteller alternates between voices, faces, and postures of a garrulous old man, a flighty young girl, and a clever peasant lad. The lordly audience of court notables and their children are enraptured by the fleeting images conjured by the comic actor's intricate storyline. All the audience that is except the regent. Though he laughs dutifully, and tries to give every indication of enjoyment and lack of concern, inside he is seething.

Telestes is alive, barely. Five wounds and yet he survives. No longer of use to Ptolemaios since Perdikkas will be of age long before the captain recovers, if he recovers. The plot to kill Perdikkas is a shambles. Only Takhos is still in place. Takhos will revenge Lukon, of that, Ptolemaios is certain. The thought offers little reassurance.

Whispers are sweeping Pella. Whispers as swift as a hawk's flight as it plunges to strike its prey. All those in the know are distancing themselves from the regent.

Queen Eurudike is away. She will not know yet of the turn of events. Small comfort to Ptolemaios since the news will reach her before he could. And while no one can say certainly that his hand guided the plot, she will have no doubt.

The notables gathered here for an afternoon's entertainment really seek to see how Ptolemaios behaves. These are the courtiers who sway in the wind, the fingerlings that count for little. No one of real importance attends, not even Arkhelaos.

Ptolemaios fights down a moment of panic. There must be a way. There is Takhos. He could order his mercenaries to attack Perdikkas' stronghold here in Pella. Even if he prevailed, he could not win the civil war that would follow.

He considers fleeing into exile. Many a man has done the same. Exile is a way of life. He could be like Argaios or Pausanias. He could wait for the next opportunity to return, to take vengeance on Perdikkas. Exile requires money. Ironically, he is blocked from the treasury by Amuntas Plousias, the very man he recalls from exile to restore the depleted wealth. Everywhere he looks there is a noble re-aligned with Perdikkas. With Telestes gone, he is not even certain of his own bodyguard.

The panic bubbles within him. He pushes it down, angry with his own weakness.

Another sally by the performer creates an uproar of laughter. Ptolemaios is caught unawares, not having heard the joke. Even if he goes into exile, Perdikkas will doubtless send assassins to kill him. Better to make his stand here in Makedonis. Momentarily, he thinks about the green mountainsides of Makedonis. The wealth of timber. The horses, spread in pastures across the plains. He does love this land. Only exile to the Persian court would be reasonable. He won't do it, not for this boy, this princeling. He will kill the son-of-a-bitch himself before he will flee from him.

On the far side of the hall there is movement as one guard goes off duty and another comes on. What startles Ptolemaios is that he does not recognize the new guard. Ptolemaios stands to see the guard better. Around him laughter ends at the regent's abrupt standing. Realizing, Ptolemaios sits again and waves the performance on, "Please continue, a momentary distraction."

Some of the courtiers continue to stare at him, but the storyteller resumes his tale and the children and then the adults are soon enthralled again. Ptolemaios wants to scream, to order his men into action. Only the new guard is not his, and he is too late.

ζ

By gestures and with what Hellenic speech they share, Pikoros and Petalouda load the cart with the prince's belongings. To be more accurate, Pikoros lifts and arranges the filled leather bags, amphorae, baskets, furniture, cookware, and other impedimenta, while Petalouda directs. Sometimes shrill, sometimes conciliatory, but always with good humor, the young woman keeps Pikoros in motion. The many months in the often disapproving household of Pammenes *Palios* has seen these two draw closer, relying on each other for sympathy to withstand the discomfort of their plight.

Watching from the stable gate, Philippos realizes that Petalouda should be mated to Pikoros. Perhaps it's the gladness bubbling within him that allows him to see what should have been obvious before. Why make himself dissatisfied with her illusory warmth, when he can gain greater loyalty and cooperation from them both by letting them have each other? All three of them will be happier.

Beyond the yard wall, Philippos can hear Pammenes *Neos* calling his name. The prince bellows back, "Here, Pammenes, at the stables."

Soon Pammenes and Kleomenes stride into the yard. "Looks like you're about ready, Philippos," calls Pammenes. "Father is short on time and asks if you would join him now. He has the council meeting to attend but would like the family to carry out our own sacrifices for your safe journey home."

"That's good of your father," answers Philippos. "My horses and mules are ready. Pikoros should be done shortly. Now's a good time."

"You won't get far on the road today. It will be midday before the full column of Makedones assembles in the marketplace," says Kleomenes.

"You may be right. Still we're well organized. I have deputies hurrying our people along. Arrangements have been in place for days. I think we can shave our departure time down. If we make it out of the city and perhaps 35 *stade* or so to the coast, I will be satisfied. I have sent Kleitos and Lamakhos ahead to secure a camping ground. The ships are waiting. If we reach them the day after tomorrow, that will be fine." Philippos is truly pleased with this day and can find nothing wrong with it. He is going home. After years—three years—he will see Perdikkas again, see the land of the Makedones. He cannot dwell on the thought less his delight overwhelms him.

Walking with his friends to the main house, Philippos considers Pammenes *Palios*' need to attend a council meeting. The summons must have come early this morning. Either the need is more news about the Arkadians and Eleans in the Peloponnesos or it's word of Timotheos the Athenian, who besieges the Persian garrison on Samos. Probably the south, news sent by Epaminondas. That is a matter close to Theban interests. For Philippos, the activities of Timotheos are far more interesting, since that general replaced Iphikrates over the winter in commanding Athenian forces in the North Aegean. The prospect of being home has whetted the prince's appetite for any intelligence touching on the Makedones and the north.

Even so, the thought of the war in the south unleashes a flow of memories. There was a supper one evening, hosted by Pammenes and attended by Epaminondas, Pelopidas, Ismenias, and others, to which the host's eldest son and Philippos had inexplicably been invited. Philippos suspects it was at the suggestion of Pelopidas.

The great men of Thebai talked openly that night of their concerns for the city and of events and personages throughout the Hellenic states and in Persia. They debated policies and argued alternatives. They talked of peace with Korinthos, the marvel of retaining Oropos in the teeth of Athenai, the trial of Kallistratos in Athenai, the satrap Mausalos' half-hearted siege of Ariobarzanes in Lydia and the role played by Agesilaos of Sparte, the advantages accruing from the murder of Lukomedes the Arkadian. These and many more events were thrown in the air and winnowed for their importance to Thebai. Of course, as often they spoke of the theater, of the price of pork, the comparative merits of different varieties of grapes, the uncertain investment in trading with Sikili and the west, of the prominent political opponent who was so wonderfully befuddled by a new bedmate, and other lesser subjects. Wit and ideas ornamented the evening.

For the younger Pammenes and Philippos it was all heady. Despite being wary of again revealing his detailed knowledge of the Makedones, Philippos was enthralled—listening carefully, ardently, but rarely speaking. The highpoint for Philippos came when Epaminondas asked him about the differences between Makedon and Thessaliote use of horsemen on campaign and in battle. The men were debating the merits of horsemen as a striking force, when the question arose. Unlike most Hellenic states, Thebai and the Boiotian League make good use of their elite horsemen. Yet the phalanx of the middle class provides their fighting strength. In Thessalos, the numerous horsemen are as likely to act as a hammer in battle as the phalanx. And in Makedonis, there is no longer a phalanx unless it is hired. Horsemen are the spear and shield of war in the north.

One of the guests, Ptoiophanes the Stammerer, stated that Makedon horsemen could only be effective in the unorganized fighting against hill tribes. The implication of barbarians fighting barbarians was clear if unstated. Then Pelopidas brought up the use of Thessaliote horse. Even there, though, it was acknowledged that if proper care were taken for the flanks of the phalanx, the horsemen had no role. Hearing from Philippos about the differences between the wedge and the diamond formations, Epaminondas mused aloud that the horsemen could exploit any gap that could be created in the phalanx ranks. Others dismissed the idea, saying such a gap would be so fleeting among a disciplined force that to take advantage of it would require more luck than is reasonable for a planned attack by horsemen. To Philippos, the idea was not absurd. After all, one wouldn't use the weak southern horsemen. Any sustained gap would occur between formations, not within a single phalanx.

"King Perdikkas must be eager for your return," says Kleomenes.

His brother's name brings Philippos back from his reverie, "Yes, we are both eager, Kleomenes."

Pammenes laughs, "Your brother has sent a dispatch every day since taking the throne. Shipping all of the hostages, I mean guest-friends of the city, back to Makedonis is a heavy expense."

"All but Philoxenos, son of Ptolemaios," comments Kleomenes.

"Philoxenos is invited to return with us," says Philippos. "He chooses exile here in Thebai."

"Is he so afraid of vengeance, being Ptolemaios' son?"

"No one would harm him." Philippos shakes his head at their blood-thirsty view of the north. "Philoxenos is better suited to the south. His is not a nature that accords well with the magnates among the Makedones. Here he can build his library, spend his days considering the soul of man, hire dancers whose style is sufficiently fashionable and ornate." Besides, thinks Philippos, no one here would manipulate the fool into being an opponent of Perdikkas.

"You mean if the great poet, Pindaros, were alive the two would discuss the finer points of acclamatory poetry," interjects Pammenes.

"Exactly, they would be equally windy." All three laugh as they enter the courtyard of the house.

At the sight of the entire household assembled to do Philippos honor, they become serious. Pammenes *Palios*, smiling and dignified, steps forward and invites Philippos to stand at the altar for the sacrifice of parting. Philippos must blink to hold back the sudden tears that threaten to shame him. For three years Philippos has pined for home, yet this good man has made exile bearable, has opened his home, and his family to a stranger. Philippos thanks Zeus for Pammenes *Palios*.

η

The ceiling is intricate, layered and carved and brightly painted. In the center is the Temenidai sun, its spikes radiating from the center orb. Gold set in an azure sky. Each spike points to one of the twelve gods, depicted in human guise and with their identifying emblems—Zeus with his thunderbolt, Demeter with her wheat, Artemis with her bow and arrows, on through the twelve. In three corners of the ceiling are additional single figures—Hestia, Hephaistos, and Herakles. In the fourth corner are the three Moirai, the fates—Klotho, Lakhesis, and Atropos. The effect of the whole ceiling is radiantly cheerful when all the lamps are lit and somehow forbidding when the lamps are dimmed.

"Well, what do you think of it?" demands Perdikkas, standing back from his brother and pointing with evident pleasure.

Looking up, trying to take it all in, then giving up and examining each figure in detail, Philippos is gaping, "I've never seen the like," he shakes his head. "When did you have this done?"

"I've been planning it for several years. I had the land cleared, gathered the stone, timber, and other supplies, even arranged contracts for some of the workmen. I gave the order to start within two hours after I had Ptolemaios' head on a spear. Less than three months, once they began.

Tomorrow this temple will be dedicated and the sacred fire lit. I have been waiting for your return." Perdikkas smiles broadly at his younger brother, "I know exile was hard. I believe living here under his rule was harder. Planning this little building was my escape from all the slights and plots. Whenever I was uncertain, I would work on the design of this temple." Perdikkas holds out his arms and the brothers embrace.

Arm in arm the two walk about the sanctuary. Perdikkas points out the stonework, the fine casting of the statuettes in the grottoes, the inlaid silver that brightens the dark lintels of the doors. Finally, his display done, Perdikkas walks Philippos through the columns of the portico and down the broad front steps.

Philippos finds Perdikkas to be bigger than he remembers. Not so much physically as mentally larger. The king is alive with joy, interested in all and everything. More pious than in the past, but not dour like some priest or fanatic—simply happy.

The two brothers grin at each other. "You'll have to visit mother, you know," says Perdikkas.

"How is she?"

"Retired from public life, almost a peasant farmer. You'll find her on her estate near Herakleon."

Philippos whistles, "She's well away from Pella."

"I think the rural life will suit her now. She can visit Aigai, but she no longer has the freedom of Pella."

Philippos considers his mother's fate. Perdikkas is her favorite, yet he's the one to banish her to a far corner of the realm. Perhaps only he could do that act and have it be accepted by her. "I'll travel south after the festivities."

"Good. Then I'd like you to travel over the mountains and see Derdas of Elimiotis. Actually, I'd like you to tour all upper Makedonis. Renew your friendship with the Lunkestoi and Pelagonoi, especially Parmenion. Size up Orestis for me. Then come back to Pella."

"What happens when I get back?" asks Philippos, suddenly curious about his brother's purpose and his own future.

"You can tell me if there's a suitable wife for me up in the hills. If not, then you can travel our lowlands and tell me what you find." Perdikkas is close to laughter.

Bewildered, Philippos asks, "Are you joking?"

"Only in part. I want you seen with a retinue of nobles and warriors. I want you to carry our banners through the land. You go south; I'll go north. We'll meet at Pella in early autumn, then you carry on north and I'll carry on south. We come back to Pella for the new year. We visit every-one of importance, down to the villages. We take the temper of this land. We talk about the future. We survey the yields and herds, the men capable of bearing arms, the extent of the forests and mines, the number of ships and the size of fish catches. We learn all there is to know of our people. We let them learn about us. If Illuriotes or Paiaones or Thraikiotes raid, we lead our riders out and punish the raiders. I am king and you are prince. We make our people know this." Perdikkas reaches out and catches his brother's shoulder, "We must end all the seething, hidden distemper. No more factions. You do well, Philippos, and I will give you lands to rule. You will raise the phalanxes you have so wanted to raise. Train the horsemen to fight together, in proper order, so our strength grows. Let me handle the high nobles. We will make the Makedones strong."

Astonishment seizes Philippos at the vision offered by his brother and at the trust this brother and king reposes in him, a youth not seen for years and a potential rival were that Philippos' character. Astonishment becomes a warmth of thankfulness, felt deeply as tears and rush are choked back. He is truly home. If no one else, Perdikkas is the hearth-stone of family. "I will do well for you, Perdikkas," swears Philippos.

"I know you will. On your journey, there are certain daughters I would have you visit and assess. I will be doing the same. Assess the fathers as deeply as the daughters. Next year, I will take one wife."

"Only one, Perdikkas?" teases Philippos.

"For a start."

CHAPTER TEN

Perdikkas

364 B.C.

α

Shilippos towels himself down after twenty laps in the pool. He feels refreshed, his muscles loose again. The morning exercises on the field had left him dusty and bruised. Now, though tired, his body is rejuvenated.

Since his return to Makedonis there has been little time for reflection. His journey across the kingdom took over three months. Even as he traveled, Perdikkas had him oversee the timber shipments to Thebai. Couriers would find him along his route, give him dispatches, then dash off taking his written instructions to the foresters, to the king's agents, to the river men and shippers. Always there were problems. Working them out long distance, with the delays of travel, had been exasperating. Still, the god Hermes protects travelers, and so the work was fruitful.

Perdikkas knew how big a job he'd given Philippos, since the king had the same responsibility under Alexandros. Then shipments had gone to Athenai. The Athenian agents were more experienced, making selection and shipping easier. Under Perdikkas, timber, pitch, ropes, and other products go to the Boiotian League. In fact, the shipments go to the port of Larymna in Lokris Opuntis, an ally of Thebai. There, north of Boiotia, Epaminondas builds his fleet. An idea born over dinner at the house of Pammenes, the fleet that will allow the Thebans to challenge Athenai in the North Aegean. None too soon for the Makedones, given the current bedevilment of Athenai.

In truth, it is the details of journey itself that still press in on Philippos, rather than the constant annoyance of the timber harvest. The sheer distance, the riding nearly every day, coming over the crest of a hill to see the length of a valley. Coming across herds of horses or cattle, or flocks of sheep or goats. Making camp with the shepherds in the high mountains. All of the festivals and banquets in village after village or in the occasional town or walled city.

Some incidents of the trip are vivid to him. Seeing his mother after three years of absence. She had been in awe of him. Gone a boy, back a man. And he in awe of her—she a beauty despite being in her late forties. But that wasn't it. What amazed him is her happiness. He expected to find her bitter in her semi-exile. Instead her household was filled with laughter and with reverence for the gods.

When they breakfasted and had the opportunity to talk without others around, he discovered that she had lost none of her interest in the kingdom and the ways of power. Her interest was no longer bound by the conflict between her children and Ptolemaios. *(Thank Zeus the son-of-a-bitch is dead, thinks Philippos.)* Rather she works to rally support for Perdikkas. Not in the old way, when she tried to be a faction leader. Instead she acts through her leadership in the temple associations that women form. In her words, she "...brings together the most active and notable women of the realm, from whatever walk-of-life, to share the joy in honoring Hera, Demeter, and Hestia. And in so doing, emphasize that we Makedones do not make servile the role of a woman. We are as responsible for the well being of the realm as for the good of our individual families and communities. A child learns first at home how to behave and what to value. Through the full extent of family and clan, the child learns to broaden his concerns from the household to the community—whether tribe or city. When the full pattern of connection and interaction is understood, the child realizes that the kingdom is his safeguard, just as readily as the garden patch he weeded when little."

Philippos came close to teasing her about formerly worshipping Aphrodite rather than Hera, but the taunt died on his lips. As he thought about his childhood, he recognized that much of the day-to-day activities of his boyhood—the demands of tutors, the requirements of religious ritual and court ceremonial, even the daily tumult of the exercise field and the careful diet he had eaten—were planned by his mother, Eurudike, even if left in the hands of Lady Kleopatra to direct.

Though he might have longed for the open affection Eurudike gave Perdikkas, he must acknowledge that she always cared for his progress and good health. Regularly as a youngster, Lady Kleopatra prepared and escorted him into an audience with the busy queen. How they must have held their laughter at his childish reports and solemn efforts. Both women were there to encourage him.

Seeing his mother in this light, he finds there exists in him a love for her that is much like the love he holds for Lady Kleopatra. Suddenly it is easy to be with the Queen-mother Eurudike, to share ideas and hopes. He is impressed with the real influence and even authority she has regained through her promotion of the temple associations.

As fascinating to him is the fact that Perdikkas did not exile her as he thought. She chose to withdraw herself from Pella. Pieris is the religious heart of the Makedones. Here is ancient Aigai, where the Temenidai kings are buried. Here is Dion, sitting below sacred Mount Olympos, the site of the annual games to honor Zeus and the other gods who dwell on Olympos. And now in Pieris is mother. Women of the old priestly families acknowledge her as their leader, not in a spiritual sense, rather with an emotional commitment derived from her good works among them and among the common folk. With all the good she organizes and does, the envy of the Temenidai once common to these old proud Pieric families is dissipating. Potential disaffection for Perdikkas is gone.

Dry now, his toweling done, Philippos sits on a cool stone bench. He remains pensive. Yes mother does well. The highlands are another story. Derdas of Elimiotis seems distant, not unfriendly, simply no longer identifying his interests with the lowlands. And his boys are no longer royal pages at the court of Perdikkas. Only the daughter, Phila, was interested in the visiting prince.

Further north it became worse. Orestis makes no acknowledgment of Perdikkas. Instead they look to the Molossi kings in Epeiros. All are allies of Athenai with whom Perdikkas is at odds. Lunkestis is dominated by Bardulis of the Illuric Dardanoi. There, if Aeropos belches, it is Bardulis who pardons him. And even Pelagonis, under its new ruler, is aligned with Athenai. Well, tonight he will learn more about Pelagonis since Parmenion, son of Philotas, now in exile, will be at supper with Perdikkas and select companions.

How all this will bear on the war with Athenai remains to be seen. Timotheos, the Athenian commander in the north, possesses an energy not seen in Iphikrates. Now the Athenians seem more menacing than ever.

Despite the delight Philippos felt on his return to Makedonis, the cares of the kingdom press on all sides. Well, he will not shirk. Whatever Perdikkas wants of him, Philippos will give.

β

"I tell you Timotheos is the most dangerous general Athenai has sent north in a generation," declares Korrhagos the Elder. Red in the face, with sweat glistening his brow and grey beard jutting around yellow teeth, the man is vehement in making his point. "Last fall he takes Sestos and Krithote, securing the Khersonesos for Athenai. This spring he seizes Torone. Now he is besieging Potidaia. He will make the Aegean an Athenian lake. Then he will squeeze us like a lemon. I say it's time we buy off Athenai, time we offer her our support against Amphipolis. I know Epaminondas intends to send a fleet into the Aegean, but when? Between the Arkadian-Elean war in the Peloponnesos and the threat Alexandros of Pherai poses to Thebai in Thessalos, I doubt we will see help from that quarter."

Athanaios yells back, "Don't count out Boiotia. Epaminondas will launch his fleet soon. And Pelopidas will deal with Alexandros of Pherai. That's a grudge match. The Boiotians ready an army even while we're arguing."

Another companion, Kharikles, one of Perdikkas' new men, lurches to his feet, "Foreigners won't save the Makedones. We must do that ourselves. That means we must ..."

Whatever Kharikles thinks must be done is interrupted by a bowl being thrown at him by one of Athanaios' supporters. At that, Perdikkas stands and waves the others down, "Before this supper degenerates into food throwing, let me remind you that I asked you to consider the question of the highlands. Shortly we have several highlanders joining us, Parmenion, son of Philotas, and Alexandros of Orestis. Both come seeking our help. Both are exiles from their lands, supplanted by other branches of their families. Both will be beholden to the Makedones for any aid we provide that helps them regain their positions."

Perdikkas looks about him, standing tall, easily in command of the room of nearly thirty men. "Yet Amuntas Plousias points out how empty is our treasury. Antipatros reports on the slim strength of our army. And at great length, we hear of the Athenian presence."

Philippos watches, admiring his brother. He whispers to Periandros, who is sharing his couch, "Perdikkas is a man to be followed." Periandros nods his assent.

The king continues, "My father taught me that Makedonis is strong when our back is secure. Philippos Arkouda, you will lead an embassy to Derdas of Elimiotis. Parrhasios and Theophilos will accompany you. Remind him that his pleasure in ruling Perrhaibis, and his hopes for his sons following him, results from the efforts of my father and brother. Certainly Athenai and her allies—Alexandros of Pherai, the Molossi, Orestis, and Pelagonis—have no interest in him ruling Perrhaibis. Or in ruling Elimiotis for that matter." The men chuckle.

"Let us send an embassy to the Molossi kings as well." Perdikkas points to Antiokhos, "You get along with King Neoptolemos. He's more reasonable than his brother, Arubbas. Perhaps we need to hint at a marriage between a Molossi princess and a Makedon king or prince. Isn't Troas of marrying age?" Perdikkas makes a wry face and the men laugh.

Parrhasios stands, "When I was in Dodona, there was talk that Neoptolemos agreed to his daughter marrying his brother."

"Do they think they are Aigyptians?" calls out Antipatros.

Another new man, Balakros, adds, "Don't they worship snakes in Epeiros, just like the Aigyptians?"

More soberly, Antiokhos asks, "Parrhasios, what is the temper of the Molossi? They prevented you from taking your men into Orestis."

"You can see why," Parrhasios answers. "The Orestoi now say the Aiakidai kings of the Molossi have always been their overlords. They deny the Temenidai."

"Which brings us back to where we started," comments King Perdikkas. "The truth is that the Orestoi fear that Bardulis intends to expand his Dardanoi kingdom down the highland basins. He dominates Lunkestis. The Orestoi expect that soon he will attempt them. They recognize our weakness and so turn to the Aiakidai kings for protection, just as does Tumphaia." He pauses, raises a mug of wine in toast, "As for Princess Troas, may she find happiness with King Arubbas. That the Aiakidai consolidate their line of succession may be wiser than we profligate Temenidai. Neoptolemos and Arubbas are half-brothers anyway. Besides, I hear she is a terrible shrew." He shudders dramatically, and the men laugh dutifully.

Again Perdikkas turns to Antiokhos, "Still, I think a mission to King Neoptolemos is needed. Let's discuss it tomorrow in my chamber. Tonight we have all been too free with the wine to think it through as clearly as it deserves."

Raising an arm for silence, Perdikkas continues to the larger group, "Let us clear the room of food and drink. Alexandros of Orestis and Parmenion of Pelagonis join us to state their respective cases. Stay attentive to them. Philippos, will you escort them in?"

* * *

The story told by Alexandros makes it clear that a strong pro-Makedon party exists in Orestis. Despite the similarity in dialects and in way of life between the Epeiriotes and the Orestoi, the Makedon claim on Orestid allegiance is strongly felt. The question is as simple as Perdikkas has put it. The highland chiefdom will align with either the Molossi or the Makedones, depending on which offers greater assurance against the encroaching Illuroi.

The truth is that the Orestoi would rather go their own way. In winter their flocks descend to the Epeiriote side of the mountains, so they must cooperate with the Molossi. Their lands are more open to penetration from the Makedones of Eordaia, the Elimiotoi, and the Lunkestoi, so they must cooperate with their highland neighbors. Their dilemma is evident.

Philippos feels that Perdikkas has it right. The key to solving the highlands muddle is to strengthen the lowlands and secure the historic alliance between the Makedones and the Elimiotoi. So Orestis must wait upon events. Let Neoptolemos and Arubbas have the trouble and expense of defending the highlanders for the time being.

The next subject is Pelagonis. For Philippos, the status of their northern neighbor causes more than intellectual concern. Philippos admires Parmenion. He killed his first man riding to war with Prince Parmenion. Where Orestis is distastefully associated with Ptolemaios, and Alexandros of Orestis is a cousin of the dead regent, to Philippos' mind, Pelagonis is the land of stalwart heroes who maintain their homes despite the surrounding Illuroi tribes.

Of course, he knows that the image of uncouth Illuroi that he holds in common with his fellows is not wholly accurate. Cities exist among the tribesmen and they field an excellent hoplite force when required. One could argue that the Pelagonoi are as uncouth. Save that the Pelagonoi speak a western Hellenic dialect, so that while a southern Hellene might see them as barbaric as any Illuroi, for Philippos they are of the same blood and worship the same gods as he and his.

Parmenion rises to speak. In his mid-thirties, he is a renowned warrior and leader of men. Standing erect, with noble bearing, he possesses an air of command and competence. "King Perdikkas, thank you for the opportunity to address you and your companions. Since it is late, I will not speak at length. My family has ruled the Pelagonoi from time immemorial. Where other peoples have legends of how their ancestors came to occupy the lands they hold, our people have legends only of our own mountains and valleys. We know nothing of the wanderings other peoples have experienced."

"Yet, like many families, over time there have been differences between brothers or cousins, between uncles and nephews. In my childhood there were three lines to our royal clan. My father's line, the Philiotai, was the junior line. The rivalry and bloodshed between the two senior lines sundered our people. Angered by the blood feud, a party of shepherd chiefs appealed to Zeus Naios and Dione at the oracle of Dodona. Zeus answered that the taller crooked branches of our family tree were obscuring the growth of the younger straight true branch."

Smiling, Parmenion explains, "The people called upon my grandfather and made him king in place of his cousin. In turn, my father, Philotas, became king. Still the strife did not end."

"Despite the authority of the prophetic Zeus, my distant cousins continue to seek the throne. Some of you joined us in expelling those of our family who denied my father. Philippos Arkouda, we rode together. Periandros, you as well. Prince Philippos, son of Amuntas, you fought against our foes. You all helped to bring peace and right to our valleys."

"As many of you know, while I was overseeing our trading at Epidamnos on the Adriatic coast, my father died. I had left my father a vigorous man of fifty-six. They say he sickened and died in a day. I do not know whether the gods called him or my cousins." Parmenion's tone is solemn. His calmness demonstrates a resolution that should give his cousins concern.

"Menelaos, son of Arrhabaios, grandson of Menelaos, great-grandson of my father's grandfather, last of his line, proclaims himself king in my father's place. To give his claim weight, he has mercenaries paid for by Athenian silver. Raised in Athenai himself, he knows less of our people than any shepherd on a hill."

"I am cut off from the treasury. I have some means as a result of the trading in Epidamnos. My friend Leonidas has brought me sixty men from

209

Pelagonis. I have twelve of my own. So we are a small band of exiles, too few to contest with Menelaos and his mercenaries openly."

Parmenion smiles again, a smile Menelaos should fear, "So my choices are these. One, I can accept exile. Two, I can return to Pelagonis with my horsemen, stay in the hills, and bring civil war on my people. Three, I can seek aid that is so overwhelming that Menelaos cannot dispute my return."

"I will not accept exile," his tone becomes fierce. "I do not want to re-ignite the cycle of endless civil strife, to cause the deaths of my country-men, to ruin their prosperity. I would choose the third option. I seek your aid, Makedones."

In an instant Perdikkas is on his feet and embracing Parmenion, "Prince, you have our pledge. We will do all we can to restore you. Tomorrow, come to me and we will plan your return."

For Philippos, the scene is indelible, suffused as he is with happiness that his good brother will help their noble friend. Yet the calculating half of Philippos is already asking, *what does Perdikkas have in mind? An expedition to Pelagonis could be poking a stick into a hornet's nest.*

γ

Wrestling is a pleasure for Philippos. Though boxing is acknowledged as the roughest sport, Philippos prefers the demands of strength, agility, and thinking imposed by wrestling. Imposed, that is, by wrestling according to accepted rules. Upright wrestling requires you to throw your opponent to the ground three times. Ground wrestling requires pinning an opponent—wearing him out and immobilizing him until he surrenders. The third form, *pankration*, is free form. Anything goes except biting and eye goug-ing. You fight until one of you gives up. Even boxing blows are permitted in *pankration*.

Today Philippos is taking on Lamakhos in *pankration*. The slave Pikoros has oiled his body, grinning hugely the whole time. Philippos has noticed that Pikoros likes sending him into battle, whether wrestling or practice swordplay or mock phalanx scrimmages. *Does the big fellow like to see me hurt?* Wonders Philippos in amusement.

At a signal from the gymnasium coach, Philippos moves into the ring drawn in the sand. Lamakhos steps forward, crouches and begins circling. Already Kleitos and Antigonos are yelling encouragement to Philippos, and other young men crowd about the ring giving their wolf whistles.

Philippos waits, letting Lamakhos move. Tense, standing lightly, ready to rush, Philippos eyes Lamakhos as he circles closer. Lamakhos has filled out since their exile in Thebai. He is proud of his new strength and new height. Philippos figures his opponent is still awkward with his new growth.

From stillness, Philippos darts to the left. Lamakhos is startled and mis-takenly draws back. While his footing is uncertain, Philippos is on Lamakhos.

They grapple. Lamakhos is not so strong as the Theban Hermiodos. Still he breaks free and lands an elbow across Philippos' nose. Ignoring the bright pain, Philippos slams a powerful right upper cut into the center of Lamakhos' chest. Lamakhos stumbles back and falls.

Philippos follows, intent on landing atop his opponent. But something is wrong. Lamakhos is down, gasping for breath yet unable to breathe, his face is red and both hands are clutching his upper chest. His body heaves in pain. His eyes roll back. Philippos kneels beside Lamakhos, trying to help but feeling helpless. The grizzled coach pushes Philippos aside and drops heavily by Lamakhos. Without hesitation the coach strikes each side of Lamakhos' ribcage, then starts vigorously rubbing the youth's chest. "Keep him from swallowing his tongue," he instructs Philippos.

Together, the two work on Lamakhos. From among the men crowding round, Alkimakhos brings a pitcher of cold well water. The coach splashes half over Lamakhos. Philippos whispers, "What are we doing?"

"We have to shock his heart into working," mutters the coach, without letting up his efforts. He pounds Lamakhos' ribcage again. "Massage his heart. Do it roughly," he orders Philippos. Kleitos puts his hand in Lamakhos' mouth, taking control of the tongue.

Nothing seems to work.

The effort seems endless. Stesidamos is crying silently. Alkimakhos is praying. Antigonos is cursing.

"Ouch!" cries out Kleitos as Lamakhos bites down on his hand. Turning on his side, coughing, the young man returns to life.

"Thank you, Hades, for giving Lamakhos back to us," calls out Philippos.

Slowly Lamakhos sits up. His chest is already livid with bruises. He is white-faced but he is alive. "Not Hades," he whispers hoarsely, then clears his throat and spits to one side. "Thank Orpheos. It is Orpheos who led me back from the fires of Tartaros."

* * *

"These tunics are becoming threadbare, master," says Petalouda as she sets the folded clothes into the leather satchel.

"They will do for riding and exercises," comments Philippos, who is deciding which scrolls to take with him.

Without warning, the door to the room bursts open and an angry Perdikkas strides in, trailing Periandros and a guard. "What is this? What is this?" exclaims Perdikkas.

"I am going to Samothrake," calmly answers Philippos.

"Now? This instant?" rebuts Perdikkas.

"The festival of the Kabiroi begins soon. I vowed I would attend as a thanksgiving for Lamakhos' life."

"Don't we have plans? Did you not agree to head our force that aids Parmenion?" is the angry rejoinder.

"Yes, King Perdikkas, I agreed," answers Philippos stiffly. "That was before the gods intervened."

"The gods you say. Which gods? Was it not our god Orpheos?" says the king.

Philippos holds up a scroll of Orphic prophecy, "Father believed in the afterlife promised by Orpheos. I never paid much heed to the Orphic version of ritual. Lamakhos' redemption is a sign to us."

In frustration, Perdikkas waves his arm, "Enough!" Turning to the slave woman and the guard, he shoos them out. Periandros he motions to stand by the door. Taking Philippos by the arm, he leads him to the window.

Speaking softly the king begins his argument, "You know we are at a critical juncture. Makedonis is weak. I am needed here, due to Timotheos of Athenai and the fighting in the Khalkidike. Arkouda leads the embassy to Derdas of Elimiotis. Antiokhos is off to Epeiros. Our embassies succeed only if we can demonstrate our ability to aid the highlands. That is your role. You reinvigorate our footmen. You and Periandros put your force in the hands of Parmenion, and together you restore him to his throne. To succeed, you need to be recruiting and training your men, not off on some pilgrimage to an Aegean island."

"What of Antipatros or one of your new men? Couldn't they be generals for Parmenion?"

"Prince Parmenion asks for you and Periandros. His confidence in you stems from your earlier battle together. I want you to lead because you are my brother, my right arm. I don't want Antipatros seen as my chief deputy. His family is powerful enough."

Philippos' resolve is weakening. His brother's appeal and the logic of kingship are potent enticements.

Perdikkas presses further, "A vow to the gods cannot be forsworn, Philippos. I know that. Am I not the chief priest of the Makedones? I tell you I take responsibility before the gods for your vow. It is for me that you delay. You may make your pilgrimage to the Kabiroi next year. On your return from Pelagonis, visit the tomb of Orpheos in Pieris. Praise him, thank him. Let him know that I bear for you any burden the gods would lay on you for postponing completion of your vow. And next year, do your journey to the Kabiroi."

Philippos nods his assent. Perdikkas puts his arm around his younger brother, "Between us, tell me, why the Kabiroi?"

"I don't know. When Lamakhos spoke of the fires of Tartaros, the image that came to mind are the god-smiths, the Kabiroi. They are of the earth, like Hades. Perhaps they mediate for mankind. I never had much use for Orpheos. He is too gentle."

"Pay him more mind. Father came to see him as a guide to the divine. We all know the power of music. It can speak more truly than prayer. He is a true teacher."

Philippos smiles, "Brother, I am glad you are my king."

δ

"No, no, Alkimakhos," yells Philippos. "I want them moving faster. They're not tortoises; they're men."

"Well they're not horses, either," yells back Alkimakhos, who then turns on his *syntagma* of 256 men and bellows, "You heard the Prince. We do it again, only faster. On my signal, you will advance to the midpoint of the field, then swing to a right oblique and double your pace to close quickly on your opponents." He motions down field, where a second *syntagma* awaits their advance.

Alkimakhos bellows, "Okay, officers, line them up. On my signal, we advance." Quickly the file leaders organize the *syntagma*. Eight men are in each half-file, and the formation is sixteen files or *lochoi* across. The two half-file deep rectangles of men are soon standing at ease, with a grass hallway of about twenty paces or *bema* between the two rectangles. With the talk of the men and the clatter of their armor, the noise is a din. At the signal, talk stops but the clanking rises and is reinforced by sound of hundreds of hard feet hitting the ground. The men are moving faster.

As Alkimakhos and his men march off, Parmenion leans down from his horse to say to the sweating, earnest Philippos, "If you want them to move faster, you must lighten their load."

"I know," answers Philippos. "I've been thinking layered linen or leather instead of bronze for their corselets. That would quarter the weight."

"Won't withstand a strong spear thrust. Your men may be slow, but at least they have the confidence to fight when protected by bronze."

"I've watched the Thebans train. They're good, you know. They wear boots. You would not call them fast, but they are brisk."

"So you're thinking of boots?" asks Parmenion skeptically.

"For winters," answers Philippos.

"Winters? You would campaign in winter?"

"The Paiaones raid in winter, as do the Thraikiotes and the Illuroi. We answer. Riding them down if we can." Philippos looks up at his older friend, "That is simply raid and counter-raid. What if we marched into their towns in winter and torched them all?"

"Carts don't move in winter. How do you provision your army on the march?"

Philippos laughs, "Prince Parmenion, there are answers to all questions. Think about what we do to lighten the army. If we move fast enough, before our enemies expect us, we have the advantage. Carts are impossible in winter? Then we cut out as many servants and haulers as possible. Make the army as lean as we can with fighting men. No luxuries like the southern Hellenes glut their armies. We use mules instead of carts. We get muleteers from the foresters and miners."

"And you leave thirty *minai* of bronze a man behind," says Parmenion in delight.

"You see it, don't you?" answers Philippos.

"I see the reason for the speed," replies Parmenion soberly. "You still haven't countered my spear thrust through you linen cuirass."

"Let me make it worse for my men before I make it better," says Philippos with a grin. "What's the next heaviest item in any hoplite's armor?"

"The shield."

"Right, that great heavy shield—three feet across, bronze plated. A shield on your left arm and spear in your right hand." Philippos shakes his head, "Look at them." Pointing down the field at the mass of the *syntagma*, Philippos shakes his head again, "It won't do, you know."

"Actually, it does very well." Parmenion smiles, "No army can match the Hellenes. Persia is eager to hire us to fight their wars. For all their tens and tens of thousands, we go through them like an arrow through parchment."

"For a stand-up fight, you may be right. In great battles between states to decide their fates, maybe, just maybe you're right. Certainly not for raids or for the kind of fighter we face. To cross mountains and come down on our enemies quickly. No, they won't do as they are now." Philippos looks pensive for a moment, "Prince Parmenion, you will regain Pelagonis. Your ideal is to overawe Menelaos so he doesn't put up a fight. A great battle, a Leuktra or Plataia, would create many deaths and maimings that will give rise to bitterness between the Pelagonoi for years."

Parmenion swings down from his horse and embraces Philippos, "You do understand. There is more that I am doing than enlisting aid from your king. My agents are there now. A hint here, a promise there, is doubt instilled. A mercenary who disappears—deserted? Dead? Pinpricks only. But each pricking is followed by another, and all together they throw Menelaos off-balance."

"That is important," agrees Philippos. "Yet for all that, what you have in mind is to march into Pelagonis at the head of a respectable number of horsemen and at least two full phalanxes of heavy hoplites. Isn't that your desire? And if you had the silver, you would hire it done."

"I would like Spartans. Oh, I know all this talk of Thebans. Nothing inspires fear like phalanxes of Spartans," says Parmenion in self-mockery.

Philippos laughs again, "You must settle for Makedones. We suspect Hellenes who have no reputation as hoplites. Will we even overawe the few mercenaries Menelaos has hired?" Then Philippos turns fierce, "I tell you. Parmenion, that we Makedones will make Spartans quake with fear before I am done."

Parmenion looks at Philippos, assessing him. He has known Philippos boy and man. Of the three brothers, it is Philippos who has always impressed Parmenion. An experience Parmenion shares with Philippos Arkouda, Periandros, and others. What Prince Philippos says he will do, he will do. Nodding thoughtfully, Parmenion says, "All right, tell me about the shield."

"The *hoplos* is too heavy and too large. It requires the use of a shoulder, arm, and hand" Gesturing with his hands, Philippos indicates a smaller diameter, "I say we decrease the size and lighten the load. Let it be worn by a strap from the shoulder, freeing the left hand. Now our man has two hands for his spear. So we can lengthen the spear. We can make it twice the length of a normal spear, make it twice the height of a man or more. That allows us to level our spears for four ranks instead of two. By opening our files a little, all four spear points are attacking the enemy. Our file leader's protection isn't some heavy shield dragging his advance but four spear heads stabbing and jabbing at his opponent's face." Philippos is excited, talking rapidly.

Parmenion thinks about the possibility. There is merit. He looks down the field at the two *syntagmai* going through their dance of mock battle. "You made your basic phalanx unit 16 men by 16. The Spartans use 12 by 12. I thought yours would be unwieldy, and figured you were trying to emulate the Thebans. But you have your own system in mind, don't you?"

"Yes. We can perfect it, you and I. I think the Hellenes throw away too much mobility on the field. The horsemen fight. Then the hoplites fight, each man a turtle in a shell. Then the *psiloi* and other light troops are used for pursuit or to protect the withdrawal. I believe we can make them all work together. You said you want to keep Menelaos off-balance. That's what we need to do on the battlefield. Let them wonder where and how we will strike. Or, better, let them think they know then strike differently. We must have speed, we must have discipline, we must have coordination, we must fight in a way that answers their strengths but doesn't allow them to answer ours. That's what I want to accomplish. I will give to Perdikkas a sword he can use to make our kingdom strong and protect it from all comers. Behind that sword, our people will prosper. Not behind a shield."

"Training is the key. Otherwise your men will have no confidence in your innovations."

"Training and experience," says Philippos in agreement. "Otherwise I won't have confidence that we're getting it right. We must learn from every exercise and every action."

"If you succeed in what you intend, there will be no room for the small highland kingdoms," says Parmenion thoughtfully.

"When Xerxes the Persian occupied all the north, he gave the Makedon king, Alexandros the First, sovereignty over the highlands. He saw that the security of the lowlands demanded that highlands be brought into obedience. That lesson has never been lost on a Makedon king since," says Philippos.

"Yet you would restore me. I will make a stronger king of the Pelagonoi than Menelaos can ever be," challenges Parmenion.

"I do not want the highlands weak. I do not want them open to intrigue from Athenai, Thebai or Bardulis of the Dardanoi. I want them unified, strong, partners in the welfare of all the Makedon peoples."

For a bleak moment, Parmenion considers killing the young prince standing before him. Almost as if Apollo gives him foreknowledge, he knows this Philippos will succeed as the general of the Makedones. Restoration as chief of the Pelagonoi will be hollow for Parmenion, knowing that the Makedones will make Pelagonis' independence a shadow. If Philippos is dead, then who among the Makedones would possess the vision and ability to make strong their kingdom?

Parmenion touches the hilt of his sword. Philippos—good looking, alert, energetic, decisive—stands easily before him. With a wry smile, Parmenion asks, "What of us little kings? Derdas of Elimiotis, Aeropos of Lunkestis, Orestis, Pelagonis? Do we let this happen?"

"Parmenion, you will rule Pelagonis. Outside of Pelagonis, I seek your alliance with the Makedones. My brother seeks the same. Within Pelagonis you hold sway. Outside you march as partner to King Perdikkas."

Without knowing fully why he is trustful, almost without his own volition, Parmenion stays his hand. When King Perdikkas and he had talked, this was not the bargain he thought he was making. Philippos thinks in stronger, starker terms than Perdikkas. Or, maybe, Philippos looks further into the future in deciding what's good for the Makedones. The temptation to back away from Philippos is there. Parmenion could find his own way to his throne.

Down the field the mock battle comes to an end. Alkimakhos and the other *syntagmatarkh* are trudging back to Philippos. All those men recruited within a few days. Others are still coming to fill new *syntagmai*. Men come from Arkouda's clan, from Periandros' and Korrhagos' clans, from most clans of the Makedones. Even citizens of Pella and other communities who are outside the clan structure, even Kretans off a merchant vessel in the harbor, within days they gather at the call from this youngster, this Prince Philippos.

Maybe this Philippos, son of Amuntas, of the Temenidai of the Argeadai Makedones, maybe he owns a grander vision than Parmenion, son of Philotas.

Parmenion looks Philippos in the eyes and asks, "May I call you brother, Prince Philippos?"

The tension eases within Philippos. The death of one of them had been in the balance. Philippos smiles and offers his hands, "Brother."

ε

The trilling laughter of the young women seems like music to Perdikkas. It's washing day in the Korrhagos household and the women go about the task happily enough. Washing day takes them out of doors. Somehow the younger ones manage to get wetter than the work demands. The songs that accompany washing are full of allusions to unclothing and to bed sheets. No maid remains ignorant of the facts of life once she's done the washing.

For Perdikkas, though he puts a good face on his role as king, being on a country estate is a relief from the councils, private arrangements, and worrying news that are his life in Pella. Not that this isn't a kingly task. Ostensibly here to hunt with the great magnate Korrhagos and the chief members of his clan, the king's real purpose is to find a wife.

Of all the suitable women of the realm that he, Philippos, and the Queen Mother have identified, the field has narrowed to three choices. The first is Phila, daughter of Derdas of Elimiotis. The second is Erinna, youngest child of Iolaos, and half-sister of Antipatros. The third is here, Telesilla, granddaughter of Korrhagos, an orphan raised by her great-aunt, Arkhedike.

Left purely to personal choice, Perdikkas would have Phila. Or, truth be known, none of these suitable young women. Instead, there is a widow from Olunthos, living in Pella, who has been Perdikkas' comfort for years. She—Polugnota—is his love truly. He likes rolling her name off his tongue.

What choice does a king have? Who he wives is political. He must seek allies rather than pleasure or heart's comfort. The men of the Temenidai get their Makedon wives from one of the three lines he is considering, or occasionally a fourth, that of Periandros' clan. Right now there is no woman of the right age and antecedents from Periandros.

An exception could be made, of course. Only exceptions are fraught with danger. Look what happened when Perdikkas the Second took Simikhe as bride.

Phila is a biddable beauty who combines appealing shyness with a bright intelligence. And Elimiotis is a thorn that must be grasped. Derdas has become unreliable. His sons have little to recommend them. Somehow Perdikkas and Philippos must settle that problem before it becomes too much of a problem. How to secure Elimiotis? In his mind, Perdikkas has consigned Elimiotis to Philippos to solve. Phila is somewhat old for the prince, not that it matters. She is reported to admire the boy.

As for Erinna, daughter of Iolaos, she is a shrew. Like all that clan, she seems to feel she knows more or better than anyone else. Perdikkas works hard to make Antipatros a friend, and often must grind his teeth in silence. Being brother-in-law as well would be too much. Kingship is a balancing act.

A girl from the Onomokritidai, from Periandros' family, would be good. He shrugs his shoulders. The fates do not allow. So that leaves Telesilla. A girl he knows only from his mother's report.

"Ah, here you are," booms the voice of old Korrhagos. The heavy red-faced man steps out onto the porch. Crossing he places a hand on the king's shoulder, "Have you picked her out yet?" Nodding beyond the porch rail to the activity of the working woman in the yard.

"I am guessing that she's the red-haired girl who keeps glancing up at the porch," answers Perdikkas easily.

Korrhagos' laughter is a wheeze, "That's Aristoklea. They're best friends. No, Telesilla will do no peaking at you. She's there at the far end, with her back to you. A fine girl with a proper sense of decorum."

Perdikkas feels a mild disappointment. The red-haired girl had intrigued him. Telesilla has raven hair and a fine figure. He had noticed her moving about, but since she seemed sad, he had dismissed her. Now he examines her more closely. She is stately. And she does laugh, only softer than the others. The redhead says something that sets the others tittering. Telesilla offers back a wry smile and a shrug. They must be teasing her.

"I tell you her spinning is fine and her loom-work is tight. She works hard. Old Arkhedike would not have less. Do you know Lady Arkhedike? Now that is a woman you don't want to cross." Korrhagos launches into a reminisce about how Arkhedike is the terror of the marketplace, but Perdikkas is only half listening. Watching Telesilla, he keeps finding more grace than he expected. Perhaps mother is right, perhaps Telesilla is a good match.

Interrupting Korrhagos, Perdikkas asks, "When we return from the hunt, Telesilla will be done with her chores?"

Korrhagos likes the king's interest in the girl. "Yes, yes, we will make an exception and invite the women to join us in a meal. Outside by the orchard, where we can keep it informal, casual. A happenstance. Later there will be time for formality." Then Korrhagos turns sly, "I warn you, though. You will need Arkhedike's approval for this match. She guards the girl jealously."

"Surely being wife to a king offers some recommendation?"

"You would think so. I tell you, though, Arkhedike is not to be trifled with. Whatever I say, whatever you think you offer, you will be left whistling if Arkhedike decides no." Korrhagos brightens, "You're a personable lad, Perdikkas, even if you are king. What girl's head wouldn't be turned by you? As for Arkhedike, she admires solid strength. Treat her and her niece well—not lightly, with respect. Do not come on too strong. Ask Arkhedike her opinion of the type of girl who could meet the demands of being queen. She will only be able to think of Telesilla."

Perdikkas turns back to the yard. The eyes of Aristoklea are on him. Telesilla is turned away. Admitting to himself that he is flattered by the interest Aristoklea shows in him, he wonders that Telesilla seems indifferent. Is it pretended or real?

*   *   *

The haunches of venison and boar turning on the spits are not from today's hunt. Korrhagos has opened his larder, offering well-hung meats.

218

None of his reputation for stinginess is in evidence for the king's visit. Instead the afternoon banquet in the orchard is lavish in food and drink. Perhaps too much wine, watered less than is usual, is drunk by all and sundry.

The king's visit is more than a feast day for the household, as many freeholders have been invited from surrounding estates and more humble homesteads. The king's party alone numbers upwards of twenty men. Easily a hundred men, as many women, and even more children, fill the orchard with their chatter, calls, laughter, and squeals. This mixing of sexes and ages makes a festival atmosphere even more than the king's presence.

Of course at the orchard's center, where lounge Perdikkas, Korrhagos, and the older folk, there is more restraint and civility. Lady Arkhedike is certain she does not approve of this gathering, but she is disposed to be tolerant for the sake of her brother-in-law, Korrhagos, and the young king. Still she resolutely refuses to look beyond the immediate group or even imagine what liberties are being taken on the fringes of the orchard. Fixing Perdikkas with her habitual glare, Arkhedike asks, "Will these differences with Athenai continue, King Perdikkas? The best prices come from Athenai and Korinthos. This trouble is affecting my ability to ship stock."

Perdikkas considers the question, then answers, "I could argue, Lady Arkhedike, that privations are necessary when the kingdom is threatened. Yet I know that the well-being of the kingdom rests as much on the prosperity of its people as it does on safeguarding our borders. I must be judicious, balancing the needs of individuals like yourself with the good of us all. To use a light metaphor, as king I must be as nimble as a market day acrobat. As Korrhagos here knows, we seek to forestall Athenai from dominating our coasts. Let me offer you this, if by the coming spring we have not settled our differences with Athenai, so you are prevented from shipping your stock, then I will purchase your horses at the prevailing price in Athenai, less the cost you would spend on shipping."

"Well said, Perdikkas," bellows Korrhagos. "Now is that a handsome offer, Dame Arkhedike?"

With a grudging smile, Arkhedike acknowledges the king's offer. Within, she is elated. Her worries are resolved by the word of the king. He neither offers her too much nor too little. Now she can give her full support to the effort against Athenai. "What will you do with my horses, King Perdikkas?" she asks.

"If our conflict with Athenai continues into spring, I will need horses as remounts for my squadrons. At the same time, you will have the incentive to raise more horses for our future needs."

A king with foresight, thinks Arkhedike. A wiser fellow than his brother Alexandros, more like his father, the divine Amuntas. On impulse she calls out to the younger folk beyond the circle of elders, "Telesilla, come here. You have not given greeting properly to your king."

From among the group of tittering young women, Telesilla stands. For the first time Perdikkas looks fully at her face. The girl is a beauty. Not a light beauty of smooth flesh and giddy excitement, but an abiding beauty of well-structured bone and dignified command. Perdikkas struggles quickly to his feet. Thoughts of Aristoklea die away on seeing Telesilla in full.

The woman walks purposefully to them, her face composed, her eyes bright with her own curiosity about Perdikkas. Stopping at the edge of their group, she bows her head and says, "King Perdikkas, I am Telesilla, daughter of Dionusios. Welcome to the home of my grandfather Korrhagos. You do us all honor." She looks up, up into the topaz eyes of Perdikkas.

As for the king, his breath is caught in his throat; he drowns, looking into the depth of her eyes. The others look at one another with the beginning of amusement. Catching hold of himself, Perdikkas bows his head in turn and manages, "Mistress Telesilla, your grandfather's counsel is of great value to me. Your father was a man of good repute. A king needs about him people of strong good character, on whom he can rely. You are a woman of an honorable family."

Then Perdikkas continues, to the astonishment of his companions, "Telesilla, let us not pretend. I want you for my wife. I pledge that whatever are the demands of kingship, you shall remain my first wife, whose children will follow me on the throne. More, I pledge to be a loving husband who will always bless this day that we have met."

Arkhedike is rigid with consternation. This is not how it is done. See what comes of odd doings in an orchard.

As for Telesilla, she smiles. The smile is rich with gladness, which promises much happiness for Perdikkas and her. "I would be your wife, King Perdikkas. As soon as we can do so in all seemliness." Then looking about her at the bemused elders, she continues, "Perhaps now that you and I have agreed, we can proceed more formally."

Perdikkas laughs, his delight an infectious contagion, "Sometimes a king must cleave quickly to the heart of a matter."

"So you have done, Perdikkas, so you have done," trumpets Korrhagos with pleasure.

ζ

In a sense the boundary between Pelagonis and the Lower Makedonis is the stretching peaks of Mount Boras. When the ancient Makedones defeated the Almopes and took their lands, the Makedones became neighbors of the Pelagonoi. Though neighbors, they can respect one another for Mount Boras prevents anyone other than shepherds or the most desperate individuals from journeying immediately north into Pelagonis.

The regular route to Pelagonis from the south travels through the Makedon highland canton of Eordaia and into Lunkestis. The track from the lowlands skirts the western reaches of Boras and the northern end of Mount Bermion, climbing beyond Edessa, then coming down near Lake Bigorritis. Once beyond the lake and over the hills that separate the Makedones Eordaia from Lunkestis, the traveler enters the western valley of the Erigon River. There, as the traveler wearily walks north, the Pelagonoi are to his right and the Lunkestoi to his left. Another people, the related Deuriopes, live west of the Pelagonoi, occupying the eastern valley of the Erigon, where that river abruptly turns as it strikes Mount Boras and flows northeast into the great Axios River.

The Axios offers another route from the south to Pelagonis. If a Makedone, this eastern route is more dangerous as it lies exposed to the Paiaones and the Illuroi. And it is longer for you to go north along the Axios River, past the eastern extremity of Mount Boras, then head west through the lands and cities of the Deuriopes along the eastern Erigon. One could even march farther up the Axios valley and not turn west until reaching the next major tributary. That would mean marching through lands of Paiaone and mixed tribes, such as the Argestoi.

Tribes of Paiaones hold these middle reaches of the Axios, all the way east to the Strymon River. Beyond the Paiaones and stretching far west above the Pelagonoi and Lunkestoi is the Dardanoi confederation of Illuroi tribes under King Bardulis. Effectively the Dardanoi and other independent Illuroi tribes represent the northern limits of Makedon contact. Occasionally news of peoples and events beyond the Illuroi reach Pella, but the meaning of the news is distorted, muted by distance and the passage of time.

The question that faced Parmenion, Philippos, and Periandros was how to take their force of over two thousand footmen and near two hundred horsemen to Pelagonis without causing a reaction from King Bardulis or, if using the eastern route, from King Agis of the Paiaones, and still confront Menelaos of the Pelagonoi before he is prepared to meet them.

Periandros argued the traditional route. Among the points he extolled were the advantage of using Eordaia as a supply base, the greater security for their line of march, and, in the event of failure, their ability to extricate themselves from Pelagonis and quickly fall back on safe territory.

Parmenion preferred using the Deuriopes as their base. That people, he felt, would be sympathetic to his cause. His father always respected their independence while securing their cooperation against raids from Illuroi and Paiaones. In contrast, the Menelaos' branch of the family cultivated and sought support from the civilized elements among the Illuroi, as well as the Lunkestoi and Epeiriote tribes of the west.

Young Philippos yearned for an approach that would permit them to completely surprise Menelaos. He toyed with a diversionary strike over Mount Boras. Between the third and fourth peaks of the mountain's five major peaks was a saddle that might be negotiated by a formed body of light troops. Not a pass certainly. A lower stretch of rock through which shepherds sometimes move smaller flocks from the southern watershed to the northern.

While Periandros and Parmenion acknowledged the surprise such a march would cause, they argued against its practicality. In the end, it would bring the troops into the Erigon's eastern valley. And at what cost in possible losses as the near impossible march exhausted horses and men?

Next Philippos suggested they march to the western tributary of the Axios above the Erigon so they could come down on Menelaos from the north. Philippos acknowledged that this was a risky plan and could only offer surprise if their journey up the Axios valley was unusually swift.

Parmenion agreed the plan had some merit, provided they could gain the secret agreement of King Agis to permit the ascent. The Paiaones principal king might not possess sufficient influence among his cousins lying close to the Dardanoi lands to gain their acquiescence. At best the diplomatic necessities of the route would delay them a month.

In the end, they adopted Parmenion's plan. By easy stages they marched north along the west bank of the Axios River. The four phalanx battalions grew accustomed to the march. Each day the march lengthened, and few men fell out ill. The end of the third day's march saw them camped well beyond the steep "gates" cut by the Axios off the eastern end of Mount Boras. The fourth day brought them to a tributary of the Axios lying below the Erigon. There they turned west, on the morning of the fifth day. By day's end they were in the country of the Deuriopes and had reached the Erigon.

Parmenion's messengers had alerted the magistrates of the Deuriope cities. As he predicted, the cities received him with enthusiasm. The small army was readily re-supplied. The Deuriopes added to their numbers, providing some 30 horsemen, 128 hoplites, and roughly 450 poorer men to serve as peltasts and *psiloi*. All were welcome, especially the fast-moving peltasts, with their javelins and wicker shields. They would serve as the hinges on either flank of the phalanx. Together with the rudely weaponed *psiloi*, they would link the slower phalanx with the faster horsemen.

After a day of rest and celebration and another day in which the growing army marched the length of the Deuriopes lands, Parmenion led his force into the southeastern corner of Pelagonis. There, agents previously sent ahead met Parmenion. Their reports confirmed that some measure of surprise had been achieved. Menelaos was calling in his mercenaries and forcing the young men of Pelagonis into ranks. If Parmenion marched on Menelaos immediately, the false king would not have time to fully form his army. As important, the lion Bardulis still slept in Illuris. That would have been impossible had they followed Periandros' advice and marched via Eordaia and Lunkestis.

Parmenion ordered the advance. Periandros went forward with the scouting horsemen. Philippos led his phalanx. Parmenion was everywhere, assuring that everyone knew their task, that all was in order, and that all were encouraged. Confidence flowed like a river among the men under the clear leadership of Parmenion.

Each league they marched brought Pelagones to their ranks. Whenever a noble Pelagone would ride in with a retinue of warriors, there would be wild greetings and echoing cheers. Parmenion and his chief lieutenant, Leonidas, quickly organized the new arrivals. The ill-armed became Pelagonid *psiloi*. The better-armed or more stalwart were formed into a hoplite phalanx. As needed, stores brought by Parmenion on mule back supplemented their arms. The nobles and their companion horsemen joined the questing Periandros.

At the end of that intoxicating day, eight full days out from Pella, Parmenion's army occupied a series of low hills above a stream that flows west into the Erigon. In the meadows on the other side of the stream stood the ranks of Menelaos' mercenaries. The day was too advanced to initiate battle, but all the combatants knew that on the morrow the fight for Pelagonis would occur.

*　　*　　*

Sleep had eluded Philippos. Now, on foot, standing behind the ranks of his four *syntagmai*, he waits—expectant, both eager and afraid. Leaving camp an hour past, he had quickly formed his men. The four *syntagmai* stretch in a line. Alkimakhos leads the first *syntagma* with its 256 men. Demetrios, older brother of Antigonos, leads the second. A member of Periandros' family, Nikiandros, has the third. The fourth *syntagma* is led by Makhatas the Elimiote. After months of drilling and better part of a *dekades* on the march to Pelagonis, Philippos is confident of his commanders. So are the men, for Philippos can hear the nervous laughter and bright chatter in the ranks.

Further right are the Deuriope hoplites, and beyond them their *psiloi*. To the left are the Pelagonid and Deuriope peltasts, with Pelagonid *psiloi* on their flank. Included there are the heavily armed Pelagones, too unused to fighting together en mass to be called a phalanx. The left is anchored on a turn in the streambed. The right on dark forest. Periandros has a troop of horsemen forward of the foot on the left. As a reserve, behind the *psiloi* on the right, is a larger body of horsemen led personally by Parmenion.

They are ready. False dawn has left, full dawn is here.

Antigonos walks over to Philippos. The prince has made his giant friend his herald for this fight. "Philpa, you want me to climb a tree and get a better look at what's going on over there?"

Philippos nods his assent, "That could help. Or have someone lighter go up a tree and you send word back to me."

"You remember Little Korrhagos? That fight was easy, fast. This will

223

be a battle, not some nameless skirmish." Antigonos is talking easily, smiling. Yet Philippos recognizes the fear underneath. The prince wonders uneasily if Antigonos can see the same fear lurking within him.

"Go climb a tree, Antigonos," he answers gently.

What is Menelaos doing? The mercenaries have broken camp across the narrow valley. They are formed and waiting. As for the Pelagones in Menelaos' army, they seem fewer than yesterday. Still there are Pelagones there by the many hundreds. Philippos supposes they represent Menelaos' own family and the more northerly Pelagonid clans. Who else would stand by the false king? Yet if Menelaos prevails today, will he still be a false king? Who has a right to the throne?

Philippos remembers the lessons taught by the Lady Kleopatra. Bloodlines may offer candidacy. Gaining a throne comes from a combination of good fortune, guile, and might. Keeping a throne is harder. Vigilance, cooperation, and stern but fair discipline are the keys she numbered.

Of course if the gods turn away from you, nothing else matters. You are lost.

The image of his father comes to mind—Amuntas as king. Does he rest easy now? Can he see his son standing here with twelve-foot spear and helmet? What would the old man think of this phalanx? No heavy round shields, no bulky breastplates. With that thought, fear lodges in the back of Philippos' throat. Not fear for himself, but for these men who trust him. Has Philippos trained and led them to slaughter? Will these innovations only lead to their bloody deaths?

Maybe eighteen is too young to be a general. Grimly he laughs at himself. If he lives today, he'll be nineteen soon.

Oh ever renewing god, both Zeus and child Dionysios, guide us today, protect us, give us your strength and we will do our human best by you. Philippos feels easier for his prayer.

The traditional sacrifice had been offered just before dawn. The diviners with the army say today is a good day. Still Philippos would feel better if the cloud cover broke and the sun of the Makedones was shining. Then he would know the strength of Zeus is with him.

"Menelaos is sending a herald," says Antigonos, startling Philippos, who marvels at how quietly the big man can move. "His army is in full formation now. I think we'll start soon."

"I'm moving forward. We'll go up by Nikiandros," Philippos waves over his trumpeter and signaler. Pikoros, the slave, trots forward too. The five men stride to the front between the two middle *syntagmai*. The men in each unit fall silent as their general goes forward.

"Ho, Nikiandros, what say?" calls Philippos.

The older man leaves his position in the line to meet Philippos, "We're ready. Either it starts soon or his army will break up. I don't think he can hold his warriors if he doesn't give them a fight soon."

Philippos likes this dour old man. Greybeard and seamed face, with a jutting nose—a man as plain as an apple and just as worthy. Periandros and Nikiandros have so many kinsmen in the ranks of this *syntagma* that it's a family reunion each morning when they shake out their hides and blankets and rise to their feet. Five sons of Nikiandros march with their father. When Philippos Arkouda and Periandros pledged their clans to Philippos, those long years ago, the pledges had not been idly made even though made to a youngster.

Pointing, Antigonos says, "There, Parmenion is sending someone out to meet Menelaos' herald."

The men watch the exchange of courtesies. The two riders separate each back to his comrades. From across the valley trumpets blare. The enemy is in motion.

Philippos shades his eyes, watching their advance. "Very deliberate," he comments. Turning to Nikiandros, he says, "Shall we go out to meet them when they reach the stream? They will expect us to be as deliberate for fear of disordering our ranks. We will run down on them instead." Turning from Nikiandros, Philippos grabs Antigonos' arm, "Go quickly to each of my commanders. On my trumpet signal, all advance on the run. Just as we practiced. Three trills and a long blast is the signal. I want us to move slightly oblique. We hit them on their right first. Let's open their ranks and give Parmenion space to enter with his horsemen. Understand?" Antigonos repeats the orders. "Now go," says Philippos.

Turning to Nikiandros, the prince says, "You heard my orders?" Nikiandros nods assent, then walks back along his file leaders giving each instructions to pass along the column. Antigonos is already jogging over to Alkimakhos.

Waving over his signaler, Philippos repeats his plan, has the man say it back, then sends him on the run to find Parmenion's couriers so that all commanders on the field will know what he is doing.

With orders in motion, Philippos waits again, watching, gauging the enemy's march. He feels no doubts now. Especially as he sees how the enemy Pelagones on the left are lagging. They must be unsure of their allegiance. Those flanking the mercenary phalanxes on the right are true to the advance. Probably people whose futures are entwined with Menelaos.

A rabbit runs brokenly across the field in front of the enemy phalanx, trying to find escape from all those marching feet. Near the stream it disappears in the bushes.

Philippos reaches out and pulls his trumpeter close. "When I say," he whispers in the blond man's ear. He tightens his grip on the trumpeter's shoulder, "Get yourself ready." The trumpet is up resting on the man's meaty lips. "Now," says Philippos. A mighty breath and then the high trilling tones followed by the great blare.

Philippos tosses his shield on his shoulder, holding it tight with the strap under his arm. He lifts his spear in both arms and runs easily down the slope, beside the third rank man of the *syntagma*'s far-left file. Behind follows Pikoros, his three javelins in one hand and a wicker shield in the other.

Within minutes, spear points thrusting ahead of the columns, they reach the mercenary formation. The enemy has braced to meet them, but the inertia of the downhill run is too much for them, and the Makedones are already among their foe. Spears work furiously, seeking throats and eyes.

Fighting now from the front rank, Philippos engages a large set hoplite. The man is good at his trade, but has never met this reckless speed in an opponent before. Philippos evades the enemy spear, slips aside the big hoplite shield and runs his spear into the other man's groin. Pulling free, he slashes a neighboring hoplite across the man's eyes with the butt end of the spear. Already deep into the enemy phalanx, Philippos raises a keening cheer. Around him other Makedones take up the high-pitched cry. Philippos sees Pikoros' grinning face. His javelins gone, he too carries a long Makedon spear. There is not time for thought, as Philippos hurtles himself at the next foeman.

Who knows how long the struggle lasts? By hoplite standards, it is not a long fight. By hoplite standards, it is a crazy fight. Who are these Makedones? This is not the weak footmen traditionally fielded by the horse-valuing Makedones. This is something new. Stolidly, together, the mercenaries retreat. If their flankers had held and gone back with them step by step, all might have been well for them. But with Menelaos' people swept away, the ranks are exposed. Soon horsemen are at their rear. The mercenary file closers face about. They fight more fiercely than the front ranks. Surrounded, stalled, they are being chewed alive by these Makedones, Deuriopes, and Pelagones. Calling out their surrender, the mercenaries lower arms. Spears fall to the ground. Men drop to their knees as supplicants. Shortly the killing stops.

Parmenion rides through the ranks of captured hoplites. Most are sitting, some still stand leaning on shields or reversed spears. Breaking through the clot of dead on the forward face of the fight, Parmenion comes to Philippos. He steps down from his horse and sweeps the young man into his arms. "Thank you for my throne, dear brother," he says in the midst of that tight embrace.

The two part, stare at each other, grinning. "You are most welcome, King Parmenion," answers Philippos. "What of Menelaos, son of Arrhabaios?"

Parmenion spits, then says, "The coward got away. He launched his army, then rode away with his closest supporters. Leonidas is following them north, but I doubt he catches the son-of-a-bitch. He'll fly away to Athenai, welcomed back by that mistress of deceit." Parmenion's anger is abiding, a rumble in his chest, a burning in his brain.

ALLIANCE WITH PELAGONIS

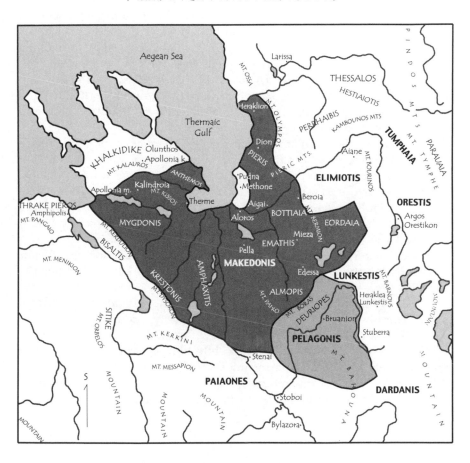

For Philippos, the words turn this victory into ashes. They had conquered leaderless men, men who fought well but without conviction. The slaughter was for nothing. Parmenion was already king before the first spear struck a man.

Looking about him, Philippos can see the cost of victory, broken bodies and blood-soaked ground. The *syntagmatarkhs* are already counting the dead and wounded. All of them except Makhatas, a second cousin of King Derdas of Elimiotis, who is down from a spear thrust in his side.

Philippos knows without an official count that too many of his men were lost this morning. They crushed the first ranks of the enemy phalanx with their charge, but lost formation themselves. In the cut and thrust that followed, speed often prevailed over armor, but not often enough. Maybe in putting aside the protection of hoplite shield and bronze corselet, he threw caution to the winds.

Parmenion follows Philippos' gaze. Gently, he touches the young man's face, drawing the eyes to him, "Prince, you and your Makedones fought like lions of the mountains. Never have I seen such speed in a phalanx. All that you theorized was realized. Like that old story told of your namesake, King Philippos, when he and his people came down on the Almopes and Illuroi, beat them and hunted the remnants. A vengeance and a righteousness. You trained your men hard and it showed."

Tears leak from Philippos' eyes. He tries to speak, sorrow overwhelms his words. All those good men gone. He steps back, shakes his head to clear his eyes.

"Master," says the raspy voice of Pikoros, "the *syntagmai* are formed again. They await you." Pikoros is smiling broadly, proudly.

Philippos turns, seeing the assembled formations of his four *syntagmai* in the valley. At his turn, they salute him, spears clashing against shields, their roar of acclaim raising the hairs on the nape of his neck. Whatever he thinks of this morning's fight, the men in the ranks have no doubt as their shining faces and tolling praise exclaim.

η

"Well, it wasn't for naught," says Perdikkas. The king is at ease, seated in a broad chair, idly plucking the *kithera* on his lap. The tones of the strings seem to underscore his statement.

Philippos sits cross-legged nearby, his back to a cool pillar. The dispassionate voice of his brother offers no sustenance for the need felt by Philippos for purpose in the sacrifice of his Makedones in distant Pelagonis.

Impatiently Perdikkas says, "How could you know that events in the south would weaken our ability to withstand Athenai? It was a good plan to strengthen our hold on the highlanders' loyalty. It is still a good plan. Philippos Arkouda spoke to good effect in his embassy to King Derdas.

You have restored our friend Parmenion to the throne of Pelagonis. Neither Bardulis of the Dardanoi or Aeropos of Lunkestis can take us for granted. Even Antiokhos had some success in Molossi Epeiros. All good." He sighs, "We take two steps forward, then must retreat a step. Well, what is new about that? In real terms, we are stronger today than we were a year ago. If we work steadily, beneath a shield of cooperation with Athenai, there will come a time when we can challenge her."

"You join Timotheos the Athenian against Olunthos in ten days time. You help him gain his prize. You help Athenai secure our coast with the bronze prows of their warships."

"Philippos, Philippos, listen to me. Why this bitterness? We must be in accord. While I am gone, you are regent here in Pella. You guard my back." Entreaty is in Perdikkas' voice.

Rubbing a finger along the joints of the floor's mosaic stones, Philippos says nothing. There is no question in his mind over supporting his brother. He is impatient himself with this lassitude that has come over him since the battle in Pelagonis. The news of Pelopidas the Theban's death has not helped. Still that's no explanation for whatever is broken inside of him.

"You liked Pelopidas," says Perdikkas matter-of-factly.

The prince nods, "Yes, a man of action. Sometimes hot-tempered, but full of ideals. Epaminondas and Pammenes will feel his loss as if he were a piece of themselves. He had that way with his friends."

"The Thessaliotes did for him the highest honors offered a mortal man."

"Well, they should. Even in his death, he freed them from the army of Pherai."

Dryly, Perdikkas answers, "Philippos, you have become all emotion. Where is that thinking part of you that I need and rely upon? Yes, he and his Thessaliote allies defeated Alexandros of Pherai. That defeat had less impact than the army Thebai marched north to avenge Pelopidas. It is they who hem in Alexandros. Their commanders, Malkitas and Diogeiton, dictate terms to Alexandros." He taps his fingers on the *kithara's* strings, the succession of tone form a shepherd's melody. "What matters to us is that with Pelopidas dead, there is no senior Theban interested in the lands north of Thessalos."

"True, for now. But Epaminondas persists in his efforts to put a Theban fleet in the Aegean."

"If he succeeds, and if he can upset the stranglehold of Athenai, then we can take an independent line again. Until then, let us play the Athenians. We will pluck the notes they want to hear. Our warriors will be with them at Olunthos. We will even aid them against Amphipolis." Perdikkas grins, "Though we will also send secret aid to the Bisaltai and other tribes that help Amphipolis. Our agents will give the Olunthians every detail of Timotheos' plans for their defeat. We will eagerly eat the food gathered to sustain the Athenian army and we will be laggards in doing the fighting." Perdikkas plays the *kithera* with more purpose, offering an ancient Makedon hymn to Zeus and Herakles.

Philippos begins to smile, his love for his brother surfacing, "You would have me rebuild my phalanx?"

"Rebuild? You exaggerate. Do add to it, hone your men, and perfect their training. Experiment further if you will. So you are not satisfied with your first battle? Then improve. Talk with your officers, with the men. What worked, what failed? Strip away anything that hindered success. And drill. Drill until you and your spearmen drop."

"All of my *syntagmatarkhs* have suggestions. Demetrios is particularly vocal. And there's Antigonos and the others, they press for an even longer spear, a pike."

"Good, good—I want two of your *syntagmai* with me. You work with the rest. Use them as a core and raise two additional *syntagmai.* Who should I have with me?"

"Nikiandros is reliable. And I think Demetrios. He is very good." Philippos considers, "I need to work more with Alkimakhos. Makhatas must be replaced. He mends but will not serve again."

"That was wise of you to see that he had a strong escort home and the best physician in attendance." Slyly Perdikkas adds, "You know Lady Phila is very fond of her kin."

"I know that we are very fond of Elimiotis," responds the prince.

"You sound like yourself, brother. Then I need have no fear for Pella while I am away?"

Philippos answers his king very seriously, "You need never fear for your back while I am guarding it."

θ

The clumps of doubting older men stand to one side watching as Alkimakhos puts his *syntagma* through its paces. Many shake their heads in dismay. One, Lagos, calls over to Philippos, "All very well against Paiaone peltasts or Thraikiotes, but it won't do, Prince Philippos, against the best hoplite pha-lanx. Yes, I know you succeeded in Pelagonis. Those ragtag men-for-hire that Menelaos could afford were surprised by the novelty of your attack. Besides, they were already a mob without a general. And look at the losses you took. Nearly one in ten killed or wounded. No, it just won't do."

Kleitos growls in his throat, beginning a rebuke of Lagos, but Philippos restrains him with a touch. Instead he calls to another older man stand-ing at the fringe of the onlookers, "Lusias, I need your assistance."

The old trainer comes forward, surprised at being summoned before these notables. "Philpa, what would you have?" he asks.

"Would you have arms in the field shed for these doughty fighters?" Philippos indicates Lagos and the dozen or so men accompanying him.

"Sure, more than enough."

"Friend Lagos, would you consent to arming properly as a hoplite? You as well Antiokhos? Korrhagos? Antipatros? All of you? Good, good." To Lusias, Philippos says, "You join them as well. You will be a file leader. Antipatros, you're younger than the rest, but everyone knows your reputation as a fighter, will you act as a second file leader?" Counting quickly, Philippos continues, "You can have two files of seven each and one of you can act as overall commander. Choose a tough commander." Turning to Kleitos, Philippos commands, "I want twelve of your men here, armed. You and I will act as our file leaders."

Before long the two groups stand across from each other, exercising. Each group is armed distinctively. As hoplites, Lagos and the others wear bronze helmets that encompass the head and neck save for eyes, mouth, chin, and throat. Some wear bronze cuirasses, but more have heavy linen corselets, reinforced with bronze plates or small scales. Bronze greaves protect shins and knees. Their most distinctive armament is the heavy shield, the hoplos. For hundreds of years this large round shield with its bronze face, broad enough in diameter to cover the torso, has defined Hellenic warfare. As offensive weapons, these hoplites have spears six to eight feet in length, butted in bronze and tipped with an iron leaf-shaped blade. In addition, most men carry an iron sword or dagger hung in a scabbard from their waist.

As the hoplites exercise, they move together from an at ease position, with spear butt and shield rim resting on the ground, to attention, spear on right shoulder, shield gripped by their left forearm and hand to cover their left and front body. At the call of "on guard", the spear is off the shoulder and thrust underhand, parallel to the ground. The files advance in this manner. At contact, the front rank of the hoplites shift their grips, raise the spear above their heads and thrust over the rim of their shields. If needing to be on the defensive, the hoplites crouch down behind their shields and thrust up with their spears. No horsemen can ride down hoplites in a defensive position.

As for Philippos and his young men, their arms include no bronze on their linen corselets. Some have dispensed with bronze greaves on their legs, while those that have them use the smaller greaves that cover the shins but not the knees. The shields they carry are half the size or less of the *hoplos*. Slung across the left shoulder by leather straps, the small shield leaves both hands free. In advance, the shields protect the upper body, no more. The most distinctive armament is the *sarissa*, the pike. Rather than a spear, this weapon is fifteen to eighteen feet in length, depending on the rank where the man stands in formation. Though long, the sarissa is relatively light for its length, being made of cornelwood. Light and strong cornelwood is native to Makedonis.

With exercises done, both groups are ready for the contest. By now, word has spread and many citizens and residents of Pella have come down to the field to watch. Among them are a group of women, led by Arsinoe, Lagos' wife. Waving across to Lagos, Philippos calls, "Is it all right if Lady Arsinoe gives the signal for advance?"

Hearing, the onlookers cheer. Arsinoe raises a scarf high, then drops it swiftly.

Instantly both formations advance. Philippos and Kleitos move at a half-run. At a cry, pikes are leveled. Across from the pikes are the opposing spears of Lusias and Antipatros, stolidly advancing. Just before striking the hoplites, Philippos and Kleitos halt the pikemen's attack. From the viewpoint of Lusias and Antipatros, four pike blades apiece are in their faces, for extending beyond Philippos and Kleitos are the pikes of the three ranks immediately behind them. Even if those hoplites pushing from behind Lusias and Antipatros still need convincing, these two are now believers.

Antipatros lowers his spear and rests his shield, "I'm glad you stopped, Philippos." Smiling wryly, the stocky man adds, "I believe I was about to gain a third eye."

"What do you mean," demands Lagos, shoving forward. "This was no true contest. We haven't even come to the push of the fight."

Korrhagos seconds Lagos, "I don't see this as proving anything."

"If you don't mind me saying so," puts in Lusias, "if it had come to a push, it would have been over my dead body."

Ignoring Lusias, Korrhagos and Lagos continue to argue for tradition. Most of their companions agree, though several look thoughtful, as if wondering where this change could take them.

After good-naturedly seeing the arguers off the field, Philippos puts an arm each around Lusias and Antipatros, "You two see the worth of what we're doing. Lusias, if I have Alkimakhos and Kleitos take you through the finer points, would you consent to train our recruits in the new methods?"

The old man is delighted, "I'm in good shape, Philpa. Maybe a little slower nowadays, but I still can put youngsters through their paces."

"I remember well the paces you put me through, Lusias. And I want the same honesty from you that you always gave me when I was little. If you think something we're doing is nonsense, then say so. I don't think we have this method of fighting right yet. Maybe we come on too fast, misaligning our front." Patting the old man on the shoulder, Philippos releases him into Kleitos' care.

Philippos and Antipatros continue walking together. Nothing is said for a time. Antipatros waits for the prince to begin. Reaching a bench under a fine spreading tree on the far side of the field, the two sit. "Antipatros, you have known Perdikkas and me since birth. Your father and mine were close friends, not simply companions. Your family, your clan, has always supported the Temenidai. Yet I do not feel I know you well. You are like some distant cousin of whom one hears much but not the essence that is the real man. I feel we should close that gap. I would have you be as dear to Perdikkas and me as was your father with mine."

Tugging lightly at his beard, Antipatros takes a moment to respond, "With two strong brothers, with many friends in your own age class, you have not needed to know me. When you were younger, our age difference probably seemed insurmountable. And there was your unfortunate exile to Thebai, absent from Makedonis for three years." The eyes in the broad bearded face light with the man's smile, "I agree that it is time we knew each other well; it is time we become friends."

Antipatros continues, "Your brother and I have drawn closer. There are also a lot of new men who have become his companions. There is his future father-in-law, Korrhagos, and that whole clan. Those people are not favorites of mine."

Philippos nods his understanding, "There are many legends from the beginnings of our people. While most say that the first Perdikkas had two brothers, others say that Guanes and Aeropos were not brothers but chieftains in their own right. I know that your family traces its line through Guanes. If Guanes was Perdikkas' older brother, then your blood runs back to Temenos, to Herakles, and to Zeus. If Guanes was not Perdikkas' brother, then yours was a ruling family of the Makedones when Perdikkas came down from the highlands. In either event, your ancestor made common cause with Perdikkas the First against mutual enemies. Either way, your family and mine are inextricably linked. We are two of the three pillars that hold up the edifice of this kingdom. I urge you to press your friendship and good counsel with our Perdikkas. If you find, at times, his other companions uncomfortable, then come to me. We shall hunt, hawk, ride, eat, and share together. You are forever welcome at my fire."

ι

The resemblance between Queen Eurudike and Lady Kleopatra is clearer to Philippos with each passing year. While Eurudike now is something more than half the age of that venerable woman when she gave her friendship to the child Philippos, already Eurudike evidences that beauty which becomes stronger with age rather than fading. Oh, the lines are there, and gray is there. They are nothing compared to the warmth, the alertness, the keen intelligence, the obvious compassion, even the sheer physical vitality and handsome features. Philippos is enlivened watching his mother laugh and be hostess for her son, King Perdikkas.

"This is a great occasion, Prince Philippos," says Korrhagos in distracted good humor. "Look, there is old Agerrhos! I must greet him. You do not mind?" Korrhagos lumbers off bellowing welcomes in the direction of a frail man trailing a host of relatives who have just entered the marriage hall.

Philippos is content to hear the laughter, raised voices, and high cheer. The entire kingdom seems ready for Perdikkas to marry. Philippos is happy for his brother. That the king nearly swoons at the sight of Telesilla is a bit comical, but years of marriage will answer for that. What is wanted is an heir. Perdikkas is popular among the people. Still, until the future is guarded with several strong sons of the king, the people will be anxious. They want no more strife as occurred between Alexandros and Ptolemaios, or those lesser contestants, Argaios and Pausanias.

As for Philippos himself, there have been several sexual partners of late from both sexes. Marriage can be an inconvenience to a young man curious about the manifold ways humans behave sexually. True there is no one he is dandling now. Well, no one unless you count Telesilla's friend, Aristoklea. But then who is dandling whom in that instance? When that lady marries, her husband will gain a wife with practical experience.

"Philippos, why are you keeping to yourself?" asks his mother, coming up beside her son and giving him a peck on the cheek. "Go, talk with your brother's friends. There is Philippos Arkouda and his boys. Take a flagon of wine to Arkouda."

Handed the flagon and pushed genially by his mother, Philippos crosses over to Arkouda, glad to see his friends and their wives. Arkouda and Philippos embrace, and in turn, Philippos embraces Arkouda's sons, the wine passing from man to man as each toasts the occasion and drinks.

"Save some for Polemaios, Antigonos," kids his sister-in-law, Stratonike. In truth, the overgrown bear seems too thirsty, but he leaves enough for his younger brothers.

Demetrios taps his wife light-heartedly, "Look out, here comes your father."

Stratonike groans in mock concern as Korrhagos bulls his way through the crowd. "What now, father, surely you've already done enough toasting," she cries in greeting.

"Never, daughter. Tonight I would drink the moon," laughs the red-faced Korrhagos. "Good to see you, Arkouda," and they embrace. Then Korrhagos turns on Demetrios in mock concern, "Boy, are you keeping this wench in hand? Remember what I told you on her wedding day, beat her once a week to make her mindful."

"Father," shrieks Stratonike, "you are an awful old man."

Demetrios laughs, "And I thought your advice was to make love to her once a day to make her appreciative."

"That too, that too. Nothing contradictory in that advice," booms Korrhagos. A little more seriously Korrhagos says to Stratonike, "Your mother tells me that Telesilla has been asking for you. Ever since Aristoklea started following Philippos around, she's not been much of a companion to Telesilla." The old man laughs to see Philippos' discomfiture.

Another couple joins the group. Korrhagos welcomes them boisterously,

"Lagos, for a hoplite general, your spear is dragging. You need a full wine cup."

"He's upset over the wine he spilled down his cloak. We were jostled in the crowd. You needn't worry, though, about his spear. I can get it up," answers Arsinoe with her usual deadpan ribaldry.

"Shush, woman," says Lagos in annoyance, then more brightly, "Let us do you honor, Korrhagos. And you, Demetrios, as you are kin through Stratonike. With this marriage, you secure connection to the king."

"What were you saying about Aristoklea?" asks Arsinoe.

Korrhagos chuckles, "Just giving young Philippos a ribbing."

Arsinoe turns her cool green eyes on Philippos. The prince smiles and bows his head lightly in return. "So, has Aphrodite favored the two of you?"

"Apparently rumor gives that speech. I must defend the lady's honor by saying that while her gifts would be welcome, they remain in her hands." Philippos lies deftly.

"So do you like receiving gifts?" responds Arsinoe.

"As do we all. But today is Telesilla's gift to Perdikkas. Let us celebrate their good fortune and future."

"Rightly said," adds Arkouda. "Demetrios, send off Stratonike to Telesilla. We want this ceremony to begin almost as anxiously as does Perdikkas."

* * *

The leaves are falling. The night wind is cool. Soon the new year will be here. Philippos looks up at the sky, filled with its myriad pinpricks of light. Focusing on them, he begins to discern their patterns. From Orion, a shower of stars seems to fall as if Father Zeus were flinging points of light in celebration. *Oh great god, thank you for this day. May Perdikkas and Telesilla enjoy your blessings,* intones Philippos in a whisper to the night air.

He is drunk, of course. Not reeling, singing, wildly drunk. Nor somnolent, inert. Just drunk enough to feel melancholy. Drunk enough to distinguish between the two voices in his head—his own, feebly, soddenly, and the more precise amused voice that must be the god Dionysios.

He supposes that by now Perdikkas and Telesilla have consummated their marriage. He smiles in memory of his brother's all suffusing happiness. Telesilla. His brother is right. She owns her own form of beauty. They will do well together.

The breeze gives him a chill. After the heat of drink, dancing, the crowds —this quiet, this coolness, feels good. He loves the intensity of dance and the full fellowship of his kin and friends. On a day like this kinship and friendship are extended as widely as possible. Now, though, he is ready for peacefulness.

The shuffle of a step behind him makes him think that Arsinoe may be continuing their private dance of desire, begun this evening, but turning he sees his mother. "I thought you had gone to bed long since, mother."

"No, son. May I sit with you?"

Philippos shifts, making space on the broad balustrade. She sits, and takes his hand in hers. For a long time they sit together with nothing being said. There is no need.

"It's coming right, isn't it?" she finally asks, though whether to Philippos, the night, or the gods is hard to know.

"I think so, mother," Philippos replies.

Nothing more is said, until Eurudike rises and kisses her son's forehead, then says, "Good night, son. Or is it good morning now? Pikoros and Petalouda were searching for you earlier. They didn't want you to be one of the drunken bodies waking up on the floor tomorrow."

Philippos smiles, "I think I shall free them."

"That would be good. They will bear you warriors, you know."

He nods thoughtfully, "Yes. They have been good to me. I can be good to them. I will go to the temple tomorrow, today, I guess. I will free them and give them the choice of staying in my service or of having a homestead of their own."

"'Tis a good night for giving," she answers. Then tousling his hair, she steps back into the palace.

Yawning, Philippos stretches. He must go in too. There are many things to do tomorrow, today. With a rush he realizes his melancholy is gone. He is happy.

CHAPTER ELEVEN

Arsinoe
363 B.C.

α

She is eager as a nubile girl first discovering sexual pleasure. He is amazed at how this sophisticated woman of the
court, with her careful clothing and intricate manners, becomes all animal within the privacy of their embraces. Though she never knew, initially
Philippos was intimidated by her cultured nonchalance, her seniority of ten
years over his age, and her apparent worldliness in understanding men.
Now it is her passion that is intimidating. The ferocity of her attacks upon
his body; the squeals and moans, that come close to howling in climax; her
raking nails and the punctures of quick severe bites. He can master her
needs, but only after exerting himself and bringing forth his own sexual
savagery. No wonder Lagos has relinquished this role to Philippos, however
unwittingly.

So long as she is unclothed, he finds he loves her—or, at least, she
evokes in him a tenderness during that brief period when they are spent
and before they resume their separate lives. As she clothes herself, combs
out her hair, touches her face with make-up—as she again becomes self-
absorbed—she hardens into the lady of the court, a tease, a sophisticate,
an intellect. And she becomes someone he cannot love.

Yet if he goes too long without seeing her, his mind begins whispering
to him—Arsinoe, Arsinoe, Arsinoe. He will be marching beside his phalanx
or in the midst of a private banquet, a *symposion*, lying next to his king-
brother or swimming laps at the gymnasium or straddling a bench at a
council called by Perdikkas—wherever—and the whispering begins in his
inner ear, Arsinoe. He becomes distracted. Others must call him back to
the task.

Worse is when they meet but cannot acknowledge their passion, at
the home of a mutual friend, at the market, during a temple ceremony. If
their eyes chance to touch, and their eyes always chance to touch, he must
hide the sudden awkward hardening of his private member.

237

He does not like being in thrall to her. He suspects she does not like their strange bondage either. For the first time he understands what his mother, Eurudike, must have gone through with Ptolemaios. Is this what Aphrodite does to a man who trifles with love? Or is it a darker sister, perhaps Hekate, who casts this spell?

Shivering at his thoughts, Philippos turns his eyes back to the woman sleeping lightly beside him. Moonlight allows him to see her muscled back, her face turned away, half hidden in the tangle of hair, lips open. This cannot continue, he thinks. Then softly he strokes her across her shoulder and down her spine. She sighs, murmurs his name. He glides down, tucking himself to her buttocks. He begins the ancient rocking rhythm. Before awakening she is already responding to his stiff member. Arsinoe, Arsinoe, Arsinoe—when with her it is no whisper, his mind is shouting lustily, joyfully, Arsinoe!

β

"Look at me, Philippos. Pay attention," commands Perdikkas. The king holds up a hand and ticks off his points, "Thebai and Boiotia are on the march. They have avenged Pelopidas and confined Alexandros of Pherai to his city. With that they gain the Thessaliote votes in the Amphiktyony of Delphoi. Epaminondas sails the Aegean leading a Boiotian fleet. All the Aegean is astir at the possibility of throwing off the yoke of Athenai. Kos, Rhodos, Byzantion, Khios and others talk of revolt. No, do more than talk. Is not Kos already free?" The king's excitement increases as he speaks, "And where is Orkhomenos? The city is gone, no longer able to defy Thebai and play truant within the Boiotian confederacy. Every man slain by the Thebans. All women and children sold."

Philippos interrupts the flow, "You see how their power befuddles them. You would think they were Athenians."

Antipatros laughs, "As if you would not do the same if a city within your realm denied you."

"We are a kingship. We rule through the favor of Zeus and to the extent that we are good shepherds to the flock under our care. Sometimes the shepherd must cull the flock. If an animal has contagion, it must die to prevent the contagion spreading. The shepherd owes as much to the flock. But the shepherd never rejoices in such a death."

Warming to his subject, Philippos continues, "Thebai says it is a republic and only the senior member of the Boiotian federation. In a republic, debate is allowed its citizens, and differences are expected, and a certain measure of defiance by the minority is acceptable. The Boiotian federation was established on those same principles. But Thebai is like Athenai. They move from being the leading city to being the master city. They brook no disobedience. Thebai has the power, so Thebai destroys her inveterate rival, Orkhomenos." Philippos pauses, then adds softly, "I despise the hypocrisy of the southern states like Thebai."

"As a stranger in your midst, permit me to suggest that the point King Perdikkas is making is just that—Thebai has the power."

The half-dozen Makedones turn their eyes to the genial Athenian philosopher who sits to the left of King Perdikkas. Euphraios is no exile from Athenai. He is one of a number of southern Hellenes invited by Perdikkas to assist in strengthening the kingdom and the kingship. In the instance of Euphraios, his teacher, the renowned Platon, who always maintains that a philosopher knows best how to rule, dispatched him. Rarely does the world agree with Platon.

"I believe the point being made is that Thebai is in ascendance. These examples, both those that benefit its fellow states and those that do not, prove the point. I might add further that Thebai in truth is no democracy such as we enjoy at Athenai. At Thebai, it is a narrow group of families and an occasional new man who rule. In Athenai, a balance exists between the righteous families and a strong demos or people's party. The key with us is the moderation resulting from that balance."

Perdikkas asserts himself, "I am not speaking solely of Thebai. Look at what is happening to the east of us. The Odrusai king, Kotys, takes advantage of Athenai's disarray to attack her allies, the coastal ports in Thraikios. Iphikrates leads the Odrusai army on behalf of Kotys, his father-in-law. Is Iphikrates still an Athenian or is he now truly a Thraikiote?"

Philippos Arkouda nods at Euphraios, "An Athenian sees no oddity in serving the interests of another state opposed to his city."

Smiling, Euphraios answers, "You see the strength of democracy. We know no doubts in the superiority of our mother-city. Yet we do not automatically believe her to be right for we also know fallible men direct her rudder. We set a middle course—some see that middle course further right or further left than others. Democracy is self-correcting, for though our course is never dead-on, by constant adjustment, it is also never far off."

"Right now, your ship of state is adrift," calls out Amuntas Plousias. The others laugh.

Philippos considers the ways men are governed. The Athenians make great noise about the superiority of democracy, but noise seems to be their most singular characteristic as they lurch from one contradictory policy to another. And who among her politicians cannot be bought?

The Spartans argue for tradition as if it were religion and make a state as severe as can be found. They weaken because they cannot admit that the majority of their population has as much stake in their policy as the thinning inbred caste that rules.

Thebai is an oligarchy. When a constellation of admirable men lead her, as in Pammenes, Pelopidas, and Epaminondas, then she is admirable. When lesser men emerge as leaders, then Thebai is as vain and foolish as her leaders. Still, as a second-rank power she offered her people generations of stability, compared to other cities. Will she do the same now that she is in the first rank of powers? Already there is an arrogance that reminds all Hellenes of Athenai and Sparte.

What of kingship? Excesses can clearly be seen as in Persia where men worship the king, exalting him above themselves. Where, within the court, knives are kept sharp and a eunuch may rule a puppet king. By contrast, those called king among the Hellenes and related peoples, the *basileiai* of the highlands say, are little more than chief magistrates. Among barbarians, an exceptional man, like Bardulis with his vast Dardanoi confederacy, may loom large and dominate his neighbors but is no more than a bubble in the cauldron of time.

Perhaps it is a question of balance or reverence. Philippos knows the weight that kingship rests upon a man. He's watched his father and both brothers bear the weight. If a man is not seasoned, not trained or readied, the weight will crush him and crack apart the kingdom. His father was as able a juggler as any traveling entertainer. Alexandros was not and was killed. The people believed in Amuntas and worship him today. Few if any extended such trust to Alexandros. Perhaps a king must understand that personal glory or even personal interests are secondary to the welfare of the kingdom. Kingship is duty. The king had best be humble under the eyes of the gods.

"From today, we no longer support Athenai. Timotheos will receive no further aid against Amphipolis or the Khalkidike League. We will pursue our own interests openly. Unlike King Kotys of the Odrusai, that does not mean we move against the coast cities protected by Athenai. It does mean we will conclude an alliance with Thebai," declares King Perdikkas.

Athanaios stands and applauds his king. Long the advisor on Theban affairs, Athanaios at last feels vindicated. The others stand and join the applause, all save the philosopher, Euphraios. He understands that the Makedones have traveled a long road since the days when Ptolemaios of Aloros would speak in favor of Athenai. There is no Makedon voice here in favor of Athenai.

Euphraios continues to sit and smile. He believes it right for the Makedones to seek to benefit their citizens. He is unconcerned about the illusionary success of Thebai. He is certain that he can guide this young king into concordance with Athenai in the future. In the meantime, it doesn't hurt to curb General Timotheos and his faction in the city. Euphraios is intrigued by Philippos, though. He liked the shepherd speech. Maybe this boy should be given a district to govern.

γ

The squealing and deep grunts of the pigs as they thrust against each other to reach the slops amuse the watching prince. The sight reminds him of the notables at the wedding feast of his brother, Perdikkas. The swineherd dumps another bucket and the animals surge and whirl to get at the additional swill.

"You have no idea what it is to bring a shipload of pigs across the Aegean," sighs the sailor, Andromitos. His Kretan accent sounds too sibilant to Philippos.

Their companion, Pakhes Mikros, laughs, "Your fee should redeem the experience." The short, thin man continues, "Notice, though, the size of the sows and the number of piglets. This single shipload is sufficient to improve our stock. If we breed them to our native animals, I hope to gain the hardiness of ours with the meat of theirs."

Realizing that the prince's interest is not strong, Mikros continues, "I know they are not horses or cattle, not even sheep or goats. But they eat anything and they are prolific. You like well-smoked pig meat as much as the next man, Philippos."

Smiling Philippos waves a hand in acknowledgment, "I may like their meat but I cannot love themselves."

"Nor I," says Andromitos of Lato, "never again will I sail with pigs as my cargo. The crew is still cleaning the ship's hull."

Mikros gestures his defeat, "Do not love them, then. Just pay me in the king's silver when I deliver fifty talent-weight of well-cured pork a year from now."

"Oh you will get your money, Mikros. I like your scheme and will advance you the tetradrakhm you need to get yourself established. If you are successful in breeding them, I want one-quarter of the offspring to strengthen other men's stock. When the time comes, my steward and yours will alternate in selecting the pigs that are mine." Philippos turns away from the pens, putting a hand on the small man's shoulder, "A further thing I want is one of your sons for King Perdikkas' school of pages."

"Is your steward or mine to pick him?" says Pakhes Mikros sharply.

Genially Philippos answers, "That's a father's prerogative."

"What becomes of the son I give up?"

"He will serve in the king's household. Learn the ways of the court, and be offered the opportunities that the sons of other leading men receive. He will be tutored. He will work as hard at court as he would in your own yard."

Mikros sighs, "And he will be useless with pigs." Then in a proud voice the man says, "I have five boys, you know. Five boys and three girls. Are you sure you couldn't use one of the girls?"

"Perhaps, if Queen Eurudike or Queen Telesilla takes a liking to one of your ladies. For King Perdikkas, I want one of your boys."

They walk along in silence, up the slope, toward the stone house. Andromitos trails a bit behind to allow the prince and the landowner their privacy. After a bit, Mikros says, "My oldest girl practically raised the others after their mother died. Now for this past year, I've had a housekeeper my sister picked out for me. She's a woman of the Limniadai, a widow. She's a good woman, understands farming and stock breeding, she's right useful. I want to marry her, but my daughter, Stakheira, is opposed and swings the other kids around to her view. Take Stakheira off my hands and you can have the best of my boys, though they're all good."

Whose household has need of a headstrong girl? thinks Philippos. He likes Pakhes Mikros and would like to help him. Mikros is proud, a typical Makedon landowner. He will accept no charity. Every exchange must be bargained. The lands Mikros holds are modest, though productive. He is struggling to feed the many mouths his household claims. Honoring one of his boys acknowledges the man, and relieves him from a measure of need. That part of this bargain must remain unsaid.

They reach the house without Philippos replying. Coming in from the back lot, they enter through the kitchen door. They walk in on an argument. A middle-aged woman is belaboring a younger woman for allowing porridge to stick to the kettle. "If you had done as I told you and added the fruit later, this wouldn't have happened," yells the widow of the Limniadai.

"A lot you know. We like the fruit cooked so the flavor is stronger."

"Fine, then you clean the kettle yourself, this time." The widow's eyes are blazing, and she is clearly more upset than the incident warrants. At the sight of Mikros, she sighs and in a calmer voice says, "I know this is a bother, but she opposes me in everything. Nothing is as her mother did things."

Mildly Mikros says to his daughter, "Go serve the others, Stakheira. Don't shame us before guests."

The girl bows woodenly and leaves with the kettle of porridge and the ladle. Philippos sighs inwardly, thinking this is no girl for the court. Older than he expected, he knows that neither queen will readily welcome an addition to their households so rudely raised as Stakheira.

The gods often provide answers in unexpected ways. Andromitos is stricken. "You said nothing of your daughter being of marriageable age," manages the Kretan sailor.

Mikros and Philippos turn to Andromitos in surprise. Mikros catches the drift before Philippos. "I have no aim to see my daughter carried off to Krete," he says severely.

Now it is Andromitos' turn to be surprised, for his reason is lagging behind his emotions. Looking at Mikros' intent face, then glancing at the doorway through which Stakheira had stepped, Andromitos accepts his fate, "Then I must stay in Makedonis."

Mikros still searches the Kretan's face. While Andromitos is no stranger to Pakhes Mikros, there is a huge step from trading with a man to accepting him as a son-in-law. Equally, Andromitos is looking at Mikros with a set of intentions he never anticipated. The young man is almost bewildered by this willful act of the godling Eros. Mikros smiles,

"Go to her, Andromitos. Tell her she has a husband. Gently, man, so she knows she's truly desired."

* * *

"No, don't touch me," says Arsinoe angrily.

Philippos is puzzled. His paramour's resentment is so unlike her usual welcome on his return from traveling that he's not sure what to make of it. She stands facing away from him, arms crossed, gaze averted, her lower lip trembling. Her agitation is greater than the occasional pouting he's experienced before from her. Sighing to himself, he asks, "What is the matter? You are upset about something. Tell me, so we can deal with it."

"What is there to say? You have no heart for me. All I can expect from you is a stolen moment here and an odd night there. We have nothing, you and I." Arsinoe at least is looking at him now, though her glare is hardly a comfort.

"Arsinoe, what would you have of me? You are the married one. You are the one who sneaks away from her husband."

"You see! What did I expect? Do you know how to comfort a woman? All you want is my legs spread at your convenience." She turns furiously away from him, "Well, I won't be a plaything. Something discarded when your eye is caught by another bird's plumage."

Now Philippos is getting angry, but not so angry that his mind has stopped trying to solve the puzzle of her behavior. "What are you saying? When have you not been as eager as I to make the double-backed animal? And who says there is anyone other than you, Arsinoe?"

"You don't know what it is to betray your husband's trust. As much as I want you, I feel the pain of lying to him. Even you feel contempt for me, even as you urge me into your arms," she is practically spitting her words at him.

Thinking of Lagos, a man Philippos has never liked and has come to despise, the prince cannot imagine why Arsinoe clings to her married state. Thinking of Lagos fuels his anger, "You could break from your husband at any time and come to me." Yet as he says these words, he feels a flare of fear in his stomach. Surely she will not accept his offer?

"Come to you? Come to you? How easily said. And what would I be, Prince Philippos, your concubine? No thank you! How pretty a thought for you and how ugly an existence for me." She is facing him straight on now, her face contorted by her fury, "And how long would it be before you take a principal wife? Some king's daughter to help further the precious Temenid ambitions."

He stops, steps back, considers. *What is this all about?* Holding up a hand, and in a reasonable voice, he asks, "What do you want of me, Arsinoe? We have shared so much already. Are you telling me that it's over? Is this how you end our sharing?"

Staring at Philippos, she takes a few shuddering breaths. She regains self-control however shakily. "You came down river with a girl in tow," she accuses.

His puzzlement evaporates, "You mean Stakheira, daughter of Pakhes Mikros?" He shakes his head, clearly relieved at how trivial is her concern. "She is not in tow for me. The ship's captain, Andromitos, is her betrothed."

"So some people say. Others say that's a convenience for you. Gives you another man's wife as your ladylove, just like me." The bitterness is back in her voice.

"People say? What people? Who whispers about you and me?"

"Who does not? We make Lagos and ourselves into a laughing stock." Inadvertently he voices, "Lagos is a laughing stock."

"May Hermaphroditis shrivel your genitals," she vehemently curses.

He reaches out to her forearms and pulls her close to him. He is laughing softly, "Is that what all this is? You are jealous of a farm girl betrothed to a sea captain? Is it that they can marry and we cannot?"

She turns her face away as he tries to nuzzle it. "There is nothing to laugh about. What I say is true. Everyone talks of us behind our backs. We cannot go on like this. Soon Lagos will no longer be able to ignore what he knows. Either he will kill you or you him."

This is a more serious idea. Much as Philippos might be willing to see Lagos dead of natural causes, he knows a killing is no solution. Lagos, like Arsinoe and Philippos, is part of a wider weave of relationships and obligations. Catching the lesser thought, while he considers the heavier, the prince comments, "So Lagos knows. I've thought as much."

"You will not marry me," she says calmly, "even if I left Lagos for you." She pulls free of him, "He loves me, you know. Many think he is a silly man. Well he is not. He may not be Prince Philippos but he is a good man. He is a good father, and will be again."

"Again?" His head comes up, "What are you saying?"

Tears well in her eyes, "I am pregnant."

For a moment he is eager, "My child? You carry my child?"

She shrugs, "Perhaps. Yours or my husband's. I do not know. Does that matter to you?"

Philippos says nothing. He tries to understand what he feels. As so often, his feelings slip away as soon as he tries to examine them. A child, well he has not begotten a child before, at least, that he knows. But what if it's only Lagos' whelp?

Arsinoe steps further away, "I have my answer, don't I?" She hangs her head sadly, "Sometimes I wish you were born earlier or me later. Perhaps then you and I would have been husband and wife. What is ten years between us? Nothing, were you the woman and I the man. Maybe nothing in itself—everything in words already said, promises made, and acts done." She sighs, "I guess I thought I meant more to you than I do. You are right, I was eager to have you love me. You could have stripped and ravished me in the *agora* before all the people of Pella if you would then have stood by me and defied the world."

She turns and walks away from him. He stands there emptily, still puzzled, but over himself now and not Arsinoe.

δ

Eurudike sits spinning wool. She is humming softly. The spindle whirls between her fingers. She wants the thread to be fine and yet the wool soft, appropriate for a baby. She doesn't see herself as a grandmother, doesn't think of herself as being so old, yet she is excited. Watching Telesilla's figure become rounder with each passing month has made her eager to hold the coming newborn. Yet the irony is not lost on her that she'd been less pleased to give birth and be a mother than she is happy to be a grandmother.

Perdikkas has already decided the child must be a boy and that he will name him Amuntas. Well, it is right to name the first son after his grandfather.

Another surprise of these past years is how fondly she remembers old Amuntas. What she put that man through, yet how unfailingly good he was to her. As for Ptolemaios, she no longer comprehends the passion she felt for him. She is obscurely shamed by the memory of him. It was a madness. Maybe it had as much to do with her resentment at being a passive woman. At least with Ptolemaios she took risks, weighed chances, and acted the queen. But none of that was worth the loss of a son. Nowadays she aches for her failure with Alexandros. Not that she dwells on him. But when she is reminded of Alexandros, the memory comes sharply with pain.

What a scandal Philippos has gotten into. Eurudike always liked Arsinoe. Saw in this younger woman that spark of rebellion and discontent that is a sign of intelligence ill-used. And the girl had the good taste to pursue Philippos. What good came of it? She is carrying the boy's child while proclaiming it dull old Lagos' spawn. Nothing good can come of a royal bastard. Still, so long as Philippos will not acknowledge the child, it can be the son or daughter of Lagos. The child has wealthy, noble parents. He or she will do well enough without a prince for a father.

Maybe, though, it's time to see Philippos properly wed. His sexual urges will only lead him into further scrapes. They say he can't resist any handsome boy or beautiful girl. He needs something to do besides teaching men to lift and thrust pikes.

Well, what color should the wool be dyed? Her favorite color is red, but for a baby the color could be less brilliant. Perhaps a golden yellow, almost a tan.

Perdikkas is doing well as king. Popular without losing respect. The break with Athenai is welcome, though she doubts it will prove so simple. He has fought well in the Khalkidike in support of Olunthos. The Athenians are off-balance. Who would have thought her chubby, grinning toddler would make so formidable a king?

The obvious choice for Philippos is Phila, daughter of King Derdas. Tie the Elimiotoi to us, thinks the queen mother. Her own highland origin is momentarily forgotten as she thinks of her son's welfare.

This philosopher-toad, the Athenian Euphraios, urges Perdikkas to grant Philippos a district to govern. The boy could certainly use the responsibility, but what is the Athenian after? Does he hope that once Philippos holds a power base he will split with his brother and weaken the kingdom? Well, if that's the plan, the philosopher underestimates the two brothers. Those boys can practically see into each other's minds. They act in concert in all things. There will be no splitting the kingdom by dividing them.

Not that there aren't others out there hungry to bite if her boys should weaken. Pausanias still hovers, turning the city of Kalindroia in Mygdonis into his private refuge. Argaios sulks in brave Athenai, and will readily play the puppet. There is Arkhelaos and his brothers—restless, bitter at being denied, and with a rural following of like-minded rough peasants.

She smiles to herself, holding the fine wool threads up to the light. An heir will be born to Perdikkas. The way Telesilla holds her back, with her great belly thrust out, is a sign of a boy child. Though it is tempting repercussions from the great gods, as grandmother, Eurudike could not resist going to the seers of the ancient brooding fates. They declare the child a male, as well.

Amuntas, son of Perdikkas, grandson of Amuntas, of the Temenidai of the Argeadai Makedones, may your future be bright. May the sun of the Temenidai shine when it is your turn to reign over our people.

A hymn of praise comes to mind, and Eurudike begins humming again. Humming, smiling secretly, nimble fingers spinning fine wool.

ε

"You see that the balance is off. The butt spike must be heavier to offset the weight of the pike shaft and blade," Philippos is patiently explaining what he wants to the artificers. The smiths and their novices huddle around the prince.

"We have a couple of choices," answers one of the older smiths. "Since the butt spike is bronze, we either make it longer or we keep it the same size but create a lead core."

"Try both ways. And in making the butt larger, try both a wider circumference and a longer spike. I want to know the steps you take for each solution and the difference in cost for the metals and for the making."

Philippos considers, then adds, "And tell me how long it takes to make each type."

"You want it quick, cheap, and more serviceable," says a younger smith.

Philippos laughs, "You find me the right balance, so that the pike is easy to wield while holding it with two hands at three-quarters along its length. You find me that balance for all four pike lengths."

"Why not try altering the pike head as well?" asks the same smith. "And what if cornel wood is not always available? Do you want us to experiment with other woods for the shafts?"

The chief woodworker interrupts, "Look at what you are demanding. You want as strong a wood as you can find; you want as light a wood as you can find; you want a long straight wood; you want a wood that is readily worked, to keep the costs down and limit the effort; you want a common wood, easily found. You nearly want too much. So we have cornel wood. A compromise, true, but it fulfills your conditions better than any other wood. What other woods might we use? Boxwood? Hornbeam? Rowan? Apple? Ash? Cherry? Pear? Those are the choices. Everything else doesn't come close. None of the other hardwoods—alder, birch, chestnut, cedar, ebony, beech, holly, walnut, olive, plane, white or red oak, willow, lime, or elm—will do."

Philippos holds up a hand, to stem the flow, "You're right. I nearly ask too much. The Kouretes of the forests are dancers not warriors. What need do these deities have for pike shafts?" Still smiling, Philippos puts an arm around the woodworker, drawing him close, "I tell you with your knowledge of wood, you could select the two likeliest alternatives. Get shafts made from those woods as well, so we can know how each best balances."

Squeezing the woodworker tight, Philippos adds, "And you forgot durable. I want a wood that lasts. We will be out in any weather." Smiling innocently, he says, "And try not to use the fruit trees. They serve us well already."

Turning back to the younger smith, Philippos says, "Certainly try some different blade designs. I want it sharp enough at the tip to enter between metal plates or links, and strong enough and broad enough after the tip to thrust those plates aside. The leaf blade is an old design because it works so well." Then grinning, Philippos adds a challenge, "How tempered can you make the blade edge? I want sharp and strong."

"We will make you the best pikes the world has ever seen," asserts the young smith with an answering smile.

"Good, we will need them." Turning, the prince calls, "Pikoros, Lusias, we have other duties. Let's be off."

Standing at the enclosure gate are King Perdikkas and a small group of his companions—Kharikles, Parrhasios, Amuntas Plousias, Antipatros, Balakros, and Euphraios the Athenian—and several of the king's bodyguards. The king is smiling at his brother, "Ho, Philippos, join us."

Philippos strides over, with Lusias and Pikoros trailing him. The king and his companions are waiting expectantly, the prince can see. His brother calls out again, "Still worrying over pikes and armaments?"

"Sure, there is no perfect answer," gesturing over his shoulder to indicate the smiths, Philippos adds, "They will come as close as they can."

As Philippos reaches the group of men, Perdikkas steps forward and briefly hugs his brother. Then turning so the two of them face the group, Perdikkas says, "I brought you all down to the workshops where I knew I would find Philippos so you can be witnesses. I am proud of my brother and all that he has done since returning from Thebai. Close on two years he has labored to strengthen our army. King Parmenion of the Pelagonoi can testify to his valor and to the worth of his efforts. I believe it's time my brother took on greater responsibility. From this day forward, in my name, Prince Philippos shall govern the lands of Amphaxitis and Anthemos. He will be responsible for relations with our neighbors in Krestonis and Mygdonis, including the Bisaltiones. With Anthemos goes responsibility for our border with the Khalkidike League. Philippos, you face all our eastern enemies and occasional allies. The Paiaones, the Thrakes, and Olunthos are the nettles you hold in your hands. While Amphipolis and the Athenian attempts on her remain concerns vital to me personally, you will take on the day-to-day tasks in support of Amphipolis. We will sustain Amphipolitan independence."

This sweeping charter is not unexpected by Philippos. Increasingly Perdikkas is interested in the north and west. He wants to take on Bardulis. By getting the Illuroi off the backs of the Makedones, he would be in better position to confront Timotheos and the Athenian fleet. Still, Perdikkas is not so wild-eyed as Alexandros was. He continues the tribute payments to Bardulis. But he prepares for the day. He has mused to Philippos many times of late, that if Philippos can hold the east and south in equilibrium for three years, Perdikkas will have the time he needs to defeat Bardulis.

Yet the timing of this announcement has taken Philippos by surprise. In the autumn, at the close of the year, was when he supposed Perdikkas would act. Make a solemn ceremony elevating Philippos, within the context of all the religious symbolism of that season. Instead here in a work yard, before hastily assembled nobles, his brother confers the governorship.

Even as the men crowd around Philippos offering congratulations and as he answers with effusive thanks, his mind worries at the question of timing. Catching the eye of Perdikkas with a questioning look, the king answers with a lift of his eyebrows and a quick nod that says later.

*   *   *

"My spies tell me that Timotheos withdraws both from before Amphipolis and from the Khalkidike. Oh, he leaves a strong garrison at Potidaia confronting Olunthos. The settlers Athenai sent to strengthen Potidaia provide a thousand spearmen. Tell me, what is Timotheos' game? Will he strike at us for sending troops to help hold Amphipolis against him?" Perdikkas muses aloud to his brother. "You see, I want to be free of the east to be able to respond to the Athenians. You will hold the east in my stead. If I'm wrong and Timotheos attacks elsewhere in the North Aegean, then I can turn my attention to Bardulis."

The two young men are huddled together on the steps leading down to the hot bath at the gymnasium of Ares Nikenor. Around them is the tumult of men bathing, jostling, laughing, and yelling to one another across the echoing chamber. No one could begin to hear the private conversation between king and prince.

Calmly Philippos asks, "What do you think Timotheos' spies tell him."

Perdikkas chuckles, "At least one tells Timotheos that I am loath to be away from Pella while Lady Telesilla is near to giving birth. Another swears that I am convinced that Timotheos is feinting and that he will strike hard at Amphipolis if I relax my watchfulness. A third tells Timotheos that if enough silver were sent my way, I would sell the Amphipolitans to Athenai in exchange for Potidaia."

"Do you think we know all his spies?"

"All?" Perdikkas pulls his beard gently. "Who can say? Treachery surrounds us. I trust you, Philippos. And mother, Telesilla, Amuntas Plousias, Antipatros, some of the others. Certainly good Arkouda. So, if there are a dozen whom I trust, some few with all my soul, there are others I trust to varying degrees. There are even some companions that I do not trust at all, save that I can rely on their venality and can play upon that."

"So that is what kingship is?"

Perdikkas gently pats his younger brother's cheek, "Don't play the fool, Philippos. You know as well as I what kingship is. Did not Lady Kleopatra tutor you from an early age?" The king sighs, "If Alexandros had a touch of common sense, he'd still be king. Then you and I would be his generals."

Perdikkas leans close to Philippos' ear, "I'll tell you a secret, though. For a Temenidai, the only thing worse than being king, is not being king. Look at how we all thrust and kill to hold the throne. Pausanias, Argaios, Arkhelaos are all wolves who'd tear out our throats to hold the kingdom as we do. Only you, dear brother, have the sense to know that a man is a fool to be eager for kingship. You can thank Lady Kleopatra."

Philippos nods, "Do you have instructions for me, then?"

"We have a lot to go over. My secretaries have a lot of it documented. Who we pay in Amphipolis. Those among the border tribes who share our interests. Those tribesmen who oppose us. We will cover all that later." The king stretches, losing the wrap that covers his strong shoulders, "You can take your footmen with you."

Philippos is surprised, "Won't you need them to counter Timotheos?"

"Not fast enough. I must rely on horsemen."

Philippos shakes his head, "I tell you we must organize the horsemen. They must train together so they act in concert on the field."

"We ride together three days of every month," protests Perdikkas.

"Ride together? Perform, you mean. So every lady can swoon for her favorite young warrior. And when you go to war, each man brings his own servants and followers. Each man has his own mounts so that the quality and care of the horses is uneven. Each gathers his own food. You are not a force of horsemen, you are a tribe on the move."

Mildly, Perdikkas says, "You may be right. I can tighten our marching ranks. That would speed our march." He brightens, "You cannot deny our prowess in battle. Look at what we accomplished in the Khalkidike against the Athenians."

Moodily, Philippos agrees, "Yes, individually, they are a capable body of men. They respond well to you. So long as you lead them, you have no cause for concern. But you cannot be everywhere, and where you are not, they bicker, they stall, they sulk, they go off on their own harebrained tangents."

"What would you do, brother?"

"Curb your nobles. Create ranks, with clear authority. Whoever balks —punish, exile if necessary. And train every day."

"I summon them and they come voluntarily. We are not talking about paid mercenaries."

"True," Philippos nods. "Recognize that all preferment flows from the king. You are the source of lands, wealth, and recognition. Obedience gains your pleasure and rewards. Recalcitrance causes your displeasure."

"We are not Persians," says Perdikkas in exasperation. "Our people are heterogeneous clans and occasional cities. We are Hellenes, even if liberally mixed with many wild tribal bloods. Ruling the Makedones requires balance."

"Let it go then," acknowledges Philippos. "I tell you, though, you must find the right balance that gives you the discipline and obedience you need in your army while still getting their enthusiasm and willingness."

"Do you want to be king, Philippos? Should I give you the throne?"

"You are the acclaimed, the sanctified. I follow you, Perdikkas," says Philippos with real humility.

Perdikkas gazes steadily at his younger brother as if weighing the young man's response. Then he smiles, "Forgive me, Philippos. I know you have our best interests at heart. I hear so much advice. Everyone feels he can advise the king, and set a better course than we follow. Most have their own interests in mind, naturally. Usually the loudest, most persuasive, are those who are most keen for their own welfare no matter how they appeal to the commonweal."

He looks away, watching the antics of the youths by the pool. He points, "You see my cadets. Each the son of a man I cultivate. Most of their fathers ride with me. A good lot, their fathers, though some are touchy of their pride, others foolish with their wealth, some besotted of wine or boys or religion or women or silver. Still, by and large, they're brave and more often than not they do what I tell them."

He sighs gently, "You're right, of course. They need more discipline." Then he brightens, "We ought to be able to do as well as the Thessaliotes. If we model ourselves on our cousins to the south, surely our people will accept instruction."

"That's a start," agrees Philippos. "The best of them will recognize the need, and the rest will follow. If your companion horsemen are a stronger body, I will feel safer for you while I'm marching east with my footmen."

Perdikkas adds, "I will coax Derdas out of the mountains to help me take a hand with my companions."

"Good," says the prince.

Slyly the king adds, "And I will talk to Derdas about his daughter, Phila. We will set your marriage date."

Philippos thinks about Phila. He likes her. How well would that survive a marriage?

"I suppose you will want to fulfill your vow before taking up your duties in the east?" asks Perdikkas.

"Yes, while the *syntagmai* march over land, I will take ship to Samothrake. The timing will work."

"I don't want Timotheos snapping my brother up at sea. Makes sure that all and sundry know you are marching east with your men. Keep your shipping arrangements quiet. Keep your vow, but be quick."

ζ

Who can understand the gods? Or is it as Kerkidas taught, as Orpheos taught, that behind the many facets of the gods there is a unity of one divinity? What the peasant in his fields believes is in the multiplicity of deities and in their awful powers for mischief, for ecstasy, for tragedy, and for apotheosis. How else can he understand the cycle of life and death that surrounds him in his fields and among his flocks? The gods are everywhere and all around us. Or the one god makes himself known everywhere and all around us. If there are many gods, you may propitiate one to offset the anger of another. You have hope. With a single god, what hope is there? Who can live as a man and not sometimes offend a god? How do you understand just one god—a god who might kill your child with disease while giving you the best harvest of your life?

Philippos does not know the answers. He does know the questions. He smiles to himself at that thought. *At least I know to question.*

When Lamakhos came back from Tartaros with the words of Orpheos in his mouth, Philippos knew he must pay homage to the Kabiroi of

Samothrake. To call it a vow does not seem accurate. More like fulfilling a command. So here he is.

The island is a temple. Oh, yes, there are villages—toilers of the sea, shepherds, miners, and smiths—the islanders. But mostly the gods are here. If you sit still you can feel them around you. Some places are like this—more holy than other places.

The prince feels himself to be a penitent, though he is not clear of what he is guilty. So while Pikoros bustles in the lodgings they've taken, Philippos sits quietly on a hillside. Behind are the higher rocks of the upthrust mountain; below and stretching away is the sea. Ever changing and always the same. Is the sea the clearest sense of the gods? Always in motion—beneficent and dangerous.

The hut Pikoros found for them is modest. That's what comes of keeping arrangements quiet. The island is filling with travelers come to participate in the festivals that begin before dawn tomorrow. The largest contingent is a royal group from Epeiros, King Neoptolemos and his family. They say the king is ailing and seeks relief.

So King Neoptolemos must also sense that the Kabiroi mediate between us humans and the great god Hades.

Now is the time to stay quiet. Tomorrow the early ceremonies will be solemn. After noon, the processions will grow progressively wilder. Then in the night will come the ecstatics, hunting for release. The hills will rush with frenzied groups. Couplings and mutilations. Danger and blessings. Pity the lone man or woman unless they seek transformation.

Within Philippos is a flame of excitement. Not being sure why he has come here, knowing that the gods summoned him, knowing that the gods are mysterious in their purposes. No one understands the gods. Trite and true. Sometimes, though, in some places, in brief moments, whether through contemplation or intoxicating rapture, you can be one with a god. And Philippos is compelled to find that moment and be within that god, whether one or one of many.

* * *

"You know of the god, Zalmoxis, master?" asks Pikoros.

"Ruler of the underworld among many Thraikiote tribes?"

"Yes, he is the one," agrees Pikoros, as the two men walk the steep path to the small village that surrounds the shrine they seek. "He was not always the god of death. First he lived in the sky. Then he lived on earth. Only later did he descend to take up residence in the underworld." Pikoros pauses, leaning on his staff, "But all that's not what I wanted to tell you about."

The prince stops and waits. Usually silent, when Pikoros does talk, often it comes slowly. Philippos feels no impatience. This man who was a slave is now his friend.

"One of my early memories is of a procession. I think it was for Zalmoxis, because I remember the masks worn by the marchers. And the keening sadness of their songs." Again Pikoros falls silent, remembering.

"I don't know why I should remember that. It's a fragment. I don't remember who I was with—my mother, I suppose. Just the procession, slow, swaying. There seemed so many of them walking along. It was cold. There was a wind, some rain. So many and so sad." Pikoros nods at his memory, then shakes himself free of it.

"Seeing the morning's processions was like that. Slow, sad. Then, by midday, the crowds became happy. Everyone's face brightened, especially when the sun glimpsed out between the showers of warm rain." Pikoros marvels at the sights he's seen today, "Was it the music that changed the celebrants from happy to something sharper, hungrier?"

Philippos says, "The expectations, I think. Day is passing and they want more than simple happiness."

"What I think of is the music, the drums louder, the pipes faster. Everyone dances, twists, cries out. No one is audience, all are celebrants, the processions disintegrate into dancing, chanting believers."

The scene comes readily to Philippos' mind. He had danced as happily, then as wildly, as anyone. Well, almost anyone. There was the young girl who out danced even the goatmen. The Princess Myrtale, they said. Never had a girl so young enflamed his mind more. Yet she had been oblivious to anyone but the gods. Her feet whirled. She had shed clothes, with only necklaces flying above her small breasts. Eyes raised to heaven, beating her tambourine, and dancing as if the ground beneath her feet were on fire.

It was for her sake that Philippos climbs to the shrine of Bendis this night. That was where they said the Molossi Epeiriotes were to go. Still, Philippos is listening to the gods this day. If Pikoros wants to talk until the moon goes down, and they miss those celebrating with Bendis, so be it. He follows the will of the gods.

"I lost much anger today, dancing beside you," says Pikoros. "I thank Zalmoxis." The big man looks at the prince, "You cannot be a slave without anger."

"You are not a slave, Pikoros," answers Philippos.

"Yes," smiles Pikoros briefly, "you freed us. But we had not freed ourselves yet. I think Petalouda came to it sooner than I. Having a child does that for a woman." Pikoros nods, "Even she was a gift to me from you. She was not my choice. Now, of course, I would choose no other, so your gift was wise. Still, for a long time, my anger held against you, against all men, against the gods." He looks down, staring at his feet, thinking.

Raising his eyes back up to Philippos, he says, "When you put a pike in my hand and turned your back, I lost my anger against you. Whether you knew it or not, you trusted me not to kill you." Pikoros reaches and touches Philippos' hand lightly, "You have made me your friend and companion, you who owned me, who freed me. You who have nobles and princes as friends."

Pikoros stares up the path, through the dim light of dusk. "Well, I am no longer angry with the gods. Let us go celebrate the goddess Bendis. Let us celebrate all the gods." He starts up the path, leaving Philippos standing.

Philippos' thoughts now are on Pikoros and the power of divinity, not on a young girl. Whether he knows it or not, Pikoros has helped Philippos become ready to receive a god.

*   *   *

The village is lit with torches. Drums offer a low-toned heartbeat. A ratcheting sound punctuates the drumming. Philippos and Pikoros are in time for the ceremony.

The shrine itself is no more than a cairn of rock next to a tall wind-bent tree, a kind of pine. Before the cairn is an altar. At each of eight points in a wide circle around the shrine are a large stone and a wooden statue—they define the shrine's precinct. The statues are all of young women, except the largest. That one depicts the goddess as a mature woman armed with a bow in one hand and holding a sheaf of grain in the other. There is nothing Hellenic about this shrine, save the majority of the worshippers. How ancient can this shrine be, wonders Philippos.

Encircling the shrine are women, most of whom are wearing the peaked cap of the goddess and all are shuffling in slow dance to the drums. They offer a moaning lament, though the priestess leading occasionally calls out a prayer that ends in a shriek. The language of the prayer is unintelligible to Philippos.

Outside the precinct are the men. They form their own rough circle. The village men hold wooden lathes that they rub in time to the drums, providing the whispering ratchet. Most men, visitors to the shrine, stand silent, waiting. Philippos and Pikoros join one group of men near a standing stone and its attendant statue. The men are Molossi. Philippos recognizes King Neoptolemos. Silently, they greet each other.

"This is the childbirth," whispers the man next to Philippos.

From the midst of the women there is increasing agitation. The moaning rhythm is more insistent. The pattern of shrieks becomes the crescendo for each moan. The drummers among them are beating with sharper blows, raising the tone of the drums.

Suddenly, from the center of the shuffling line bursts a woman, an infant upraised in her arms. The baby's cries are intense as the woman rushes past the statue of Bendis, through the recoiling circle of men and out of sight.

Philippos looks questioningly at his informant. The man whispers, "Any man she touches, the woman kills. That's why they leapt out of her way."

The dance is ended, but not the expectancy. The women are silent, but not motionless. An exaggerated shiver runs through their ranks. Philippos notices Princess Myrtale in their lines. She is too young to participate, yet there she is. He points her out to Pikoros and their neighbor. The man whispers, "The chief priestess added her to the dancers. Her menses began this month, so technically she qualifies. My guess is her father made a suitable donation. Myrtale wanted to dance, and he usually gives her what she asks. It's easier that way."

A line of torches abruptly light the hillside above the village. The line comes on swiftly, and with the light comes the energetic notes of the pipes. A dozen priestesses dance into view, each with a torch. In their line are four young men dressed as goats and playing the pipes. Beside them, a young girl leads a large pure white goat.

Within the precinct, the women are wild in their welcome. Their singing is a joyous keening. The shivering motion is gone, replaced by a wild stamping skip-like dance. As the spirit moves a woman, she dances out from their lines to do a frenzied improvised dance of her own.

As the line of torchbearers and youths reach the precinct, the women dance back, giving the newcomers space to reach the raised altar. Once at the altar, the four youths lift the goat and the young girl onto the broad sacrificial stone. A hush descends. Only the drums can be heard, low again, pulsing. The chief priestess chants a prayer, its cadence increasing and tone rising as she prays. As soon as she ends the prayer in a great shriek, an arrow flies out of the night, striking the goat in its breast. The priestess instantly completes the sacrifice by slicing the animal's throat. As it writhes in death, all the women intone a loud answering prayer.

"Now it really starts," says the new-found companion of Philippos.

Knowing the man's mind is on the upcoming mass copulation for which the ceremony is known, Philippos still has time to wonder, "That was an amazing shot. Any deviance would have struck a worshipper."

"I guess it used to be easier, when the target was a man." The Molossiote looks at Philippos, grinning, "Many years ago, generations back, the arrow took the girl instead of the goat. The people suffered seven years of famine—nothing from the sea, nothing from the soil, no lambs among the flocks. They do not miss their shot any longer."

During that interchange, the ceremony has altered character. Dancing is wild. The drums, pipes, ratchets are eager. Groups of women dance out to the edge of the precinct, catch a man and drag him into the circle of dancers. If a group of men resist, and succeed in pulling a woman into their midst, then she is lost in an orgy of sacrificial rapes. Those women eager for the night's lust dance out in small groups. Those who would dance until exhausted, take their men by dancing out in a large group.

In truth, most men become neither dancers nor rapers, but the possibilities make all men dry of mouth and uneasy of mind. Philippos is astonished at how much his reaction is like waiting for battle. Not the intensity of fear, of course, but the haunting breathless uncertainty.

A large group of women, perhaps the largest to dance out, reaches the Molossi men. Most of the women are Molossi themselves. There is great laughter and comic effort as the men and women surge, each trying to pull the other.

Myrtale dances in uncontrolled leaps and whirls, though she is not so reckless as to be in the forefront of the group. Still one young man darts to the edge of the precinct to try and reach her. With great glee, the older women smother the youth and drag him into their midst. At that, Myrtale, as if offended at being rescued, crosses the precinct line. She dances through the men as if magically protected. Before her father, she puts a hand out to pull him into the dance. At his resistance, she frees him and dances away. She hesitates as she dances by Pikoros, but on seeing Philippos, she reaches for the prince's arm. Knowing how foolish it would be to pull her to him, yet feeling the temptation to ravish her, Philippos, all unresisting, dances away with her into the sacred precinct of the goddess Bendis.

*   *   *

Late, so late that the new dawn will soon arise, Philippos lays on a hillside looking up at the myriad of stars. He is tired. Beside him sleeps Pikoros, cloak drawn over the big man's shoulders for warmth. Tomorrow —no, today—they must be away to Makedonis. His new duties await. His brother entertains Derdas of the Elimiotoi. In some time he will marry Derdas' daughter, Phila. Yet in his mind is this young girl, Princess Myrtale. What an untamed filly she is. Even so young she is intoxicating. And then, there is Epeiros. Traditionally aligned with Athenai, the Molossi kingdom in Epeiros marches to the west of the highland Makedones. Were the lowland Makedones and the Molossi united in alliance, then the highlanders must follow their lead. Even the Thessaliotes would see a great alliance across their northern and western borders. Bardulis of the Dardanoi would be matched.

Marrying into Elimiotis is necessary. Marrying into the Epeiriote Molossi would offer new avenues of possibilities.

For all that, it isn't the security of Makedonis that dances nakedly through Philippos' mind. Small, high jutting breasts and slender waist over wide hips. At twelve, Myrtale takes his breath away. What would she do to him if she were twenty-four, he wonders.

Not once during the long day did he feel he was one with the god. Yet he knows that the gods led him here. What else but for Myrtale? The calculating rational part of his mind adds, what else but for Epeiros?

η

Perdikkas knows he is drunk, and for what good cause. Every man of his companions has toasted the king on the birth of his son, Amuntas. He has seen the boy, all complete and healthy. Has kissed his good woman and wife, Telesilla. Been praised by Eurudike for fathering an heir. This is a glorious day. A shame that Philippos could not be here. He does well in Amphaxitis. Now he's up north, near the Paiaones, keeping those bastard raiders in their place.

The king smiles, thinking of the small hands of his newborn son. Best not let the old gods know how delight dances through him. They could become jealous. In a few days Perdikkas can dedicate the boy to a great god. By month end, he and Telesilla can officially name the child Amuntas. Children are a chancy thing. Be best if he fathers another son in a year. Other kings would find a second wife, so that a second heir would be here all the sooner. Perdikkas has no interest in any woman but Telesilla as mother of his children. A foible, the magnates would say.

A dance tune drifts into mind. Humming and clapping his hands lightly in time, Perdikkas dances. Here in the privacy of his chamber, away from all the notables, companions, even guards, he dances his joy.

*   *   *

The pounding on the door of his room matches so perfectly the pounding pain in his head that the king does not immediately separate the two actions. Shaking his poor head, Perdikkas calls, "Who's there?"

"Arise, Perdikkas," answers a muffled voice beyond the door that the king recognizes as his friend, Balakros. "You must come at once."

On his feet and alert already, the naked king unscabbards his sword. "What is the matter?" he loudly asks.

"We've lost Methone," comes the reply.

"Methone. How?" *Timotheos, of course,* thinks the king. *But why no warning? Can only be due to betrayal.* Perdikkas hauls open the door. "When we take Methone back, every pro-Athenian there will be exiled," he declares.

The sight of his naked king holding a naked blade momentarily startles Balakros, but not the certainty in the king's voice.

Perdikkas has no time for hesitation, "Summon the horsemen, Balakros."

"Done already, Perdikkas."

To the guard at the door Perdikkas says, "Rouse out my scribes while I dress." Turning back to Balakros, the king asks, "What details are known? Who brought the word? How many men did Timotheos put ashore? Is the city with him or is it a handful of traitors?"

"The scout, Evagoras, brought the news. He says Timotheos marches his main force against Pudna, since Methone is secure with its own citizens stiffened by a small garrison."

The pain in Perdikkas' head intrudes. He ignores it as he laces up his boots. Why was there no word of the landing? Methone lies too close to the sea. When he gets it back, he'll move the whole city. Let them have a port on the sea, but the city will be on the further side of their lands. Damn Hellenes, the whole lot of them. Only Makedones are truly loyal.

The three scribes, all tousled with their rude awakening, stumble into the room. Beyond, in the corridor, half the household stands awake. Torches flare, creating strange shadows on the anxious faces. Already Perdikkas is dictating instructions for one officer after another, plus dispatches to the notables. Yet buzzing in the back of his mind is the desire to recall Philippos. Whatever his brother touches turns out right. The king knows it would be folly to denude the border when the human wolves and ravens beyond are ready to pounce on his people as prey. Perhaps Timotheos timed his strike to coincide with the incursions of restless Paiaones.

Derdas, the Elimiote king, thrusts himself through the crowd, followed by several of his men. The Elimiote comes fully armed, ready to ride in support of his kingly cousin. Thank Zeus for the irascible ally. "So you've heard, Derdas," says Perdikkas.

"You need to clean house, Perdikkas. This should not have caught you by surprise. Someone was lax."

"True words, my guest-friend," answers the young king, "yet you know many of my best men are in Eordaia to keep watch for Bardulis." He addresses the problem, "For now, we will mask Methone. Let us succor Pudna as quickly as we can. If we can isolate Methone, we can counter Timotheos."

I should have known, thinks Perdikkas. And the king must acknowledge that he did know really. Timotheos must do something dramatic to recapture the attention of his fellow citizens. If the Athenians dwelt on his failure at Amphipolis and his narrow success in the Khalkidike, then the politician-general might as well save himself the trip home and go on into exile. Well, taking Methone and Pudna and whatever else he has planned will do to secure the general's reputation in Athenai and all Attika.

"We ride in three hours," says Perdikkas to Derdas. "There will be a hundred and twenty of us, plus your contingent. These dispatches will get us another hundred, maybe a hundred and fifty, by tomorrow night. The rest must catch up in the days to come. We should assemble over four hundred horse, not counting your people. The local levy bands are ordered out in Pieris and Bottiaia. In ten days, we can have three thousand foot at Pudna."

Derdas doesn't speak his thoughts, although Perdikkas can guess them easily enough. The highlander doubts their success. Timotheos has stolen a march on them. Yet all is not undone.

Derdas beckons Perdikkas aside. The king follows to the alcove where the statue of Herakles stands. The Elimiote urges, "We are in motion in the northwest. We build our armies to confront Bardulis. I beg you not to let Methone and Pudna distract you from our main purpose. If we fail to act this year in the highlands, it will be harder to gather the support we need in the future. Methone is a stone in your boot. How will things differ in the long run? They will remain the primary port for timber shipments whether independent or under Athenian control. No doubt you'll pay more to ship through Methone. And I understand the threat the Athenians pose if they were to expand inland. You know they won't. A day's march from their ships is all you need worry about. They are never successful far inland. Your ports may be in jeopardy but not your lands or your throne. Only Bardulis threatens our very existence."

Perdikkas considers what Derdas is saying. While there is a measure of truth in the highlander's words, there is also a fair measure of self-interest. Bardulis is not a threat so long as the yearly tribute goes out to him. True the tribute burdens the realm—and cripples the king's efforts to modernize the kingdom—but it is bearable. For the Elimiotoi and other highlanders, the threat is nearer and the tribute proportionately higher. Perdikkas aches to shake off the grasp of the Illuroi but not at the cost of ignoring his other responsibilities.

The Makedon king answers, "First, let us go to succor Pudna. If we succeed, then Methone is isolated and I can deal with that fact. If we fail before Pudna, then I may need to renegotiate with Athenai. How all this affects what we intend against Bardulis, I do not know. You do know my purpose, and you can assure all our cousins in the highlands. The time will come to end the tribute to the Dardanoi kingdom. Whether it's this year, the next, or the year after, will wait upon events. Be certain that the time is not some distant, never-to-be-attained future. Now help me contain Timotheos." With that, he turns on his heels and rejoins his companions.

θ

Steam rises from the dish of greens, bringing their tart aroma mingled with the fragrance of olive oil, vinegar, and marjoram. Beyond is a plate of warm, soft flat breads. Pikoros sets a platter down, heaped with roasted marinated meats. With that, Philippos, Eurulokhos, Alkimakhos, and the others jostle to get at the meal. Pikoros stabs his knife into the tabletop and roars, "One at a time, one at a time." Meekly the prince and his friends let the surly Pikoros serve them. The redhead mutters about their respective upbringings as he heaps their plates.

Philippos begins chuckling and soon they are all laughing, Pikoros included. "Oh, serve the wine, and let us serve ourselves," says the prince.

A day trooping along the river Axios, high where it emerges into Makedonis, has made them all hungry. Their return to the village that serves as their headquarters was late. Then they dealt with the horses and getting their men settled. Now, quite late, those officers who have come off duty are getting their first meal since the paltry march feed at mid-day.

Still they are in a good mood. This day went well. Nothing spectacular: they assisted a merchant with his pack animals through a mire. The man regaled them with tales of the Dardanian court and other northern peoples. Across the river they had seen distant riders, armed and in quantity. The riders turned away to the northeast at the sight of their column. Perhaps only hunters, perhaps some internecine Paiaone happening, or perhaps raiders thwarted due to Makedon vigilance. Though little enough, the two events broke the monotony of the march and offered proof that they march for good reason.

On the frontier here, they were dispirited when news came of the Athenian capture of Methone and Pudna. Even word of the king's newborn son failed to dispel the gloom. Philippos wondered at the time whether the outcome at Pudna would have been different had his *syntagmai* been in Pieris rather than here.

Tomorrow Philippos and Pikoros travel south to visit another command post. Eurulokhos and Alkimakhos do well here. The next stop is with Demetrios and his brother, Antigonos. They are responsible for the lifeline to Amphipolis.

After that, it may be time to probe east. They will go in the guise of envoys to the various Paiaone and western Thrake tribes. They will go in force so that the tribes understand that the Makedones are strong enough to defend the border. Probably they will march beyond the river Strymon and back.

The secret dispatch from Perdikkas makes this eastern show-of-force more urgent. The king wants half the *syntagmai* to go west. One will be posted at Pella, and the other will march all the way to Eordaia, the Makedon province in the highlands. Since reading the dispatch on his return to the village, Philippos has pondered the redistribution of his forces. In some ways the recall is good. Time to see how Demetrios and some of the others do independent of the prince's direct command. Supplying the *syntagmai* is easier here, along the river, than it will be on the march. Only the column due for Eordaia will need to draw supplies en route.

Should he raise an additional unit here along the border? It might need to be of mixed blood.

Pikoros and he will be on the road themselves for nearly three days before they reach Atalante, where Demetrios is stationed. There Philippos will need to catch up on his duties as civil governor. Say five days there before they ride east to the Bisaltai. That tribe will be hospitable, more so than the tribes in the Strymon valley.

Stuffing into his mouth the savory lamb, Philippos catches the eye of Eurulokhos, who is grinning at him. The officer calls across, "Did you receive word of Lagos?"

Not able to respond at once, Philippos thinks of the note his mother sent. Arsinoe delivered a boy, large and lively. Despite the end of their affair and the months of her pregnancy, she still comes to the prince in his dreams. He grins as he chews, then calls back, "You mean about the proud poppa's new son?"

"He names the boy Ptolemaios," says another officer.

"A common enough name," says Philippos mildly.

"A dangerous name for a Temenidai," comments Alkimakhos dourly.

"Is the boy a Temenidai?" asks the prince. "If so, only by a lengthy stretch back in the family's roots. Some of you probably have as much right to call yourselves Temenidai."

"If you say so, Philippos," laughs Eurulokhos.

Though Philippos probably should feel anger at their jibes, in fact he feels some pride. The child is a boy after all. Only Arsinoe knows, outside the gods, but the boy is likelier his than Lagos'. That bodes well for the children he gets from Phila. Children whose paternity are not in doubt. He chuckles, "Lagos claims the boy as a father should. After all, he dotes on his Lady Arsinoe."

By his ear, Pikoros stage whispers, "You did more than dote."

Philippos spews bread and meat as he laughs out loud. Others are laughing as hardily. Standing, the prince raises his mug of wine, "Let me be the first here to offer a salute. May young Ptolemaios have a long, fortunate life. As for his father, may he prosper, too."

The others recognize that the prince is not jesting, even if the reference to the father is still ambiguous. They rise and in turn offer their toasts to the well-being of the infant Ptolemaios.

CHAPTER TWELVE

Phila and Elimiotis

362 - 359 B.C.

α

Derdas, *basileos* or king of the Elimiotoi, married the older sister of Orestes. Orestes was the boy-king of the Makedones whose half-uncle, Aeropos, poisoned him and usurped his throne. The sister, like Orestes, was the daughter of King Arkhelaos and was named for Arkhelaos' mother, Simikhe.

When Derdas married he was quite young and the princess some years older. King Arkhelaos was alive then, and Derdas' father, Pausanias, felt it expedient to marry his son to a princess of the lowland Makedones. That marriage, like earlier dynastic marriages, marked the close connection between the two families. The long-standing alliance between Elimiotis and Makedonis is realized as much through marriages as through other acts.

The coming marriage between Philippos and Phila is but one of a long series.

Though linking two dynasties and two *ethnos* or peoples, the marriage of Philippos and Phila is not intended to disrupt the rule of Derdas' family in Elimiotis. Phila is the eldest child of Derdas and Simikhe. Two sons follow her: Derdas the younger and little Makhatas. In her honorary uncle, Makhatas, lives another line of the family, the same Makhatas crippled in the fight to restore Parmenion in Pelagonis. If deserving, the younger Derdas is expected to succeed his father when the time comes to be Derdas the Fourth.

The marriage is important. For this King Derdas is like no other. His alliance with the Temenidai is more personal than was true for earlier kings of Elimiotis. As a youthful *basileos* at the court of his cousin— Amuntas, son of Arkhelaos and Kleopatra, half-brother to Simikhe—he was angered by the haughty manners of this Makedon king little older than himself. On an ill-fated day, the foolish Amuntas scoffed at the worth of highlanders, asserted a right over the Elimiote throne, and doubted the legitimacy of Derdas. Enraged, Derdas killed that Amuntas.

The murdered Amuntas was that same sad royal son that Lady Kleopatra mourned when telling Philippos of her life.

On killing King Amuntas, Derdas fled. There was no possibility of escaping to the highlands. What Derdas needed was the protection of a great noble opposed to the faction that supported Little Amuntas. The *basileos* sought sanctuary from another Temenid magnate, old Amuntas, son of Aridaios and Adea. Together, old Amuntas and Derdas the Elimiote forced the Makedones to accept the elder Amuntas as king. Assistance and recognition came from many quarters, most notably Queen Kleopatra, mother of the murdered king. And duly, Derdas was absolved of the murder of the new king's predecessor.

From that time on, Derdas was the chief companion of old Amuntas, rivaling in influence the noble Iolaos. The bond between Derdas and the Temenidai weakened after the death of Amuntas the Third—Amuntas the Wise—especially during the reigns of Alexandros and Ptolemaios of Aloros. To neither of these men did Derdas give much respect. In Perdikkas, Derdas sees the resilient strength of the Temenidai. Close alliance again is attractive. For more than a year Perdikkas and Derdas have worked together to restore their mutual influence in the highlands. They intend to confront and defeat Bardulis, king of the Dardanoi confederacy. And in Philippos, Derdas sees a warrior prince who is a fitting husband for his Phila.

Curiously, for a man so short-tempered and pragmatic, Derdas is a gentle, patient father to Phila. His two boys he holds to high standards and is constantly disappointed in them. With Phila, he takes time to explain, includes her in his confidences, delights in whatever she achieves, whether cooking, riding, weaving, singing, or conversing. In turn, she never disappoints him for her standards of behavior may be higher than his.

Perhaps that is why she is unmarried yet, though older than is typical for one of her station. He considered her for the eldest son of Aeropos of Lunkestis at one time. He found he could not marry her off so lightly. Now he is glad he did not squander her on a highlander. Since the return of Philippos from Thebai, Derdas has kept an eye on the young man.

With the marriage looming—now less than a fortnight away—Derdas finds he possesses fewer anxieties for Phila than he expected. Prince Philippos' visits to the Elimiote court over the last several years gave the two youngsters the opportunity to be introduced and to take to each other. Not in any unseemly way, but in forthright manner as occurs between fellow huntsmen.

Generously, Perdikkas has given Derdas full say over the wedding arrangements. So the marriage takes place in Aiane, principal city of the Elimiotoi. To the Hellenes and even to the lowland Makedones, the towns of the highland are scarcely cities or *polis.* In the view of the southerners, cities are the grounding for civil life. Without cities, what distinguishes a Hellenic tribe from barbarians?

Derdas is proud of Aiane and his people. Aiane's walls have surrounded the town for a hundred years. For longer than two hundred years, the kings of the Elimiotoi have adorned the town with many civic buildings. Terraces built into the side of the hill accommodate the *agora*, temples, and palace that mark a city.

Elimiotis is a well-ordered kingdom. Rather than a countryside of citadels and fortifications, Derdas relies on the vigilance of his horsemen to give his lands security. His horsemen, the occasional mass levy of the men of the kingdom, and, mostly, astute diplomacy, guard his people. A resurgent Makedonis could be an enemy, but Derdas makes certain that Perdikkas is a friend and that the young king's energy is directed against Bardulis.

Aiane will be decorated and literally scrubbed clean to bedazzle her people and to signal the delight Derdas takes in giving his sweet Phila to valiant Prince Philippos. In times to come, Philippos will general the Makedon army. An army the young prince is making stronger. Perhaps as strong or stronger than the Makedon army as it existed under King Arkhelaos. Through this marriage, it will be as important to Philippos to protect Elimiotis as it is to protect Makedonis.

Derdas nods in pleasure at this thought. Staring into the fireplace, he thinks about being fifty years old. No more hiding from his mortality. If his sons don't cease their wastrel ways, well, there will be grandchildren from Phila and Philippos. If the gods grant him twenty more years, and he piously thanks them for his life thus far, then there is time to sort out who best follows him to the throne.

β

Phila blows across the steaming cup of licorice root tea. The brew is nearly an addiction for her each afternoon. How she likes the sweet earthy flavor. True, its taste lingers long so anything eaten even a few hours later cannot compete. One must take the good with the bad, like this man, Philippos.

He will be her husband, and she has little say in the matter. Not that she is displeased. Given whom she might marry, this prince shows well. That Phila would rather not marry at all is of no notice to anyone but her.

She sips the tea, burning her tongue in her eagerness. Holding back from sipping more, she assesses her prospects with Philippos. He will be kind. His vices are few and go with most highborn Makedones—too much wine, too much hunting, too much rough company. Her father all over again, except sweet-tempered rather than irascible. They say he beds all and sundry. And he has caught the Theban habit of liking young boys, yet still retains the Makedon trait of bedding women, any woman. Well enough, then he will take pleasure in bedding her though she is plain-featured. And if he takes pleasure, they say he gives pleasure as well. That's better than most men.

He is a good-humored man, though with a tendency toward the sardonic.

Vigorous. Ambitious, like all the Temenidai. Keenly intelligent, and better educated than most as a result of his Theban captivity.

She sighs, and cautiously sips again. Well, then, what is he getting? She tries to think of herself as someone else would see her, a difficult chore. As much farmer's wife as princess. Always with the horses. Though that will be in her favor with Philippos. Known for her general happiness and ability, with an occasionally too blunt tongue.

Does he even care what he is getting, besides the friendship of Elimiotis? Probably does, to do him justice, though he would marry the princess of Elimiotis were she a loathsome shrew.

They will have children. That is a central requirement.

Secretly she is afraid of having children. She is marrying in her twenties, older than most. Children have never interested her. Bawling, soiling themselves, ever a drag on their mother or wet nurse. Older children are all right, if not spoiled. Well, girls, at least, are all right, from age eight to age twelve. They do say that your own child is infinitely more precious than anyone else's child. Bearing a child is supposed to stimulate all the traditional feelings of motherhood. She can't imagine it.

Truth is, she would be a man if she could. Dionysios holds the power to transform. Were she to worship him, would he transform her?

His followers are many among the Makedon women, highland and lowland. Somehow he has never attracted her. All emotion, whereas she likes the reasoning of men. Yet she barely thinks these thoughts for fear Dionysios will notice her impiety and deliver her into madness.

She and Philippos have met on three occasions. The occasions were informal, they talked about horses and dogs. He made her laugh, talking about how a dog's master comes to take the attributes of his dog, and illustrating the point with members of the Elimiote court. She likes him well enough. Likes him better than her own brothers. Would willingly see him as her brother. As her husband?

She would like him to make love to her. She knows he won't truly love her, as she does not him. But sex, well, that would be fine. She's been restless lately with the thought of it.

Princess Phila of Elimiotis, she thinks. I am my father's possession, given as a pledge of friendship. I am also myself, and can make a life with this man they make my husband. He will not have all of me, no matter what these men think. Anyway, this man is not so foolish as to demand all of me. And he is a man of goodness who will give me something of himself.

γ

Some believe that marriage is a solemn sacrament—two people dedicating themselves before the goddesses Hera and Hestia. Couple that with all the seriousness of linking two noble families in an event that has more to do with lands and power than with love or simple caring. Those few guests who expected solemnity did not know the two brothers, Perdikkas and Philippos.

Not that they treated Derdas, Phila, or the marriage frivolously. No, but treat them with joy, good-natured levity, and a hearty salute to both future children and the activity that precedes them, that they did.

The marriage ceremony was brief, though intense. Phila was surprised by the fierceness of Philippos as he pledged himself to her. His words, almost harshly spoken "...and to thee, dear Phila, I give myself as husband, so that you will ever have an honored place by my side and in my heart..." thrilled her. Words unexpected, "...in my heart..." For the first time an unnamed feeling welled within her. This man had need of her. And so her pledge, in turn, held more in it than she thought to give "...shall cherish my place with you, in all that I do and feel." What odd words, "cherish," "feel." What did she mean by them and how did Philippos take their meaning? Well, she meant them, they were heartfelt for sure and she could have added from now on. No qualifiers, for none are needed. From now on, she is his wife and his concerns are hers.

If the ceremony was brief, the celebration was not. Dancing and drinking. Games, jokes, and drinking. Toasts. Mingling with guests, asking about this or that, answering what? Who remembers. A whirl of conversation. Too much drinking.

Perdikkas, what a bear. If he stepped on her feet one more time while dancing she would have knocked him to the ground. She grins to herself. How grand that the king of the Makedones is her brother-in-law and is clearly happy to see his brother and Phila wedded. The happiness the king feels with his queen, Telesilla, and infant son, he is certain will be the happiness Philippos and Phila experience.

Even father surprised her. She was worried that in his sadness at giving her away, his behavior would be grudging. She needn't have felt concern. Never had her father been more gracious, more light-hearted. Some time along this day's journey, she realized that Derdas feels relief. A father's obligation is done in seeing his beloved daughter safely in the arms of a man capable of her proper care and certain to provide that care. Like a ship's captain come ashore after an arduous voyage with the cargo intact and no hands lost.

At one point, late in the festivities, near drunk herself, she watched Philippos reel, as he led a line of dancing men, all bellowing some merry song mocking the lovelorn. She'd thought, *he will sleep like a log and wake in remorse. I will be a lonely bride this first night.* Then he had looked at her across the room and winked. With sudden good cheer, she realized that he was not so drunk as the men around him. He simply acts as they expect.

Softly she thinks of Philippos. He will come to her soon. He's ushering the last ribald, drunken guest out of the house.

Lying there, tired herself, spinning with strange emotions, having drunk more wine this day than she is accustomed to drinking in a month, Phila feels no fear. Only the Fates know the future. A mere human knows that there will be pain and sorrow—for there is always pain and sorrow in life—yet she shall have more. She shall have pleasure and joys. That's not it. How important are they? She will have yet more, she will have purpose. Even the idea of children no longer scares her. From now, this day, with this husband, this Philippos, she understands that they are a cord twined together that is one part of the weaving that is their ancestors and posterity. Death is illusion. The weaving is continuous. The Fates do not cut the cord of life, though they measure each individual's span.

The door to the room eases open, and Philippos enters quietly. Seeing her awake, he says gently, "How are you, Phila?"

She raises herself, smiling, "I am radiant, dear husband."

His head goes back in laughter, "Your radiance dazzles my eyes."

"I thought all Temenidai were used to looking at the sun."

"Isn't the moon the realm of women?"

"Perhaps for most women, but a woman worthy of the Temenidai must be worthy of the sun."

Phila's teasing is becoming a statement between them, for with her words, Philippos becomes serious, "You are most worthy, Phila of Elimiotis. I am glad to be your husband."

They stare at each other across the room until she beckons him to her. He sits on the edge of the bed, and begins to pull her to him. She resists, putting a finger to his lips. Surprised, he sits back. "Listen to me, Prince Philippos. We need to talk about what we are together." She smiles at his puzzled look.

She continues, "You remember that day at the stables, when we talked about horse lines and breeds of dogs?"

He nods but does not interrupt.

"We knew then that we were betrothed, that we would wed. Yet we did not talk about it." She hugs her knees, thinks for a moment on how to say what she wants to say. "Today, we did say words, promises. I can tell you that those promises meant more to me than I thought they would. I hope the same was true for you." Again, he nods silently.

Holding up a hand for him to see, she begins to tick down her fingers, "I think we need to say to each other that we are husband and wife in several ways. We are husband and wife because we are Makedonis and Elimiotis. In consequence, there will be demands on us, pressures, that have to do with titles and power." She ticks a second finger, "We are husband and wife in order to have children. Again, we are part of two dynasties." Here she grins at him, "I expect the making of those children will be fun." More soberly, she adds, "And you will spend your sexual self on others while expecting me to be your vessel alone." She shrugs, "Part of the bad bargain of being a woman."

She ticks down a third finger, "I think we can be husband and wife and friends. I thought that the day we talked at the stables, and I think it still."

He takes her hand in his, "I believe that, too, Phila. Whatever comes, let us be friends."

This time she nods, the she adds, "Husband, we may be more. I find myself caring, concerned for you, more deeply that I supposed I would. I hope you find yourself feeling the same."

"Phila, you are beautiful in your honesty. Since we are starting with truth, let it always be so between us. That I care for you, I know. How deeply? How will that caring grow? I do not know." He is silent for a time, holding her hand in his. Then he adds, "Perdikkas and I are contemplating that I wed again, a daughter of the Molossi king of Epeiros. I do not know whether it will come about. There would be a long betrothal."

He sighs, then says, "Perdikkas and I have vowed before our ancestors, back to father Zeus, that we will secure the Makedones. We will work unceasingly so that our people no longer are the prey of Illuroi, Paiaones, Thraikiotes, Triballi, Olunthians, Athenians, Thebans, Spartans, and even Persians. I do not know what sacrifices the gods will demand of us."

She reaches and strokes his forehead, "Then let me add my vow, husband, that I will aid you in whatever you ask, and to the extent of my strength and capacity." Though she likes this man, she is glad there will be other wives. All the easier to be herself and not be sucked dry by him.

He pulls her to him again, and this time she allows it,

δ

Months later, the heat of summer is full upon the land. Day after day, Helios burns brightly. No cloud obscures the blue sky. What was dry is now dust. Grass withers. Streams become trickles with occasional slimy pools. Philippos is worried for his horse herd.

"We can cut a ditch from the west branch of the Ekhedoros so its waters irrigate your land," suggests Thalorion, the steward of this estate.

"How will that affect our neighbors downstream?" asks Philippos.

"They won't like it, but what can they say? Your word is law in Amphaxitis," answers the steward.

Philippos looks searchingly at this retainer, making the steward suddenly uncomfortable. "That is not the solution. Their herds and grains are needed, too."

Abruptly deciding, Philippos says, "You will drive half the herd north in easy stages to my estate at Gortyna. That will give the grass here some peace. For the remainder of the herd alternate stored fodder with the range. Make it two days of range for each day of fodder. Send the mares and younger horses north."

Then smiling thinly, Philippos adds, "And find a way to give aid to our neighbors, especially the smallholders. They won't possess other estates to

ALLIANCE WITH ELIMIOTIS

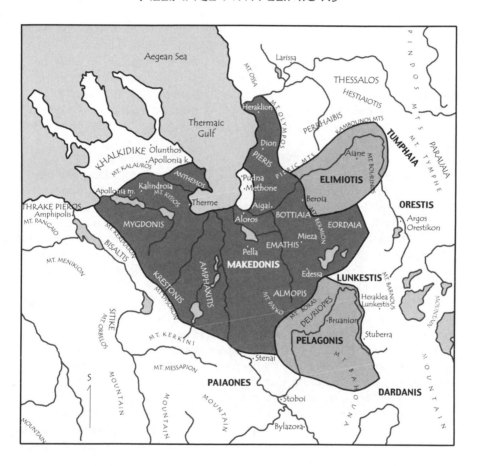

provide relief. Let them know the aid you give is in my name. Be generous, Thalorion."

Turning away from his man, Philippos mounts his own horse, Kapnos, a gray. Though as often Philippos refers to the horse as *pachos katsarida,* Fat Cockroach. The gelding is a good animal for riding all day as he tends to his duties as landowner. Perhaps an animal better suited to do his duty than Thalorion is to his.

Ambling along, the man and horse fall to quiet reflection, as the heat requires conservation of effort. Oddly, Philippos realizes that he is happy. He offers a brief thanks to the great god for the benison of this day. Tomorrow he must be active, for he will rejoin his commanders for the monthly march and encampment along the borders. Today though is his.

A halloo banishes his peaceful thoughts. Ahead, cresting the rise comes Pikoros, eager with some news. Philippos waves acknowledgment and sets his heels to Kapnos.

The two meet midway. "What is it, Pikoros?"

"News from the south. The battle the Thebans were seeking has been fought in the Peloponnesos. They and their allies beat the Spartans, Mantineans, and Athenians, but they lost Epaminondas."

"So they lost more than they won."

"Thebai still has Pammenes," answers Pikoros. When a slave staying with Philippos in the household of Pammenes, Pikoros had been desperately unhappy. Even so, he was not oblivious to the merits of the master of the household. He respects Pammenes to this day.

Philippos nods absently, remembering Epaminondas. Thebai's renowned general is now a shade. The risks of a life given to war. Still a terrible loss for the city and its confederacy. With Pelopidas killed fighting Pherai several years back, Thebai depended on Epaminondas as if he were their only spear. Oh, Pammenes is a good officer, but he is a sword to Epaminondas' spear. The city has no trouble making new *Beotarkhs,* generals. Who among them is likely to own the strategic and tactical genius of Epaminondas? Who among them is likely to inspire, with the fierce noble spirit of Pelopidas?

What does all this mean for the Makedones? Asks Philippos of himself. As if answering, Pikoros says, "The dispatch brought direction from King Perdikkas. You are to return to Pella for a great council."

"Good. Send word to Eurulokhos that he will make the monthly march without us. You and I will ride for Pella. The day is early enough yet, we can get a good ways today."

Pikoros grins, "I've brought your traveling bag. Fresh horses and baggage mules will be at the crossroads. A rider will be waiting there for your orders to Eurulokhos. The escort will be only two men so we can move quickly." Pikoros leans back and pulls a scabbarded sword and belt free from the bundle behind him, "Here, put this on. I hate it when you ride out with only a knife."

Accepting the mild scolding as due, given all the care and anticipation Pikoros has taken, Philippos slaps his companion's upper arm, "Let's ride then."

ε

When away from Pella, Philippos misses the gymnasium, especially the swimming pool. So here he is now, snorting like a sea lion. Though most men either swim laps or get briskly in and out of the water, Philippos likes to play. Today he and several others are diving for coins tossed into the pool.

The bottom is bright with a mosaic, so the coins lay hidden in its pattern. Groping along the floor of the pool, with eyes and hands busy searching as the strain of being underwater pushes harder at his lungs, the prince collides with another searcher, young Polemaios. They tussle as they spot the same coin. The burly prince grabs the coin and eludes Polemaios' groping hands. They burst to the surface, laughing and gasping for breath.

Philippos hands the silver coin to Polemaios, "That's enough for me. You keep the prize. You fought hard for it." With a heave, Philippos sits on the side of the pool. For a bit he watches the half-dozen boys and young men continue the game. One of the boys, Peithon, seems a likely youth. Tall and slender for his age, yet with definite musculature. The prince watches him with appreciation.

A towel snaps him across the shoulders. "Caught you ogling the children," says Antipatros, sitting down next to Philippos. The prince smiles his greeting.

Together they dangle their feet in the water, letting the loud antics around and in the pool wash over them. Finally Antipatros taps Philippos lightly on the ribs, "Your brother is in heat. Says that now is our opportunity, with Thebai prostrate over Epaminondas and Athenai dealing with opposition from Byzantion, Khalkedon, and Kyzikos."

Philippos grunts non-committally, his eyes following two young boys chasing a third. The leader dives into the pool, with the younger two right behind. "Do you like children, Antipatros?" asks the prince.

"How do you mean? I prefer women as lovers," says the older man, beginning to bristle.

Philippos laughs, touching Antipatros' knee in placation, "No, no, I don't mean that as you think. I simply was asking if you like children— little boys and girls."

Antipatros settles back down and shrugs, "Some, my own. I like them better when they're past the toddler stage, when you can talk to them." He considers further, "Boys take more effort, but it's of use."

Turning and looking at Antipatros fully, Philippos wonders about this

271

gruff man. He has known Antipatros all his life. They are not close, yet their family interests lie together. Perdikkas has grown to rely on Antipatros. "How many children is it now?"

"Me?" Antipatros shrugs again, "Two girls. We lost the boy, some damn fever. That's why I don't give much attention when they're young. You lose them too easily." The pain is there to see on his face, then he hardens, "There will be more, even if it means taking another wife or two." He turns to Philippos, "Why do you ask? Has Phila announced herself pregnant?"

"No, not yet. No doubt it will come." Philippos considers the impulse that made him first ask about children, "You said my brother is in heat and that made me think of his son, Amuntas. I find I like being an uncle."

Antipatros starts to say something about Arsinoe's boy, Ptolemaios, but thinks better of it, "Being an uncle is easier than being a father."

"Making the Makedones secure we do for ourselves, to honor the gods and forefathers, and to offer a patrimony to our children. Perdikkas is in heat for all of those reasons. I can think of no better reasons," says Philippos softly yet forcefully.

Nodding thoughtfully, Antipatros responds, "So what Derdas and the king propound, you agree?"

The prince stands, looking down on the bearded face of Antipatros. "The timing may not be perfect. We could use additional revenues to raise mercenaries to support our own troops. Still, yes, with all the southern powers occupied, it's time to bind the highlands to us. Then we can face Bardulis."

"Your brother even has a scheme for raising revenues. Another of those Athenian exiles suggests we increase the harbor dues in all our ports." Antipatros stands as well, "Why is it that Athenians always think of ways of harming their city when in exile and of harming all other cities when they're in power?"

"Custom dues on timber, cattle, and horses will see the greatest increase, then?"

"Of what goes out. Incoming pottery, wine, and olive oil will be raised, too." The two men are of a size and can look each other squarely in the eye. Antipatros is dark, his face swarthy from working out of doors, although a pale body. Philippos, younger, is not so burly. Beard and hair are a lighter shade, become a brown since his youth. His body is more fully tanned from all his running and athletics in the nude. Strong men, both of them.

"You've not said your thoughts about the highlands," mentions Philippos.

"With Athenai facing rebellion from her allies, I think we should move against Methone and Pudna. Bring them back in the fold." He pulls at his beard, "I do see the wisdom of gathering the highlanders so we can get the Illuroi off our backs. I fear, though, that Bardulis is not a trifle. We'd best know what we're about and be ready for a massive fight."

"Are you speaking for yourself, your clan, or all the country notables?"

"Certainly for myself, for I have estates in Eordaia, too, you know. As for the clan and the country folk, you know our feelings. If we are going to war, it had better be worth the dead we will harvest." His voice grim, Antipatros adds, "This won't be like countering King Agis of the Paiaones. Not the odd raid. When you fight Bardulis of the Dardanoi, you fight as if your back is to the wall."

Now it is Philippos who nods thoughtfully. What Antipatros says is true. They'd better be prepared to fight a savage war. And Perdikkas will need the enthusiastic support of Antipatros and all those he represents. For this year, though, all they need do is intervene with Orestis and Lunkestis. That and continue to ensure the alliances with the Pelagonoi and the Elimiotoi. "I will talk it out further with Perdikkas and Derdas."

"That's all I ask, Philippos," says Antipatros seriously.

As they walk together to the dressing room, Antipatros adds, "You understand that while I can speak for many of the country notables and smallholders, there is a faction led by your half-brothers. Arkhelaos is a popular man. They oppose any wars outside what they call the ancient kingdom. You and Perdikkas tend to underrate Arkhelaos. Besides his country faction, there are priestly families at Aigai who listen to his interpretation of the Temenidai's divine descent.

"Perhaps there needs to be a focus for rural discontent," muses Philippos. "Has there ever been a time when numbers of country folk are not in debt or want? The sons of Derdas are forever bleating about their gambling losses. Yet their gambling is nothing compared to the risks run by peasants and herders against drought, depredations, and blight."

"Spring was too wet and now summer is too hot and dry," agrees Antipatros.

"We must see what royal aid can be offered. Perhaps we should guarantee planting seed for next spring." Philippos smiles at Antipatros, "Arkhelaos is not formidable. Better he should serve as the touchstone of grievance than some others I could name. Still, let's bring this to Perdikkas and see what reasonable plan can be devised to assist the people."

"And what about Bardulis?"

"Perdikkas will refuse to pay tribute at the beginning of the new year. He will temporize long enough in the fall so that Bardulis cannot launch an attack before winter sets in. So, it will be next spring that we fight. In the meantime, we have nine months to complete our preparations and to enlist Orestis and Lunkestis on our side." Philippos grins at Antipatros, "We can do it, friend."

"You two have kept your timetable tight within your fists."

"Oh, yes," answers the prince dryly, "we do not know everyone who is in Bardulis' pay."

Antipatros feels mildly insulted that the king has not included him in his confidence, yet here is Prince Philippos revealing a portion. "Who else knows that the king is in earnest?"

"Why, Antipatros, there is the king, Derdas of Elimiotis, Parmenion of Pelagonis, you, and me."

The simple statement eases the tension in the noble. So the royal Temenidai still hold the family of Iolaos closest of all the Makedones. "Then there is still much to do."

Philippos reaches out and lightly pulls the tuft of hair on Antipatros' shoulder, "You are right, and we are the five who can make it happen."

ζ

Overtures to Aeropos of Lunkestis and Orontes of Orestis are well-received. Aeropos in particular remembers the young Philippos and the good will between his boy Alexandros and the prince. Orontes is less enthusiastic, perhaps keeping in mind the fate of his distant cousin, Ptolemaios of Aloros. Orontes listens carefully to the embassy, but prefers to shelter his people under the mantle of the Molossi of Epeiros.

Both *basileiai* agree, though, to provide troops to Perdikkas for the Makedon army come spring. While their small contingents will be tokens, it means neither will support Bardulis. This makes a promising preamble to the campaign.

Perdikkas takes the next step, refusing tribute to the Dardanoi king. Not outright refusal, but a quibble over complaints brought by shepherds. A request for negotiations. A pleading that the Makedones are strapped for coins and will bartered goods do? And how will these goods best be valued? How transported? Until winter sweeps snow down from the north.

Meanwhile Perdikkas readies the army. The militia levy in Eordaia receives improved pikes, and supplies are stockpiled in the canton's principal city. Lagos accepts command of the local forces, for he is from a prominent Eordaian family. Following the examples of Derdas and Parmenion, the squadrons of Makedon horsemen train. Philippos Arkouda, Periandros, Antiokhos, Korrhagos, Balakros, and Parrhasios each lead a squadron. In addition, Perdikkas trains his personal *agema*, the men of his own squadron. Prince Philippos and his commanders put the four phalanxes through their paces. Recruiting agents are sent south to raise two hoplite phalanxes of mercenaries.

How Bardulis of the Dardanoi must smile in his capital city. How much the brothers Temenidai underestimate the old wolf. For Bardulis does not wait for spring. When the ground is frozen so movement is not impeded, Bardulis leads six thousand men south into Lunkestis. Aeropos capitulates. Orontes of Orestis flees to Dodona, capital of Kings Neoptolemos and Arubbas of Epeiros. Parmenion is isolated, bottled up in his valleys.

Will the Makedones and Elimiotes fight? There is not time, as Bardulis overruns Eordaia and his horsemen probe into Elimiotis.

Perdikkas and Derdas know they must come to terms with Bardulis. The tribute will increase, making Bardulis smile broader. If they cannot defeat Bardulis, there is no choice. If Bardulis lets his army linger in the highlands deep into spring, then it will eat up all that the people saved to see them through. Early spring is always the time of hunger. This year it could become a time of starvation.

Two Makedones and an Elimiote are chosen as envoys to the Dardanid king. Athanaios, who is an experienced diplomat, having been the chief ambassador to Thebai. Philippos, son of Makhatas, and a prince of the Elimiotoi, represents Derdas. And Prince Philippos, brother of King Perdikkas, for the Temenidai must humble themselves.

The meeting place is a small village just beyond the Eordaian side of the Kara Burun pass. If Bardulis were to lead his army through that pass he would be in Emathis, one of the heartland provinces of the Makedones. Poised there, waiting, the Dardanoi king knows he is putting irresistible pressure on King Perdikkas.

For Philippos, riding north with the small entourage of the envoys, there is wonder at the success of Bardulis. He looks forward to meeting this menace for the first time. For all of his life and for much of his father's, Bardulis' sword hand has shadowed the Makedones.

Athanaios rides forward to join Philippos and continue the argument begun last night, "You look as if you are eager to see this barbarian."

"Well, you have met him before. For me, this is like meeting the Hydra or Sphinx, some mythical evil beast."

"You have that right, a beast. You are sure to be disappointed." Athanaios smiles, "After all, you've met the likes of Epaminondas, Pelopidas, and Pammenes, true warriors and gentlemen."

"Bardulis may not have the cultured manners of the south, but he is as true a warrior."

"We go through this every seven or ten years, you know," says Athanaios. "We Makedones become restless and try to loose the limits placed on us by the Dardanoi confederacy. Then Bardulis marches in with an army and says boo. We trot out as envoys, add more coins to the annual tribute, ransom our prisoners, and he goes away."

The third envoy, Philippos Makhatou, joins them in time to overhear Athanaios' last comment. He answers, "Athanaios, you sound as if this is some game."

The older man turns to their new companion, "Well, it's not Pelagonid stick ball. I say it's not as serious as the Athenians holding Methone and Pudna."

"Perhaps not for you lowlanders. For those of us who inhabit the highland basins, what Bardulis decides to do is more important than any southern city. Perhaps the southerners touch the highlands once in twenty years, while we pay Bardulis every year. And it's not simply the tribute. It's the knowledge that if he chooses he could take our principalities, one after the other, and share them out as he decides."

Philippos considers that idea, "He could take them, but could he hold them? Not without taking Epeiros or Makedonis. Otherwise, he's a turtle with his head stuck out."

"Maybe," acknowledges the Elimiote noble. "He's holding them now, all saved Elimiotis. I don't see either Epeiros or Makedonis chopping through the turtle's neck." He looks across at his two fellow riders. Athanaios is a figure of the court. An old man used to tact and intrigue. If need be he could fight and not be useless, but is no general. Prince Philippos is a likely enough fellow. Yet his war experience is shallow, a single campaign in Pelagonis. Successful, true, depending on how you count the losses. His phalanxes seem promising but are largely untested. The new weapons and tactics he's adopted echo the work of Iphikrates in Thraikios, so they may prove sound. "You're right this time. He'll withdraw if we pay him enough. He's planned his own campaign for spring against the coastal tribes of the Adriatic Sea."

"You are well informed," comments Athanaios.

"We must be. We have agents at his court and in his cities."

Prince Philippos looks keenly at Philippos Makhatou, "That's why your uncle wanted to strike this year. He expected Bardulis to be occupied."

"The opportunity seemed to be there. You lowlanders were willing to accept the challenge, with Athenai and Thebai caught in their own turmoils."

Athanaios comments, "So much for opportunity. Hat in hand again, pleading our poverty, pleading misunderstanding, pleading our good intentions. We will be serious, polite, genial if he'll let us. And Bardulis will go away."

"I think you miss the point being made by Philippos Makhatou," says the prince. "Bardulis does not go away. He simply withdraws while remaining a threat. We buy him off for now, but that doesn't end the threat." Nodding at the Elimiote, Philippos adds, "You highlanders are right to fear the Illuroi. I've spent more than a year on our eastern borders, and there they fear the Paiaones and Thraikiotes. I pledge to you that we will eliminate these threats even if I spend my life as my brother's general fighting these three peoples. I swear we will make them afraid of us."

Philippos Makhatou looks curiously at the prince. There is steel in this young man. Maybe Perdikkas has learned the right priorities. Secure the borders, then deal with the southerners. At least the king's brother understands the proper priorities.

*　*　*

Fortunately the tent set up by the Illuroi is huge, for it is crowded with men. That too is good, for though ill-smelling there is warmth, particularly near the center fire where sit the negotiators. All of the Makedon entourage is there, save the servants who care for the horses. With the three envoys are the two interpreters, three scribes, two guards, and one servant. They are outnumbered three or four to one by the Illuroi in the tent.

The procedure agreed among the envoys is being followed. Athanaios speaks for the lowlanders, Philippos Makhatou for Elimiotis. A scribe copies down all that they say. The primary interpreter, a mixed breed of Lunkestoi and Illuroi stock, states their words in the Dardanoi dialect to their opponents. The second interpreter tells the negotiators and the second scribe what the Illuroi are saying. Prince Philippos is observing, sitting to one side. The third scribe, Tyros, is with him. If Philippos has a suggestion or comment, he quietly says it to Tyros, who then takes a note to either Athanaios or Philippos Makhatou.

Across the fire, on the Dardanoi side, four men are active negotiators. Though introduced civilly at the outset, their respective roles are uncertain to the Makedones. One is a son of Bardulis, named Agirros. Another is the king's nephew, Epidios. The third is some sort of priest, Ziraios. And the fourth is a mystery, a slender youth, dressed as a Hellene, who speaks rarely, named Epikados. They also have interpreters and scribes.

Bardulis takes no direct part in the discussion, yet misses nothing. He does not seem to require an interpreter. Philippos had expected a grim, huge, evil man—not the jovial, small-statured, and potbellied grandfather that is Bardulis.

He also had not expected the Dardanoi to be so well informed about everything in the highlands and the lowlands. For every assertion made by Athanaios or Philippos Makhatou, the Dardanoi delegation responds with questions that inevitably lead back to the false note within the Makedon statement. *If these are barbarians, the gods protect us if they become civilized,* thinks Philippos.

Another series of Dardanoi questions about silver mining in Makedonis makes Philippos realize that the Hellene in their delegation is their treasurer. With that thought, it all falls in place. The priest is responsible for the Illuroi agents in the highlands and Makedonis. The son and nephew are generals, of course, but it is the nephew who is the senior officer. The son, Agirros, then, must be the king's heir.

Bardulis has many sons, nephews, cousins, collateral cousins, consanguinial and affinal relatives. Much of his power rests in the extent of his family connections. He has taken many wives through his long life and fathered many children on each. Half or more of the men in this tent are likely his kin. That this son is a negotiator must indicate his favor in the king's eyes. Why are there two warriors among the negotiators? Speaking softly to Tyros, Philippos sends a note to Athanaios with his observation.

Abruptly Bardulis claps his hands twice. All the Illuroi fall silent, and Athanaios' voice sputters to a halt. The king stands and approaches the fires, "Enough of your lies, Makedones. Do not try to be Athenians, you're not good enough at half-truths and prevaricating righteousness." The heavily accented Hellenic is perfectly understandable, if in the western dialect.

He waves Athanaios down, and the envoy sits. "I will tell you how much you will pay. You will pay half again as much as you owed before, and you will pay in coin. The coinage will be pure, silver or gold. I want no bronze or other copper coinage. As for our prisoners, each man is three silver *tetradrakhm* to redeem, except the leaders. They are two gold darics apiece. We have 973 prisoners, and five men we count as leaders."

Gone is the image of a rustic grandfather. Somehow Bardulis has grown taller, leaner, sterner. This is a king who demands obedience.

"You, Athanaios, son of Arkhutas and you, Philippos, son of Makhatas, may sign the treaty representing your peoples. You, Philippos, son of Amuntas, brother of King Perdikkas, you will sign for the Temenidai and for King Perdikkas. I know your wiles, and I want testament from both the Makedon king and people."

Athanaios glances anxiously back to the prince. Philippos stands and answers the Dardanid king, "You shall have our affirmations, King Bardulis, but at one-third higher tribute, not one-half. There is no need for you to press us so severely that we cannot comply. If you would have us honor this agreement, then it must be at a rate that we can bear, year-in and year-out."

He pauses to see the effect on Bardulis. "The rates for the prisoners, we accept. Since you did not mention women and children, those individuals will be restored to their homes at no cost." Philippos folds his arms and stares at the king.

The tentful of men are silent. Bardulis stares back at Philippos, the pale eyes gleaming yet betraying nothing. Then the king says, "Done" and laughs. Immediately the tent is full of chatter again, and Bardulis is again a jovial grandfather.

Philippos feels let down. Yet he knows that he's learned much today. Some he must sort out as he reads what the scribes took down. Some he carries in his head as observations of the interplay among the Illuroi.

He and Perdikkas must hunt down Illuroi agents, and given the extent of Dardanid knowledge, some agents number among the realm's notables. Ziraios the Priest seems to be a priest of the Dardanid version of Ares. So perhaps Perdikkas should begin his search with the priestly family in Aigai dedicated to Ares.

Making a vow to himself, Philippos promises that some day he will have the head of Epidios at his feet. If Epidios is their principal general, then Epidios must die.

With the simple treaty written in quadruplicate, Philippos is called forward to sign. Standing beside Bardulis, he quickly signs each copy. The Dardanid king smells of herbs and garlic, strong but not unpleasant. The king leans close to Philippos and says so softly that only the prince can hear, "Do not take it so hard. Some future day we can cross swords. Then you will find out if your phalanxes can do as well against the Dardanoi as they did against renegade Pelagones." The king pats Philippos gently on the arm, then strides away, bellowing harshly to his followers.

η

"We do it again, Philippos. That is the only answer that serves," says Perdikkas. "There is no sense in waiting. Only this time we do not rely on Lunkestoi, Orestoi, and Pelagonoi. This time we rely on ourselves and the Elimiotoi."

"I advise you waiting another year, maybe two. Let us build our strength further," Philippos is anxious that they do it right this time.

"The mercenaries will be here this month. Bardulis is lulled, and has begun his Adriatic campaign. Persia has no interest as he deals with rebellious satraps. Athenai lost her grain fleet to Byzantion. She also faces King Kotys in Thraikios. Thebai grinds on in the Peloponnesos, without brilliance or the possibility of overcoming Sparte. And now we hear that Neoptolemos, king of the Molossi, is dead. Perhaps Orestis and Lunkestis, and even Tumphaia, can be weaned from the Molossi if we are victorious."

The two men sit on a bench in the garden, enjoying the spring sun, weak though it is this time of year. Many varieties of birds have already returned. Buds, shoots, and early flowers abound. The cold, bitter events of winter seem past.

Knowing his brother's reluctance, the king presses, "You've heard Lagos since his ransom. He is ardent against the Illuroi for the humiliations they visited on him and his men. All of our magnates and notables are thirsting after the blood of the Dardanoi. Have you ever seen them so heated? To be expected of a Parrhasios, even an Antipatros, but Lagos? Why even Arkhelaos and his brothers offer to lead a contingent against Bardulis."

"Do we know any more about their agents in Makedonis?"

"I doubt it's the priests of Ares," says Perdikkas shrugging. "We have some names from Eordaia and among the Lunkestoi. None of my companions, nor any notable in the lowlands."

"Perhaps we're looking at this the wrong way round. Perhaps we should not be searching for a Dardanid agent. What if someone at court is reporting back to another Makedon notable, not knowing where the information is bound? What prominent man does not have sources? Perhaps there are no threads leading to Bardulis. Only one man or a few men who gather what they learn and pass it along to Bardulis."

The king considers, "That does sound likelier. I doubt there's a cross-section of our citizens catering to the Illuroi. Some one person may be making himself favorable to Bardulis. Someone hopeful of preferment if Bardulis intervenes directly. That I can believe."

The brothers look at each other. "Shall I say it or you?" asks Philippos.

Perdikkas laughs, "I will have Arkhelaos, Aridaios, and Menelaos watched more closely. Why not set a trap? We feed them a tidbit and see if the tidbit ends up with Bardulis."

"Who will you put on this?"

"Theagenes. He's a clever fellow, the one from Skotussa in Thessalos.

You've met him. He's an actor, a bit disreputable. Would prefer to be known as a poet, though he hasn't the gift. As an actor, he's decent. Probably what makes him a good agent. In fact, I think you should run him."

"Why me?"

"When I march with the army, you shall be my regent in Pella."

Philippos is keenly disappointed, though he sees the sense in Perdikkas' decision. His boy, Amuntas, is a toddler and Telesilla is too sweet to be a regent. To choose the father-in-law is too dangerous. Philippos is glad of the confidence Perdikkas reposes in him. One advantage is that Philippos need not act directly in repudiating the treaty, sworn before Hellenic and Illuric gods. All that said, Philippos despairs at not leading the men he has trained these past several years.

"There is something else," adds the king, seeing his brother's dismay.

"Yes?"

"On our success in the highlands, you will reinforce Amphipolis. Time we shooed the Athenians away from our ally."

"What force will I have?"

"I'll leave you two of your phalanxes. You can raise more this year. Is it possible to manage another four? Are the funds available? Let me discuss that with Kallistratos the Athene. He's finding ways to raise money that Amuntas Plousias never considered."

"You need every man you can get to face Bardulis."

"Not yet. Not until Bardulis ties up his campaign. I can steal a march on him. And I will have the mercenaries, your other two phalanxes, my horsemen, the Elimiote horses, and levies from Eordaia and Elimiotis. Plus each notable has pledged a contingent. The clans support this war."

"The clans lack discipline."

"True enough." The king sighs, "Philippos, you always want things to be perfect. Life does not lend itself to perfection. I tell you now is our time. When else will all our chief opponents be in such disarray? And we must appease that faction that still sees Athenai as our chief threat. This year, both the highlands and Amphipolis will be gained."

Why this sense of foreboding, thinks Philippos. He watches a sparrow alight on a tree limb. Then lands a second, a third, the fourth. Others of the flock arrive in the garden. Perhaps it's only his dissatisfaction at missing the action. He does indeed want to cross swords with Bardulis, and has not forgotten his vow to take Epidios' head.

"A wind is coming up. Time to move back indoors. Telesilla and Phila want some of our time today. With Phila now pregnant, she hangs on every word Telesilla says about birthing Amuntas," comments Perdikkas, stretching his legs.

Thinking every woman who ever gave birth feels free to advise a woman pregnant for the first time, Philippos answers, "I will be glad to see your boy. He's so comical when he walks."

"Mothers says I always ran as a child. All Amuntas can do is waddle."

"Give the boy time, Perdikkas. He will grow straight and true."

"Spoken like an indulgent uncle."

Another thought occurs to Philippos, "We share suspicions of Arkhelaos. Let's not neglect our dear cousins, Pausanias and Argaios."

"Pausanias cultivates the Thraikiotes, Argaios the Athenians. I doubt either is in league with Bardulis. We do keep watch on them as it is."

"We can probably exclude Argaios. But the barbarians have formed pan-ethnic conspiracies before. Kotys is on the march, as well as Bardulis. Even King Agis of the Paiaones is reported restless. Just a thought."

"All right. I'll use some of my Amphipolitan contacts to see if Pausanias is up to anything unusual."

"Good." Philippos smiles for the first time today, "Let's go see our ladies."

θ

The march east to Amphipolis was done in haste. Word had reached Philippos in Pella that the renewed siege by Timotheos was close to success. A sally by the citizens, which burned much of the siege works, recoiled to their disfavor when Timotheos counterattacked, killing many and seizing a portion of the outer walls. Only the obdurate resistance of the citizenry had prevented the Athenian's complete success.

Not able to follow the direct route, which would have exposed them to attack along the coast road, the Makedones marched inland, over the hills of the Bisaltai, skirting the swamps and lake in the Strymon valley, and down the east side of the river to enter Amphipolis from an unexpected direction. Their reception was tumultuous. Where the citizens dreaded that the next day or the day after would see the fall of Amphipolis and the terrible vengeance of the Athenians, the arrival of Philippos with over five hundred hardened, expert phalangists meant the end of Timotheos' threat for this campaign season.

Not only the citizens, but Philippos is elated at this success. Timotheos is foiled doubly, for in this Athenai is thwarted and the general's reputation is diminished. The Makedones demonstrated their ability to succor an ally. A Makedon garrison, small though it is, is introduced into Amphipolis. No, the word introduced is inadequate. Rather, they are welcomed by the jubilant citizenry. The Makedones possess a handhold on the city without bloodshed. The question the Amphipolitans have not begun to consider is when will the Makedones depart.

The men of the phalanxes themselves give pride to Philippos. They marched league after league in long swinging strides, burdened with packs and weapons, day after day. They marched with less complaining than singing. The task set them by Philippos and urged by their officers and file leaders was cheerfully met. And they arrived ready to fight. The memory of a long ago day teased at Philippos. A downhill run, a race, in which only he had arrived spear in hand. Now he had a body of men who could race and arrive with pike and shield in hand.

The *syntagmatarkh* of the first small phalanx is Alkimakhos. When a childhood friend grows to become an able companion and officer, there exists a familiarity that can either ease the understanding of common purpose or be a barrier due to reluctance to accept commands. Because Philippos was always the prince or because of a natural leadership long established, for Philippos and Alkimakhos there is no barrier.

So, as the two men stand together on the wall of Amphipolis, watching the Athenian encampment, they share their thoughts. "You intend to leave us in place even if Timotheos withdraws?" states Alkimakhos, his question largely rhetorical.

Philippos nods, "Help me come up with logical reasons for the Amphipolitans."

"There is Kotys."

"Yes, that is a possibility. He seems intent on throwing the Athenians off his coasts. No reason he might not make Amphipolis his next target."

"Is it true he's hired Kharidemos as general?"

"Yes," Philippos grins. "Why are we always surprised when an Athenian takes money to turn on his fellow citizens?"

"Not only an Athenian, any southern Hellene, with the possible exception of a Spartan."

"Sparte sent one of her kings to Aigyptos. Agesilaos is the more able general of the two kings, so the Spartiate sent him to earn money for the state," comments Philippos.

"Who's he fighting for, Pharoah Takhos or the pretender Nektanebo?"

"What does Sparte care as long as it returns them money?" Philippos shrugs. "Takhos did the hiring."

"Look, Philippos, they're striking their tents on the far slope," Alkimakhos points down valley.

Philippos stares intently at the distant figures, trying to discern the import if any of their actions. "Do we know what part of the camp site that is?"

"According to Rhesos, the Pieric Thrake the Amphipolitans use as their chief agent, that far slope is where Timotheos placed his supply depot."

"So is he shifting his base to attempt a new move?" says Philippos, thinking out loud.

"If you were going to take Amphipolis, where would you strike her?"

"Timotheos has tried the south, the east, and the west. He never tried north, thinking that it's too hard. I would come in from the west, with diversions against the other sectors. The attack would be before first light, and it would be silent." Philippos turns to look at Alkimakhos fully, "Truthfully, though, I don't expect to assault Amphipolis without first buying some help on the inside."

"Well Timotheos is no fool. Why is that not his plan?"

"Never underestimate the arrogance of an Athenian aristocrat," laughs Philippos. Then more seriously, "Who could the Athenians buy inside? The Amphipolitans know how bitter are the Athenians. Likely all men would be killed, all women and children sold into slavery, and a new colony of destitute Athenians would be planted here."

The two turn back to watch the Athenians and their mercenaries. "You hate Athenians, Philippos."

Surprised, Philippos answers, "Hate? No, who can hate a city that produces such playwrights and pottery? I simply value a wider range of ideals than do the Athenians. They do not understand how small a state they are." Then grinning again, "Still their olive oil is superb."

Knowing Perdikkas and Philippos well, Alkimakhos asks, "The king and you have sworn publicly many times that you will make the Makedones secure. Where are the limits of security?"

"The fates grant us a single lifetime. If you are a Puthagorean, you might believe in more. If there is rebirth, it must be at a spiritual level and not at the level of sentience or self-knowledge and purpose in this world."

Clearly Alkimakhos is puzzled by this answer, but Philippos continues, "What Perdikkas and I have sworn, what we asked you to swear and every companion and officer, is to a kingship that meets the approval of the gods and fulfills its role as leader and protector of our people. Security comes from strength. To be strong, the Makedones need full partnership with our highland kin and full respect from neighboring states, cities, and tribes. We need a people united in purpose, inured to adversity and hard working to assure prosperity. We need an army enlarged and more competent; officered by men who are skilled, brave, and eager to achieve our vision."

Philippos drops the hand raised to show his vision, "Can we accomplish that in one lifetime? I do not know, Alkimakhos. If we raise sons who share our vision, it will be achieved." He laughs ruefully, "What does all that mean?"

Alkimakhos is silent, offering only a questioning look.

"How many men do you command, Alkimakhos? You have 256 men and your supernumeraries. We call your *syntagma* a phalanx. We have four such units. Perdikkas authorizes me to raise four more. Well and good." Then fiercely, "Where we have eight *syntagmai*, I would have eight time eight. A phalanx of more than sixteen thousand men would please me, but it is not enough. We need two or more such phalanxes."

"Where would the manpower come from?" protests Alkimakhos. "How would they be rationed and paid?"

Philippos waves his hand, "Not yet, I know. Give us time, Alkimakhos. Give us the favor of the gods. You will see such an army. And it will be an army that will make the Makedones secure."

ι

Perdikkas summons Philippos to Pella. Despite the continued presence of Timotheos before Amphipolis, despite even the news that the Odrusai monarch of Thraikios, Kotys, has been murdered, Perdikkas needs Philippos at Pella. Leaving Alkimakhos in command at Amphipolis, Philippos hurries to his brother's side.

Entering the great chamber of the palace, Philippos joins the small group of men attending the king. Perdikkas stands and warmly hugs his brother, "Thank you for making such haste. Were you a raven you could not have come more swiftly."

"You said urgent, Perdikkas," answers Philippos.

"What news of Amphipolis, Philippos?" asks Antipatros.

"I believe Timotheos is abandoning the siege."

Korrhagos pounds on the table with the flat of his hand. Amuntas Plousias and Balakros join him in sounding the praise. "Good news, that," bellows Korrhagos.

Looking around, Philippos realizes that none of the king's foreign advisers are here—no Euphraios, Kallistratos or the others. "This is a council for Makedones alone?"

"Bardulis has left off his Adriatic campaign. He will invade the highlands again. We are going to meet him in battle. No more tribute, Philippos," says Perdikkas.

"Who do you have there now?"

"Arkouda and Derdas are in command. Most of the horse, the mercenaries, and two of your phalanxes," states Antipatros.

The king interrupts, "We are deciding what levies to invoke. Eordaia naturally. Who else can get there in time?"

"And we need to set defenses in the passes, in case of a reverse," puts in Amuntas Plousias.

"What is my role?" asks Philippos.

"Here, of course," answers Perdikkas. Then to the men around him, the king says, "Prince Philippos is my regent here in Pella. Should, as Plousias says, we suffer a reverse, he commands the kingdom on behalf of my son."

"You have no more than 3,500 men assembled so far, and most of those are mercenaries," comments Philippos. "Antipatros, what will Eordaia provide?"

"Of the better armed, something more than a thousand. Of *psiloi*, many more if we want them."

"Derdas has five hundred peltasts on the march already, led by his nephew," adds Perdikkas. "We bring another thousand from the northern cantons. You can see to the redistribution of forces in the rest of the lowlands so that the passes are covered."

"Lusias and Stesidamos wrote that the recruiting of the new phalanxes is going forward," says Philippos. "They have two bodies training, and a third formed, and the fourth partially filled. Do you want them with you as well?"

Perdikkas considers his brother's offer. The temptation to bring every possible man to bear is strong. Bardulis outnumbers them and will be leading an experienced army. Yet a king must think of the whole kingdom. If Perdikkas fails, his brother must have enough strength to retain control of the heartland. "Keep your men, you may need them. Each noble has his own entourage as well."

"Two of the new *syntagmai* were recruited out of Pella and the surrounding villages," says Antipatros. "That means the local levy is made up of the youngest and oldest men. You already have the prime men in training."

Nodding in acknowledgment, Philippos asks, "That puts your army at something over six thousand men, maybe seven thousand depending on the clans. Have you sent for Prince Parmenion of the Pelagonoi?"

Korrhagos butts in, "Says he's ill. Maybe he is. Maybe he's trying to play safe."

"He is sending three hundred horsemen under a cousin," says Perdikkas. "I trust in his good faith. There is no point, however, in looking to Aeropos of Lunkestis or Orontes of Orestis. Lunkestis will lie down for Bardulis again. Orontes is a coward."

More mildly, Antipatros says, "In truth, the Illuric tribesmen dislodged by the Adriatic campaign of Bardulis have fled south into Epeiros. Arubbas has his hands full, and has called on all his subchiefs to send men. Orontes has complied. He will always look to the Molossi king before the Makedones."

"So, the army you will have is either in place or en route already, save for some local levies," comments Philippos. "You expect Bardulis to muster the larger army. Anyone know of his losses on the Adriatic or what detachments he must leave behind?"

Perdikkas says, "He's dented. He can't bring his full force against us."

"So he'll be larger but not overwhelming. You intend to stand on the defensive?"

"Would you?" asks the king.

"I would want to know where he is, how fast he is traveling, whether he's split his army into separate columns. Then pick a ground that forces him to confront me where I choose. A narrow place where his numbers offer no advantage." Eyes alight, Philippos sweeps on, "Your proportion of horse to foot is higher. If you break his formation, your horse can wreak havoc on him. So pick a spot and put all your muscle to it."

"Thus speaks the strategy of Thebai," says Balakros.

Philippos glances at his brother's friend, uncertain whether the man spoke sarcastically or in support.

Balakros smiles, "A good plan, Prince." He gestures to himself, "Your brother appointed me to command the mercenaries. That's where our muscle is."

Philippos wishes he knew Balakros better. Does he have the steel of a Philippos Arkouda or an Antipatros? Does he have the timing of a Periandros or Parrhasios? "Then you will know when and where to push hard."

Stoutly Balakros says, "We will make the crows happy." The phrase brings to mind the birds and beasts that feed on the dead.

* * *

Later, in Queen Telesilla's weaving room with its three looms, Perdikkas spends a quiet hour with his wife and son. Laughing at the boy as he chases yarn balls on his chubby legs, Perdikkas tells Telesilla, "Philippos asked permission to name his son Perdikkas, if Phila gives birth to a boy."

"What did you say?"

"That he ought to use the name of Alexandros, if he wants a brother's name, or Aridaios, after our grandfather. I think I want to keep Perdikkas as a name for our next son."

"So we are to have another son?" says Telesilla with false archness.

Perdikkas reaches to her, "If we can put this boy down for a nap, we can start that next son now."

Giggling, Telesilla slaps his hand away, "Not before baby Amuntas."

"Shall I call the nurse? I will not be here tonight."

Anxiously, Telesilla looks at her man, "You will be in my prayers, Perdikkas."

"I won't pretend that this will be easy. But we are much stronger now. We will prevail, with the blessings of Herakles and Zeus." Briefly Perdikkas is in earnest, then smiles, "I want that nurse, Telesilla. Send for her, so I can say goodbye to you in a way we both like."

Quickly his wife goes to the door to fetch little Amuntas' nurse.

* * *

At the townhouse Philippos maintains, there is much laughter and mirth. Phila's younger brothers are visiting Pella, and their friends fill the rooms with noise. Though Philippos would rather have his wife to himself, he is gracious to the guests. Knowing that he is being patient, Phila grabs his hand and smiles up to him, "I'm glad you are home, even if the cause is Bardulis."

He leans down and pats her huge belly, "You two are looking good."

"This condition—pregnancy—is not gladsome. I can no longer ride a horse, garden, or do most activities. I must endure boring lectures from any woman who is or has been or hopes to be a mother. At least I'm past the nausea stage."

"You feel well, then?"

Before Phila can answer, her brother lurches into the room followed by several companions. "Hoa, Philippos, back from the borderlands. Does not my sister seem the size of a mare?"

"Derdas, how early do you start drinking?" asks Phila.

"I never seem to know whether I am starting early or never stopped from the day before," Young Derdas replies easily. "You own a reputation as a drinker, Prince Philippos."

"When it's time to feast, I can drink with the best of them," says Philippos politely.

"T-t-then we o-ought to have a feast," stammers the younger brother, Makhatas. Their companions laugh.

"When King Perdikkas returns, victorious over the Dardanoi, we will enjoy such a feast as all Pella will talk about for years," answers Philippos.

"King Perdikkas and our father, King Derdas," says Young Derdas.

"You are right, for the Makedones and Elimiotoi prosper together." Philippos smiles, "Your father might well use you seven in his band."

"F-f-father prefers we p-protect his paternity by staying in P-pella," says Little Makhatas.

"Is that what you prefer?" interjects Phila.

Annoyed, Derdas demands, "Do you slight our willingness to take risks?"

Innocently Phila responds, "Oh, no, haven't you already wagered when my baby will be born, what its sex will be, and whether its hair will be dark or light? I'm sure you've risked your silver on the outcome of the battle."

"We are recruiting men for the phalanx," says Philippos. "Would any of you be willing to join?"

"Certainly not," responds Derdas haughtily, "we are nobles and would ride to war."

Yet among the Elimiote companions, one youth stirs and timidly asks, "Are you seeking officers?"

Interested in the young man's response, Philippos says, "Whether an officer or a man in the ranks, you learn to drill with a pike."

Looking cautiously first at Derdas, and seeing neither dissuasion or encouragement, the fellow says to the prince, "Who would train us?"

"If you join, you train under me."

With increasing confidence, the youth says, "Then I would apply, sir."

"And why? Has Derdas not said you are horsemen."

Derdas and the others have stepped away from this companion, or perhaps he has stepped forward to Philippos. "You may not have meant to impugn our honor, but I felt it nonetheless. King Derdas sends his sons to Pella for safekeeping, but my father gave no such order to me. Since I am here, though, and not in Eordaia, then it is under your command that I would prove my worth."

"Your name?" inquires Philippos softly.

"Theodoros, son of Pausanias Daskolos," the youth smiles. "My father's family is the Makheridai; my mother is from a noble family of Tumphaia."

"Then you are from western Elimiotis," replies Philippos.

"Where sheep herding is the only livelihood," comments Young Derdas with a certain acidity.

"I'll make a bet with you, Derdas," says Philippos decisively, "for two gold stater that your friend Theodoros learns the pike drill to the standard set by the trainer Lusias faster than you or anyone of your other companions here."

The youths look at one another as if guessing which one will be set to match Theodoros since they all know Derdas will accept the gamble. Derdas smiles and grabs the largest boy by the arm. Whispering in his ear. The big fellow is reluctant, but Derdas is obviously insisting. Grudgingly the big kid nods, and Derdas announces, "Nikias, here, will accept the challenge on my behalf. When do they start and how long do we give them?"

"Why they can start today if they're both willing. We'll give them ten days, until the festival of Hephaistos."

"I'm willing," states Theodoros.

"All right," says Nikias.

Derdas snickers and claps Nikias on the back, "Shall we walk down to the fields?"

"Shortly. First though, Theodoros I want you to pack your belongings. You will be moving into the field house we use as a barracks for the Black Bull *syntagma*. Nikias, you are welcome to do the same."

All the boys head for the bedrooms, whooping with anticipation. Phila reaches out to Philippos again, "You may lose your gold. Nikias is a noted athlete while Theodoros is best known for his verses."

Philippos grins, "For ten days neither boy will drink. Even your brothers will be occupied by preparing for the outcome. Nikias is not pleased while Theodoros is determined. The drill is not too demanding. Theodoros will ache, but ten days is long enough to get him past the rough spots. I'm guessing I'll gain two officers out of this gamble."

"A lot to spend for two officers."

"Perhaps, depends on their quality. Over a lifetime, it may be a good price." Then Philippos shakes his head, "I was hoping that your brother would accept the challenge himself."

"You should have challenged Makhatas. He's worth more than Derdas, though he doesn't know it."

"You don't like your brother much, Phila."

She's silent for a moment, thinking about Derdas. Then, "Once upon a time I doted on him. He was a good baby. Somehow he became a fool— a conniver and a coward. Yet Makhatas believes him a hero." She looks at her husband, "Some day you should wager Derdas for Elimiotis. Believe me, he would gamble his patrimony away."

"Do you regret that your gender prevents you from being King of Elimiotis?"

"If you were to become king of my country, I would be its queen," she replies serenely.

К

Perdikkas has joined his army in Eordaia and Philippos is regent in Pella by the time the feast of Hephaistos arrives. Though one of the twelve high gods, Hephaistos is not prominent among the Makedones, except for the smiths and miners. Still his temple is adorned and its priests lead a dawn procession which culminates in an impressive sacrifice of twin white goats and a great brown bull. Standing in for his brother, Philippos attends the festivities.

From the ceremonies and feast, he walks the breadth of Pella with many others to be at the mid-morning contest between Theodoros and Nikias. The marching field is filled with spectators, drawn from the men of the several phalanxes as well as the townspeople and courtiers. Though no one else's wager matches the size of Philippos', the crowd engages in lively betting. A trio will judge the event: Lusias, who is the judge selected by Philippos; Lagos, chosen by Young Derdas, who is aware of the long-standing dislike between the prince and the noble; a mercenary officer, one Liontaros Polemos, chosen by Theodoros and Nikias.

The two contestants stand side by side. Both appear limber and ready. The betting favors Nikias as his physique is the hardier.

With them are fourteen other members of their *syntagma*, who will participate in the exercise. Together, they form two ranks. At a command from Stesidamos, the sixteen come to attention. Pikes are upright, small shields slung from their shoulders, all fully accoutered as Makedon phalangists. What follows is a series of commands in which the shields come down from shoulders and the pike is advanced from shoulders to successive positions until parallel with the ground and thrust forward. Then up again, and thrust overhand. Then down again, and the ranks advance from loose order to close order to locked shields, then back. For half an hour the men step through their evolutions. Finally, Stesidamos calls them back to attention with the butt end of their pikes grounded.

Their fellows from the phalanxes begin cheering, and though the non-phalangists of the crowd do not appreciate the nuances, they are equally impressed with the precision displayed not only by Theodoros and Nikias, but by all sixteen men.

Philippos is grinning, delighted with the performance. Regardless of what the three judges decide, the skillful demonstration will bring in more recruits.

Standing in a knot, the three judges are talking heatedly. Lusias, the loudest, can be heard to swear. The crowd murmurs and calls out advice as it awaits the decision. At length, Liontaros steps forward and calls for silence. The crowd complies. Calling out in a high carrying voice, to reach as many in the crowd as possible, Liontaros announces, "The judges are unable to distinguish any significant difference in the performances of Theodoros and Nikias. Both fully acquitted themselves. They are identically capable in their drill." Then adding an opinion, Liontaros declares, "May I say that the other fourteen men displayed equal skill. Never have I seen a better showing."

Young Derdas steps rapidly out from his supporters, "Where does that leave the wager? Did not Philippos bet that Theodoros would outperform Nikias? He has not, so I win the bet."

Derdas' supporters applaud, while many others in the crowd groan or hiss. Philippos steps forward, arms raised and waving down the crowd's noise, "Derdas, son of Derdas, speaks correctly. The gold staters are his. Yet I tell you that I too have won, for these are men I will lead into battle. Their skill and confidence will win in battle as well as on this marching field." The crowd applauds, but Philippos waves for silence again, "I have another gold stater here for refreshments for any of those among you who will spend the next half-hour going through the same passage of arms you have just seen."

A roar of approval from the crowd, then hundreds upon hundreds form ranks. A few have pikes, some have practice poles, and others shoulder nothing but step into line. With Lusias, Stesidamos, Liontaros, and other experienced officers leading, the whole march through the passage of arms.

Beside Philippos, Pikoros says, "Your cook has sent a runner. The food and drink are ready on trestles beside the horse stalls."

"Then march them all over there after they ground their pikes. See how many new men you and the others can recruit." Looking at the many marching men, Philippos judges, "Have the cook send for another steer and whatever else he thinks necessary. I think there are a hundred and fifty more than we planned."

"Don't think to see Derdas there. He took the gold and left the field with a half-dozen of his fellows."

Philippos shrugs, "Then we don't need him. He left many of his people behind."

"Isn't two gold staters a lot for what you achieve here?"

Philippos smiles gently, "It's nothing. We will get another full *syntagma* or more today. As for the gold, I will simply bet Derdas again on something else and win back the gold. He cannot stop betting."

λ

Perdikkas told Philippos to expect him to be away from Pella for an entire season, or even a month longer. Much depends on how severely the king is able to defeat the Dardanoi, and what follow-up needs to occur after the climactic battle. Assuming there is a climactic battle. Conceivably both parties could maneuver at length, marauding and probing, but not find the advantage needed to come to grips. Dispatches received from the Perdikkas indicate that Bardulis is coming on fast and has gathered a larger army than expected. Looks like the Dardanoi king intends to confront the Makedones.

Acting as his own general leaves Perdikkas little time to deal with the more mundane concerns of the kingdom. Plus many of the ablest men and notables accompany Perdikkas, each with his own command. Thus much devolves on the regent, Philippos.

Rather than use the great hall, Philippos chooses to deal with the business of the city and wider kingdom from a suite of rooms in a house situated close to the *agora*, the main marketplace. Using the palace smacks of acting the king, and Philippos wants no suggestion that he seeks to usurp his brother's prerogatives. There is another advantage to working from his own offices, he can use his people rather than relying on his brother's staff of officials and servants.

Pikoros continues to act as his ombudsman for the common people. How they know to approach Pikoros is a bit of a mystery, yet they do.

Though Philippos has stewards on his various estates, now that he's taken on the work of regent, he appoints one man to administer the workings of his personal holdings. Ephrastos was steward for Philippos' brother, Alexandros. During the ascendancy of Ptolemaios, Ephrastos traveled the Hellenic cities of the south. Home again and not employed in a suitable capacity, he eagerly joins Philippos' household.

Philippos must deal with the many officers of his growing number of *syntagmai*, and with the governors he appointed for his two cantons of Anthemos and Amphaxitis, as well as with the councils of the various cities and towns in those cantons. For the military, he appoints a pair of lieutenants: a kinsmen of Lagos, named Hippasos, and Philippos' friend, Antigonos. Hippasos, while kin to Lagos, is respected among the older citizen-soldiers and officers. He seems oblivious to the mutual aversion between Lagos and Philippos, and is hard working. Who knows, his appointment may ease some bitterness with Lagos. Antigonos is a firebrand, eager as always to be of value, and hugely popular among the younger men.

The governors of Anthemos and Amphaxitis are friends of the king, suggested by him from a list of candidates and accepted by Philippos. Both are older men, not incompatible with Philippos but of no special sympathy. To work directly with them, Philippos chooses a citizen of Pella, a former councilman, named Demokedes. Whenever Philippos had occasion in the past to attend a city council meeting, admittedly rarely, it was Demokedes —fat, humorous, shrewd, honest—who attracted Philippos. Now the genial man can keep an eye on the eastern cantons and cities.

Today is typical. First, a dispute over encroachment on meadow lands in Anthemos must be decided. The larger problem with the dispute is that it involves a Bottikene landowner from the neighboring country. The Bottiaoi are a Thrake people, or possibly some earlier blood than Thraikiote. Though the dispute itself is a simple, common boundary argument, its international context requires it to be referred to the king or his governor. Second, a money-lender of Pella is accused of knowingly using false weights when repaid. The weights are undoubtedly off, yet by a slim margin. They seem to accord with the measure used in certain Paiaone cities. To complicate the matter, while the weights favor the moneylender, he is known for generously rounding in his debtors' favor. The individual bringing the accusation is a vitriolic sea captain, who's reputedly a sharp dealer himself. Third, Stesidamos will lead a newly trained *syntagma* to the northwestern city of Edessa, near the pass into Eordaia. They are posted there to stiffen the local militia. If Perdikkas needs to call on them as reinforcements, they will be closer to hand. Before they depart, Philippos will officiate at the sacrifices and purification ceremony. Other matters will present themselves as the day progresses.

While Philippos listens to Demokedes present the Anthemite case in the boundary dispute, he watches his nephew Amuntas play in one corner of the crowded room. The toddler is in the care of two young boys from noble families and a nursemaid. Between the three of them, they keep the little prince amused. When Philippos suggested to Telesilla that her son spend an occasional day at his offices, the young mother was skeptical. Yet the arrangement is proving admirable, giving Telesilla some time free of motherly responsibility and, equally, giving even so young a child some time away from women's concerns.

The death of his infant daughter after struggling for life for three days underlay the suggestion made by Philippos. Phila handles her grief in private. Philippos displays no grief, but holds within himself a melancholy that little Amuntas assuages.

"...a claim made based upon events occurring after the Argeadai destruction of the city of Amydon, when the Bottiaoi fled these lands where Pella and its neighboring towns now stand." Demokedes is concluding his speech. "Fled to the hills and mountains we now call Bottikis, supplanting earlier inhabitants or absorbing them into their own *ethnos*. Fled not to the river valley of the Anthemos, which was already controlled by the Hellenes. Now if Treres wants to claim Hellenic descent, perhaps some great-great-grandmother impregnated by a wandering demi-god, so common to the Hellenes of that distant day, we might feel empathy for the plight of his sheep when they, in turn, wander into our client, Kratippos', river meadows."

As ever, Demokedes manages to insert a comedic reference in his peroration. While several men in the crowded room applaud with laughter, and as many more, like Philippos, find themselves smiling, the opposing party ignores the jibe and prepares in all seriousness to respond.

Interrupting the start of the opposition's speech, a dusty dispatch rider steps into the room. Thinking this may be some command of the king's, Philippos waves him over. Seeing everyone waiting, Philippos calls out, "Continue, continue. My scribe is taking notes."

The Bottikene voice begins to declaim loudly, as the rider comes to Philippos' side. The regent hands his own mug of watered wine to the rider. After two quick gulps and a swipe with the back of a grimy hand to dry lips, the rider whispers, "I bring word of the Odrusai kingdom. General Alkimakhos sends that the court there is following the will of the dead King Kotys after all. The kingdom is to be divided among three of his sons. Berisades rules between the rivers Strymon and Nestos. Amadokos has from the Nestos to the Hebros. East of the Hebros to the Bosporos rules Kersebleptes. Further, both Berisades and Amadokos are elderly, and Berisades in particular is not well. He has three vigorous sons, Ketriporis, Monounos, and Shostokes. Amadokos has two sons who would contend at his death, Teres and Amadokos the Younger. Only Kersebleptes, child of a later wife of Kotys, is known for his vitality and he's likely to rule his portion of the kingdom at length."

An echo of Alkimakhos and his passion for the intrigue of ruling families reaches Philippos in the rider's words. Yet Alkimakhos is right to make this known quickly, for the powerful Thrake kingdom of the Odrusai is completely sundered. When word reached them earlier of Kotys' murder by two Hellenes from the coastal city of Ainos, who would rule in his stead was unclear. For months the rival princes argued their rights, and allowed their retainers to fight. Not one of the three is strong enough to hold the whole of the kingdom.

From power to impotence on the death of one man, this is news indeed. This news must reach Perdikkas as quickly as riders can find him. If any power will take advantage of these events, it will be Athenai. Persia is not a concern, for many of his western satraps are in revolt against the Great King. Though Athenai is having difficulty with some of her erstwhile allies, this outcome in Thraikios should allow her to conclude its war of several years with the Odrusai. Each brother king will now seek his own treaty with Athenai.

It is Berisades who most concerns the Makedones. Between the lands ruled by Berisades and the Makedones is the city of Amphipolis and various small peoples, like the Bottiaoi. Of course, the Khalkidike confederacy will be as concerned as the Makedones. Like Athenai and the Makedones, they will want to seize the advantage in this disintegration of a powerful kingdom.

What ambitions do these sons of Kotys harbor? Each has waited long to reach a throne. None can be happy that the throne held by their father is so diminished. The parallel between these events and the division of the Makedones kingdom on the death of Alexandros the First is not lost on Philippos. Then Alexandros wanted his able younger son, Perdikkas, to inherit, but would not bypass the older Philippos and Alketas. In Thraikios, it is the younger Kersebleptes who must inherit, but not without a patrimony for Berisades and Amadokos.

Another small city existing in the lands between Makedonis and Berisades' new kingdom is Kalindroia. Its effective ruler is Pausanias the Exile. Kalindroia is in the Mygdonis lands, where marshy Lakes Bolbe and Koronia separate the Bottikis highlands from Bisaltiones territory. The city lies near the main road that runs from Amphaxitis to Amphipolis. Pausanias has acted as an ally of the small Thrake states and independent cities of the region. He too will pursue his advantages with King Berisades.

These thoughts of Philippos follow rapidly on hearing the rider's message. "You will pass your message to a man of mine so that we may send it on to King Perdikkas, then you may rest a day and return to General Alkimakhos." Philippos catches the eye of Pikoros, who quickly joins them. "Follow Pikoros now." Turning to his companion, Philippos adds, "Have two riders readied, the first to go immediately on memorizing this man's message. The second will follow after this matter of the Bottikene's claims are settled today. He will carry my thoughts on this matter to Perdikkas, as well as our recommendation regarding the Bottikene. See that this man is made comfortable, and receives a reward for his efficiency."

With that done, Philippos turns back to the boundary dispute. He has long since grasped the essentials of this case, so while he makes a show of interest, his mind is already playing with the ramifications of a shattered Ordusai kingdom.

μ

That same day, far to the west, in the highland basin that comprises the chiefdom of Lunkestis, the armies of King Perdikkas and King Bardulis find each other. Rather than concentrate the Illuroi horsemen in an attempt to sweep aside Perdikkas' scouts, Bardulis chose to spread his cavalry widely, masking the true march of his army. Then, instead of the traditional march into the Lunkestis heartland, Bardulis moved east into Pelagonis. Reaching the foothills of the Barnous mountains, that divide Pelagonis from the Almope canton of Makedonis, Bardulis turned west, re-entering Lunkestis along its southeastern border with Eordaia. Thus at dawn of this day, Perdikkas is surprised to find the Dardanoi army so close, with his army dispersed searching toward the northwest for Bardulis.

Reacting quickly, Perdikkas sends in swarms of horsemen and light foot to harry the the Dardanid advance. The troops with Perdikkas back down the wide valley slowly, while messengers speed to find and recall the dispersed columns. By nightfall of that first day of contact, Perdikkas is again feeling confident. What at daybreak had seemed an avalanche of barbarians is now slowed. His own people arrive all through the night, until close on six thousand men are again assembled.

Tomorrow comes the great battle. No, really it will be today—for it is nearly time to make the daily sacrifice to Zeus and the ancestors of the Makedones, the Argeadai clan and the Temenidai family. Though a daily ritual, this ceremony is the heartbeat of the priestship held by Perdikkas. This sacred trust given him by the Makedon citizens, assembled in their ranks, is both that of king and chief priest.

Slapping a dozing Parrhasios on the arm, Perdikkas says, "Time for me to honor Zeus. Gather our generals. We will sacrifice for battle immediately. Then a quick council of war. Balakros stuck his head in earlier to say the men are bedded down. By now, they've had an hour or two of sleep. Those who choose to sleep the night before a battle." Perdikkas laughs. The weary Parrhasios heard at least the command to assemble the generals. Picking up his helmet, yawning, Parrhasios stumbles from the tent to carry out his errand.

A tired army. Still the strategy is sound, thinks Perdikkas. We face a foe who outnumbers us. We screen the length of his line, but concentrate on his left. We must break his left quickly, for we haven't the strength to hold the whole of him. Once his line opens, we pour our horsemen through. Well, he has fooled me and given me a scare, but he scattered his horse across Lunkestis to do so. We will dominate in horsemen. Perdikkas nods decisively. The plan will work.

The men have done well today—yesterday, whatever—thinks Perdikkas. No panic at the surprise. Steadiness in the ranks. The light foot, *psiloi* and peltasts, performed well, especially the men of Eordaia. For once Lagos was staunch. He is a good man in battle, all his strangeness and hesitancy gone. Eordaic battlecry on his lips, he and his levy ambushed the advancing Dardanoi again and again. And our losses were not heavy for a day of sporadic fighting.

Perdikkas smiles, today will be a glorious victory. Praise the gods.

$$* \quad * \quad *$$

Sun's up, though still early. Hours gone by in marshaling the line of men. Across less than a *stade* of rolling meadow stands the army of the Dardanoi. Better armed than the Makedones have seen before. More Dardanoi formed into hoplite phalanxes, as if they would be Hellenes. On the wings of their phalanx line are the light foot. Beyond are more ranks. The same here among the Makedones—mercenaries and the phalanxes trained by Philippos creating the center, then the local hoplite warriors as a phalanx, and to either side the peltasts. Except behind the Makedon right are the additional *syntagmai*. And behind and to one side are squadrons of horsemen.

King Perdikkas turns to Balakros, "Advance your line slowly. Keep your alignment. When you come to grips, push so they are engaged. You need to secure them for twenty minutes to a half-hour. By then Antipatros' wing should be grinding up their left. Arkouda and I will bring in the horsemen. You need not worry about your flank, Lagos will keep it safe with his peltasts. Okay, off you go."

Nervously licking his lips, Balakros nods his understanding, then strides to his waiting men. The shrill pipes give signal, and the line lurches into motion.

Perdikkas mounts and trots to the waiting horsemen. His squadron, the *agema,* is made up of the best young men of the realm. Well-seasoned but not past thirty years in age, like the king himself. They cheer as he reaches them, their affection genuine. He is one of them.

Across the sward stands a second squadron, aligned on the *agema*. Their commander is Philippos Arkouda. Most of his men are his clansmen. A wider range of ages in their ranks—fathers and sons, brothers, cousins, sons-in-law. Two of Arkouda's sons are not with their father. The eldest, Demetrios, commands a *syntagma*. Antigonos, Arkouda's young giant, serves the regent. Even without his two boys, Arkouda's kinsmen here number 140. No squadron has a better reputation in the entire army. Wherever Arkouda leads them, they go.

Gently, Perdikkas waves them all forward. At a slow walk, the horses follow the footmen. Behind the two lead squadrons follow the other squadrons.

Ahead are the Dardanoi. Their line is motionless, except for the unit banners that wave languidly in the morning breeze. Perdikkas tries to pick out the clot of men that would surround Bardulis. He cannot, too far away, already too much dust.

After an eternity of walking, though in fact quicker than Perdikkas expected, the Makedon army is within range of the Dardanoi. Already slingers on the flanks throw stones to down the unwary. And the opposing peltasts are flinging javelins at each other, trying to uncover a flank of the heavily armored foot. Just out of reach of each others spears, the two lines dress ranks, then with a cry on both sides, they hurtle forward.

The crash is enormous, echoing out beyond the contending armies. Screams mark the unlucky. Those down are stepped on as their fellow spearmen pace forward. Yelling insults or praying at the top of their lungs or occasionally laughing deliriously, the men smash shield against shield, jabbing, poking, thrusting with their spears, seeking to wound, to kill, to find some advantage, to force the enemy to flee.

Those in the rear ranks press blindly forward, pushing on the backs of their mates, so that the front rank must force the enemy to give or be crushed themselves. How desperately the front ranks struggle.

The *syntagmai* created by Philippos are doing well. Their long pikes outreach the Dardanid spears. The Makedones are doing what they intend, boring into the left side of the Dardanid line.

Arkouda's son, Demetrios, and his fellow *syntagmatarkhs* lead by example, for they hold the most dangerous position in the line, the extreme right front of their rank.

Judiciously, Antipatros readies the second half-files of eight into the assault. They must enter the fray at the point where the first eight ranks are ebbing in strength but before they truly falter.

That time comes as, on the Illuric side, the left is reinforced. Yelling encouragement and striding forward with pike in hand himself, Antipatros leads the second half-files into battle to bolster the thinning numbers of the first half-files.

Standing high in the saddle behind the foot fight, Perdikkas tries to judge the momentum and drift of the combat. Always when phalanx fight they drift to the right. The shield arm, the left, is their defense. The right thrusts the spear. As opponents strike at each other, they close to the right, bringing their shields up, and taking a half-step. Whole lines can wheel and end up fighting in the opposite direction from where they started if a fight goes on long enough. Not able to make out what is happening, Perdikkas waves one of his young horsemen forward. "Ride to the west end of the line. Bring me word of what's happening. Be quick." The rider spurs away.

Unexpectedly, from the woods to the east, pour several squadrons of Dardanid horsemen, interspersed with Illuric peltasts and *psiloi.* The Makedon light foot on that flank begin to give way. Seeing this, Arkouda waves the three squadrons to his rear over to reinforce their flank footmen.

Arkouda sends a rider to inform Perdikkas. Perdikkas grins at the news. If that's the worst old Bardulis can do, then we will prevail, thinks the king.

Much rests on how well Antipatros is doing. No one, save Arkouda, is more tenacious in a fight. The Dardanid left cannot stand up to this punishment much longer. How long has passed since the fight began, wonders Perdikkas. No sure way of knowing, but longer than he'd hoped.

Out of the dusty haze, the youth sent west earlier rides up to Perdikkas, "Lord Lagos is pressing back the Illuric light foot on their right. Our center is strained; they have pushed into us and are pressing us back. I found an officer who thinks they will hold another quarter hour. Oh, and Balakros is dead."

Time is up, thinks Perdikkas, sending the boy back to the squadron. Do I send my last *syntagma* of foot to the center or do I push it forward here to ensure the collapse of their left? Not wanting to see the plan fail, knowing that he has only one plan for success, Perdikkas orders the final *syntagma* forward, much to the surprise of Antipatros, who considered those men his reserve.

Suddenly the Dardanoi left recoils. There is a gap. Elation and relief wash through Perdikkas. At his command, and with a cheer, the *agema* and Arkouda's squadron charge for the gap. Dardanoi retreat, like a gate opening. The king and his lead squadrons are through. Before the following squadrons can reach the gap, the gate swings shut.

Now Perdikkas can see Bardulis. Up the slight slope, the grim warrior is urging forward rank after rank of spearmen. This is a trap, screams Perdikkas' mind. Still his arm does not cease thrusting his spear into Illuroi fighters. Around him, his horsemen fight individually. The charge is exhausted and the horsemen mill. Too few entered the gap. Like a pack of dogs overwhelming a great bear, the Dardanoi bring Arkouda down.

Perdikkas urges his men back. They must break free and reach the security of their lines. Slapping the rump of a neighboring horse, Perdikkas sends his men crashing back through the lines they've just entered. With a few others to guard this retreat, the king swings round to face the Dardanoi onslaught. The Dardanoi cheer, recognizing their quarry. For a moment, their eagerness to reach the Makedon king impedes their attack. Then they are on Perdikkas and his half-dozen companions. So many spears slice into the king's horse that the animal slides down in its own blood. The king's death follows the horse's.

* * *

With the center gone and their king dead, the Makedones flee. The Dardanoi and their allies hunt. Those groups of Makedones who remain steady, like the men under Antipatros, are rocks that the sea of Illuroi crashes against, then washes around. With defeat occurring by mid-morning, the Illuroi have a long day to enjoy slaughtering Makedones.

By nightfall of that terrible day, Antipatros has emerged as the hero of the army. Most of the two thousand survivors cling to his steadiness. Retreating stubbornly, they block the road that leads over the pass into the lowlands. Nor has Antipatros forgotten the *syntagma* of Stesidamos, waiting in Edessa. Orders are sent to bring it forward to the pass, to meet the retreating army.

As importantly, Antipatros has the presence of mind to dispatch multiple riders to Prince Philippos in Pella. At least one rider must get through as soon as possible.

* * *

And by nightfall, at the site of the battle and for many *stade* south, lay the bodies of more than four thousand Makedones and Elimiotes. Those who at morning led the kingdom by night are thinned to a few—Perdikkas, Korrhagos, Balakros, Parrhasios, Arkouda, and many others are now carrion.

CHAPTER THIRTEEN

Rivals

359 B.C.

α

Telesilla will not bring the boy to the assembly-in-arms," says Eurudike. Her words are empty of intonation. They could be stones dropping onto sand. Grief makes grey this day, and color exists only when memory insists on thrusting the once-live Perdikkas to mind. While feeling great pain, she functions, which is more than Telesilla can seem to manage.

"The boy must come," answers Philippos softly yet firmly. "Until he is acclaimed, all must wait." He pauses, seeking a reaction, "You must bring Amuntas if his mother will not."

"She says she does not want her son to be king. King's die too young."

"She is beyond reason, mother. What she wants does not matter. The army declares him king. They are as eaten with grief as she, and no one will do for them but the son of Perdikkas."

"You must talk to her then." Eurudike touches his arm, "Philippos, her fears are not groundless. The boy is four years old. You will rule, not him."

With a touch of bitterness, he asks, "Does she think I am Aeropos and her son Orestes?"

Eurudike gestures in despair. She wants to say something consoling, something encouraging, but her favorite is dead and before her stands the son she loves least. She is as certain that he will be king as she is certain that life bears pain. Twenty-three years old and he possesses more of the Temenidai traits than anyone—all ambition and capability, touched with the favor of the gods. What hope is there for little Amuntas? Amuntas the Fourth he will be, but for how long?

Seeing her thoughts in her gesture, Philippos says fiercely, "Amuntas, son of Perdikkas, need not fear me. I pledge to you, mother, that I will assure his survival."

Who can guarantee what is in the hands of the gods? thinks Eurudike. "Go to Telesilla. Take Phila with you so Telesilla sees your gentle side.

Persuade her that her son is king whatever she wills, and that you will answer before men and gods for his well-being."

"You know that Amuntas is safer with me than with any of the pretenders. Arkhelaos, Pausanias, Argaios—he would not see age five if any one of them becomes king, nor would I see my next birth date." Philippos is in earnest, for the kingdom seems to stand on sand, not rock.

"See that they do not, son," says Eurudike dryly.

His laugh is bitter elation, "They will never get another chance."

β

First there is Bardulis of the Dardanoi. The victorious Illuroi must be met and forestalled. Whatever they want will be promised. The defeat of Perdikkas leaves four thousand dead warriors of the Makedones and Elimiotoi. Even with every Makedon city, town, and village armed, they are not the trained force that can face the royal army of the Dardanoi confederacy. Antipatros holds what remains of the field army at Edessa, blocking the direct route to the lowlands. Bardulis need only lurch forward with his army and the lowlands will be overrun.

Second are the Paiaones. King Agis takes advantage of our disarray and leads his raiders down the Axios valley. They, too, must be bribed to turn away.

Third are the pretenders. Pausanias has the support of King Berisades of the western Thraikiote Odrusai. Thank Hades that King Kotys is dead or Pausanias might be a true threat. The new Thrake kinglets are more concerned with each other than about the Makedones. Still Berisades will launch Pausanias at us, if for no other reason than to keep us off-balance while he deals with his brothers Amadokos and Kersebleptes.

My older half-brothers finally reveal themselves. Arkhelaos parades the support of Olunthos and the Khalkidike League. That will gain him nothing in the eyes of the notables, but his peasant adherents are all for leveling the notables.

Then there is ancient Argaios. Athenai makes its play through him. If all reports are correct, they assembled a fleet and are sending three thousand hoplites to support Argaios in his candidacy for the throne. His is the most serious threat of the three pretenders.

With the acclamation of the assembly done, Amuntas is king. With the sad funeral procession for Perdikkas over, culminating in his burial and dedication, Philippos can act against their foes. Returned to Pella from Aigai, Philippos has called a meeting of the chief companions. He considers what he will say. He paces. Are there any that will not support him and King Amuntas? They all know the extent of the crisis. He wishes Antipatros were here, and others in the army at Edessa. Even Lagos. Only the old men and men from his garrison are here in Pella. Well, so be it, he will make them all believers.

With that thought, he smiles. He calms. He prays to his father and all his father's fathers back to omnipotent Zeus: *Guide me, father and all you who are my forefathers. Help me to safeguard the Makedones. Protect King Amuntas. Let me know what is right to do.*

* * *

Iolaos looks grey. He is dying, it's written on his face. Yet he is here to support the Temenidai. Old Agerrhos has come as well. Another ancient. Antiokhos is here, near enough in age to Iolaos. His cousin, Agathokles, as well, only a bit younger. Other grey beards are here.

Then there are the youngsters, like Antigonos and Polemaios, mourning their dead father. Hegesias, on leave with his wounds, sits beside the Arkouda brothers. Young Derdas of Elimiotis, bored and little interested but here to represent his father. Several others who are suddenly clan heads after the harvest made by the Illuroi, like Hipponikos and Lakudes.

And there are men who owe their presence here to Philippos. Hippasos, the cousin of Lagos, is certainly acceptable to the old men. Even the city politician, Demokedes, must seem reasonable. Inwardly, though, the old men must be wondering about the Kretan, Andromitos of Lato, the steward, Ephrastos, and the former slave, Pikoros.

To still these concerns Philippos motions for silence, "I prayed to Zeus, to Herakles, to my father, Amuntas the Wise. The promise for ourselves and our people, embodied in my brother Perdikkas, will not be lost with his death and the deaths of our many kinsmen, friends, and companions. As regent for my nephew, King Amuntas *Neos*, it is my duty to him, to you, and to all Makedones, to lead us through this crisis where we are assailed from all sides. In carrying out my duty, I will call on all the resources available to me, whether traditional clan heads, councils of cities and towns, or friends from all walks of life, who in their love for us and our people will work and fight to free us from our foes."

"Today we seem weak. Our enemies gloat. They gather like ravens and wild dogs. They do not know our true strength. You all will help me and our people find our true strength."

"First we must lull them. We will spread honey on warm bread and let them eat; we will offer strong fine wine and let them drink." Philippos looks searchingly into the eyes of the men about him, and adds softly, "Then we will kill them."

Evenly, full voiced, Philippos continues, "Our honey and wine will be silver and gold. Antiokhos, Hipponikos—I ask you to take responsibility for King Agis and the Paiaones. Find their price, load them with valuables, and send them home."

"Lakudes, through your maternal grandmother you have connections to the royal Odrusai. Learn what you can about King Berisades' needs. Ephrastos and his agents will assist you. Find the key that will cause Berisades to disavow Pausanias the Exile."

"Agathokles and Hippasos, your responsibility will be Olunthos and the Khalkidike. Divide them from my half-brother, Arkhelaos. Demokedes should be able to help you." Philippos smiles at the politician, "Demokedes, you introduced the widow Polugnota to Perdikkas. Her family has great influence in Olunthos. I understand that she is beholden to you."

Demokedes nods, a bit red-faced, and answers, "Polugnota is devoted to the memory of Perdikkas. She will want to help. We are friends of old."

Philippos smiles, "I remember my last meal at Polugnota's. How that woman can cook. And how merrily she laughs."

"She makes fun of herself, never of others," says Demokedes.

A memory of Polugnota with Perdikkas comes to Philippos. The two standing in the vestibule of her house, laughing. Perdikkas alive, truly alive.

Polugnota is a short plain woman, with more weight than you would expect Perdikkas to admire. In truth, one was never concerned with her appearance. Always in motion, always making others feel better, clever in her speech, quick of mind, yet not a sour word or a disparaging remark for anyone. Her stories turning on her own missteps or those of the old mule she kept, though never for sympathy. You could not imagine anything she would not try. Forthrightly herself, she would not exchange her widowhood for the strictures of another husband. No wonder Perdikkas and Demokedes and a dozen more men treasure her. There are those who criticize her virtue, especially women. Little did they know that men love her for her warmth of character more than any erotic gymnastics.

Coming back to the present, Philippos simply says, "You all must know my tasks. I will face Bardulis and will find a way to deal with Athenai and her puppet, Argaios. Antigonos, Pikoros, and I leave for Edessa tonight. We will see Bardulis soon. Young Derdas, you are welcome to join us, although I'll understand if you need to report back to your father."

"While I am away from Pella, I ask Iolaos here, with my mother, Queen Eurudike, to guard the welfare of the king. Call on Polemaios and Andromitos if you need force of arms beyond the local levy. They each have a *syntagma* under formation."

Looking about him, Philippos asks, "Do I have all your assent?"

The rumble of agreement is heartening. Prince Philippos knows these men as they know him. He has carefully balanced the assignments. They know he has taken the hardest tasks, which is his due as regent. Where he sees greybeards and youths, they see a young man of average height, broad in the shoulder, softbearded, handsome, but saved from prettiness by a slight skew to his face. Doubtless they see these features, but the features mean less than their knowledge of the character of the man. As Platon of Athenai would say, they see beyond the surface to the reality. This man, this young prince, is the bedrock of the kingdom. On his determination, intelligence, and skill, they will all depend. And they will depend with confidence. He is a man larger than his physical presence.

γ

How did he ever think Bardulis looked grandfatherly? The armored king, with his deep lined face, old scars, and heavy grizzled beard, looks like a god of war. Not some youthful muscular warrior swinging a bright edged sword—not that simple—no, a man of cunning, ruthless, who has seen all and knows more. A man who launches all those mindless muscled warriors into whatever endeavor he wills them to do.

Philippos is silent, considerate of the hostility he faces. As once before, he leads an embassy of supplicant Makedones to the Dardanoi. This time there is no huge busy tent bustling with the comings and goings of self-important Illuroi. Instead they are in the bleak remains of a burnt out hall, some notable's manor—perhaps that of the dead Balakros who came from hereabouts. Only Antigonos and Pikoros, the scribe Tyros, the interpreter Pinnes, and the bodyguard Andros, formerly Perdikkas' man, are with Philippos. Bardulis is as simply served—a scribe, an interpreter, the general Epidios, the priest Ziraios, and four guards.

Bardulis is speaking, "There is no surprise in betrayal. The breaking of oaths is expected of a Makedone." Here he spits on the streaked cracked mosaic floor. "Still, you might expect the weak to serve the strong. Now, if not before, Makedone, you know your weakness." Then with a mocking gesture of invitation, he adds, "What do you offer to fill my wagons that I cannot fill myself by sending my army into Emathis and Mieza?"

Epidios is grinning at the Makedon discomfiture. You can tell that he would like little more than to lead his warriors into the lowlands.

Calmly Philippos says, "There is nothing I can do to prevent your march. And yet, let me ask what you would gain? You can ravage our lands. You know, though, that the lowlands are not the highlands. There are more cities into which our people can safely withdraw. Though you have killed many Makedones, in the lowlands there are many more. Your own line of advance will lengthen and must be protected. You are further from your source of strength. You will be like the long ago Thraikiote King Sitalkes when he invaded our lands, not knowing who conspires behind you when you are gone so long in enemy country." Barely pausing, the prince-regent continues, "What is best for you now is what was best before. Tribute sent to you year in and year out. The same is best for us. Death and devastation rewards no one."

"Young prince, you gave me your word before the gods," accuses Bardulis. "What reliance can I place on your words now?"

"Now when I speak, I speak as regent of the Makedones. The decisions are mine to make."

Bardulis looks searchingly at Philippos. Perdikkas' little boy is king in name. He won't truly be king for many years, if ever. Within, Bardulis can admit to liking Prince Philippos. The man is solid, not a fool, not frightened, not a willow to the wind. He is a man who earns respect. What

Bardulis wants to do is bind the Makedones to him. Not simply gain tribute but gain their services. And after the Makedones, then Bardulis wants the Molossi. With the northern Hellenic kingdoms part of his confederacy, he would make all the Hellenes tremble at his command.

"How long will you be regent, Prince Philippos?" asks Ziraios suddenly. Answering his own rhetoric, the priest says, "Only so long as little Amuntas is king." He shrugs, dismissing the boy, "Why should we not treat with your brother Arkhelaos or your cousin Pausanias? Or even Argaios, whom Athenai pushes forward?"

After hearing out the interpreter's translation of the priest's words, Philippos responds, "All three aspire to be king. All three have support outside the kingdom. I command from within, the army and the people support me. None of the three will ever be king."

Where does this confidence come from? thinks Bardulis. There is no boasting here, and no hint of defeat or despair. And the young man is right. Bardulis does not want his army entangled in the lowlands. If it were truly profitable to march into Emathis, the Illuroi would already be there.

Well, Arkhelaos is a nonentity. Good for mustering peasants for slaughter. Argaios has Athenai and does not need the Dardanoi. So the choice is between Philippos and Pausanias. But Pausanias will never knit the Makedones together. Isn't that good, a weak divided kingdom? For tribute, perhaps. For providing a strong Makedon contingent in the Dardanoi army? No. If Bardulis wants the Makedones as a useful subkingdom, then Philippos is the answer.

The silence stretches. Bardulis eyes Philippos steadily. The prince waits easily, returning the king's gaze.

Abruptly Bardulis commands, "The tribute will double and be made in semi-annual payments. Do not try to bargain with me." The king pauses to see the effect of his words. The Makedones do not flinch, and the prince nods agreement.

For the first time, Bardulis smiles, "Prince Philippos, you answer readily for each of the three pretenders. How ready would you be if I chose one of them to be king of the Makedones?"

Now it is Philippos' turn to consider. With the weight of the Dardanoi, added to the support each pretender possesses, any one of them could be made king. "King Bardulis, I acknowledge that you can make any man you choose the king of the Makedones. But only King Amuntas would remain king the moment you withdraw your army. Do you want to commit your army to the Makedon lowlands for many years?"

Impatient, Bardulis reacts, "Let's not talk of King Amuntas. When he is of age I will be prepared to treat with him. There is the regent Philippos. There are three possible kings: Arkhelaos, Argaios, and Pausanias. These are the choices before me. Which man will enter into alliance with me, give me his pledge as his overlord, deliver the full tribute when due, provide me with well-armed and provisioned warriors when I demand, and follow my lead where I direct?"

These words do not catch Epidios or Ziraios by surprise. Eyes do not widen a hairsbreadth. The Dardanoi want alliance and have decided beforehand with whom. *And it must be me,* thinks Philippos, *else why this meeting. They seek to size me up, but they lean in my direction. So I have them while they think they have me.*

"You know the answer to your question, King Bardulis. Only I speak for the Makedones. At best, Argaios will say what Athenai wants him to say. And Athenai speaks with the whim and arrogance of its people. Arkhelaos, if he knows how to speak, will echo Olunthos and its League. And Pausanias will always consult King Berisades before King Bardulis."

"Perhaps you are right, but can I rely on you?" Bardulis demands, "So, Prince Philippos, do you give me your word? Do the Makedones follow you into alliance with me?"

Without hesitation Philippos says, "Yes."

"Deliver the first half of your tribute to me. Kill your brother Arkhelaos. Then we will seal the bargain. You will marry my granddaughter, Audata. I will support you against Pausanias and Argaios." Bardulis grins with satisfaction, "Do it all quickly, Prince-regent, for I will have further orders for you."

δ

"You are working quickly, Philippos," growls Antipatros. "I must have received a dozen dispatches in the past day and a half."

"There is much to be done," answers the regent, handing another letter sealed with his ring to a runner. Around them are several subscribes under Tyros' direction making fair copies of the latest dictation. Riders wait in the courtyard, the stamping and snorting of their horses is faintly audible in the large hall.

Antipatros follows the runner with his eyes as the youngster sprints for the door, "You are sure this will work? The city's a great treasure to give up."

Philippos laughs lightly, "We are dealing with Athenai here—a democracy. The likelihood of them agreeing on anything quickly is remote. So they will be cautious. They will feel certain of only one thing, that I am weak."

"So why wouldn't they push harder? Why not put a puppet on the throne if you are so weak?"

"Better a ruler who has the support of his people and yet is pliant to their needs than a puppet whom they must prop up by force of arms."

"The same argument you used on Bardulis," nods Antipatros. "You are promising yourself in many directions."

"Promising?" Philippos shakes his head and looks Antipatros in the eye. "I am promised to King Amuntas and the Makedones, all else is sub-terfuge. We withdraw our garrison from Amphipolis and send overtures of friendship to Athenai. We protest their support of Argaios. Where is any-thing promised?"

Tyros steps over, "They are done writing, Prince Philippos. The riders are away."

Philippos smiles, "Good, good. Send your scribes to get a bite, to get some sleep. We will be on the road again after the judgment. Get some rest yourself, Tyros."

"What of you, Prince?" he responds.

"There will be time to sleep tomorrow night." Philippos turns back to Antipatros, "I want to be in Pella the day after tomorrow. I will want half your horsemen."

Antipatros grunts at the thought of losing three squadrons. Bardulis has been quieted, perhaps it's all right. Antigonos stays with the Dardanid king until the first tribute payment is made. If the Dardanoi become rest-less, Antigonos will send word. News from the east is that King Agis accepted his bribe and the Paiaones return to their lands richer for their raiding. There is the judgment this afternoon. Another problem solved. That leaves Pausanias and Argaios. "I regret not capturing Aridaios. We should have had him, too. Pure negligence on the part of my officer, and he is reprimanded."

"No doubt Aridaios went south to the Khalkidike. Menelaos was in Olunthos three days ago. He's further east now. Maybe at Stagiros. Aridaios will join him. After this afternoon they will be official exiles. Without Arkhelaos, they are no more than clods of dirt."

"What of Pausanias?"

Grimacing, Philippos says, "Negotiations with King Berisades are trick-ier than is needful. The man wants too much. Fortunately, Pausanias is making little progress recruiting. Mostly he's got border scum—outlaws, men of no allegiance. His core people have dwindled. No money left for mercenaries. He knows, and the people around him know, that the Odrusai king is wavering. Our march on Kalindroia went well enough. Pausanias had to run to Berisades."

The regent considers, "Still, I think giving up Amphipolis will do it." He touches Antipatros on the arm, "You see the beauty of recalling the garrison? We win three ways. Athenai sees the gesture as a gift. Berisades sees me delivering the Strymon valley to his authority. The Amphipolitans see us honoring their independence. And what have we really done? Consolidated our strength until we are powerful enough to return."

"Athenai never found it easy to put a garrison into Amphipolis," objects Antipatros.

"Why do by force what you can do by silver? When the time comes, Amphipolis will give us her allegiance."

"Berisades will give up Pausanias?" asks Antipatros.

"That's uncertain. I can get Berisades to hobble Pausanias, but not to surrender him." Philippos tightens his grip on Antipatros' arm, "Ephrastos is working on the problem."

Antipatros nods. Philippos always has more than one approach in mind to solve a problem. No matter that Berisades continues to protect Pausanias. The Thraikiote may think he can keep Pausanias safe in the event he wants to trot the exile out as a threat to the Makedon kingship. Ephrastos will find a way past that safety. Pausanias will turn to dust in Berisades' hands.

*   *   *

The assembly at Edessa shows some regrowth in the army since the disastrous battle under Perdikkas. Using drill instructors forwarded by Philippos from the *syntagmai* at Pella, Antipatros has already improved the competence of the raw men drawn from the local militias.

Of the footmen who escaped the terrible pursuit by the Dardanoi after the battle, most belonged to the *syntagmai* raised and trained by Philippos. Their cohesiveness and fighting ability allowed them to withstand the flood of Illuroi warriors. These strong cadres speed the integration of the new men.

The survival of so many who consider themselves personal adherents of Prince Philippos makes this army his in a way few Makedon kings have experienced. That fact, coupled with the high loss among the notables, clan heads, and their followers, means that the loyalty the army feels to him is stronger for the absence of many parochial pulls. True, the army can feel emotional over little King Amuntas, but only as a symbol for his dead father. The army looks to Philippos for leadership.

Acting for the king, Philippos ordered this assembly. The citizen-warriors of the royal army are judges of the prosecution Philippos presents against his half-brother, Arkhelaos. The regent presents his arguments and offers evidence and witnesses. For more than ten years Arkhelaos gave King Bardulis every scrap of knowledge he could glean of Makedon plans, policies, and preparations, hoping to gain the Dardanid king's favor. Since the death of Perdikkas, he actively sought to overturn the army's acclamation of little Amuntas as king. He allied with the Khalkidike confederacy, promising them territories and tribute for their aid in putting him on the throne. He armed retainers and misguided country folk in his effort to become king. His full-brothers, Aridaios and Menelaos, who are equally culpable, even now are in the Khalkidike attempting to raise an army. These treasons are proven, Philippos declares. It is time for the citizens to call out their judgment.

Arkhelaos stands before the many ranks of warriors. He is not craven. A robust man, past middle-aged, grizzled, he looks more the Temenidai today, despite his chains, than ever in the past. He is arrogant in his pride, sustained by his hatred of Philippos. His defense is simple. He is the eldest son of good king Amuntas. The throne is his by right.

Raising his voice, pitching it high so it will carry down the rows of men, Philippos responds, "Citizens, you hear what Arkhelaos, son of Amuntas, says on his own behalf. You hear the words from his own mouth. He claims the kingship as his right." Philippos pauses dramatically, then screams out, "Who acclaims the king? Who is it that acclaimed good king Amuntas, my father—Amuntas the Wise? Who is it that acclaimed young king Amuntas, my nephew? Who acclaims a king?"

The roar back echoes widely, "We do! We acclaim! We acclaim the king!"

Pointing at Arkhelaos and answering the army, Philippos yells, "Has this man committed treason? Has he betrayed his king? Has he dishonored your rights?"

"Yes, yes!" There is no doubt in any man assembled here. Already many take up the call, "Death! Death to Arkhelaos. Death to a traitor."

And it is done. Condemned as a traitor by the army, Arkhelaos is marched beyond the perimeter of the camp, and well outside the city walls. There, the elected representatives from each unit of the army kill Arkhelaos. The temper of the army can be told by the size of the stones used. The larger the stone, the more easy the death. For Arkhelaos, small stones are thrown and the dying is hard.

ε

The ships of Athenai carry the pretender Argaios and the Athenian general, Mantias, as well as three thousand hoplites, the adventurers and exiles that have joined Argaios, and the sailors of the fleet. Coasting by day and ashore at night, it takes many days to sail from the Attikan port of Piraios to the city of Methone on the Pieric shore of the Makedon homeland. First sailing southeast from Piraios to clear the jutting promontory of Mount Laurion. Then claw northeast, ignoring the inner channel between the mainland and the long island of Euboia to sail beyond Euboia into the full Aegean. There the fleet turns northwest, following along Euboia's east coast to the northern Sporades, which they pass to enter the arm of the Aegean known as the Thraikiote Sea. Then an easy reach into the Thermaic Gulf to Methone.

Off the sloping shore, the hoplites splash into thigh-deep water then trudge to dry land. Tenders on the ships' sea side are used to offload weapons, armor, tents, and other supplies. The citizens of Methone help enthusiastically. The arrival of the fleet means much money for the city. Once unloaded, the triremes are beached and hauled above the storm line.

After sacrifices for their safe arrival, after hearing welcomes from a delegation of the city's leadership, after assuring the proper setup of their encampment, after seeing that the men are fed, Mantias is ready on the morrow to start the second phase of the operation. Already he's dispatched a column south to Pudna, for that small city is the second anchor for his beachhead. With five hundred men each strengthening the defenses of these two cities, and leaving the sailors to guard the ships of the fleet, Mantias has two thousand reliable troops to march inland with the odd mix of men who accompany Argaios.

They are a confident force. What is there to oppose them? The whole Hellenic world knows that King Bardulis destroyed the Makedon army in Eordaia.

Mantias and Argaios have a good plan. Instead of striking immediately at Pella where Prince Philippos is likely to concentrate his adherents, they will march on Aigai. Old Argaios assures Mantias that the ancient religious capital of the Makedones, founded by his namesake the second king of the dynasty, does not support this upstart branch of the Temenidai. By seeking the allegiance of the priestly families first, and the elders of the Argeadai clan, Argaios gathers to himself the legitimacy necessary to win the realm. The Makedones are profoundly conservative in their religious awe and observation. They will heed Aigai. Once Argaios consolidates his hold on Pieris, they will march on Pella. If Philippos is foolish enough to attack them in Pieris, they will destroy him here.

What is there to fear? Their army will be augmented by the citizens-in-arms of Methone and Pudna. As Argaios rallies his people, the population of the region will add to their strength. Pieris remains the homeland of the Argeadai Makedones.

So as Mantias, Argaios, and their senior officers enjoy the feast offered them by the Methone council, they cannot resist boasting and delighting in their easy success. To many there, the hardest part is done. They have braved Poseidon's grace, that stern god. But then Poseidon often favors the hardy sailors of Athenai.

After the feast, Mantias' host and a second leader of Methone seek a private audience with the general. Gruffly the soldier-politician hears out the two men. The older man, Sousarion, is the owner of the house, prominent in the city's politics, and a noted wit. The younger man, Thersandros Komos, is from the senior family of Methone, descended from the city's founder. They represent the city's ruling class.

Sousarion is asking Mantias about the speech he gave during the banquet, "Your words were stirring. A martial cry for restoring King Argaios, wrongfully deprived of his throne by old Amuntas, whose family are usurpers still. Who are we, here in Methone, to deny that Argaios is in the right?" Slyly the lean grey-beard eyes the bulky Mantias, "Still, we cannot help ask, what is it to Methone who rules the Makedones? Granted we are allied with Athenai, and are guaranteed our independence from the Makedones through the support of your citizenry. If Athenai wants Argaios, son of Saturos, to occupy the Argeadai throne, is that not reason enough? Certainly, if the good citizens of Athenai will sustain that throne for Argaios."

Again Sousarion smiles, "Methone thrives when the forest harvest of the Makedones flows through our port to meet the needs of Athenai's navy. We would have the Makedones and Athenai always be friends. Argaios is that friend Athenai so earnestly wants to see be the Makedon king. We will support you in your endeavor, so long as you can assure us that even after Argaios occupies the throne, you and your army will remain in Pieris or at Pella."

Mantias purses his lips, considers his reply, "I ask no more of Methone than is in the city's own interest. You need field no men beyond the lands you and neighboring Pudna claim. That will suffice to safeguard my line of supply and communication. Your lands reach north to the Haliakmon River and east to the foothills of Mount Pieric. Aigai is a day's march beyond."

"Then we need not be identified as giving aid to Argaios, only as playing our part as allies of Athenai," bursts out Thersandros.

"Is that so important?" asks Mantias.

"What latitude are you allowed in your orders from the council of Athenai?" counters Sousarion.

Puzzled, Mantias asks, "There is something you are not saying. Spell it out for me."

Guessing, Sousarion says, "You haven't heard that Prince Philippos withdraws his garrison from Amphipolis. He offers to negotiate with Athenai."

"Amphipolis!" exclaims Mantias, quickly considering the implications. So the Methonians fear that Athenai will abandon Argaios if Philippos offers enough. If they are active in supporting Argaios, and he is not sustained, they will look ill in the eyes of Philippos. Amphipolis is one of the touchstones of Attikan politics, possessing a symbolic value far beyond reason. The people of Athenai would willingly drop one barbarian for another if it gains them their prize. "Is this hearsay or do you have proof?"

"We have received an official herald from Prince Philippos. Our own merchants in Amphipolis confirm the withdrawal. Some of our people saw the ship Philippos sent to Athenai with his delegates," blurts Thersandros.

"What type of ship?"

"A light penteconter with a picked crew out of Therme," answers the genial Sousarion. "Must have reached Piraios not many days after you set sail. Word is they each are to receive a gold daric over and above their fee if they break the speed record in reaching Piraios."

"A fortune if counting every oarsmen," exclaims Mantias.

Sousarion laughs, "Philippos will double the sum if they break the record returning as well. There is no doubting he is a generous master." The old man looks shrewdly at Mantias, "You see why we are not certain that serving Argaios is in the interest of either Methone or Athenai."

"I have my orders," answers Mantias.

"Which is why I asked you how much latitude you were given. Must you march on Aigai tomorrow? Might you not send for instructions?" asks Sousarion.

Mantias is silent. Delay gives Philippos an opportunity to respond to their landing. Yet the Prince has already stolen a march, for by relinquishing Amphipolis and seeking peace with Athenai he may well have made this expedition hollow. Mantias knows just how likely it is that Athenai will abrogate Argaios. If Mantias marches out tomorrow to give the kingdom to Argaios, he will look foolish indeed to his fellow citizens if they have decided against Argaios. Finally he says, "The sea voyage has been long. My men need to find their land legs again. They need exercise and good food. We can march in a few days."

*　　*　　*

Fury etches the face of the proud old man, "You delay! Well, I won't delay, Mantias." Argaios is nearly spitting his rebuke at the Athenian general. "My people and I march on Aigai today." He eyes each Athenian officer standing with Mantias, "Now is the opportunity. Surely you must see that. Why let Philippos gather his forces? No, I go today."

Mantias smiles, "That is your choice, King Argaios. My men need time to recover from the sea voyage. I suggest you wait until we are all ready to march. If you insist on going, then you and your followers may secure Aigai. There is nothing to fear in that direction."

"Time?" sneers Argaios. "You do not fool me. I've heard the whispers and rumors about Amphipolis. You Athenians seek your advantage. Why shouldn't you, save for your promises? Do not expect me to wait out your faithlessness."

His neck reddening at the spare old man's words, Mantias retorts, "You do what you feel you must do, King Argaios. I know my responsibilities and must judge how to safeguard the trust and interests of the citizens of Athenai."

With a snort of disgust, Argaios abruptly turns away, motioning to his aids to follow him. He is certain as he stalks away that behind him the Athenian officers are smirking. *Well, they will see what a Makedon king can do,* thinks Argaios. He has not come this far, back to his native land, to be thwarted by the crosscurrents of Athenian perfidy. In truth, he owes much to the generosity of individual Athenians. As individual friends, there are none better and many are among his followers. But as a people, as a state, they are untrustworthy—a city of avarice.

He can count on something over three hundred men. His friends, companions, and kinsmen, plus the 256 mercenaries he personally hired. Enough to wake up sleepy Aigai and announce his return. As he walks to the quarters assigned by the city council for his personal following, he is blind to all around him. Instead he imagines the scene of welcome in Aigai, as clan head after clan head comes forward to swear allegiance. He can barely restrain grinning at the thought of that sweet day.

Melankhros, the old man's son-in-law, catches up to the quick striding Argaios. "Father Argaios, what do we do without the army?"

"It's better this way, boy. Much better," the thin face creases in a grin. "Now we act on our own. When the Makedones acknowledge me, we will not be beholden to Mantias."

"Will it be that easy?"

Testily, Argaios snaps back, "Of course not. Do you think I don't know the temper of my people? There will be some who will oppose me, whose interests are tied to the family of old Amuntas. And some will hang back waiting to see how the wind is blowing. That's why we have Sadokos and his mercenaries."

Then Argaios smiles, "This is not a question of bloodshed. We will prevail because the gods want us to prevail. Right is with us. For thirty years I have corresponded with my supporters here. How many times have they urged me to come? Well I am here." He grasps Melankhros' arm, "Boy, if we march fast, we could be in Aigai tomorrow morning at the latest. We landed yesterday. Philippos and little Amuntas won't have time to react. By the time we face them, we will have overwhelming strength."

ζ

In Pella, word has reached Philippos of the landing. Fishermen saw the fleet arrive and sent the news. Before the last hoplite set foot on dry land, the regent received the message.

The news was expected and plans had been made. The prince's chief scribe, Tyros, quickly sends fast riders carrying orders to summon army units to pre-arranged assembly sites near Aloros, Beroia, and Pella. The main army under Antipatros will march south from Edessa, along the road that connects the towns in the Bermion foothills, to Beroia, which is west of Aigai and north of the River Haliakmon. The levy of Bottiaia and the units already at Pella will march for Aloros via the marsh road. Aloros lies on the north side of the Haliakmon, close to the estuary of the Thermaic Gulf. Philippos will lead that contingent. The more distant units will march for Pella to protect King Amuntas and provide a rallying point in case of defeat.

The relief felt by Philippos is immense. Until now the Athenians were a threat of uncertain proportions. With the landing, the Athenians have fixed their position. The prince's agents are in Methone cautioning the Athenians to delay until the results of the negotiations between the regent and Athenai are known. They will work hard to disengage this man Mantias from old Argaios.

Signal relays are being established so the prince can monitor actions in the Methone lands. If the invading army marches north, they will probably cross the Haliakmon at either Aigai or Aloros. Aloros is closer and on a more direct route to Pella. Thus, the prince goes to Aloros. If the enemy marches on Aigai, Antipatros can either confront them directly or maneuver until Philippos can come west so that they fight Mantias together.

The first task is to secure Aloros. For that purpose, Philippos is taking several squadrons of horsemen to reach the city quickly. The small militia garrison there will be reinforced from the immediate countryside. More time is needed before the *syntagmai* from the capital or more distant levies can be expected to reach Aloros.

By dusk, Philippos, his immediate companions, and the squadrons are riding south. The marsh road is not an easy route. Wending its way around Lake Borboros, it slogs from hillock to hillock, with mud and seepage through the split logs laid down between the rises impeding fast travel. Road maintenance is the responsibility of each local village, but in the marshes villages are few and far between. They will cross the River Loudias at the only ford from the lake to the sea. This time of year the ford is passable.

Starting out in high spirits, the riders grow quieter and wearier as they ride. Every few hours Philippos calls a break to rest the horses. Then he pushes them on again. By dawn, they are out of the marshes. Aloros is close, and they pass cultivated fields. Already peasants are out, and they stare at the long column of horsemen.

As he rides, head down, Philippos muses on the lands hereabouts. Ptolemaios had his major holdings through his mother in Aloros. Ptolemaios of Aloros, now just scattered bones, with all ambition gone. *Ah, Perdikkas,* thinks the prince, *would that you were alive and king. Well, we shall see where ambition takes old Argaios.* The old man has tried to be king of the Makedones twice before, with some success. King Amuntas, the prince's father, always defeated him in the end.

Is there anyone out there among the Makedones who would still see Argaios be king? Argaios believes it, is here to prove it. He must have some basis for it, some agents and contacts giving him encouragement. Who among the notables still see their well-being tied to Argaios or to Athenai rather than the regent? He comes to Pieris first, to the oldest homeland. Because of Methone, for the Athenians need a safe base. Also because of Aigai, Aloros, and Dion? Because of the old families of the Pieris? Are the loyalties in the old homeland so divided?

Down the road come several riders, splashing through the odd puddle left by the recent rain. Pikoros and his scouts, whom Philippos sent on ahead to find out if Aloros is still loyal. Pikoros calls out, "Hola, Philippos, all is well."

Philippos halts the column and sends word down its length to take a short break—to clean gear and dress the ranks—so when they enter Aloros they impress its citizens. At the same time Pikoros sums up the situation in Aloros, grinning the whole time, "You needn't have worried. Your mother is in Aloros and has all in hand. The town council and militia are bowing and scraping to the tune she plays. The first of the country levies have begun to arrive. The crossing of the Haliakmon is well guarded."

"Mother?" says Philippos in surprise. "I thought she'd stay put on her estate or go south to Dion if she felt threatened." He considers further, "Did you have any difficulty with her?" Asking because his mother does not approve that a former slave is one of the prince's companions.

"None," laughs Pikoros. "She is proud of her achievement and would have you know that you can count on Aloros and the region all around."

"Did she say anything of the Athenians or Argaios?"

"She has horsemen patrolling down into the Methone lands. Her agents there say the Athenians are just sitting. No one is coming north to Aloros."

Philippos sits quietly on his horse. He tries to put himself into the mind of Mantias. What must the general be thinking? "Does Queen Eurudike know any cause for their inaction?"

"There are rumors. Maybe the voyage was rough on them. Maybe the Athenian commander waits on further orders. There is much talk of Amphipolis and how the Athenians would rather acknowledge King Amuntas and gain that city than lift Argaios to an uncertain throne."

"Good, good, that sounds plausible." Philippos muses further. He is counting on Amphipolis as his strongest argument in persuading the Athenians to accept his government. Yet not the only argument. That he is only regent to a toddler king is also an argument. The Athenians will see the weakness in the arrangement. Some of them at least will view dealing with a weak regency as cheaper than propping up an aging King Argaios. The merchants and manufacturers of the teeming Athenai think a lot about money. Then again, those particular politicians of the city gifted in secret with the regent's silver find money a strong persuader. Still, for all his goodwill, there must be something to crystallize their belief in the value of his friendship. Amphipolis may not be enough. After all, they view that city as theirs by right.

Aloud he says, "We must hurry on to Eurudike's realm. There may be more news by now." Then he adds, smiling at Pikoros, "Was she wearing armor?"

"Your mother? No, no, she need not pretend to be a man to rule. She may be a grandmother, but no one mistakes her mettle."

η

The bullock carts slowed the march to Aigai. With the fall of evening, Argaios and his men were still short of their destination. Not overly concerned, Argaios set up a careful camp. The carts were used to mark the perimeter. Sentries were posted. The mercenaries were feasted with a whole ox, but little wine.

With the dawn, Argaios sent riders ahead to Aigai to announce his arrival. Within the hour, he had the whole column on the move again. Soon they came over the brow of a hill to see the river valley before them. With Aigai in sight, Argaios' heart rose with gladness. All the years as exile in Athenai gave color to this journey, this progress to assume his throne. Aigai—ancient capital of the Makedones—where generations of kings are buried. Truly this city is home.

But the closer they come to the city, the more disquiet is felt by Argaios and his companions. Where are the crowds? Where the welcoming citizenry? Why haven't the town fathers come out to greet him?

Now, hours later, standing on the steps of the council house, with the *agora* or central market before him, Argaios feels an abiding angry embarrassment. There is no one. Houses are shuttered. The better people have fled the city. The poor are here, having nowhere to flee, but they are nothing without leadership. He is tempted to loose Sadokos and have the mercenaries loot the city. His anger is that strong. But he is a Makedon prince. This city is the religious heart of his kingdom. True, Dion to the south is the cult center, but Aigai, sacred Aigai, has held his dreams too long. He will not profane her.

He has sacrificed to the gods of the city. He has sacrificed to his ancestors. He has summoned the few senior men still in the city. They have nothing to offer him. Poor old Panaitios, with whom Argaios has corresponded for a score of years, came forward joyously to greet him. To no matter, for the old man's mind is gone, and he greets Argaios as if the past thirty years have not happened.

For many of the Athenian adventurers accompanying Argaios, the wandering mind of liver-spotted Panaitios epitomizes the sheer futility of this expedition. Remarks about a king who commands a single fool circulate among them. Where they hoped to find riches as rewards for gaining Argaios a kingdom, they now find nothing more than the weary toil of their wasted march.

Argaios realizes resolution is needed. What does not come easily, can still come through hard work. Time to go back to Methone and use Mantias and his army to gain the kingdom. Defeat Philippos and all the fawning notables will return, eager to court the favor of King Argaios. With this bitter scene in mind, Argaios turns to Melankhros and gives the command, "We return. Have Sadokos call in his men. Get the rest of these nincompoops started. We must make war on Philippos before the notables will love us."

Melankhros salutes his father-in-law casually, then hurries down the steps to get the band of adventurers and mercenaries in motion. He recognizes the frustration in Argaios, and also the nerve. His father-in-law has ruled this land before and expects to again. Argaios will not hesitate to bring his people around by the sword if that is required. Hopes for a euphoric reception from the notables in Aigai may have vanished, but nothing has diminished the determination in Argaios.

θ

Scouts bring in the news of Argaios to Philippos—the lack of success at Aigai, the size of the force with the pretender, and the route of their return march.

Philippos has already assessed his strength. The three squadrons of horsemen number roughly eighty men each. He has another dozen companions. The rest of his small army are footmen, though none of his trained *syntagmai*. Aloros offers a hundred and fifty men, well enough armed. The levy has brought in another two hundred with a wide mix of arms. Most can act only as *psiloi*—with their slings, javelins, daggers, and farming tools. Within hours many more ill-armed men, loosely organized, will be here. Some few will be bowmen. The two *syntagmai* from Pella, under Polemaios and Andromitos, will be at Aloros by mid-morning. Their phalangists will be the first men here who can stand toe to toe with Sadokos' mercenaries or with the hoplites of Mantias, should that general prove aggressive and leave the protection of Methone.

Once Argaios has rejoined Mantias, there will be no prizing him loose from Athenai. Even if the Athenians accept the peace offered by Philippos, Argaios will be safe and available as a future threat. Back in Athenai again, it is doubtful if even Ephrastos and his agents can touch Argaios given the Attikan politics.

No, this is the only opportunity. Now as Argaios leads his men back to Methone.

Deciding, Philippos addresses his captains, "We will ride him down. Surround him, dog him, slow him, until I can bring up strong enough forces to face him in line. We won't trade him blow for blow until Polemaios and Andromitos join us."

"What about Mantias?" asks Liontaros Polemos, who commands the first squadron.

"Hippasos, will you lead the Alorites across the river into Methone lands?" asks Philippos.

"Whatever you want, Philippos," stoutly answers the regent's companion.

"Take Evagoras to scout for you. He's the best." Philippos smiles gently at Hippasos, "Try not to fight. Just make a lot of noise. Make Mantias think you are the advance of something bigger. Don't go too far south. Take all the *psiloi* as well."

"I can do it, Prince. We will be all the bears in the wood," laughs Hippasos.

"We will strip Aloros of its fighting men. If need be Queen Eurudike can stand at the gate and bar our enemies," says the prince-regent. The men laugh dutifully and truly. None doubt that she would do it if called upon. "All right, then, we will leave Hippasos to his responsibilities. Liontaros, Theodoros, Hipponikos, mount your men."

* * *

By mid-morning the mists are burnt away. The men in Argaios' column feel the sun on their brows. They trudge on. Marching in even half-armor is wearying. But Argaios wants them prepared. There is no fooling him now, he knows he's in enemy country and vulnerable until he rejoins Mantias. Better slow and steady than unready.

Just after fording one of the several small streams, they catch site of a line of horsemen barring their path. Argaios halts his men, calls in his rear, and spreads his van into a facing line. The horsemen trot away. The march resumes.

Again the horsemen appear. Now not only a line in front, but along both sides too. Not a lot of horsemen. Nothing to fear. Still, Argaios has Sadokos shake out half the mercenaries into a square to face the enemy. Time passes. The horsemen make no hostile move. Cautiously Argaios orders the mercenaries to advance. The horsemen to the front wheel and fall back. Sadokos' men cheer, the first sign of good morale since seeing Aigai yesterday.

On the left, a curving line of horsemen gallops down on the column's flank. Warnings are shouted, but the scrambling men of the column think only of their own safety. The horsemen throw a shower of javelins, and then they are away. Few casualties occur within the column. Two dead and a half-dozen are injured, mostly from their own panicky flight into the ranks of their fellow warriors.

Argaios is furious. He orders Melankhros to the rear to assure discipline along the column. Sadokos pulls his men back into the column. They halt for a time, to distribute arms and full armor from the bullock carts. Argaios orders them to eat as well, for after this halt he is determined that there will be no more stopping until they are within the protection of Methone. Calling out to two of the Athenian adventurers, he orders them to ride hard for Methone to bring out Mantias in force.

Grinning at each other and at the lark of escaping the slow column, the two youths salute Argaios and race on ahead.

Distantly, still within sight of the column, Makedon horsemen confront the two riders. Neither escapes. There will be no word to Mantias.

* * *

"Timing, Pikoros, timing," chuckles Philippos. He watches the long slow column, like a wolf eyeing a sheep herd. About him are Pikoros, young Peithon, the burly Andros—his self-appointed bodyguards—as well as the 84 men of the second squadron under Theodoros. Across the valley floor, Liontaros has led his men into a swoop against the column's rear. Hipponikos' third squadron is barring the column's front. These past four hours of harrying Argaios has raised the level of caution and discipline among the enemy. They remain a force to be reckoned with, but are visibly tiring.

317

Now with the enemy attention fully on Liontaros and Hipponikos, Philippos gives a screaming yell and charges. They dig in their heels and gallop for the center of the column.

The prince is the first to reach the column, with Pikoros an instant behind. They cut a furrow among the enemy like a plow in easily worked soil. Screams, obscenities, savage prayers. They thrust, then cut, laying about them, harvesting a grim crop. A spear thrust from a mercenary brings down Philippos' horse, but not before the prince cuts off the enemy's arm. Down now, free of the horse and on his feet, Philippos is in danger of being overwhelmed.

With Andros there and Peithon beside him, Pikoros rides down an officer rallying the counterattack. The prince is up behind Peithon, and the boy spurs through the column. He is laughing wildly. Philippos yells in his ear, "What is it, Peithon?"

"I love this, dear Prince, nothing is better."

They are clear now, and Philippos slides to the ground. He turns to see how the squadron fares. They are all through, they have cut the column in half. At a cost, though. Until now the Makedones had suffered few losses. Closing with the column meant more have fallen. But what a swath they have cut. The dead and wounded among their enemies are many. For the first time, Philippos thinks he may not need to wait for Polemaios and Andromitos.

One of the loose horses is gathered in for Philippos. He's uncertain whether it's from the column or one of the fallen Makedones. The mare responds well to the strong will of its rider.

In command again, Philippos trots parallel to the column well out of harm's way. A quick count shows they lost five in that skirmish. Looking about for Hipponikos and Liontaros, he halloos them, pointing ahead. Soon all the horsemen are riding for a crossroads up beyond the column. There they turn and face the slow moving footmen. Excitement runs through the Makedones. They grin wolfish grins at one another and call out taunts to their enemies.

*　　*　　*

Sadokos confronts Argaios, "This is no good. They strike us without fear. If we keep up this running fight they will tear at us the whole way. Surely Mantias must know what's happening. If we fort up, they can't touch us. Mantias will come to our relief."

Argaios says nothing, stares at the experienced mercenary, sees the fear in the man's eyes. With the death of Melankhros, ridden down by some huge Makedones, there is no one Argaios can truly count on. Argaios nods assent, can say nothing. He feels no fear, only a numb resignation. Herakles, Zeus, his own Posis Das, whom others say is an aspect of Zeus, all have turned away from him. Never before would he believe the gods

318

could abandon him. There is nothing one can do. The sun favors these young Temenidai and not him. His day is past. Again he nods, acquiescing in Sadokos' command.

Within minutes, Sadokos has his troops turned, lumbering heavily in their armor toward a nearby hill. The others follow the mercenaries. The wounded in the carts cry out as they lurch off the pathway onto the rougher ground.

Seeing the column turn away and make the climb to the low hill, the horsemen ride to intercept the footmen. The front ranks of the mercenaries reach the top without interference. The rear of the column is not as fortunate. Leaning low from their saddles, the riders slash and stab at the footmen.

Again and again, the riders canter away as resistance stiffens, only to sweep back the moment their enemies return to the march. Though filled with inner lethargy, Argaios acts to save his followers. On foot himself now, with shield and spear in hand, he guards the rear with a few stalwarts. Ahead, on the hill, Sadokos organizes a defense.

Finally all the surviving marchers are in the perimeter set by Sadokos. The riders circle the hill. Mounts as tired as the marchers from the long day, no riders will charge up the hill despite its gentle slope. From the hilltop to the pathway is a litter of weapons, armor parts, bodies, dying bullocks, stalled carts, and other debris.

Only a few hours of daylight remain. The hilltop is a temporary haven at best. No water, only what food might have been carried during the agonizing scramble to its safety. All that Argaios and Sadokos can hope for is the sight of Mantias leading the Athenian army.

*　　*　　*

Peithon walks his horse over to Philippos. Under one arm is a helmet filled with water. "Thank you, Peithon," says the prince, drinking deeply.

Pawing the ground, Liontaros' horse snorts at the smell of water. His master says, "We cannot get them down ourselves."

"We need not," answers Philippos. Raising his voice to carry to many of the riders, Philippos calls, "You have done well this day. You have done all that I asked. Like hunting dogs, we have treed our prey. When the phalanx comes, the hunt will be over." Softer, he says to his officers, "Let your horses and men rest. Keep one in three on the line around the hill. Rotate them so all rest, eat, drink. I want twenty back as a reserve, in case anyone up there tries to break out."

Turning to Pikoros, the prince adds, "Take two others and ride toward Aloros. Guide Polemaios and Andromitos here." Then to Andros, "Take several men as well. Ride east toward Methone, spread yourselves out and watch for any relief from there."

Time passes slowly now, though slower for those on the hill. The Makedones number their dead, bind their wounded, care for their horses, keep watch, recount the day, share their provisions, resharpen blunted blades, wait. There is a bustle as two horsemen are sighted. Philippos recognizes Evagoras and waves him in.

"What news, Evagoras?" he calls as the taciturn scout trots up.

"Hippasos sent me. We passed through the outlying villages north of Methone. Mantias does not stir. Hippasos is careful to seem like more than he is."

Philippos considers, trying to understand the situation from Mantias' view. The Athenian must be fretting over Argaios. Nothing from the west, and a seemingly strong force from the north. Why isn't the general pushing scouts forward to learn what he can?

Evagoras clears his throat, sips water brought to him by Peithon. "Hippasos had word from Methone. An Athenian penteconter came in this morning with orders for Mantias to await instructions."

"Where are his scouts?"

"Some have tried, but we gobbled them up." Smiling for the first time, Evagoras says, "My men are in a band from north to southwest. Nothing will get through without my knowing."

Abruptly Philippos says, "Then it's done. Mantias won't come and they can't stay up on the hill." He nods toward the hill.

Evagoras shades his eyes against the lowering sun, "How many up there?"

"Maybe three hundred. We drained away nearly a hundred of them," Peithon says eagerly, proudly.

"Evagoras, you and Liontaros ride up closer to them. Let them know that Mantias is not coming. Convince them. Liontaros, let them know I have a phalanx of more than five hundred men who will be here in the morning. Tell them to give up," says Philippos flatly.

Liontaros answers, "As you command. Could be enough to cause them to charge down that hill and continue to Methone."

Shaking his head, Philippos says, "No, they are defeated. They gave up when they left the road. We don't have to wait any longer." He considers further, "Mount all the men. We'll be ready if any up there are still brave."

As Philippos says, the Hellenes are broken. Argaios argues for perseverance, but the men are through. Perhaps they sense how little faith Argaios has in his own words. Leaving weapons behind, they come down the hill two by two, between the lines of fervent, belligerent horsemen.

Peithon asks Philippos, "What will become of them?"

Thinking, Philippos says, "We will send the Athenians home, eventually. No ransom for them. The rest of the mercenaries we'll ransom or take into our service. Those who have no one to redeem them, and refuse service, will be sold." He adds softly, "We will try Argaios for treason, as we did Arkhelaos."

Surprisingly Philippos feels little of the elation that surges through his men. Argaios has been a lifelong enemy of his father and his family. Yet the old man is of the Temenidai. With a little thought Philippos could state exactly how closely he and Argaios are related. Arkhelaos, Argaios, and, if Ephrastos is successful, Pausanias—all three are Temenidai. The Lady Kleopatra was so right about the cost of kingship.

Looking at the men stumbling down the hill, Peithon says, "What an amazing day, dear Prince. How the gods favor you."

Recalled by Peithon's words to the thanks Philippos owes, he intones a short prayer praising Zeus and thanking Herakles, and promising a fuller sacrifice before dawn. Yet his mind adds, not only have the gods favored us, they did not favor Argaios or Athenai. Neither the gods nor the strong sword arms of the Makedones.

CHAPTER FOURTEEN

Paiaones

359 B.C.

α

Bardulis grows impatient," states Antipatros.

Looking at Antipatros, Philippos nods slowly. For the first time, he notices that Antipatros' hair is thinning on top. How old is Antipatros? Forty years old? The beard is grizzled and the face is creased. Yet Antipatros wears well. You have to look close to realize his age. If battle doesn't kill him, he'll last a long time, like his father.

"Then my son had best arrange a date for the wedding," answers Eurudike. "You are not ready for war, Philpa." She stirs in her chair, leaning forward to emphasize her point.

Briefly Philippos thinks about the necessity of marrying Audata. As briefly he thinks of his good wife, Phila. She will not care. The princess of Elimiotis understands the requirements of states, and already knows her place in his regard. There is the little princess of the Molossi. Young Myrtale may not be as uncaring. The thought of her sends a shiver through his loins. Fierce little Myrtale, she will be sixteen now. He means to have her for his wife.

"How far off can we safely place the wedding?" asks Philippos of his mother and the two men.

Antipatros looks at Periandros. Periandros ventures, "You agreed to act quickly, Prince. Arkhelaos and Argaios are dead. Pausanias is in flight from Berisades' court. The Paiaones are home with their loot. He will see nothing standing in your way that is more important than honoring your agreement and marrying his granddaughter."

Across the terrace, shadowed from the summer sun, Pikoros calls out, "And it's time to redeem Antigonos. He must be tired of being guest to the Dardanoi."

Philippos smiles at Pikoros, there as bodyguard rather than counselor. "What Pikoros says touches deep. I miss Antigonos." He turns to his mother, "What preparations do we need to make before you welcome another daughter?"

"Leave that in my hands. You wed at the Dardanid court. My work will be simple," she smiles. "Remember that being your wife is no fault of the girl's. You will treat her as a princess and member of our family once you wed."

Though he understands her meaning, Philippos nearly laughs, thinking of his executed half-brother and cousin. Being a member of the family has its risks. "Mother, you know me."

She sighs, "You'll father a kid on her before the first week is out."

Antipatros and Periandros laugh at Philippos' discomfiture. Yet this marriage is distasteful to all of them. With it, Philippos acknowledges the subordination of the Makedones to King Bardulis. In particular, these two clan heads do not want Philippos breeding a Temenid child on Audata.

Though reddening, Philippos asks calmly, "Do we know anything of Audata?"

"She was betrothed before, to some prince of a northern Illuroi tribe. He died in battle before they could wed. She is said to be handsome, though melancholy," says Periandros. He shrugs, "She's no admirer of the Hellenes —a pure barbarian."

Abruptly Philippos says, "I mean to chastise the Paiaones this winter. They won't expect us. I never want them entering our lands as raiders again. So it will be fierce, grim work we'll do."

The others wait to hear the thread of thought that connects Audata and the Paiaones. Philippos considers his words, "If the wedding follows the harvest and the new year, then I will not be back to Pella before midwinter. A possibility is to strike the Paiaones from west and south. Antipatros leads an army up from Pella. I come down with my wedding retinue from the north." Unspoken is the idea that Parmenion and his Pelagones will strengthen the thrust from the west.

"So you use your new status with Bardulis to crush the Paiaones," says Antipatros with a touch of excitement in his voice.

"The Paiaones will plead for peace if they think the Illuroi and the Makedones cooperate in their destruction," agrees Queen Eurudike. "King Agis could ally with Berisades and all the small tribes of the borderlands if he learns of your scheme in advance."

"King Berisades has no love for Paiaones, is still arguing with his brothers, and has taken our silver to betray Pausanias. I doubt Agis will find him a stable ally. And without the Odrusai, what are the small tribes? If we can achieve surprise, the border tribes will not be a factor." Philippos speaks with certainty, "King Agis will only know that the weak Makedones bend their knees to the Dardanoi king. He will not expect war."

Turning to the general, Philippos says, "Antipatros, your troops must be assembled on the march. We station men along the frontier between now and year-end. You bring them together at the last moment. Stay away from the border yourself."

"I can return to Edessa," answers Antipatros.

"For now, yes. But with the new year rituals, you would normally be back here at Aigai. Instead, be in Pella. On the day of the wedding, march north."

Periandros speaks up, "Who conducts the rituals? You will be with the Dardanoi."

"King Amuntas. Queen Eurudike and the elder magnates can guide him—Old Agerrhos, if Iolaos cannot make the journey, will instruct him in the ceremonies. I'll teach him the specifics of the Argeadai rituals."

The others look uncomfortable. Eurudike says softly, "He'll only be five. Will the gods accept his devotions for the nation?"

Before Philippos can answer, Pikoros speaks up, "He is the king."

"He is acclaimed, he is king. The gods and ancestors know this. They will forgive a five-year old his fumbles in the ceremony. They may not forgive any one who acts for the king," says Philippos.

"Will you let Bardulis know that you intend attacking the Paiaones?" asks Antipatros.

"If I tell him, he will decide it requires his permission. And he'd likely deny us. He can learn about the attack at the same time as King Agis," states the prince flatly.

Antipatros smiles broadly, "He won't like it."

"All of you will work hard through the autumn. All the commanders —Alkimakhos, Demetrios, Eurulokhos, Kharikles, Liontaros, Polemaios, your senior officers, yourselves—all the officers will train the town militias and select levy. I want ten thousand men under arms by early spring. Under arms, trained, and ready to fight in phalanx wielding the *sarissa*. I want at least six hundred horsemen. I will call on Derdas of Elimiotis. I will want the regular levies, as well, for peltasts and *psiloi*." Philippos glares, not at them but at the future he confronts. "We will put the fear of Herakles and the Makedones into every Paiaones' heart this winter. And in the spring, we will do the same to Bardulis and his confederacy."

With this plan, the marriage to Audata ceases to be a necessary humiliation. The marriage becomes a stratagem to gull and destroy their enemies. Already Antipatros and Periandros are afire with anticipation. Pikoros is grinning. Philippos looks into the eyes of Eurudike and sees her pride and agreement. At last the old Queen has found a ruler she will follow.

β

Derdas, *basileos* of the Elimiotoi, sits tightly in the corner of the parapet, feeling the warmth of sun-beaten stone against his back. His daughter dangles her legs over the edge of the wooden walkway. They can see into the courtyard below. They are talked out, having spent an hour catching up with each other's news. They are content together. Derdas watches Phila, his Phila, home at last from Pella.

"Father, what would you say if I chose not to return? If I stayed here in Aiane?"

The king cannot see her face, though her voice sounds wistful rather than purposeful. Still her question takes away his relaxed mood, "You keep your husband's household. How can you do that in Aiane?"

"If I ask him, he will let me." She turns her head to see her father, "He would not be sending me home in divorce. He needs me more here, than with him."

"Is he so uncertain of Elimiotis?"

"Not while you are *basileos*," she answers firmly.

Derdas grunts, thinking over the unspoken questions of his health and the succession. There is a palsy in his left arm that he cannot control. Not that the twitches and tremors are all that noticeable to others, or so he had thought. This slight weakness does not prevent him from performing his duties. When he first noticed the malady, fear froze him. He loathes his aging body, this deterioration. No man is immortal. He knows that and doesn't fear death, only the manner of dying.

Knowing his own temper and rashness, he always assumed he'd die in battle. As a king should. How glorious to have been Perdikkas, though better if he'd died in victory. Poets already sing of Perdikkas charging into the gap in the enemy lines, then holding open the trap so his companions could escape, finally dying as overwhelming numbers of barbarians cut him down.

True there are poets who question whether such a death has purpose, has virtue. Poets who emulate the ancient Arkhilokos the Thraikiote.

He sighs. He supposes it is the fault of city life. A country man, whether herder or cultivator, knows the virtues even if he does not practice them. The gods are closer to such a man, for he sees their actions plainly every day. He understands the privileges gained by those who guard his livelihood. The guardians, in turn, understand that they are honor bound to one another, to those they protect, and to the gods. Bravery is a virtue less in deed than in its intention. A bad man can be brave. One can even applaud that a brave bad man possesses some measure of self-mastery. How much more meritorious is bravery performed for good purpose. The poets know that when they sing praises, they say to all who hear them what is important, what is laudable, and what is not.

Poets should sing the deeds of great kings. Kings who were the good shepherds of their people. Kings who inspire their warriors to protect the herder and cultivator from depredations and murder. Poets should praise kings.

Derdas sighs again. One day the kingdom must pass to another. And his boys are not worthy to be kings.

"What is it, father?" asks Phila, concerned over her father's long face and sighs.

"Your husband protects a small boy. As the boy grows he will turn away from so strong a protector. He will feel no gratitude. There will be many who will take advantage of any dissatisfaction the boy shows. Minor rifts will be wedged to become wide faults, maybe chasms." Derdas bows his head until his chin rests upon steepled fingers, "Elimiotis is no better. My eldest child, my daughter, could be a great king, and is denied by her gender. My two sons can turn all they touch into loss. What hope is there for Elimiotis and for the Argeadai Makedones? Bardulis and his like, Athenai and her like, surround us."

Phila reaches and touches her father's foot. They stare at each other. Slowly Phila says, "My Philippos would be a strong *basileos* for our people."

"Dispossess my line?" snorts Derdas, waving his hand in dismissal. "I could live to see a son of mine raise a worthy grandson. Or seek from your cousins, from a collateral line."

"If Philippos is *basileos,* I would govern Elimiotis," states Phila serenely.

The old man is silent, mulling over her words. Then he glances up at the sun, "Getting late, time I got back. Tonight there is a *symposion.* We men will talk of this, drink, talk of that, drink, talk some more, drink some more. All very weighty stuff, about sheep and goats, young boys, some women, Bardulis, my governance of Perrhaibis, Athenai, wine, olives, cheeses. You know, all that weighty stuff that matters to my companions. Your brothers will be there, your husband, some of his companions."

He stands, reaches down to give his daughter a hand. She reaches up, comes to her feet, and embraces her father. She says to him softly, "You will live many more years. Grandsons will be born and raised to do you honor. Philippos will retain the affection of young Amuntas. Together, you and Philippos will defeat Bardulis. Amuntas will come of age in a secure kingdom. Whatever you and my husband command will please me."

Derdas smiles, tousles her hair, "I thought that's why Philippos is here. He wants to talk me into another war with Bardulis." He tugs once more on her hair, "I will think about what you said. If I die before a grandson is born, perhaps Philippos should become *basileos.*" He takes her arm, "I have a long night ahead of me. Your brothers will be drunk and on the floor tonight before Philippos talks to me about Bardulis."

"At least a woman avoids the aching head and sour stomach that comes the morning after one of your *symposions,*" she laughs. She touches her head against his shoulder briefly, allowing him to feel the love she bears him.

γ

Each city and town sends its contingent to the royal army. Mostly young men used to the soft drill of their local militias. Some have no training, being substitutes sent in place of wealthier townsmen. The rural districts, too, send men, raw to discipline even if used to the rigors of their labor.

Through the hot dusty days of summer they toil. Enduring blisters, muscle cramps, chafing, fatigue, and, hardest, the harsh orders of the experienced officers. Quick march, halt, dress ranks, slow step, up arms, thrust, push. Up arms, thrust, push. Up arms, thrust, push. Again. And again.

The weak are lost to sickness, those who can toughen remain. Hands harden. Awkward steps become certain. Slowly joined ragged formations become rapid, integrated evolutions. Small unit drill is succeeded by drill with ever-larger numbers. Mock combat becomes fiercer as both cohesions and rivalries build.

And still they drill and take long marches as the rains begin, and the nights grow cooler. Days are shorter. The men are released to their homes to help gather the harvest. When the granaries are full, and the new year begins, the regent will call them forth.

All the while Philippos engages in diplomacy. Envoys to Athenai arrange the return of their citizens who are now his guest-prisoners. Seeking peace with a proud city takes time. Envoys to King Berisades of the Western Odrusai seek the head of the Pretender Pausanias. Envoys to King Bardulis of the Dardanoi offer assurances and prepare for the wedding with the Princess Audata. Envoys to Olunthos, capital of the Khalkidike *Koinon*, identify common interests in the face of Athenian ambitions and suggest the expulsion of the half-brothers, Aridaios and Menelaos. Envoys to the Molossi kingdom in Epeiros lay the groundwork for his suit of the Princess Myrtale. Envoys go south to Larissa in Thessalos and Thebai in Boiotia. Envoys and agents coming, envoys and agents going, envoys received from other states. Talking, bargaining, spinning threads connecting one possibility to another. All the words having the same purpose as the gathering army, the security of the Makedones.

Nor is that all. The regent must have more money, not only now but also in the future—larger sums than ever before. The expanded army requires arms, supplies of all kinds from ground oats, wheat, barley, and rye to mules and horses to lead for sling bullets to goose feathers for arrow fletching and horsehair for helmet crests. Diplomacy is as demanding in coins—expenses for travel, for feasting and entertainments, for gifts and tokens, for bribery and the purchase of information. The kingdom itself must run, so harbors can be dredged, so roads can be resurfaced, so rivers can be bridged. Also, so that those in need can have recourse to the king's largesse and so notables are rewarded for their allegiance and services.

What is there to pay for all this outflow of money? Traditionally, through the king, the kingdom owns the forests, the sea-lanes and river routes, and the mineral wealth of the lands. In addition, the king, the queen, the queen mother, and the prince-regent all have their personal estates. For Philippos, this demand for money means the mines must be worked more efficiently, the tree harvest must gain top price, the minting of coin must return a value, the harbor dues must be scrupulous. Still he must secure loans from his wealthier magnates, the merchants in Larissa, Olunthos, Amphipolis, Methone and other cities. He mortgages the kingdom's future.

For all the frantic activity, there is elation felt by Philippos. His elation communicates to all around him and from them into the widening circle of the populace. There is planning and purpose, there are visible improvements in infrastructure and military strength, there is a transformation among the people, a coming together, that is turning defeat and fear into willingness and confidence. Before all else there is reverence—recognition that while the gods required the sacrifice of King Perdikkas and thousands more, now they honor what the Makedones achieve in the face of that loss.

Soon it will be dawn. Philippos stands in the courtyard of the temple, that reverence strong within him. King Amuntas, the little boy, is with him. Together they will conduct the rituals and sacrifice of the Argeadai rite that start each day for a Makedon king.

Noticing that Amuntas is shivering, Philippos asks, "Are you cold?"

"Yes, Uncle," the boy smiles, "But soon we'll light the fire."

"You will light the fire, Amuntas. You are the priest here."

Goat hooves clicking on the stone floor of the yard interrupts them. Pikoros leads the animal to the altar.

Philippos takes its halter and brings the goat round so it stands by their side. A young and docile animal, carefully chosen. Philippos gently pulls the razor sharp knife from the sheath on his belt. Prompting the four-year old, the two begin reciting the prayers. Words as said generations earlier. With the little boy's hand in his, both their fingers holding the knife, Philippos cuts the taut neck of the goat quickly, turning the animal in the same motion so the blood sprays away from them.

For another quarter hour the ceremony continues. Full dawn is here. Amuntas followed every step, cheerfully taking direction from his uncle. The boy likes the importance of this ritual, likes being the center of his uncle's attention.

As they walk back to the palace, the boy's fingers in the regent's hand, Philippos says, "You did very well today, Amuntas. You're growing up fast. The gods are pleased with you. Today will be a bright sunny day because you did so well."

Amuntas chuckles with delight, "Then I can play outside today."

Philippos laughs, "Yes you can, and so can other boys and girls of the kingdom." Then more soberly he adds, "You know I leave this afternoon. Tomorrow you must usher in the sun with the help of Agathokles and Agerrhos."

The boy makes a sour face and his uncle laughs again, "Treat them well, nephew, for the gods are watching. You must please Father Zeus, so that our clan and our people prosper."

"You go to marry the barbarian," says the boy.

"Yes, the Princess Audata."

Suddenly concerned the child asks, "What about Auntie Phila?"

"Auntie Phila will be all right. She remains my honored wife, but she goes to live in Elimiotis. Her father needs her. From time to time, I will join her there."

"Mother will be sad when Auntie goes away," says Amuntas.

"Yes." Philippos considers the boy, "What would you think if your mother married again, Amuntas?"

"Would I still be king?"

"You are acclaimed by the citizens of the army. Only they can choose another to be king."

"Would it make mother happy to marry again?"

"I think so, Amuntas. In time. There is no hurry. In time, it would be best if she married again. You and I will find her a good man to be her husband."

The boy pulls on his uncle's hand, "Was father a good man?"

"He was the best of men," answers Philippos truthfully. Both find the answer satisfying.

δ

There are many tribes among the Illuroi and their subject peoples. Those known to Philippos include the Dessaretoi, Eordi, Bylliones, Parthini, and Taulanti in the lands north of Epeiros. The folded mountains protect the coastal Taulanti from the Dardanoi. The Parthini and Bylliones generally are in alliance with either the Taulanti or one of the Epeiriote tribes south of them. The Dessaretoi occupy the area west of Lake Lukhnites and are subject to the Dardanoi. In turn, the Eordi are their clients, being a remnant of the people conquered by the Makedones in ancient times.

Northwest of the Dessaretoi are the Atintanes, a large tribe. They are partners of the Dardanoi, choosing to share in Bardulis' success rather than oppose him. Definitely subject to the Dardanoi are the Enkhelioi and Penestai to the south of their kingdom and the Khelidones, Labiates, and Grabaoi to the west. In the east, the small tribe of the Argestai is also subject, while further east the Agrianes and Maidoi tribes maintain a tenuous independence, so long as they, like the Makedones, provide tribute to Bardulis. Beyond the Dardanoi to the north is the powerful Autariatai confederation. Relations between the Dardanoi and the Autariatai are tense. Above the Autariatai are tribes with whom Philippos is unfamiliar, for Illuroi lands extend far north.

Another tribe of which Philippos has heard and which restricts Dardanoi expansion to the northwest, are the Ardiaoi on the Adriatic coast, north of the Taulanti and near a great lake, Lake Skutari. They may be the same people as the Abri, or the Abri may be their subjects. Other tribes dominated by the Ardiaoi, or perhaps are subtribes of the Ardiaoi, are the Dassarenes and the Seleiitani.

Illuroi are the inveterate enemies of the Hellenes. Fortunately, they are so divided into warring tribes, clans, and septs that in ancient times they rarely posed a threat to the Hellenes. Indeed, the Makedones and Epeiriotes, especially the Molossi, expanded at the expense of the Illuroi. The Makedones fragmented and expelled the Eordi, when the Argeadai Makedones crossed Mount Bermion and established their own canton in the highlands.

In the last several generations, though, the situation has changed. Instead of isolated tribes, the Illuroi adhere into ever larger confederations. Their trade, particularly with the west, has given them wealth and weapons which allow them to challenge the Hellenes. At times, western Hellenes in the Greater Hellas of Sicily and Italia have assisted the Illuroi to make war against the Hellenic city-states and kingdoms of the homeland. Dionysios of Syrakuse provided five hundred sets of armor and two thousand mercenaries to the Illuroi of the Adriatic coast some twenty years earlier. With that aid the Illuroi destroyed a Molossi army of fifteen thousand men.

Today it is Bardulis and the Dardanoi who dominate the southern lands of the Illuroi. He extends his reach into Epeiros and the Makedon highland kingdoms, even to the Argeadai Makedones, the lowlanders. The old man has come a long way from his common origins as a charcoal maker in the forests of his fatherland. His prowess as a warlord, coupled with his generosity in rewarding his warriors, enabled him to enlarge his rule from a few narrow river valleys to a wide region. As important are the many marriage alliances he has effected, for himself and his children, so that all the neighboring tribes are linked to him. The children from his several wives number more than twenty.

The sons of Bardulis known by report to Philippos are Agirros, Skerdis, Annaios, Kleitos, Mallias, and Grabos. Philippos has met Agirros but none of the others. Two nephews are also prominent, Epidios, whom Philippos met with Agirros, and Dasios. There are many other important men in the confederation, chiefs of various subtribes, renowned warriors, renegade Hellenes like the treasurer, Epikados, and priests, like Ziraios. Of chiefs, Philippos knows of Apludos, Seio, Pleuratos, and Beuzas. The champion of Bardulis' army—known throughout the north—is Bato. Other well-known warriors are Panios, Pravaios, and Karrios.

How many of these men Philippos will meet at the wedding, he is unsure. Certainly every scrap of knowledge he can gather about the Dardanoi and the wider Illuric *ethnos* will help him. As he rides north, he rehearses with his companions their roles. They are to be more than polite, they should enthusiastically participate in all the feasting and drinking. Join the dances. Raise voices in singing. Wrestle, run, and race in the games. Make the Illuroi love you, is Philippos' command. And note everything.

Count the warriors. Number their horses. Find out the sources of their grains, their wines and beers, their pigs and goats, their wives and slaves, their armor and weapons, their gold and silver. Find out everything you can—not awkwardly, inquisitively, but as a natural outcome of embracing your hosts for their generosity, for the wonder of their strength and wealth, for beauty of their women and the extent of the slaves.

Learn who attends the wedding and who does not. Learn on what terms the Dardanoi exist with their neighbors, and with their neighbor's neighbor. Learn who has a high reputation among them, and who a low, and why for either. How do they recruit their army, how is it trained, how do they fight? Who do they fear? Hatred of the Kelts is known, but who does not hate a Kelt. Do the Kelts press on them or their neighbors? And what are their feelings about the Paiaones, the Triballi, the Thraikiote tribes? Learn everything.

Philippos says nothing to his immediate companions and his larger entourage about his plans for King Agis and the Paiaones. Among those traveling with Philippos, only Pikoros, Alkimakhos, and Hippasos know that a winter campaign is coming. Still, every man in the long train is well-armed and well-provisioned. Twenty horsemen, more than two hundred foot, and a leavening of some sixty non-combatants and women form the entourage, along with forty or more carters, servants, and slaves. A well-protected marriage party, slow moving with all its carts, and with Queen Eurudike, who decided to come after all.

Philippos allotted enough time to reach the distant Dardanoi capital. Time enough, in fact, to visit King Parmenion, for their route takes them first to the Pelagonoi before entering the realm of Bardulis. Parmenion and his counselors can tell him far more about the Dardanoi than is known among the lowland Makedones. The Pelagonoi and Deuriopes live tucked between Illuroi and Paiaones. Their survival depends on their knowledge of their foes.

*   *   *

So on the tenth day out from Pella, Philippos leads his cavalcade into the small city of Bruanion on the River Erigon. The town is old, but under Parmenion it has been refounded, its walls expanded and dressed in stone. Though not formidable by the standards of the south, the town is becoming a city of the southern pattern. Ordered streets, a large market surrounded by new buildings in stone—two temples, a porticoed structure fronting offices and store rooms, a rebuilt fountain—and a strengthened citadel.

Having sent word ahead, Philippos is not surprised to see Parmenion, Leonidas, Asandros, and other companions of the *basileos* waiting on the steps of the stoa. The delight evident on Parmenion's face does much to dispel the disquiet this journey gives Philippos.

After suitable greetings and a ritual refreshment, the main party of travelers are guided to an encampment. Most of Parmenion's counselors disperse. Hippasos stays with the Makedon main body as camp marshal. Parmenion invites Philippos to his house on the road leading to the citadel. Alkimakhos and Pikoros accompany Philippos, as Leonidas and Asandros walk with Parmenion.

Soon the six men reach the ruler's home, a dwelling unexpectedly modest. A manservant greets them at the door, and is quickly sent scurrying at Parmenion's bidding to bring out his son. "You will see, Philippos, what a strong boy he is," exclaims the proud father.

Soon the king's wife comes bearing the infant. Parmenion takes the baby gently from his wife, then holds him up for all the men to admire. "You see, teeth already. You can count all four if you are careful to lean his head back and avoid his bite." Bald and crying, but with teeth, the infant Philotas is unsure he wants all this attention.

Laughing, Philippos reaches out and Parmenion slips the baby into the prince's arms. Immediately the crying becomes a screech of highpitched anguish.

An indulgent uncle, Asandros, rescues Philippos. He soothes the baby by offering a fingers for chewing. Wincing from the strong bite, Asandros says, "We must teach him to be gentler with family and fiercer to our enemies."

"May I?" asks Pikoros, who offers his arms to the baby boy. Surprisingly the boy responds to the wide smile of Pikoros, and grins in return, then lurches from his uncle's arms into Pikoros' outstretched hands. Soon Pikoros is crooning some soft barbarian melody that is punctuated on the high note by a gentle tap on the baby's nose. With each tap, the tiny Philotas chuckles.

Soon enough, the arm holding the baby's bottom becomes damp, causing son and mother to withdraw from the men. Then the six men settle in the *andron*—the room in the house where guests are entertained by the household head. The manservant brings in watered wine, fruit and a fried sweet nutty biscuit peculiar to the Pelagonoi. For a time discussion is general as they catch up with one another while sharing the food. Parmenion interrupts the genial flow with a pointed question for Philippos, "What will you owe your grandfather-in-law for the privilege of marrying Lady Audata?"

"King Bardulis demands the cooperation of the Makedones in his endeavors as he chooses. We pay annual tribute, as does Elimiotis. He has a free hand with Lunkestis. When he wants, I provide horsemen and footmen for his army." Philippos is smiling, "And in honor of the old man, I try to get him a great-grandson on Audata, who, in due course, will succeed to his father's honors among the Makedones."

Alkimakhos growls, "Will he want the child raised in barbarian ways? Are the Makedones to be come Illuric instead of Hellenic?"

"Little to fear there, my friend," says Philippos. "We Makedones, like our

Molossi cousins and the our companions here, the Pelagones, are the true Hellenes. We are as like the heroes of Homeros as you will find in the Hellas. We are not like southerners, mixing our blood with the aboriginal Pelasgiotes. In fact, I sometimes wonder if you are not Aias, son of Telamon, or, perhaps, Akhilles, son of Peleos, come to life again."

The men laugh. Parmenion holds up a hand, "In truth, we Pelagones are Hellenes. The question might well be, though, who any longer is a true Pelagone. We marry the Deuriopes. Ancient Brygi, Geneatai, and Dostones are part of our population. No doubt some Almope blood still runs in the veins of some of us. Though I know that the core of my people is of the Hellenic *ethnos*, I must admit we are Hellenes because we choose to be Hellenes. Our religion, our speech, our way of living, our education is Hellenic, of the older, true tribal Hellenic. Today we are the furthermost reach of the Hellenes in the European lands, abutting the vast expanse of barbarians. I tell you, it was not always so for we are part of the original homeland of all Hellenes, not some Kretan fool living on a sun-drenched isle or some Attikan sharpie squatting before his wares in great Athenai, counting his *obeloi.*"

Asandros breaks in excitedly, "The people of Boiotia, of Attika, of the Argolis, even of Lakonia will say nay. They will say you Pelagones, you Makedones, you Epeiriotes are not Hellenes, for Hellenes are city folk. They forget the kings that led their ancestors south. We northerners, and I include the Thessaliotes, cherish our origins and our distinctions. We must, for we are surrounded by barbaric tribes."

More realistically, Philippos asks, "Yet do we not all want to emulate the south? I see Bruanion becoming a city of stone that any southerner would recognize even if he scorns its inhabitants as barbarous."

"So what is a Hellene?" asks Pikoros, the non-Hellene among the six. "Now I speak as a Makedone. I serve a Makedon prince. My wife and I live as Makedones in the city of Pella. Our children are raised as Makedones. Though my bloodline is not Hellenic, though I have not forgotten my youth, I could no longer live as I did then. I can only live as a Makedone."

Philippos reaches across and grasps his friend's hand, "Have we not adopted you as you have adopted us? When my forefather wandered north in exile from ancient Argos, he found his fortune in the service of a Makedon chief. The clear favor of Zeus caused his adoption by the Argeadai clan. Only the gods know what fortune will play out among the descendants of Pikoros and Petalouda."

"Once I was an Atintane. My family was betrayed because we were of the faction that detested Bardulis and the Dardanoi. I was sold south. You redeemed me, Prince Philippos. And when the time comes, my shield will protect you as our pikes cut into Dardanoi flesh." Pikoros' tone is gentle, as when he spoke to the babe, but not his eyes or the set of his lips.

"Your companion cuts to the quick of the matter," comments Parmenion. "You tell us what Bardulis wants. What do you want of Bardulis?"

"Six months, perhaps seven," answers Philippos. He grins, dispelling the somber turn of the conversation. "First, though, I will give my attention to the Paiaones."

"Your timing will be good, now that King Agis is dead," says Leandros.

"Dead? Truly?" asks Philippos.

"You haven't heard? Of course, you've been journeying." Parmenion nods, "When was it, Leandros? Six days back? We had word two days ago."

Alkimakhos, Philippos, and Pikoros grin at each other. How much easier will be their raid now. Quickly Philippos is calculating, perhaps he can reduce the force he plans to use. Why show Bardulis more than necessary? Enough to overwhelm the Paiaones but not so much to cause the old man to mobilize.

"Was he murdered?" asks Philippos expectantly.

"No, he died peacefully enough. Some coughing illness," provides Leandros.

Disappointed, Philippos asks, "So there will be no confusion over the succession?"

Parmenion laughs, following the prince's line of thought. "If you hurry, you'll be all right. The Paiaones' funeral practice requires thirty days to placate the man's shade and see it into the afterlife. So Lyppeios cannot formally take the crown for almost a month." He explains, "As important, not all their cities and clans will instantly accord Lyppeios the allegiance they gave Agis. You can expect the Paiaones to be divided again. Forget the eastern Paiaones and attack the western tribe."

"Will you join us?" asks Philippos.

"Did I not give you my pledge to follow you in all regards outside my kingdom? We are ready to fight beside you." Parmenion grins hugely, "I never doubted you, Philippos. I knew you would not abide Bardulis. I admit I thought it would take you longer. After your wedding, we punish the Paiaones. In the spring, we hunt the Dardanoi."

The men raise their wine bowls in heartfelt toast. Tossing back the wine, Philippos is elated. Being who he is, he must act immediately. "Parmenion, could your man send to the encampment? I need Hippasos, Tyros, and my scribes. I have messages to send to Antipatros, Eurulokhos, and others."

Without listening for a response, Philippos turns to Alkimakhos, "We will move quickly now. I will have Hippasos turn around the heavier carts. Your footmen can march up the Erigon to be in position to strike the Paiaones. I won't need you among the Dardanoi." Turning back to Parmenion, Philippos asks, "Do you have mules we can use?"

Parmenion nods assent, then turns to Leandros and Asandros, "You see? What did I tell you?" Addressing the prince, "Philippos, you will stay the night?" Parmenion laughs.

Ruefully, Philippos chuckles as well. "Yes, the night, we will enjoy your feast. In the morning, you and I can work out the details for both the winter and spring campaigns. By tomorrow afternoon, my party will head north. We can get a few hours of marching in before we stop again."

Parmenion says, "I did not intend to attend your wedding. I feared for your humiliation. Now I would be honored if you would invite me, for I will not accept Bardulis' invitation."

"King Parmenion, please join me as witness to my wedding to the Princess Audata," answers Philippos instantly.

"I am charmed to accept," says Parmenion lightly. "I cannot help wondering, though, if Bardulis has given any thought to the fact that his great-grandson from you and Audata might as easily occupy the throne of the Dardanoi."

ε

Philippos comes up spluttering, water spraying all about him. Bardulis sits in the corner, doubled over in laughter. The priest, Ziraios, prepares to dunk the bridegroom again, but Philippos is saved by the intervention of Pikoros and Hippasos. The roomful of Dardanoi have enjoyed the joke of this ritual bath hugely. Pikoros hauls Philippos free of the massive earthenware tub and begins toweling the prince down briskly. "Great Zeus, I hope the women are gentler on Princess Audata," mutters Philippos.

Catching the words, the treasurer, Epikados, repeats them in the Illuric tongue to the crowd of men. They whoop with laughter.

Grinning through his bad teeth, Bardulis steps forward and hugs the dripping Philippos. In his thickly accented Hellenic, he says, "I'm glad you are concerned for my granddaughter. Do not worry, though, for she is a hardy girl."

Picturing a hardy granddaughter of Bardulis, Philippos restrains a grimace. He likes slim-waisted, small-breasted, well-muscled women. Undoubtedly Audata will be a big-boned, brawny woman with breasts so large they knock you over when they swing against you.

Still hugging Bardulis, Philippos is tempted to chew off the man's ear. Instead, he calls out, "Have you warned Audata about what she's getting? One of us soft-living Hellenes?" And he lifts Bardulis off his feet and swings him lightly around in a circle before letting the king down.

After hearing a translation, the girl's father, Skerdis, bellows something back. Epikados explains, "He says she has stopped mourning now and is resigned to her fate. She is consoled that you are at least a Makedone and not some truly effeminate southerner. She hopes to have children."

The men around Skerdis find this funnier than does Philippos. Perhaps some nuance is lost in translation.

Bardulis interrupts, urging all to hurry. Unlike the leisurely pace of Hellenic weddings, in which several days of ceremony are required among wealthy families, Bardulis wants this marriage made quickly. Since timing is important to Philippos as well, he is pleased to get this thing done.

From the bath, they all move to the robing room. Although Philippos is well-accustomed to being naked in the presence of other men at the gymnasium, he feels much more vulnerable as the only naked man who is the center of attention for twenty or so loud barbaric strangers, many of whom are armed with more than a dagger, most of whom have obviously not bathed in some time themselves, and all of whom are drinking a brew that combines an anise flavor with a heavy beer. Apparently the brew is a festive wedding drink. To a wine-drinking man like Philippos, the taste is foul.

The heavy white marriage robe is a relief to wear in this company. Before they join the women, Ziraios chants an incantation to one of the strange Illuric gods. To Philippos, it sounds as if the god being addressed is Tomor. If he remembers correctly what Pikoros told him, Tomor is the creator god of the Illuroi.

Feeling some relief when the chanting ends with Ziraios sprinkling herbs on the fire, Philippos is bustled out of doors for a short walk to Skerdis' house. If this were a Hellenic marriage, Philippos and Audata would ride in a chariot from her home to his. This marriage is not occurring in the close confines of a Hellenic city. These people have their own rituals.

From Skerdis' house, after a long draft of some herbal concoction, with the women dancing about the couple and keening in high accented tones, Philippos and Audata walk hand in hand, amidst the crowds of Illuroi and those Makedones who accompanied the prince north. The walk is slow, measured, to the beat of small handheld drums. Audata, whom Philippos is meeting for the first time, is veiled and wears multiple layers of light linen. Philippos is relieved to note that her figure is not heavy. Tall, she is likely of equal height with the prince. Wryly Philippos guesses that Audata is as curiously noting details of him.

The walk seems endless, especially as the combination of licorice beer and the herbal drink has filled Philippos' bladder to the full. They come to a sacred grove. The trees are tall, ancient—not secondary growth left from tilling or charcoal production, but the true forest of origin. Entering the grove, the laughing joyous throng falls silent. The great trees demand no less. From sunlight, they walk into permanent dusk. Birds do fly above, but few compared to the nearby fields. Following the path around a bend, the party comes to an opening in the woods where stands an old woman, dressed in white like the bridal pair, tending a small fire on an altar.

This priestess takes their hands and speaks an incantation, her words carrying in the silence despite the softness of her utterances. Then she gives them an apple and bids them to eat. Audata lifts her veil, and for a moment Philippos is awestruck. A calm face, with grey wide-set eyes, lips even and full below a graceful nose. Maybe the eyes are too wide for beauty, the lips too full, the nose a trifle long—yet together the features are in harmony. The high cheekbones redeem each feature, individually unusual, but together so striking. With barely a glance at Philippos, the young woman bites into the apple. Philippos bites as well, tasting the sweet juice.

With more prayers, the priestess takes the apple from them and sets it in the flames. She takes their hands and passes them through the flame. The heat is so quickly felt it gives no harm. The perfume of cooking apple rises. The priestess presents the couple to the crowd. While the grove is too solemn a place for cheering, the many witnesses call out their individual well-wishes. None calls more heartily than Bardulis.

What began as a necessity for Philippos, and become an artifice of war, and through the bathing ritual dangerously like a prank, now feels real to him. What matter if the rituals vary and the gods be named differently? He and Audata are married. Eurudike is right. The fault is not in Audata, and Philippos will treat her as his wife.

Catching the eye of his mother, standing in the crowd, he feels encouraged. To one side is Parmenion, elegant and formidable. Pikoros, Hippasos, and other companions are witnesses. Not only is this marriage taking place among a wide set of strangers, it is taking place before family and friends of his. This marriage is no less than the marriage to Phila.

With the help of the maiden girls in the gathering, Audata is freed from some of her close bound linens. The maidens eagerly seek these rectangles of cloth.

The march back to town is faster, happier, with the drumming beat quickened, and now accompanied by pipes and horns. The bridal couple must dodge and duck from the rain of nuts, raisins, and pieces of sesame cakes thrown by the partygoers. Soon all are practically running.

While the dowry has already been carefully negotiated, today the more casual gifts are given. Philippos' offerings filled a small cart and the backs of three mules for the journey here. Amidst the feasting that followed the marriage, the gifts are exchanged. To Skerdis, Philippos gives a gold armband, intricately engraved with the scene of Odussios slaying the suitors, and a long heavy sword, with ornate pommel and strong blade. Skerdis smiles for the first time without mocking his son-in-law. To the other sons and notables holding fealty to Bardulis, gifts are provided. No one goes unrecognized, from Posantion, and exiled prince of the distant Delmatai, to the treasurer, Epikados, whom Philippos thinks of as a turncoat.

One would expect Philippos to give Bardulis the richest gift, but all he offers the king is a simple iron ring. The king takes this as a sign of the Makedon subjugation, and is more delighted than if the prince provided gold. After all, he already receives an tribute of gold, silver, and kind semi-annually.

Thinking back over the lengthy bargaining for the dowry, Philippos especially enjoys giving the king only that iron ring, like those made at any smith's forge. Let Bardulis make what he will of it, Philippos knows it is a promise to himself to feed the king a lengthier and sharper iron. In the end, of course, Audata comes to Philippos with ample wealth. Bardulis would do no less. No doubt he recompensed the sour Skerdis in some way.

The feasting goes on until late, with the women participating as fully as the men. Unseemly to a Hellene, this participation suggests that all the wives, mothers, and sisters of these barbarians are courtesans, *hetairoi.* At last Bardulis sways to his feet and proposes a final toast to the couple. Then with a roar of pointed humor, those in the hall still sober enough to stand, escort the prince and his bride outside and walk them to the house given by Bardulis as a gift.

As instructed, the Makedones have stayed on their feet and form the core of the escort. Their presence keeps down most of the ribald chivvying and outright obscenity that would normally be the chorus for this walk to the bridal chamber. Still, when Philippos hoists Audata off her feet to cross the threshold, even his mother calls out a "fair mounting gives a fine child."

Alone in the room, Philippos sets Audata down on the pallet that is the bridal bed. Instead of straw, the cloth of the pallet is filled with herbs and late flowers, giving the room a glorious scent. As she makes herself comfortable, she crushes more of the herbs within the mattress, creating fresh perfume. He kneels beside her, gently removing the garland that encircles her forehead. Her eyes seem large, unknowable. Her face is serious. He feels inadequate to the task. Too much to drink, too puzzled by his response to her, too pushed by the expectations of the day.

This is no happy mating as he had with Phila. While both marriages are policy, this is with an enemy. Indeed, this is but part of his war. Fine to say that the woman bears no fault in the actions of her grandfather. Or that the kingly grandfather uses the girl. Philippos can send her off to some house in Makedonis on his return. After spring, this marriage will not matter.

She reaches across the night. Her fingers touch his cheek, stroke the soft beard along the line of his jaw, then reach up and free his head of his garland. She speaks, but he does not understand her Illuric words. She tries again, her northwestern Hellenic rough in accent and phrasing, "What we do, we must."

He recognizes that she is seeking understanding, trying to come to terms with him. She is not frightened, but she is uncertain. She wants to find a common ground, trying to make contact with him. That is what women do well. He could ignore her efforts, take her as if he were forcing his will on her. Some men would do that.

He attempts a smile, and realizes that his face must be as serious as hers, maybe even grimmer. Speaking slowly, speaking Attikan Hellenic for its commonality, he says, "We are married now. No matter how it's come about. If that is enough for you, it will be enough for me."

She watches his face, mulling over his words. She nods, "Enough. Between us, no hate."

Now it is his turn to think about her words. Slowly, clumsily, he kisses her forehead, "No hate, Princess Audata."

For the first time he sees her smile. A small smile, it graces her with beauty. She is so much younger than he expected.

She pulls on him gently. "Fair mounting," she says and pats her thigh.

He finds he has warmed to her. Soon he is much more than adequate.

ζ

Snow lay across the forests and meadows. The streams that are not dry are iced. Winter is hard upon them, harder than most years.

Careful planning have kept the horses in fodder, though they still paw through the snow cover where it is thinnest to find the grasses beneath. They can become as wild as deer in winter. Like Parmenion, Philippos is becoming known for being a meticulous general. His men, his beasts, do not want when on campaign. Fewer men and animals waste in sickness and hunger. Strange how common is the general, well-fed in town, who can plan even a campaign of less than a month, say a *dekades* or ten days, and fail to remember how quickly the want of food will debilitate an army. Many men are brave in battle, but are undisciplined when hungry. Rare are generals both cautious in planning and fierce in fighting.

Days before Philippos sent the non-combatants of the bridal party home through Eordaia. They are under Hippasos' command, with a thin escort of weaker men. Curiously, Audata was loath to part from Philippos. The few Illuric men in her train elected to join Philippos in his expedition against the Paiaones.

At the outset, the army numbered some three hundred men. Mostly Pelagones and Deuriopes led by Parmenion and Leandros. Their march followed the Erigon River until reaching the easy route to the vale of the high Axios River. At the point where they left the Erigon, they joined Alkimakhos and his *syntagma*, who had been camped there all this time. With that accretion of strength, the Makedones have parity in numbers with their confederates.

Philippos calculates that he needs no more than six hundred men in the midst of winter. At least, not as the hammer to the anvil that is Antipatros and his army. Philippos' army is further from its starting point and harder to keep fed. The proportion of horsemen to foot is higher than in Antipatros' army. Its march is longer and it must move faster. Many more than six hundred would be an encumbrance.

Antipatros is already invading the Paiaone lands from the south, using the Axios valley as a highway. The general has close on to three thousand foot and several hundred horsemen. The audacity of this attack in winter amazes the Paiaones. Antipatros will keep his attack shallow. The furthest he will march is to their chief southern town, Stoboi. There he will hold the attention of the enemy warriors, freeing Philippos to wreak havoc on the western towns. The Makedones are ignoring the eastern Paiaones, save to send coins to certain chieftains so that loyalties remain confused.

Parmenion's scouts have brought word of fleeing Paiaones. Youngsters leading women, children and ancients, while the fighting men strike back at Antipatros. The Paiaones evidence little organization. They fight in small groups—families and clan septs. Word is that the new king, Lyppeios— properly, king-in-waiting—is calling for a concentration of fighters at a major Paiaone town, Bylazora.

Starting at dawn on this day, Philippos and Parmenion led out their men. The evening before they had reached the Axios River. This morning's river crossing awoke man, horse and mule to their soul's depth as they splashed through the icy waters. After the river and re-assembly, a looping march south brings them close to Bylazora. Though not marching far, their advance had taken time for they moved over high rough ground, through paths in the forest, guided by Parmenion's scouts. Anyone they came across was secured or cut down. And they succeeded, for Bylazora lay unsuspecting before them.

The town is situated in part on a hilly spur of the same high ground the invaders used on their march. Below the hill, the town spills down to the river. The fields that feed the town parallel the river and stretch north and south between the floodline and the forest. The roads on either side of the river are thick with Paiaones. Mostly refugees from the south, all bundled and with slow moving carts and small flocks of sheep and goats. Here and there among the families are groups of warriors, presumably answering Lyppeios' summons.

A wooden palisade set on a stone and earth wall surrounds the part of the town on the high ground. Two watch towers stand above the close-set fence, one to the west, facing the river, and the other to the northwest, on the town's highest point. To the south, a ditch and winding earth mound bolster the town's defenses. An additional palisade crowns the mound until the mound merges with the hill.

From the forest edge, Philippos watches. Parmenion, Alkimakhos, and Kleitos are with him. Not far away stand Pikoros and Andros, self-appointed bodyguards for the prince. "On my signal, the horsemen go forward with a man running on either side. I want them across the open ground and to the dead ground below the palisade quickly. The footmen running with the horses are to use the battering rams and axes to hole the wall. Kleitos, are the mules for hauling the logs ready?"

"Aye, Prince. Waiting this past half-hour," says the dour officer and friend.

Parmenion says softly, "We'll have word from Leandros shortly." His second-in-command is placing the far wing of their horsemen.

"Then, Alkimakhos, return to your column. You'll need to hustle your men onto the open ground and into formation after the horsemen and *psiloi* attack. Yours is the only formed phalanx for this fight. With luck, your men will be idle, but we fall back on you if they are too much for us.

Keep them alert. If I summon you forward, you are to come quick." Philippos is emphatic.

Alkimakhos salutes casually, "You need not fear. Keep the snow in mind, though. It will slow us." With that, he and Kleitos walk back through the brush to join their commands.

Pikoros comes to Philippos' side. "Maybe two hours of good light left," he comments.

Parmenion answers gently, "We have time enough."

Smiling, Philippos turns, "Pikoros, have our horses brought up. We'll start soon."

The brush parts a few feet away, and Leandros' messenger rushes to Parmenion, "We are ready, King."

Mounting, Philippos adjusts his reins. Pikoros hands up the lance, then mounts his own animal. Parmenion is astride his horse. Philippos waves over the trumpeters. The four trumpeters gulp breath, then blow a peal of brazen sound that cleaves the winter air.

Immediately Philippos spurs his horse. Andros runs at one heel, holding a leather strap tied to the saddle. On the other side runs one of Audata's Dardanoi. The Illuric warrior has been ordered by Audata to watch over her husband. Along the length of the tree line, other trios emerge, crushing through the snowdrifts around the bushes until reaching the clearer ground on the ridge crest. Soon the horses are trotting and the accompanying foot are running.

From the town, there's little Philippos can see. Figures in the nearer watchtower are pointing. The alarm can be heard clanging in the town. As he closes in on the wall there is less he can see. Some warriors have appeared on the wall, their heads and upper shoulders showing in the palisade's crenels. Soon Philippos is in bow range. Andros and the Illuroi —Verzo is his name—are running easily, despite weapons and a brush pole each carries.

Philippos wonders for the tenth time whether Verzo is really Bardulis' or Skerdis' man, rather than Audata's. Pikoros rides slightly to Philippos' left rear, with no runners clinging by thongs to his horse. Pikoros is there to kill Verzo at the slightest sign of treachery. The irony of one Illuric warrior watching another is not lost on Philippos, but he trusts Pikoros in full.

They are at the wall. Like all the other *psiloi*, Andros and Verzo toss their brush poles on the fast-growing pile. Those among the *psiloi* who are archers or slingers are already sending their missiles to clear the warriors from atop the wall. Their success is mixed, for arrows and stones are raining on the attackers.

Soon the mules are up. Logs are rolled on top of the brush pile and quickly heaved into place. The pile grows to the base of the wooden palisade. *Psiloi* clamber up carrying the two huge logs that will serve as battering rams. Without enough space to swing the ram properly they begin battering the fence. Occasionally a man falls, brained by a stone or trans-fixed by an arrow. But the defenders are losing the exchange and fewer missiles come down. The pile is broadened into a platform and the rams are swinging true.

Behind them, coming down the ridge at a steady pace, is Alkimakhos with his *syntagma* in phalanx formation. Leaving Kleitos to direct the hol-ing of the palisade, Philippos races his horse to the right to find Leandros. The Pelagone has all in order, protecting their flank with his horsemen. Parmenion does the same on the left. Riders have also been sent around the town to strike at the river gate. This diversion will create great tumult among the refugees and perhaps confusion among the Paiaone warriors.

Cheering draws Philippos back to the center. The palisade is breached. Other sections of the fence are on fire, though again as a diversion rather than as an essential. As ordered, the log platform now is a narrow ramp. Pikoros leads horsemen up the center, while on either side swarm *psiloi*. With one last look over his shoulder to check on Alkimakhos' progress, Philippos takes his horse up the ramp.

Patting the roan gelding as they cross the breach, Philippos sees the extent of the drop they must jump. Without hesitation he touches his heels to the horse and they leap to the muddy ground. The horse buckles but does not fall and quickly recovers. Spurring forward, Philippos calls to the men around him to take the town.

Many of the nearer huts are in flames. Ahead can be heard screams, the clash of arms, and the rough shouts of the fighters. Riding down one of the many lanes, his men running alongside, they hurtle the still bodies of the fallen. Soon they are among the living Paiaones. What moments of resistance offered the Makedones are instantly overcome, as much through the panic of the fleeing women and children as by the force of their arms. No one is spared in a running fight.

Reaching the town center, with its more substantial buildings, Philippos finds the Paiaones cohering. Not yet an organized force, they have begun to realize their weight in numbers. Soon their shields will form a new wall. That must not happen, even though the very rapidity of the attack has thinned the Makedones and Pelagones. Many are hunting down survivors in the houses leading back to the breach. The horsemen have outrun all but the fleetest and determined *psiloi*. Yet there can be no stopping or the Paiaones will become as formidable as their attackers.

Drawing his sword with his right hand and holding his lance in his left, directing his mount with the pressure of his legs and heels, Philippos charges the Paiaones. He is not conscious of his own screaming command, but all about him Makedon, Pelagonid and Deuriope riders respond. The prince's lance head disappears into the chest of a brawny Paiaone. The sword blade slashes down on the shield arm of another warrior. Laying about him in a fury of violence, Philippos cuts deep into the mass of

Paiaones. Cuts through the warriors and is amidst the women and kids. His horse's hooves crush a girl's foot as he wheels to charge back into the warriors. All around him his other riders are doing the same.

Philippos sees Pikoros on foot wielding his sword in two hands as their enemies try to put him down from all sides. Swearing an oath to Herakles, Philippos rides through the struggling fighters. His own horse slides, its footing lost. The horse is down heavily, but Philippos jumps clear. Back to back with Pikoros, they fight the enraged Paiaones. The echo of a long ago day in Thebai plays in Philippos' mind, only this is in earnest. Within seconds the pressure eases as more Makedones reach the main fight.

Verzo reaches Philippos' side, leading someone else's horse. With a heave, Philippos is mounted. Whatever resistance the Paiaones might have made in the town's commons is gone. Everywhere they are fleeing and the pursuers offer no mercy.

Discovering Andros by him, Philippos says, "Find a mount quickly. Ride back to Alkimakhos. Tell him the town is cleared and he can march his men around to the main gate."

His horse bucks a moment, and Philippos quiets the nervous animal. The horse is mired up to its fetlocks in mud, snowmelt, blood and other gore. Its fear or disgust is understandable. Looking about, Philippos sees that the killing edge of the fight has swept on. Those Paiaone survivors in the commons are being gathered.

Pikoros leads up two prisoners, wealthy-looking Paiaones. One appears far gone in shock. The other can still reason. "Look what I found hiding in the temple."

Philippos asks, "Who are they?"

"The loony one is Lyppeios' younger brother. This one's the *arkhon*," Pikoros prods the man with a spear butt.

"Where's Lyppcios?" asks Philippos of the town magistrate.

"He isn't here. He went east to get help from our people in the Pontios valley."

Philippos nods, considering. Antipatros will have the valley of the Pontios River shut off from the Axios by now. The eastern Paiaones are not likely to intervene. By the time they assemble adequate forces, it will be too late for the western Paiaones. "Fortunate for him. Who commands here?"

The *arkhon* says, "Does it matter? He lays over there." Pointing toward a thick clot of bodies near the main road to the town center.

"Who was he to Lyppeios?" insists Philippos.

"Brother-in-law. Pitakos was his name. Not much of a general," says the *arkhon* with mild contempt.

"And you? What is your name?"

"Mezekias."

"Well, Mezekias, it's time to stop the killing and begin numbering the living. I'm going to want your help," says Philippos.

A look of incredulity greets Philippos' words. Before Mezekias can say anything impolitic, the other Paiaone screams at Philippos, "You butchering whoreson! You bloody-handed fiend! The gods saw all this, they saw what you've done. All of you. Never will it be forgiven."

Mildly Philippos considers the young prince. Pikoros motions, asking silently if he can cut the young man's throat. Philippos denies Pikoros with a shake of his head. "Mezekias, get him under control before my men kill him."

The *arkhon* grabs the Paiaone prince roughly, slapping him harshly back and forth across the face. Blood sprays from broken lips. For a moment it's as if the magistrate is taking his anger out on the youth. Until the princeling crumples sobbing into the *arkhon*'s arms, who absently smooths the young man's hair. Looking up at the mounted Makedon prince, Mezekias asks in a subdued voice, "What else will you have me do?"

* * *

For a half-month Philippos leads his army from town to village to town among the western Paiaones. Nowhere else is there slaughter as at Bylazora. The tale of Bylazora traveled too widely for others to offer resistance. Those few who do, die.

Instead Philippos exacts tribute. The prince-regent is careful to make the tribute no more than the value of what the Paiaones themselves had taken as loot and ransom from the Makedones. Everywhere he goes, he states the same message. This is restitution for the marauding done by Paiaones. Friendship with the Makedones is possible. The two peoples may live side by side in harmony. If any Paiaone attempts vengeance for this restitution, then all Paiaones will suffer unless the Paiaones themselves punish the transgressor.

Finally, even Lyppeios comes in and swears peace with the Makedones. Twenty some days and it is done. The Paiaones must suffer a Makedon garrison at Stoboi, north of the iron gates—the mountain passage of the Axios before the river enters Makedonis. The iron gates separate Paiaones and Makedonis. Some hostages travel south with the Makedones to take up residence in Pella.

The peace is fragile. Perhaps no more than a truce, but for now the Paiaones are cowed.

DEFEAT OF PAIAONES

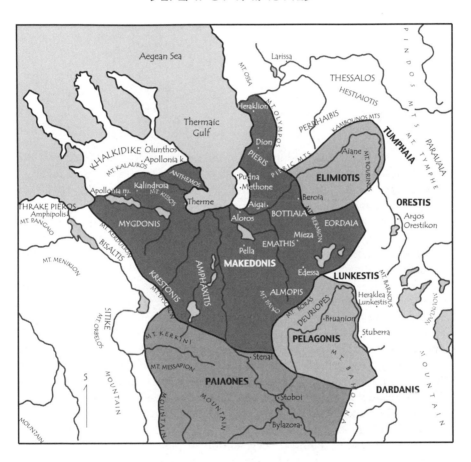

CHAPTER FIFTEEN

Bardulis

358 B.C.

α

T he sharp slap of the flat of his hand on the arm of his chair calls the room full of men to attention. "Stop talking," Bardulis commands loudly. "I will tell you when you may talk." He glares at them all, his generals, chieftains, priests, and warriors. There is no doubting the authority of the stout old man. "Now, Epikados, read to me again the response I receive from Prince Philippos."

The treasurer glances down at the parchment, "He starts with all the titles and compliments. States that Princess Audata is pregnant. Assures you of his good intentions. Like his last letter, he states that the attack on the Paiaones was just retribution. Agrees with your demand that he send you men in the spring. Asks how they will be used, what he should prepare them for, what supplies will be needed. Asks if this loan of men will discount the tribute owed. Apologizes for not being able to confer with you himself, but says he will send a trusted general. Offers you felicitations. All said very politely, even a little flowery. Some nice turns of phrase." Epikados looks up into the seething eyes of the Dardanoi king, "What part do you want repeated word for word?"

"First, exactly what does it say about the men?"

Epikados reads, "In accordance with your request, I will direct that the three thousand foot you seek will be in place for spring. In fact, if I may demonstrate my zeal, I pledge you four thousand men or more. They will be assembled in Eordaia by the tenth day of *Artemisios*. If you will let me know how you intend to use the men, I can better prepare them for the expedition. Do you wish them fully armed? In the Makedon or Iluric manner? For how long will they be in your keeping? What supplies will you want from me for their upkeep?" Epikados stops reading and asks Bardulis, "Is that what you wanted to hear?"

"Why does he offer me four thousand? Is he boasting? Does he have so many men that an extra thousand matters little to him?" muses Bardulis. He looks at Epikados, "Find his excuse for not meeting with me."

BARDULIS (358 B.C.)

"Regretfully, I am unable to join you at Skupai by the new moon of *Xantikos.* The annual festival of Athena, who as you know is a protectress of Argos, home of my forefathers and is revered by my family, occurs then. The rituals of my family, the Temenidai, must be held, as must the Argeadai rituals of the clan of which my family is chief. You will understand the demands of the gods being a king."

"I can send to you a trusted general. I recommend to you Antipatros, son of Iolaos, who has my confidence. If Antipatros does not suit you, then may I suggest Periandros, son of Marsuas, or Athanaios, son of Oloros, both of whom are Makedones of noted reputation, clan heads, and close companions of myself."

Skerdis interrupts Epikados, "A skein of lies and half-truths. Do not trust this man, father. Call him to his obligations to you."

Bardulis considers his son, a man in his fifties, but does not answer or rebuke the interruption. Turning back to Epikados, he says, "Enough. This princeling is a weasel." He looks about him, at the many men, almost as if counting them. "Skerdis and Agirros stay with me. You, Epikados. Send for Ziraios, I want his advice. Apludos, Seio, Epidios stay, as well. The rest of you, get out. Come back for the eating and drinking tonight."

With a rumble of disappointment and speculation the many make for the doorway. One, the hulking warrior Bato, is last, trying to linger, sulking at his exclusion. Seeing him, Bardulis hides a grin, waits until Bato is through the door before calling, "Has anyone seen my faithful hound, Bato? A king is not without his bodyguard."

Bato is back instantly, importantly, acting as if he had merely been ushering the others out. He takes his place behind the king's sword arm.

This comedy done, Bardulis gestures the chosen few to attend him. "I repeat, this Prince Philippos is a weasel. We will be chastising the Makedones again, mark my words." His tone is grim. "We do have other concerns. Apludos, how goes our preparations for attacking the Taulanti?"

The chieftain hunches forward, "The Parthini will come over to us. We will be able to march through their lands unhindered. We should leave a strong force with them to ensure their cooperation in the event we suffer a reverse. Their betrayal of the Taulanti will be a surprise. My agents have caused the Taulanti to be suspicious of the Bylliones, not the Parthini. When we march in late spring, the Taulanti will be isolated. Their quarrel with the Epeiriotes continues."

Skerdis comments skeptically, "The Taulanti are not so trusting. They know we are coming."

"They think we intend to raid," says Agirros, as always disagreeing with his brother.

"They will not be expecting the Makedones," comments their cousin, the general Epidios.

"Which brings us back to Philippos," states Bardulis. "Philippos used

347

nearly as many men in his campaign against the Paiaones as he promises to bring to me. His losses in defeating the Paiaones were light. He is a formidable young man. As a whole, his kingdom can field perhaps twice that number, so he has made good the army his brother led to destruction. And that has been done a good three years earlier than I expected."

"They're Makedones, though. What real good are they?" sneers Skerdis.

"Why don't you ask the Paiaones?" answers Agirros.

Bardulis holds up his hand which stills his sons, "We know the tactics Philippos employs. He emulates Iphikrates by making his phalanx light so that it moves quickly compared to hoplites. Interesting, especially since he arms them with long spears. To be effective requires months of training."

Epidios adds, "Their speed can confound an uninformed opponent, as happened in Pelagonis. The Taulanti won't be expecting the novelty of their attack."

Skerdis grunts, "His casualties there were heavy despite the surprise. And that was against men fighting half-heartedly since Menelaos had already left the field."

Seio speaks for the first time, "You can be sure that the men he sends you won't be his best."

"If I insist that he leads them and not this Antipatros or Periandros, he will have his best with him," assures Bardulis. "The real question is can we trust him not to bolt in the spring? Will I have to put my army in motion against him instead of the Taulanti?"

Before any can answer, Ziraios enters the hall, his necklaces of finger bones, stones, and bronze figurines announcing him with each step he walks. Bardulis waves the priest over, "We are debating the reliance we can place on Philippos the Makedone."

"None, in my opinion," says Ziraios. "You wasted a granddaughter on that one. Better if we had marched to Pella after we killed Perdikkas."

Bardulis chuckles, "Ziraios, Ziraios, I want your intervention with the fates. Look to the future, don't dwell on the unchanging past."

"Wrong time of the month," says Ziraios slyly.

"What are you, a woman or a seer? Do you need some trinkets to look inside yourself? Should we have incense, a boiling cauldron, throbbing drums? Be what you claim you are and tell us what you see. Just what you see, not what you think. Thinking I can do for myself." Bardulis ends his tirade.

Now Ziraios is amused, for this chafing of each other has a long history between the two men. "At least show me the courtesy of being quiet."

Skerdis drags a chair over to the priest. Bato arranges a bearskin on the chair. Ziraios sits and begins a low, deep humming. All the others are silent. The humming goes on and on, the pitch rising and falling, rising and falling. Seio glances at Epikados and raises an eyebrow. The Hellene shakes his head.

In time the humming softens and stills. The priest sits slack limbed, mouth agape, almost as if asleep, save that the eyes are open, twitching slightly, with only the whites showing. Bardulis leans forward, "Oh, great Tadenos, we ask that you speak through your servant, Ziraios. However unworthy is your servant, however unworthy are we, we beseech you to hear our earnest plea. You know already the depths of our thoughts, the sadnesses, worries, and questions. We are open to you, please reveal what we need to know of the future."

Bardulis pauses, licks his lips, seems to be waiting on some sign. A palsy begins in Ziraios' lower limbs. The shaking moves up his frame, until his head lolls back and forth. Froth appears at his mouth. A voice speaks through Ziraios' lips, not the gravelly tones of the priest but a pleasant baritone voice, a young man's voice. "Ask, Dardanai. You are in my keeping."

"A prince of the Makedones, Philippos, promises to honor his agreement with us. We doubt his word. We ask, Tadenos, that you lift the veil of the future and say whether Philippos, son of Amuntas, is a man of his word and will fulfill his promise to us."

"What was given in iron, will be kept in iron. Thousands are numbered, led by a prince, who honors Herakles. Not yours to command, yet eager to embrace you."

Bardulis sits silent, head on his knuckles. What do the words mean? Ziraios is now in ragged sleep, the god has departed. Epidios clears his throat and ventures softly, questioningly, "Embrace you?"

The words tumble in Bardulis' mind—"not yours to command", "kept with iron." He thinks about the iron ring given to him by Philippos at the wedding.

"Well, we know he's coming then. With the numbers you summoned," says Apludos.

"Aye," agrees Bardulis warily. "Epikados, I want a letter taken to him. Hold him to his promises. He is to lead his men. If he comes in the spring and joins the campaign against the Taulanti, well and good. If he attempts anything else, we will punish him and his people. My army will be assembled in any event."

β

"You have your treaty with Athenai," observes the old man, Antiokhos. "You paid for it with Amphipolis."

The others in the room stir at the implied criticism. Though Philippos is only the regent by virtue of being uncle to the king, no one is unclear about who rules. Yet Antiokhos and many older men here have decided that it is time to put Philippos in his place. He is not the acclaimed king, he is only the first among equals. Before launching the Makedones on a possibly suicidal campaign against Bardulis, he needs to heed the counsel of the most experienced notables and clan heads of the realm, not just his cronies, like Antipatros.

"Amphipolis?" responds Philippos smiling. "Yes, that's one view. Yet Mantias still sailed and Argaios marched." He stretches his arms and scratches his bearded throat. "Certainly Amphipolis is bait. Remember that before Athenai accepted, I had to kill Argaios. Surely, you would not rather that Argaios, son of Saturos, be in Pella instead of King Amuntas, son of Perdikkas?"

Hastily Agerrhos speaks up, "That is not the point Antiokhos is making. All Makedon citizens joined in raising young Amuntas to his father's position. For that matter, all of us joined in creating the regency you hold. That is the point. We all acted together. Now you act alone or with a few. You do not consult with the elders of the realm. We recognize that you must act expeditiously when there is a clear emergency, as when Argaios crossed the border between Methone and Pieris. Then there was no time to confer."

He looks about to draw support from his fellows, "But when you invaded the lands of the Paiaones, or now with this scheme to beard Bardulis in his den, there is time to assure concurrence. If you had sought agreement on this treaty of yours with Athenai, then the treaty would have been ours, not just yours."

Philippos considers Agerrhos. The spindly man is like some grey crane. Nose a beak, thin lips, beady eyes—eyes that water, waver. Lines seam his face, a countenance made longer by his wispy yellow-white beard. Never a close companion of the prince's father. Always on the fence in the politics of the kingdom. So why is he coming on so strongly now?

With Agerrhos are Antiokhos, Lagos, Agathokles, Athanaios—maybe even Derdas, clutching a cloak over his shaky, weak left arm. Lined up with Philippos are Antipatros, Periandros, Amuntas Plousias. Others haven't decided, men like Kharikles and Theophilos. Each is the leader of a major clan, though Periandros now leads two clans since marrying the widow of Philippos Arkouda. And strictly speaking, Derdas of Elimiotis is a foreigner, even though he is Philippos' father-in-law and a highland Makedone.

Realization strikes Philippos. They have understood ahead of him that the kingdom and, therefore the kingship, is not the same as before. While he as regent is intent on securing the throne for his nephew, these old men see him curtailing their local power. They fear this new army and all his innovations more than they fear Bardulis. Why cannot they be as wise as King Parmenion? Well, the safety of Amuntas' patrimony comes first.

"You are right, in your way, Agerrhos. I do take it on myself to speak for the king because he is too young to speak for himself. I believe that is the responsibility I bear. And so I treat with Athenai's envoys, and even conclude a treaty with Athenai. Many years ago such a treaty would have been signed not only by the king, but also by all the senior men of the Temenidai. The archives show such treaties. King Alexandros the First, his five sons, and even his eldest grandsons sign a treaty." Philippos shakes his head sadly, "Where are the Temenidai?" Still speaking softly, the prince says, "I am the only male adult Temenidai surviving from the sons of King Alexandros the First who is not in exile."

The names of the exiles echo in everyone's mind—the half-brothers, Aridaios and Menelaos, and the cousin, Pausanias. Soberly they stare at Philippos. His life is all that guards the sacred kingship, that of the Temenidai, which secures on behalf of the Makedones the beneficence of mighty Zeus. Until Amuntas Perdikka Makedonon reaches manhood, Philippos Amuntou Temenidai Argeadai is the living bond with Zeus, Herakles and the line of kings who are his forefathers for hundreds of years back. No one in this room would have Aridaios, Menelaos, or Pausanias take that role.

Having seized the high ground, Philippos continues, gently, with the slightest smile, "I take counsel with my companions, Agerrhos, as is the custom. I value my friends for themselves and for their opinions. For certain topics, I even listen to my mother and other senior women. I seek the most experienced, the most knowledgeable, the wisest where forest are concerned or harbors and shipyards or the raising of horses, of sheep, of cattle, of goats, of wheat, of barley, or for the mines, mints, smelting, and all to do with metals, or the building of temples, bridges, fortifications, markets, houses or for the letting of contracts and the settlement of disputes. I seek advice, facts, ideas. And then I decide. And then I act."

He looks around at the circle of men, "Agerrhos, Antiokhos, all and each one of you, I invite you to be my friend. Know that I expect my friends to challenge my ideas in counsel if their knowledge and opinions can improve my ideas, to set me straight if I misunderstand a fact, to share in the work that needs doing. When I decide, when I act, I expect my friends to act with me, to do all in their power to make that decision and action successful. Together we can achieve the security of the king and the kingdom. We can go further and assure the prosperity of our people and the well-being of the king as he reaches manhood and takes the kingdom into his own hands. By doing so we gain our own security and prosperity and honor. We can do these things together." His tone becomes sterner, "What we cannot do together is pull in a dozen different directions. What we cannot do together is be concerned solely for our own parochial interests. What we cannot do together is place our own interests above the king's."

They are nodding, Agerrhos' eyes are wider. They have not co-opted the regent, he has co-opted them. There is nothing to be done but offer this young man their friendship.

Seeing their acceptance, Philippos continues, "Of course, the king or his regent cannot make all decisions alone. Who shall be king, for example. Or whether a citizen has betrayed the king and the Makedones. Some decisions are of such momentous import that they need the confirmation of the Makedones. As regent for King Amuntas, I am ready to put the question of whether we should contest with the Dardanoi for our independence before our citizen warriors and veterans."

"All of the army is not here in Pella," points out Lagos.

"We have time. Orders will be sent assembling as many men as is prudent. In Eordaia, the local militia can hold with no more than a stiffening from the royal army." Philippos laughs easily, "I'm glad, Antiokhos, that you raised the question of the Athenian treaty." Assembling the army will give ample time for the adherents of Antipatros, Periandros, and Philippos to convince the remainder that they have the strength to throw off the coils of the Dardanoi serpent. Philippos knows the royal army desires the coming fight. Confidence beams from the twenty-three year old regent.

γ

The hillside undulates with the casual movement of thousands of men standing in rank after rank. Men in arms, pike heads high, shields on shoulders, helmets offering their dull shine. The royal army is here, nearly in full. To one side of the army stand those men of Pella who are veteran citizens not in the serving ranks. Many of these are men called by the regent to duties in the palace or in governing the kingdom.

For Philippos, on the podium below the hill, the sight of this army gives a sense of awe. Although he's worked hard for months to create this army from the remnants left of his brother's force and from the amalgamation of disparate units, levies, and town militias, this is the first time they are assembled together. Royal purpose, pay, weapons and drill are molding these men into one army.

In the forefront is his personal *syntagma* of foot companions. These, with the *agema,* the royal squadron of horsemen, are his elite.

If Philippos is awed, how much more impressed is the ranker standing on the hill. The Makedones are a phoenix, for from the destruction of Perdikkas comes an army larger, better trained, and with disciplined officers. An army made more from the cities and towns than from the clans. Defeat has tempered the Makedones in fire.

With Philippos is the boy-king. A dozen counselors, men like Antiokhos and Agerrhos, stand with them. Also a handful of older royal pages to act as bodyguards to the king. Antipatros, Periandros and other officers stand with their men. Philippos touches Amuntas' shoulder, "We are ready."

Together the little king and his uncle-regent step forward. Philippos raises an arm. The vast murmuring of the huge assembly takes time to still.

The boy is trembling next to the prince. Philippos places an arm around his nephew's shoulder. He whispers to the king, "Open the assembly, Amuntas."

In a small voice, the boy begins, "Citizens, as King of the Makedones, I declare this assembly opened." Nothing happens, so with a squeeze from his uncle's arm, the boy repeats himself, speaking louder. This time he's heard far enough for the callers to repeat his words up through the ranks.

When all have heard, Amuntas next declares, "We have before us a matter that requires your assent if it is to go forward. I ask my uncle, Prince Philippos, who is regent for my kingship, to put the question to you." With that, young Amuntas has played his role. The rest is up to Philippos.

Boldly, loudly, pitching his voice higher than normal so it will carry to as many as possible without the aid of the callers, Philippos begins, "You all know why we are here. For a generation we have paid tribute to Bardulis, King of the Dardanoi. When my brother, King Perdikkas, attempted to end our humiliation, war ensued and we suffered the loss of our king and so many of our fellows that few households did not mourn."

Pausing, Philippos turns to Amuntas, touching him lightly on the head, "Bardulis is certain that the Temenid King is too young to challenge him. He is certain that the Makedones are too cowed to face his army again. And I have not dissuaded him from that illusion. We have sent him tribute. I have married his granddaughter. Though, I tell you, she is fast becoming a Makedone as the child within her grows." This last sally provokes laughter that ripples up the hill. "Why has it been important to leave Bardulis shrouded in his beliefs of us?"

A few men call out answers. Philippos waits, hearing increasingly bellicose responses. Then he calls back, "Yes, you are why it has been necessary to deceive Bardulis. We needed time for you, all of you, to step forward. Time for all of you to harden in your resolve as the strength and skill in your arms grew. Who are you now?"

Nodding, Philippos answers his rhetorical question, "You are what you were not a year ago. You are warriors of merit and more. You are an army, fighters who battle in concert. For you have a discipline and skill no other army can match. You are the royal army of King Amuntas Makedonon. You are now truly Makedones. You are what Bardulis fears, you are a terrible vengeance on the Dardanoi."

Philippos' arms are thrown wide. The gesture embraces the whole hillside, and the men stamp their feet and pound their pike butts into the earth, their voices roaring back down the hill in relish at Philippos' depiction.

His arms wave them down into quiet again. He raises his voice, "Have I told you how tough, how hardened, are the fighters who make up the Dardanid army? Does anyone think a fight with the Dardanoi will be easy? Is it any wonder that I ask the Elimiotes and the Pelagones to join us in throwing back the Illuroi? You know your own strength, but to answer the question I will propose fairly, you must know your enemy's strength. Is their army large? Yes. Is it experienced, having campaigned and raided afar? Yes. Is it led by men who know much of war and are merciless in their killing? Yes." They are somber out on the hill. Men listening intently.

"I will promise you victory. I cannot promise you that there will be no Makedon widows. I will promise you honor. I will promise you the heartfelt thanks of our women and children for all who partake in this redemption. The gods—Zeus Dios and all his lordly kin and progeny—will recognize all that we do. Who you are to your family, to your fellows, to your king, and to the gods may well be defined by what you do in gaining that victory. What name will you bear into the future? How would you have yourself known? Think on that a moment."

Philippos waits, his eyes searching the field of men. "I put it to you, then. Shall we deny Bardulis the tribute he claims from us? Shall we fight him and his army?" Philippos has no doubt that most will choose war. What is critical is the margin of their approval, especially if those who do not approve are concentrated in particular units.

Those who approve are to remain standing, while those who disapprove are to sit down. Already men are looking about them to see who is not standing. The callers canvas the ranks.

From below, Philippos scans the hillside. Here and there he catches sight of seated men, but inevitably their comrades around them urge them to stand again. Soon it is obvious that the army is united and the war against Bardulis is hugely popular. Though he was confident of the outcome—or he would not have put it to a test—the extent of enthusiasm impresses even him. The callers have not a single dissenting man.

The men begin a chanting praise of victory. Pike shafts against shields are used to beat a rhythm. Though Philippos feels some inner alarm at this tempting of the fates, he cannot repress the elation, the wild pride he feels in this army. From ashes to a citadel of brawny strength in a year.

δ

The woodpecker hammers at the dead tree limb. Other limbs of the tree are already uncurling from buds to light green leaves. How easy is the woodpecker's work in finding larvae-rich dead wood when other limbs show live growth.

Philippos watches the bird a moment longer. If Aristoteles were here he would already declare the exact type of woodpecker, whether male or female, and how healthy it is. Philippos smiles remembering his thin-limbed friend. The latest dispatch from Athenai gives much news while still capturing the curious logic of Aristoteles' unique mind. The anti-war party in Athenai is still in ascendance. Though that means only so much in the fickle city. Still, it helps to know that Olunthos and the Khalkidike remain at odds with the Athenians.

Beside him stirs Audata, stretching her legs on the wide, thick linen square spread on the hillock's slope. Philippos feels the stir of his own manhood as she brushes her legs against him. She is not so far along with child to prevent lovemaking should they want it. Audata estimates she's at four months.

Yet there is a lassitude within Philippos. This will be the last gentle day for some time to come. Though some would say his quiet days are more active than most men's busy days. His friends and he drank until late last night. Later still was the company of a youngster, one of the royal pages attending the king's court.

Dispatches read, council of commanders held—now there is time for Audata. Her suggestion of a camp nap, spent out-of-doors, sounded good. He feels drowsy after the midday meal. So here they are, with Audata dozing off and on. Soon, he'll need to move along, to drill again with his *syntagma.*

What will he do with her after the fight that's coming? Simple if she weren't with child. Boy or girl? What if her father or grandfather is killed? And the gods willing, they will be. Pack her home? No, she is his wife. But she's no Phila, who can be trusted to hold his interests in his absence. Phila in Elimiotis makes sense. She more than counterbalances young Derdas and his little brother, Makhatas. But Audata? Audata in Dardanis? No. He glances at her affectionately. No political ambition or skill animates her. Her genius is purely domestic. Probably why old Bardulis chose her.

She rubs a foot along his leg and again he feels a response in his loins. She turns to him, opening one eye sleepily. Gently he brushes his lips over her high cheekbone. She tugs at his hip. Soon they are in a slow, languorous lovemaking that seems to keep them in their own world for a long time. When his climax comes it is surprisingly heady, and he hopes hers is the same.

They sleep. Not for all that long. Pebbles thrown lightly at Philippos jolt him awake. At the bottom of the knoll stand Pikoros and Antigonos. The jovial giant is about to toss another small stone when Pikoros stays his arm. Philippos rises, grabbing up his tunic, and strides down to his waiting men.

"You said to send for you in time for the drill," says Pikoros apologetically.

"Quite right," answers Philippos. He smiles and grips Antigonos' arm. Antigonos is chuckling, "You often do this kind of thing outdoors?"

Before Philippos can answer, Pikoros says, "The prince does this kind of thing wherever he can." Both men guffaw, and with a snort of dismissal Philippos walks past them down to the brook and steps into the cold water. Stooping, he quickly washes.

Coming back, he dons his tunic. Nodding toward the sleeping Audata, he asks, "Where are her ladies?"

"Beyond the trees," indicates Pikoros. "I'll fetch them." He jogs off.

Philippos and Antigonos follow more slowly, "So what news do you have from the highlands?"

"Antipatros says to tell you he's ready," answers Antigonos. "Under anyone else all that mud of this season would have slowed the schedule. Not with Antipatros, that man is a driver."

Philippos grunts his acknowledgment. That's why Antipatros is in command in Eordaia and not someone like Lagos. Word came two days ago from Parmenion that he is ready as well. Time to close down this encampment and get his men on the road to Edessa. Alkimakhos was sent off yesterday with his troops. From other encampments, men are in motion for the highlands. "Food and fodder all arranged?"

"Yes," says Antigonos impatiently. "You know that."

"Doesn't hurt to check again," says Philippos mildly.

"When are you going to give me something to do besides seeing to supplies and exchanging messages?"

Philippos looks at his hulking friend, "Didn't you ask me for a position of responsibility?"

Antigonos nods warily.

"I won't say fighting is the easy part. We both know that battle is hard enough, and it's harder still to direct men in battle." Philippos pauses, thinks about his words, "Getting men in place to fight, and in condition to fight, is as important as the fighting. And fewer officers do that part as well as the fighting. You have the makings of a good general, Antigonos, not just a good fighter." He gives his friend's shoulder a light shove.

"All right," says Antigonos. "All right for now. But I'll want a full phalanx, like my brother Demetrios, in time."

"Your time will come," Philippos smiles broadly. "Of that, I'm certain." For a moment he hesitates, unsure whether to say more, "I don't want to presume too much on the gods. In the end, it's in their hands. As much as men can do, we've done. We are going to defeat Bardulis. The only question is how hard and at what cost. When it's done, there will be changes. I will need you then, even more than I do now."

Antigonos now is smiling as broadly as the regent. The frustrations of all the petty details of gathering pike shafts, hay, red wine, linen strips, and innumerable other supplies are set aside. With Philippos, one is always confident that the future will be good and that you will have a hand in that future.

ε

Bardulis rubs uneasily at an old wound. What more can he do? Word came days ago that the Makedon army is marching north from Eordaia. The perfidy of Philippos enrages the old man, though by now he's used to the idea and can draw strength from his rage when he needs to. He tried to gain time—sending envoys to Philippos offering to share power, Dardanoi and Makedones each commanding the cities and peoples in their spheres. Philippos the regent will have none of it. *The arrogance of the puppy is unbelievable. He orders me to withdraw to Illuris. Lunkestis is mine; I've made it so with the point of my spear.* Bardulis grins to himself, *I've been killing Makedones, Epeiriotes, and others thrice longer than this pup's been alive.*

Then the thought catches in his mind, maybe more than three times, closer to four. A shiver passes through him. He cannot remember the number of men he has personally killed. Men taken down in battle, in ambush, in heroic individual combat, and in stealth. In truth, even men murdered. The fates made him indomitable. How else does a charcoal burner become a king?

These Makedones, he spits into the campfire, cursing his enemies with the sizzle. Their rulers call themselves Hellenes, these Temenid upstarts and some others among their magnates. Most are the same sheep and goat herders that wander the Pindos range. What difference is there between a Taulanti, Molossi, Lunkestoi, Orestoi, Makedones, and, for that matter, a Dardanoi? All the same.

The Argeadai Makedones are as pretentious as the Pelagonoi of King Parmenion, another whelp. King, as if being a chieftain over the Pelagonoi and Deuriopes compares with being King of the Dardanoi and all our confederates.

Bardulis picks up a stick and stirs the fire. The sparks climb. Watching them rise, Bardulis notices how light the eastern sky is becoming. *Well, we settle it today,* he thinks. Need to get the men up. He pulls his cloak tighter around his broad shoulders, hugging the warmth by the fire. These last years he's needed the warmth more. Too many aches and odd pains—feeling the pains and being alive is better than feeling no pain as a shade. *When you're ninety years old, if that's what I am, I deserve the warmth,* he thinks to himself. Another thought tumbles in as quickly as the first, *You didn't get to be ninety by hogging the fire.*

Slowly he stands, knees creaking. Better to be upright. He looks about him. Mostly sleeping forms on the ground, like fallen dead. Some, though, are stirring. And there are others, like Bardulis, who haven't slept this night. He coughs deeply, wonders how long it will take him to piss today. He curses the gods softly so they won't hear—why age a man's body while keeping the mind alert.

A boy is beside him—a great-grandson—and says anxiously, "Your sword and shield, sir?"

"No, not yet. Time enough for that when we form our lines. Send off for my generals. Let's get this army moving, boy."

ζ

The mists have cleared from the river bottoms. On the narrow plain above and west of a branch of the River Erigon, the two armies face each other.

The mutual taunting between the two sides is already a loud roar, but it is a quiet sound compared to the din of battle that is coming when the two armies close.

The two armies are of equivalent size, give or take a few hundred men. The Makedones have a preponderance of horsemen, thanks to the Elimiotes and the Pelagones—six hundred horsemen. Most are on the left flank but several squadrons are on the right. Parmenion is on the left and Derdas to the right.

The foot will carry the main fight. Philippos has forty *syntagmai* or slightly more than ten thousand phalangists. A few thousand more men, drawn from the baggage train, act as *psiloi*. Like the horsemen, the *psiloi* are relegated to the flanks, to tie the Makedones line to the river on the right and the forested hillside on the left.

Already the officers are quieting the men, so that orders can be heard. Philippos stares across the open ground that divides the two armies. The way seems even enough not to disorder the ranks. He decides to keep the advance in open order—about an *orgyia*, the full stretch of both arms, across—until the last twenty paces. Then he will order the ranks closed to half that space per man for the clash.

At sixteen men across and sixteen men deep in a *syntagma*, in open order they occupy a square roughly fifty paces by fifty paces. The interval between the first eight ranks and the second adds some depth. Behind the first line of twenty *syntagmai*, Philippos has placed his second twenty. He hopes this formation makes sense in this fight.

Never having fought in a battle with so many men, let alone commanded them, he feels inadequate. In giving his directions to his generals and officers, he keeps a calm, confident poise. A facade, he's never felt such fear.

Parmenion and Derdas command the flanks. Antipatros leads the front left ten *syntagmai*. Philippos has the right ten. Behind them are Periandros and Demetrios, each with ten. Good men, all of them. Yet it all feels so experimental. Having devised this formation, Philippos now doubts it and himself. Ten *syntagmai* seem too much for a man to control. On the drill field it seemed to work, but here, facing the Dardanoi, it seems too many.

The sun is high enough. We do not win by waiting. He lifts his eyes to the opposing line. A traditional hoplite phalanx, perhaps even more traditional than the Thebans, being a newer form of fighting for Illuroi. From the flags and commotion at their center, it appears that Bardulis is there on horseback, though at this distance it's hard to tell. No horse for Philippos today. Today he marches in the front rank.

Keeping his face impassive, though his mouth is dry, Philippos turns to his trumpeters. He can only nod. The blare lifts the hair on the nape of his neck. He raises his arm, then on its drop, immediately steps forward. The weight of the pike on his shoulder is familiar. He glances down the front rank. They are stepping out beautifully. And it comes like a soft garment slipping over him, how beautiful this sight, how terrible a beauty. Armed men marching, deliberately, solemnly, filled with bloody purpose.

Far to the left, Parmenion's squadrons are thundering down on the enemy horse. The fight begins there. All dust and swirling horses. Little of the action can be seen or understood from where the prince-regent marches.

Close by are the officers of this *syntagma*, calling down the ranks, keeping the men in step. Not too fast, not too slow, even measured steps —like a procession. And the thought is instantly formed, a funeral procession, vast and intensely personal to each man that marches.

Near Philippos are Pikoros, Peithon, and the Illurian Verzo. Though they are as familiar as brothers, now with helmets down, shields up, greaves on marching legs, each paces forward with private faces, their thoughts their own. Even with his visage as armored as theirs, Philippos cannot help wondering if they know how afraid he is. Afraid not for himself, but for his fellows, afraid that this whole scheme of war he has devised is not as good as the tried and true methods they face. Afraid that he is leading men to be slaughtered through his own pride in his cleverness.

They are close now. Already some arrows are reaching them, usually bouncing off helmet or shield, but occasionally pulling a man down. He raises his arm. Trumpets blare again. They halt. Lines are redressed to close order. Behind them the second line comes up to fill the intervals created by halving the spacing.

During this wait, Philippos can see that Derdas has led his horsemen forward as well. Many of the *psiloi* are running along side the horsemen. Whatever is happening on the left under Parmenion is now out of sight. The prince-regent must await what word the runners bring.

The fight led by Derdas is clear enough. The Elimiote king wisely held off until Bardulis reinforced his horsemen opposing Parmenion. With the enemy flank in front of him weakened by the shift, Derdas advanced. Philippos can see that Derdas is gaining the upper hand. Bardulis' riders are fleeing.

Already there is movement in the Dardanid lines. They are stepping back slowly, while still facing the Makedones. The foot on their flank are pulling back more rapidly. Suddenly it's obvious. The Dardanoi are forming a new line at right angle to their front line. While a part of their horsemen still hold Derdas, the foot are avoiding being lapped.

Time to attack. Philippos calls to his trumpeters, "Play the advance. We must attack now." The notes blare and lift into a distinctive trill. Philippos pulls his helmet down to enclose his face. Across the first five ranks pikes come down level. They advance to catch the Dardanoi.

The men are yelling. The battle cries vary from *syntagma* to *syntagma* depending on the city or region where each unit was raised. Philippos forgets his fears.

Pike outreaching spear, Philippos hammers at the enemy footman opposite him. Pike head grates across the bronze curvature of the enemy's shield.
Philippos grunts, pulls back, and thrusts forward again. He can feel the
push of the ranks of men behind him. The clash and clatter is enormous.
Yet he works his pike and shoulders his shield within the solitude of his own
efforts. Beside him are many, yet he is alone with the hard thrust of his own
ash pike. The weight is in his horny hands. Though he is thrusting in fierce
haste, though all is noise and dust and heat and deadly assault, he is coolly
doing what he has trained himself and all these ten thousand other men to
do. Thought is suspended in the muscled serenity of the thrust.

A spearhead slamming into his helmet jars him back into furious
reality. This is no exercise. He must be alert, he must feel the danger, he
must kill. And he does. The Illurian opposite him goes down when the pike
pierces through his eye. No pause. Philippos duels the next antagonist.
Pike shifting, pulling, thrusting, searching for an opening while the opponent's big shield blocks and his spear as eagerly seeks Philippos' death.

The footing is slippery. And a misstep by the foeman gives Philippos his
second kill. There is no relief or pleasure. Another Dardanian forces the prince's
pike aside and, using his big hoplite shield as a ram, smashes Philippos off
his feet. Little Peithon rescues Philippos, leaning over the prince and taking a slash across his back. From the Philippos' right side and from behind
the prince, Pikoros and Verzo simultaneously slice the big Dardanoi down.

Philippos realizes in that moment that his companions are spending
more care protecting him than themselves. He must do the same for them
and for the whole ten thousand. On his feet again, he hefts his pike. Other
men in the ranks have pressed forward. He gestures to his companions,
"Lift me." Standing on the dead Dardanian's hoplite shield, Philippos is
lifted by his companions so he can see above the immediate fighting. An
officer rushes over, holding high the prince's banner. "A runner came, sent
by Antipatros. The enemy has formed a large square. Parmenion keeps the
horse in hand so they threaten, but he can do nothing. The enemy front is
quartered by their squaring."

Philippos acknowledges the tidings. From his vantage he can discern
the square. He can also see that there is no more advance. There is only
a desperate cutting edge to the fight, where men grind away at each other.
He waves himself down. Turning to the officer he says, "Send messages.
Antigonos should have an adequate number of runners. Keep rotating the
men in the first five ranks. We keep the pressure on them, on the Illuroi."

Philippos lifts off his helmet to wipe the sweat from his eyes. They
have been stinging for some time. He smiles at Peithon and pulls him into
an embrace. The boy—young man now—winces due to his back wound
but smiles. Philippos lifts his pike, kisses the shaft. "Let's take our turns
at the front again," he says to Pikoros and Verzo.

For what seems like hours, Philippos struggles from the third rank.

He thrusts across and around the shoulders of the men in front of him. Every opening he sees he speeds to fill with the head of his pike. Once he gets a true touch, though whether a kill or not he does not know. He could feel the pike blade go in. His arms ache. Around him, men wheeze with the effort. The sudden killings of the start are gone. Now all is closed shields and visored faces. The enemy is as strong as the Makedones. Still, if a man on either side goes under, the opening creates frantic attacks until sealed by another man behind a shield.

Opportunity occurs most often due to a stumble or fall. Bodies or parts, lost helms, broken shafts, the front ranks fight in a litter of death. They step in mud made of blood. Even with fresher men rotating to the front ranks, this battle cannot go on. Too much fatigue. For Philippos, the drumbeat in his mind is that they are losing. His confidence is eroding under the constant clips and slams of enemy spears. Though fighting is continuous and ever fiercesome, the lines are static. Neither side is backing down. It's becoming harder to fight with the dead underfoot.

A Makedone steps beside Philippos and thrusts down the alley between the shields. Philippos is relieved and can step back out of the first ranks. He does so wearily, yet watchfully. He keeps his pike to the front, taking each backward step carefully so that none of his fellows is endangered by his withdrawal.

Out of the melee, he looks for his bannerman. A different officer than before, older, comes up. A footman beside him holds the banner pole. "Where's Hippolutos?"

"He took an arrow," answers the officer. The fellow looks searchingly along the battleline, "I've never seen such a fight."

Philippos knows the man now. One of the mercenaries, Old Pamphilos. "What of any runners?"

"Demetrios says his men are faltering, they need a rest."

"How long ago?"

"Not long. We sent in men to relieve your section when we got word."

"Anything else?"

"Antipatros is on the far side of their square. Periandros along the forest side."

"If they break, they'll have to get across the river."

Pamphilos smiles grimly, "Yes, lots will die then." He looks Philippos in the eye, "Will they break?"

"Not the way it's going now," answers the prince. He considers the predicament. The Dardanoi are holding. What to do?

Coming across the swale is Antigonos on horseback. The giant makes the horse look like a small ass. Before Antigonos can reach them, Philippos comes to a decision.

As Antigonos reins up before them, Philippos asks, "You have enough runners to reach my generals and all forty *syntagma* commanders?"

"Aye, we can press in some additional men," answers Antigonos.

"I want reliable runners."

"You'll have them, Philip."

"Send to all commanders to disengage. They step back on three blasts of the trumpets. Step the men back keeping their fronts. Then I want a runner to Bardulis."

"I'll do that myself," says Antigonos.

Philippos looks at him evenly. Going to Bardulis will be dangerous, possibly suicidal. "All right then. You do it. I want a truce, a time out to collect the dead and wounded. We can hardly reach other for the bodies. Once he accepts the truce, we act fast. Get our people cleared away as quick as we can. Those not collecting the dead are to stand to arms. When I order the attack trumpet call, we go back in fast. Double the quick pace. I don't want any mistakes or their taking advantage of us."

Antigonos grins at him, "You want to take advantage of him."

"Of course I do," answers Philippos mildly.

Pamphilos says, "Will he take a truce?"

"Yes. He must need a respite as much or more than we do," says Philippos with instant decision. Then more warily, "Herakles knows we need a truce. Even a short span will liven the men."

Pamphilos glances up at Antigonos. All three turn to look at the battleline. The ranks are leaking. Dead down, wounded helped aside by comrades, the faint-hearted edging back from the fight. The truth is there to see, the Makedones could break. "Hurry, Antigonos," says Philippos tersely.

η

Bardulis stares down at the big Makedone standing there with his live branch indicating a truce. He knows this man, this boy. Antigonos they call him—Antigonos, son of Philippos Arkouda. One of the regent's companions. Feeling phlegm in his chest, the king hawks and spits to one side. Breathing dust for hours will do that. "He wants to clear away the dead, huh?" says Bardulis absently. *Wants a rest, truth be told. Means they're close to breaking. Maybe we should just advance and smash into them, through them.*

The wild elation he'd felt when the Makedones began disengaging is gone. The bastards did it well. Lost a few in the process, but they kept their formations and got clear. His men couldn't have done it. There they are, facing us. Look just as tough now as before. Can't be though if the puppy wants a truce.

His boys need a rest, too. They stand there sagging on their shields and spear shafts. They need water. The river side of the formation is mostly clear. While the truce is on, they can take time to send for water and distribute it.

Bardulis rubs the neck of his horse, looks up at the sky, considers. More than three hours of daylight remaining. Say an hour for the truce, then push hard at them for two hours or so. Need to come up with a stratagem to throw the bastards off balance or we'll end the day like this—a standoff.

He turns back to Antigonos, "Okay. You tell him he's got his truce. Until the sun makes our shadows another pace in size."

With that Bardulis turns his horse to ride west to find Epidios. Calling to Ziraios, he says, "You heard. Send word about the truce. Then bring my sons and chiefs to me. I will be at the southwest angle of the lines with Epidios." The priest calls to his runners as the king trots away, with his bodyguard, Bato, trailing behind, bobbing to stay on his horse.

After a short ride, Bardulis greets his nephew the general, "Epidios, you look like you've got a third eye."

The man touches the gouge in his forehead, his fingers coming away bloody, "Their fucking pikes are long."

One of the nearby warriors, the famed Pravaios, laughs, "Long, but you can chop them easier. Leaves the fucker standing with only a big stick in his hands." Other men around Pravaios laugh as well.

The good cheer heartens Bardulis. He laughs with the men. "They need a truce. We're breaking them. By agreeing, we can clear the field a bit so we can get at them better. Our bearers will be bringing water to the lines."

The men raise a quick cheer of appreciation for their king. Epidios, though, does not look as pleased.

Seeing this, Bardulis slides off his horse and gestures to Epidios. The two men walk deeper into the square, with Bato following a dozen steps behind. Bardulis puts his arm around his nephew's waist, "You look as sour as a crabapple."

"If they're so close to breaking, why are we giving a truce?"

"How close are we to breaking, Epidios?"

The tall man sighs, touches fingers to his head again. "Water will be good. My head feels like it could splinter into a thousand pieces." He closes his eyes and leans against the king. In a lower voice, he continues, "You're right. We need the rest, too. Most of our boys aren't Pravaios."

"Sit down Epidios. Lower your head, relax. I'm pulling our chiefs to us. We need to think clearly and devise a way to seize the advantage. Either that or I need to turn this truce into a longer peace and divide the highlands with that son-of-a-bitch, Philippos."

Soon the others begin arriving. Apludos is first, then one of the sons, Agirros. Other men come in. Several have wounds, like Epidios. The dozen men look weary, but sound. "Where's Skerdis?" asks Bardulis.

"Took a pike head in the groin," says Seio.

Bardulis grunts, surprised at his own pain at the thought of the grumpy Skerdis dying. Never thought much of the boy. Not a good head on his shoulders, always resentful. Still, my own flesh and blood. A spurt of anger touches his heart, the gods damn all Makedones. "Anyone else?" he asks tightly.

"Many, too many," says Dasios. But then Dasios has always been softhearted.

Apludos answers more properly, "Someone said Beuzas was killed. His son is holding their people together."

"Well, we don't have much time," says Bardulis. "We need a way to overcome them. Can we shift men from any part of the line to build greater weight elsewhere?"

"The river side," says one. And the others agree, calling out for shifting the men holding the river side of the square.

"Where will we put the extra strength?" asks Epidios.

"Here, along this south facing line. Philippos will have his best men with him, down the line. His troops here have fought just as long. They'll be as tired here, and they're not his best." Bardulis is getting excited by the prospect. "Put Pravaios and Bato in the first rank. Find Karrios, too. Let's get our best men here. Thin out the river line, down to six or even four ranks. Place twenty-four ranks along this line."

"That's how the Thebans beat the Spartiates at Leuktra," says Dasios approvingly.

"There's no time to waste. Dasios, take my horse. You, Agirros, take Bato's. Get across the square and hustle them here. Epidios, you place them." Bardulis is grinning, almost jumping from foot to foot as the image of the breakthrough takes hold in his mind.

Dasios and Agirros are away, and Bardulis feels a burst of impatient anxiety. Already he wants the men pouring into the ranks to thicken the line.

A call from the front line interrupts the chieftains. Pravaios is hallooing them. "What is it?" asks Bardulis restlessly.

Epidios looks toward the line. The men there are waving, pointing to the south. Something is happening. Are the Makedones withdrawing? Then with a curse he realizes.

"What is it?"

"They're coming. The Makedones are attacking."

"It's too soon. That son-of-a-bitch. I should have had him strangled when I could," says Bardulis in a fury. "Get to your positions, get back to your men. Hurry!" He waves them away. Soon only he and Bato are left where the generals and chiefs conferred.

θ

Around the perimeter of the Illuric square, the Makedon phalangists jog forward. Like rain falling at a slant, the pikes come down until parallel with the ground. Illuroi are scrambling to regain their ranks. Warriors drop the wounded and bodies. File leaders are screaming. On the river bank, bearers mingle with spearmen. Gaps exist in the Dardanid ranks facing the river.

The Makedones are on the Dardanid army before they can fully recover their formation. Derdas leads his horsemen in at the charge, coming up from the shallows of the river. Of the phalangists, Philippos' ten *syntagmai* reach the Illuroi first.

In the front rank again, Philippos lunges forward as they reach the enemy line. His blade strikes an Dardanian officer in the side, skewering the man. The convulsive arch of the dying man's body rips the pike from the prince's hands.

Philippos continues running, pulling his sword from its scabbard as he goes. The pike heads of the men behind and beside him cover his rush. With sword free, Philippos is in among the Illuroi. Slashing, cutting, piercing, Philippos is war's incarnation. He is through the enemy line and around him are his comrades. This section of the Dardanid army is fleeing.

Yelling, "Where is Bardulis?" Philippos pursues the foe. Suddenly, among the fugitive enemy, a new Illuroi line is being formed. A Dardanian general or officer is grabbing men and shoving them into position. Another officer does the same a pike's length away. Looming behind them is a man ahorse. Philippos knows no hesitation, yelling an inchoate warcry, he is in their midst.

As quickly, Pikoros, Peithon, and Verzo lead their files against the nascent line. Where Philippos fights savagely with sword, the others still carry their pikes. They shatter the new line, sending their adversaries reeling. And they must run, themselves, to stay up with Philippos.

Philippos hurtles himself upon the horsemen, bearing man and horse to the ground. The prince's forward-balanced blade slices through the enemy's neck. The vaguely familiar face of the foe is awash with blood. Dasios. Rolling free and on his feet again, Philippos scans for his next opponent.

Pikoros is panting beside the prince. "Form the men, Philippos. We're too disordered if they have a counterstroke."

"They have no counterstroke to this," the prince-regent points as Elimiote horsemen ride down hapless Dardanoi. Around him, officers of the *syntagmai* are pulling, shoving, and pushing their men back into ranks.

Old Pamphilos comes up to stand by Philippos, "Parmenion sends to say they are streaming north parallel to the river. He's letting them run for a bit, using his men to keep up their panic."

"Bardulis must still be here. He's too old to run," pronounces the prince grimly. He turns to Pamphilos, "What of Antipatros, Demetrios, Periandros?"

"Their line to the west held the longest. Slowed up Periandros. Antipatros was with Parmenion last I heard. I've had nothing from Demetrios."

Philippos looks up at his banner. Somewhere Bardulis has a flag. If the enemy rallies, it will be there. The line around him is ready. He gives command and they all step out deliberately. No headlong rush like before. No matter how brave are the Dardanoi, nothing they have left can resist the Makedones now.

The very pressure of the Makedones on all sides forces desperation on the Illuroi. Those trapped, unable to flee, fight fiercely. Sometimes a surrender is accepted. The line passes small groups of disarmed enemy. More often, no quarter is given. The foes go down in a fury of plunging pikes.

The only courage the Makedones need now is to be blind to their foes' humanity.

A rider reaches Philippos. Antigonos, leading a second horse. He leans over the prince, "Bardulis is making a stand on a slope in Demetrios' sector. I figured you'd want to be in on the kill."

Mounting quickly, Philippos is ready to ride when Pikoros grabs at his leg. "Not without me," yells the redhead.

"Get up then."

Verzo scrambles up behind Antigonos, and the two heavily laden horses trot toward Demetrios' portion of the battle. Within minutes they can see the slight slope where the Dardanid remnant stands. Bardulis' raven flag flies above them. Lines of Makedones surround the knoll. There seems to be a parley in motion.

"Looks like you can take Bardulis alive, Philippos," calls Antigonos.

An idea the prince had not considered—Bardulis alive. Useful?

They rein up beside Demetrios. "Who's talking?" asks Philippos.

"I sent Andromenes to them, see if we can do this without losing any more Makedones."

"What's holding things up?"

"Bardulis is bargaining."

Philippos snorts, "He's got nothing left to bargain."

Pikoros whispers in Philippos' ear, "I was an Atintane before you made me a Makedone. I want no Dardanoi king alive."

Answering, Philippos says, "I have no use for a Bardulis who still thinks he can bargain."

Pikoros slides off the horse. Philippos dismounts more regally. "Call Andromenes back. We will need pikes, Demetrios," says the prince.

On the knoll they have seen Philippos. Have seen him dismount. See the pike put in his hands, see him pull his helmet down to enclose his face. They know what is coming. Pravaios begins a death chant. One by one, the others on the knoll take it up.

All save Bardulis. The old man is coughing. He has little sentiment anyway. Spitting into the dust at his feet, he says, "Bato, let me have your spear." Then raising his voice, he bellows to his thirty-seven companions, "My kingdom when I'm gone to the man who kills Philippos the Makedone." Around him the others cheer.

The half-*syntagma* led by Philippos advances first. He moves them at a quick pace. The pikes of the first five ranks are lowered. The other units surrounding the knoll lurch into motion. Before ten breaths are taken, Philippos and his rankers are on the Dardanid shields.

Raising his pike above his head, Philippos brings it over the shield of their frontman. A second thrust takes the Dardanian in the throat. The weight of the column behind him shoves Philippos over the dead man and onto the next Dardanoi. They crash together, and Philippos can smell the man's fetid sweat. A sword hilt smashes against the prince's helm from the Dardanian on his flank. Losing his grip on the pike, the prince tries to protect himself with his small shield. Frantically, he finds his dagger and does a rolling dive below the hoplite shield before him. Coming up, he slices along the length of the man's inner thigh.

Now he has time to bring out his sword. With his shield hanging on his shoulder and back, the prince attacks with dagger and sword. He staggers over the wounded Illuroi to find himself facing Bato.

Before Philippos can react, Bato smashes him aside with his huge shield. Rather than killing the prince, Bato leaps over him screaming, "Traitor!" The massive warrior attacks Verzo.

Philippos scrambles to his feet and sees Bardulis running toward him. Pikoros is past Philippos in a rush and catches the Dardanid king in the abdomen with his long pike.

Feeling danger, Philippos whirls to find Bato trying to reach Bardulis after downing Verzo. This time the prince is standing ready. They trade blows, and Philippos steps forward into the warrior's next swing. Hammering, slashing, taking blows by dagger and sword and sending them back, Philippos is forcing Bato down slope. At last there is an opening and Philippos stabs deep, his lunge gaining power from the slope. Panting, Philippos stands over the fallen Bato. Raising his eyes from the dead warrior, Philippos sees the Makedon pikemen standing all around him, grinning. They cheer his win.

Antigonos steps up and wipes the sweat from Philippos' face, using cloth from the Dardanid royal banner. "To your victory, Prince Philippos," says the beaming Antigonos. Pikoros stands beside him, holding the dripping head of Bardulis by its beard.

DEFEAT OF DARDANIS

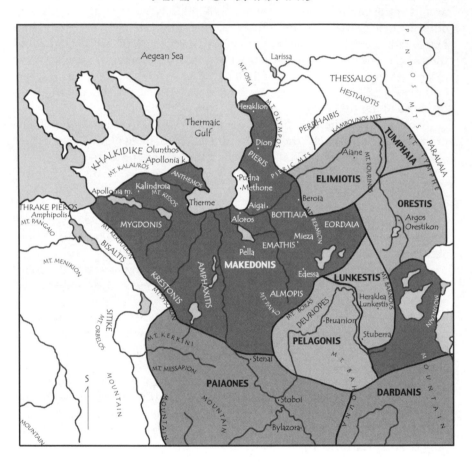

PART THREE

To Secure the Kingdom
358 - 356 B.C.

CHAPTER SIXTEEN

The Aleuadai

358 B.C.

α

Aiane, capitol of Elimiotis, is abustle for market day. Though the streets to the agora are filled, they do not compare to the crowding that occurred a handful of days before when Prince Philippos came to his wife, Phila, to announce the great victory over the Illuroi. What a strange day that was—a day that mixed exhilaration and sorrow. The Makedon prince had succeeded as none before him, killing the wicked Dardanoi king and slaying thousands of enemy warriors. Yet the prince brought his father-in-law, the dying *Basileos* Derdas, back to his daughter and his people.

Still, for all that happens to kings, princes, and warriors, life goes on for the people. Sheep are sheared and wool is spun. Seed is planted and sprouts are weeded. The sun comes up, arcs through the sky, and is hidden by night. The gods require propitiation. The baby sucks. The old wither. Daily life is more urgent than great events, though the mighty seldom think so. Daily life is a broad river that carries all before it.

There is time in a day, though, to wonder, what will become of us. To hope that the new *basileos* of the Elimiotoi will be as good as was this Derdas. Or, at least, no worse.

The great folk return today from the old hill town that is ritual center for the Elimiotoi. The libations, the sacrifices, the other burial rites— rich and solemn for a king—are done. Time to raise a new king.

There are those that whisper that the new king already rules and she is Princess Phila. But men will have a man for king.

More important to most is the price a good fleece will get at market, or what a brace of doves command. Grain is still dear, this early in the spring. Cheese, eggs, and olive oil, those are essentials.

The people do pause when the retinues of Princess Phila and her husband, Prince Philippos of the Makedones, ride through the gate, followed in turn by young Derdas and little Makhatas, as well as other notables, like

Xenokleitos. Some people even cheer and wave. After all, many have cousins or friends in the retinues of the magnates. Not that the notables lack popularity or adherents, it's just that this is market day. You must be intent to gain a bargain.

And that afternoon, in the palace on the hill, the decision on the kingship is enforced. Philippos the Makedone is declared the new *basileos* of the Elimiotoi. When he is absent, his wife, Princess Phila, will be his regent. All the chief men of the kingdom are pleased, save for young Derdas, his brother, Makhatas, and the few young men who stand with them.

Noting the anger of Derdas and Makhatas—the obvious abiding nature of the hatred they feel for Philippos and their elder sister—the first act of the new king is to banish his brothers-in-law. Xenokleitos and other clan heads, senior men and companions, approve this first act as readily as they had the anointing of Philippos. The threat the young wastrels represent to the good and prosperity of the Elimiotoi is gone with a command. The kingship is safely in the hands of an able man. Better, this man Philippos will not often be here, so governing rests with Phila and her council. The council members are the very men who have made this arrangement. Xenokleitos leads the council.

Following the evening feast, when the guests have withdrawn to their rooms or lay soddenly on their couches, Philippos joins his Elimiote wife. She sits on the carved wooden rail of her bedroom's balcony. As Philippos comes to stand beside her, she asks, "Have you ever tried to count the stars in the sky?"

"No, there are so many," he answers, stroking her arm.

"Yes, so many. And the moment you think you've counted them up in just one quadrant of the night, you realize there are more, faintly, barely discernible, and you guess that there are more yet that a hawk might see but that are too dim or, maybe, too distant, for the human eye."

"You are philosophical tonight, Phila," says the prince, smiling at her profile as she stares up at the night.

"Cannot a woman be philosophical? A woman who has just bade farewell in this life for her father?"

"I do not know much about women," answers Philippos truthfully, "but you can be whatever you want. I know you are a pragmatic person. You and I have just exiled your brothers. I do not know whether I'm your figurehead here, or you are my cat's paw."

She turns to him now. Reaches out with a finger and traces the length of his cheek, "Does it matter? You will have whatever you need from Elimiotis."

"We seem unlikely to have children, you and I. Your father wanted that."

She thinks of her stillborn child, "Who knows but the fates?" She shrugs, then says fiercely, "You will bed me tonight, Philippos. Not one of your young boys."

He laughs aloud, "Truly, gladly."

Then she laughs, too, as surprised as he by the vitality of her desire. Then more somberly she says, "You are right, though. Father wanted his line to continue on the throne, even if through his daughter."

"I am king of the Elimiotoi in my name, not in my nephew's. There will be sons of mine."

Briefly she wonders if he thinks of Ptolemaios, the boy that he or Lagos got on Arsinoe. Another thought occurs to her, "Your people call the Princess Audata by the name Eurudike since your victory."

"She will never be an Illuroi again. Time she had a Makedon name. And since she is soon to be a mother, I thought to give her my mother's name."

Phila purses her lips and asks, "What does your mother think?" That formidable woman is one of several reasons why Phila prefers to reside in Aiane than in the Makedon capitol of Pella.

"Since Eurudike Audata may give birth to my heir, mother is delighted at the compliment."

Phila shivers, "A bit early to talk of heirs."

"Tell that to my brothers, if you could." Philippos sighs, "The king's mother, Telesilla, remains convinced that I will kill my nephew for the throne. Where once she and I were friends, now she will have none of me." Hurt is in his voice.

"Why not marry her?"

"She is a Makedone. I best take my wives outside the lowland kingdom. If I marry into the clans, then much of the old intrigue would start again." He leans forward and kisses Phila lightly on the cheek, "Besides, in her fear, she would not have me. You are my fortress, and Eurudike Audata is my brood-mare."

"You do need to be king of the Makedones, Philippos." She looks up again at the stars, as if reading them. "You see your destiny? Whether you know it or not, you sealed your fate by killing Bardulis. What other king but you would the Makedones follow now?"

He is silent, his thoughts shying away from her direct challenge.

She slides off the rail and embraces him softly. In his ear, she whispers, "Do not think I suggest killing little Amuntas. You must set him aside. You will find a way to make it happen. Your natural kingdom is larger than Elimiotis."

He pulls from her, steps back, then leans onto the rail to stare at the town below. He remains silent for a time, until she steps to him and strokes his back. He says quietly, "The fight was terrible, you know. Oh, the bards can sing about strong arms cleaving bronzen helmets. I tell you it was blood and hunks of human flesh. We lost close on a thousand men. And in the battle and pursuit, we slaughtered seven thousand of them. Have you ever seen a river flow red?"

He turns to her, holds her arms in his hands, "And it was a good fight. I mean we fought for a good reason. A generation will pass before the highland and lowland Makedones need fear the Dardanoi."

She kisses his brow, "You control Lake Lukhnitis. All the highland chiefdoms do you homage. You build fortresses in Lunkestis. Orestis turns from the Molossi to you as protector. We are all flowers and you are the sun."

"You don't see my point. War against the Illuroi is a good war. But war among the Makedones can never be good. Everything would be lost if the kingdom becomes divided."

"Then listen to my point, Philippos," says Phila angrily. "The highlands do homage to you. You are the Makedones. You are the sun of the Temenidai, the favor of Zeus shows through your acts. Every chief man, whether highland or lowland, knows it. You think becoming *basileos* of the Elimiotoi, you think exiling my brothers, would have been possible without your victory? A victory won by an army you built, led, and inspired."

"There are times you remind me of my mother," he answers.

She shivers again, not certain whether his words are compliment or curse. "Philippos, *basileos* of the Elimiotoi, prince of the Makedones, husband, be what you must be—king of your people. You are cleverer than your friend Aristoteles and are more king than either of your brothers could be. Do not do injustice to Amuntas Perdikka. He will never be the king you already are in everything except name. If he remains king, there will come a day when he will have your death because he will be unable to compare with you. Give him, yourself, your people, the gift of deposing him."

He thinks about the puzzle. He will be no Ptolemaios of Aloros, killing his way to the throne; no Aeropos, the rapacious uncle dealing death to a nephew. Yet he knows her words are true. How to depose the king without needing to kill the boy? Can an anointed king be undone? In a sense, isn't that what happened to Argaios years ago when father retook the kingdom? "I will think about what you've said, Phila. I see no clear way now. Were the citizen Makedones to depose King Amuntas, it must be due to vital necessity and it must be done while he is still quite young."

She stops his words, kissing him warmly on the lips, "Never mind now. You will find a way. Take me to bed, husband."

β

Within a *dekades*, Philippos is back in Pella. In this time, he's come to a decision about how to best secure the highlands. Yet he knows how unpopular will be his plan. Even a man as practical as Antipatros shies away from implementing the regent's idea. For the moment, this new predicament looms larger than Philippos' worries over the kingship and Amuntas Perdikka.

The regent is determined to hold Lunkestis so that the invasion corridor through the highland chiefdoms is closed to the Illuroi forever.

Building a citadel and outlying posts in Lunkestis is not enough for him. By itself, it's too passive a policy for Philippos.

In addition, Philippos would move Makedones from the lowland kingdom to Lunkestis. In turn, he would transfer border populations to the homelands of the Makedones. Some Illuroi, some mixed breeds, some Lunkestoi, some of whatever other peoples occupy the frontier. The outcry among the Makedones is shrill.

In council, Parmenion argues fervently in favor of the regent's course of action. But Parmenion is an outsider, a Pelagone, and many of the regent's companions are suspicious of his motives. They listen to Parmenion in silence, seeing only Pelagonid self-interest in his words. For what Philippos proposes would benefit the Pelagonoi and Deuriopes as readily as the Lunkestoi, Orestoi, Elimiotoi, and the Makedones of Eordaia.

Philippos is meeting with a delegation from the three towns chosen to move north from the communities of Pieris. The elders seek to reverse the regent's decision. Several chief men of the realm are speaking on behalf of the towns as well. For more than three hours Philippos has listened, sitting with his head resting on clasped hands, seeming intent on the arguments.

"...traditions will be lost. We no longer will be able to carry out the annual rites at the graves of our fathers. You would cut us off from our patrimony. You make of us barbarians, men of the hills..." The senior elder from Baye is in full tirade, face flushed at the indifference he sees in Philippos.

At the height of the old man's peroration, Philippos straightens in his chair and holds up a hand to stop the flow of words. "Thank you, Thersandros of Baye. I apologize for interrupting but time presses."

The regent stands and says to the delegation and their backers, "All of you have spoken eloquently. Facts are more demanding of me than eloquence. Were there another way that would be as effective as this transfer of populations, I would seize it. While your arguments are well-chosen for your purposes, none answers my purpose. None offers a better means of securing the Upland Makedones."

A voice calls out from the side of the chamber, "Upland Makedones? You mean Lunkestoi, Orestoi, Elimiotoi, Pelagonoi, and Deuriopes."

Seeing the speaker, Philippos turns to the vehement young man, though addressing everyone, "Let me make plain to you that when I say Upland Makedones that is what I mean. As in the day of King Alexandros the First, the people of the highland basins are united to our kingdom. No longer is there a separate Lunkestoi kingdom. While we do distinguish Pelagonis, as King Parmenion rules there, he has made perpetual alliance with us, sworn down through future generations of Pelagonoi and Makedones."

Sweeping his arms out to encompass everyone standing in the hall, Philippos says, "Look about you. Here you see highlanders as well as lowlanders. Here is Alexandros, eldest son of Aeropos of Lunkestis. Here

Philippos of the Elimiotoi. Here Pausanias of Orestes. Who fought at the River Erigon? Do you think, you people of Pieris, that lowland Makedones won that battle alone?"

Raising arms to the heavens, Philippos continues, "We mingled our blood that day. Together we gave sacrifice to high Zeus and savage Ares. We are one people. We are one in origin and we are now one in deed." He glares at the crowd, "You talk of the graves of your forefathers. I tell you that none of you are more pious than I. None honors his fathers more than I, a descendant of Zeus, I know the spirit of our fathers. That spirit is more precious than dirt. When was Pieris made our homeland? Who led us down from the mountains, down from the very highlands we now secure? You follow the Temenidai of the Argeadai clan. Why? Because great Zeus honors our family, because Herakles, our forefather, was made divine, because we Temenidai are the shield behind which you prosper." His angry voice fills the hall. He glares. Men drop their eyes before him. Some few stare back, eyes shining with excitement.

Then softer, he says, "Do not think I'm unaware of the pain and effort my command costs you. I understand your lament, and am filled with its haunting. We will aid you. You are given a bounty, and will be fed as you migrate. The army escorts you so not a sheep is lost, not a seed dropped. You are free of taxation for five years to give you time to build and regain your prosperity. I place forts on the frontier to give protection. We build a new city of Heraklea, expanding the ancient Lunkestoi town, and site a strong citadel there. You will have a city worthy of your civilization."

He smiles, "You will make good my promise, for with the Lunkestoi who remain there, you will create one people. Future generations will be unable to distinguish between those who were once Lunkestoi from those whose fathers journeyed from Pieris. And why is that so necessary? So that the borders of our lands are as strong as the heartland."

Though Philippos' words help, there is no mistaking the heavy burden felt by Thersandros of Baye and the other delegates. At least they now understand the reasoning of the young regent. They can see the vision he professes, and realize it's not punishment he visits on them, however close it may feel. Understanding offers some small consolation to the Makedones of Baye, Dobera, and Kellion. But why them and not those of Dion, Petra, Phyla or other Pieric communities? Still, they will do as Prince Philippos orders.

γ

In the early morning hours, before the dawn, before even the ceremony of sacrifice that Philippos and little Amuntas offer each day—the ceremony that binds the Makedones to the Temenidai and to Zeus—there is less certainty in the prince. Though the victory over Bardulis is a validation of all that the regent strived to accomplish these past 18 months or so, the aftermath confuses him. He fought the direct threats to little Amuntas— his half-brother Arkhelaos executed and Olunthos thwarted, the pretender Argaios executed and Athenai denied, Bardulis dead in battle and his confederacy sundered. Even Pausanias the Exile dead, strangled. As the regent's steward, Ephrastos, promised, the killing is blamed on King Berisades of the Western Odrusai. Any perfidy can be blamed on a Thraikiote. So the field is clear and Amuntas Perdikka can thrive.

The treaty with Athenai is being honored. A watchful coexistence is maintained with Olunthos and the Khalkidike confederacy, though it rankles that Philippos' half-brothers, Aridaios and Menelaos, shelter in Olunthos.

Philippos is ambitious to free the Pieric coast of Athenian influence. He desires the cities of Methone and Pudna, those allies of Athenai. And there is Amphipolis, with its precarious independence, under threat from Athenai. When the Makedones take Amphipolis, he intends to advance up the valley of the Strymon River. For now, the highlands are enough. Time is required to make them the willing participants in the Makedon kingdom that he requires. No doubt the Illuroi and Paiaones will require further chastisement. They will inevitably test his resolve and ability.

He should feel satisfaction with is successes, yet he feels the pressure to sustain what has been accomplished. And these current achievements are so much less than his ambitions. He cannot stop himself from musing on the Thraikiotes and the weakness of the divided Odrusai kingdom. He has his marital suit of Myrtale of the Molossi to complete. And there is Thessalos.

The prince smiles at the thought of Thessalos. To the greater world of the Hellenes, Philippos and his family are Hellenes. His forefathers are identified as nobles of proud Argos in the Peloponnesos. Identified as Hellenic Dorians who succeeded in seizing that ancient land in a distant past.

True, there are detractors who whisper that the noble Temenidai are no more than a family from Argos Orestikon, capital of the highland chiefdom of Orestis. To Philippos' mind, it's more likely that the first Perdikkas and his brothers, exiled from the Peloponnesos or elsewhere, founded the city in the highlands before leading the Makedones into Pieris.

There are other legends kept within the family. Philippos and his ancestors are Hellenes. Of that, he has no doubt. But the secret legends speak of those distant brothers—Perdikkas, Guanes, and Aeropos—coming out of Thessalos, not the Peloponnesos or Orestis. In a past more distant than most imagine, before the taking of Ilion by the Hellenes as sung by Homeros, the first Argolid was in Thessalos. Thessalos is the cradle of their people, of their genius, their civilization. And he dreams of ruling that ancient cradle, of gaining the lands that truly knew his forefather, Herakles.

As regent he has perhaps ten years to achieve his ends. A few more years possibly, depending on the mettle of young King Amuntas. The prince's ability to direct events will wane as Amuntas Perdikka rises to his majority. Even in the best of worlds, he will turn over his achievements to his nephew. He will be lucky to escape the regency alive—to retire respected and safe into the highland canton of Elimiotis.

So he sits here on the cold stone of this bench in the dark, hugging his knees, wrestling with himself. Though he longs for a sign from the gods themselves, he is not a lesser man who requires such signs. He could go to his closest companions and talk out his troubled mind, although they would likely be cowed by his vision save for Parmenion and, probably, Pikoros. He has already given the Makedones a kingdom that is greater than they expected. They would find that enough. Only the outsiders like Parmenion and Pikoros, one the king of another land, the other the ex-slave tolerated solely due to the prince's favor, share his restless ambition.

He knows what Phila says. Yet how bound up is her counsel in her own ambitions for Elimiotis? To whom else can he confide? He would make plain his conflict between his hopes and desires and his true allegiance to the boy-king, his nephew whom he loves. To whom can he talk out his dilemma? There is only one person. He must talk with his mother, with old Queen Eurudike.

*　　*　　*

On a day that can't decide whether to clear and be sunny or completely cloud over and rain, Philippos finds his mother in her garden. She is hoeing, her face shadowed by a broad-brimmed straw hat. He comes upon her from behind. "Ho, mother, is that you?" he calls out.

She turns to see him, pushing up the brim of her hat with her hand, leaving a smudge of dirt on her forehead. "Hot work," she answers. Eurudike looks about at the herbs, some flowering white or purple-blue or yellow, with their leaves all shades of green in rich profusion. Bumblebees are already harvesting. She sighs in satisfaction, "Here are tastes and salves and tisanes and dyes." She waves her hand to indicate the length and breadth of the garden. "All of it useful," she smiles.

"Careful the villagers don't take you for a witch."

"Who do you think I learn my herbals from?" she retorts, laughing. "What would you know of herbs? Can you tell fennel from anise from rosemary from tarragon from lovage from horseradish from sage from savory from dittany from madder?"

"I can by taste," he says.

"Well, don't eat the madder."

He points at a plant, "Parsley?"

"Oregano," she answers.

He prowls the garden, "Sage?"

"Lucky guess," she laughs.

"Dittany?"

"No, another variety of sage."

At that, he laughs as well, "All right, mother. I'll leave the herbs to you." He links his arm in hers, "Can I borrow you from your gardening?"

"Of course." She looks about for one of her servants but none are in sight.

"Midday, mother. They're sleeping. Not everyone is as determined as you to wring the day dry."

She shrugs, leans her hoe against a sturdy branch of the garden hedge, unties her hat, and leaves it dangling from the hedgerow. "We can talk by the spring. The water will taste good."

They walk the path to the spring, arms linked, without exchanging a word. For Eurudike, it is enough that they are together, that her busy son has taken time to visit. For Philippos, the subject of his visit is unpleasant, he would rather linger with the laughter over the herbs.

At the spring, she kneels and cups the water to her mouth. She takes the water where it leaves the rocks to splash into the pool. The spring is small, though quite cold and refreshing. She drinks several draughts greedily.

Philippos sits nearby, watching her. Idly, he tosses a pebble into the pool.

"I hope you offered a prayer to the water nymph before disturbing her repose," says Eurudike.

The prince is uncertain whether she is serious or teasing. He decides she's more serious than not.

"You know, Philippos, I like my estate. Not large, perhaps, but with ample variety here. Horses in the meadow, goats on the high hill. Forest, a marsh. The old house and outbuildings, and the new little house. Like my garden, a bit of everything that does well here, including the bee hives, and a few exotic things I must carefully nurture."

"You have made yourself comfortable in the country to an extent I would not have guessed possible." He offers a smile, "Are you still active in the temples and sisterhood?"

"Yes, that. One needs to be with people. Needs to hear disagreement as well as agreement. Some days I get to feeling that the way I think, what I believe, is how everyone thinks. So I get off my lands and go visiting. Quickly I am disabused of my smug notions, and see that my views are more peculiar than common."

"Are you disabused of the notion that what you think is right?"

She chuckles, "Not often." Then she looks at him inquiringly, "I doubt you came to visit without a reason, my son. What is it that you want?"

Philippos looks at her steadily, the cheerfulness fading from his face, "Have I done well as regent?"

"The kingdom, and the king himself, are secure. At least, for now. While your vigilance cannot relax, you have done well," she answers.

He nods slowly, considering his words, "The kingdom is secure for now. I'm not sure I would say as much for King Amuntas."

The queen's head comes up sharply, "The boy is in danger? From whom?"

Philippos does not answer. He stares at her steadily, letting her work it out.

Abruptly her expression changes, from alert anger to a pensive concern, "From you, the regent, you mean?"

He nods assent, thinks to add explanation, but waits.

"No regent, no king, would have done better than you, Philippos. We were fearfully beset and you have freed us." She looks at her feet, will not look at him. "Amuntas is a good boy. He's my grandson. I will not let harm come to him." She looks up, stares him in the eye, "You kill that boy and the furies will tear you apart, body and soul." Her words are hissed, furious, a curse.

"I do not intend to kill him or have him killed. I am not Ptolemaios or Aeropos."

Eurudike continues to stare at him, then says, "Yet you will be king, won't you, Philippos?"

He nods agreement again, then states emphatically, "Yes, mother, I will be king. It's necessary, both because of what is needed and because it's what I need."

"If you depose him, he will still grow to manhood." The warning in her statement hangs between them.

"I cannot depose him, that the citizen army must do. As for me, he can grow to manhood and always be a trusted companion of the king."

She sits there thinking. After a time, she asks, "You believe he can accept that? That others won't use him, twist him?"

"His father is an uncertain memory for him. He is young enough now, that as he grows he will barely remember being king. He will be like my son."

"So, at your death, he would succeed you?"

Philippos gestures his uncertainty, "The fates know, not me. When will I die? What children will I have? Will Amuntas prove to be the man promised in the child? Will pestilence, war, and harm pass by him so that he is alive at my death?" He shrugs, "He is a Temenidai, he is eligible."

"There is your boy by Arsinoe," says Eurudike pointedly.

"Lagos' son?" asks Philippos as sharply.

"Well, you're likely to have more sons, even if you don't acknowledge your paternity of that cub."

"I expect to have sons." Suddenly light-hearted, Philippos laughs, "Sons and daughters, wide lands and great wealth. Aren't I blessed with a wise woman as mother?"

"I've not always been wise. Looking back, I'd say wisdom came to me slowly and at great price." Bitterness is in her voice, self-reproach. "So you want my acceptance? Is that why you come to me?"

Serious again, Philippos says, "I want more than acceptance, I want your active help in making this happen."

"You will be an able king provided you can reach the throne without dividing the people. Do not reach for the kingship through bloodshed." Her voice is harsh, she is intent.

"The citizens must make me king. I cannot make me king. They will, if the army and the people are prepared for the possibility and favor it. You can work through the temples, the sisterhoods, and your charities. Be subtle. Do not besmirch Amuntas or the kingship. All must see that the safety, the security of the realm rests in me holding the kingship. They must understand the dangers inherent in a regency, as the boy grows older." Has he persuaded her?

She asks, "When will you act?"

"I do not know. Within the next two years, any later and it will be too late. He will, in truth, be the king-in-waiting."

"Yes," she agrees, "by then a faction will surround him and he will know enough himself to realize what it is to be king. Any later and you will have to kill him, his mother's family, and many others to gain the kingship." Eurudike faces her son, "Make no mistake. I will not countenance any killing. You had best remain regent in all virtue if you have not worked this magic by then."

"Then you will act for me, until such time?"

Eurudike is silent. She scrutinizes his face as if seeking deeply into his heart. Then she says, "I give you 18 months, no more."

He nods acceptance, does not speak. He is already thinking about who to approach next. Probably Antipatros.

She watches, notes how much older he seems with the weight of the kingdom. Not aging, just a maturity. Well, good kings mature young. Eurudike does not doubt her son will be king. "What will you do with your kingship? What more than can be done as regent?" she asks, curious to know what he seeks to accomplish.

Her question brings him back to her. He looks at her in appraisal, "How far into the future do you want me to peer?" Then he smiles gently, "I possess great ambitions for the Makedones, mother. I want us inviolate. That means we must dominate the north and never feel interference from the south again. No more Theban armies in our lands; no more Athenian navies raiding our coasts, constraining our commerce. No more tribute to the likes of the Illuroi." He sighs, "I do not see exactly how to do this, but I think I see the next few steps. The Makedones, Thessaliotes, and Epeiriotes must act in accord. And I would eliminate the threat of the Thraikiotes while they are weak."

"War on Thessalos and Epeiros would be folly," she says sharply.

"Who spoke of war? Words and exchanges first." He pulls at his ear, "War on all Thessalos would indeed be folly. Rescuing Thessaliote freedom from the grasp of Pherai? That we can do."

"Your brother tried," she replies dryly.

"Alexandros had the right idea but inadequate means. He acted intemperately. The army I have built offers greater means. And I will not act without full cooperation from Larissa, Pharsalos, and other Thessaliote cities threatened by Pherai." He sits back, looking happy, "As for Epeiros, young Princess Myrtale will become my wife."

"I doubt you'll find much common interest going that route, knowing her uncle, King Arubbas."

He shrugs, acknowledging her point, "I had a thought, no more than a thought, that Arubbas should share power with his brother's heir. After all, Neoptolemos was the senior of the dual kings. Myrtale has a younger brother."

"And an older sister, married to Arubbas, which combines the lines in their sons. I don't see him letting lose one bitten nailscrap of power."

Philippos taps a finger to his nose, "Nor do I, mother. To be truthful, I'm not certain how to proceed in Epeiros. I will start with a marriage and the knowledge that I need the Molossi kingdom in Epeiros as a partner."

"Well, you're young enough, Philippos, to see if your plans bear fruit. You are more capable than were your brothers. And you seem favored by the fates." She stands and arches her back to ease the pain from hoeing, "Let an old woman get back to her gardening. Go be a good ruler to our people."

He would like to ask her how she intends to go about her task of winning support for him. Her mind is already back to her herbs and not with him. He's seldom held her attention long. Perhaps it's best if he simply leaves her to it. She is a quite capable king in the realm she's created for herself.

δ

By way of the coast road, one would walk 610 stade from Pella to Larissa. The coast road leads south through Pieris until coming to the vale of Tempe, where it turns inland to march in an arc along side the River Peneios. Of course, this direct route would take the traveler across the homelands of Methone and Pudna, city-states allied with Athenai. To bypass these lands adds another 65 to 70 stade to the distance.

An alternative route would be to use the mountain roads. From Pella, the traveler would journey west to cross Mount Bermion, then south to Elimiotis. Crossing a second mountain chain, the road enters Perrhaibis. Once in the valley of the River Europos, a tributary of the Peneios, the route leads southeast. After the city of Mulai, the traveler crosses the hills to the east that separate the Europos and the Peneios valleys. This longer route to Larissa is about 725 stade, depending on which mountain trails were followed.

There is a shorter mountain route that leaves the coast road to cross between Mount Pieric and Mount Olympos, but the traveler must be prepared for steeper ascents and descents. Besides, to reach that road means entering the Methone and Pudna lands.

A simple traveler has these three choices. The possibilities narrow if leading a Makedon army. Entering the lands of Methone and Pudna with an army likely means renewing the war with Athenai.

For the Aleuadai, the ruling family of Larissa, these distances matter. The number of stade between Pella and Larissa is a factor in how quickly Philippos the Makedones can support the Aleuadai in their war with Alexandros of Pherai.

Not that the family is in accord over inviting the Makedon regent to intervene. Memories of the highhanded actions of the regent's older brother, Alexandros, remain vivid. Alexandros outstayed his welcome and might have been as threatening as Pherai.

The Aleuadai are a large clan. The proud Aleuadai trace their descent from the hero Thessalos, progenitor of all the Thessaliotes. Some say that Thessalos was the son of Haimon and the grandson of Zeus, others that his parents were Iason and Medea. That is the Iason who led the legendary Argonauts in their exploration of the Euxine Sea. The latter line of descent for Thessalos is claimed in Pherai, while the Aleuadai adhere to the origin in Zeus.

Whatever is the truth, what is indisputable is that Aleuas the Red was the first to unite all the Thessaliotes and be proclaimed *tagos* or high magistrate. Under Aleuas, the Thessaliotes were organized into their four cantons: Thessaliotis, Pelasgiotis, Hestiaiotis, Phthiotis. Larissa is the traditional capital of Pelasgiotis. In the time of Aleuas and his Aleuadai successors, the neighboring lands of Perrhaibis, Magnesia, and Akhaia Phthiotis came under Thessaliote control.

These aristocrats, like the Makedon Temenidai, are descended from generations of noble magistrates and leaders. Though they lost the position of *tagos* to the Ekhekratidai of Pharsalos due to the intervention of Sparte more than 120 years ago, they have never failed to assert their claim to the primacy of the Thessaliotes.

That Iason of Pherai was the last man to successfully unite Thessalos and secure the title of *tagos* is cruelly bitter to the Aleuadai. Alexandros of Pherai strives to emulate the success of his half-uncle. The Aleuadai are determined to resist.

Pherai's advantage is its location. The city dominates the Thessaliote coast on the Pagasaian Gulf. Their port city of Pagasai is the finest port in the north Aegean. Trade makes Pherai rich. Trade and, even, manufactories.

Besides controlling the best port and the gulf, they control the best road to the southern Hellenes.

Trade provides the monies that allow Alexandros of Pherai to hire mercenaries. Mercenaries who hammer on the independence of Larissa and, more importantly to the Aleuadai, on the dominance of the Aleuadai in Pelasgiotis.

Though controlling estates far and wide, with many thousands of serfs, collectively the Aleuadai do not have the means to carry on the war with Pherai continuously and alone. When the other principal clans and cities of Thessalos are free to join in opposing Pherai, outsiders are not needed. But Pherai has whittled the opposition down, forcing Pharsalos, Krannon, Skotussa, even far Trikka and Gomphi, to bow. That leaves Larissa and the lesser cities of north Thessalos resisting encroachment.

And so now the Aleuadai elders debate. The choices are clear. They can invite Thebai, Athenai, or the Makedones to intervene. No one else has sufficient power. For the moment, though, Thebai and Athenai are not attending on Thessalos. Instead, their focus is on the island of Euboia. There the populace is growing restless under Theban arrogance. The long, large island spanning the northern coast of these states is strategically crucial.

Beyond that distraction, Athenai has proven incapable of protecting her own allies against the piratical depredations of Pherai. Or so argues Eudikos, standing before his kinsmen.

Medios retorts, "If not the Attikans, why not the Boiotians?"

"You would have Thebans here again?" asks Eudikos incredulously. "Pelopidas and Epaminondas did well in putting Pherai in its place, but they couldn't resist tampering with our freedoms as well."

More dryly, Simos observes, "Pelopidas and Epaminondas are dead. There is no one of their stature in Thebai now."

"I tell you, Thebai will favor Pharsalos at our expense. They have always favored the Pharsalenes," answers Aristippos. "They created the role of *arkhon* in place of the *tagos*, and appointed Agelaos of Pharsalos."

"Little good it did them or Agelaos," mutters Medios.

"True, but because of Pherai, not us," replies Eudikos. "I say we make alliance with Philippos of the Makedones. He understands rule by nobility, unlike the democrats of Athenai and the oligarchs of Thebai."

Simos nods, "We can work with him. The people will see him as a natural choice given his destruction of the Dardanoi."

"Are you forgetting what his brother attempted?" says Medios harshly.

They all stare at Medios. The oldest of them, Medios once favored the Makedones. He has never forgiven King Alexandros' betrayal of his trust. None of the rest of them have either. Still, Philippos is not his brother Alexandros. They weigh the risk.

Simos breaks the silence, "We do not require his army. We only require the ability to call on his army when and if needed."

THE ALEUADAI (358 B.C.)

"You mean trumpet an alliance, and make it clear that if Pherai tries to grab anymore we can call down the Makedones on him," suggests Aristippos.

"Yes. Invite Philippos and his leading companions, but not request armed intervention yet," says Simos in concurrence.

Again there is silence, while all consider the idea. The youngest, Thoraxios, inquires, "What does he gain?"

Medios laughs his phlegmy old man's laugh, "The Makedones are obsessed with security. Philippos may have crushed the Dardanoi and chastised the Paiaones, but he still has plenty of enemies. Athenai meddles on his coasts. The Khalkidike are uncertain neighbors, and harbor his half-brothers. The Thraikiotes believe that Makedones are their natural prey. The Illuroi and Paiaones won't stay quiet. Like all rulers of the Makedones, Philippos wants a safe southern border. We want a safe northern border. We make good allies one to another, the Aleuadai and the Temenidai." Combing his beard with his gnarled fingers, Medios continues, "If it weren't for the rashness of King Alexandros, I'd have no doubt of alliance with the Temenidai. We had no trouble with the father, old Amuntas. But if Philippos shares his brother's ambitions, we'd best find other allies for he has a better army to enforce his greed than did his brother."

"Medios, we all share your concern," says the tall Aristippos. He stands and stretches, "We've sat and talked long enough. I think Simos has hit on the answer. We make an alliance with Philippos, but use him and his army only in the last resort." Aristippos taps Eudikos on the shoulder, "How old is your girl, Philinna?"

Suspiciously, Eudikos asks, "Why? What do you have in mind?"

"You're right, Aristippos," says Simos with a chuckle, "They say Philippos can't keep his hands off anyone who's comely."

"No, no, Philinna is promised," wails Eudikos. The sight of big bluff Eudikos in distress always amuses his cousins.

"Promised? Yes, to my sister-in-law's boy," answers Aristippos. "Well, I release you of your promise. Now, let's get envoys sent to Philippos. Pherai is not idle, nor should we be. Alliance sealed with a marriage, Aleuadai and Temenidai." Aristippos looks at Medios, challenging his uncle.

Medios nods reluctant agreement, though he adds, "Don't say I didn't warn you."

Thoraxios smiles at the timeworn phrase of the old man's. Aristippos winks at the younger man.

Eudikos sits heavily on the side couch, still absorbing the blow to his household. Simos slaps Eudikos on the shoulder and says, "Don't worry about Philinna. She's a capable girl, and they say he's good to his wives even if he does tomcat around."

*   *   *

Easy for Aristippos to say, thinks Eudikos as he walks back to his house, torchbearer ahead and bodyguard behind. *Marry Philinna off to this barbarian prince. Not even a king! Never see the girl again, or rarely. One of several wives to a hulking chieftain from over the mountains—a Makedone. Where Philinna might have married young Diodoros, combining their lands near Atrax, good grazing lands, with tillage and woods as well. What a heartbreak for the girl, and what will her mother say?* Eudikos winces when he thinks of his wife, with her sulks and petulance when he fails to consult her opinion. Life is not easy, even though Eudikos would be an easy-going man.

Coming to his gate, he kicks at the bronze plate affixed to the gate's lower edge. The sharp clatter rouses the gatekeeper. Passing into the courtyard, Eudikos dismisses his yawning servants and makes his way to his front door. Unlocking the door as quietly as possible, Eudikos slips into the gloom of the house. He stands listening. No one stirs in the household. His eyes adjust to the dimness. Slowly he skirts the stairs, fearful of waking his wife. If he had drunk less he might have stepped more confidently. As it is, he creeps along interminably. One of the dogs has found him and sniffs at his legs. Navigating by hand outstretched and shuffling feet, Eudikos makes his way down the dark hall. At least two of the dogs are with him now. With a grateful thank you to the gods, he reaches the threshold of his room.

"Poppa," hisses a voice from behind him.

Eudikos gives a start, but is pleased it's his Philinna and not his wife, Aristomeda. He glances back down the hall, perceiving the dim white form that must be his daughter. He should be indignant that she is up and in his wing of the house. Instead, as ever, he's simply glad to see her. "What is it, Philinna?" he whispers back.

"You're out late tonight. I was concerned for you," she answers. Although the truth is she heard gossip today from her cousin that something was going to be said tonight by the elders about her. Curiosity and anticipation filled her since afternoon. When the dogs fled her room to find her father in the dark, she had rushed along behind them.

What a blessing the girl is, thinks Eudikos, *so unlike her mother.* His smile, though hidden by the dark, can be heard in his voice, "How kind of you, Philinna. I am fine, you can go back to bed. Don't let your mother find you running about after bedtime."

She comes up close to her father and asks, "Did you talk about anything important tonight, Poppa?" She wants to say...anything important to her?

"We always talk of serious things, daughter," replies Eudikos. He considers how much to tell her. Best left until morning. He must talk with Aristomeda first; persuade her that this marriage is for their common good.

In the dimness, her father's face is a lighter patch whose features can't be made out. The timbre of his voice tells her more than his words or expression. Something talked of among the elders concerns her. She grows insistent, "Poppa, Kreisis says you were going to talk about me. Will my marriage to Diodoros come soon?"

"You'll not be marrying Diodoros," blurts out Eudikos.

Prayers to Hera and Aphrodite are answered. Joy turns instantly to apprehension within Philinna. Who will she marry? Surely not one of the elders, like old Medios.

Hearing her sharp intake of breath, Eudikos fears his clumsiness has caused her pain. He rushes to reassure her, "Your future husband is of high rank. You will be an instrument of our mutual trust. All of the Aleuadai will honor your..." He stops short of saying sacrifice.

The words tumble in her mind. The dread in her father's voice almost panics her. Is she to go to the house of Pherai? Or, perhaps wed to a Molossi prince, though their Alexandros is a small boy. Surely not an Elimiote High Rank? Realization strikes her, Philippos of the Makedones! Who else has been on everyone's lips these past months? She ventures, "Am I to wed Philippos of the Makedones?"

How prescient is the girl, how remarkable, what a gift of the gods, thinks Eudikos as he answers somberly, "Yes, Philinna." Heavily he adds, "We must preserve our alliance with the Makedones. They can serve as our bulwark against evil Pherai."

Quickly she embraces her father. A happiness has blossomed within her. She had so despaired at spending her life in thrall to that sniveling liar Diodoros. Tears spring to her eyes.

Holding his daughter tightly, Eudikos has difficulty holding back his own tears. What a terrible fate it is to give away one's daughter for some purpose other than her own good.

ε

Eurudike Audata gives birth to a baby girl. Philippos is not present, though his mother and the other royal ladies, Phila and Telesilla, are in attendance, with several companions and maids. The birthing is a festive event, although Phila's presence is pure luck, since she rarely visits Pella anymore.

Telesilla's participation is due to Queen Eurudike. The old queen has worked hard to placate the widow's fears for her son, the young king. Most of Telesilla's family has come round, entering into full partnership with the regent. Telesilla still distrusts her brother-in-law.

Even Telesilla admits now that her distrust has less to do with Philippos personally than with the fact of a regency. Though her fears for little Amuntas seem extreme, to her they are the rational outcome of the logic of kingship. Her relief that Audata has borne a girl, ineligible for the throne, is palpable to all the ladies.

The ritual bathing of babe and mother are done. Audata can rest and the infant can suck. Leaving the two in the care of Audata's personal companions, the royal ladies find their way to the palace garden. By then old Eurudike has dispersed their retinues. Some have duties but most can now retire after the long night.

In the garden, Eurudike finds a bench and pats the stone surface to either side of herself to indicate that Telesilla and Phila are to join her. Phila is commenting on the name, "Did Audata choose the name herself? Has Philippos heard the name?"

"Kynnane is a pretty enough name," suggests Telesilla. "Girls' names should be interesting."

"Philippos has more on his mind than naming a daughter," answers Eurudike. "Audata's not a first wife."

"True, but he likes her," says Telesilla simply.

Phila snorts, "Of course, he likes her. She's good-looking and places no demands on him."

Eurudike chuckles, "Is that jealousy, Phila?"

Looking confused for a moment, Phila answers, "Maybe. Perhaps for having a child. Who knows? You know Philippos and I are more like brother and sister than husband and wife. He relies on me, and without his understanding and support, I would never be able to..." And she stops.

Eurudike smiles gently, "Were you about to say, rule in Elimiotis?" The younger woman nods. Eurudike continues, "You needn't worry. Your place with Philippos is safe."

Phila waves a hand, dismissing thought of any concern, "It's not that."

"What is it then?" asks Telesilla. Her fears for her son make the subject of Philippos fascinating to her. She wants to know all there is to Philippos. She waits anxiously for any hint of duplicity in the man.

Phila leans around Eurudike to look at Telesilla, "You and Perdikkas had a true marriage. There was more to it than respect and affection. I know everyone thinks I'm all horses and governing my people, but I am a woman too. While I wouldn't change places with anyone, sometimes I wish things were a little different."

"You love Philippos?" tries Telesilla cautiously.

"Love? I don't know," Phila shrugs in confusion. "What is that? My big brood mare, the bay, Bomianatoli? That horse I love. If I were a horse, I would be her. But Philippos? I guess I wish it were in me to love a man, to love him."

"Aphrodite can make love a madness or a refuge or a living vine," interjects Eurudike. "You and Perdikkas were fortunate, Telesilla."

The young woman looks unhappily at her hands, "We did not have long together."

"True," replies Eurudike, reaching over and holding the girl's hand. "What Phila is telling you is that you had more in your short time than she will have in her life."

"Do you hate Philippos so much?" asks Phila of Telesilla.

Telesilla thinks about her brother-in-law, picturing the vital muscular man—a man usually cheerful, alert to others, decisive. A man others long to have as a friend, to imitate, to gain his approval. Even before he became regent, just because of the kind of man he is.

She despises her own fear of him, can feel the weakness, the sickness in it. Yet all she has to do is picture her son, her Amuntas, fruit of her loins, son of his father, her dear Perdikkas, and fear coils within her. In truth, the fears are not only of Philippos, but of all the grasping men that surround the throne. Even wider, her fears encompass the Illuroi, Paiaones, Thraikiotes, everyone who threatens the kingdom and her boy, the king. Faltering, Telesilla states, "I do not hate Philippos. I hate the regency; I hate that Amuntas is king. I never wanted that for him while he is a child."

Phila turns to Eurudike, in seeming innocence, "Does Amuntas need to be king?"

"He was acclaimed. The magnates accepted him and presented him to the army. They called for his kingship. Now, though only a young boy, he understands that he is king," says Eurudike craftily.

Telesilla grasps at her words, "The chiefs and notables accepted for him. It was not an act he took."

"True," replies Eurudike, "but he is training to rule. He expects to reach his majority, dismiss his uncle, and rule in fact."

"Some say that Philippos should be king; that Amuntas is too young and we cannot wait," says Telesilla desperately. "If they depose Amuntas, they will kill him." All her anxiety is in full flow.

Eurudike considers her response, "There are ways that will not harm Amuntas. He could abdicate in honor of his uncle. If the magnates and the army understand that he does not want the burden, they would freely offer it to Philippos."

"Philippos vowed his faithful tenure of the regency. Would he agree to such a turn of events?" asks Phila coyly. "If Amuntas desires the kingship or is even uncertain, Philippos will be his guarantor."

"I can get Amuntas to deny the kingship," asserts Telesilla. "He's only a small boy. He doesn't want me to be unhappy."

"If he abdicates, he may never have the opportunity to be king again. Are you sure that this is what you want? You deny not only young Amuntas, but the claims of your grandchildren and their children," states Eurudike firmly.

Telesilla stares at the two queens. The means to save her boy are at hand. What else matters? Philippos may be honorable, but events will force nephew and uncle to be at odds. The conflict is inevitable. Telesilla recognizes the competence and strength of Philippos. She has no faith that Amuntas would survive a confrontation with his uncle. Telesilla will save Amuntas any way that's necessary. She says softly, "Let Philippos be king."

ζ

The small boy, Amuntas, stands erect, facing the wide expanse of faces. The hillside is alive with thousands of armed men. On the podium, the boy is alone save for Philippos who stands well apart from the boy. In his role as the kingdom's chief priest in honor of Zeus of the Makedones—more particularly, of the Argeadai clan—Philippos calls out the questions to Amuntas. "Do you, Amuntas Perdikka Temenidai, renounce the king-ship of the Makedones, which you hold through the favor of Zeus Argeas, the blood of your fathers, and the will of the Makedones as manifested by this assembly of citizens here before you?"

Without hesitation, and in a clear high voice, Amuntas cries out, "I renounce the kingship." The boy does not stop with the rehearsed words, turning toward Philippos, he appeals for help, "I don't want to be king. You be king, Uncle. I don't want to do this any more." And in an awkward run, arms outstretched the boy rushes for Philippos.

Philippos meets Amuntas, scoops him up and hugs him to his chest. Hot tears course down the boy's cheeks to flow into the man's beard.

Though not the solemn ceremony planned, this sudden act makes obvious to all not only the boy's true desire but the real affection between nephew and uncle. A chant of "Philippos, Philippos, King of the Makedones," lifts from thousands of throats. Spears crash against shields. Feet stamp the ground. The roar is deafening.

For the two on the podium, for the length of their embrace, there is only each other and Zeus. Within Philippos the prayer spills through his mind as readily as the boy's anointing tears touch his soul, *Great Zeus, Father Herakles, all of you who have gone before me, give me the wisdom and strength to do right by this boy, to do well by my people, to safeguard our patrimony, to make the most of my kingship, to honor you and all the gods.*

η

Riding into Larissa, Philippos leads a retinue of friends and companions —Thessaliotes and Makedones. Though armed, they are not an army. So they are welcomed, not only by the Aleuadai, but by all the people of the city who line the streets and cheers the new King of the Makedones. For all know that this marriage between an Aleuadai maiden and the warrior king means the safety of their city and its lands is secured against en-croachment by Alexandros of Pherai.

Music is playing and there is friendly laughter, blown kisses, a showering of flower petals. One would have imagined that Philippos had already slain the ruler of Pherai. Dismounting so that he can more easily reach the many hands of welcome, Philippos finds the people's joy both amusing and exhilarating. Put crudely, all he has done is agree to bed one of their women. Yet this marriage is symbolic of a more potent union. By this marriage, the Makedones recognize the primacy of Larissa, of the Aleuadai, in Thessalos. And as a new member of the Aleuadai family, Philippos, who commands a powerful army, is bound to aid his in-laws.

The Aleuadai elders come forward to meet Philippos and his party as they enter the main civic square. Eudikos, once the reluctant father-in-law, is now delighted at the union. Father-in-law to a king! What a difference, the bridegroom is no longer a regent with an uncertain future. Even in private, his wife, Aristomeda, is pleased with the foresight shown by her husband in agreeing that their daughter be offered as wife to Philippos. Perhaps there will be a prominent place for Eudikos at the Makedon royal court.

Though Philippos is all cordiality and enters fully into the happiness of the occasion, his cunning is not dulled. He understands completely why he is here from the Aleuadai viewpoint. More importantly to him, he knows clearly how this alliance fits into his own plans. He might as easily have sought a princess from the house of Pherai, or looked further to Pharsalos or another Thessaliote city. Alliance with the Aleuadai has the advantage of tradition, which pleases the Makedones. Since the Aleuadai dominate the lands on the Makedon southern frontier, alliance with them better guards the Makedones. The deciding factor, though, is that they are weaker than Pherai and need Philippos more. If the time ever comes to discard or turn against the Aleuadai, they are less likely to withstand the king's might.

Why let calculation mar the happy moment? Philippos applauds the dancing youths as readily as any man. Quaffs the wine handed to him without a thought for poison. Leads his own men in singing a hymn of praise to the city's guardian gods. Indeed, he is happy.

* * *

From the dark hallway, Philinna peeks between curtain and door frame. The crowded room before her is smoky from the flare of torches and the open braziers. She should not be watching the men. Evading her mother and aunts was difficult. Her intense curiosity proved too strong to allow her to remain sequestered. All the city turned out to greet her husband-to-be and still her mother insisted that she hide herself away for fear of offending the fates. Taking advantage of her mother being called to the kitchen, Philinna had run through the servants' quarters to reach this back hall onto the andron, the men's dining room.

A rush and breathlessness startles Philinna, but it is only her young maid, Mikrosdiana. The diminutive girl whispers, "Have you seen him yet?"

Philinna shakes her head no and puts a finger to her lips to indicate silence. Carefully she pulls the curtain back a slit from the door jamb. How will she know him? She thought he'd be at the center couch, the place of honor, with her father beside him, even though she knew they were not having a formal meal. She didn't expect all the men to be milling about, all talking excitedly, all clapping one another's backs, raising cups of wine, telling jokes, calling out to others just arriving. As many strangers as family and friends. Which man is Philippos?

"There, mistress, there," says Mikrosdiana, peering under her lady's arm. "See the one in blue, who's laughing with Aristippos?"

Not as tall as she thought he would be. Still, a good-looking man. Not so old. In his twenties to her seventeen. Good teeth.

Staring, watching intently, she realizes that Philippos is taller than she first judged. So broad-shouldered, strong-muscled. This is no idle man. A shiver passes through her. What will the first night be like? She's seen dogs together, horses, goats. Her mother says it will be all right if she doesn't let him go too fast. She should play with him, slow him, give them both time. If she's lucky, and he is considerate, she'll learn to like it.

Mikrosdiana tugs at Philinna's sleeve. Philinna bends her head and the girl whispers, "We should go back before your mother misses us. I don't want a whipping."

Philinna lets herself be pulled away from the curtain and back down the hall. Mikrosdiana will go with her to the country of the Makedones. Perhaps one or two others. She cannot expect to see her family often, probably rarely. She knows her father hopes to find a place at the king's court. She doubts her mother will live in the north.

In truth she will miss the small birds in the courtyard most. Her habit and pleasure is to leave them scraps of bread and fruit, then watch as they gather and flutter. Some timid, others incredibly bold. Who will feed them when she is gone? Well, there will be birds in Pella. All the same kinds or will some be different, she wonders.

She has fears, of course. Philippos has royal ladies already. Her mother explained that she would not be the first wife. That is the princess, now queen, of the Elimiotoi. A barbarian who mucks out her own stable. An even more barbarous woman, an Illuroi, has given Philippos a daughter. Well, she can hold her own with those two. What, though, of the king's mother? Tales are told of Queen Eurudike, who had her eldest son murdered so her lover could rule. Mother says to be careful in the company of the old queen. Be respectful. Give no cause for grief.

She grips Mikrosdiana's hand tightly at the thought of Eurudike. "When we are in Pella, I will want you to sleep in my room. I will need you to be close by at all times, 'diana."

Answering, the slight girl laughs softly, "There will be times when your good husband does not want me there."

θ

With the Thessaliote marriage accomplished, to the consternation of Pherai and the gratification of Larissa, Philippos takes his bride back to Pella. Being home is a relief for Philippos. No king likes placing himself in the hands of others, even friends.

Philinna also seems pleased to have the journey over. Though Philippos is not so well-acquainted with her to see far beyond her apparent courtesies and small gaieties. The Aleuadai girl is no beauty, having the long nose of her clan. Still, she has the comeliness of youth and is seemly. First night caused her less trepidation than he thought likely. Eurudike has now taken the girl under her wing. *The well-bred girl will do well enough,* he thinks complacently. She is biddable and quite meek under Eurudike's gaze.

Actually it is the girl's young maid who's caught Philippos' eye. Just a sprite of a girl, like the wife of a mercenary captain who so took Perdikkas' fancy long years ago. The sprite reminds the king of the blithe spirit and lithe form of Myrtale, Princess of the Molossi. And there reaches Philippos' next ambition. Envoys sent again to the court of King Arubbas seek Myrtale's hand for the king. Perhaps in another month or two negotiations can be settled. Arubbas drives a hard bargain, but he is a hard man, not a man to Philippos' liking.

Not that liking Arubbas matters. Once there is alliance with the Molossi, then their country of Epeiros will guard his back so that he can finally deal with Amphipolis, Methone, and Pudna, which is to say deal with the grasping reach of the Athenians. When that is done, the kingdom will be rounded out. He will need to be alert, of course, to future dangers, but he will have achieved the full measure of the kingdom as it existed under the first King Alexandros. Though, in truth, Alexandros achieved that success through the patronage of the Persians rather than through the bright edges of his own spears and swords.

Philippos completes another lap in the pool. Swimming eases his muscles, refreshes him, and gives him time for thought. He holds the lip of the pool while he catches his breath. There's not time for more. He needs to join his officers in taking Pella's garrison through their paces.

He heaves himself out of the pool. From the corner where his companions have been dicing with knucklebones, Peithon calls out, "Are you wrinkled as a prune?" Alkimakhos, Pikoros, and Antigonos stand from their gambling huddle.

Philippos catches up a dry cloth to towel himself, "Who's the winner today?"

Antigonos grins, tossing the bones lightly in his huge hand, "Is there any question?"

"Send him off to his brother, Philippos," says Alkimakhos with a touch of sourness. Alkimakhos hates losing.

"Demetrios should have the garrison marching. We all need to go out and meet them. What tactics should we rehearse today?" asks Philippos as he begins donning clothes and then armor. Peithon helps tie the straps of the corselet.

"Left refuse, then wheel back," suggests Alkimakhos. "Like a feigned retreat and counter-advance."

Pikoros starts to make a suggestion, but Antigonos shushes him, "Pikoros, you always want the same thing, a charge across the field by everyone."

Not offended, Pikoros answers, "I was going to say we should divide the garrison. Let's batter at each other. Push the pikes until one side gives."

Straps done, Peithon steps back, "You could practice a combined attack, horse and foot."

Looking at Peithon, Philippos thinks it's time the young man took an officer's role. Though not wanting this ex-lover to think he is unappreci-ated, still the time has come for him to go. A frontier command would be proper. *I will need to reward him well and let him know the respect and affection I hold for him*, thinks Philippos. "Peithon, you command the horse today. We'll let Demetrios advance against you. Take advantage of any gaps in the line. Later we'll split the foot and try Pikoros' game. We'll give Alkimakhos half the men. He can do his maneuver if he's able and the men don't fall into confusion. That should be a long morning's work."

"Antigonos heard the plan. We won't fool Demetrios," complains Alki-makhos.

"Antigonos can be a judge with me today. So can Pikoros. Demetrios won't be in on the secret," replies Philippos, leading his men outdoors. Coming down the slope to the fields, they see a courier trotting toward them. The man's horse looks tired. With the courier is Demetrios, running alongside. For the officer of the watch to be with the courier means the news is out of the ordinary.

"What say?" bellows Pikoros.

Demetrios waves, and as the two parties close, they can hear his answer, "Alexandros of Pherai is dead. Cut down by his brothers-in-law."

Antigonos turns to Philippos, "Looks like you got your Aleuadai wife and alliance just in time."

Philippos responds, "Pherai and Larissa will be at each other's throat no matter who rules in Pherai." Still he hurries forward to learn more details. Who does rule in Pherai now?

CHAPTER SEVENTEEN

Myrtale of the Molossi

357 B.C.

α

Philippos hefts the silver coins in his hand. Bright, newly minted coins—made to the standard used in the Khalkidike, the old Phoenikai standard, instead of the Persic standard used by Philippos' predecessors. Minted from silver mined at Damastion. Mines formerly controlled by Bardulis of the Dardanoi and now controlled by Philippos. Ah, what satisfaction there is in holding your own silver coins in your hand. He clenches his fist over the five coins.

Hundreds of such coins are stacked neatly on the table. Leather bags filled with coins sit in a row on the floor along the wall. Amuntas Plousias finishes filling another bag. Using two hands he tosses it down so it lands heavily at the end of the row with a satisfying chunk.

"You've had practice doing that," comments Philippos.

Plousias glances at the long row of bags, then smiles, "Today's shipment. You pay a lot of money out, Philippos."

Philippos grunts his agreement. A lot is being paid out—rewards to companions, all the normal running of the kingdom, and all the extras: mercenaries, spies, politicians in other states. Though this shipment is special, payment to King Arubbas of the Molossi. Payment for alliance and for the Molossi king's niece.

Still, there's more silver mined each day. Is there enough? Well, when is there ever enough? He needs to look into that. Is there a way to improve the output from the mines? His needs are growing each passing month, so a better way needs to be found. A question for the miners? Probably too set in their ways. Still, he will ask. Maybe no one has bothered to ask them if they could do it a better way, or provided the means if they know. And he'll not just ask them, he'll set it as a problem to some of his bright young men, like the Thessaliote Polueidos, who so likes mechanical problems.

The king pulls his cloak tighter around him. Cool in the treasury, though the sunlight pouring through the high windows promises a beautiful day.

Fog must be burnt off by now. After days of gray and harsh rain, the sun is welcome.

"You'll be done soon," says Philippos, pushing back the stool and standing.

Plousias nods pleasantly.

"I am raising new units of foot in the highlands. We will be scratching a bit to pay for them. What you have here would do the trick."

Plousias looks up from his counting, "Then the Molossi better be worth as much as your new phalangists."

Philippos purses his lips considering. He wishes he could trust Arubbas. The man's a weasel. The image of the young Myrtale comes to mind—of her dancing at the ceremonies on Samothrake so many years ago. Is this alliance driven by necessity or lust he asks himself again. Then he smiles, it's good when lust can be accommodated by necessity.

He waves casually to Plousias, "I'll send down the carters and guards. They can start loading."

β

Far to the west is Epeiros, beyond the Makedon highlands, across the Pindos Mountains, which reach like a spine down into the Hellas. If the Makedones guard the northeast for the Hellenes, then the kingdom of the Molossi in Epeiros does the same in the northwest. Not that the Molossi are the only Hellenic tribe in Epeiros. They are but one of fourteen tribes. Besides the Molossi, the Khaones and Thesproti hold extensive lands. Still, the Molossi are the paramount tribe, dominating the central plateau.

The capital of Molossis is Dodona, an ancient town located below Mount Tomaros. Though situated where its citizens control the routes north to south and east to west in Epeiros, Dodona is best known for its oracle. This most ancient of Hellenic oracles is the sanctuary of Zeus Naïos and his consort, Dione Naïa. Some say that the sanctuary was first dedicated to Dione, mother of Aphrodite, and not until later did Zeus become her consort. Certainly, long ago, priests served the divinity until the Molossi Aiakidai dynasty reformed the sanctuary generations earlier. Since that time, three priestesses, known as the Doves, serve in the grove of Zeus Naïos and Dione Naïa.

And it is to these priestesses that Myrtale has come. At nearly eighteen, Myrtale is a beauty. Slimmer and shorter than the standard of the day, she makes up for her flaws by her startling eyes, erect carriage and high breasts. Few, though, stop to consider her features individually. They are held instead by her sheer vitality—the passion that she pours into all that she does. Nothing is moderate in her.

"I must consult the Naïa," insists Myrtale, flinging her hand out in a beseeching gesture. "My question cannot wait."

The Doves look to one another. The eldest ventures, "The day is not a propitious day. The Naïa answer when they choose. This day they are still."

Myrtale will not be thwarted, "Surely they understand the human heart, the human need. While we may not command their attention, they see and respond to our devotion and desperation." To underscore her own need—for what desire of hers is not a need?—the girl gestures to her five companions. "You see what I have brought them? Oils of lavender and of hyssop. The finest fleeces and parchments. Golden amber from the far north. Wines of both Thasos and Rhodos." She waves her hands at the bearers.

None of the Doves miss the richness of the offerings. Not only the offerings, but their containers too—the exquisitely decorated urns for the wine, the gold of the perfumeries holding the oils, even the finely woven and painted baskets for the fleeces are unusual and tasteful. The whole effect is extravagant. More than would be offered by the envoy of a great city-state or the king of a large ethnos. More, perhaps, than does honor to the Naïa. One does not bribe the gods.

Still the Doves know well their Aiakidai princess. They have no desire to feel her rage. The youngest ventures, "We can ask. Let us begin the ceremonies. If the Naïa respond, then your piety is rewarded. Whether they respond now or not, you can take comfort in knowing that your question is asked and the answer will come in time, with your homage recognized."

"Surely we can do more than ask. We can beseech, we can implore, ..." Myrtale stops herself. Even she would not go so far as to say demand of the gods.

The middle Dove smiles for she likes Myrtale's spirit. She takes Myrtale's hand and leads her to the grove.

Soon the ceremonies are underway. Though the day had been still, now a light wind begins to play among the tree tops. The birds of the grove grow restless, cooing and flitting from tree to tree, some circling up and above the tall oaks. While intent on their mysteries, the Doves can see that the Naïa take an interest in Myrtale.

Myrtale awaits the lead tablet. Her earlier impatience is gone. Now she would attune herself to the gods. The Naïa are not her beloved Dionysios, yet she feels an affinity for them, especially Dione. With eyes closed, Myrtale sees the goddess wearing her high headdress. Will the queen of the heavens point her scepter to left or right?

Tapped on the shoulder, Myrtale stops swaying and takes the lead tablet in hand. She expected it to be cold, but the lead is still warm from its form. Immediately she begins scratching her question with her stylus into the soft metal. She's had plenty of time to word the question in her mind. *Is it best that I marry Philippos the Makedon King?* Questions put to the Naïa are answered by a yes or no. Unlike the oracle at Delphoi, where the answers given by Apollo are famous for their ambiguity. Here, the questioner in framing a question causes any ambiguity.

After surrendering her tablet, Myrtale again is in haste for a response. The measured tones of the eldest Dove, as she restates the question in the archaic language required by the Naïa, calm Myrtale. While her urgency recedes, anxiety enfolds her as the question ends and all eyes are on the swaying trees.

The force of the wind has grown. No birds circle now. The treetops bend, swing, swoop.

Staring, straining to understand what the Doves can comprehend, Myrtale watches the swaying trees intensely. Save for the wind and the rushing, rustling leaves, all is quiet. Myrtale has to blink her eyes to keep from slipping into a trance.

First one Dove begins singing. Then the second raises her voice. The third's song entwines within and around the first two. The voices rise and fall. The three become silent at the same time.

A shiver passes down Myrtale's spine. She feels a momentary guilt at importuning the gods on a matter so trivial to them. She takes comfort in knowing that Dione will understand a woman's fears.

The three Doves encircle her, arms extended, holding hands, dancing lightly to the right. Myrtale feels relief, the answer is yes. She waits for their song to confirm the direction of the dance and she is not disappointed.

γ

Kneeling beside the little boy, Philippos sticks a twig upright in the dirt they have mounded before them. "That will be the citadel's standard," he says to the five-year old. "When we knock it down with our stones, the citadel is ours."

The boy nods solemnly. Together they step back the seven paces to where they piled their pebbles. "You go first," offers Philippos.

Rummaging through the pebbles with his fingers, the boy selects a chestnut-sized pebble that fits his grubby hand easily. Aiming carefully he throws. He's put more power in his throw than is needed, and his pebble flies high and well beyond the dirt mound with its twig standard.

"Good shot," says Philippos. "You were centered on it, just too high." He leans down, casually grabbing up a stone. As casually he tosses, and the stone hits the mound without disturbing the twig.

"Your shot's good, too, but wide," answers the boy, surprising Philippos who barely hides his grin.

As seriously as with his first pebble, the boy picks his second stone. Flatter than the first, though heavy enough for its purpose, the pebble satisfies the boy. Eyes narrowing, he weighs up his throw. With a hard pitch he hits the twig at its base and sends it flying.

"Superb, Alexandros," exclaims Philippos, impressed that a youngster so young can make his throws so sure.

Alexandros laughs with pleasure, "Can we do it again?"

A stir at the palace gate interrupts their play. King Arubbas, his immediate courtiers, and some guards cross the yard to the pair. The Molossi king looks out of sorts. Philippos is not concerned, for the grumpy man is often out of sorts. Deep-chested but quite short, Arubbas looks up at the world in anger whenever he must walk instead of ride.

Coughing, Arubbas strides up. "Let's get this done, Philippos," he growls, as if Philippos were the cause of delay. He cuffs at the boy, who is his young nephew, "Should you be here? Get back to the women."

"I asked Alekos to accompany me," responds Philippos. "We have been amusing ourselves until time for the ceremony."

"Well, it's time now. I'm here," blurts Arubbas testily.

Inwardly, Philippos sighs. True the other man is ill, but he lives with a sense of grievance. His older brother, Neoptolemos, had been a man of worth. Too bad the wrong brother died. Outwardly, Philippos smiles, "A beautiful day for a wedding."

"What's this I hear that you're changing Myrtale's name?" says Arubbas accusingly. "Myrtale's a good Epeiriote name."

"You and I agreed that your niece would be my primary wife. She would mark that fact by bestowing a marriage name on herself, one congenial to her royal role. She has chosen the name Olympias."

Arubbas grunts willing acknowledgment of the logic. Yet he cannot resist a remark, "She aims high, choosing such a name. Let's hope the gods don't feel she compares herself to them."

Though Philippos feels the name too august, he doesn't betray his thoughts, "Your niece has a fine spirit. The gods know that already."

The Molossi king knows his niece better than Philippos. He's happily rid of the girl. And he's happy this Makedon puppy is so besotted with her. They say this Makedon king rules from his crotch. Though he wasn't so besotted that the negotiations were easy.

Arubbas is dissatisfied with their agreement. Having Philippos settle the borderline between their lands is a hefty price. For now, Philippos is the dominant king here, it's his army that holds the highlands and keeps the Illuroi at bay. That and this sickness raging through the Molossi kingdom that sends too many to their graves. Arubbas coughs harshly and spits. The warmth of the coming summer will see them right.

Abruptly Arubbas motions his men forward. They will proceed to the king's townhouse, lent to Philippos for the occasion. From there Philippos will ride a chariot to the home of Myrtale's maternal aunt, where the women have gathered. Myrtale and Philippos will return to the king's house riding the marriage chariot and leading the procession. Queen Troas, wife of Arubbas and older sister of Myrtale, planned today's events.

Philippos cannot help but compare the proceedings at Dodona to his three earlier marriages, to Phila, Eurudike Audata, and Philinna. Now Myrtale, soon to be Olympias. Elimiotis, Dardanis, northern Thessalos, and now Epeiros—each one is worth a vow. Yet for Philippos this Myrtale is more than an acquisition and accommodation. Though each of his wives holds a distinct place in his thoughts and feelings, none of the others arouse such a turmoil within him as Myrtale. He's not even sure he likes how she stirs him. He cannot think of her without a lust more enslaving than hearty.

No one knows that save he. Well, truthfully, no one but he and Myrtale herself, for she seems to read it in his eyes. Worse, she will not hesitate to use that knowledge. He knows this, yet would still go forward. Not only due to needing this alliance, for were there no alliance, he would still want her.

He glances down at the boy walking hand-in-hand beside him. How small the effort to win this boy to him. How the boy wants a father. Arubbas could easily have done the same, except being Arubbas he also cannot. Well, the Molossi king does not recognize that it matters. A day will come when the loyalties of his nephew, Alexandros of the Aiakidai, will matter very much. Then the boy and Philippos will impress the fact upon the short-statured, ill-tempered king. Philippos smiles to himself. He's glad he likes the boy. It makes winning the boy to him so much easier.

Interrupting Philippos' thoughts, Arubbas declares, "Where the border runs in the Tumphaia region has been on my mind. I don't like what you've suggested. The border with Elimiotis should be further down the Beneikos valley."

How like the king to haggle over something already decided as they walk to the wedding that is meant to demonstrate their agreement.

δ

As regent in Philippos' absence, Antipatros must decide how urgent is the news of Athenai's alliances in Thraikios. He stares at the dispatch in his hand. Setting it on the table, he begins pacing.

That Athenai intends to isolate Amphipolis is obvious. The alliances establish peace with the three Thraikiote kingdoms, giving Athenai's allies on the Aegean coast—cities like Abdera, Maronia, and Ainos—security. Most important to Athenai, the terms of the alliances grant her a free hand on the Khersonesos peninsula. The exception, the holdout, is Kardia, the large city at the narrows that join the peninsula to the mainland. Well, if Athenai can find the means to come to terms with Byzantion on the Bosporos, then her grain fleets from the Euxine Sea need fear only the weather. Still, the Athenians' war on Byzantion has dragged on for years, though now activity flares only occasionally.

Running his fingers through his beard, he considers. What are Athenai's intentions for the Makedones and for the Khalkidike confederacy? In seeking friendship with the Thraikiote kings, is Athenai rejecting the idea of friendship with us?

Then an uncomfortable thought occurs to Antipatros. What if Athenian envoys are negotiating with Olunthos, the chief city of the Khalkidike? Certainly the enmity between Athenai and the Khalkidike runs deep, but not any deeper than Athenai's ambivalence over Kersebleptes, the most powerful of the Thraikiote kings. Antipatros decides to send for word from Olunthos. Let's make certain our agents there are not napping.

Before calling his scribes, he picks up the dispatch again. That the kings Berisades and Amadokos are Athenian clients is easy to understand. Without Athenai, Kersebleptes would overwhelm them. The Athenian commander, Khares, must be crowing at his success in forcing Kersebleptes to the table. The thought makes Antipatros grimace. Though with Kersebleptes hobbled, muses Antipatros, do Berisades and Amadokos need Athenai?

Now is not the time to explore that possibility, in the teeth of three treaties. Nodding to himself Antipatros is sure Athenai will overstep her bounds. She always does. Look at this war with Byzantion, her erstwhile ally. Other allies are said to be restless.

With sudden pleasure Antipatros decides to recall Philippos. Time the king were home, Antipatros grunts to himself. While he knows the need for the alliance with Epeiros, he still believes King Arubbas is more scavenger dog than lion. Philippos is probably ready to return with his newest wife by now anyway. A Molossi woman, Antipatros shakes his head in derision. Philippos should marry into the Makedon nobility, a daughter of a man of true blood, some connection to the house of the Iolodai, to Antipatros.

ε

"I hate this place," says Philinna to Mikrosdiana. "I'm no more than a brood mare or a prize sheep."

"That will change, mistress," answers Mikrosdiana complacently.

The Aleuadai princess kicks at a stool with her bare foot, sending it spinning. Then she rights it, and steps up to peer out the window. Across the vegetable garden behind the house is the wall that surrounds the property. Beyond the wall she sees trees and hills. Birds flit from the trees to the garden and back. "The sparrows and wrens are free to come and go. Here I wait on a man who has no time for me," Philinna is sullen, aggrieved.

Mikrosdiana suppresses a sigh. "The king does not know you are pregnant, Philinna. When your child is born, you will have his attention."

"Little good it's done for Eurudike Audata," mutters Philinna.

Mikrosdiana shrugs, "She's an Illuroi and her child is a girl. What do you expect?"

"And will I have a boy?"

"That's what the market seeress predicts. We have done everything to ensure a boy. We timed your coupling to the most auspicious phase of the

401

moon. You drank the potion and wore the amulet. You sacrificed and prayed to the Fates. And now see how the baby sits, deep inside of you. Most have not guessed you're pregnant yet, only the Queen-mother."

Mikrosdiana jumps down from the storage chest on which she'd been sitting and crosses the room to take Philinna's hand, "Be patient, dear lady. He will sate himself on this Molossi princess. They say she is high-strung and demanding. He will tire of her."

Unbidden comes the thought to Philinna that the king is already tired of her, his Aleuadai wife. She pulls herself free from her companion. "Have the escort assemble, 'diana. I would go riding this afternoon."

"Yes, ma'am," answers the girl with a quick bow of her head.

Running down the back stairs to the stable yard to summon the escort riders, the thought occurs to Mikrosdiana that she might divert the king's attentions from Olympias. Before he left for Epeiros, she had often felt Philippos' eye on her. She would like to bed the king. How to make that happen? Perhaps it's time he learned of the pregnancy. His courteous nature would cause him to visit Philinna.

* * *

Philippos lifts Philinna off her feet in a hearty hug, "So you're to be a mother, Lady Philinna." He laughs and swings her back to the floor.

Mikrosdiana bobs from behind her mistress, beaming at the king's joy and the flustered pleasure of Philinna. Spreading the word of the young queen's pregnancy succeeded in flushing the king from his new wife's bedroom.

Eurudike, the Queen-mother, seated on a small chair in perfect composure, asks "Have you thought about names yet?"

"No, no. I haven't had the opportunity to speak to my husband," replies Philinna in a rush.

"You say it's a boy?" demands Philippos with a smile.

Eurudike interrupts, "Who can say at this stage."

Mikrosdiana blurts out, "All the signs indicate a boy, my lord. Do you remember the night of the great storm when you and Lady Philinna went abed early? That was the night, I'm sure. Most auspicious for a boy, sir."

Philippos eyes the slim young woman, even shorter than Olympias. Smiling he asks, "Do you keep track of all our couplings?"

Mikrosdiana blushes and mumbles, "I am my lady's confidante."

"Hush, 'diana," says Philinna, touching her companion's shoulder. Speaking to Philippos, she says, "We all so earnestly hope for a son. Your good mother is right, though. Prayers, the right diet, and the counting of days may not be enough. If the Fates will a girl, then a girl it will be. Still I believe with 'diana that I will give you a son, husband."

"Then may he be strong and survive childhood, for a man needs sons. None more than a king," replies Philippos, chucking her lightly under the chin. He grins at them all, "I must be away to my duties, Philinna. Mikros-diana, take care of your mistress. Ease her pregnancy so both she and the child do well. I charge you with this."

Though his tone is genial, the look he gives Mikrosdiana tells her he is serious. Suddenly she shivers at the responsibility he places on her.

ζ

Myrtale, now Olympias, is not pleased. That Philinna is bearing the king's child is to be expected, she supposes. That the king should show such interest in the mother and her growing belly is not desirable. Aren't pregnant women to be shut away? Olympias would have thought that this whelp of the Aleuadai, simply an expedience of political maneuvers, would be of no more concern to the busy king than his infant daughter by the Dardanian, Eurudike Audata.

Everyone around Olympias knows of her sulks and are skittish as they serve her. In the harsh tongue of the northwestern Hellenes, she scolds her people at the least misstep or inadvertence.

She vows to herself that on the king's return she will regain his attentions. For now, though, he is gone for more than a month. He is off on his royal progress, riding the lands of the Makedones, from city to city, from one magnate's estate to another, holding court here and there.

Olympias is one more wife left behind. Though she can console herself with the vigor of their lovemaking the night before his departure, she is not deceived. He will be in the company of men, and some youth will serve him well.

She realizes that Philinna being pregnant does not compare to his infatuation for herself. Clearly he is delighted in her. That she knows. But it is in this time of delight that she must clinch his acknowledgment of her as his chief wife. All must see that she comes first in the king's regard and in his dignity. She feels that the timing of Philinna's child could not be worse.

In truth she is surprised at how much Philippos pleases her. His ambitions for the Makedones are limitless. Yet their success can occur only through alliances. What he has done in small scale with Parmenion and the Pelagonoi, he would do in large scale through her with the Molossi. She welcomes this since it accords with her own ambitions.

She does not understand her own wants truly. They are too vast, too wide to be encompassed by a single objective. So wide and so unattainable. She yearns to be what a man can be, though she has no desire not to be a woman. She would rule. She would experience more—she would possess such renown and accomplishment that even the gods take notice.

Though, of course, they do notice. For what can be without the thought of the gods? Is she not under the special favor of Dionysios?

Though she is beautiful, it is not enough. Many women are beautiful, strong in health, bright in mind, those attributes are not unique. And they pass. Having a soul fit for a god?

Her thoughts skid away from the idea, from any blasphemy. She knows herself to be unique, as was Herakles. No one understands her.

Shaking her head, she brings herself back to the room in which she stands. This palace room where she tries so hard to ignore the servants tiptoeing about. She must be practical. The king wants a son. Then she must bear him a son—a son more brilliant than any offspring a mere Thessaliote wench produces.

The king wants a submissive Epeiros. Then he shall have that too. She has her own following among the Molossi. Her weak older sister, Troas, and that toad Arubbas ought not to rule the Molossi. The ancient blood of the Aiakidai flows strongest through her veins. Though her sex excludes her, she could rule through her own tool. Who better, when the time comes, than her little brother? She is amused that Philippos does what she has done, binds the boy through affection. A boy without a father needs a lot of affection.

Like Philippos, the boy Alexandros pleases her. Her brother would do anything she asks of him. He is a good boy.

First, though, she must give the king a son. She must seek the wise women who will know how to assure a man-child.

The thought brings to mind the pregnant Philinna. Her child must not win the king's favor. How to make certain of that?

She taps a fingernail against her teeth. Perhaps one of the wise women will know an herb that will do the trick? Then how to introduce the poison? The king has ordered Philinna's dwarf-sized companion to guard her health.

Suddenly Olympias knows she is going about this all wrong. She should not be moping or fretful. The king admires strength. Then she must make the palace a place of steady achievement even in his absence. Instead of shunning his other wives, she needs to embrace them and lead them. She must be the example all look to. And in the care she offers Philinna there will be opportunity. If something goes wrong with the pregnancy, then Mikrosdiana will take the blame. Olympias smiles in satisfaction at the image in her mind.

η

The dozen or more goats possess long, shaggy coats, with odd tufts of hair. How uncomfortable they must be in the summer heat. Soon they will be eased as the young goatherd and her two companions comb the coats. Not that the purpose is to ease goat suffering. The youngsters will be collecting the dark resin that has collected on the goats as they browse the rocky coastland.

A twiggy evergreen shrub abounds in this rocky area. As the sun bears down their leaves exude a gummy, aromatic resin called labdanum. Used in soaps and perfumes, the resin has value. And in this poor district, anything of value is not wasted.

Standing with the peasant father of the young goatherd, Philippos cannot help musing that this method of gathering the resin seems haphazard. Why not collect the resin directly from the bushes? Why even rely on bushes that are wild, scattered here and there? Why not plant the bushes purposefully, cultivate them for their economic value?

Philippos says nothing of this to the peasant. Doubtless the man would be horrified. There will be a nymph presiding over the shrubs. Or something older, perhaps the god Hykanthos holds labdanum in his regard. Certainly there will be some divinity that accords the traditional method of harvesting labdanum with sanctity.

Still the idea bears thinking. Perhaps he will raise it with one of those proud landowners whose avarice will see the merits of lowly labdanum and whose cunning piety will find a means for assuaging a god.

The waiting ends, for Philippos can see the dust raised as several men cross the headland from the sheltered inlet where the ship had landed. He turns to the peasant, "Thank you for your courtesy. Remember, your oldest boy does service in the local levy for two months in autumn. That is compensation for your use of these hillsides for grazing." With obedience muttered by the peasant, Philippos waves to the young goat combers and walks across the stony yard to his body of horsemen.

"Done playing herder, Philippos?" laughs Hipponikos, one of the column's officers.

"Your estates are large and many, Hipponikos. You can afford to be casual. But this man has his old mother, his wife, two sons, a foster-boy, two daughters, and several serving girls. Count his goats. Look at his small fishing boat. Is it any wonder he scratches at anything he can turn into food that will feed his dependents?" Philippos looks about the small homestead.

Gruffly the black-bearded Kleitos interrupts, "You make us brigands for eating the bread and cheese his wife offers us."

"Not brigands. They offer hospitality gladly, as well they should. And as gladly, we will gift them before we depart," replies the king.

Stirring in his saddle, Antigonos adds, "You could give this man wider lands on the Illuric or Paiaone frontiers."

Mounting his horse, Philippos responds, "No doubt he'd appreciate it more than the townsmen I transplanted to Lunkestis." Memory of their protests chides Philippos, giving him hurt. Though he considers himself too soft, for the necessities of the kingdom weigh more than any subject's desires, still such decisions require him to reaffirm to himself that he met the greater good. The plight of those displaced touched him.

"Their sons will have fairer prospects in those lands than competing for their patrimonies on the closely held acreage of Pieris," answers Antigonos thoughtfully.

"We will gain more lands yet," says Kleitos fiercely. Eyes alight he says what the king wants to hear, "If rumors are true, we will have all Thraikios at our spearpoint."

Ephrastos, who held himself apart from the others, calls softly, "They are in sight."

"Call your men together. Let's go hear what the Amphipolitans have to say," commands Philippos, pointing to the path from the headland where three men can be seen toiling along.

The officers call to their horsemen. Soon the king, his companions and some thirty horsemen swing away from the homestead. In the lead, the king touches heels to his mount and canters away. The spy-chief, Ephrastos, stays close to the king despite his awkward riding.

Ahead of the others, Philippos slows to let Ephrastos reach his side, "This man Rhesos brings to us the cousin of Philon of Amphipolis?"

"He does, sir," says Ephrastos. "But they are enemies, Philon and Eriguios. You may rely on Eriguios to oppose Philon."

"And I can rely on Philon to oppose me," says Philippos dryly.

"Just so, sir." Unsaid is Ephrastos' disapproval of the king's way of meeting Eriguios. The spy-master would have a quiet meeting, yet here they are with a cavalcade. He is uncertain why the king insisted on an armed force. It's not as if Philippos needs to impress Eriguios with his strength.

Calling out a greeting, the king trots ahead to meet the trio of men, who have halted as the king comes up.

Antigonos and Kleitos, exchanging glances of concern, spur forward to minimize the king's exposure to these strangers alone. The whole column quickens its pace.

Soon horsemen surround the men on foot. Dust and the clatter of hooves on the stony path make talking impossible. With a bellow of impatience, Philippos orders his party to split. One part goes forward to where the path crosses the crest of the headland. The other part falls back, to a wide stretch where the slope flattens towards the sea, accommodating the bulk of the horsemen. Philippos is left with the Amphipolitan trio, Ephrastos, and his three officers.

Rhesos is a Pierosic Thrake. Philippos knows him of old, for he has long been a useful agent shuttling between Amphipolis and whoever rules the Makedones. The man is distasteful to the king for he brings to mind Ptolemaios of Aloros, the man who authored the murder of Alexandros, the king's older brother. Ephrastos finds him useful, though. So then does Philippos.

The other two the king does not know. Eriguios must be the richly dressed man, perhaps thirty years of age. The older man is probably the ship's captain. Certainly he is a seafarer, from his weathered features, patched clothes and curious gait. His sword is good quality, though, as is the armband of gold. Barbarian probably or mixed blood, from some Asian port.

Philippos dismounts and Ephrastos does the same. The king waves his officers out of earshot, but within easy reach in case somehow this turns threatening. Addressing Eriguios, the king asks, "Can you tell me how things stand in Amphipolis?"

Eyeing the king and all his company, it's plain that Eriguios did not bargain for all these warriors. He clearly feels concern at the potential for betrayal so many men represent. He looks questioningly at Ephrastos. "Answer King Philippos," is all the response Ephrastos offers.

Nodding reluctantly, Eriguios launches in, "The citizenry are elated over the withdrawal of the Athenians. After news came of Athenai's alliance with King Kersebleptes, we were cast down, especially following the Athenian success in Euboia. Arguments for capitulating ran hot." Eriguios smiles nastily at the memory.

The Amphipolitan continues, "Then came news of the revolt. No one knew what it would mean. Candidly, it seemed so distant and preposterous. Rhodos, Kos and Khios against Attika and all her loyal allies. Then the Athenians were defeated at Khios—Khabrias dead, Khares withdrawing to the Hellespont. Suddenly the war was not distant. With Byzantion joining the rebels, and fighting now occurring on Samos, Lemnos, and Imbros, this could mean the end of Athenian dominion. The garrisons and ships at Eion and Galepsos are withdrawn. We no longer need to run a blockade." Eriguios grins, "The pro-Athenians are in disarray in the city."

"So Amphipolis is safe and you may pursue your trade without interference," says Philippos lightly.

"My cousin, Philon, raises a new threat to cow the people into Athenian protection," answers Eriguios grimly.

"What threat is that?"

"You, Philippos of the Makedones."

"Am I a threat, Eriguios?"

"If Amphipolis is to remain independent, then anyone who would constrain her is a threat. Athenai, you Makedones, the Khalkidike Confederacy, the Thraikiotes under King Berisades or worse, King Kersebleptes if he reunites Thraikios under his kingship, even the Paiaones upstream on the River Strymon if they were to combine. We are surrounded by real and potential foes."

Philippos considers, "You name your neighbors, many of whom are your trading partners."

"Often a man who trades with you when you are strong is a pirate when you are weak," replies Eriguios. He gestures to the sea captain,

"Neanthes here brings an offer from Mausolos, Satrap of Karia. The Satrap would have us join our strength with the rebels who fight Athenai, just as Byzantion has done. He offers gold and silver for mercenaries. He says he understands how weakened our city is after years of blockade by Athenai. Now is our opportunity to revenge ourselves."

Ephrastos interrupts, "What is Philon's reaction to the offer?"

With a dismissive snort, Eriguios says, "Philon and his friends—men like Hierax and Stratokles—would have expelled Neanthes from the city. Philon, though, does not control the council, much as he tries. The council is so divided as to be useless. The oldest men cling to the idea of an independent Amphipolis. They grasp at the Karian offer. Philon and his faction would betray us to Athenai. Others argue that we should join the Khalkidike Confederacy. Amphipolis and Olunthos would be twin anchors for the Khalkidike."

"What of you, Eriguios?" asks Philippos softly.

"The days when a city of our size could truly be independent are long past. So I ask myself, who among the contenders would possess the sense to be our protector yet allow us to flourish? Who would honorably take responsibility for our defense yet allow us a maximum of freedom internally?"

Folding back his elegant cloak, Eriguios ticks on his fingers, "Not Athenai, we know her record. This rebellion is proof of that. Not Mausolos, despite his interesting offer. He is a distant ruler who serves his own mysterious agenda. Whatever he does, ultimately he is subject to Persia. Not Olunthos, for she is heavy-handed within the Khalkidike and would be no less with us. Her word would only be good until the next shift of politics among her oligarchs. Certainly not the Thraikiotes. The ailing Berisades cannot last much longer. With Athenai distracted by rebellion, it's likely Kersebleptes will gobble up the neighboring kingdoms."

With four fingers pointed down, Eriguios smiles at his thumb, "That leaves you, King Philippos." He looks into the king's eyes, gaze steady. "Were your nephew still king, I would not come to you. I believe I can place my trust in you. I can entrust you with my city, with my family, with my friends. You have demonstrated that the sun of the Temenidai is again rising."

Philippos gazes as steadily at Eriguios, his face composed. Inwardly he is elated. How easily fruit falls to hand when it is ripe. "I value your friendship, Eriguios. You can be certain of my friendship in return."

"Do not think I deliver the city to you summarily, King Philippos," says Eriguios. "The factions holding for independence or for Athenai are too strong. If you want Amphipolis, you will have to fight for it. I can, however, make the fight easier. And when the fight is over, I can persuade the people and many of the notables to accept the outcome and cooperate fully with your sovereignty."

"I understand your position, and will not ask more of you than you can give," replies the king smiling. He takes Eriguios by the hand, "Let us eat and drink. We can talk through how we might best proceed." Turning to Ephrastos, the king comments, "Perhaps you and Neanthes should talk as well. What Mausolos offers Amphipolis may be of use to us." Gesturing widely, Philippos sweeps Rhesos and his officers together. They turn toward the larger contingent of horsemen, some of whom have erected a tent, started a fire, and are laying out food.

θ

Even this late, men still stagger to their feet to proclaim a toast to Philippos and to the health of his newborn son. Though he is suffused with happiness, Philippos is weary. Stuffed almost to pain with food and drink, tired of the revelry, still he finds the toasts satisfying, even the drunken mismouthings make him smile. Especially significant are the toasts of the many Thessaliotes who are present, for they pin their hopes on this child, born of their kinswoman, Philinna.

Most of the five dozen men invited to the feast remain. The abstemious ones have departed, those few, like Antipatros, who have no taste for wine. Of the men still here, fully a third lay sprawled out or sit slumped, sodden, oblivious to the dwindling festivities.

Philippos almost pities the musicians whose fingers must be numb by now and whose efforts are ignored. Their melodies are less gay now, having passed to hymns or the slower, maudlin drinking songs.

Time to call a halt and bid his guests depart. They have their gifts, the royal largesse. Tomorrow it will be mid-morning before any of them make it to the exercise fields.

The thought of a swim sounds good to Philippos. Maybe it will revive him enough to check on the new mother and his son. A son. Think of it. Though his little girl by Audata gives him pleasure just by her comical walk and baby talk, he knows she is of small value to the kingdom. A son, on the other hand, is a kingly treasure. True his mother is from an odd branch of the many-branched Aleuadai. Still, if the boy grows to healthy manhood, the succession is assured.

He stands, swaying slightly. Holding out his hands, he ends any more thick-tongued toasts. He thanks them. He bids them goodnight. Only Pikoros follows him out.

Feeling somewhat fuddled even though he stopped his own drinking some time ago, Philippos asks, "Pikoros, companion of mine. What would you think of a midnight swim? Let's rid ourselves of these poisonous vapors."

Reaching out a hand to steady the king, Pikoros answers, "You are certain you can find the pool and if you find it, that you won't drown?"

"You're sober enough. You would save me."

"Yes, I would, dear Philippos."

Arms around each other, the two make their way down the hall. Suddenly Philippos stops. Nausea almost overwhelms him. Had he drunk so much? He waits. Pikoros is patient beside him. The feeling passes. "No noble bodyguards tonight. All too drunk. Only you, faithful Pikoros. You possess your own nobility."

Smiling, Pikoros leans into his king, "I am your knife." Leaning back again, Pikoros adds, "I offered no toast tonight. There were enough said already. I want you to know, though, how pleased Petalouda and I are for you. We have our own boys. We know what this means to you."

The words warm Philippos. They are true words, unlike some of the speeches earlier. "I sacrificed and gave thanks. All is in the hands of the gods. Yet we must do what we, as men, can do. Raise this boy to be strong and wise. What a threshold lies before him." Philippos grins, imagining the boy's future. He invokes the boy's name, "Arrhidaios."

* * *

Later still, they sit on the edge of the pool, letting their feet dangle in the cool water. They are silent, side by side.

Philippos thinks on the future. He feels blessed that he lives today and not in his grandfather's time. The possibilities for the Makedones are so open. Who knows what he can accomplish and bequeath to his son? Who knows what Arrhidaios himself will achieve? Long ago Philippos resolved to make the Makedones strong so they would never again suffer the impositions faced by his father and brothers. With a son, now he feels further ambitions stirring within him.

Given the rebellion that sunders all that Athenai holds, the opportunities are bright. Perhaps Athenai's power will fade as has Sparte's and Thebai's. One must reckon with them, but they no longer threaten the Makedones.

Though some hate Philippos for the relocations of people he ordered, the policy is a success. The highlands will never be the same. Before twenty years are out, he will have made the highland and lowland Makedones indivisible. Even he is surprised at the pace at which these moves have strengthened the kingdom. If he can keep the Illuroi off-balance, never again permitting an Illuric prince to gather power the way Bardulis once wielded it, then the north is secure. With his marriages to Philinna and Myrtale—no, he must remember to say Olympias—the first steps are taken to make the west secure. That leaves the east and south.

While the Thraikiotes are divided they pose no real threat from the east. Only they will not remain divided. King Berisades is ailing. He divides his kingdom further, making each of his three sons heirs: Ketriporis, Monounios, and Shostokes. The resulting small kingdoms will be too splintered to withstand their neighbors, Amadokos and Kersebleptes. And of those two, Kersebleptes is the more dangerous. Left to themselves, the Odrusai will be re-united by Kersebleptes and they will dominate all the other Thraikiote tribes within ten years.

First, Philippos must have Amphipolis. The city will hold the Thraikiotes from crossing the Strymon into Makedon lands. With the Athenian League self-destructing, Amphipolis will be his. He can count on Eriguios and others. Taking the city will require fighting, but it can be done.

Second, he will dispossess Berisades' heirs. After that, well, it will depend on Amadokos and Kersebleptes.

To do all this, he must neutralize Olunthos and the Khalkidike. He must think on how to accomplish that measure. Just as he still must determine what additional steps to take in Thessalos. Those efforts are key not only for his push east, but for his security in the south.

Pikoros digs an elbow into the king's ribs, "You're not falling asleep, are you?"

Laughing, Philippos answers, "No, just thinking. You are right, having a son changes things. Lifts your eyes from yourself to your descendants."

"I suppose a girl carries your blood forward down generations," muses Pikoros, "but not the same. Like the difference between a pitcher and wine. Girls are a vessel, while boys are the precious cargo."

"Are your feet cold enough?"

Pulling his legs out of the water, Pikoros says, "At least they're clean."

"I think I shall find my way to Philinna. You should go to Petalouda," Philippos shoves his friend gently.

"Philinna will be asleep. Go to Myrtale, she's the one who will be tossing and turning tonight."

Since returning from his journey to the coast, it's been pleasant to find Olympias free of her sulks. All the palace, all the court, seems brighter for her wit and pure liveliness. She has even charmed Philinna and Audata. Still, Philippos suspects some calculation there. But why not take advantage of her sudden generosity? The thought excites him.

Her happiness is important. Not only domestically, but also as policy. Philippos nods, stands by pushing a hand against Pikoros' shoulder, "You're right. I will visit Olympias. Philinna needs her rest. Tomorrow there will be much ado over the newborn."

CHAPTER EIGHTEEN

Amphipolis and Pudna
357 B.C.

α

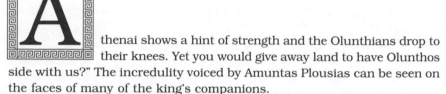 thenai shows a hint of strength and the Olunthians drop to their knees. Yet you would give away land to have Olunthos side with us?" The incredulity voiced by Amuntas Plousias can be seen on the faces of many of the king's companions.

Philippos knows that Plousias speaks his true views, but the king also understands that Plousias' post as the king's treasurer shapes his views. The older the treasurer gets, the greater his parsimony. Relinquishing the Anthemos region to the Khalkidike confederacy is relinquishing revenues for the treasury.

Others here who are opposed to the king's plans are less forthright in their opposition. Even so, their disapproval may well be harsher than Plousias'. The king finds the usual division in opinions. The younger men support Philippos, even when they are uncertain of his purpose. The older men are against any change, against innovation. Well, not all of them, he can count on Antipatros and, generally, Periandros. But as for Agathokles, Lagos, Athanaios, Antiokhos, Kharikles, and lately even Theophilos, they keep forming an opposition, a faction of sorts. The more cautious, conservative men follow their lead.

None of this is a surprise. Philippos expected this before he asked the clan heads and his chief companions to assemble. Though they must follow the king's command, he would be foolish not to hear them out. He may need to modify his intentions to gain the acceptance he wants. In truth he would rather be on the exercise field or in the marketplace just outside this great hall. His wants matter less than his duties. He waits to see who will champion him in answering Plousias.

Seeing that Philippos wants someone else to reply to Plousias, Demetrios, son of Arkouda, speaks out, "I do not understand the argument you are making. If the Olunthians are appealing to Athenai, then all the more reason to bribe them to our side."

Plousias snorts in derision, "We don't need to bribe Olunthos. The Athenians will boot their envoys out of Attika. They don't trust Olunthians, nor should we."

Speaking on the king's behalf, Eurulokhos interjects, "You may be right, Plousias, in saying that Olunthos sends her envoys in vain. Still, Athenai could as easily decide that while she's faced with rebellion from her allies, securing the Khalkidike would make a demonstration of strength and avoid the rebels enlisting aid from Olunthos."

Agathokles takes up the counter-argument, "The Athenian mob—I mean people—don't see themselves as weak. Look how they enrolled all the Euboian cities in their alliance less than twelve months ago in the face of Thebai's troops. Now they are placing garrisons on Andros and Amorgas. They outfit a second fleet under Timotheos and Iphikrates to subdue the rebellion. This is not lost on her allies, most of them are standing firm by Athenai. Plousias is exactly right. The Athenians will give nothing to the Khalkidike. Olunthos and her confederates will turn to us without our disgorging Anthemos."

"You say most of her allies stand by her. I say most are waiting to see if Rhodos, Khios, and Kos succeed. Then Athenai will be engulfed in an avalanche of defection," replies Eurulokhos.

Having let the opinions be aired, Philippos now intervenes, "We are all in agreement that in order to move on Amphipolis, we must keep the Khalkidike quiet. We want them in alliance with us, not with Athenai." All the men nod or mutter their concurrence. The king continues, "I want all of you to look two years into the future. Why two years? Because I estimate that is how long this rebellion against Athenai will last. Two years, three at the outside. Either the city will prevail or the rebels will succeed or Persia will order the outcome by the end of that time. That is how long we have to eliminate the Athenian enclaves in our midst. That is how long we have to secure our borders. In that time we can take actions so repugnant to Athenians that Athenai must declare war on us, actions like seizing Amphipolis."

The king looks around him, staring into the eyes of his companions. He sees no dissent to his propositions. Softy and firmly, he states, "I agree with Plousias that the Khalkidike deputation will fail. We know that many within the Khalkidike were unhappy that the envoys were sent. You can be sure the men who run Athenai know this, too. The chief reasons the Khalkidike make an untrustworthy ally are the differences in views between the federation's cities, and the degree to which Olunthos is able to dominate the confederacy at any given time. Athenai sees itself in Olunthos. Knowing itself, it knows to fear Olunthos."

The men laugh at the king's aphorism. His warmth of tone engages them. "Now, let's consider Olunthos. We have friends there and we have violent enemies. We are not alone in this. The same can be said by every city in their confederation. The weakness of the confederacy is Olunthos, even while she is the strongest member of the league. Without her, all the other cities are dust to either Athenai or us. Yet the same can be said of Olunthos, for without the league, she could not withstand a strong power. Her leaders know her weakness so they would force the other cities to follow her without question. The member cities, in turn, find every reason to excuse themselves. Olunthos and the league cities balance one another. Thus Olunthos shops for an ally to strengthen her hand in the league."

All follow the king's reasoning. He continues, "The Athenians hold Potidaia, the only city of the Khalkidike to openly defy Olunthos. Sitting on Olunthos' doorstep, a port that could readily serve her big sister city, instead Potidaia invites in the Athenians so she can stand up to Olunthos. If for no other reason, Olunthos should be forever opposed to Athenai. Yet she sends envoys to Athenai and not to us."

The king pauses, making sure all are with him. "You see it now as clearly as I do. Olunthos fears us so much that she turns to her enemy before she comes to us. What have we done to make her fear us? We put our house in order, we raised up an army the like of which has not been seen before among the Makedones, we destroyed the Dardanoi confederacy, we restrained the Paiaones, we joined the highlands and the lowlands. She sees our new strength and she knows her own guilt. She remembers the wars she brought on us, the impositions made upon us— all when we were weak. Guilt leads to fear, fear leads to hate."

Impatiently Agathokles interrupts, "All you say is true. All the more reason to distrust Olunthos. Why not attack the confederacy? Let Amphipolis wait."

"Who is stronger, the Khalkidike or Amphipolis?" the king asks the grizzled magnate.

"The Khalkidike," answers Agathokles. "All the more reason to eliminate their threat. Why add to an enemy's strength? Why give them Anthemos?"

For a moment Philippos feels frustration rising in him. Why can't they see it? Are they so blinded by their holdings in Anthemos? He would like their understanding without spelling out his plans, since what's said among so many is likely to be known throughout the kingdom and by their neighbors within days. His face shows none of his irritation. Smiling gently, he says to them all, "Amphipolis is the stopper in the amphora that is Thraikios. The opportunity that exists is due not only to Athenai's disarray. The splintering of the Odrusai in Thraikios is unlikely to persist. It is the conjunction of these two events that makes possible our success. Now is the time to take Amphipolis."

By bringing the group back to Amphipolis, he has them nodding agreement again. "To set the army in motion against Amphipolis without first ensuring that any appeal by the Amphipolitans to the Khalkidike will go unanswered is to invite failure. We will not fail. Athenai spent its wealth and more than a generation trying to regain Amphipolis. We will seize her in one campaign." This last is said fiercely. The king glares at his companions, as if daring anyone to contradict him. His look cows Agathokles and those standing around the noble.

"We buy cooperation from the Khalkidike because we must. That is the only way we will win their neutrality when we strike at Amphipolis. They will share Anthemos among themselves. By sharing, none of the league cities can claim the region for itself. They will hold the region only for the duration of our treaty. As for Olunthos, we will add a sweetener, to Olunthos will go Potidaia."

At this last statement, there are exclamations among the companions. Several call out, "Potidaia? How?"

Philippos grins, holds up a hand, and the room quiets. "All in good time. Let me repeat. I intend to eliminate all the Athenian enclaves or potential enclaves." He holds up his hand and ticks off his fingers, "Amphipolis, Pudna, Potidaia, Methone." Then he adds a sweetener for the men here, "Consider that the lands will be spear won. They will be in my gift. And it is to you I will be grateful." At that each man is with him, each and every one of them. He can proceed as he intends.

β

The defenders send a flight of arrows toward the advancing ram. Their effect is useless. Wicker mantles protect the crew heaving the ram forward. From behind these light broad shields, Kretan archers and slingers fire back at the men on the walls.

Watching from a distance, Philippos grunts in satisfaction. The Kretans are worth their pay, just as Andromitos said they would be. Still, it will be full dark before the first ram will reach the base of the city wall. When all three rams are up, the wall will take a pounding.

Even with the rams and the miners, Philippos estimates it will take most of a month to make the breach. In provisioning the army, he has allowed four months for the campaign, and already the first month has passed.

Time flows so fast. Bringing the army together, driving in the Amphipolitan patrols, investing the city—squeezing it in on all sides so that no food or allies reach the walls. Constructing the defensive palisades around the camps, then building the mantles, rams, and catapults. Clearing the ground and filling in declivities to allow the rams to move. Time rushing by, as if a strong wind were blowing and time is no more than the seeds of dandelions.

He must succeed, and within his four-month limit. Yet who among the Hellenes has take a well-armed, well-supplied, fortified city in that time?

This is Amphipolis—the city that's defied Athenai for more than a generation. Philippos tells himself that he is certain he will succeed. He spurns his own doubts. After all, there is the treachery proposed by Eriguios. The king is confident Eriguios will act. He's less certain the traitor will win. Perhaps he will. The king, though, cannot afford to base his plans on Eriguios. Philippos is determined to take the city whether or not the traitor lends his strength.

Planning, preparation, a trained army well-provisioned and largely free of disease, the finest siege equipment, the best engineers—these are the ingredients with which Philippos will cook this stew. He turns to his color bearer, "Signal Kleitos to move the second ram forward. Then signal Eurulokhos to fire his scorpions to clear the wall."

Soon the long arrows of the scorpions slice toward the city. Though only one man is transfixed and falls, all on the wall scramble for safety. Between the scorpions and the Kretan archers the wall is cleared. Not that the Amphipolitans are much threat at this stage, not like when the Makedones were clearing the approaches to the wall. The losses then were higher than Philippos had expected. When the rams reach the walls they will be vulnerable to burning pitch and dropped stones. If the walls can be kept clear through fear of the scorpions and archers, then the huge rams will do their work.

With the rams safe for now, Philippos can visit his lines on the far side of the city, where the stone-throwing catapults batter at the north gate. Hipponikos should be reporting in soon on what the horsemen have found on the scout east. Ephrastos should be up from the coast by midday to report on the state of the stores, and news his agents have sent him. When the afternoon sun is high, and most are asleep, the king will meet with Tyros. Right now Tyros and his scribes are annotating the king's digest with whatever dispatches have come in from army commands and from around the kingdom. With that information in hand, along with the confidential matters provided by Ephrastos and his own observations, Philippos will dictate his orders. That will not preclude the nightly gathering of the senior commanders. Somewhere in this day, the king must fit in his pike exercise. Maybe Pikoros can put him through his paces.

The image of a youthful noble from the highlands flits through Philippos' mind. Young Leokhares possesses a courteous manner, a pleasing face, and a lithe body. He seems a willing fellow. Philippos smiles in anticipation—so many are willing for a king, not all are so fine bred. The king finds he prefers a male lover when on campaign, no squalid female camp follower or refugee for him.

As Philippos turns to call up his mount, a tumult near the walls snatches his attention. He calls to Pikoros, "What is it? Can you tell from here?"

One of the bodyguards answers first, "They are making a sortie. There must be a hidden gate in that tower beyond the ram."

Pikoros adds, "Looks like the ram's crew and supports are running."

"Colors," bellows Philippos. The signalman runs to the king's side. "Hoist the flag for Polemaios. Send in the horsemen."

"Lamakhos is launching his *syntagma*," calls out Pikoros. In the fields near the camp, the pikemen are already in motion. Officers are quick marching the formation.

"He won't reach them in time," Philippos is furious with himself for not keeping a formed body of pike closer to the rams. "Let's mount. If Polemaios reaches the attackers in time, he may delay them. We may be able to aid him."

Within moments Philippos and his immediate companions are riding recklessly down the slope and across the broad sands. Despite the speed of their response, it's doubtful they can save the ram. Already smoke is rising from its frame. With the distraction at the ram, the enemy has manned the walls again. Now their arrows find targets among the retreating crew and Kretan mercenaries.

From the river, Polemaios leads his horsemen down on the enemy party at the ram. But his column is strung out, having reacted hastily. Though they don't have the force of a well-executed charge, they could cut off the enemy from safety.

Eurulokhos is awake to the danger from the walls. His crews work their scorpions as quickly as possible. The long arrows hum in flight.

Yet on the wall the defenders do not flinch. Despite losses, their arrows fly faster than any scorpion can be worked. A flight brings down a number of horses among Polemaios' riders.

Kleitos is the savior. From the second ram, he leads his crew and mercenaries at a dead run against the sallying force. His improbable attack rallies the first ram's crew. Besieged and besieger are soon swinging blows at one another. As the fighters mix and melee, the bowmen on the wall must shoot more cautiously. Arrows still find bodies but no longer in massive flights.

Now Polemaios and his front riders are in the melee. More horsemen ride into the mass of milling men. Striking down, they break the resistance of the enemy line.

Kretans begin answering the fire from the wall again. Coupled with the slinging bolts from the scorpions, the Makedones again make headway against the defenders. The failure of the sally is enough for the opposing commander to call off his archers.

Riding through the disorganized troops, Philippos calls harshly to the officers to reform the men. He is pleased to see the ram's carriage is safe, the attempt at firing it already doused. Much of the disorder is caused by the surrender of the enemy party. Weapons are gathered and disheartened prisoners are being marched to the investing lines. Coming up to Black Kleitos, Philippos calls out his praise, "Well done, Kleitos, well done. They made a good try but you were a lion."

Swinging out of the saddle he hugs his old friend to him. All around, officers and men are watching the king. With his arm around Kleitos' shoulder, the king raises his arm to still those about him, "This is what I expect. Courage, determination, quick action. Kleitos is a warrior we can all admire." Loosing his sword from its scabbard the king hands it pommel first to the burly man, "You are my sword, Kleitos. What do I have for this blade when you are on the field?"

All about him the men cheer. What better man is there to serve than Philippos, king of the Makedones?

γ

In Pella, daily life is dull. The king and his companions are off to their campaign against Amphipolis. Olympias feels restless. As if there were an itch she cannot scratch. This boy of Philinna's, this little Arrhidaios, princeling of the king's, he is one source of her mood. A placid child, though growing quickly, already he is bigger than most his age. And that despite the illness of his second month when they all thought he was lost, the fevers burning him for days, scalding hot. Arrhidaios, though, is only one small part of her mood.

Routine is another element. Who can bear routine?

She stretches her arms, and the gauzy Aigyptian cotton folds slide to her shoulders. She touches her finger to a nipple that pokes up the taut fabric over her bosom. A shiver runs through her. How sensitive her breasts seem lately.

She misses him. She's not sure she likes how much she misses her husband. She hates any sense of dependency in herself. Even so, his absence is like the loss of her arm; no, worse, like the loss of some part of her vitality, her soul. She grits her teeth wanting to spit. A wave of longing and lust and sheer anxiety grabs her throat. What if something was to happen to him?

The Amphipolitans fight. For more than two months, they have fought—seven *dekades* now, they have fought. And Philippos is in the thick of it. The wounded who survive and return to Pella talk of the king. They all admire him—his energy, his certainty, his care for them, his strength of arm, his raw courage, his crafty stratagems. She is sick of hearing about him and yet eagerly seeks out each man that returns. What of the king? Tell me, tell me, tell me all that you can.

Philinna has her Arrhidaios; Eurudike Audata, her Kynnane; Phila, her chiefdom of Elimiotis and her horses. Only his mother, the dowager queen, Eurudike, must feel as she does. Who would guess how much the mother and Olympias share in torment?

Sitting up, Olympias puts her feet to the rugs and furs surrounding her sleeping couch. Normally she loves the richness of their touch—the

418

softness, the subtle tickling pleasure, of thick woolen rugs and heavy furs. Her feet can distinguish one animal's pelt from another. This is bear, this mountain lion, this fox. The sensations are too much today, they cloy. Quickly she rushes to the bare flooring by the window. Even the wood is too smooth. She sits on the wide windowsill so her naked feet can feel the cold stone of the wall. Better, much better, she feels the uneven gnarls of the stone. She should be with Philippos, sleep on the ground, share his blanket.

No one should love a husband, be in thrall to him. Is it not enough that he has his authority over you? Why voluntarily put yourself in slavery? The image of Aphrodite laughing at her flits through her mind. She is a sardonic goddess who mocks Olympias' pretensions. Aphrodite sees beyond the identity of Olympias the Queen to the young girl, Myrtale, hidden within. Who says love is voluntary? asks the goddess.

No wonder Myrtale prefers the ever-changing god Dionysios. A god who can be embraced, who will burn you with the heat of his desires, his intensities, his purpose. For a moment she wonders if Dionysios exists in the guise of her husband, Philippos. Instantly she dismisses the notion.

The year ends soon. Already the harvests have begun to be gathered. The moon of autumn is huge. There are festivals coming. These she looks forward to. The ennui of the court will be overwhelmed by the sanctity of ritual and sacrifice. He said he would have Amphipolis before the year-end. He will be here to honor Zeus, and the ancestors of his Argeadai clan and Temenidai family. The gods, the spirits of his ancestors, and the people would expect no less.

She has heard whispers, though, that Philippos intends another campaign the instant he succeeds at Amphipolis. A quick campaign before winter settles in. Antipatros, and at the thought of the magnate Olympias purses her lips in distaste, comes to Pella, leaving his command in the highlands. That brute, Antigonos, gathers arms and supplies here. Recruits are being drilled. The king enlarges his army even as he fights on the eastern frontier.

A clatter and knock at the door interrupt Olympias' musings. Her women are at the door. The day must begin. She promised to take her little brother, Alexandros, riding today. The queen-mother is to arrive in Pella and must be appropriately greeted. Olympias must also do her rounds to her sister-queens, Philinna and Audata. Thank goodness Phila has returned to her mountains and her stables.

The knocking is light but persistent. Time to start the day. And it is the thought of time—as if time were a separate being, a god in its own right—which causes her to abruptly swing to the floor. How long has this campaign gone on? When did she have her last monthly flow? She takes a breast in each hand, running her fingers over her nipples. She knows the itch now. She has quickened. The king's running visit to the capitol to squeeze more money from the treasury. She counts back. That sudden mounting, after so long an absence, that was it. Here for a day, then Philippos is gone back to the fighting.

A child, she is with child. Panic slices through her. Her mother died in childbirth.

The knocking at the door is louder. She can hear their rising voices, their concern. For a moment longer she lets them wait. She controls her panic. Consciously she beats it down and substitutes the image of a healthy son, a prince who overshadows all the king's other children. She imagines the heir to the throne come from her loins. Perhaps Dionysios does at time inhabit her husband. And now the god is within her. She will give birth to a lion, a god, a crown prince of the Makedones.

δ

The council chamber of Amphipolis is ornate. A frieze runs along the inner wall, near the ceiling. There the gods crown the achievement of the city's founder. The city's ostentatious self-congratulation no longer seems in place as Makedon phalangists ground their pikes on the stone floor. The well-armed phalangists line the chamber. The surviving city councilors are assembled between the warriors, facing the dais where Philippos and several of his generals sit idly chatting.

The city councilors are sullen, afraid, silent save for occasional whispered muttering. They eye their conquerors with expectant apprehension. What will become of them, of their city?

Philippos does not appear to notice the assembly's fear. He leans toward Kharikles, tapping him on the knee, "Well, the joke is soon known to Athenai."

"How anyone could be deceived of your intentions amazes me," answers Kharikles.

"The Athenians believe so in themselves that they think all others must appease them," interjects Lamakhos. "The king tells their ambassadors that he will hand over Amphipolis to them and they accept the offer as a given."

Eurulokhos strokes his beard, "Doubtless they did not believe we could succeed where time and again they failed. Even under commanders like Timotheos and Iphikrates, whose reputations are for boldness, at least."

Philippos smiles gently, "Any one of you could manipulate the Athenians. You must provide them with a reason not to act, even if it's flimsy or specious. Then the faction that calls for immediate action is sure to be opposed by a faction that seizes on the pretext you provided. You must give them cause for talk, for their endless speechmaking."

The men laugh. More dourly, from the back row, Kleitos says, "Well, it's war with them now."

"We are well-suited for war," responds Philippos mildly. He grins,

"They will be hard put to fight us over Amphipolis while facing their rebellious allies. We will make them howl even louder before we're done."

The hall ushers begin closing the great doors as the last few Amphipolitan councilors scurry in. What little was being said among the councilors now quiets.

Philippos stands. He surveys the many faces turned toward him. The virulently anti-Makedones cluster together around Philon, a smaller group of pro-Makedones stand with Eriguios. Between the two parties are the many cowed but uncommitted councilors. Some of these men are simply bewildered, uncertain where their best interests or the best interest of the city rests. Yet all the councilors, even the anti-Makedones, are impressed by the discipline of the Makedon army and are surprised that the city was not plundered and its citizens were not savaged.

Stepping forward, Philippos addresses the city fathers, "You and your people have shown courage. You can take pride in your defense of Amphipolis. As citizens of an independent state, it was your duty and your devotion. You have long withstood your enemies in the past. Many of you believed you could again."

"While I admire your courage in fighting me, I now want you to show another form of courage. I want you to recognize, accept, and commit yourselves and your people to my stewardship of Amphipolis. In time, I hope you will take the same pride in that stewardship and in your city's partnership with the Makedones as you have taken in your city itself."

No response is evident among the councilors, except for the fury of the anti-Makedones. All are listening intently but even the pro-Makedones appear at best solemn and at worst downcast.

"Let me be clear why I fought you and conquered your city. Your city was divided. Four principal parties contended for power. Those who believed Amphipolis could maintain her freedom. Those who believed the city would be safest if surrendered to Athenai. Those who wanted to join the city to the Khalkidike confederacy. And those who had come to recognize that the city could prosper under my care."

"In the past you have appealed to the Makedones for succor against Athenai. Yet when my brother died, and all the world seemed ready to partition Makedonis, I withdrew our garrison from your city. Had I abandoned you to Athenai? So it must have seemed."

He can see some faces nodding. He continues, "Until I killed Bardulis and destroyed the Dardanoi confederacy, how could you believe that my strength could shield you? That event frightened some of you. Had the Makedones become too strong? There were some in this chamber who argued here or at dinners shared in wealthy homes, that if Amphipolis were not to be free, it should be ruled by the civilized and democratic Athenians. Those same voices declared that we Makedones are barbarians, and they called us despicable."

421

At this Philon turns his back on Philippos, and one by one his faction does the same. A gap of a few paces opens between that faction and the rest of the councilors.

"As my achievements grew, so grew the fear of me in Amphipolis, here among you. I saw the hostility grow towards my people. Outrages occurred, a beating here, a rape there, even a pillaged homestead on your borders, with a man killed. Beyond these events were your official actions, like raising the tolls, then closing your markets to Makedones. Is this not true?" The last is barked at the councilors, forcing them to acknowledge the anti-Makedon passions that had risen like a flood this past winter.

"I could not stand idle as you became hostile to me. My coasts are already in the hands of Athenai and her allies, how could I allow you to sell yourselves to her servitude? Yet that seemed likely as you felt squeezed by the Khalkidike, by Athenai, and by me."

The king shakes his head wearily, as if remembering the errant ways of the Amphipolitans. "I know how great a city you are. Think how prosperous you could be if your shores were freed of Athenian blockade. I know that cooperation between us can create strength and wealth for Amphipolitans and Makedones alike. How could I see you betrayed by a few men who would be oligarchs propped up by Athenian spears?"

"I struck. You fought. Good, stalwart men have died on both sides. Their blood flows together. Their sacrifice pacifies the gods. We are now one people." This admonition is said with great force, as Philippos drives a right fist into his left hand then raises both hands with fingers interlocked.

"I could rule you as spear-won land, with all rights residing in me. That is what victory permits." He sternly gazes down on them, he sees no disagreement with his statement. Some bow their heads in resignation, others look hopeful having heard the word "could".

"Why would I destroy a city and people who, in accepting and working within my care, would increase my well-being and theirs? If you willingly give me your allegiance, you have nothing to fear. You may retain your civic institutions and govern the internal affairs of your city. War, diplomacy, external trade will be in my keeping. You will help shoulder the burden of the kingdom, but only in measure with all others who share that burden. You need fear no reparations. This is what I offer you." With that Philippos closes his speech. He turns to his generals and motions them off the platform. He and they all step down and aside. The dais is clear, open to the Amphipolitans.

The councilors look to one another. Voices speak out, clash. The senior magistrate mounts the dais. He quiets the Amphipolitans. He looks anxiously toward Philippos and his officers. The king remains impassive, though inwardly he is laughing, looking forward to the fruits of his planning.

Straightening, the magistrate raps his staff on the platform floor, calling his fellows into council. Eriguios immediately proposes a motion accepting the king's gracious conciliation. With several brief speeches in support, the Amphipolitans vote their allegiance.

Eriguios then launches a motion exiling Philon, Hierax, and Stratokles with their families and dependents. Let the instigators of King Philippos' wrath be gone from Amphipolis. Let the lovers of Athenai find their way to her. Let them be glad their lives are spared and their families not reduced to servitude. Tell them to depart within two days. Their lands are forfeit. All they hold is forfeit. All that belongs to them is stripped from them.

The motion carries. How eagerly the majority seek to please the king.

With that motion passed, the Athenian faction is a hen flapping, its head severed. Ready to be eaten by their hungry Amphipolitan neighbors. Philippos has no need to be harsh. While his proponents take a necessary revenge, they can also take any blame for their exactions. Philippos can be just and restrain their zeal.

Raising an arm, the king stills the council, "Amphipolitans, I approve your legislation but ask that you show mercy on Philon and his friends. Exiled they must be for the good of Amphipolis. Let them, though, depart with their personal belongings. Allow them the means to possess dignity in the city of your enemies. By your forbearance you will gain respect among the Hellenes. This I ask of you."

Quickly the earlier ruling is amended. Exile—the loss of their city gods, homes, and lands—is enough.

Philippos is well satisfied. The city is truly his now, not a sullen, defeated people seething with hatred, waiting for his back to turn. They have much to learn to be comfortable under his rule, but they will endeavor to serve him. The garrison he leaves behind can be discrete. The people here no longer need fear Athenai or the Thraikiotes, nor need they fear Philippos.

ε

The New Year and all its festivities will soon be upon them. Winter will follow, but today the sun is shining. Throughout Pella, the people are out-of-doors eager to enjoy one of the last days of good weather before spring. The marketplace is full of city dwellers and country folk. This late morning is a respite for the king. For this brief interlude he can simply be a family man. Up ahead, Philinna and the nurse each give fat baby Arrhidaios a finger to hold as he staggers forward between them. Beside Philippos strolls Olympias, just beginning to show that she will bear a child come summer. Somewhere in the crowd is Eurudike Audata, trying to catch up with the scurrying Kynnane, with the help of the king's nephew, Amuntas. Trailing behind are three guards and the king's young brother-in-law, Alexandros of Epeiros.

Though not as rare as a family outing like this would be in Thebai or

Athenai, still it is unusual for the women of the king's household to shop the public market. The freedom enjoyed by a Makedon peasant woman is far greater than that of a princess or a magnate's wife. The more one conforms with the mores of the city Hellenes, the more restrained is a woman.

Philippos stops at a booth to pick up a turnip. He turns to Olympias, "Do you know how many days I ate a soup or stew with turnips while we besieged Amphipolis?"

"As many days as you fought its citizens?" asks Olympias.

Seeing her derision, Philippos mildly replies, "A turnip may be humble, but it feeds the army that permits our ambitions to succeed."

"True, though the men of the army would prefer bread or even porridge with a few morsels of mutton," spars Olympias smiling. Lightly she touches Philippos' arm to take the sting from her opposition.

Tossing the turnip in the air to catch it in upturned hand, the king realizes how much he likes turnips. Not so much for their taste as for their sturdy plainness. He likes them for their essence, their very commonness and hearty sustenance. They are very much like the rural men who haul them to market, and like the farmers' brothers and cousins who wield the long pike in the ranks of his army. Yes, turnips will do quite well.

"I suppose you will be going to the sheep stalls next?" says Olympias.

"I'm more interested in horses today."

Horses are royal and near divine, so Olympias will willingly examine horse stock, "Shall we find the horses by way of the goldsmiths?"

Philippos looks about him to locate Philinna and Eurudike Audata. Olympias turns away to hide the touch of irritation she always feels at being one of her husband's several wives.

Alert to Philippos, Audata nudges Kynnane in the direction of the king. The toddler is shy of her father, who rarely has time for her. The girl is eager for Olympias, whom she sees and plays with regularly. Though disdaining her sister-queens, Olympias does enjoy their children now that she's pregnant. The little girl hurries as fast as she can to her honorary Aunt.

On up ahead, Arrhidaios' nurse tugs at her mistress' sleeve. Philinna has stopped at a booth to admire finely woven cloth imported from Asia. Her baby son is on the ground next to her, propped on a pile of woolens, a tiny fist stuffed in his mouth. Philinna reacts to the nurse's pull by first looking for her companion, Mikrosdiana. No doubt her friend is at the perfumery.

Catching Philinna's eye as she looks about her, Philippos points toward the alley leading to the stock yard. The queen from Thessalos nods her understanding and gestures that she will follow.

Dryly, Olympias says, "She wants her Mikrosdiana. I have never seen one woman so dependent on another."

"Who are you dependent on, Olympias?" replies Philippos.

For an instant, Olympias considers flattering Philippos but dismisses the notion. The king can be susceptible to flattery when he considers it both his due and honestly given. From her, he does not like fawning, "I am dependent on the divine Dionysios, Lord my husband."

Philippos laughs at the ironic 'Lord my husband', "We are all dependents of the gods. Though, for their existence, I sometimes wonder if they are also dependent on us."

"Don't blaspheme, husband. You betray your Orphic speculations," Olympias smiles mischievously.

"Even if you don't like the pieties attributed to Orpheos, you seem to like his music."

"Music? Who does not like music is a dullard," she answers. The thought of Antipatros, with his poor ear for song, comes quickly to her mind.

Kynnane has stumbled, fallen, gotten up, charged further, nearly fallen again, but in full motion comes colliding into Olympias' legs. Stooping, the queen from the Molossi picks up the girl, "Ready to see the horses, my pet?"

"'Pia come, too," commands the small princess. Her name for Olympias always brings a smile to the queen's face.

"Where is Amuntas?" asks Philippos as Audata comes up. "Telesilla will scold me if I lose her boy."

In her slow, awkward Hellenic, Audata says, "He's coming. He went to the stalls of the armourers."

"That's where my brother is headed. They're by the goldsmiths, we can meet them on the way," directs Olympias. Eurudike Audata respectfully bows her head to Olympias, and takes Kynnane from the principal queen.

Around them the crowd parts easily to let them pass. Though the Makedones offer their king less deference than a king receives in Eastern lands, they have enough respect and affection for Philippos to show a ready courtesy. They do not hesitate to greet him, many calling him by name without title. Yet they are not so familiar that any observer would mistake their greetings as disrespectful. When the king chooses to go about the city privately, as this morning with his family, he and his receive a polite fiction of privacy despite being the focus of discreet attention from all about them. In truth, there is no possibility of Amuntas or any of the children becoming lost.

Looking back, Philippos can see Philinna and Mikrosdiana coming along, hand-in-hand. Trailing behind is the nurse, carrying a drooling Arrhidaios. Something about the way the nurse holds the baby's head up catches Philippos' eye. He stops to stare.

Olympias assumes he is eyeing Mikrosdiana. A slice of rage cuts through her mind. She wants the court rid of the wanton Thessaliote. The girl is too clever and too attractive. Olympias sees too much of herself in Mikrosdiana. She comments, "Isn't it time Mikrosdiana were married off?"

Philippos grunts, his attention refocusing to Philinna's companion. He

425

has long recognized the desire he feels for the diminutive Thessaliote, and that he can slake his lusts more safely elsewhere. He responds, "Philinna seems to need her for now." Then he states his real concern, "Have you noticed anything odd about Arrhidaios?"

"Not particularly, he's an infant."

"I seem to remember Kynnane growing faster, more alert and attentive."

Olympias starts to say he sees Kynnane so infrequently, of course she seems to grow quickly, but she holds her tongue. Instead she offers, "Kynnane did not have a serious bout of illness like Arrhidaios."

Audata interjects stolidly, "The baby is slow."

Philippos stares at Audata, trying to understand what her statement implies. "Slow in what way?" he asks.

Audata thinks about her words, wanting to find the right Hellenic term, "The boy is simple."

A flash of fear pierces Philippos. This is his only legitimate male child. This is his heir. He wants to shout that it cannot be true, only he knows with immediate comprehension that it is true. The disquiet he's felt about the boy since returning from Amphipolis is now so obvious.

As suddenly Olympias sees that Audata is right. The barbarian's insight is accurate. What Olympias has attributed to a long recovery from serious illness is the natural simplicity of the child. Though she experiences a moment of sorrow for Arrhidaios and Philinna, her mind quickly passes to joy. When she bears the king a son, her child will not be slow. And fiercely she knows this child she carries within her is a boy. Her son will rule when Philippos can no longer.

Innocently, Philinna and Mikrosdiana approach the waiting group. Philinna is tittering at something her companion is saying. The nurse trudges behind them, carrying the king's son, who is oblivious to so much around him.

ζ

Pudna was founded on the western coast of the Thermaic Gulf some three hundred years earlier by Ionian settlers from Euboia. The small city is one of many sites in the North Aegean and Euxine established in the last period of widespread Hellenic colonization. Back then, the Makedones had held Pieris and the Thermaic coast for no more than a generation. The Euboians settled on lands they considered barbarous.

Welcomed by the Makedones, the Euboian settlers created a trading port that served the hinterland. The newly arrived Hellenes also helped deter Thraikiote and Paiaone raiders.

Still, Pudna never prospered to the extent of its neighbor to the north, Methone. Under King Arkhelaos, the Makedones refounded Pudna, strengthening it in its rivalry with Methone. The opportunity to trade through several centers was important to the Makedones. Without their aid, Pudna might have dwindled further, leaving Methone to monopolize trade.

That influx of Makedones under King Arkhelaos mixed the population of Pudna. A definite affinity for the Makedones exists in Pudna that is absent in Methone. Depending on the nativity of the citizen, the city is called Pydna or Pudna. The former is the Ionic dialect and the latter the Makedon.

That relationship was not strong enough to withstand the pressure exerted by the seafaring power of Athenai. Today Pudna is a firm ally of Athenai. The Athenian general, Timotheos, saw to that some eight years earlier by seizing the city and settling Athenian citizens there.

Not that the Athenian leadership values the little city all that much. That fact is clear as Philippos listens to the offer of the envoys dispatched by the Athenian council.

"...and in receiving Pydna for Amphipolis, you gain a city at your heartland rather than a city on your frontier." The Athenian envoy, Kharidemos, looks pleased with the delivery of his logic. His younger associate, Antiphon, nods enthusiastically to points made in the speech. The tall florid Kharidemos continues, "In summary, King Philippos, you gain in three ways. First, you gain a useful port without a people resentful of your rule, for are not many citizens of Pydna cousins to your people? Second, you avoid the trying financial and military responsibilities for maintaining a garrison in a restive city, known for its stubborn independence, far from the center of your power. Moreover, Amphipolis is a city that faces constant threats from the encroachments of neighboring Thraikiote tribesmen. Third, you regain the friendship of Athenai, the most powerful and renowned city of the Hellenes. The friends of Athenai enjoy the prosperity of her trade and share in the benefits of her naval strength. The enemies of Athenai tremble at her wrath and fear her chastisement. Linking the destiny of King Philippos with the genius and resilience of our democracy makes all the North Aegean and the lands along its coast our mutual and natural allies."

Philippos smiles gently to hide the real mirth he feels, "Good Kharidemos, your argument is persuasive. Rarely have I heard such logic so brilliantly and clearly expressed. If I could recapitulate in my own rough words—I gain friendship and alliance with Athenai if I exchange my spear-won lands of Amphipolis for the gift of Pudna?"

The slim Antiphon speaks up, "Exactly so, King Philippos."

Turning to his only two companions in the room, Philippos asks, "Amuntas Plousias and Antipatros, do you find the points made as interesting as I do?"

"If Amphipolis proves a drain on the kingdom's finances, then exchanging her for the certainty of revenues from Pudna and her port would be an advantage," says Plousias quietly. As the king's treasurer, Plousias has already estimated the increase in revenue the king gains from Amphipolis. Offsetting the cost of the city's defense is the flow of goods from all the peoples inhabiting the River Strymon's valley and watershed. That does not count the added silver and gold from mines on Mount Pangaion. But if the king wants to bemuse these foreigners, then Plousias has no difficulty dissembling. Although given this Kharidemos' ability to declaim over an Aegean-wide alliance in the face of hardy rebellion against Athenai, Plousias doubts that it takes much to make Kharidemos hear what he wants to hear.

Antipatros is slower to respond as he decides how best to support the king's game. "The army has many responsibilities. We guard the highlands from the Illuroi and we guard our borders to the north and east from the Paiaones and Thraikiotes. Friendship with our neighbors to the west in Epeiros and to the south in Thessalos and the Khalkidike is essential. Friendship with Athenai would be advantageous, as well, for our coasts are open to her fleets and our borders porous were she to excite her allies, the Thraikiotes, against us."

Attentive to the envoys, Philippos gestures, "You see how my counselors are sympathetic to your views? There is much in what you say. I see only one flaw, but you may already have an answer. I do not believe the citizens of Pudna are aware of the exchange you propose."

Kharidemos replies, "You are correct, sir. Why concern an ally unless our proposal has merit in your eyes? Their concurrence is our responsibility. After all, you would not consult the Amphipolitans, King Philippos."

Eyeing the tall Athenian, Philippos wonders if all people look small from his height. Certainly he acts as if the concerns of others are small. Still the king is careful not to disagree openly, "Then you have considered all the issues, good Kharidemos." He stands, facing the pair, "You may return to Athenai and say to your colleagues in the senior council that you may initiate the exchange. Inform Pudna. We shall ready the Amphipolitans."

Both envoys are grinning. Antiphon begins an effusive encomium until cut short as Philippos pleads the press of other business. Kharidemos suggests the agreement be reduced to writing but is also put off by Philippos, who asserts the need for secrecy. Calling in his steward, Philippos has the happy pair ushered out.

All this time Plousias and Antipatros are silent, waiting. With the pair gone, Antipatros begins chuckling. Plousias wears a grin as wide as those envoys wore. Philippos starts laughing as well. "What a pair."

"Where do Athenians get such hare-brained ideas?" sputters Plousias. "How could they believe you would give up Amphipolis?"

"They want to believe. And, after all, I gave up Amphipolis once before."

"But for Pudna?" says Antipatros. "A ripe plum that falls into our hand the moment we stretch out an arm."

"We hold off Athenian action for another few months with this nonsense. If word of the Athenian betrayal reaches the Pudnaians soon, in the worst possible light, how much easier is our task."

Plousias grins, "I think I can guarantee that word will reach Pudna."

"Would that all our enemies were as inept as the people of Athenai," says Philippos with a good-natured laugh.

η

The attack on Pudna is timed to follow the change of year and its attendant ceremonies. Makedones from all over the kingdom congregate each year at the religious centers of Dion and Aigai in the Pieris for the festivals of renewal. Nothing in that to alarm the Pudnaians. That this year so many more come and so many are warriors seem only the consequence of the kingdom's expansion and the several years of war in which it has engaged.

This year-end comes early in the season, with the harvest of some crops still waiting. Philippos and his generals feel no impiety at using festivals dedicated to the gods and ancestors as cover for their approach on Pudna. Philippos decided long ago, under the tutelage of the ancient and pious Lady Kleopatra, that his progenitor, Perdikkas the First, was a practical man for all the favor showered on him by Zeus. The king is certain his ancestors praise the cunning.

With the first day of the year not two days past, Philippos leads the invasion army across the Pudnaian border. The initial object of the main column is to cross the Mitys River at Hatera. From there they march up the coast road to strike Pudna from the south. A smaller column, all of horsemen, ride from Aigai to reach Pudna from the northwest and cut the city off from its neighbor, Methone.

A squadron of Makedon ships sails from Therme. On board are the siege engines. The Makedones hope to close Pudna's harbor with their seaforce. They're uncertain whether they can be in place long enough to help force the city's surrender. If the Athenian's northern fleet is alert, the squadron will have to flee as soon as they complete unloading the siege engines. At sea, they are no match for the Athenians. The king's advance column can protect the landing from the shore side.

Though three forces must coordinate, Philippos is confident. He views this operation as little more than training. Certainly as an expedition it pales compared to the war against Bardulis, the advance into Thessalos, or the siege of Amphipolis. Still he wants it to be flawless and fast, both to forestall the Athenians and to impress the cities of Methone and Olunthos.

Philippos is with the main column, slogging through mud as he leads his horse. Doesn't hurt for his royal footmen to see the king march beside them despite the pouring rain. If all goes well, the siege will be a sham. The king's adherents in the city will see that the gates open with a minimum of battle. The young men marching in this long column don't know that. They expect a sharp action even if they don't expect the fierce fighting that occurred at Amphipolis.

Out of the corner of his eye, Philippos can see the young fellows pointing him out to one another. A bold pikeman calls to him, "Lord King, were you to march barefoot like us you'd feel more comfort than in your riding boots."

"So would my horse when I remount him and urge him to canter," calls back Philippos.

Another footman calls, "If you keep your feet bare, they'll be so tough, the horse won't be able to tell the difference." At this sally, several rows of men laugh.

Taking the challenge, the king points upslope where stones, briars, and nettles aren't buried in mud. "I'll take off my boots if you win a race with me to the top of the hill."

"I'll race you sir, if you take your boots off before we start."

"Will you race with your pike and shield?" asks the king.

The first pikeman calls out, "Will you race carrying your horse?" Again laughter resounds among the men.

By now an officer from the head of the column has come back to learn the cause of the laughter. Seeing the king, he starts to order the men into respectful silence, but Philippos waves him off. Calling to his challenger, the king says, "We both run to the top of the knoll and back. Both barefoot. If you win, I give you my horse. If I win, you become my horse's groom."

"Where's the advantage in that? Either way I end up caring for the horse," answers the young challenger. Again the footmen laugh.

Philippos grins, he likes the spirit of these men. "If you win and don't want to keep the horse, I'll buy him back from you for the cost of her upkeep for two years."

At this the men start pushing their hero to the king's side. All around they chant, "A race! A race!"

Philippos unlaces his boots and pulls them free. He stretches and jogs in place a moment. Beside him the challenger hands off his pike, shield and accouterments to his friends. Philippos asks, "Your name?"

"Pantores." The young man smiles shyly and offers his hand. They grip each other's wrists in greeting. The youngster is well muscled.

"Who will call the mark?" asks Philippos.

"Me," says the burly fellow who first called to the king, pointing a thumb to himself. "You both ready?"

They nod, side by side facing the knoll. The rain has lifted a bit and the top can be seen clearly now.

"Then on my count of three you run. *Ena...thio...tria!*"

Head down, Philippos spurts forward. Arms pumping. Legs flying. He does not intend to lose. Yet when he looks up the younger man is ahead.

The king puts more speed into it, leaping rocks, dodging thorny bushes. Does not matter, his feet are already abrading. He ignores his feet, he ignores the effort. He wills himself faster, steadier. The run is long enough to need more than sprinting.

Pantores is well ahead of the king. Seeming to run easily. His body is fluid motion, like a horse or antelope. If man is made for walking, how is it that this Pantores runs so well?

The king does not despair. He has the rhythm now. His feet have numbed. He no longer dodges small bushes and rocks. He finds himself gaining on Pantores.

Laughing in exuberance, Pantores reaches the top of the small hill. He pauses, jumps to stamp both feet solidly on the tiny peak, then pivots to make his run downhill. Surprised at how close the king is, he immediately dashes for the roadway and his brothers-in-arms.

Philippos spins at the hilltop and runs flat out for the road. He focuses on his horse, standing docilely amidst the men. He pays no attention to Pantores, to the path he runs. He focuses solely on his goal.

The cheering men see that Pantores is beating the king. Their own betting has stopped, as the outcome is clear. They recognize that the king continues to cut Pantores' lead. The race will be closer than most thought likely.

The win by Pantores should have been inevitable. Would have been had he not looked back at the king. Would have been had he not stumbled in looking and fallen. Would have been if the king had ever lessened his determination one iota.

Scrabbling back to his feet, Pantores bursts for the roadway. Now he and the king are neck and neck. They thunder down the last of the slope and cross the roadside together. All along, up and down the road, the royal footmen cheer. Helmets fly in the air. Arms pound neighbors' backs.

Panting, hurting, walking off the tightness in his legs, Philippos is smiling hugely. Pantores is laughing, as well, ruefully. "So who won the race?" asks the king.

Some call his name, others Pantores. Some of the gamblers are already squabbling. A bellow cuts through the noise, "A tie! Was a tie. There is no winner. They must run again," the burly companion of Pantores proclaims.

Pantores staggers over and places his arms around his companion, "Not again, Oloros. The king will beat me surely and I'll lose what honor I have left. Let me groom the king's horse for a year." He is laughing at the outlandish situation.

"Do you ride, Pantores?" asks Philippos.

"I have ridden. I can stay on a horse."

"Then the horse is yours provided you become a messenger, a dispatch rider, for me."

"I go nowhere without Oloros," says Pantores loyally.

Philippos eyes the beefy pikeman. Oloros looks glum at the prospect of losing Pantores to the king. "You don't look like a rider, Oloros."

Shrugging, Oloros nods agreement with the king's statement. "Not much use for a horse tending goats, your honor."

Knowing the requirements for being recruited into the royal foot, the king guesses Oloros' father must own several large herds of goats or have other wealth. Clearly the young warrior is a man of the soil and not the horse.

Loudly the king says, "Then Pantores, here is a gold coin for the race you should have won. Stay with Oloros. A man should be true to his family and friends. Let me offer you this. Do well at Pudna, be among the first that enter the city and I invite you both to be members of my household."

Nods and murmurs of appreciation sweep the crowd of warriors. Here is a king who knows how to reward. A king who shares in the trials of the campaign.

In softer voice, hugging Pantores to him, Philippos says, "Learn today's lesson, Pantores. Do not falter in your purpose. Stay the course. Had you done so, you would have won. Had I not done so, you would have won." With that, and a pat on the young man's back, the king takes back the reins of his horse.

The officers soon have the men back into their column. The march resumes.

*　*　*

Pudna does not require storming. The siege is barely in place when the gates swing open. The populace acknowledges Philippos, and only a few need exiling. The Athenians among the people are cordially sent back to their homeland with no mention of ransom or slavery.

The gesture does no good. Athenai declares war.

By the time word reaches the king of Athenai's decision, Pantores and Oloros have joined the king's household.

Chapter Nineteen

Krenides

356 B.C.

α

urrying, a filled krater of wine in his hand, the slave bumps the edge of the dining couch on which Philippos' reclines. Wine slops across the king's robe. Glancing down, Philippos asks conversationally, "A local wine? Or something finer?"

Eriguios is on his feet berating the old man, "Look what you've done this time, Old Fool. Set down the bowl. Get water to rinse the king's robe."

Mildly, Philippos waves Eriguios down, "Needn't be concerned. The robe is already red." At that the king laughs, realizing as he does how fuddled he is with drinking.

The slave is gone, no doubt fetching a jug of water. Mollified, Eriguios sinks back down on his couch.

Across from them, Eriguios' cousin, Nikophanes, and the young king's friend, Leokhares, share a couch. The cousin resumes his droning about trade, wanting Philippos to ease restrictions on ships going east along the Thraikiote coast. Leokhares knows that the man has long lost the king's attention. No need to state the obvious or restate the complex to Philippos. Leokhares winks at the king.

The king is staring at the floor's mosaic. Looking up, he smiles, "Excuse me, good Nikophanes. Eriguios, who constructed your mosaic?"

Eriguios thinks a moment, his mind slowed by wine. He turns to his cousin, "Do you recall, Nikophanes? Oh, it was a Thasian, Kandaules or Kharmides, something like that. My father favored him. Rough work compared to what you see nowadays. I've often thought it's time to plaster it over and have something put in its place. Is there an artisan you would recommend, King Philippos?"

Philippos rather likes the mosaic. Rough, no; but rustic. A vigorous design, a good hunting scene—see how the bear turns on the three hunters. The horse is rearing in fear. What horse would get that close to a bear? Strange there are no dogs. "Taken from an incident in life or is it imagined by the artist?"

Now they are all examining the mosaic. "That's how our grandfather died," says Nikophanes. "Surprised a bear when on the road to Murkinos, coming down the Angites River beyond Mount Pangaion. He'd been trading with the Edones."

"The way the story goes, he lost his seat on the horse and was dumped at the bear's feet. Fortune had abandoned him," adds Eriguios.

A draft causes the flames to flicker in the oil lamps. The bear seems to move. Philippos shivers, "Not a good way to die."

"Is there any good way?" mutters Nikophanes.

For a moment, in the tight warmth of the room, thick with wine, Philippos absently starts to agree with Nikophanes. Then he realizes that he does believe there are good ways to die, "At the end of a long life, with much accomplished, with children and grandchildren who are able and strong. Or, in battle, striking down your enemies, guarding the realm. Yes, there are good ways."

The trader inwardly scoffs at the king's willingness to die for the realm. Perhaps the former premise is true, though the trader doubts whether he and the king would agree on each other's definition of what much accomplished means. Maybe it's good for a man who is king to believe in the ideal of giving his life for his realm.

Leokhares offers, "What of laying down your life for your lover?"

Eriguios laughs, knowing who the young man's lover is, "Youth will think so. When does an older man die for a younger?"

A spurt of anger rises in Philippos, but he controls it. These two Amphipolitans are among the dozen or so he uses to manage the city. Now, in winter, he visits his conquest to see how it fares. Does the mood of the people hold any danger? For months now the city has been under his rule. His garrison commander, Black Kleitos, reports all is well. Other agents of the king tell a more complex reckoning of loyalties and fears. Being here in the city helps build confidence among the people in Philippos. The attention he gives them makes them feel honored members of the kingdom.

That is one reason for visiting Amphipolis. Another is to learn what is happening among the Thraikiotes. War lies east of Amphipolis. King Kersebleptes is coercing his fellow kings, seeking to widen his rule to encompass what his father, Kotys, had held. King Ketriporis is said to be the target of the crafty eastern king. Philippos may need to prop up Ketriporis. Can't have Kersebleptes getting his way.

Then again, Philippos admires Kersebleptes more than Ketriporis, son of Berisades. All three of Berisades' boys seem weak compared to Kersebleptes. How does the Odrussai dynasty flow? Philippos tries to remember, his wine intake not helping: Teres to his sons Sparadokos and Sitalkes, with Sitalkes the greater king. Then Seuthes, son of Sparadokos, is king, bypassing Sitalkes' boy, Sadokos. Seuthes fathers Rhebalos and Kotys.

King Kotys fathers Berisades, Amadokos, and Kersebleptes, though not by the same mother, of course.

Old Seuthes married into the Temenidai, to Stratonike, daughter of the second Perdikkas. Strictly, then, Temenidai blood flows in the dynasty even if much diluted. None of the Odrussai have attempted to push a claim on the Makedones.

Berisades is dead, leaving his boys to divide his patrimony, just as Kotys divided his. Wonderful, this splintering of the Odrussai. So now Ketriporis, Monounios, and Shostokes hold Berisades' small kingdom. Given that Ketriporis is the ablest of the three, he's the only one Kersebleptes need defeat.

Between Ketriporis and Kersebleptes is Amadokos' kingdom. Amadokos with his two stalwart sons, Amadokos the Younger and Teres, defy Kersebleptes with admirable grit. The cunning eastern king now tries to leapfrog Amadokos to destroy his half-nephew, Ketriporis. Then he can squeeze Amadokos from east and west.

There are other Odrussai dynasts from that sprawling, brawling family—a younger Seuthes and a younger Sitalkes for two. One is connected to Rhebalos' line and the other to Sadokos' line. The king shakes his head wearily. Why worry this bone tonight?

For this evening, the king is relaxing. That he dines with Eriguios is known outside these walls. Though nothing of state is being said here, the mere presence of the king as guest-friend bolsters Eriguios' standing in the city council.

"Do you have anything sweet?" asks the king.

"Some pastries," answers Eriguios, suddenly the eager host.

"Tart walnuts contrasting with honey and held together by thin layers of crisp dough or the same type of dough enclosing a light egg custard or..." Leokhares' voice trails off, knowing the king asks for sweets for him. Knowing that in this way, Philippos is answering Eriguios' sally about the older lover, though the host is too obtuse to realize.

"Let us have sweets," says the king happily.

β

Lacing her fingers across her broadening belly, Olympias thinks about her son. Within her, the boy grows. He is king already in her mind for he is god conceived. She smiles at the thought. She remembers the vivid dreams she had portending her son's conception. She feels no contradiction in ascribing that conception to both Philippos, a mortal and royal father, and to Dionysios, the immortal god. She feels no doubt that Dionysios possessed her husband at the moment of ecstasy.

A snake flows heavily, silently over her foot. Cool and dry, the slithering creature winds its way among the furs and pillows on the floor.

Others are in the room. The queen likes to keep the sacred creatures near her. Soon she will need to send them to the temple. Philippos will be returning and he cannot abide her snakes.

A few days back she was riding with her ladies. A peasant woman, old and burdened with a huge bundle of firewood was shuffling across the roadway. Olympias would have ridden on by save that she noticed the snake curled around the woman's shoulders and waist. Halting, the queen asked, "Auntie, are you in need of help?"

The crone stopped and looked at her closely, staring intently, "You will bear a singular son, my child. Take care that he grows true to his father. His will be a life of a warrior-king, and will see him renowned without peer. He will honor his mother always." Then she reached a hand up to touch the queen's knee, "Don't think you will escape sorrow. You will live longer than you should though not so long as you would want."

All this time the snake's head is by the old woman's ear, forked tongue tasting the air. Olympias was dazed at being confronted so suddenly with prophecy. "Who are you?" she asked.

"'Tis enough that I am the seventh daughter of a seventh daughter," replied the crone with a disquieting chuckle. Then the crone raised a finger, pointing beyond to a large raven alighting on a tree limb, "You see that black hungry mouth on the ash tree? Wherever I go, he comes. He seeks to greet my death. But I cheat him, I cheat him." Again, the light soft cackle of laughter.

Then looking back up at Olympias, and ignoring the queen's whole entourage, the crone whispers, "Have you no experience of the gods? The portents are all about you if you but look and see. Raise your son well, good lady." With that she shuffled on across the road, then followed the faint path that led downhill to a far woods.

Reliving that experience causes a shiver of wonder in the queen. Was it Athena in disguise? No, a more ancient goddess, maybe Hekate. Whomever, the words were true. All about them are the portents and signs of the gods. How blind are men that they do not realize what they see.

When the time comes they will recognize in her son all that his birthright commands. The prophecies foretell the truth. She sighs with pleasure.

γ

Toddling beside Petalouda as she packs the king's travel kit is her young daughter, Dori. The girl will be two years old soon and is into everything. Petalouda sighs loudly, but does not scold as Dori reaches and pulls free a bundle of the king's clothes. She will be glad to get the child back home to Pella. Dori travels everywhere with Petalouda. And Petalouda follows her husband, Pikoros. When Pikoros stays with the king on the road, Petalouda again becomes Philippos' trusted servant as long ago in Thebai.

Odd to see Philippos and Pikoros together, former master and former slave, and just as odd to be wife to Pikoros having been owned and taken by the king. She knows both men's bodies, though memory of the king's fades as time goes by. Her freed husband is a close companion of the king, yet here she is in her old role, gathering up clothes for Philippos.

No wonder so many of the magnates and notables say little to Pikoros. Not that the king concerns himself over the oddity of an ex-slave being a companion. Like a man who is confident of his manhood and has no need to proclaim it by appearance or extravagant deed, the king's nobility is not threatened by making a companion of a former slave. Just as those less certain of their manhood must show off, compete loudly, boastfully, seek reassurance in other's admiration, then those of less illustrious family or of recent position, must distance themselves from an ex-slave and disdain his counsel.

What then of the queen? Why does Olympias feel such animosity for Pikoros?

Is she simply one of those women jealous of any affection her husband has for another—whether man or woman?

Petalouda finishes refolding the king's clothes, "Come along, Dori. We have more to do."

What a dear child Dori is, unlike the conniving Kynnane or the dull Arrhidaios. How unfortunate is the king in his children. Quickly she mumbles a prayer to ward off any baleful influence that might take advantage of her love and pride in Dori. *Mother Hera, please protect my daughter, Dori.*

"There you two are," calls out Pikoros, striding down the corridor. He leans down and scoops Dori up to his shoulders. "Are you mother's helper? Are you being good?"

Dori nods vigorously, points to herself and says, "Good."

Pikoros laughs. To Petalouda, he says, "There is a delay. We must put off the journey. Perhaps for only a day."

Petalouda questions with her eyes.

Softly Pikoros adds, "A delegation is meeting with Philippos. Depends on what he decides after hearing them out. If he grants their request, then his plans change." Though no one is about, Pikoros is cautious with his explanation. Petalouda knows that if she wants, he will tell her all tonight when they are abed. Often, though, she isn't all that interested in the comings and goings of the court, and sometimes it's better not to know.

Even softer Pikoros continues, "I think he's already decided. He sent messengers to Antipatros, Parmenion, and others. Plan that we will go east and be gone for maybe a month."

"Is there danger?" asks Petalouda.

Pikoros shrugs, "Some, perhaps. When is there not? It should be all right. You and Dori can travel with us."

Petalouda nods thoughtfully. She knows that the king's next campaign was to be in the Khalkidike. Going east is unexpected. Yet coming here to Amphipolis raised the possibility they would visit the Thrake kingdoms. "Well, Dori, come help me unpack."

δ

Say Krenides and it conjures up an image of a tough mining and trading town isolated in a vastness of barbarian tribesmen. Though founded by good Hellenes out of the island of Thasos, the generations have seen it survive through the admixture of many people.

The city is sited in the foothills of a Thraikiote mountain sometimes called Mount Bounestos, midway between the Aegean coast and the Angites River valley. The Angites flows west and parallel to the coast to join the Strymon at Lake Prasios, north of Amphipolis. Between Krenides and Amphipolis lies Mount Pangaion, a high stretch of rock rich in mineral wealth. While some of the refined ores go west to Amphipolis, more goes east to Krenides due to the mines' locations. From Krenides a road leads south to its seaport, Neapolis.

King Ketriporis levies tribute from the small city although it is loosely affiliated with Athenai through its parent, the island-state of Thasos, and through its port, Neapolis. Ostensibly Ketriporis rules the Thraikiote tribes from the River Strymon to the River Nestos. The small Hellenic ports that stud his coastline are leagued with Athenai. In addition to Neapolis, these ports include Gelpsos, Apollonia-in-Thrake Pieros, and Oisyme.

East of Ketriporis, his uncle Amadokos rules to the River Hebros. And further east, from the Hebros to the Athenian dominated Hellespont lies the kingdom of Kersebleptes. With Athenai weakened by the rebellion among her allies, Kersebleptes seeks to dominate all the Thraikiotes south of the Haimos Mountains. His raiders pressure Amadokos and Ketriporis. Amadokos was forced to withdraw from Hebros valley. Ketriporis faces incursions coming down from the north.

The miners and traders of Krenides are not immune to Kersebleptes' warriors. Neither Ketriporis nor Athenai seem able to protect the city and its mines. Now word comes that Kersebleptes has gathered an army and intends full-scale invasion.

Who to turn to save Philippos? The Makedon king holds Amphipolis and patrols the Strymon valley. That puts him no more than 300 stade away, whether by the coast road or the valley road. That puts him two days away by horse. More like four days if his army marches with all the impediments of a Hellenic army.

So the city fathers of Krenides argued and convinced themselves that appealing to Philippos was better than putting their city in the hands of Ketriporis or submitting it to Kersebleptes. Look how generous was the King of the Makedones to the Amphipolitans, even after he took their city by storm.

And their appeal echoes in the mind of Philippos. *Kersebleptes is like the man-eating Nemean lion. Are you not a son of Herakles? Is not the burden of Herakles to kill the lion?* Who can resist comparison to a demi-god and forebear, even if it is the grossest flattery. Flattery aside, it is a true demand. The Temenidai are more than simply proud of their descent from Zeus through his son, Herakles. That descent is an important justification for their monopoly of the Makedon kingship. Being of the royal bloodline means accepting its burdens even as one accepts its privileges.

Philippos is pleased with this burden. Though not part of his plans, the appeal is opportune. The army is already preparing for the next campaign. Placing Krenides under his protection puts Mount Pangaion and all its wealth under his control. He weakens Ketriporis, as well as Kersebleptes- . And it all comes when Athenai cannot intervene.

Krenides retains its autonomy while accepting a Makedon garrison. In effect, the city becomes an advance post warning of any Thraikiote approach to Amphipolis.

Soon Antipatros and Parmenion will be here. Philippos is undecided whether he or Parmenion should lead the portion of the army he sends against Kersebleptes. Antipatros can continue preparations for the war against Potidaia. Perhaps Parmenion ought to command in the north. Philippos wonders if he's stretching his forces too thin. He needs to quicken the mustering of Amphipolitans into the army.

His is a large army by the standards of the Hellenic states, though quite small compared to Persia. He knows he's more than a match for any state of the south, however exalted. Athenai, Thebai, or Sparte—not one of them can match him. Yet he faces diverse opponents. Will the Illuroi and Paiaones remain quiet? Not without his forces on their borders.

A mix of peoples occupies the newly acquired regions stretching from Amphaxitis and Mygdonis, east of the Axios River, to Amphipolis. The Bisaltai may be problematical. They seem uneasy and can use Mount Kerdulion as refuge if they raise the war banner. Others north of them could turn Mount Dysoron into a bastion. Well, let's not imagine unnecessary fears. Unless the whole border flares up, the smaller tribes are unlikely to rise. Besides, he is carefully courting the elders of the Bisaltai.

Yet the thoughts do not rest easily. War in the Khalkidike could also cause unrest among the Bisaltai, he muses. The treaty with Olunthos should keep the region still. Wryly he shrugs to himself. The treaty costs him the Anthemos valley. He uses the treaty to strike at the Athenian colony at Potidaia. It will have to do for now.

The Khalkidike is an odd conglomeration of states and people. Half-Hellenic and half every refugee people forced east by generations of Makedon expansion. No wonder they hate us. Someday there will be war between us.

He glances out the window at a drum roll of thunder. The rain will slow his generals' arrivals. Lightning shears the sky again. He loves storms, the more violent the better. A memory of his brother Aleko comes to him. Philippos couldn't have been more than seven or so at the time. He'd been allowed to go camping with his big brother. They were hunting doves when a heavy storm caught them out in the hills. Skaros and his brother's attendant were with them, as he remembers, though not his brother Perdix. He doesn't recall why Perdix was absent. Skaros tried to set up a tent, but could do nothing in the driving rain and high winds. Even a fire was impossible.

The young Philippos—Philpa then—kept climbing to the top of the bare hill to watch the lightning and feel the wind and rain. Skaros and Aleko would pull him back to the hollow where they huddled. They warned him of lightning, but he would not believe that Father Zeus would strike him. Finally Aleko took him by the hand and together they stood on the hill's brow and faced out the storm. Never again was Alexandros afraid of thunder.

Alexandros and Perdikkas—an ache cuts through Philippos as he thinks of his brothers. He knows the burdens of being king. Then he thinks of Lady Kleopatra and how she taught him his duties. Would Alexandros have made a better king under Kleopatra's tutelage? Father—old Amuntas —was too easy with Alexandros. Without love, a man becomes worse than an animal; with too much love, and not enough discipline, a man becomes —what? Too weak, too arrogant, too blind to others, too blind to duty?

What about this boy that Olympias says she will bear him? He's dreamt of this boy, dreams that bother him. He must find time to consult a seer. He thinks about Olympias, and his loins warm. He's been away from Pella too long. Well, it will be longer yet for the duty of a king takes him east to Krenides.

ε

The column of weary footmen and following pack train is strung out for several stade along the road to Krenides. The word road is a compliment for it's little more than a broad path sited well up the slope of the first foothills that fringe Mount Pangaion. The valley bottom is too swampy along much of the meandering river to bear a road.

Out ahead, as well as on the flanks, Black Kleitos has scouts riding. Some lancers tail the column providing security to the rear. Still, Kleitos is uncomfortable with the straggling formations as each unit struggles to keep up. In this heat, the term unit seems inaccurate, more knots and tendrils of men. He expects a rebuke from the king at the slow pace and lack of cohesion. They are in enemy country and responsibility for the column is weighing heavily on Kleitos.

In truth the king is dismayed at how quickly garrison living has sapped the men's endurance. The day is hot and humid. That does not offer reason enough. The Pelagones who accompany Parmenion don't show the fatigue like the others for they spent the past two months patrolling the Paiaones' country. Philippos resolves to implement a program of marches for men when in garrison. Obviously formation exercises are not sufficient.

That's for the future. The problem now is this column's panting crawl. This small army must instill confidence in the citizens of Krenides and deter King Kersebleptes. Philippos mustered only a few thousand men for this march. His main army gathers near Pella under Antipatros in preparation for the campaign against Potidaia. Garrisons stud the highland borders and occupy key cities, like Amphipolis. That leaves little strength for a Thraikiote adventure.

The king turns on his mount to Pikoros, "Ride to Kleitos and his guides. Ask when we should reach the next clearing or settlement. The next with good water. We'll call a halt there. Unless it's too far to reach at this rate today. If that's likely, then have him call a halt soon so we can send a party to the river for water."

Next he waves Tyros over. The scribe looks faintly ridiculous sitting on his huge mule, but the man disdains horses for the light loads they carry. With his three mules, he keeps up with the king and carries the necessary correspondence and records of the kingdom. Suppressing a smile, Philippos reaches over and scratches between the ears of Tyros' mule, "The heat doesn't seem to bother Kleftis the mule, Tyros."

"He's holding up well. Better than the horses." Tyros points at the troop of drooping horses being led at a slow walk by their masters. Leokhares commands these fifty companions, and they are half the heavy-armed horsemen Philippos has with him.

"We'll camp before too long and see if we can't sort out this army. I'm thinking of sending the weaker men and animals back to Amphipolis. We'll tighten the march and be in Krenides sooner."

"How many warriors does Kersebleptes have out?" The scribe's question is as close to criticism as Tyros will come.

Again Philippos suppresses a smile. He understands the scribe's concern. "Many more than we do. Though not trained as we Makedones."

Tyros comments, "The mule train is doing well too. The half-dozen carrying the goods for gifts are close up to the column."

"If we were dealing solely with Hellenes some of these gifts might be confused with bribes. As it is, we deal with Thraikiotes, Paiaones, and mixed fragments of ancient peoples, and whatever Hellenic blood still flows among the Krenideiai. A shepherd king is generous. He is a father and gifts those children who kindly submit to his care. All the woolens, blades, combs, needles, and drinking vessels packed on the treasure mules are, in their way, warriors as mighty as any man wielding a pike in this column."

Now Tyros laughs, "Then our strength is more than doubled."

* * *

Despite their real concerns on the march, Philippos, Parmenion, and Kleitos bring the army safely to Krenides. Their entry is tumultuous, boisterous, festive. No harvest procession has offered greater joy or spectacle, for the citizens of Krenides truly feared for their prosperity and lives.

Philippos arranged for the city elders and much of the population to meet the column on the road nearly ten stade out from the city. His men respond to their reception with pride in their step and an easy camaraderie with the citizens.

For the people of Krenides, there is emotional release at their rescue from Kersebleptes. Yet, as devised by Philippos and the dual city magistrates, Lukambes, son of Ladmon, and Euenos Nevrikos, the display has a larger purpose. Agents of King Kersebleptes will undoubtedly carry news of the glad alliance. While the Odrusai king will already know of the Makedon expedition, the sheer enthusiasm of the populace is as important as the number of Makedon warriors.

Quickly the Makedon lancers and psiloi reinforce the cordon of Krenideiai patrols watching the Odrusai army. The bulk of the enemy forces are encamped above the Angites River crossing some thirty stade away.

Had Philippos or Parmenion led the enemy army, they would have prevented the juncture of the Makedones and Krenideiai. But Kersebleptes had not expected the rapid response of Philippos to the city's appeal. The Odrusai king is undecided whether to fight, negotiate, or withdraw. The reputation of Philippos and his new model army is high after defeating the Paiaones, the Dardanoi, and Amphipolis. Can the Thraikiotes and their mercenaries drive away the Makedones without sustaining unacceptable losses? And if Philippos survives, will he simply return with his main army? Kersebleptes ponders these questions, while fearing that he's not yet prepared to take on the Makedones.

Philippos is already decided on how to proceed. The decision was made in broad terms before launching the expedition. He will offer Kersebleptes a choice. The Odrusai king will withdraw with many respectful gifts or he will feel the cutting edge of the Makedon pikes.

Kleitos is already ordered to lead the Makedones, in company with Euenos Nevrikos and the Krenideiai foot, the short way to the Angites River in the morning. Parmenion, in the meantime, leads the embassy to Kersebleptes. With Parmenion is an escort led by Pikoros and a string of gift-laden mules directed by Tyros.

Curiously Philippos finds he does not care which decision Kersebleptes makes. Thinking it through, Philippos realizes it might be better to defeat the Odrusai king now far from his homeland rather than give him and his tribesmen several years of peace in which to ready themselves for war. On the other hand, this whole Krenides episode, welcome as it is, is a distraction from his immediate plans to eliminate the Athenian enclaves on the Makedon coast. Further, this army of alliance has never worked together. How brittle is the bravery of the Krenideiai? The fight will not be easy. Perhaps young Amuntas will be king again shortly.

Morning will bring the enemy's decision. He can be calm now. If it is a fight, then come the dawn he will be afraid until the fray begins. He knows he can command his fears and none will know of them save himself and the gods. With that thought he snuffs the oil lamp and turns on his side to sleep.

*   *   *

The meadow above the river crossing is not all that broad or all that dry. It is enough to permit the allied army to unfold across its restricted space. Makedon phalangists to the right, long pikes carefully aligned. Krenideiai hoplites, behind their large bronze-faced shields, stand in ranks on the left. Peltasts with their javelins and small wicker shields are on either flank, where the meadow becomes woods. The tight frontal space causes the units to form in depth.

All night and through the early morning hours, the light horsemen and the ragged *psiloi* have skirmished with the enemy. Losses are trifling. Hard to judge, but the Thraikiotes may have gotten the worst of it.

Parmenion, back from his embassy, holds his Pelagones as a reserve. Philippos has a second reserve in his companion horsemen.

If Parmenion is right, there won't be a battle. Though many of the enemy warriors want to fight today, feeling cheated of their honor and rewards by these upstart Makedones, Kersebleptes accepted the gifts and fine words. Parmenion clearly stated the unique relationship that now exists between Philippos and Krenides. Also clearly stated was the distinction between this city, with its Hellenic foundation, and those Thraikiote communities of the region like nearby Drabeskos and Datum, or the larger town of Serrhai above the Strymon River. Kersebleptes realizes that the dependency of Krenides on Philippos is not being advanced as an argument for Makedon protection of the western Thraikiote tribes.

Philippos is taking no chances. The crafty arrogant Kersebleptes is fully equal to lulling an embassy while planning to attack. And as a king, he is not free of his warriors' desire for battle. Philippos smiles to himself for he, too, has lulled his enemies before. Kingship demands more than fairness and honesty.

Waving a hand to clear the spiral of gnats he's ridden into, Philippos urges his horse forward. Though early, the day is heavy with humidity. The king is growing concerned at the absence of word from his scouts. Pikoros is out there with the furthest light horsemen. He won't let me be surprised, thinks the king.

On the far bank of the river are posted a group of *psiloi* under a junior officer. Though armed with little more than staves, slings, and knives, the *psiloi* are effective in advance of a fight and in its aftermath. Like the whiskers on a cat, they sense approach and departure. A hint of disturbance in their surroundings and they are alert. Philippos can just make out this small group by shading his eyes with his hands, and they appear agitated. He should know why soon. He calls behind him to the page on duty, "Meleagros, have my runners brought up. Have the alert banner raised and send for my trumpeter."

At the far riverbank the junior officer is waving his shield from side to side. That means the Odrusai army is withdrawing. The tension eases within Philippos. He won by simply being here.

ζ

Riding together, apart from the slow column of the returning army, Philippos and Parmenion are discussing their northern frontier. "I do not trust the Paiaones," Parmenion is saying. "They think they surrendered too easily. That they were unnaturally weak when the old king died and you caught them unexpectedly in winter. They're sure they can give you a better fight."

Nodding Philippos says dryly, "No doubt they can, though not enough of a fight to give them a chance of succeeding. Surely they see that?"

Parmenion looks into the eyes of the younger king. The Makedone returns his gaze steadily. Parmenion says, "They are searching for allies."

"And they approached you?"

"Me?" Parmenion chuckles. "No, they accept that you and I are bound brothers. They make no distinction between the Makedones, Pelagonoi, and Deuriopes." More somberly, "I'm not sure all Pelagones and Deuriopes feel the same. Enough blood flowed in securing my place as *basileos* that there will always be some nugget of hatred for me among certain families and their connections."

"Carrion eaters always surround a throne," says Philippos, echoing advice heard long ago from Lady Kleopatra.

"True enough," replies the Pelagonoi king. "It's not my people I am concerned about. Killing Bardulis of the Dardanoi left a hole in the tapestry of the Illuroi. Others seek to stitch themselves in. I think King Lyppeios of the Paiaones will find an ally among the more ambitious Illuroi chiefs."

"Do you advise we move against them now?" asks Philippos.

"Too soon. Let's let the hens sit on their eggs. That way, when the time comes, we catch the chicks as well as the hens."

Amused at the imagery, Philippos asks, "Are you turning peasant on me?"

Sheepishly the older warrior answers, "Hens and eggs came to mind."

"If you were truly worried about the Paiaones you would have thought wolves and pups or bears and cubs."

Changing the subject Parmenion comments, "We reach Pella the day after tomorrow. Will you move against Potidaia immediately?"

"While we were being feted in Krenides, word came of events in the south. Curious events. The Thebans are accusing the Phokians and Spartans of sacrilege before the Delphic Amphiktyony."

"Why should that concern you?"

"Thebai seeks to take advantage of a distracted Athenai, just as we do. The Theban leaders feel confident enough to challenge Sparte directly. As you know, Thebai controls a majority of the votes in the Amphiktyony. That is so long as she can rely on the Thessaliote votes. Thebai demands fines be imposed on Phokis and Sparte for their sacrilege against Apollo's oracle at Delphoi. The fines are purposefully too heavy for the Phokians to pay. Thebai and her Boiotian League will move to crush their Phokian rivals."

Parmenion pulls on his lip, feeling glad he need concern himself only with the northern frontier. Deciding who is your enemy in the north is an easier proposition. He sees why Philippos may need to move cautiously as the situation in the south shifts. He asks, "What of Athenai?"

The king does not answer immediately. Memories of his years of exile in Thebai crowd his mind. While there are individual Thebans he admires and, even, loves—Pammenes for one—those days have left a residue of bitterness in him. He knows the feelings are not truly fair to the Thebans. The feelings are as much a reflection of his own behavior then, and of the death of the faithful Skaros. Still Thebai causes him distaste.

Who he is today is a contrast to who he was, a hostage youth lost in rage. There has been so much to take pride in since Thebai. Look at this bloodless triumph over Kersebleptes. The victory is doubly sweet for it sets a clear boundary for the Odrusai king's ambitions while securing the obligation of the Krenides citizenry. Now it seems the gods grace him. In Thebai, they nearly drove him to madness. A prayer comes to mind offering praise to Zeus. An Orphic prayer now that he thinks of it.

After the celebration at Krenides and the tour of the nearby mines—especially the gold mine of Asyla—Philippos left a deputy and military escort to bolster the city. Not enough to be called a garrison. Certainly the magistrates, Lukambes and Euenos Navrikos, were as glad to see the bulk of the Makedones go as they were happy to see them arrive when threatened by Kersebleptes. It will take them some time to understand that they gifted Philippos with their city permanently.

Another thought intrudes. An idea first thought when he saw the Asyla gold mine. Krenides granted him a portion of the gold production for the security he offers. He needs to help them up their production to increase his take from the mine. Did he have Tyros note to send engineers to Krenides?

An uneven step by his horse causes Philippos to break from his reverie. "What did you ask, Parmenion?"

Parmenion was not made ill at ease by the king's silence. He knows what webs of thought are always spinning within his friend. "What of Athenai?"

"Their General Khares has been reinforced in the Hellespont. They will attack Byzantion."

"If they put down Byzantion, what does that do to your plans?"

"We'll see. They're only plans and we can always make new plans. What will not change is my purpose." Philippos reins in his horse, "I think I'll walk for a while. Give old Astion here a rest." He pats the horse's neck as he slides down from the saddle.

"You do like ugly horses."

"Astion is almost a mule. Strong if short, good for long distances, not a horse you want to ride in battle. He's a good trail animal." The king nuzzles against the gelding's muzzle, then looks at Parmenion and grins, "A horse for each task. At least, as king, I can be wealthy in my horses."

Parmenion almost says it's the same with men, that Philippos uses them each for a purpose. Instead he dismounts after taking a look around. The main column of marching men on the path below is trudging with weariness. Time they had a break as well. The king's escorts are halted at a respectful distance, waiting to see if they'll be summoned. Distantly, ahead, can be seen the advance guard. Presumably the scouts are on beyond, as well as back and around the column. Parmenion approves the king's instructions to maintain security on the march even though they are well into friendly land. Parmenion admires good generalship.

Truthfully Parmenion is uncertain whether Philippos is simply beguiling Olunthos and the Khalkidike or fully intends to take Potidaia and give it to Olunthos as he's promised. Parmenion's responsibility is the north. Antipatros watches over the Khalkidike. Philippos may be undecided. Much may depend on whether Athenai is successful in reasserting her control over Byzantion and the rebellious Aegean islands. Probably as much depends on the prevailing attitude among the Khalkidike cities. Parmenion would have thought the king would be more concerned about the Athenian campaign than about the machinations in the Delphic Amphiktyony.

Yet for all the questions that occur to Parmenion, he has faith in Philippos and feels no need to press for answers. The king relies on his judgment in dealing with the north. That is enough for Parmenion. For all that, it does sometimes puzzle Parmenion why he feels such strong loyalty to this man, this still young king, nearly twenty years his junior. Maybe because the Makedon king gives fidelity in return. And though Parmenion does not consider his piety as overly superstitious, maybe because the Pelagone suspects that Zeus truly does favor at least this one member of the Temenidai.

Philippos is watching the lengthy files of men, tramping along with pikes aslant on their shoulders. Each set of files marks off a unit. The men know the king is watching them. They straighten, their steps become firmer, some grin or raise a hand in recognition. "Everything is a balance. Have you noticed that in life, Parmenion?"

"How so, Philippos?"

"How much should a footman carry and how much baggage should follow? How long should we ride and how long should we lead our mounts? Whether tonight is a night for drinking too much wine or it is best left for another night. Whether this summer I take Potidaia or is it best left for the fall or even next spring."

"A man of moderation, such as yourself, will find the right balance," replies Parmenion with some mockery.

"I am a man of moderation," asserts Philippos defensively. He sees amusement in Parmenion's eyes. "Well, perhaps not when it comes to handsome youths and intelligent women. You see that is proof of my moderation. For if I am to be balanced than where I overreach it must be in a sphere that's harmless. Not like the Thebans. They would punish the Phokians for failing them in their fight against Athenai in Euboia. Do they confront Phokis over a failed alliance? No, they create discord in the Delphic Amphiktyony. Their anger causes them to use any means to get at Phokis. Don't they see that they trifle with Apollo?"

"It's not the first time the council has been used for political ends," says Parmenion.

"True, nor will it be the last. Had I the power there I would likely use it as well. After all, in one sense, the council is only men representing the twelve Hellenic tribes. Politics exist wherever men are. Apollo understands that, so long as the council achieves the god's needs. The shrines of Delphoi and Anthela are in the council's care. They are among the sacred mysteries that bind Hellenes together, that make us Hellenes. They transcend politics, like the Olympiad. So long as the Thebans honor Apollo and make their accusations of sacrilege for his purposes and not theirs all should be well. You can see that they do not. Their proposed punishments are too severe. They do not act moderately."

Looking beyond Philippos, Parmenion says, "Looks like Tyros is coming with a courier. He'll put you to work, my most moderate brother-king."

Philippos laughs, realizing how intense he sounded. He's not certain why this news from the south gives him such a thrill of dread and excitement. He senses opportunity, but does not want to trifle with the gods as the Thebans are doing. Save for the impact on Thessalos, there's little place for him in these events. Time enough to see what occurs. For the moment Tyros demands his attention, "You won't be interested in whatever Tyros is bringing me to do."

"Then I'm returning to my men. I'll catch up with you at camp tonight."

The two part company with a wave. Philippos leads Astion down the slope to greet Tyros. Walking down he has another thought about moderation. Not all the gods admire moderation. Take Dionysios, the god of ecstasy espoused by Olympias. He is a divinity of passion, of illusion, of overwhelming spirituality rather than of reason and intellect.

To Philippos, who identifies himself strongly as a Hellene, there is a foreign quality to Dionysios. Few among the Makedones would agree. All the accretions of Thraikiote, Illuric, Paiaone, and other stock among the Makedones make his people peculiarly open to many gods, especially the ancient dark goddesses and their consorts. Though in truth, there are many Hellenes who embrace Dionysios, particularly the Asian Hellenes.

Lately Philippos finds himself attracted to the gods of life. Apollo personifies his sense of wonder at the many unknowns of life. Or, maybe as Orpheos taught, that greater unknowable wholeness of which life and divinity are aspects.

Wryly Philippos winces as he thinks more about Apollo. The truth is that no god is always temperate, not even Apollo. Maybe moderation is the wrong sense. Maybe he was right to begin with when he said balance. Balance encompasses more than moderation. Balance can include extremes.

Enough of this, Tyros has more practical matters to present.

η

"You can expect Olympias to be out of sorts," says Eurudike lightly. "The great sag of her belly pulls every muscle into aches and pains. You did this to her so you can put up with her whims and fatigue."

Philippos shakes his shaggy head over how women invariably side together when the topic is pregnancy. Truly this is the heart of the female sisterhood. Inevitably the male is blamed for the pregnancy, as if no woman ever enjoys the frolic of sex or never initiates seduction. Still Philippos holds his tongue. Why provoke hornets?

Alexandros of Epeiros, the eight-year old brother of Olympias, is not so reticent. "She takes on so, as if being pregnant has only ever happened to her."

The Queen Mother is far more tolerant of the boy-prince than she would be of Philippos. "Alexandros, son of Neoptolemos, be sympathetic to your sister. This is her first child. Life has not given her much pain before so what little she bears now looms large. After she's given birth, she'll have more perspective on these aches and grippes."

Not especially mollified, Alexandros sniffs, "Well, I'm staying away from her until she's done giving birth."

"You're due back in Dodona before that's likely to occur," comments Philippos mildly.

More slyly Eurudike points out, "Your sister says her son will be named Alexandros like you."

KRENIDES (356 B.C.)

The three are sitting on the steps of the temple of Zeus that presides over the marketplace of Pella. Since returning to the city nearly a month back, this is the first day that Philippos has spent time with his mother. He and the boy accompanied the elder lady to the market. Now, with purchases made and dispatched home with the servants, the three are relaxing.

Midday soon, with the high hot sun. Not that the sun will touch Eurudike, wearing a broad-brimmed low-crowned straw hat. Philippos marvels that the older his mother gets, the more she turns away from elegance to become the practical and rustic manager of her country estate. Maybe all the tribulations of the past cause her to scorn what she once was. He asks, "You're staying in Pella past the birth, mother?"

"Oh, yes. Someone with sense needs to be here. You won't be."

"Olympias is best left to you women. I can be more useful to the kingdom in the field," he says defensively. He has no intention of awkwardly awaiting the birth that's a month or perhaps more away. Or of enduring any more petulance from Olympias.

Since realizing that his boy, Arrhidaios, is feeble, he's not felt much interest in children. Yet he is keenly aware that he must secure his line for the sake of the kingdom. This boy Alexandros of Epeiros and his nephew, Amuntas, are the only kids he has time for now. Besides he likes a sturdy, active boy eager to learn. As Amuntas could yet be King of the Makedones, Alexandros could be heir to a strong kingdom if the fates don't favor his uncle, King Arubbas and the Molossi king's sons. Since Philippos despises Arubbas, and needs a friendly Epeiros at his back, he'd be willing to give the fates a nudge.

Not being interested in babies, Alexandros asks, "You will be running a horse at the Olympiade this year, brother?" The word brother is said awkwardly since Alexandros is often confused whether he should call Philippos the respectful uncle the man's age indicates, the more familiar brother due to Philippos' marriage to Myrtale, now Olympias, or even cousin as their respective ranks of Molossi prince and Makedon king might suggest. Alexandros likes saying brother when he thinks of Philippos. Yet he would never call Arubbas more than uncle, even though his father's brother is also married to a sister of the boy.

"A horse? Not a horse, not just any horse!" Philippos exclaims with mock severity. "I tell you that my Trekhonike is a horse like no other. His heart is boundless. His strength and endurance—well, it is enough to say that he is all muscle save for his mind, which is as agile as his hooves. Among horses he is smarter than my friend Aristoteles is among men. Did I say he was fast? If you stand too close when he goes by, he pulls you into his wake. The rider need not guide him for Trekhonike always knows the best stride, the best path, the possible pitfalls. He is unbeatable, saving the gods' grace."

Alexandros grins at the king's enthusiasm, "Then he is a horse from Thessalos?"

"His stock is from Thessalos, but he was bred and coursed here among the Makedones."

Breeding interests Eurudike, "I thought his grandfather came down from the north, from the Skythoi?"

"That, too," admits Philippos. "Like all animals he has two grandfathers."

"I would like to see him race."

"You can, Alekos," smiles Philippos. "There will be a race here before he goes south to the Peloponnesos."

"Will he win?"

"At the Olympiade?" The king shrugs, "I would not tempt the fates. He is a fortunate creature. No other horse I've seen is better in a race."

"The rider matters, too," points out Eurudike.

"True, and I have not decided who will ride Trekhonike at the Olympiade. That is why he races again soon. We'll see who gets the best from him."

"A win at the Olympiade will be honored by all Hellenes," says the dowager queen. She is pleased when the southerners acknowledge the northern and western Hellenes.

Knowing her feelings Philippos grins again, "Oh, as king they see us Temenidai as pure Hellenes readily enough. They're not so sure of the people we rule." He snorts his derision of southern pretensions. Turning to his young brother-in-law he asks, "Did you fear for your sister when she went to live among barbarians?"

"Fear for Myrtale? Better you should fear."

Philippos laughs aloud. As he laughs he spots a distant figure threading his way through the market crowd. His eyes narrow. A royal messenger searching for the king—if sent by Tyros or Antipatros, then the message is urgent. A summons from his idyll with his mother.

Soon Eurudike and Alexandros see the man, too. Philippos stands so the messenger can find him readily. Already several individuals in the marketplace are pointing out the king.

"Work to attend to, mother," says the king.

"We've had a good morning of it. I'm surprised no one's come for you sooner," replies Eurudike.

*　　*　　*

Antipatros looks grim, "Athenian promises, Athenian silver, that's what it is. Their cunning words are busy building walls around us." The general is angry, always an impressive sight. "They will thwart us. Always seeking to keep us fragmented, threatened—they would bend us to their will."

Reading the dispatch from Black Kleitos, Philippos responds mildly, "They are at war with us. We have loudly announced our campaign against Potidaia. In their place, we'd do the same."

"Loudly?" snorts Alkimakhos. "We conclude an alliance with Olunthos and all the world knows its details."

"There's little enough Athenai can do. Since their defeat at Embata what force do they have in the north? Silver and words are all they have. They squabble among themselves. Khares points fingers at Timotheos when the truth is that Khares' own rashness caused their losses. Byzantion and the other rebels are stronger than before." Philippos holds up the dispatch to his senior officers, "This is another act of rashness. Ketriporis attacks Krenides. Why does he suppose he's stronger than Kersebleptes?"

"Then you will succor Krenides again? We were to launch ourselves against Potidaia," growls Eurulokhos.

More equably Demetrios asks, "How do we divide ourselves to face Grabos of the Illuroi, Lyppeios of the Paiaones, and Ketriporis of the Western Thraikiotes?"

"We postpone again our advance on Potidaia. No reason to be concerned with that delay. The city will still be there when we have leisure to give it our attention." The king turns to his spymaster, "Ephrastos, you are certain we can hold our partisans in Olunthos to the alliance? If Athenai is offering silver to Illuroi, Paiaones, and Thraikiotes, she must be offering gold to the Khalkidike."

The thin balding Ephrastos smiles faintly, "No need to be concerned. Your advocates are many and for many reasons. Some are in our pay, others we hold by securing their secrets, some truly love you over Athenai, and still others receive diverse inducements, catering to vices or virtues depending on the need. Olunthos and its Khalkidike confederacy will hold for you so long as Athenai is distracted by her rebels."

"Fair enough," grins Philippos. Turning to the others but addressing Antipatros, he asks, "How many men can we field? How well-trained? How well-provisioned and for how long? Be sure to count Parmenion and the Pelagones."

Setting to the task, Antipatros recites, "We are as strong as we have ever been. You have the full royal phalanx you demanded, over 16,000 pikemen in 64 *syntagmai*."

"Actually 16,348 well-trained and eager pikemen," interjects Demetrios.

Antipatros continues, "For horse, among the Makedones there are four squadrons of heavy-armed, each of 128 men, plus your double-sized guard squadron. That makes more than 700 horsemen. The Elimiotes can field another squadron, or even two if pressed. The other highlanders can offer yet another squadron." Ticking down his fingers, "You have your mercenaries—hoplites number about 1,400, the Kriti bowmen and slingers add another 1,200. Then we have the engineer and sappers, call them 300. Finally, you have the town militias to form more pikemen if need be, say another 4,000. And you have the rural levy if need be for peltasts and *psiloi*. Plus there are our allies, the Pelagonoi, Deuriopes, Lunkestoi, and even some loyal Illuroi and Paiaones. All told they must add another 800 to 900 heavy foot and another squadron or a bit more of horse. Actually, maybe a hundred heavy horse and a hundred light-armed horsemen. And they can give you more light foot if you want them." The heavily bearded generals glances at Demetrios and Ephrastos, "So what's that total?"

"Better than 24,000," says Demetrios with satisfaction.

"We can get more men from the highlands than you counted," responds Philippos. "Tumphaia owes us its strength now. The Lunkestoi are ours as well. For Tumphaia, Simmias is chief there. We can use his people against Grabos. The Lunkestoi chief, Aeropos, is past campaigning but I can rely on his son, Alexandros. All the highlanders we will lend to Parmenion."

Antipatros frowns at the idea of Parmenion leading in the north independently. Gruffly he says, "You would give the fight against Grabos to a foreign prince?"

"Against Grabos, yes. Defeating the Illuroi is always in the interest of the Pelagonoi. And my Elimiotes will provide weight and balance. You, Antipatros, will defeat Lyppeios."

"Leaving you to deal with Ketriporis, Philippos?" asks Antipatros.

"Yes, let them see me rescue them again. And I can bring men out of Amphipolis to help. Best if both cities see me as their war leader." The king looks at Eurulokhos, "You'd best stay in place in Mygdonis, to keep an eye on the Khalkidike. You'll have two *syntagmai* and a squadron of horse." He waves away the protest before it begins.

"My young nephew, Amuntas, will be regent in Pella under my mother's direction and that of Demokedes and Hippasos. Alkimakhos, you will be by their sides with the hoplites and two *syntagmai*. Oh, and keep the engineers and sappers here."

The king turns back to Antipatros, "You will support Parmenion by lending him ten *syntagmai* and a third of the bowmen and slingers. With the highlanders and his own warriors, that should more than suffice."

"A respectable force—more than 4,000 men with his own Pelagones," comments Eurulokhos.

"Closer to 5,000, as I said the highlanders will provide more as will his own people," replies the king.

"What does that leave Antipatros?" asks Eurulokhos.

"Parmenion can give us our pikemen and mercenaries back after chastising Grabos. If Antipatros needs to move against Lyppeios before then, he'll still have twenty *syntagmai*, three squadrons of horsemen, and a third of the Kriti. That gives our redoubtable Antipatros more than 6,000 even if he goes in early and takes some of his clansmen as *psiloi*, as well."

The older general nods his acceptance. It's now obvious to all how delighted Philippos is with their prospects. Where they saw encirclement and possible contraction, he sees opportunity and a wider set of conquests.

"We can leave the town militias and rural levy in place. In the unlikely event the fates turn against us, we'll need them then. Anyway, we'd have to feed them if we had them along." The king's eyes are alight, "That leaves me with 30 *syntagmai*, my royal squadron, and a third of the Kriti, plus what Amphipolis and Krenides provide. Demetrios, you'll be my second-in-command."

"When do we go?" asks Antipatros.

"The army is ready for campaign, only the target has changed. We need to shift to the north and east. We strike quickly, we strike hard, we strike before they expect us." Then Philippos smiles broadly, "The Pelagones are already assembled. Send your reinforcements to him, Antipatros. By the time they reach him, the Elimiotes and other highlanders will have joined him."

"Then you knew this was coming," exclaims Ephrastos.

"A king hears from many mouths," Philippos enjoys his spymaster's surprise. "Grabos will be going for the mines at Damastion. Only if he seizes them will he have the gold and silver to buy enough allies and mercenaries to hurt us. Parmenion will prevent his success."

Looking at Antipatros, Philippos says, "You will find an ally in Mezekias the Paiaone. He recognizes our strength and is prudent with the lives of his people. Since he opposes the recklessness of Lyppeios, you can use Bylazora as your base."

Demetrios says, "The 8,000 men you take east, Philippos, is more than you used to overawe Kersebleptes."

"My intention is not to overawe Ketriporis. It is to overwhelm him. He can submit or he can die. Our eastern border will be the River Nestos not the Strymon."

"What of Krenides?" asks Eurulokhos.

"Krenides will be an honored ally, enfolded in the embrace of the Makedones. What better fate for a city we rescue twice?"

The men about the king have lost their doubts. What had seemed confusion now seems a part of the king's plans. Though they know he could not have foreseen exactly how events would unfold, they also realize how readily he turns events to his favor. Strong, able men in their own right, they understand that the king is stronger and abler still.

As for Philippos, he fully understands the effect his commands have had. That within himself there remains uncertainty, he conceals. All that he attempts can come unraveled. Grabos can prove stronger than anticipated. The Paiaones could be swept by a fervor of retribution so that all their subtribes and factions unite. Ketriporis could slow Philippos long enough to defeat Krenides and use its gold to buy a flood of mercenaries. More likely than any of these possibilities is that the anti-Makedon leaders within the Khalkidike will take advantage of his distractions to push the league into war with the Makedones. Eurulokhos and Alkimakhos haven't enough force between them to seal that breach.

Philippos knows the risks he runs in confronting all his enemies simultaneously. He calculates that to wait and take them one at a time gives too much opportunity for their growth into formidable threats. In some ways the greatest risk is the small force at Pella under Alkimakhos. He must hold Pella regardless of what reverses occur anywhere else, for the king's heir, young Amuntas, must survive.

θ

By comparison to the previous march to Krenides, the Makedones speed to the city. The advance is eased by the improvements made to the road during the return to Pella, coupled with the several supply depots established at dispatch waystations since then. The thirst and hunger of pack animals and war horses is accommodated with fewer delays and no reroutes. No longer are they marching into lands known in detail only to guides of indifferent loyalty.

The citizens of Krenides are sobered by this second need for help in as many months. What seemed an unusual event before now seems all too regular. Many of the leading citizens conclude that some permanent arrangement must be made with the Makedon king or they may well be making arrangements with the Thraikiotes.

The knowledge that the Makedones came fast at the first request despite raids and bloodshed on their northern borders speaks both to the importance they place on this alliance and to the depth and resilience of their resources. While the citizenry welcome the Makedones with less frenzy than the last time, the gratitude is more strongly felt. As the citizens arm and prepare to march beside their rescuers, they know what is expected of them. Most find it comfortable to stand, spear in hand, as companions to the pike-wielding Makedones.

Recognizing the prevailing sentiment, the magistrates Lukambes and Euenos Navrikos come quickly to terms with King Philippos. The city will be refounded by the king with a colony of Makedones. Nearly doubling the population of Krenides will do much to make it secure. The city will be a free state, like Amphipolis, subject to its own laws save for issues relating to the larger world of trade, military service, diplomacy, and war. And the city will be renamed upon its new dedication. Krenides will become Philippi. These arrangements, of course, are dependent on Philippos defeating Ketriporis.

The day after the populace acclaim the treaty, the king leads out the army, now raised to nearly 10,000 with the Amphipolitan and Krenideiai additions, though many of these are peltasts and *psiloi*. Scouts have already fixed the current location of Ketriporis' army.

Surprised by the rapid approach of the Makedones, the Thraikiotes recoiled from Krenides to a stronger position. Now their army is held north of the Angites River. They offer a tougher prospect than did Kersebleptes, for knowing their own country better than did the Eastern Thraikiotes, their army is better placed.

Ketriporis has fortified a narrow valley that allows him to cover the road north to Drabeskos and the route west to Serrhai. With his two chief towns covered, he awaits Philippos. The Thraikiote king expects the rough terrain leading to the valley entrance to disrupt the phalangist's formation.

Grudgingly Philippos admits that Ketriporis is proving a wily opponent. He has his scouts bring in as many of the country folk as they can find. He personally questions each to learn about the valley. How far does it extend? Whose sheep eat its grass? Who knows the ways in and out of the valley?

Philippos decides how he will dislodge Ketriporis. The king, with Black Kleitos, will lead the main assault against the fortified valley mouth using two-thirds of his phalangists hinged at either end by local *psiloi*. Under Euenos Navrikos, the Krenideiai hoplites will form a local reserve, along with the peltasts. Philippos will advance them to support any breakthrough.

Demetrios will take the remaining phalangists, the Kriti, and the Amphipolitans over the lower hills at the valley's midriff. For this purpose, the phalangists will put aside their pikes and attack with three javelins apiece, much like peltasts.

Finally, Leokhares will take the royal squadron down the Serrhai road, then cut across to the north end of the valley. They are to force an entry through the valley's high pass after the frontal and flank assaults draw all the Thraikiotes into battle.

Philippos regrets the absence of professional archers and slingers in the frontal attack. He is loath to commit his pikemen against the Thraikiotes manning their earth slope and palisade fortification. But the men under Demetrios need that support more as they go in without their pikes. What he would give for something he could ram through those walls up ahead.

With that thought, a further refinement occurs to the king. In the Hellenic manner, the Amphipolitans and Krenideiai came to war with carts to carry their armaments and supplies. For every hoplite, there are two or three servants. Though the morning is already advanced, Philippos orders a dozen carts brought forward loaded with wet straw, green wood, and flammables. He wants more smoke than fire.

Phalangists and hoplites stand at arms waiting. The king knows the wait must seem interminable to men about to go into battle. Their nerves will already be keyed up. This trick, however paltry, may save the lives of some of his men, so they can afford to wait.

By midday a dozen filled carts are trundled to the front of the line. Servants and slaves push the small wagons in place. Fires have been lit, and the sweating, pushing men are coughing whenever the breeze is fitful. For the most part, though, the breeze blows from the south into the faces of the Thraikiotes.

On his order, the trumpet blares and his banner waves. Soon the unit pipes and pennants take up the order. His men step forward in an oblique line. The right end will reach the Thrake wall first. Lurching ahead of the right flank are the smoking carts.

The sight has excited the enemy. Stones, javelins, and arrows rain on the carts. The enemy's aim is poor as eyes smart and water. To the Thraikiotes, smoke masks the head of the Makedon line. They are confused, uncertain how to counter this strange attack, fearful of what might appear out of the smoke.

Dismounting behind the center of his line, Philippos takes up a pike and jogs to the front. Beside him jogs Pikoros, faithfully covering the king's left side. Slightly behind is the king's trumpeter.

As the carts are being shoved up the slope towards the palisade on the far right, Philippos has his trumpeter blow the call. The several center *syntagmai* advance at a steady trot, soon outstripping their comrades. They close on the wall. The foemen manning the wall here are thinned to meet the perceived threat of the smoking carts and oblique advance. The feint to the right has served well, the enemy center is off guard. Working quickly, the phalangists help one another to scramble up the slope and boost each other over the palisade.

Philippos steps on the shield held between Pikoros and young Axiokhos, his trumpeter. Raising the shield lifts the king to the top of the palisade. With two hands holding the rough poles of the palisade, Philippos swings his legs up and pulls himself erect. Uncomfortably straddling the wall, he reaches back for his pike.

Other phalangists are already up and over the wall. Some have chopped and pried their way through the hastily built palisade, using the leverage of their pikes and the edge of their short swords.

Everywhere there is tumult and the clash of arms. Though fewer here, the Thraikiotes are stubborn in defense. They seek to cut down the phalangists before the pikemen can reform inside the walls. The long pikes are proving cumbersome in this type of fight.

Having gained the narrow walkway behind the palisade, Philippos thrusts into the mass of men below. Behind him, Pikoros uses the long shafts of his and the trumpeter's pikes to shimmy up the wall. Axiokhos follows. Soon they are beside Philippos and thrusting as eagerly at the Thraikiote warriors.

To rally the phalangists, Philippos yells to Axiokhos to blow his trumpet. Before the youth has a chance, he is cut down by a spear thrust from below that hamstrings his right leg. The trumpeter collapses and falls from the walkway. Pikoros puts his pike through the enemy's throat.

With a cry of exasperation, Philippos jumps from the wall into the melee. There is no rational thought to the act. The king is failing his duty by being an archaic warrior and not a general. Yet sometimes a general must give an example.

Pikoros fights his way to the king's side. Behind them, weakly, a trumpet calls. Axiokhos leans against the inner palisade and tries again. The trumpet blares. On the wall behind them is the king's bannerman as more of their *syntagma* reach the walkway. Their fellow phalangists drop to the ground to fight beside the king.

A huge Thraikiote attacks the king with a bellow, followed by a rush of warriors. Pikeheads slice into the enemy chieftain from several points before he can reach Philippos. The phalangists are in line and their steady thrusts are forcing the foe back.

Pulling a phalangist officer to his side, Philippos yells in his ear, "Take command here. Keep pushing them." Then the king steps back out of the line. He looks around for his runners.

The trumpeter is still blowing his horn. Its brassy cry goads the Makedones. Sections of the palisade are splintered open and the phalangists crowd through, then spread quickly to extend and reinforce their line.

Grabbing a runner, Philippos bellows, "Go to Euenos the Magistrate. I want his hoplites and peltasts here. Quickly, man." The king clambers back up the palisade to the walkway. Looking east, he tries to understand what is happening where Black Kleitos led the advance behind the smoking carts.

Coming down the valley to join the fight are a thousand, maybe 1,500 Thraikiote warriors. The battle at the valley's gate is drawing Ketriporis' fighters. Where is the enemy king?

Though the palisade is pierced in many places, the fighting here is uneven. Many phalangists have yet to funnel into the fight. The Makedon line is strong enough to hold for now but not strong enough to deliver victory.

Philippos needs the mid-valley attack to go forward. Why is there no word from Demetrios? At least it appears that Black Kleitos and his men are over the wall on the right.

"King Philippos, sir King!"

Philippos sees one of the royal pages calling up to him from the south side of the palisade. "What is it, boy?"

"Black Kleitos has sent me. He has three *syntagmai* advancing, sweeping in a pivot toward the enemy center. He has a few *psiloi* on either flank."

"Good, boy, good. Tell him we have breached the palisade here and are holding the Thraikiote center. They have reinforced. As soon as our ranks are formed, we will advance."

The boy turns and runs. Philippos feels some satisfaction. Still the battle is not won. And despite the stratagem of the smoke carts, Philippos fears that his losses are heavy.

It could be worse. The enemy is fighting in clan, sept, and tribal groups. No overall hand is directing them. Wherever Ketriporis is, it's not here. Philippos can identify Edones, Odomantes, Pieres, Dersai, Sapaei, and Satres among the Thraikiotes. Undoubtedly other subtribes are represented. Ketriporis pulled together a strong alliance with his Athenian silver.

The heavy-shielded mass of hoplites is climbing the earth slope to the palisade. Now all the Makedon phalangists are within the wall. Pikoros, Antigonos, and Hegesias have the phalanx in hand. Philippos would feel better if he had word from Demetrios or from Leokhares and the horsemen.

Philippos drops off the palisade walkway. He quickly finds Euenos. "I want you to form your men on my line's right. Kleitos will be to your right. Right now the Thrakes lap us at either end. We need your people in place before we advance far from the palisade."

Euenos acknowledges the order and moves the hoplites to the right with alacrity. Philippos finds himself liking the junior magistrate more and more as they have worked together. A solid man, perhaps less intelligent than is desirable, but always reliable under direction.

A runner stands panting next to Philippos. "Yes, son, what is it?"

"I am from Hegesias, sir. The phalanx is ready. We are holding the Thraikiotes and the general says we can break them with an advance."

Something peculiar about this fight. Where is Ketriporis? Why aren't they under more pressure from the tribesmen? What is happening up the valley? If this defense, stubborn as it is, is a diversion while the main body of Thraikiotes escapes, then it will all need to be done again. "Take me to Hegesias, boy."

Soon the king has a pike in both hands again and stands behind Hegesias, helping to thrust and push at the enemy swordsmen. Yelling in Hegesias' left ear, the king says, "Take the line forward."

Hegesias signals his piper and the shrill trill of the notes play repeatedly. The trio of ascending notes followed by a break and a single high piercing note commands a steady single step by single step push forward. Some stumbling and disorder mark the first several pushes. Then the whole phalanx is in motion. Pikes stab, thrust, cut into the enemy ranks. As a front-line phalangist tires, another steps into his place.

Philippos is in the front line. Sweat beads his brow. The pike is smashed forward, skidding on a shield. Withdrawing it quickly, he then slices back into the enemy's shield with all his might. This time the blade skids past the curvature of the foe's shield to take the man in his upper right arm. Again the king withdraws the pike quickly and as quickly thrusts forward. The injured warrior is weaker and pike's blade again passes along the shield to pierce the leather of his tunic below the bronze plate that covers his right breast. The man is down. Philippos steps a pace forward seeking his next opponent.

Beside the king, his companions advance a step. A quick side-glance tells Philippos that it's Pikoros again guarding his left. "Hard to keep up with you," calls the redhead.

The remark strikes Philippos as funny given the circumstances. The king's wild laughter causes the enemy before him to shrink away. The opening is enough for Philippos to slice the jugular of the next man in line. Enemy blood fountains over him.

In that instant, the Thraikiotes break. Where the Makedones had faced spears, javelins, and swords now there is scrambling running backs. An insistent trilling of the Makedon pipes urges pursuit.

The king stops and slumps to his knees. Anxious Pikoros bends over him. "It's nothing. Just weary. Look at them run, Pikoros."

"You broke their palisade and you broke their wall of blades, Philippos," answers Pikoros.

"We did, we did, all of these men of ours," says the king. And his gesture covers not only the lunging line pursuing the terrified Thraikiotes, but the litter of broken and cut bodies behind the line.

A horseman rides up. A wan Axiokhos, his leg bound, leans from the saddle, "Ketriporis attempted to escape over the mid-valley hills. Ran straight into Demetrios and the Amphipolitan magistrate. The rider from Demetrios says they were just able to hold the Thrakes until Leokhares took the enemy in the rear. That decided the fight. Ketriporis is captured. The surviving Thraikiotes are fleeing."

A great relief washes through Philippos. The fight was worth it. Much to sort out yet, but Makedonis now extends to the Nestos River. Krenides is Philippi, with all its mines. Whatever is happening in the north against the Illuroi and Paiaones, the Athenians are thwarted. The Makedones emerge stronger, not weaker, by confronting the foe.

CHAPTER TWENTY

Potidaia, Alexandros, and the Olympiad

356 B.C.

α

Carefully balancing the blade tip with his right hand on the nail of the middle finger of his left hand, Oloros prepares to flip the dagger. Around him, his companions lay their bets for or against his success. Two steps away Pantores stands still his feet spread a hand's span apart. Oloros must sink the dagger's blade between Pantores' feet to win this round of the game.

A trumpet blare sounds from the camp causing several of the gamblers to reach for their coins at the summons while others protest, urging Oloros to hurry. With due deliberation the dagger is flipped to stab into the ground cleanly next to Pantores' right big toe. Those who bet against the burly man groan as they watch their silver grabbed by the grinning winners.

Already officers at the camp are bellowing to form their men. All the men gamblers scramble for the camp. To be last in line is to be fined.

Jogging beside Oloros, Pantores is laughing, "How much did we make?"

"Enough. We won't need to water our wine."

As members of the king's household and guardsmen in his personal *syntagma* the two earn more than most phalangists. They do even better from their games of skill and chance. Yet neither is a reckless man. Each sends a tithe of one-twentieth to the temple of Zeus in Pella, and half the remainder to the same temple to be banked for the future. Each is the other's beneficiary for their temple savings.

During the campaign against the nearer Thraikiotes—Ketriporis' kingdom—from the outset through the battle of Angites Valley and for the ten days after that they spent in securing the region, the two shouldered their duties eagerly and well. These past days in camp near Amphipolis were another matter. Exercise and work details paled by comparison to the active campaigning.

Their boredom led them to contrive escapes from routine. Many of the rougher men of the phalanx—the drinkers, gamblers, brawlers, and thieves

—looked to them to provide amusement. Today's game offered a good example with its touch of danger on which to gamble and the amphora of watered wine on which to tipple.

The two jostle their way into the formation, late but not last. Some poor man coming from the privies has that dishonor.

Then Philippos the King, mounted and armored, is before the assembled ranks. The men quickly quiet. They respect the king.

Philippos calls out to them, "I bring you good news. Our general, Parmenion, has beaten the Illuroi. He has crushed the army of Grabos far to the north near the mines of Damastion. Already he has sent a part of his army to strengthen Antipatros. Soon he will follow in person with more of his men. Generals Parmenion and Antipatros will corner King Lyppeios. They will make the Paiaones suffer for joining our enemies."

The men of the ranks stamp their feet and beat their pikes against their shields to praise the tidings. The king quiets them with a motion of his hand, "Within ten days, we march south into the Khalkidike. When Antipatros subdues the Paiaones, he will march south to join us. *Basileos* Parmenion will stay in the north to assure that the Illuroi and Paiaones keep still."

"When we cross the border into the lands of the Khalkidike League, we go in friendship. We are their guest-friends, all of us. For we go to do them a service. We go to take the city of Potidaia, to give to them. Their friendship is a key to our success in defying Athenai. Their friendship is a key to our security and to the growing strength of the Makedones."

Pantores nudges Oloros. Their eyes look sidelong at one another. They are pleased at the prospect of action. Around them other phalangists are also reacting favorably. Surely in taking Potidaia some of its riches will reach them even if the city eventually ends up in the hands of the citizens of Olunthos.

β

Potidaia is a relatively young city for the Khalkidike. Founded some two hundred and fifty years earlier, maybe a bit less, by settlers out of Korinthos, where the Pallene peninsula joins the Khalkidike mainland. It was the last city of any significance to be founded in the Khalkidike. Most Hellenic cities of the region were founded as much as a hundred years earlier. And not all the cities were founded by Hellenes. The Bottiaoi founded Olunthos, though it has long since become Hellenic in culture and, to a lesser extent, in blood.

Most of the men marching south don't know the history of the Khalkidike, nor would they care much. To them, the Khalkidike—the large peninsula with its three smaller peninsulas reaching into the Aegean like a claw—is a strange land. Most of the men haven't been to the far south

461

among the Southern Hellenes. They can only recognize that the south and the Khalkidike share a common agriculture through tales told. The Khalkidike has olive trees, has grapes that differ from those in Makedonis, and has less hardy grains. Its climate is warmer, surrounded on three of four sides by the Aegean Sea.

They do know that the cities of the Khalkidike are many and rich. That is a temptation the king requires them to resist. From Amphipolis they march down the coast road. Crossing the River Pennana, they quickly reach Argilos. Then they move on to the River Aulon and the city of Bromiskos. From there they cross the border. Soon they see the great city of Stagiros. From there it's west to Apollonia of the Khalkidike, and south again to Olunthos.

The road has led them along the heights that divide the Khalkidike from the Makedon Mygdonis. Much of the way they are in the Bottike, the lands to which their ancestors had driven the Bottiaoi. That was many kings back in time, for the Makedones have long occupied the Bottiaoi's former homeland and consider Bottiaia one of the provinces of their heartland.

The Bottiaoi, in turn, had driven other Thraikiotes before them. The Sithones gave their name to the middle claw of the peninsulas. Several Paiaone and Thraikiote subtribes (Bisaltai, Krestoni, Edones, and, maybe, Pelasgians) were driven further east to the peninsula of Akte.

Riding along the column of men, with Tyros droning next to him and Pikoros dozing in the saddle on the other side, Philippos suffers a harsh headache in silence. To keep his mind off the pain, he is mentally recounting the history of this country and League. For it all has a bearing on Potidaia.

Korinthos founded Potidaia. An oddity that fact, since most Hellenes first came to the Khalkidike from the islands of Euboia and Andros. Indeed, the name Khalkidike comes from the city of Khalkis, the largest city of Euboia. Some say that the southwest coast, the Krousis, was already occupied by Hellenes, but that goes too far back in time for anyone to know for sure. And the Anthemos valley, lying in the peninsula's northwest, has its own distinct history.

The Hellenes from Euboia and Andros founded more than thirty cities, mostly along the coastline. In time, the Hellenes moved inland and through trade, some warfare, interbreeding and even through precept caused the Bottiaoi to become more Hellenic than Thraikiote. Now it's no longer easy to tell Bottiaoi from Hellene.

Today the principal city and capitol of the confederacy is Olunthos. With walls rising from the flat-topped hill it occupies, the city is strong with a large population. The new town, below the hill, was well-planned. The streets march regularly along. The blocks split by alleys, with five connected town houses to a half-block. What Philippos envies is the water supply and drainage that permits each household its own cisterns and spigots. The wealth of the city has been well used.

The Persians captured Olunthos in ancient times. They broke the power of the Bottiaoi and allowed those Hellenes of the Khalkidike who offered them water and earth to seize Bottiaic lands.

Had the Bottiaoi been as clever as the king's forefather, Alexandros the First, perhaps they would still rule these lands. Alexandros had placated the King-of-Kings, and received the highland Makedones as his reward. Yet Alexandros was clever enough to keep counsel secretly with those Hellenes who defied the Persians—notably the Athenians. In so doing, he retained the goodwill of the southern Hellenes after the Persian flood receded.

The other major cities of the Khalkidike—Apollonia-in-Khalkidike, Stagiros, Sermyle on the Tortonaic Gulf, Akanthos on the arm of the Aegean known as the Thraikikon Sea, Mende and Skione on Pallene, Torone and Singos on Sithone, and Sane and Dion on Akte—are together more than the equal of Olunthos. Singly, though, they are no match for her and so she dominates them.

Other smaller cities are numerous. In Anthemos there are Ainea, Kissos, and the city Anthemos. In the Krousis, he can number Skapsa, Gigonos, and Skolos as cities. Spartolos is the only other city of Bottike, having already counted Olunthos and Apollonia. Of course, Olunthos has its dependent port, the city of Mekyberna. Properly speaking, it's in the old Khalkidike province. Others not already named in the original Khalkidike are Assera, and Stratonikaia.

That takes care of the mainland palm of the hand or claw that makes up the region. The digits or talons of the claw, the smaller peninsulas, hold many more cities. He lists them in his mind: Pallenic Sane, Aphytis, Neapolis, Aige, and Thermous on Pallene; Galepsos and Sarte on Sithone; Thyssos, Kleonai, Olophyxos, Kharadrai, and Akrothoi on Akte.

Truly the Khalkidike is a rich land, richer than any like-sized area of the Makedones. Rich from agriculture, from the sea, from the winds that feed the trade routes to them. With so many people and such wealth, it's easy to understand why, in the time of the king's father and for several generations earlier, Sparte and Athenai contested for the allegiance of the Khalkidike.

Today, it is Philippos and Athenai who woo the League. Though, as ever, Athenai is a rough lover. Which brings the king back to Potidaia, the one city of the Khalkidike that stands apart from the League. The one city occupied by Athenian colonists. The city that the Athenians use to threaten Olunthos, and to restrict her trade through Mekyberna.

Potidaia has always stood apart from the rest. As a Korinthian foundation, it was always distinct from the other Hellenic cities. Sited so close to Olunthos, they must be rivals.

Not that Potidaia will be easily taken. Its walls are high. It is open to water on two sides. The approaches are narrow and easily defended.

In anticipation of this siege, Philippos ordered the construction of a fleet.

Not a fleet that can take on the Athenians head-to-head. Even with his new wealth, that would be too costly. Nor would he have the ability to gather the experienced seamen to man such a fleet. No, this fleet is made up of many small swift ships. Their task will be to close Potidaia's harbors. They are to flee if the Athenians come in force in their great ships.

He is counting on the war with their rebels to prevent the arrival of the Athenian northern fleet. He is counting on the prevailing winds at this time of year to prevent or delay the arrival of a fleet from the south. He is counting on taking the city swiftly. Taking it by the one maneuver considered impossible for hoplites. Taking it by storming the city.

He is afraid of his own plan. Not that anyone knows save himself.

Is he too audacious? A heavily-armored footman, a hoplite, is not trained or armed for forcing his way over a wall and then fighting house by house. Even the king's phalangists, while more lightly armored and so faster and looser, are not intended for that purpose. Instead, he has chosen a select body of men and trained them for the task.

Quite young men for the most part are in the storming ranks. Many were drawn from the best of the juniors, those who carry their elder's equipage on the march and care for it in camp. These second-sons and landless youth have been leavened with royal pages and the younger officers, even favorites like Peithon and Leokhares. Peltasts, archers, slingers, and the stone-throwing and bolt-slinging siege engines will support them.

If they succeed, he will reward them well. Already he's has decided that he will keep them in separate *syntagmai*, like a royal guard save that they are footmen and that there are so many of them, close to 1,500.

For that to happen, they must succeed. He thinks it again, They must succeed. The words form a beat in his head as he rides. They pound with the pulsing rhythm of his headache. They must succeed.

γ

Though Parmenion is not a favorite of Antipatros', the Makedon magnate readily cooperates with the Pelagonid *basileos*. Given the rapid retreat of Lyppeios and his Paiaones to the northeast and the higher wilder mountains that separate Paiaones and Thraikiotes, Antipatros needs Parmenion's support. The general is glad that Parmenion was able to smash the Illuroi so quickly. The Paiaones are proving to be wily, elusive opponents.

And so Antipatros greets Parmenion with a hearty shout and broad smile as the *basileos* dismounts before the general's tent. The two men clasp forearms then pull each other into a warrior's bear hug. Around them their assembled men cheer—Makedones, Pelagones, Deuriopes, loyal Paiaones, mercenaries, even a scattering of Illuroi and Thraikiotes who've given their allegiance to Philippos. The men know they are stronger for this combining of armies, and have less to fear now from the fugitive Paiaones.

Antipatros ushers Parmenion and his two senior officers into the tent. Waiting within are Mezekias, the Paiaone noble from Bylazora, several of Antipatros' chief lieutenants, and the commander of his scouts. Without preamble, Antipatros asks, "How many men have you brought? How well-supplied? We've nothing extra. Mezekias, here, is having his people gather and forward to us what foodstuffs he can. We won't be able to stay together long. I have two columns out in pursuit of Lyppeios. As soon as we have a clear scent, we're on the move."

Parmenion chuckles, "You are to the point, friend Antipatros." He turns to his companions, "How are we found?"

He's answered by Leonidas, "We are three thousand strong. We've food enough with us for five more days for the men. Fodder for two days for the horses and mules."

Clearing his throat softly, Mezekias says, "You can be on the upper Strymon River in that time."

"We think Lyppeios is among the Maedi now. Since he's not strong enough to face us, we think he'll cross the mountains and go either among the Bessi or the Serdi. If we don't catch him, he and his men will draw warriors from the wild tribes and come down like wolves on a sheepfold." Antipatros wipes his large hand over his face and tugs at his grizzled beard.

"Can we turn him? Push him further north, toward the Illuroi and not the Thrakes?" asks Parmenion.

"What does that do for us?" asks Apollonios Tharos, a distant cousin of Antipatros and his second-in-command.

"We Pelagonoi have good relations with the Agrianes. If Lyppeios doesn't cross the mountains, he's likely to enter their lands."

Antipatros turns to his scoutmaster, "Madena, what say you? Can we turn them north, even northwest?"

"We've said all this before. You're pushing your right column along the eastern bank of the Strymon. The left column skirts the northern foothills of Mount Massapion. We sit here in the Pontios valley. You hope to squeeze Lyppeios. To cut Lyppeios off from the Rhodope mountains, the right column needs to reach the key passes first. Sending more men behind them doesn't help to catch them, it only makes them more frantic to put the mountains between us."

"What if we withdraw?" asks Parmenion.

All the men stare at him. He smiles gently, "If Philippos were to recall us, if the pursuit were called off, what would Lyppeios do?"

"He's brave enough. He'd come back down among our people. He'd take it as his opportunity to rally more fools to his banner," there's a bitter tone to Mezekias' voice.

"Antipatros, he doesn't know I've come yet. What if I took my men north. Go among the Agrianes, while you go west. You could return to Bylazora. Let your right column withdraw down among the Sitike, below

Mount Orbelos. We leave the eastern Paiaones alone. Let our spies bring us word when he returns. Then I lead my men to cut off the passes, while you advance again. We'll surround him."

"It could work," ventures Apollonios Tharos.

Antipatros nods slowly, "It will if Lyppeios believes it."

The *basileos* advances his argument, "Philippos advances on Potidaia. There's no telling how long that siege will last or what strength he'll need. With Grabos and Ketriporis down, that leaves only Lyppeios in the field, and he's fleeing. Doesn't it make sense that the king would recall you, leaving only the force needed to guard the frontier?"

"He could still gather men from the Maedi and from over the mountains. And there will be more Paiaones who will join him. He'll be stronger even if he does fall for the trap." comments Leonidas.

"I don't fear his strength. I fear the king's scorn if Lyppeios does escape us," says Antipatros.

"He won't escape you," says Mezekias. "His vanity will make him eager to ride among our people and say that he outthought or outfought the Makedones."

"My good Parmenion, you advise us well." Antipatros turns to the others, "Let's make this happen. The sooner, the better."

δ

Placing a hand on her swollen belly, Olympias gently pushes back on the tiny fist or foot or elbow that's lifting a small portion of her flesh. She laughs contentedly. This boy within her is so active. How much longer? A month? Perhaps another *dekades* beyond? She'll be glad and sad when he's born. Though she hates this sense of heaviness, and the many limits it places on her, especially the seclusion that is seen as necessary for a pregnant noble, she also enjoys this fish or snake or soul, this boy child, that is within and with whom she communes.

Across from her Eurudike watches. She's glad her son's principal wife takes pleasure in her condition. She doesn't remember ever being pleased at being pregnant herself.

Still, she does remember the proud visage of old Amuntas each time he took one of his five-day olds and carried him or her around the hearth to accept the child into the family. Or the naming celebration, five days after that, another small step in making the child a reality and not some dream soul soon lost to illness or birth wound.

"Have you and Philippos talked about names?" she asks Olympias.

"Well, we're clear it won't be Neoptolemos after my father or Amuntas after his. No grandfather's name for this boy, that's decided. He wants a name important to the Makedones and to the Molossi."

"He turned down Dionusios, too, I hear," comments Eurudike,

Olympias doesn't respond immediately. She's still angered by her husband's abrupt dismissal of the name she suggested. There is no more appropriate name, she feels. The god Dionysios possessed Philippos the night this boy was conceived. Of that, she is certain. She's also irked that Eurudike knows of the incident since only Philippos could have told her.

"What name does Philippos suggest?"

Olympias smiles wanly, "Alexandros."

A pang strikes Eurudike at the sound of her eldest son's name, "For his brother?"

"Or for mine," answers Olympias. "Not really, but for King Alexandros the First who united the highland and lowland Makedones. And for the echo it carries among the Molossi, with our family having its share of ancestors bearing the name."

Eurudike wonders if the shade of King Alexandros the First is jealous of his name. If he curses any Temenidai who carry his name, who would equal his exploits. She dismisses her musings as nonsense, Philippos has already surpassed his famous forefather. No, it wasn't any ancient king who cursed her murdered son, Alexandros. If it was anyone, it was she, and how she regrets it.

"What do you hope for this son you're bearing the king?" asks Eurudike with a smile.

"That he always makes his father and me proud. When the time comes, that he succeeds his father, and then goes on to surpass the deeds of his father. For if he does, then how much more would that honor his parents and his ancestors." She laughs lightly, yet within is a resolve that her son be the greatest of the Makedon kings.

Eurudike smiles as well even though she perceives the ambition within the words not only for the son but also for the mother.

ε

The agora of the new town section of Olunthos is wide and handsome. On one side of the marketplace, the city fathers erected an imposing council hall. Beautifully-built temples flank two other sides. On the fourth side are the main fountain house and the huge market building. The marketplace itself is often crowded with the tents and awnings of merchants, traders, and craftsmen. On those days, the people of the city throng the market, fingering goods, cajoling bargains, and bringing their bright energy to the give-and-take of buying. But not today—for today, there is ceremony in the agora as the magistrates, council members, federation representatives, and the citizenry welcome Philippos and his generals.

With the Makedon army safely encamped southwest of the city, towards Potidaia, it is only the king and his retinue who attend to the people of Olunthos. While only a small number of men are with the king, it is not lost on Philippos that this ceremony is in the new town and not on the hill of the city's heart, not within the citadel of Olunthos. Allies, yes, yet duly cautious.

He endures the speeches and says solemn words, almost pompous, of his own. They are the kind of pieties and promises the people want to hear, to reassure themselves that the decision to make common cause with the Makedones was wise. He knows he does this kind of thing well.

The king takes note of everything and everyone. As he has always done. His mind works to unlock the stories and secrets that surround him, for each individual is a story and each one's thoughts are seemingly secret. Gestures and facial expressions, interactions and placement, clothing, weapons, and jewelry, hairstyles, appearance—health, cleanliness, care or its lack—there is so much that is as telling or more than the words uttered. And there are the words themselves, like so many coins. When words pass through another's mind do they possess the same value, the same meaning, as in your own? Which are mouthings, devoid of content; which are unguarded, said honestly; which are traditional, heartfelt but unexamined; which are whimsy, attempts at humor or acts of exuberance that are only of the moment; which are true, reliable, valuable, to be treasured as the measure of the speaker's worth?

This morning it seems as if every politician of the city and some of the wider federation have spoken at length. Of the two magistrates, who in effect rule both city and federation, Leukippos seems the stronger and abler. His co-magistrate, Aristeas, is an older man who thinks only of Olunthos and cannot see beyond its walls. As for the many councilors and federation representatives here, watching them has added to the impressions the king gained on the march to Olunthos as he listened to Tyros read Ephrastos' report identifying and assessing each one. The florid Apollonides leads the anti-Makedon faction, with support from young Ophellas and the lean Kallisthenes. The pro-Makedon faction is lead by shrewd Pherekydes and the arrogant Lasthenes. Other leaders include Nikandros, whose stubby body and blunt ways remind Philippos of a fist, the energetic Euthykrates, and sly Aleuttes. The latter speaks for that part of the population that still maintains some traditions of the Bottiaoi. By tagging each man with an epithet, Philippos more clearly keeps him in mind.

There are two men not here who Philippos would learn more about. The first is Didymos Hierax, the mercenary general employed by Olunthos to command their army. Often simply called the Hawk, his reputation is formidable. He is in the citadel now guarding the city's heart—its treasury, granaries, and religious center. The second is the ancient Ixion Pistisos, who is revered throughout the Khalkidike as a teacher, healer, and disciple of Dionysiac and Orphic beliefs. Presumably this elderly man is at his home, which doubles as his school. A transplanted Thessaliote, Pistisos is related to Polugnota, who was Perdikkas' lover.

Finally, the rituals and speeches in the agora come to a close. The public spectacle is done. Yet the magistrates require one final ceremony, to be witnessed by themselves, the city councilors and federation representatives, and the king's generals, and to be conducted by Philippos and the priests of Artemis.

Philippos will be glad when all these tedious but necessary acts are completed. Doubtless the patience of Alkimakhos, Eurulokhos, Antigonos, Attalos, and his other men are suffering. None of them, he included, are men who delight in such lengthy rituals. Alkimakhos is pious enough but these are foreign ceremonies and not the daily ritual of one's own household and clan.

The procession winds its way to the temple precinct. They are going to the temple of Artemis. Though Artemis holds many aspects—warrior as Artemis Agrotera, protector of women and children as Artemis Eileithyia, huntress and protector of nature as Artemis Parthenos, and, here in the Khalkidike, is often identified with Hekate, in both her benign and terrible forms—it is as Artemis Throsia they seek her today. The Artemis who consecrates and before whom one makes agreements or dedicates oneself. It is in this temple's grounds that the Olunthians raised the stele on which is cut the terms of the agreement between Philippos and themselves. Even the affirmative answer Apollo gave Olunthos at the oracle of Delphoi when they submitted the question of the alliance to the god is inscribed on the tall stone stele.

Finally, they are there. Philippos and the priests make the sacrifice of the wild boar and the deer, an unusual sacrifice for Hellenes to make, though not unique in sacrifices to Artemis. Again Philippos swears to uphold the agreement. Inwardly he thinks the witnesses simply can't believe he will take Potidaia and give to them, even though they already enjoy Anthemos as his gift. So they insist he repeat what is agreed.

Yet it is so simple to Philippos. He seeks to expel the Athenians from the Thermaic Gulf. So Potidaia must fall. The federation has not succeeded in quelling Potidaia themselves, and would never permit him to hold the city once he takes it. So the answer is to take it for them and gain their thanks.

* * *

From the Makedon encampment Potidaia can be seen in the distance, a scant twenty or so stade away. The citizens of the city can as easily see the extent of the camp enclosure and the smoke from the many campfires. They know a host has come to besiege them.

The citizens know all about the king's promise and the stele proclaiming the same in the courtyard of Artemis. They have sent to Athenai for help. They have appealed to the gods. They have armored their bodies and stand in turn, watch-by-watch, upon the ramparts.

Grim jokes are told in Potidaia. They make light of the Makedones, and reassure each other of Athenai's mighty reach. Yes, Makedones are capable when fighting barbarians. Yes, Amphipolis and Pudna have fallen to the king—though only through treachery within. There will be no treachery at Potidaia. The citizens of Potodaia are well used to the hatred of their neighbors in the Khalkidike. The Potidaians return the favor, despising the Olunthians. They think it weak of Philippos to need their foes so much that he pays them for alliance with his own people in Anthemos.

They know their own strength. They count their unity in the face of enemies, their stalwart warriors, their strong walls, their own catapults, and the ships in their harbor that will help keep the city fed by bringing in the grain they will need. True, the Makedones have mounted a watch by sea on the Thermaic Gulf with their new ships. That is but one seaway.

The Potidaian commander, Heraklides, is less sanguine than the many citizens who are boasting to one another. He was with Timotheos seven years ago when Athenai recovered the city from the Khalkidike. The same Timotheos who, with Iphikrates, is being tried for treason in Athenai now on the accusation of General Khares, that misbegotten whore's son. Potidaia can be taken, that the commander knows. Will Philippos be willing to pay the price?

That's the question that plays in Heraklides' mind. How can he make the king's attempt so bloody that the king recoils? How long will the city hold out? Two and half years as did the Potidaians more than seventy years earlier? That siege cost the besieger, Athenai, 2000 talents of silver and the lives of many men, more to plague than to enemy blades. Even a matter of three months would be enough, for by then Athenai can bring its strength down on the king. At least, that is what Heraklides hopes.

Heraklides stares out from the high walls at the distant encampment of his enemies. He may be less eager for the fight than his compatriots but he is as determined as any man in Potidaia. He believes he fights for his country—*khorā*—and his personal honor—*timë*. For him, his country is Attika not Potidaia.

* * *

Watching from the hillside, with the slanting sunlight of late afternoon, Philippos can take in the sweep of sea from Potidaia to Mekyberna and past to Sermyle. The king smiles in satisfaction. The squadron of Makedon ships under Andromitos is taking station off Potidaia's eastern harbor in the Toronaic Gulf. Confederation ships out of Mekyberna, Sermyle, and Torone should join them soon. Both watergates to Potidaia are closed. Now the siege can truly begin.

Philippos turns to Didymos Hierax, "Well, my friend Hawk, what say you?"

"You advance your men in the morning?"

"We'll ferry troops to Aphystis, and march them up to Potidaia's south walls. Then I'll advance from here to the north walls. Another two days we'll spend in assembling the siege towers and engines. Then we'll attack, three days from now, four days at the outside. If fortune smiles, they'll attempt a sortie to burn the siege equipment. I'll have horsemen posted to cut them off from the city. If we catch them, we'll destroy them."

The mercenary general eyes the king, "And you want no help from us?"

"How is it a gift if you and your men share the dangers?"

The Hawk grunts, thinking the king foolish not to avail himself of the confederation army. As it is, Olunthos supplies the food and fodder for the king's army. Why not men, as well? And if the Hawk and his men join the siege, they share in the plunder when the city falls. Thinking to sting Philippos, the general asks, "Half your army is in the north chasing Lyppeios of the Paiaones. Aren't you tempting the fates?"

Philippos believes he is tempting the fates or, perhaps, testing the favor Zeus bestows on him and the Temenidai. Yet he sees little advantage in adding the Khalkidike army to this siege. His tactics will work without that help. If not, then it will be a long siege. Time enough then to consider the option and the price Olunthos would demand. "How many hoplites can the Khalkidike field?"

"Olunthos and the League can put ten thousand citizen hoplites at my command. In addition, there are my mercenaries, their horsemen, and plenty of *psiloi*. They can hire thousands of peltasts out of Thraikios. In extremity, there are other cities that would aid them if permitted by the Athenians." The last is said to unsettle the king.

"You are from Oreos in Euboia, Didymos Hierax?"

"Long ago," the scarred face grimaces. "I've not been back for many years."

"You've fought for and against the Persians."

"Yes. The Persians pay well, better than Athenai or the cities of coastal Asia."

"How well do they fight?"

"They can't stand up to us man for man. That's why they hire Hellenes. But war is more than standing toe to toe. They are sly vipers. I never rest easy there."

The Hawk strokes his chin, then adds, "And there are so many of them from so many nations. I said we could raise ten thousand hoplites. For every one, there could be twenty or more in Persia's western army."

"Do you rest easy here?" laughs Philippos.

The Hawk chuckles, "Why not? We're not at war. You're the scrapper here, Philippos. You tweak Athenai's nose. Amphipolis, Pudna, Potidaia, and no doubt you're greedy for more. She won't always look elsewhere first. Your turn will come."

"You sound as if you know."

"I am a Euboian. Thebai and Athenai make us the playground of their fighting. Worse, I'm from Oreos. So the tyrants of Khalkis are my foes. Who funds them but Athenai. Great lovers of democracy are the Athenians, so long as it's only their democracy they need consider."

Philippos is certain that someday the bitterness of the Hawk could be useful. Haters of Athenai are to be treasured. "You are my guest, if you so choose and your duties permit, through the siege. You are welcome to come and go as you please."

"There is nothing you would hide from my paymasters, Philippos?"

"There is nothing I would hide from you, Didymos Hierax. What you say to Leukippos and the others is up to you." Philippos places a hand on the others shoulder, "You are a man of wide experience. Wider, in truth, than mine when it comes to fighting. I would value any advice you give."

Though he doesn't show it, the Hawk is flattered. And Philippos is known to be generous in his pay and gifts for those who serve him. Aristeas, the magistrate, in particular does not trust the king and urged the Hawk to learn all he could. Where better than at the king's side?

ζ

Much relieved, Lyppeios leads his small army out of the high mountains. Several thousands strong, they are heartened by the return to their homeland and to the families they left behind when they fled Antipatros. These eastern Paiaones, these men who have stood by Lyppeios, are fierce fighters. Only three years back they raided among the Makedones, contemptuous of their foes. The weak kingdom bribed them to withdraw.

Then in the following winter, Philippos came on them with his riders like a pack of wolves on an undefended sheepfold. Everyone in the long column of warriors suffered loss that winter. Not one cannot name a father, brother, cousin, or, even, one of his womenfolk gone in that hard season. When Lyppeios raised his banner, they were glad to come. Glad to know that Ketriporis, Grabos, and Lyppeios fought in company. How thwarted they felt when forced to run from the steel hard Makedones.

As for Lyppeios, while he knows he was right to flee when both Ketriporis and Grabos were lost as allies, the necessity was bitter. Truthfully, he had little desire to go to the Bessi as a suppliant. It was enough to flee to the Maedi. When word reached him of the withdrawal of the Makedones it was a godsend. Praise Shurdi.

The stay with the Maedi was worthwhile. He smiles at the thought of his young Maedi princess. Their wedding symbolizes the alliance. Though the many Maedi warriors gathering at the Stone Ford crossing of the upper Strymon are more to the point. When his band and theirs are joined, even the western Paiaones will flock to him. If he can turn all the Paiaones against the Makedones, then he has no fear of them.

The thought of the traitorous Mezekias' head on a stake causes

Lyppeios to grin. He hates that lying viper almost as much as he hates the Makedon king and his Pelagonid servant, Parmenion.

A rider, the Paiaone king's chief of scouts, comes crashing out of the timber, his horse lathered and ready to drop. "Ho, Drakon, here," calls Lyppeios. "What is it?"

"Turn the column, Lord. Form in line before the Makedones are on us," screams Drakon.

Fear pierces Lyppeios' bowels, "What are you saying? Where are the Maedi?"

"Not at the ford. It's Parmenion coming down on us, Parmenion with his Pelagones and Makedones."

"How many?"

"Many more than we are!"

Those warrior chiefs and men near them have heard Drakon and are already scrambling back. The more level-headed men are uncovering shields, loosing swords, gathering by their leaders. Most though are turning, running, yelling at those in their way.

Lyppeios looks frantically for his banner man and his signaler. One of the war band leaders is bellowing at the panic stricken, beating at the men around him to form them into a line. A handful of riders are coming through the woods. They are the rest of the scouts. In their haste they smash through the disorganized foot, scattering the rough formation.

Drakon reaches a hand to Lyppeios, "You must run for it, Lord. It's too late. There's not enough of us and there's not time."

"What happened to the Maedi?"

"I don't know. They weren't at the ford, they never reached the ford. Only Parmenion and his men were there."

Why was there no warning of this? Could the Makedones outride word of their coming? No, it must be treachery. Now there is no time to discover the truth. Most of the foot will not escape the Makedones. He must ride away from them, get to the high hills with at least the horsemen.

Calling to the bellicose war leader, Lyppeios says, "Teutaros, you and your warriors must hold the Makedones. Gain what time you can for the rest of us. If we can reach the Red Hill, we can set an ambush there."

Teutaros yells back, "Lend me Drakon and his riders, King Lyppeios. With twenty men here, you'll have a moment. With fifty here, you may have time to get away. With a hundred here, you may make your ambush there."

With his trumpeter up, Lyppeios has the man blow several peals. The Paiaone king calls out, "Who will stand with the stalwart Teutaros? Who will give your king time to make a victory?"

Some few respond, joining the knot of men about Teutaros. Most dodge around them and continue to run. With Teutaros willing to be sacrificed, other war leaders are running with their men.

"Drakon, take your men and cut the column. Use your blades if need be. Turn enough back so Teutaros can make a stand," orders Lyppeios.

Drakon stares at his grim-faced king, then abruptly nods his assent. He puts heels to his tired horse's flanks, waving his riders to him.

Soon the van of the column is cut, though not without some bodies on the ground. Perhaps two hundred men are forced to join Teutaros.

Lyppeios trots past them, trailing his signaler and bannerman. Several men jeer at the king, calling "Come take my place." Lyppeios is tight-lipped with fury but continues resolutely on. He must catch up with the bulk of his army, though the thought of just riding on, gathering what horsemen he can, is hard to ignore. Yet he is also desperate to believe that if he can pull enough men together to ambush the pursuing Makedones, there is a chance he can turn the day around.

Behind him he can hear the warcry of the Makedones. They are already upon Teutaros. He does not look back. He slashes the rump of his horse with his switch, overtaking the fleeing footmen. He must escape, and for the first time panic wells within him.

η

Softly singing, Mikrosdiana strokes the forehead of little Arrhidaios. She wills the boy to sleep, though he is restless and cranky. The boy is not so witless, thinks the young woman, as not to know when his mother ignores him.

Since the realization that the boy is feeble, his mother will have nothing to do with him. The pain this causes the child fills Mikrosdiana with a surprising hatred for Philinna.

Though Mikrosdiana knows Philinna's reaction is as much due to her loss of favor with Philippos, and the ascendance of Olympias, this does not mediate Mikrosdiana's anger with the young mother.

The lullaby is working. She looks down on the boy, admiring the fineness of his skin and light-colored hair. As surprising as her hatred of Philinna is the tenderness she feels for Arrhidaios. She cannot believe it is his fault that he is Hera's fool.

Truly, it is time she left Philinna. Time to go home to Larissa. The yearning to be among her kin, to hear Hellenic as spoken in Thessalos, to eat the foods made there, to be away from Pella is almost overwhelming. It's time she wed. Only now does she realize how lonely she's been. Especially with that Molossi witch, Olympias, watching all that she does. The queen is so jealous for her husband, fearing that he takes any interest in the girl.

Well, she need not fear. Mikrosdiana will depart.

For today, there is no one watching Arrhidaios or Mikrosdiana. The Molossi witch is in labor. A hard labor that's already filled the day and is continuing into this evening. Well, the girl will wish no evil on Olympias. Let the child be born blessed. More blessed than wretched Arrhidaios, she thinks.

If there was a reason not to go home, go to Thessalos, it is this little boy. Who will care for him if she leaves? Philippos is not harsh to the boy, but he's a man and a king. What does he know of a small boy's needs, let alone one so burdened as this child? The king is doing what king's do, fighting his enemies. Expect no gentleness there.

Yet even as she thinks this she knows it's not true. The king's daily report always includes news of his children. Trinkets arrive from wherever the king has traveled. There is a peasant nurse to feed the child, to clothe and clean him. Though the wench feels no love for Arrhidaios she is not rough or unkind. That, too, is at the king's word for Philinna would have abandoned the boy.

Would the king let her raise the boy? Not in Thessalos, that is certain. Feeble he may be, but he is a Temenidai. And what man would want her for a wife with a feeble-minded child in tow? So she must part from the boy.

Will the king let her go? The king made her responsible for Arrhidaios when Philinna was pregnant. He has never released her from that obligation. No matter how much Olympias despises her, still she bears the king's regard.

The boy's breathing is even and deep. Asleep you cannot tell his condition. If prayer could heal the boy, if Apollo or Artemis would touch him and awaken his wits, what then would this boy become?

Immediately, she thinks, then Olympias would see him dead. As she would like to see me.

θ

Within the wooden tower the heat is stifling, the noise deafening. Outside the hide-clad timbers of the tower is the roar and screaming of men, the clatter of sling stones and arrows, the heavy workings of the catapults with their distinctive screeching of tightened sinews and crash of thrown logs and rocks. The tumult within the tower seems no less, as men scramble for the interior ladders, some falling from clumsiness or, from the top fighting platform, with wounds. All are frantic to climb the ladders and get out. To fight is better than this fear of being trapped inside if the tower is fired or toppled.

Philippos is unprepared for this fear. For how unnerving it is to be within the tower. The shaft of the short spear he grips, so light compared to his usual long pike, is slick with the sweat of his right hand. He restrains himself from shoving the man in front of him, from trying to hurry the ascent and breaking its rhythm.

Earlier Alkimakhos and Pikoros had pleaded with him to leave the attack to Eurulokhos who commands the specially trained men. General Eurulokhos has the best young officers—men like Peithon, Antigonos, and Leokhares—and the pick of the men, at least of the second sons and other strivers most eager to make names for themselves.

Yet the king could not allow himself to wait on the outcome. To be passive, when so much depends on a quick resolution of this siege. To let other men risk when it is his unorthodox plan they follow. So Eurulokhos commands the assault, and Philippos leads one column, one tower filled with warriors, one tower out of eight.

He didn't think it would be this bad. Oloros is ahead of him and Pantores behind him, both instructed by Alkimakhos to lose their own lives before harm comes to him. As if Alkimakhos could protect him from whatever the fates have decided. The first file of men, already fighting on the wall, is led by Pikoros. He insisted his file go before the king's. And Eurulokhos and Alkimakhos made sure of it.

Mounting the last ladder, Philippos feels the first breath of clean morning air since entering the tower. It clears his mind. Emerging on the top platform, he no longer fears. He swings his shield in place on his shoulder, grips the short spear, and takes his place beside Oloros. An arrow clings to his helmet but he barely notices. Four abreast, he and his immediate companions lead their file across the plank bridge and over the wall.

* * *

Weary now, so tired and aching he can barely stand, the king feels relief that he is alive. The stench of the burning city is about him. Standing on temple steps, he is above the writhing bodies of his wounded. Bearers are tending them, separating those unlikely to survive from those for whom there is hope. Wounds are being sewn together or cauterized or bound. Herbal water is being dispensed. As many as can be saved will be. He planned for this.

He feels surprise that he bears no wounds himself, though he has enough bruises and scrapings to make pain real to him even if none of the wounded around him were screaming or sobbing. His mind keeps circling back to the scenes he's seen. Of butchery, of savage slaughter as his men finally broke the Potidaians and were loosed on the people. Oh great Zeus, is there anything worse than a siege, than a city lost.

Like a tongue exploring a rotten tooth, he thinks again of what to tell Petalouda. Pikoros dead. He will honor him, see that his children are never in want and never forget the worth of their father. Others, too, Peithon gone, that beautiful body broken and torn, that generous heart stilled.

For all the sorrow he feels, there remains a glowing ember within him. The city is his, done quickly and at cost, but done.

What to say to Petalouda? Nothing will comfort her.

There is a stir. Eurulokhos is riding into the square with a handful of companions. They halt at the far side of this sea of wounded men and dismount. No horse would pick its way.

Philippos raises an arm to greet his general. Oloros stands up next to the king, despite his injured leg that still seeps blood. They can see Pantores with the general. He has guided Eurulokhos to the king.

A flight of crows comes screeching, but several bearers shy stones at the birds to keep them off the dead. Ignoring the macabre moment, Eurulokhos walks steadily towards the king.

Philippos calls to him, "You and your men have done all that was asked of you. You have my thanks, Eurulokhos."

Eurulokhos nods acceptance, his expression somber. It is too soon for elation, with the grim cleanup still to be completed. "As you ordered, we have separated the Athenians from the others. How do you want them dealt with?"

"Now that they're unarmed, deal with them tenderly."

"And all the others?"

"You can be gentle with them as well, for their fates will not be kind."

Philippos will sell the locals. The slavers of the Khalkidike are gathered at Olunthos awaiting word of Potidaia's fall. As for the Athenians, he intends to create wonder in Athenai by returning them without even asking for ransom. Let them make what they can of his act. His magnanimity should confuse them more, dividing their counsels, help turn some to view him favorably.

Eurulokhos says, "Didymos Hierax has two *syntagmai* of hoplites on the beach. He would take possession of the city on behalf of the Khalkidike."

Philippos grimaces, "They waste no time."

Eurulokhos shrugs, as if to say what do you expect. Then he smiles, "While you were in the tower a dispatch rider came in. You have more cause to celebrate. You have a new son. May Zeus and Hera protect him, my king."

A son, so Olympias was right all along, maybe she is a witch. The news lifts his spirits. He grins, "A boy. Well, wonderful. I am thankful to know I do all this for good reasons. We Temenidai still possess the favor of the gods and our ancestors, and so, then, do the Makedones."

Even as he says it, he cannot help but think of his other son, Arrhidaios. What if this new child, this Alexandros, is no different? What if Philippos can only father feeble children? Yet his girl Kynnane is as lively a child as anyone could desire. And so is Arsinoe's son, though that's small comfort since he could be Lagos' get.

Around him the men are offering congratulations, praising the gods. The good news seems even to enliven the wounded, and they manage to raise a cheer. And well they should, for it is good when an able king has a son to follow him.

ι

The feasting is past. In the great hall some men still lie on couches or on the floor, too drunk to make their way home or back to the encampment depending on whether a citizen of Olunthos or Makedonis. Most though have departed, however uncertain their gait. The triple celebration—for the fall of Potidaia, the birth of the king's son, and the defeat of Lyppeios—was good cause for drinking. The feasting began in the hour before last light and continued far into the night.

Now in a small room off the main hall, on four couches, recline eight men still conversing and sipping watered wine. A flute girl plays quietly from a corner. Two senior servants occasionally enter to top off any chalice or mug, or to offer exquisite tidbits and morsels saved for this quiet gathering.

Philippos is here with his officers Alkimakhos, Attalos, and Antigonos. The Olunthians attending are the magistrate Leukippos, the pro-Makedon counselor Phenekydes, their general Didymos Hierax, and the teacher or philosopher Ixion Pistisos. It is the latter who reclines on the couch with the king.

None of these men engaged in the drinking games during the feast in the great hall. These men knew this private *symposion* would follow. The king, of course, had to join uncounted toasts. He'd been careful to take the smallest of swallows while giving every appearance of quaffing deeply. A drunken man is an object of derision. Woe betides a king who allows himself to be an object of derision.

Occasionally their conversation becomes general, but for the most part they talk with their couch companions or their immediate neighbors. There is no great policy being discussed. Rather this is relaxation and conviviality ostensibly honoring Attalos and Antigonos for their outstanding bravery at Potidaia, while also acknowledging the two politicians of Olunthos who are key to the alliance with the king. For Philippos, this is an opportunity to talk at length with Ixion.

As for Ixion, he felt no surprise at the invitation to join this select party. Though not greatly vain, he understands the part he plays in ornamenting Olunthos by living here. All Hellenic states strive to attract the finest intellects and most gifted artists. At Olunthos, it is his time—for now and for a number of years past and, if the fates are willing, for some years into the future, his is the keenest mind and clearest voice when one considers the gods, man's place in existence, and the measure of a life.

That this young man, this most successful of the Makedon kings, should want to drink from the cup of the philosopher's wisdom seems appropriate given the favors showered on the king by the gods. Or so thinks Ixion Pistisos.

"...and they are now living in the Isles of the Blessed," asserts Leukippos, speaking of the Makedon officers who died leading their men at Potidaia.

Alkimakhos, who shares the magistrate's couch, nods in pious agreement. But Antigonos, from a farther couch, having heard the remark in one of those lulls that makes one man's voice seem loud, calls back, "What of Heraklides? Didn't he fall at the head of his men, resisting our advance? Is he, too, gone to the *nesoi makaron*?"

"Certainly not," replies the magistrate. "It's not enough that one is brave. One's heart must be pure, and one's cause right in the eyes of the gods."

"With all due respect, friend Leukippos, do not the gods have conflicts? Cannot both sides be in the right, as viewed by some of the gods?" answers Antigonos, who would prefer a more sardonic response were he not enjoined by Philippos to be polite to the Olunthians.

The white-bearded Ixion feels they trespass on his expertise, and so he interjects, "Let us not descend into the common view of the gods. It's best to understand that there is one divinity of many aspects. Within that divinity there is no conflict. How men come to relate to the various aspects of divinity is what seems a conflict. The fault lies in the misunderstandings of men."

There's a moment of silence. Then Antigonos says, "Sage Ixion, what is your belief then? Does Heraklides join Pikoros, Peithon, and the others?"

The old man stares across the couches at the powerful young warrior. He hears the challenge in the other's voice. "Do my beliefs matter to you, young sir? Or is it only your own opinions that you hear?"

Before Antigonos can respond, Philippos speaks, "Heraklides was an honorable man. He was as brave as the best of our men. Though I mourn Pikoros, Peithon, Makhon, Antinoos, Patrokles, and the others, I do not fail to note the worth of my enemies."

"Well said, Philippos," states Didymos Hierax, who has spoken rarely during this symposion. The mercenary general is certain there will be a day when he must fight the Makedones. He doubts he'll survive and is glad their king respects his foes.

Phenekydes seeks to change the tenor of the talk, "Philippos, what you set out to do, you do. Ketriporis, Grabos, and Lyppeios are all undone, and Athenai thwarted. Potidaia is taken, and generously given to the Khalkidike. Your queen bears you a son. What more could the gods give you to prove their favor?"

"My horse, Trekhonike, could win at the Olympiad," as soon as he says his jest, Philippos regrets it. Why tempt the fates?

The others laugh, save Ixion. What if Phenekydes speaks the truth? What if this man is favored? Truly, this young king is remarkable, but there are many remarkable men. Ixion is, himself, a remarkable man. Though the fates have been kind to Ixion, for which he is grateful, he is not beloved by Zeus. That much he knows. Being loved by a god is not necessarily a blessing.

So Ixion offers, "If your horse wins, then you will cap this year with yet another success. You have had an extraordinary year. Yet let me say a word of caution. You are young. With the blessing of the fates, you have many years ahead of you. You must keep a sense of balance. All your years will not be so extraordinary. At least some will visit you with failure. How you behave when all goes your way, how you behave when nothing goes your way, and how you behave during the normal twists and turns of life determines your worth. Character matters more than anything else."

"Does that make sense, Ixion?" asks Leukippos. "Even a bad man can accomplish good things."

"Though I sometimes feel I know nothing of the gods, other times they give me glimpses of the divine. The divine cares more about who you truly are than they care about your position, your riches, and your accomplishments." The old man would say more if words could convey his meaning. He tries, "In the end, we all stand alone, as we truly are. Yes, it's possible that a good man can do a horrible wrong and a bad man can do a wondrous good. Notice, though, that despite their deeds, even we know one is a good man and the other bad. Even to us, when judging the man, while we may admire or deplore a deed, we judge on intent, purpose, character."

Philippos has been disappointed in Ixion Pistisos. The long white beard, the watery blue eyes, the fine cloth of his cloak, his perfumed hair, but most of all the pretension do not match Philippos' preconception of a philosopher and teacher. Kerkidas of Tanagra, the king's teacher in Thebai, comes closer to the image. Or even the king's friend and contemporary, Aristoteles of Stagiros, who is now studying in Athenai, comes closer with his questing mind. This pronouncement of Ixion's, though, bears the ring of truth. Perhaps there is something to this old man. Yet there is pain with this truth, for Philippos is not certain who he truly is. He is a king, and so must have many guises.

Antigonos stands, holding his drinking cup high, "You say rightly, Ixion Pistisos. And I say that I serve Philippos not only as my king and friend, but as a man of worth. Were we shepherds, I would give him my allegiance."

"Antigonos, are you drunk?" asks the king.

"Yes, but that's not important," and the king's friend sits down heavily on the couch to the genial laughter of his companions.

Κ

Olympias is laughing. She is supremely happy for here is her husband, home from his wars, admiring her marvelous baby boy. Philippos has gently tickled the infant awake. Instead of crying, little Alexandros is staring at this looming bearded face. A small hand tries to catch the jutting beard. "Well, King Philippos, what do you think of our son, Prince Alexandros?"

"Why he is perfection, surely you can see that?"

She laughs again in pleasure, "He is, is he not?" What satisfaction to know the boy is no Arrhidaios. That Philippos is delighted and proud is evident. And he should well be, for Dionysios has favored him in conceiving the child.

"I'd forgotten how small they start out. I could hold him in the palm of my hand," says the father.

Looking at those broad tough scarred hands, it's hard to imagine that one day the boy might have hands just so.

"And you, my queen, are you well?" he turns to her with his question smiling in his intense eyes.

"Would you inspect me, sir? See if I am as perfect as your son in your eyes?"

"Oh, Olympias, when you are able I will do more than inspect you with my eyes."

She can hear the lust in his voice, and is momentarily thrilled until thinking where he might slake that lust since she is not yet able. Either Eurudike Audata or Philinna will likely offer him a splendid welcome home from the Khalkidike.

The baby gurgles, pulling her thoughts back to child and husband. The tiny fingers have found the beard. "He has your face, Olympias," says Philippos.

"Perhaps, it's too early to know. He has a lot of growing to do. Your mother thinks he has your eyes because he can stare so intently."

He straightens slowly to not startle the child. "Will we do well by this boy, Olympias?"

She is puzzled by the question, "Of course, Philippos. He will have the best of everything."

"That may not be wise. If he is someday King of the Makedones, his raising cannot be soft."

The word 'if' catches her. This boy will be king after Philippos, of that she is certain. No one will be permitted to come before him. She says, with just a hint of command, "When he is old enough, you will become responsible for his upbringing. But for the next few years, he is all mine, Philippos, and he will have the best of everything."

Behind his ready smile, there is a moment of cold consideration. This boy could become a tug-of-war between them. He answers, "You mother him, Olympias. Safeguard him so he grows strong and healthy. In due time, he can begin to learn the rigors of a kingdom."

*   *   *

A few days past two *dekades* after the new moon that follows the summer solstice, word arrives in Pella from the 106th Olympiad. The king's horse, Trekhonike, has indeed won the race. Philippos is again blessed, and now can wear the wreath of an Olympic victor.

The celebration will be grand, even if quickly arranged. Most of the king's companions are in Pella anyway, summoned to a series of meetings as the king plans his next campaign.

Only those who guard the borders, and those with the expedition under Eurulokhos will be absent. Eurulokhos' reward for his work in the Khalkidike is to seize the Hellenic cities along the Thraike Pieros coast, below Mount Pangaion. He is to destroy Apollonia-in-Pieros and Galepsos. What plunder is gained will be the king's gift to Eurulokhos and the army. The third Hellenic city, Oisyme, will survive to serve the region's need for a port, but it will receive a new foundation of Makedones and be renamed Emathia. That eliminates the final Athenian holdings that disturb trade from the Strymon valley.

There will remain two more Athenian targets to consider. Methone on the Makedon Pieric coast is the sole surviving Athenian ally on the Thermaic Gulf. The other is Neapolis, an Athenian ally on the mainland opposite the island of Thasos. If reinforced by the Athenians, that city can threaten Krenides, now named Philippi, as well as trade from the Nestos River.

With those two cities in the hands of the Makedones, Philippos figures his conquests will be rounded out. As Methone is the far larger, tougher and closer city, its defeat comes first. The king and his men are plotting that end, and will be until it's time for the cycle of festivities and rituals that follow the harvest and mark the New Year.

Celebrating Trekhonike's victory is only one reason to interrupt planning the Methone campaign. Another is the other news from the south. The king and several of his senior advisors are considering the news of the Phokians and Delphoi.

Antipatros is saying, "I don't see why you are so concerned, Philippos. Unless Thessalos is threatened or the Athenians are strengthened, these events are quite distant from our core concerns."

"I surprise myself by agreeing with Antipatros, Philippos," adds Alkimakhos. "The despoiling of the sacred oracle at Delphoi is sacrilege, is blasphemy, but it does not impinge on us. Thebai and her allies will surely chastise the Phokians."

Philippos nods absently, watching his advisors. From these five— grizzled reliable Antipatros, astute vigorous Parmenion, pious patriotic Alkimakhos, sly efficient Ephrastos, and the aging treasurer, Amuntas Plousias—he can hear a variety of views. Others could be here, like Hippasos and Demokedes, and offer additional views. What would it matter? Each man hears his own secrets at heart even while being fully loyal to the king. How else could it be? He could tell them what they would advise him before they say it. Yet a king must be seen to take counsel, to weigh many views, before deciding on a course of action that others would see as too ambitious or too radical.

The king is not ready to say what lies beyond Methone and Neapolis. Certainly the borderlands will always require attention, especially the Illuroi and the Thraikiotes. Opportunity exists in Thraikios that is apparent to all of these men, and closer to their hearts.

Yet Philippos knows they are foolish to think this fight between Phokis and Boiotia is too distant. Here is another opportunity and a danger. The Phokians loot Delphoi not out of greed. They loot to gather the gold and silver they need to hire mercenaries. As many mercenaries as it will take to defeat Thebai. Not just Thebai, they must take on many of the states of the Amphiktyony, and that includes Thessalos. How can we not be drawn into this?

Parmenion jabs at the floor tile with a cut green stick, "Who knows what the fates will demand? I would not hazard. I would guess, though, that if we believe the interests of Thessalos are our interests, then we'd best watch and listen closely to all that happens between Phokis and the Amphiktyony."

Glad that at least one of these men sees some of what he sees, the king says, "We could say let Apollo punish this trespass. And leave it at that. Then we, too, will have trespassed."

Alkimakhos looks startled, clearly not having considered that idea, "I would not be party to sacrilege."

"Nor I, nor I," states Amuntas Plousias. "Yet I would hasten to add, like Antipatros, that these events are distant for now. They bear watching, of course. And here is Ephrastos to do the watching. If Thessalos requests our aid then I would act."

Ephrastos nods agreement but adds, "In a sense, there is no Thessalos. There are instead a handful of powerful families controlling key cities. If the summons comes, it will not be from all of Thessalos."

"Are you all underestimating Thebai and the Boiotians? With Athenai still facing her rebels, who will stand by Phokis?" Antipatros demands.

"How much is the wealth of Delphoi?" asks Philippos.

Amuntas Plousias whistles, "It's immense. Nowhere else is more wealth gathered in all of the Hellas. Save the mountains you own, Philippos."

"How many men would sell their spears to Phokis?" is the king's next question.

Parmenion laughs, "Every impoverished male between the age of fifteen and forty-five in the Peloponnesos."

"That would make a larger army than Persia's," says Alkimakhos. All the men chuckle.

"Ephrastos, I want you to expand the number of agents in the south. I want to know what's said in Theban councils, in Phokian camps, among the politicians of Athenai, between our friends and foes in Thessalos, even among the kings, ephors, and elders of Sparte. I want no surprises from the south," orders Philippos.

Now more somber, all the men nod their agreement.

*   *   *

The old queen mother, Eurudike, sits in the gathering twilight beside Petalouda. The two women hold hands. The silence has been long but not uncomfortable. Finally the young woman stirs, "Dori and the other kids will need me soon."

"Yes, now and for a good while to come," says the queen, patting Petalouda's hand as she rises to go. "Think on what I've said. I know Philippos assured you that you and the children will want for nothing. His word is good. Yet you and I know that's not enough. You will need a man again. Not that anyone one can replace Pikoros. But it's not enough to rely on the word of a king who will not stand down from danger. His life is no more safe than was Pikoros'."

"Philippos gave me to Pikoros, or gave Pikoros to me. Hard to say which it was." Petalouda pauses, searching for words, "I know Philippos well. He is a restless man. There is no stopping him. Whomever you recommend to me to wed, I will. But whoever he is, he will be a warrior for Philippos."

The queen feels her age, understands both the sorrow and the resolution of this young woman. A woman the queen would not know as more than a servant were it not for her son, who draws his brave companions from anywhere that breeds able men, whether a princely Parmenion or a slave like Pikoros. "Then let us leave it at that for now. You and I will know when the time has come, perhaps in a year. Your children will need a foster-father."

The young woman stands and lightly embraces Eurudike, "When you see Philippos, thank him for me." She stands back, "I do not begrudge him my Pikoros. My man would lay down his life for the king, and so he did. Philippos knows he can expect as much from me were it necessary. I know that in his way Philippos is doing the same for me and all of us. So long as Philippos is king, I will feel safe. An ex-slave still knows how dear it is to be trusted and to be able to trust."

* * *

It is late now, in the dark just before it begins to yield to a dawning day. Philippos is awake, unable to sleep. Soon he must conduct the sacrifice and ritual of the Argeadai Temenidai. Though he feels the weight of his responsibilities, the events of the past months give him confidence that he will be aided by Zeus and his ancestors in bearing those responsibilities. A healthy son, taking Potidaia, defeating the barbarian alliance, and even winning the horse race at the Olympiad, what favor he has been shown. He smiles in the dark savoring his fortune. Then as quickly, he adds a prayer to fend off any jealousy the fates or other gods might feel, *Almighty Zeus, father Herakles, and all my fathers of the Temenidai, I give you my thanks and ask that you guide me in what lies before me to do. It is you who strengthen my arm and heart, who offer me your wisdom, who know my future and prepare for the time when I will join you. Help me in this hour and in the times ahead.*

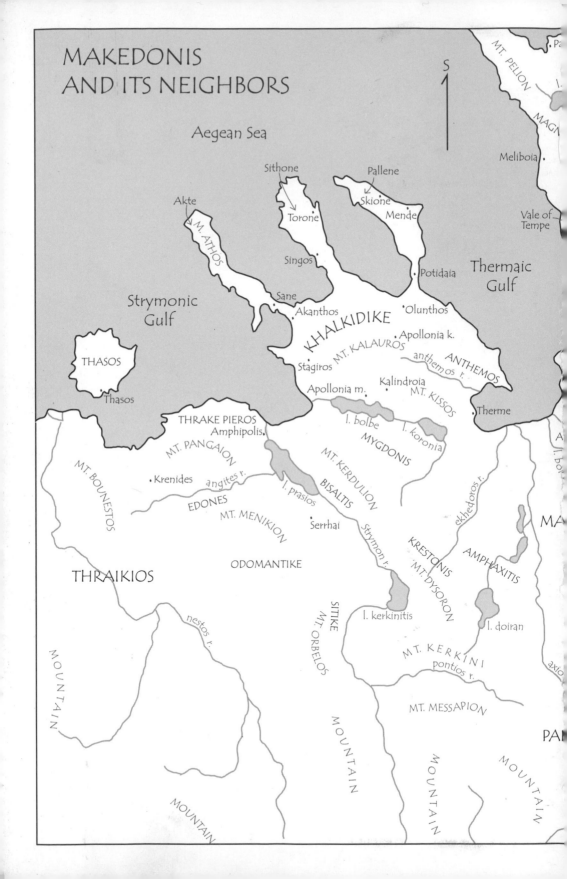

MAKEDONIS
AND ITS NEIGHBORS

Aegean Sea

S

MT. PELION

MAGN

Pa

I.

Meliboia

Vale of
Tempe

Sithone

Pallene

Akte

Skione

Mende

M. ATHOS

Torone

Thermaic
Gulf

Singos

Potidaia

Strymonic
Gulf

Sane

Akanthos

Olunthos

KHALKIDIKE

Apollonia k.

THASOS

Stagiros

MT. KALAUROS

anthemos r.

ANTHEMOS

Thasos

Apollonia m.

Kalindroia

MT. KISSOS

THRAKE PIEROS

Amphipolis.

l. bolbe

l. koronia

Therme

MT. PANGAION

MYGDONIS

MT. BOUNESTOS

Krenides

angites r.

MT. KERDULION

ekhedoros r.

MA

l. prasios

BISALTIS

EDONES

MT. MENIKION

Serrhai

Strymon r.

KRESTONIS

AMPHAXITIS

l. bo

ODOMANTIKE

MT. DYSORON

THRAIKIOS

SITIKE

MT. ORBELOS

l. kerkinitis

l. doiran

nestos r.

MT. KERKINI

pontios r.

axio

MOUNTAIN

MT. MESSAPION

PA

MOUNTAIN

MOUNTAIN

MOUNTAIN

MOUNTAIN